Lovers' Hollow

ORNA ROSS

PENGUIN
IRELAND

PENGUIN IRELAND

Published by the Penguin Group
Penguin Ireland, 25 St Stephen's Green, Dublin 2, Ireland
(a division of Penguin Books Ltd)
Penguin Books Ltd, 80 Strand, London WC2R ORL, England
Penguin Group (USA) Inc., 375 Hudson Street, New York, New York 10014, USA
Penguin Group (Australia), 250 Camberwell Road,
Camberwell, Victoria 3124, Australia (a division of Pearson Australia Group Pty Ltd)
Penguin Group (Canada), 90 Eglinton Avenue East, Suite 700, Toronto, Ontario, Canada M4P 2Y3
(a division of Pearson Penguin Canada Inc.)
Penguin Books India Pvt Ltd, 11 Community Centre,
Panchsheel Park, New Delhi – 110 017, India
Penguin Group (NZ), cnr Airborne and Rosedale Roads, Albany,
Auckland 1310, New Zealand (a division of Pearson New Zealand Ltd)
Penguin Books (South Africa) (Pty) Ltd, 24 Sturdee Avenue,
Rosebank, Johannesburg 2196, South Africa

Penguin Books Ltd, Registered Offices: 80 Strand, London WC2R ORL, England

www.penguin.com

First published 2005
1

Set in 11/14 pt Monotype Garamond
Typeset by Rowland Phototypesetting Ltd, Bury St Edmunds, Suffolk
Printed in Great Britain by Clays Ltd, St Ives plc

A CIP catalogue record for this book is available from the British Library

ISBN-13: 978–1–844–88052–4
ISBN-10: 1–844–88052–4

Philip

This one for you

Two things make a story. The net and the
air that falls through the net.

Pablo Neruda

I
Silt

I

1995

The thick front door under the sign – Devereux's Bar and Grocery – is closed. A For Sale board juts from the side wall, with a Sale Agreed banner across it. The window blinds are drawn, like eyelids pulled down. The house looks as if it, too, has died.

That's all I have time to notice as my taxi whips past. I can't tell the driver to slow down as I have already given him instructions to hurry. After we pass, I look back through the rear window. It seems nothing about the place has changed, yet it looks different. Smaller, lesser. Then the road swerves behind us and the house is gone, disappeared by a bend.

I lean forward to the driver. 'That's the chapel there,' I say and he brakes to a screeching stop, ending my hopes of a discreet arrival. At the church door, heads turn towards us and I shelter in the back of the cab for a final moment while the driver collects my suitcase from the boot. A loud slam and he is at my window, tugging the door open. 'Here we are, so.'

I put on my sunglasses, fading the world to shades of brown, and let my hair veil me from the stares turned my way. I step out. The air feels thick and hot, hardly like air at all, and nausea growls again inside me. I pay the driver and he hands me my bag. Through the open gates I walk, fixing my eyes beyond the gaping faces, onto the chapel door. Beside the crowd, the hearse sits and waits, its hatchback door open like a mouth.

As I draw nearer, people begin to recognize me. One says, 'Hello,' another, 'Sorry for your trouble.' Then there is a general murmur of greeting and sympathy. I nod acknowledgement. 'Welcome home,' says a man whose face I know, one of the Kennedys, I think, a sly fellow who used to mock me from his high stool at our bar counter. Is he mocking me still? The crowd parts to let me through.

Inside, the porch is crammed. I shoulder my way through into the chapel proper. From the altar come words I haven't heard for a long, long time: *Giving thanks to you, His Almighty Father, He broke the bread . . . gave it to His disciples . . .* The priest is a performer, wallowing in emphases and pauses. Two other clerics in purple robes stand behind him. One is Father Pat Moore, curate of Mucknamore when I was growing up, the same plump face with twenty extra years in it. Father Fat, my sister Maeve and I used to call him. The other is a stranger to me but he must have meant something to Mrs D.

The congregation is on its knees, heads bowed. It is the Consecration, the holiest part of the Mass. The *quietest* part of the Mass. So the click of my heels stepping from the porch rug onto the red-and-black tiles sounds louder than it should. People look up, nudge and nod to those beside them. The silence loosens. As I walk up the aisle, whispers swirl in my wake. The years peel away, laying me bare. I am back where I started, with the eyes of Mucknamore on me.

Father Performer genuflects deeply. *Do this in memory of Me.* The altar boy tinkles a little bell, its sound failing to cut through the buzz of the congregation. Sensing the loss of his audience, the priest comes out of his prayer-trance and looks up, his eyes narrowing to specks of stone as he watches me advance.

I hold and answer his stare. *Back off, Padre*, I tell him with my eyes; she was *my* mother. Between us, at the top of the aisle, her coffin sits gleaming on its trolley, all polished wood and burnished trimmings, topped by flowers: bunches, wreaths, circles and crosses of glossy leaves and over-perfect blooms. Funeral flowers, grown to be cut.

The priest stops the ceremony and stands still, hands together pointing heavenwards, a column of forbearance. Father Pat and the other priest behind him imitate the pose. They wait, censuring me with silence.

I am almost at the top pew, where my family is sitting. I can see Maeve now, looking thin, too thin, almost gaunt. Her hair is drawn up into a bun like a ballerina's, making me wish I had tied back my own. I watch her follow the eyes of the priests, turning to see what is causing the delay. When she finds it is me, a look of pure exasperation breaks across her face. *Now, Jo?* her expression says, before she turns her elegant neck away from me, back towards the altar. *Now?* My brother-in-law, Donal, grants me a nod. The little girl between them must be Ria, their eight-year-old daughter, staring at me with Maeve's eyes. A look that tells me she has heard all about her Auntie Jo.

At last I am there. Donal walks his knees down to make a place for me but Maeve, in one of her childish gestures, kneels firm. I put my bag down in the aisle, squeeze into the pew whether Maeve wants me or not. The wood is hard against my kneecaps. The smell of incense sends another wave of nausea undulating through me.

The priest begins again. *Heavenly Father, you gave your only son . . .*

I close my eyes. Kneel. Wait for it to be over.

Why am I here? All the way back I kept asking myself: why? Through the black night flight from San Francisco. During the taxi ride between Dublin airport and the railway station. Through every chug of the rickety three-hour trip to Wexford. And still in the final cab I took from Wexford town to Mucknamore, all the time, the same question: why? Why – when I spent twenty years *not* making this journey, when I had left it so late that I was unlikely to arrive on time anyway – why had I nonetheless organized a last-minute ticket? Why did I feel I *had* to come?

And it wasn't just me. My sister, who long ago gave up trying to get me back to Mucknamore while my mother lived, made frantic efforts to contact me once she began to die: left numerous messages, telephoned my friends, in the end sent a telegram. 'Death demands such attentions.'

We rise and stand and sit and kneel and stand sit again, through the rites. At Holy Communion everybody in our pew goes up to the altar except me, and everybody from the other pews has a good look at me on their way back. Finally, the organ springs into sound for the last time and an elderly voice begins a quavering 'Ave Maria'. I look up to the balcony: it is Mrs Redmond, chins a-wobble, Mrs D.'s oldest friend. While she struggles with the top notes, an undertaker steps up to release the brake on the trolley and glide the coffin down the aisle. The rubber wheels skim smoothly over the uneven tiles. We follow the coffin out of the church, Maeve and Donal first, then Ria and me, and everybody else behind. Maeve is crying, curling her sobs into her husband.

Outside, the heat crawls over us. The others are quickly engulfed by sympathizers, swept away into the crowd, a wall of backs encircling them. Everybody in Mucknamore knows Maeve; she has kept allegiance with the place. Seeing me alone, Donal steps across and bends to bestow a kiss on my cheek. 'So,' he says. 'The prodigal returns.'

I have met Donal only a handful of times in the seventeen years he has been married to my sister. When they were first engaged, Maeve brought him to London to meet me, and that first encounter has always stayed in my mind: how he enfolded her as we sat in the restaurant, her hand heavy with his ring.

'How is Maeve?' I ask, ignoring his jibe.

'Wearing herself to a frazzle,' he says. 'Your mother had very definite ideas about this funeral. Maeve seems to feel duty bound to carry them out to the *n*th degree.'

I think I'm detecting a sardonic note. Maeve always claimed that Donal and Mrs D. were fond of each other but when it comes to family relationships, my sister is prone to whitewash.

'I take it she's annoyed with me?'

'Your mother wanted to see you and Maeve promised her she'd track you down. When she wasn't able to . . . Well . . . you know what your mother meant to Maeve.'

I can't give him the response that leaps into my mind and find I can't think of anything to say instead. Maeve is the single thing Donal and I have in common; communication is strained when she is not with us. Just as the silence is stretching towards awkwardness, we are rescued by a loud shriek that jerks our heads – and everybody else's – around. At the church door four young women are screeching, there's no other word for it. Screeching a tuneless chant that sounds like a saw scraping across metal. The four are in costume, made up to look old, with shawls drawn up over grey-wigged heads and black wrinkles painted across their foreheads and around their eyes. Their lips strain, their eyes gape as they shriek through a string of unintelligible words. I resist the impulse to cover my ears. 'What the hell . . . ?'

'Ahhh,' says Donal, enjoying himself. 'Our keening friends again.'

'Keeners?'

'Professional mourners, one of your mother's *many* special requests,' he says. 'She wanted an old-style, traditional Irish send-off. We had a wake, too, last night, complete with those four weeping and wailing and flinging themselves on the floor. She left Maeve six pages of instructions about this funeral. Six pages!'

All around us, people in the churchyard are pointing and nudging. I look across at my sister, explaining to everybody what the sideshow is about and wonder how she can bear it. Did Mrs D. consider her at all while concocting her schemes? Probably not. Our mother wouldn't understand how funerals serve the needs of those left behind. No doubt she had visions of her celestial self scrutinizing proceedings, seeing who came along and noting how they behaved, so she would know how to treat them when they eventually caught up with her above.

'I don't think anybody will be sorry when this day is over,' Donal says, his thoughts, for once, in line with mine.

I feel a hand on my back and turn to see Eileen standing there with her husband, Séamus. 'Jo,' she says. 'Jo, I'm so sorry.' For the first time I feel something wobble inside me. Eileen worked in our shop while we were growing up and lived with us until she married. I let her hold me.

Her hug seems to give the others permission to approach me and people I haven't seen for years begin to come over and grab my hand. Faces I remember, names I've forgotten; names I remember, faces I've forgotten. They find words to say: My mother is gone to a better place. She is the lucky one now. She was a great character, one of the best. God would give me comfort. Only one old woman says something that sounds like the truth, and she gets herself dragged away by the arm for it. 'Who are you?' she asks. 'I never heard Máirín mention *you* at all.'

Then, abruptly, out of the mass of well-wishers comes a hand and a voice that I do know. 'Jo,' he says, and my heart skips. A second hand comes forward, encircles mine in a careful, caring cup. And then he is there, all of him, looking down on me: Rory O'Donovan.

I had thought about Rory on the journey back, of course I had. I knew I would meet him and had planned my opening lines and the airy way I would deliver them. But in my imaginings, we met on the beach, or on the village street. Not here, at my mother's funeral, the last place I would expect to find him, or any O'Donovan. Not here, in front of everybody. Not here.

'How are you, Dev?'

Dev. His old name for me. He is still the picture I have held in my head but blurred at the edges, like a photograph out of focus. Extra weight has loosened his jawline. His hair is gone, his long, black, beautiful hair. It used to flow down his back, soft and shiny as night-water. I used to sink my face in it, loop it through my fingers, knot it around my naked neck. All gone. Shorn and thinning now: any man's hair. And he wears a suit, any man's clothes. I look for what I used to know.

'How are you?' he asks again. Behind us, the keeners raise their wailing to a higher pitch and he winces with a smile. It is a look to share: amused and confident of my amusement. Just like the old days, us against Mrs D. A deep flush begins at the base of my neck and tracks slowly up my face.

I panic, swivel my head round to look about the churchyard, at the pockets of people, the waiting priest, the undertaker slamming the hearse door shut. I point across. 'I have to go!' I say and that's what I do, almost running from him, decamping back to Donal who stands with Ria near the hearse. It's the shock of seeing him here that has unnerved me, I tell myself as I flee. The suddenness of this new Rory sprung upon me when my mind was on Mrs D. and Maeve and everything else. But I know that's not it. I know that really it's Mucknamore. Not even back an hour and already I am regressing, coming unstrung.

Donal explains that we are to stand behind the hearse and lead the cortège to the cemetery. The old cemetery. Only when he says this do I look across and realize: my father's grave lies flat and undisturbed, no heap of earth beside it, no open cavity waiting to be filled.

'She's not going to be buried with Daddy?'

'No.'

'Don't tell me. Another special request?'

'Yup. Down in the old cemetery, with her own family.'

The old cemetery. A twenty-minute walk away. At least.

'Can't we drive?'

'Apparently not. She wanted us to walk.'

Thank you, Mrs D. I seriously doubt that I can walk that far in this blistering heat. And now here's Maeve bustling across, her aggravated-big-sister face taped on. She surprises me by slipping an arm around me and kissing my cheek. A real kiss, a close hug. 'Am I supposed to say, better late than never?' she asks.

'I'm sorry, Maeve,' I say. 'Really I am. I didn't get your messages until last night and . . .'

'Honestly, Jo, you're impossible. Why do you have an answering machine if you don't bother listening to your messages?'

I say nothing. Usually, I do take my messages as soon as I come in the door of my apartment. But these past days have not been usual.

'Couldn't you have let us know you were coming? Where were you when I rang, anyway?'

'Out.' It's what I have planned to say so I say it.

'Out!' she says. What do I mean, out? She rang me at all hours of the day and night, left four or five messages on my machine. She even telephoned Deirdre Mernagh, who told her I was home, that she had been with me on the Friday night. So where had I been since?

I want to tell her to back off and mind her own business, but I don't. Her red-rimmed eyes are ringed with black, circles gouged deep by days of distress. Scolding me seems to ease her, so I take the rap. But it's a relief when the undertaker slides across and whispers in her ear and she returns to her duties.

She lines us up in the order Mrs D. dictated: first Father Performer, whose name, I learn, is Doyle, then two of the shrieking keeners; then the hearse, followed by the other two priests, the other two keeners behind them. Then us: herself, Donal, Ria, me. Was Mrs D. expecting me when she made her plans, I wonder? 'Ria! Over here, love,' Maeve calls, with that voice that mothers use to address their children when they have an audience.

Behind us, everybody lines up in whatever order they like. The black car slips into gear and rolls towards the chapel gates. As we begin our march, the keeners lift the pitch of their noise another notch, start to hold their notes for longer. The only words I recognize are the lamentation of the refrain: *Ochón agus ochón ó*. They are a troupe of actors, Maeve explains in whispers. Mrs D. contacted them through the Arts Centre in Wexford, paying them to research the keening tradition and compile a performance that would enact that tradition at her funeral. They also performed in the house last night, at the wake. The wake was done in the old style, with stories and music and singing and Mrs D. laid out in the middle of it all in an open coffin. On all of this she had insisted. Her instructions covered everything, from the food to be eaten to the songs to be sung. She must have been planning the event for months, Maeve says, if not years.

On we trudge down the village main street. Slow progress, up a gently sloping hill. Past the two-roomed national school; past Lamberts' little farm, still the same stench of dung mingled with sea salt; past the post office, its green An Post stickers plastered all over the window. We round the curve in the road and I can see our house atop its small hill. As the road rises, my breath begins to strain again. When we reach the front door, the hearse stops. The undertaker turns off the engine, the keeners drop quiet, and now we can hear the sea surf, its sound loud in the hush. We all stand for two minutes' silence, praying or thinking. Our house. Mrs D.'s house, really. Bar and grocery in front, bedrooms above, living rooms and kitchen behind. Just a front-room bar and shop but in Mrs D.'s world it made her someone. A home that was bigger than most others around and a business that was central to village life. So central, in her mind, that when she talked about the shop, she gave it the name of the village itself.

'Mammy's talking about selling Mucknamore,' Maeve had said to me on the telephone a month or so ago. 'This time I think she really means it.'

And this time she really did. The For Sale sign went up on the dwelling that had defined her for seventy-two years, and in boom-time Ireland quickly attracted a handsome offer. But before she had time to sign the deal, she fell dead.

Dead, Mrs D. Dead. That is what you are. It's over.

*

After one hundred and twenty blessed seconds of silence, the keeners recommence their lament and we move off again, feet treading together in a slow march. Now we can see across the tops of the houses set into the cliff below. It's fresher up here, with a small breeze blowing off the sea. We pass the old police barracks, once a burnt-out husk, now a holiday-apartment block with landscaped gardens and balconies facing the sea. Around the corner, a caravan park has opened, and opposite its entrance a mini-market sells food and beach-balls and yellow canisters of gas. Next door, a silhouette of a steaming black kettle announces Kehoe's Kafé and beside that is Fryer Tuck, a fried-food takeaway.

Here, everything has changed. The older part of the village was closed and empty, but here people stand and stare and some of them bless themselves as we pass. Beyond the shops is a line of bungalows, each built without any awareness of its neighbour so they squat higgledy-piggledy along the road, like a row of crooked teeth. Many have B&B signs swinging above their gates, offering accommodation. On we go, past two holiday-home developments: Sea View and Mucknamore Cottages and beyond them two building sites in the muddy stage of excavation. 'Luxury Three- and Four-Bedroom Houses', their signs promise. 'Investment and Private. Last few remaining.'

Then suddenly the buildings stop, the road narrows and we are in a country lane. The sun bleaches the hedgerows to grey and seeks out white skin to burn. I tuck my exposed arms into my body, away from its glare. No fresh air here. My nausea now is solid, a squirming mass in the pit of my stomach, so thick and threatening I can no longer respond to Maeve's whispers. I concentrate on my breathing, keeping it regular, focusing only on the road ahead. Slowly, slowly, on we tramp.

At last, we can see the cemetery up ahead at the end of the curving road that veers back towards the coast. Old Mucknamore cemetery, a patchwork of crosses and slabs of stone staring over a low wall at the sea below. Closed now to anybody who does not already have a plot inside. The keeners separate as we approach the entrance, two standing at each pillar of the gate, their eerie, unearthly sound ushering us through.

Her open grave is up near the top of the cemetery, waiting for us. Beside it lies the pile of earth that will be thrown back in on top of her coffin, its surface cracking as it dries in the sun. Two Celtic high crosses and a simple granite slab stand sentry over the hole. The taller, thicker cross is Uncle Barney's, a memorial erected by his old IRA brigade. Its inscription is in the old Irish alphabet and therefore illegible to me; all I can read is the date of his death: 10.1.1923. The other, erected by the family, commemorates Granny Peg and their parents. And now, soon, Mrs D. The small one is Auntie Nora's, buried with Peg, not her own people.

A terrible thought strikes me and I whisper to Maeve. 'We're not having a tricolour flag over the coffin or any of that rigmarole?' Granny Peg had had a full Irish Republican burial when she died, I knew: tricolour, prayers in Irish, volleys from old IRA guns fired into the air as the coffin went down . . .

'No, no,' Maeve whispers from the side of her mouth, her eyes to the crowd. 'Nobody does that any more. Not since things got bad in the North.'

The keeners join us at the graveside, their singing even louder now. My knees long to buckle but we must stand straight and wait under their clamour while the long string of people trudges in and gathers round the grave. Father Doyle's face makes his feelings clear: he has no choice but to indulge these eccentric requests – the deceased was, after all, one of his keenest patrons – but he does not have to approve. Reluctant as I am to be on Father Doyle's side on anything, I too long for them to stop. Instead they get louder and louder, until their noise batters against my temples in time with my blood. *Shut up*, beats the pulse inside my head. *Shut up. Shut up.* Finally, at the height of the lamentation, they do, stopping abruptly and stepping back into the crowd.

Silence reverberates. A lone pair of hands starts to applaud, the claps faltering as it becomes obvious that nobody else is going to join in. Father Doyle begins to pray in the name of the Father, the Son and the Holy Spirit, his voice and the crowd's responses weak and small in the open air: *Lord, have mercy. Lord, graciously hear us.* My tongue feels dry and rough as the sand dunes below us. Nausea twists in me again. And again. I try to beat it back down but this time pressure is swelling up into my nose and ears and I know it's going to come. My heart starts knocking. My stomach constricts. My head floods until I am swimming in black.

Somebody is wailing and Father Doyle looks up from his missal, annoyance all over his face now. This is not what was agreed, this is supposed to be his time. He should have recognized that this sound is different, rawer than the ritual cries of professional keeners. Me.

I try to stumble away, floundering in the only direction free of people, and find I'm walking towards the open grave. I can see Father Doyle and Maeve and all the questioning faces of the crowd, their necks straining to see, but it is as if they are behind a gauze. Mrs D.'s cool earth-hole beckons.

As I pitch towards the ground, a male voice calls out my name, 'Jo!' and two strong arms shoot out towards me. My body recognizes him before I do, sways towards him but as it does, my stomach erupts, spurting vomit out over his shoes. I try to apologize but the next wave surges up. Again and again I retch, sick pooling on the grass around our feet, thick and pale first, then hot, clear-green liquid, stinging-sour. Rory holds me throughout. 'You're all right, Jo,' he says. 'You're all right.'

Oh, but I'm not.

When the heaving stops he places a handkerchief into my shaking hands and I wipe my mouth. I try to speak but my lips won't move and when I step away from him in an effort to stand on my own, the world comes rushing in through my ears, spinning me round, dragging me down into a vortex of black. Rory O'Donovan takes hold of me and I sag, let unconsciousness carry me off.

2

It feels like hours later when I wake. I am in bed, between two sheets, blankets pressing down on me like hands, wool making my nose prickle. Above me, on the ceiling, strips of timber make a design of squares. My old bedroom. My eyes track the pattern of wood on the ceiling in the old way, and for a moment I am a child again, trapped in the dark with the night-monsters. The adult me shivers and I turn onto my side, pulling the blankets close.

Two windows extend from the floor to the low, sloped ceiling. Their green blinds are closed but I know exactly what's out there behind them: our back garden, a long lawn, some outbuildings, a small fence. Then a stretch of grass that turns to marram leading onto sand dunes and then, the sea.

The sea. I listen for its pounding swoosh and there it is, as it always was, the backing track to my childhood. Mrs D. fought an unending battle against its encroachments. She hated the sand that clung to our skin and our hair, to the linoleum and carpets, to the end of the bath after we let out the water. She hated the searing salt wind that spattered our windows with stains and scoured paint off doors and window frames. Her voice was forever raised in high complaint about it all: 'Am I the only one who sees the dirt? Does nobody else in this house have a pair of eyes on them, a pair of hands?' The sea didn't care. On it went, forwards and back, raising its volume whenever we opened a window or door; smashing against the shore like an angry god in winter; in summer sending glitter-blue invitations to us to come out and play.

Every day, summer and winter, Granny Peg and Auntie Nora swam in the sea. 'It does Nora good,' Gran used to say. 'Nothing better for a body.' It was true that Auntie Nora always seemed more cheerful, less impaired, out of the house, out of her clothes, with her white swimming hat making a bulb of her head. So did Gran. Sometimes I would swim with them or go along to watch. The two of them would run their girlish run across the sand together then wade out, stopping to dip a hand in the shallows to make the sign of the cross. Once waist deep, they would dive together into an oncoming wave. Sitting on the grassy bank I'd watch the two disembodied heads bobbing above the waves and wonder whether Auntie Nora talked to Gran while they were out there, away from Mother and the rest of us.

Once I asked. 'Does Auntie Nora talk to you when you're on your own together, Gran?'

'Sometimes she does, pet. But not that often.'

'Why doesn't she talk more?'

'Because she can't.'

'Mammy says she's well able to talk if she wanted to.'

'No, no, that's not right. If she could, she would.'

A door is opened downstairs and a yell of laughter reaches my ears. The funeral. No doubt the drink is flowing by now, the *craic* flying, the cheap sentiment oozing. I am grateful for the queasiness that allows me to lie here and avoid it. Twenty years on, and they all seem just the same.

We've been hearing reports in San Francisco about a new Ireland and anyone I met on my journey from Dublin to Wexford wanted to talk about it. The advertising hoardings in the airport, the Irish newspapers I bought for the journey, the taxi driver: all sang this hymn of change. Dublin now has cappuccino coffee-houses and designer boutiques, theme pubs and five-star hotels, private schools and soaraway property prices. They've even had to bring in brickies from England to cope with the building boom, a man told me on the train. But I can see that the place hasn't changed, not as much as it thinks it has. The high-tech multinationals, the suburban estates, the little motorways, the out-of-town shopping malls are a touch-up, not a transformation. Beside them sit the thick bungalows and farmhouses and cottages, with their squinting, calculating windows. Grasping, grudging, judging. Still.

Everything that drove me away is still here, in this village, in this house. I can feel it, crouching in the corners, watching and waiting. I shiver again, roll myself into a tight coil inside the bedcovers and let the rhythm of the waves carry me back to sleep.

'Jo. Jo! Can you hear me, Jo?' I am being summoned out of sleep. Nausea wakens with me. I want to abscond back to my dream but the voice won't let me. 'Jo? Are you awake?'

It is Maeve, standing at the end of the bed holding a tray. Tea and toast.

'I am now.'

'I'm sorry. I didn't know whether to wake you or not but you haven't eaten a thing all day.'

I try to sit up but my head feels like it is packed with gravel and I sink back into my pillows, closing my eyes again. She sets the tray on the locker, settles her small weight on the side of my mattress. 'I'm sorry,' she says again. 'Should I have let you sleep on? I didn't like to go to bed without checking you.'

'Bed? Is it bedtime?'

'It's early yet but I'm just shattered. Ria's getting ready to go off and I'm going to follow her as soon as I can.'

Go on, then, I want to say. Go. But she is telling me how she has spent the day, serving drinks and wine, lunch and snacks, tea and coffee. How she could never have managed it all without Eileen. (A reproach here that I ignore.) 'Now there are only the stragglers left,' she says. 'The tables are cleared away, the washing-up is done, the house is clean and tidy again. As soon as the last of them clear, I'm off. I've had it.'

I have nothing to say to any of this.

She sighs. 'So how are you feeling now?'

'I don't know, a bit woozy.'

'Has this happened before? Have you been sick in San Francisco?'

I shake my head.

'I rang Doctor Woods, asked him to drop by.'

'No need for that.'

'Just in case. He wanted me to drive you to the surgery but I persuaded him to make a house call. Tonight or first thing tomorrow, he said.'

She is slumped at the end of the bed, her head bent. 'You don't look too hot yourself,' I say.

'Thanks.'

'You know what I mean . . . It's been a tough few days for you.'

'Awful. The worst.' Her eyes well up. 'Jesus, I can't stop crying! I stop for a while and I think that's it, I'm all cried out, but the bloody tears are only gathering for the next flow. I never knew it was possible to cry so much.'

Which is better, I wonder, to cry too much when your mother dies or not to cry at all?

'I can't bear to think of her, in the kitchen, on her own . . . struggling to get to the phone . . .'

That's where Mrs D.'s heart attack had struck, early on Friday morning. The tears flow down Maeve's cheeks now, in sheets. I wonder at the way she can accept them, just let them fall. After she has blown her nose and dried her eyes, I say, as some sort of consolation: 'You were very good to her.'

She was. Our mother was seventy-six when she died, severely arthritic and chronically cranky, but Maeve had converted the garage of her Dublin home into a granny-flat so Mrs D. could spend protracted visits. Every year, she and Donal brought her away on their winter holiday, and at least one weekend out of every four, Maeve and Ria drove the hundred miles from Dublin to Mucknamore to visit her.

Which is better? To see too much of a disagreeable parent or not to see her at all?

'When Daddy died,' Maeve says, 'I had a lot of regrets. Whatever else, I didn't want that to happen this—'

Her hand flies to her mouth. 'Oh, God, Jo, I'm so sorry. I didn't mean . . .'

'It all right,' I say. 'I know you didn't.'

She looks so embarrassed. Does she really think a little gaffe like that makes any difference?

'Do me a favour,' I say. 'Lift the blinds, would you? I'd love to see the sea.'

The mattress shifts as she gets up to do it. She pulls the cord, first on one window, then the other. Evening sunshine slants across the pink carpet. 'Aren't the old sash windows lovely?' she says, opening one slightly. Fresh air trips in.

Outside, the tide is out. Over to our right, the setting sun throws streaks of orange and pink and red along the sky and the sea borrows and flaunts the colours like they are its own. Mucknamore in full seductive act. People are strolling on the beach and out along the Causeway, enjoying the dimming of the day.

The Causeway wasn't always there. When Gran was a child she knew old men and women who remembered when the only way out to Inisheen was by boat. She never started a story without referring to the Causeway. Instead of 'Once upon a time . . .' her story opening was: '*Fadó, fadó*, long, long ago, when the world was younger and the road to Inisheen lay under the water . . .' A gift from the sea, she called it, this sandbar of dunes now stabilized by sturdy grasses.

After a long time, Maeve speaks from the window. 'I have a favour to ask you,' she says.

'You have? Of me?'

What she wants ('needs, actually') is for me to stay here in Mucknamore for a while to sort our mother's business affairs.

Things are complicated. Mrs D. auctioned the house and business a few weeks ago but it failed to meet its reserve price. She since agreed a sale with a German couple – who have given up their jobs in Düsseldorf to move across – but Mrs D. died before contracts were finalized. All this, on top of the usual issues that arise after a death.

'I can't stay,' says Maeve. 'I just can't. Ria needs to get back to school and Donal is up to his eyes in work.'

'Whereas the spinster sister has no life worth speaking of?'

'Oh, come on, Jo,' she says.

Yes, Jo, come on. This is the first family duty you've been asked to cover in twenty years. You've never done *anything* for your mother or for the rest of us. Now you're needed and it's the least you can do. All of this my sister conveys to me in four short words. Such is the verbal shorthand of families.

'If you can't do it, I don't know how we'll manage,' she says. 'But before you decide, there's something you should know.'

'Go on.'

'Mammy's affairs are being handled by Rory O'Donovan.'

I guffaw.

'Really. He's been acting as her solicitor for months, apparently, ever since she started to seriously consider selling.'

She is looking out the window, not at me. 'He has the will,' she goes on. 'She has arranged for him to come here and read it to us both tomorrow.'

'But, Maeve—'

'I know. I was as surprised as you.'

'Mrs D.? Telling her business to an O'Donovan?'

Talking to an O'Donovan, for God's sake. Especially to Rory O'Donovan. To *Rory*! 'I don't believe it,' I say. 'I just don't believe it.'

'He's downstairs now,' she says. 'He's been there since he . . . since you . . . all afternoon. He wants to know, can he come up and see you before he goes?'

'No!' I say, almost shout. 'No way. Tell him I'm not well enough to see anybody.'

This reminds Maeve that she should be looking after me. 'Aren't you going to eat something?' she says, pointing at the tray.

I put my hand on the blanket over my queasy stomach and shake my head.

'At least have some tea. You have to have something.'

She comes over, pours me a cup of tea, adds just the right amount of milk and hands it to me. I wrap my fingers around the warmth of the cup. In my sour mouth, the tea tastes acrid but unexpectedly comforting. I try some toast. Again, surprisingly good.

Maeve sits on the bed again, closer this time. So close I can feel the tension humming in her, and – like everything else today – it brings me right back: I remember her circling Mrs D.'s moods, senses on full alert, seeking a gap through which she might enter to say the right thing. Usually she picked her moment with uncanny tact but not always. Not always.

I wonder how she remembers it all now. We gave up talking about the past years ago; we saw it all too differently. I take a second slice of toast and she pours me another cup of tea.

She says, 'There will be money, you know, once the place is sold.'

'I suppose.'

'It should be a fair few bob. Prices have gone mad in Wexford these last few years.'

I chew my toast, the noise loud in my ears.

'You should think about what you'll do with a lump sum like that, Jo. You'd lose a lot taking it back to the States, with the exchange rate the way it is.'

'Ever Ms Sensible,' I say with a smile, hoping to divert her.

'Really.'

'Thanks for the concern, Sis. I know you think I am doomed to a miserable old age because I haven't got a pension—'

'You can laugh now, Jo, but . . .'

I put my hand on her arm. 'Maeve, you don't need to say any more. *If* Mrs D. should leave me some money, and we both know that's a big if . . .'

'She wouldn't cut you out.'

'It doesn't matter to me if she does, Maeve.'

She shakes her head. 'She wouldn't do that,' she insists.

I give up.

She sits on my bed, twisting her marriage ring round and round its finger as I finish my toast. Then she blurts out the question I realize she has wanted to ask since she came in. 'Donal said not to ask you this, Jo, but I have to. Where were you?'

A longing for sleep suddenly settles on me like a sea mist. I want to let go, to sink into oblivion, avoid the coming confrontation. She says it lightly – 'Where were you?' – but she is rearing up for attack, even if she doesn't know it. In Maeve's world everything is well ordered and controlled and nobody is allowed to go AWOL, even if they are a continent away. I shrink into my pillows.

It comes slow and soft at first. 'She asked for you and asked for you, you know. So we tried, Jesus knows, Jo, we tried. We rang one of your so-called friends after another. We left a million messages on your damned answering machine.'

The sun has dropped below the horizon and the light outside is turning navy blue. You can tell just by looking that the heat is gone from the day. The last of the walkers are headed homeward in the dusk, their evening – an ordinary evening for them – setting in.

'Where were you, Jo?' my sister asks me again.

My silence is getting to her. It always does, though this time I am not trying to. I want her to let it go. I cannot understand this need of hers to hurt on Mrs D.'s behalf.

She starts to cry again. 'Jesus, Jo, would you answer me. Is an answer too much to ask?'

'Please, Maeve,' I say. 'Please. You're only upsetting yourself.'

She fishes out a well-used tissue from her sleeve but it is torn into flitters so she sits with it in her hand, looking up at me, her big wet brown eyes boring into me. I make my face blank, a sheet of glass that bounces her gaze right back. I have to, I have to . . .

After a long time she says, 'You've something missing in you, Jo, do you know that?'

'Probably.' I keep my tone even, pleasant. 'But you have enough for both of us, don't you?'

Her face colours, searing me with guilt. She picks up the tray – domestic reproof again – and walks towards the door. As she reaches it I call to her. 'Maeve?'

She turns, two hands on the tray, her foot in the door keeping it open.

'This business of reading Mrs D.'s will tomorrow . . .'

'Yes?'

'I won't be there.'

Even the thought of it makes me boil: Maeve and I sitting at the dining-room table while Rory sits across from us reading out our mother's requests and bequests. No, Mrs D., I'm not playing your little game, whatever it is.

'But, Jo, you have to . . . If you're not there, you can't—'

'I'm not going. You can tell me all about it afterwards if you want.'

'I really think—'

'Maeve, I'm not going.'

3

So where was I? When my mother was calling for me on her deathbed, where, oh where – the hell – was I? I told you, sister dear, I was out. O-U-T.

What would you say, Maeve, if you knew that I had heard the first words of the first message you left last Friday afternoon? If you knew that when the telephone rang, I was halfway out my front door and that, on hearing its *ring-ring*, I waited only long enough to hear the answering machine pick up the call, so I could hear who was calling? If you knew that as soon as I heard your voice, I thought, No, not my sister, not now. That I heard only, 'Hello, Jo, this is Maeve . . .' before closing the door on you?

I thought you were ringing with one of your little bulletins. A new carpet, maybe, or Ria's latest school report or another promotion for Donal. And of course the always-proffered, never-requested information at the end, lobbed in regardless: 'Mammy is well.' Or increasingly, lately: 'Mammy is not very well.' And that evening, Maeve, I couldn't bear it. I know how sour and unappreciative that sounds. I know how good it is of you to keep in touch but last Friday evening I had news of my own blistering my head. I was going out. Out to one of my favourite restaurants with my favourite friend, Deirdre, who was waiting to hear me, to help me if she could. You know Dee, Deirdre Mernagh, my friend since our schooldays in Wexford. Sometimes you ask about her since she moved out to San Francisco, trying to keep your voice light, not to let your disapproval show.

You object to Dee because you think she drinks too much alcohol, smokes too much dope, sleeps with too many men. And you are right. You think she and I are a bad influence on each other but Dee has a side that you've never seen, and since my friend Richard died she is the only person who can soothe me. That's what she was doing when you called me. Twenty minutes before your voice came through on my machine I had telephoned her in a panic, and, as always, she had known just the right things to say. I was to stop worrying, to stop planning, stop even *thinking*. She would leave work, I was to come and meet her and together we would sort out what I should do next.

So that's what I was doing when you rang, Maeve. Trying not to worry, not to plan, not to think, trying to get out of my apartment as quickly as possible. When the phone began to ring, I hovered in the doorway, waiting just long enough to make sure it wasn't Dee calling me back. Maeve can wait, I told myself, when I heard it was you.

I didn't know.

And if I had? If some premonition had made me wait for your next words ('I have some bad news for you . . .'), if I had run to pick up the phone, if I had telephoned you back later that evening or the following morning? I might have got back to Ireland on Saturday instead of Monday. I might have been there *in time.*

But in time for what? I ask myself, I ask you. To visit the hospital and be confronted with a new Mrs D.: twenty years older, weak and wretched, fatally ill. To snatch a few words from her, maybe even say something myself, then watch her die. What difference would that make? Really. I am not being facetious; I would like an answer. What difference, do you think? I know how you imagine the scene: our mother looking up to see you ushering me in the door, meaningful looks passing between us all, clasping of hands, forgiveness all round. Then, reconciliation complete, you and I together watching her die, smiles and tears ushering her out of the world.

No, Maeve. No words, not even deathbed words, are that strong. Too much had and hadn't happened between Mrs D. and me. Too much was left to curdle for far too long. No last words could hold the weight of it all.

No. It was better the way it happened.

But wait, my sister would say, if I ever offered her this account (which I almost certainly never will). Wait. You've explained why you didn't return the first call but what about the other four? One from Mucknamore later that Friday night. Two more on Saturday. Another on Sunday morning. How could two full days have expired between the first telephone call and my eventual response?

She would point out, she who knows this side of me so well, that I still haven't answered her question. Exasperated by my evasiveness and determined not to be fobbed off (so wholeheartedly did she believe she had a right, a *duty* on Mother's behalf, to know, to find out, to set the record straight), she would no doubt pose her question again. Where were you, Jo?

Last Friday in San Francisco. For the first day in a while, the fog stays off and the temperature's up. At the time I am walking to meet Dee, the sky is fading from blue to purple and lights are springing on here and there. I walk along sidewalks that throb with the heat of a long sunny day, through air thickening with the smell of food.

We meet at our usual table outside Benton's, order our usual pasta bowls – the linguini for me, cannelloni for her – and a bottle of our favourite Nobile. The waiter brings the wine, pours a little for Deirdre to taste and when she pronounces it agreeable, fills a glass for me. I do not protest. 'To decisions,' she says as we clink our glasses. I sip.

So we talk about decisions, our heads leaning towards each other over the food. Dee won't let me indulge in regrets or self-recrimination. It's the main reason I love her: her placid acceptance of (my) human frailty. We don't mention the last time, because she knows, without being told, that this time is different. She knows how I see the events of my past: like stones used to cross a river, each unconnected to the other. What we talk about is my options now. Up and down, we turn the horrible facts around; in out and back again, until I am drained, until going around it all again is futile.

'Enough,' she says then, and she calls for a second bottle of wine. As she refills our glasses, we set talk aside, begin to take in our surroundings. Two men stroll past our table, arm in arm, identically dressed: red leather miniskirts and black leather jackets, fishnet tights and shaven heads. Deirdre wolf whistles and one of them blows her a kiss. We give ourselves over to people-watching and on Valencia Corridor that night there is plenty to watch. The summer spirit rises in us to accord with the rest of the world.

Somewhere down the second bottle of wine, the dead weight of my dilemma seems to dissolve. It will be all right, I think, as I smile a hazy smile on my friend, the waiter, the chrome table, the passers-by. I relish this drunken feeling, that seems almost like happiness, but even as I stretch towards it, I can feel it sliding away from me, turning into something else. And I can tell from the way Deirdre drains her glass, throwing back her head to do it, that she is on a parallel path. We are winding up to a Mrs Mernagh and Mrs Devereux night.

'Mrs Mernagh' and 'Mrs Devereux' are our alter egos: two wild and raucous women who kick into action once a sufficient quantity of alcohol has been imbibed. They do things Deirdre and Jo never do any more. Smoke. Heckle. Cackle. Pick up men. They perform, for each other, and for lookers-on. It's a routine that dates back to our teenage years in Ireland when we first discovered alcohol and the licence it gave us to misbehave. In a flourish that seemed wildly witty to us at that time, we gave the rowdy strangers who emerged when we were drunk the names of the least rowdy people we knew: our mothers.

The morning after a Mrs Mernagh and Mrs Devereux night is always a post-mortem of cringing hilarity at the antics we/they got up to: 'Remember when you . . . ?'; 'Oh my God, I didn't, did I? But you were as bad. Remember . . . ?'

It's a routine.

And if it's a routine that long ago grew stale, it's still easy, now tonight, to slip back into it. It's only a laugh, I tell myself, as we welter through another glass of wine. A bit of *craic*. A diversion. And if it's not as diverting as it used to be, if I can hear the forced note in my laughter – and am afraid to ask Deirdre if she hears it too – still it has all the comforting inevitability of a habit.

By midnight we have left talk far behind and are flinging ourselves around an almost empty dance floor at our favourite club, Araby's, singing along to Abba remixes. It's a posture, a preliminary to the main act of the evening: landing a man. We have already chosen our targets; they sit over their drinks at our regular table, in the corner among our regular crowd. Mine is Paul, a bulky guy with longish black hair (I love long hair on a man, always have). Deirdre's is Steve, newly divorced, and already involved with her in a more-off-than-on affair. Both are watching us cavort around the floor. We watch them too, but stealthily, as we twist and turn and gyrate on the dance floor, pretending to only have eyes for each other and our own good time, pretending we are not on show.

By one o'clock, we both have our arms wrapped round our quarry. Paul has a thick back and strong limbs: he feels substantial. He asks me what I work at. I pull back, look into his face to deliver my deadpan answer. 'I'm in the sex business,' I say.

I love that line. I always use it in this situation, when I have just met a man, and I assess him by how he reacts. Most are startled to silence. I love to watch them look at me hard, with new eyes. To observe their simultaneous, contrary pulls: fascination, repulsion. And as I watch them, I judge.

It's all there now, in this guy Paul's face. He pulls away from me a little, peers into my eyes. '*Really?*' he asks.

'Really.'

Silence. After a while he says: 'You don't look like someone "in the sex business", as you call it.'

'Why? Is there a look?'

He grins. 'I think so.'

'What? Big breasts, blonde hair, plastic face?'

'Something like that, yeah.'

'That's just a stereotype,' I say.

'I guess it is. Still . . .'

'Still . . . what? I don't look sexy enough?'

'Honey, not that . . . Definitely not that.'

'What, then?'

'It's just . . . Oh hell . . .'

We laugh at his tangle but behind the amusement, I can see his brain is fizzing through the options: prostitute? stripper? lap-dancer? telephone-sex operator? 'glamour' model? porn actress? Like me, he has had too much to drink. Unlike me, his thoughts slide across his face, clear to read.

'Come on, tell me,' he says. 'What is it you do?'

'Can't you guess?' I tease.

'No way,' he laughs. 'Uh-uh. I'm not guessing.'

I laugh again and I relent. My corner of the sex market, I tell him, is advice. I am Sue D'Enim. *Sue D'Enim Solves Your Sex Problems*. Read by millions of glossy-magazine readers all over the States and in Canada, Britain, South Africa and Australia too. *Sue D'Enim: the Sexpert with Sizzle*.

When I tell people what I do, the question they always ask is, 'Aren't those letters made up?' The answer is: no. Every month hundreds of dispatches arrive on my desk or into my email inbox, all hoping to be granted a place on the page, their problem aired, shared and answered.

Dear Sue, *Nobody has ever loved me . . .*

Dear Sue, *My genitals are so ugly I could never let any man see them . . .*

Dear Sue, *My boyfriend raped me last night . . .*

Dear Sue, *My penis is too small to satisfy a woman . . .* (yes, men write too)

Dear Sue, *I like to be whipped until my skin breaks . . .*

Dear Sue, *I'm crying as I write this letter . . .*

It's a non-job, I know that. I don't flatter myself that I solve these people's troubles. My value is simply in prodding them to sit down and write out their dilemma. In order to write, they have to put some order on their chaos, define it to themselves. And when I question whether that small benefit justifies the easy and ample living I make from their distress, I console myself by asking, who does heal the troubles of the world? Psychologists? Psychiatrists? New-age therapists? At least I do not fool myself.

I am a stranger, not an aunt; a hack, not a healer. I take pain and shape it into reading matter. *Sue D'Enim: Fraud.*

He starts to kiss me during the third track when I lean back my head in invitation. There was a time when I used to enjoy the preliminaries, the chit-chat and hold-off, the let's-get-to-know-each-other-first, but somewhere along the line of my life, cutting direct to the physical came to seem more honest.

I love first kisses, the soft small movements of lips learning about each other, the smell and taste of new mouth. I lean my body into his, feeling his arms close around me. His skin is slightly damp under his shirt. The kiss deepens, to the bone under the flesh, to the muscle of tongue. I reach up and touch his hair. When the slow set fades, the lights come up and the thump of dance music resumes. We pull apart, our breath thick with the taste of each other.

I say, 'Let's get out of here.'

His eyes, heavy from our embrace, spring open. A sliver of hesitation. It has been two, maybe three, minutes since we started kissing.

Then he smiles. 'Yeah, OK,' he says. 'Why not?'

Deirdre, still wrapped around Steve as if the music has not

upped its tempo, gives me a thumbs-up behind his back, happy to be abandoned. So I get my bag, say goodnight, walk out into the night hand in hand with my man, my booty.

'Where should we go?' he asks.

'Your place,' I say, my voice crisp.

'I'm out in Rockridge.'

'That's OK.'

'Where are you?'

'Haight.'

'Five miles closer.'

'No,' I say. 'That's not what I want.'

He looks like he might argue but then shrugs. 'OK.'

He hails a cab and when it stops, he gives the driver his address. We sit into the yellow car, in the back, side by side. 'Are you always so . . . certain?' he asks, as the cab pulls away. He means bossy.

'You need to know what you want in life,' I say. 'Otherwise you end up with something else.'

All this self-assurance is a lie, of course, a mask. I no longer treat each new encounter with a man as a potential beginning, especially not a nightclubbing, drink-fuelled encounter. He doesn't like it. He gathers himself into himself, tight inside his jacket. No arm around me now, no hand towards my hand, no further attempt at conversation. I sit beside him, awkward in the chill. I have misjudged again: he wants the sexual transaction on his terms, thinks he likes a woman to be assertive but doesn't, not really.

Or maybe it's just me? Maybe he just doesn't fancy me now that he sees me in the glare of the streetlights that are whipping past us (now that 'Mrs Devereux' is fading and Jo re-emerging)? This is not going to be good, I realize. I should cut my losses and go home. But I can't. Tonight I just cannot face my too-empty flat and my too-full head. I need diversion, distraction, human contact. I let the cab drive on.

His apartment is a mess, strewn with dirty clothes and dishes. He makes a perfunctory offer of coffee, which I decline. We move straight to the bedroom. Within seconds, he is fumbling at my clothes and regret is seeping through me. The only way I am going to make anything of this encounter is if I can slow him down, give myself time to relax into the physical, but already he is pulling my top out of the waistband of my trousers, slipping his hands inside, skimming his palms up and down my bare skin.

I close my eyes, reach for a response within myself, but he gives me no time. Before I can settle into my feelings, his hands are gone, darting behind my back to open my bra, then round front to squeeze my breasts, then lifting off me to unbutton his own shirt. I open my eyes, thinking to protest, expecting to see arrogance there, a we'll-see-who's-in-charge-now expression on his face. Instead, he floors me with a grin. An eager grin, excited and a little shy, expectant as a small boy. No poses, no defences, now sex is imminent, and no doubt but that I am equally thrilled by the prospect.

I should probably find this certainty offensive but instead I am touched. I should probably take him to task, holler at him to slow down, rail at him as a selfish, useless lover but I can't. Smiling back at him, I slip out of my clothes.

Sue D'Enim would not approve. Proper sexual attention is my due in this encounter, she would say. Insist on a pleasurable outcome for you as well as him. If he doesn't know how, show him. And Sue is right, I know she's right. So what am I doing spreading myself naked on this stranger's bed, pretending he's doing just fine when he isn't? Why am I careful to lie on his pillow with one knee bent upwards, a position I know to be the most flattering to my ageing body, flattening the wad of fat that rings my abdomen? We women deserve everything we (don't) get.

His chest is hairless, smooth as my own. Like me, he is past the age of looking better with his clothes off: a small beer belly strains the waistband of his blue-stripe boxer shorts. He drops them, revealing a short penis, thick and erect. Lying down beside me, he starts to kiss me again and in moments he is leaning over me, expecting entry. Again I am gripped by the urge to call a halt, to start again. But start where? Back at the nightclub? When I refused coffee? When we started kissing in earnest? Whenever, it is too late now. I open my legs to him.

Propping himself up on his elbows so that we touch only at the hips, he begins. It isn't lovemaking, or even what I hoped for when we got together in the nightclub, sexual intercourse. No, he is the fucker and I am the fuckee. Slow at first, then faster and faster he goes, ever more oblivious to the human being under him, until he comes with a smothered groan. He lets his arms go then and he slumps down onto my body, but not for long. Consciousness returning, he rolls off me.

I meet his eyes and see *that* look: surprise at his own need, now it is spent. 'That was great,' he says. His distaste is pointed in the same direction as mine: at me.

He lifts the duvet. To climb underneath it, into the hollow where he sleeps each night, feels more intimate than taking him into my body. He doesn't want me here, I don't want to be here. But it is late and I am tired. To leave, I would have to engage him in conversation, get up and dressed, organize and wait for a cab, drive all the way back to the city. And my alcohol-drenched brain is throbbing, a hangover starting before I've even sobered up. Red wine, always the same. So lethargy wins. I slip between his sheets, pull his covers over me.

After a few moments, he says 'Are you asleep?' I don't answer and he turns to the wall. After a while, I am.

And next day, when I have extricated myself and made my way back home, I open my apartment door to the red number of the answering machine winking at me: 3–3–3. Three messages now. I groan. I feel pummelled, like I've been on the receiving end of a fist-fight, too bruised to consider communication with anyone, never mind Maeve. So I let the messages lie and turn down the telephone and answer machine so any further calls won't ring through. In the kitchen I pour myself a large glass of water from the fridge and swig it down without stopping. Cold and clear, it slushes around my empty stomach. A second glassful in hand, I head for bed. My own dear, clean, soft, white, female bed.

During the rest of the day, I wake only for short moments and never completely, just enough to be surprised by the quality of my sleep before drifting back. As the day goes on, dreams begin to kick in and it is a dream that finally jerks me awake: I am walking down some grey concrete steps leading into a cellar when the handrail I am leaning on snaps and I tumble forward into the dark. I wake at the moment of impact, find I am sitting upright, my heart pumping like a cornered animal's.

It's hours since I took to my bed and it's almost dark again, yet I feel like I haven't slept at all: my brain is a ratchet, screwed too tight. Dehydration is the culprit, I know. I must get up, get out, refill my water glass.

In the bathroom, I resist the medicine cabinet and instead brush my teeth, gargle with mouthwash. The bright lights treat me to a full-frontal of my almost thirty-eight-year-old face. Around the eyes is where my age shows worst but I can see other ghosts of my future haunting the mirror today: crinkles near the mouth, slackness beneath the chin, little hairs that need tweezing at the corner of my upper lip. My face is a clock, marking time. Today, I hate it.

I am heading for forty. I'm supposed to have matured by now, acquired wisdom through experience, knowledge through reflection, equilibrium through adversity. All I feel is older. Older but as weightless as ever, like an empty wine sack that's drying out.

He shouldn't matter, Paul, that nothing man from last night. A small man, I tell myself; selfish, inattentive, weak. And a lousy lover, ha! But the jibe just makes me feel worse. If the sex was lousy – and it was – then it says as much about me as him. I know we get the sex – and the love and the life – that we accept. I am Sue D'Enim, after all.

I am Sue D'Enim. I make my living from writing but I am no writer. *You want to be a writer? So write.* That's what Richard used to say. He made it sound so simple and when he was here, with me, that's how it felt: never easy but simple. *Write. Just write.* I wrote. I filled notebooks with words and plans. I had ideas. I was moving towards something, I could feel it. But now Richard is gone and I am like a clock that's wound down. I have no writing, no man, no child, nothing that I thought I'd have by now. No child. Yes, there's the rub. But forget it. Forget . . .

The pain is fear, I know, fear beating its black throb-throb-throb around my edges, hoping to thump its way in. I waggle my head, trying to shake it loose. I should eat, I should do a hundred things that might be good for me, but instead I refill my water glass and hobble back to bed.

Saturday night into early Sunday is the worst. When the hangover tide pulls out exposing the other pain. I close myself to it but it is determined. If I am not vigilant, it will surface. I am frightened. I need help. I can't continue to fight it alone.

But I am alone. If it wins, nobody will know. It could be days, weeks, before I am missed. Not until I fail to return enough phone calls or miss my next deadline (three whole weeks away) would anybody notice. Eventually, somebody – Deirdre maybe, or Gary, or maybe even Lauren, my editor – might grow anxious and come round here to check. The police will be called and when they fail to gain entry, they will have to break in. Once inside, their eyes will fasten onto my closed bedroom door and wordlessly, they will move across to open it . . .

These are the kind of thoughts you have when you lie awake in the night, looking into the dark with open eyes. The kind of thoughts that drive you from the bed. I throw aside the duvet, put shaky bare feet to the rug. If I could fix myself a drink I'd feel better, if I could untwist a bottle top, hear the glug of liquid pouring into a glass, loud and comforting in the silent night, might it settle me? No. No. No. A drink (*a* drink?) would only make things worse. For me, alcohol is never what it pretends to be: a nice ice-tinkling treat. Anyway, all the booze is gone. Last week I poured it down the kitchen sink: three bottles of red wine, two of white; half a bottle of vodka, one of gin, one and a half of Scotch, nine bottles of beer. The kitchen smelled like a bar for hours afterwards.

Around my four small rooms I pad, barefoot, unable to settle: into the spare bedroom, neat and cold, and back out again; into the kitchen where I open the refrigerator and close it; out into the hallway. Beside the telephone, the little red message-light of my answering machine flashes at me: 5 now. 5–5–5. I press the play button, turn the volume back up and stand and wait, my forehead leaning against the door frame. I wait through a long whirr of rewinding tape, to hear who has been calling me, and why.

4

'Well, would you look at her!' Rory O'Donovan has just walked into my Mucknamore bedroom and is standing at the end of my bed. Despite myself, a smile breaks in me at the words. That phrase belonged to a guy we knew in university. In those days, we used to amuse ourselves by picking over the verbal quirks of our classmates and friends, playing them back for each other. Now his joke is on our junior selves.

'So howzit goin?' he says, pulling up a chair to sit down.

I give him the old reply: 'Howzit goin yourself?'

'Basically . . . I think, like . . . as I asked you first, like . . . that the question is over to you . . . basically . . .'

I groan when I recognize that one. 'Oh, no! Stickie Martin. Poor old Stickie. Do you ever see him?'

He shakes his head. Our eyes meet. Together, we burst out laughing.

'So, Dev,' he says, dropping the mimicry and using his old name for me. 'What's going on? Why are you receiving visitors in bed, like some sort of courtesan? You don't look sick to me.'

I am struck again by the newness of him, the short hair that makes him look unfinished. He sits down on the chair that Maeve has left beside the bed. In his right hand he holds a white envelope.

'Don't think I don't know what you're up to,' he continues. 'Lying low, avoiding the mob. Avoiding me too, you brat.'

He sounds so Irish to my ears now, a strong streak of Wexford in his accent: the nasal vowels, the singing rise and fall to his sentences but of course it's not his speech that's changed, but mine.

'So,' I say. 'You came back to live in Mucknamore?'

'Yup.'

'That must be exciting.'

'No need to sneer, city girl. It's a good place to live.'

'Really?'

'Really.'

I raise my brows into a question.

'Really,' he says. 'I like that it takes me only thirty traffic-free minutes to get to work. That my nice big house cost half-nothing compared to a similar place in the city. That after work I can go walking in clean air or swimming in a clean sea. That I drink in a pub where everybody knows me.'

'Stop,' I say. 'You're scaring me.'

He laughs, then waves towards the window. 'Look at it. Look at how lovely it is. Even you must admit that.'

It is lovely. The swell of Inisheen island against the horizon, the waves surging around the curve of the Causeway, the sands glistening with sea foam and above it all the seabirds circling high, flashing silver underwings in the morning light. 'When did you ever care about scenery?' I say.

He shrugs. 'People change.'

I feel stifled. His bulk is too near me in the bedside chair. I can see the shape of his thighs straining against his trousers.

'Maybe not you?' He leans into me. 'You don't seem to have changed a bit.'

'Of course I have.'

'You look the same. So much the same. I was surprised by that.'

'I'm twenty years different, Rory. Just like you.'

'Twenty years.' He lets out a long whistle. 'Is that what it is?'

Twenty years and seven days, I think but do not say.

'And you're happy over there? You like it?'

'Sure. I like that I'm surrounded by millions of people. That my two-roomed apartment is worth a ludicrous amount of money that keeps on rising. That I can choose from a hundred bars where *nobody* knows me.'

He tosses his head back into a laugh, his way. It's all the same: the crinkles round his eyes, the missing tooth that only shows when his lips stretch into a smile. He says: 'See. I was right, you haven't changed a bit.'

When I was a girl, I had one thing that was all mine: a secret. A secret into which I poured everything. A boy.

He lived up the road from me but we were not allowed to talk to each other, though I knew his name and he knew mine. He didn't go to the local school, my school; each morning his eldest sister brought him into Wexford town in her blue Mini on her way to work. He never came into our shop and I never walked up the side road that led to his family's farm. If he, or any of his family, met me or any of my family, our heads turned from each other.

I knew he was never given instructions in how to do this or why. I knew that, like me, he was born to it.

Outside school hours, I saw him often. We never spoke to each other, not even hello. All we did was look. When I would sneak my veiled glance towards him, across the road or the church or the beach, I often found him looking back. We would get locked in these stares but never for long; we were both too afraid of being noticed. And anyway too shy: a few seconds so intense they nearly hurt, then we had to twist our eyes away. But it was enough. While we were fastened onto each other like that, time changed its shape and those seconds leaked into all the other moments we'd had before.

At night in bed I would summon up in my mind our most recent encounter and run it through my head like a movie, milking it for every detail: what he wore, how he looked, where it happened, how I felt. Memory and anticipation carried me through from one sighting to the next.

Our connection was a secret and not just from our families. Boys and girls never mixed in those days in Mucknamore, not even brothers and sisters. I had no time for other boys, with their bruised legs and dirty hands and slow minds. Boys who always had to be in a group, jostling or jeering or running about, yelling and waving their arms. Shooting each other from behind trees with sticks: 'You're dead, I killed you.' Or punching each other for real: 'I'll kill you, I'll bloody kill you.' Giving each other cut lips and bloody noses then days later giving each other mock punches to say they were friends again. Those boys could never do what he did: walk down the road alone. He was different. Like me.

He became an altar boy and every Sunday I got to watch him following the priest around and performing his holy chores: bowing low, ringing his little bell, bringing up the water and wine, reclining on the altar steps with his good shoes and grey socks jutting from beneath his surplice, showing a line of bare shin above.

Holy communion became the high point of my week. I lived for those few seconds when I knelt at the altar, letting out my tongue for the host, knowing his hand was beneath my chin, his white surplice level with my face, close enough to kiss. As the sacrament approached, anticipation rose in me, trembling. Sometimes, my hands shook so bad, I had to sit on them.

How did Mrs D. or Gran or Auntie Nora or especially Maeve not notice, standing and sitting and kneeling so close to me? How could so much intensity have been contained by my skin?

Once, I broke the unspoken rule at home and asked about the O'Donovans, asked why the two families were estranged.

Daddy said, 'Aw, that old *scéal*. Ask your mammy.'

Mrs D. said: 'I'm up to my eyes, child. Will you don't be bothering me?'

Granny Peg said, 'Ah now, pet, don't go digging up all of that. You'll only upset your mammy. And your Auntie Nora. You don't want to upset Auntie Nora, do you?'

Auntie Nora was the key, I knew that. Miss Nora O'Donovan: his aunt really, not mine. His aunt, living with us. And like us, never ever talking to them.

*

And now his eyes are almost forty years old, like mine. And they are bouncing all over me, like they can't get enough of what they are seeing, a look that stirs feelings I don't want to have.

'How on earth,' I ask him, 'did you end up with my mother as a client?'

'You were surprised?'

'Stupefied.'

'I knew you would be.'

'But how did it happen?'

'It began six years ago, when I moved back to Mucknamore. If I was going to be living here, I decided I couldn't carry on avoiding this place. Most of the lads I get on with drink here and anyway, the whole quarrel had come to seem so stupid and pointless. So I gathered up my courage and one early evening after work, when I thought the place wouldn't be too busy, I took myself in for a drink.'

'Wow!'

'After taking the big step, she wasn't even there herself. Eileen Power was behind the counter. I asked her for a pint and she looked at me boggle-eyed, she didn't know what to do. "Excuse me one sec," she said, and she scuttled off to find your mother, leaving me standing there like a right eejit. Three or four others were in, delighted with the goings-on, on the edge of their stools to see what was going to happen next.'

I raise my eyes towards the ceiling. This is just why I left this place.

'I know. The situation was funny but I was nervous too. I thought she might make a fool of me. You know your mother . . .'

'Few would have braved it.'

'To tell you the truth, only everyone was watching, I think I'd have run out at that stage. Anyway, after what seemed like a day and a half, out she came, with Eileen running behind her. "Can I help you?" she said in her best frosty voice, and I knew then it was going to be all right because I could see that underneath the frost she was well flustered herself. “A pint of Guinness, please, Mrs Devereux,” I said. She stood there a minute. Everybody was watching. When she picked up a glass and pulled the tap, it was like the whole place let out its breath.’

‘And that was it?’

‘That was it. I’ve been a regular ever since. I even get – got – a Christmas drink. I even,’ he says, looking across at me, ‘became fond of her.’

I groan.

‘Ah, Dev, her bark was worse than her bite.’

‘Don’t *you* start.’ I never try to make anyone else see Mrs D. my way. Why do they all feel the need to exhort me? ‘What about your own folks?’ I ask. ‘They can’t have been too delighted to see you tippling in the enemy camp?’

‘I didn’t tell them at first. I knew it wouldn’t take long for it to get out. My father was given the job of tackling me. “I hear you’ve been seen in Devereux’s,” was what he said to me, as if it was a brothel or something. I just laughed, said the old feud had nothing to do with me, that what was past was past.’

‘That simple, eh?’

‘What could he say, if you think about it?’

A familiar feeling coils inside me, deep and cold.

‘So . . . A happy ending all round,’ I say. ‘How moving.’

He knows what I mean. That it could be that easy, after all they put us through. That he could just say, what’s past is past and, miraculously, it was.

He leans forward in the chair. ‘I often wondered how things turned out for you, Dev, but I never got the nerve to ask your mother. Our association – hers and mine – was very much on her terms.’

‘That sounds like Mrs D. all right.’

‘So I never asked. But I often wondered,’ he repeats, his voice soft. He leans in close to me, picks up a strand of my hair. ‘You never changed it,’ he says. ‘When you made your grand entrance into the church yesterday that was the first thing I thought: she never changed the hair.'

He tugs the curl straight, then winds it around his finger. I let him, but only for a second, before jerking my head away, pulling my hair back behind my shoulders.

'You have your own law firm, Maeve tells me,' I say, briskly.

'Yeah. I bought out old McBride's practice in Wexford when he retired.'

'So you live in Mucknamore and drive to town every day, is that it?'

'It only takes half an hour.'

'You live alone?' I ask, knowing the answer.

'No.' He tries not to hesitate. 'No. I got married nine years ago.'

Yes, Maeve had also told me that. I had a follow-up line prepared but my brain has decided to evacuate. Silence lengthens and loads. It is he who breaks it. 'We have two children,' he says.

'Two? That's lovely.' Oh, God, I think, is that the best you can do? *That's lovely*?

'Boys?' I manage after a while. 'Or . . . em . . . girls?'

'One of each. Ella, the elder one, is five. Dara is four.' His face is expanding with that look parents wear when they talk about their children.

'And your wife, is she from round here? Would I know her?'

'No. She's from Cork.'

'So you've done it all,' I say. 'Wife, kids, law practice in town, big house in the country.'

'I've been lucky, I suppose.'

Doesn't he remember us saying we never wanted all that? Maybe he is right, maybe I haven't changed as much as he has. Since my arrival in Mucknamore yesterday morning, I've been feeling and behaving like a gauche adolescent. *I am not normally like this!* I want to scream at him. I am a syndicated magazine writer! I have a des. res. in Lower Haight! Sometimes people ask for my autograph!

'What about you?' he wants to know. 'Are you married?'

'No.'

I don't elaborate. Anything I might say would sound defensive.

'So,' he says, his turn to change the subject. 'Do you know why I'm here this morning?'

'The will, I suppose.'

'Yes, the will.'

'Rory, I've already explained to Maeve. I don't give a fiddler's about—'

He holds up his hand to stop me. 'I know that, Dev. We all know that. Just listen for a second. Your mother had a premonition of her death. She said to me in January, "I'm not long for this world. I won't last the year." I just laughed it off, the way you do, but she started making plans for you and Maeve and she hired me to carry them out. So this is business. And this,' he says, reaching across to hand me the envelope he has been holding, 'is for you.'

A white A4 envelope with my name written on the outside in blue ink: Siobhán. My given, christened name, the name that only Mrs D. uses. Her handwriting, still small and neat and tight as print. At the centre, between the folds of paper: something hard.

'Don't open the letter yet,' he says, getting up. 'I've something else you have to be given first. Wait here.'

He goes out of the room and returns immediately, carrying a battered stiff-sided blue suitcase. I recognize it immediately. Six times a year, it would be filled with blankets and sheets, uniforms and games kit and driven with me from Mucknamore to my convent boarding school or back. Maeve had a similar one in red.

He heaves it onto the bed where it lands at my feet with a bounce. 'It's heavy,' he says. 'I'm always surprised by how heavy paper is.'

'Paper?'

'It's full of documents. Family papers, photographs, newspaper cuttings, that sort of thing.'

'Have you seen them?'

'No. It's locked. That's the key you've got in that sealed envelope there. You are the only one who is to have access.'

'Why?'

'I don't know. I'm just following instructions. I was to make sure to give this to you myself and I was to tell you that the contents are for your eyes only, nobody else's. She was very clear about that.'

I shake my head. 'What was she up to?'

'I honestly don't know,' he says. 'Apart from the fact that it meant meeting up with you' – that grin again – 'I treated it as if she was just another client. I've had stranger requests.'

'Why was she so certain I would be back for her funeral?'

'If you didn't come, I was to get your address from Maeve and bring the suitcase and the letter over to you in San Francisco. Make sure to put it into your hand myself.'

I imagine myself in my apartment, answering my buzzer one ordinary day and hearing Rory O'Donovan's voice coming through the speaker at me. What the hell was Mrs D. playing at? 'You can take it back,' I say. 'I don't want it.'

'Ah, Dev . . .'

'Family papers. Can't you just imagine? Uncle Barney the IRA hero. Fianna Fáil the fabulous. A dose of crap from start to finish. What would I want with any of it?'

He falls silent. Though I'm annoyed by Mrs D. and her schemes, mostly I am thinking about him, about how quickly the newness of him is passing. Already, his features are settling into something familiar. On impulse, I decide to tell him what I have told nobody yet except Deirdre. 'Remember when you came in,' I say, 'and you remarked that I don't look sick?'

He nods.

'You were right, I'm not sick. Just vomiting all the time.'

He looks at me, blank. A woman would know immediately what I am trying to say.

'Especially in the mornings.'

Still vacant.

'Morning sickness.'

'Oh . . .' The message gets through. 'Oh. Oh my God, right. Yes. I see.' His brain winds slowly around all the implications. 'So that was why you threw up yesterday . . .'

'And fainted, yes. As pregnancies go, it's been pretty rough so far. I vomit about five times a day. Not usually on other people, though.'

Lost in a spiky silence, he doesn't smile. 'The father?' he asks.

'Nobody. He doesn't know.' Everything I say bumps against the past.

'Oh.'

I put a hand on my belly though there's nothing to feel there, not yet. The changes are in other parts of me: the chaotic stomach, the tender breasts, the tiredness that seeps every muscle and bone. This is about as far as it progressed, last time.

'I feel like that line of Oscar Wilde's that everybody's always misquoting,' I say. '"To conceive once, Ms Devereux, may be regarded as an accident but to conceive twice . . ."'

He is staring at me.

'Even if there is twenty years between the two,' I add.

I'm alone now, still in bed. Before Rory left he opened the envelope, took out the rust-spotted key and put it in my hand. That was an hour and a half ago, but still it sits in my palm and the suitcase lies where he left it on the bed. On the bedspread is a letter from Mrs D., four pages covered with her brittle handwriting.

For an hour and a half, I have sat like this: key in my hand, letter by my side, suitcase of papers at my feet. Resisting. I can't believe that I am here, where I thought I'd never be again: engaged in another showdown with my mother. And that once again, she's winning. I know there's no point in holding out. Curiosity will prevail; I might as well succumb sooner as later. So I pick up the letter again.

Dear Siobhán, A letter from beyond the grave . . .

God, what a typical Mrs D. phrase. I can't read it, I just can't. I'll open the case instead. I pull it towards me, insert the key. It rotates easily, as if the locks have recently been oiled: one twist in each and – click, click – the clasps snap open. Inside is a smell of convent yesterdays and stale paper. The case is crammed with all kinds of documents. Damn you, Mrs D., I think as I begin to rummage through, reluctantly at first, then greedily; through press cuttings and photographs from every period: stiff sepia Victorians and Edwardians, family snapshots and seaside postcards, heavy daguerreotypes and colourful prints, some mounted on card but otherwise in no order of date or size or person.

I find letters, packs of them tied with faded pink ribbon, others lying loose. I find fourteen big shop ledgers, used as diaries (author: Granny Peg) and sheaves of lined paper, close covered in black ink, tied with string (author: Auntie Nora). I find pamphlets and booklets and the words of old songs and poems and ballads. I find files of notes by Gran and her mother and dispatches from them to and from various officers of Mucknamore's IRA company.

After a long time sifting and probing, I pick up Mrs D.'s letter again. *Dear Siobhán . . .*

I always hated that name Siobhán. Shove-awn. So open to schoolgirl mockery: *Shove on, you! You're in my way . . . Shove on your knickers, your mammy's comin'.* Nobody has called me Siobhán for years, decades. I was under ten when I ditched that name, around the same time that I stopped calling my mother Mammy. Yes, under ten I remember, because Daddy was still living with us then. It was on him that I first tried out my alternative.

During term-time, he and I were always up earliest in our house. He had to be at his office desk in Wexford by nine, the same time as Mucknamore National School started. Because the shop didn't open until half-past ten, Mrs D. and Granny Peg would lie on. Everything about that quiet morning time with my father was special. I loved sitting on the closed seat of the toilet, watching him wash and shave. I loved the faces he pulled in the mirror: the way he would drag the skin down from below his eyes to look at the red squishy stuff underneath. Or stick his tongue out for an examination. Pink tongue was good, white made him groan, yellow was the worst.

His tongue was pink, the morning I told him about my name-change. Pink, with his mood to match. He was humming as he foamed up his face with the shaving brush, one of his favourites: Perry Como's *Hot dickety, dawg dickety, ooh what you do to me* . . . I spoke carefully to him all the same in case he wasn't in a talking mood.

'Daddy?'

'Mmmmm.'

'I've decided to change my name.'

'Have you now?'

He sloshed the brush in the water, turning it soapy, and picked up his razor. The blade scraped through the foam on his cheek leaving a skin-coloured track behind. He wasn't really listening to me.

'I don't like my own name.'

'Do you not?' He cocked his chin up for scraping. 'Since when?'

'Since always.'

A pause.

'I'm going to be called Jo from now on.'

'Joe? Isn't that a boy's name?'

'No. Jo, like short for Josephine. Or Joan.'

'The English version?'

'Yes, but I don't want to be Josephine or Joan. Just Jo.'

'Ah now. Do you want people to think you're trying to be a fella?'

'It is a girl's name, Daddy, it is. I got it from a book.' *Little Women*, where the sisters are fond and the mother never slaps and the heroine has a name as brisk and bouncy as herself: Jo.

Daddy pulled the plug. Foamy water gurgled. He turned on the cold tap and splashed handfuls of water onto his face.

'Jo. Hmmm, Jo.' He tried it out. He had a small smile on but now he was listening. 'I never knew a girl to be called Jo around here.'

'I know. I don't mind that.' One of the things in its favour, in fact. 'But isn't it a nice name, Daddy? Don't you like it?'

'It's not the worst, I suppose.'

I took the towel from the rail by the bath, put it into his hands. 'Does that mean you'll call me that, Daddy. Will you call me Jo? Will you?'

'We'll see. We'll see.' He dried his face, then flicked the towel at me with a grin. And I knew it was going to be OK, that he would do what I wanted if I kept at him.

He forgot at first, of course, but I made it more irritating for him to forget than to remember. Not just for him but for everybody in the house. After getting over her disappointment that I didn't like my name ('Your mother and I took so long over the picking of it') and my preference for Jo over the Irish version Siobhán ('Can't you hear the music in it? How can you not love those soft, Irish sounds?'), Gran gave in. Auntie Nora never called me anything anyway and everybody else I wore down in time. Even Maeve. Everybody, that is, except Mrs D. I was always Siobhán to my mother.

6th February 1995

Dear Siobhán,

A letter from beyond the grave, what do you think of that? I got one from your granny when she passed on so I can imagine some of your feelings as you read this. However, I don't write to you just to keep up a family tradition, but because I have a proposal to put to you.

By now you will have been given the old suitcase and seen that it's full of family papers going back to my grandparents' time. Most of these letters and records were kept by your Granny Peg – I don't think that woman ever threw away a piece of paper. She even kept stacks of gibberish scribbled by your Auntie Nora. It was always in my mind that I would sort out the papers some day, destroy the rubbish and the private stuff, the stuff that nobody outside the family needs to know, and give the rest to somebody who could put together a family history.

As you know, Siobhán, you come from a family that played no small part in Ireland's fight for freedom. It is my belief that the stories of those who died for their country should be preserved and passed on to the younger generations who, I have to say, seem to take so much for granted. I've been thinking about this for a long time and a few months ago I sat down to tackle the task in earnest but I found it impossible. Everything was all mixed up together and one thing seemed to hang on another. I couldn't work out what to leave in and what to take out. After days of shuffling bits of paper in and out of different piles, I gave up.

Then one day I woke from a fireside nap with the solution: I would leave the task to you. You are used to doing writing and research and would be much better up to the task. So that is what I want, Siobhán. I want you to be the person who writes our family history. Focus on the part our family played in national affairs, there is where you'll find our glory. There is so much ignorance today about the sacrifices endured by that great generation of Irish people. Sacrifices made so that those who came after them (yourself included, I might add) could grow up in a free country.

The men who died for Ireland are half-forgotten now. The 75-year commemoration of the 1916 Rising in '91 was an unholy disgrace. It nearly killed your Gran, the things they failed to do. It's time someone reminded the young people that not too long ago, there were Irish men and women who had interests beyond the raking in of money, who had principles and ideals they were prepared to die for. You come from such a family; it would do you good to learn the details of that and pass them on to others.

That's the line I want you to take in whatever you write about them: the bravery of these great men and women. You'll be good at it, I know. You're a clever girl, you always were, and you've a lot more talent in you than you've used so far. A work like this could be the making of you.

I could never have passed these papers on while I was alive. When you read them, you'll know why. I thought I'd take their secret to the grave with me but in the past few years I've come to believe it right that you and Maeve should know the truth, now that the knowing can do no harm. So I've left it all there, every bit. (I've even left in Nora's ramblings, though to tell you the truth, I don't expect you to have any more success with that than I had – it's impossible reading, her handwriting so bad and her thoughts all over the place.) It should also help you understand why it was so terrible for me, the thought of you getting yourself mixed up with Rory O'Donovan that time.

How often I've thought over that. I've played that last evening a thousand times in my mind and regretted the pity of how we both overreacted. So many times I've half dialled your telephone number. So many letters I never posted. At the beginning, I was afraid that if we did make up and you came back home, you'd take up with young O'Donovan again. Your grandmother feared it too. It seems stupid now, that fear, but at the time it was very real. Later on, when that didn't seem so important any more, it felt like it was too late. I didn't know how to go about it.

I was always expecting something to happen that would bring you home again. Always, until Mammy died. When you didn't come back for your Granny Peg's funeral, I knew I would probably go to my own grave without ever seeing you again. That's a hard thing to do to a parent, Siobhán. But I forgive you, as I'm sure my will makes clear. Everything I have, I leave equally to you and Maeve. I'm sure you agree it's a tidy sum. Invested wisely, you'll be free from money worries and able to do whatever you want. You could afford to take time off from writing in those magazines. Better still, you could give them up entirely.

There's a danger in me doing this, Siobhán, I won't pretend I don't know it. I'm putting myself, and my mother and father, and my grandparents, into your hands and trusting you not to make public anything you find that they, or I, would prefer to remain private. Do not write anything that would upset me if I were still alive. *Share any such secrets as you come across* only with Maeve, *this is* very important. *Make your history something the family can be proud of, that can be passed on to little Ria and her children.*

I hope you'll do this one thing for me. I've never asked anything of you your whole life long and though you may have changed in so many years' absence I don't imagine you've become the kind of girl who would disregard her mother's last wish. Think of it as a way of making amends for running away, a way of putting things right between us.

I regret that I won't be here to guide you but I'll be looking down from Heaven. (Keep that in your mind as you write and you won't go too far wrong.) I'll be praying for you as I always have. Always. Because whatever you might believe, through it all I was always

Your loving

Mammy

5

Monday again, one week on. I walk along the beach, by the edge of the water, towards Mucknamore's old cemetery. Above me the sun blazes like metal in a forge and out to sea a heat-haze shimmers over Inisheen, but I am not too uncomfortable. I wear only my swimming togs and a pair of shorts, allowing the sea breeze to fan my hot limbs. The nausea that has plagued me for weeks has eased a little and is now confining itself to mornings. The water laps cool over my feet as I walk.

To get to the cemetery I walk westwards, away from the village and the crowds that congregate around the Hole in the Wall. That's where the car park is and the lifeguard hut, the trashcans and the ice-cream van. There, people settle their towels just feet apart from each other and the sea teems with bodies. There, local people look up when I pass on the sand, smile hello and resent it when I smile back but keep on walking. In Mucknamore, you are supposed to stop and talk, even if you have nothing to say. I prefer the beach further up, behind the twist in the coastline where it is empty except for an occasional jogger or walker, where I can stand alone in the shallows, looking out at a world where everything is horizontal and vast, except me.

Today, though, I do not stop in my usual spot. I walk briskly on, aiming myself at the green slope of land, studded with crosses and stones, that slants down to the sand. I am under orders. Maeve has returned to Dublin, where she telephones daily with instructions. Today's task is to look at the new inscription on the family gravestone and check that it has been done to spec before we pay the bill and the extra money the stonecutter was promised for doing it, at Mrs D.'s request, so soon.

A path divides the cemetery in two. It is stony, jagged under my bare feet so I pick my way up along the grassy ridges between the burial stones instead. As I draw near to the grave, I see it is a mess, covered in rotting bunches of flowers, with plastic wrappings still swathing some of the decayed clumps. Up close, I can smell the rot, fetid in the hot, still air. Among the wilted stalks, only a single carnation clings to a faded shade of its former colour, pink. The whole thing looks terrible, like nobody cares. But who is there to tend things like the family graves now Mrs D. is gone?

Some of the mess has slid across onto Auntie Nora's patch. I kneel to pick up the rotting stems and they shrink in my hands, oozing slime. Holding the mess away from my body, I carry it down the slope and over the wall, onto the soft sand of the beach. I dump it there, then go back up for another handful. Then another. Again and again I trudge up the path and back down until I have cleared it all away. On the beach then, I kneel and dig a hole with my hands, scrabbling like a dog at sand that is soft on top, like pale brown sugar, but darker and damper underneath. When the hole is big enough, I transfer in the stinking vegetation and cover it over, pat it down. I stand to finish the job, dragging soft sand across with one foot, stamping it flat.

By the time I've finished, I am sweating and my hands and arms are caked in sand. I kick off my shorts. The sea is flat as a table in the still quiet heat but I know it will be cold. I stride forward, not stopping when I reach the water. That's my way, to ignore the cold that licks at my calves, my thighs, my groin, getting sharper with each step. I push on until the water is waist height, then I throw myself forward into it. Cold thumps me in the heart and I gasp out loud but still I feel the joy of water under me, over me, all around me. I stretch my arms wide in a breaststroke. It begins to warm to me.

It's a week now since the funeral and I still can't believe she's gone. I had the same feeling when Daddy died, I remember. Is it like this for everybody or is it just that my parents were already so absent from my life? 'She is dead,' I say out loud, lifting my head up out of the waves to shout it across the empty sea. 'Dead. Dead. Dead.' The word skims across the water like a flat stone.

I turn to float on my back, arms stretched wide, staring into the blue eyes of the sky. The sea holds me up, small waves cresting under me, rocking me gently. Its comfort confuses me. So I pull my knees into my chest, wrap my arms around them, and let myself go heavy, let out my breath and hang in the water, willing myself down. I sink to the bottom on my hunkers, my breath trapped and swelling behind my closed eyes and nose and mouth, all shut tight. Only my ears are open, full of noise of the sea.

I stay down until the last moment, until my lungs are fissured with pressure, my heart panic-hammering and my brain about to burst inside its skull. Just before I sway towards blackness, I kick myself back up, my head breaking the surface skin of the water just in time, my head full of nothing but its gulping need for air.

I used to do this breath-holding in the bath, in the days when a full bath was almost deep enough for me to swim in. Timing myself with Mrs D.'s alarm clock, I would try to hold under for longer and longer each time. Afterwards I would feel drained. Drained and depleted but strangely relieved. Just as I feel now, heaving for breath. I have limits but I can stretch myself still.

I stay in the water a long time, until I'm cold, chilled to my bones despite the sun. When I get out, my teeth are chattering and I can't stop them. Dripping wet, I go back up the slope to the cemetery. The grave looks better after my efforts, although stubborn remnants of slime cling to the chipstones in places, and the smell lingers. Tomorrow I will bring a bucket and rinse it off with seawater.

I check the inscription on the headstone. It seems to be just as Maeve ordered: Máirín Devereux, née Delaney. Born 5.5.1923. Died 12.5.1995, aged 72. *Go nDéanfaidh Dia Trócaire ar a hAnam.* May God Have Mercy on Her Soul. The new-chiselled letters, black on the old grey stone, stand out strong and bold, so that

Granny Peg and Granddad and all the other names above it look less important. As if Mrs D.'s death is the one that really matters.

My exertions in the water have tired me so I sit down on the edge of the grave, shivering, in front of Auntie Nora's little cross. From sitting, I move to lying on my side, curled up and hugging my knees for warmth. I lie so I can see over the tops of the other gravestones, over the wall, over the waves, all the way out the Causeway to Inisheen. The island shimmers in the heat, seems to move, so it looks like a great basking whale.

I lie and imagine the baby swimming inside me and wonder whether it can feel yet, what it knows. Under my cheek, the chipstones are hot and sharp but beneath them I can smell the earth. I close my eyes. Blood rushes around my head as it always does after a swim, its noise in my ears echoing the sea, and old thoughts and memories swirl with it. Day after day here, I'm assailed by the past. Memories I thought I'd sealed away forever slide out, fresh as the day I put them away. Even more jarring are the scenes that spurt up from what seems like nowhere, where I've forgotten there was anything to forget.

I lie on my family's graveyard plot, remembering. The sun beats down from above and underneath me the stones poke at my skin. It hurts, but still I lie there, like that.

6

Ding-dong: the doorbell rings and I know it must be Rory. In my stomach, a battalion of butterflies flutter up. I lay aside the newspaper cutting I have been reading – an article from the *Wexford Weekly* of June 1921 that describes my great-uncle Barney's and Rory's great-uncle Dan's trial for leading IRA manoeuvres. I stand up, take three deep breaths.

He is in his suit, on his way home from work, his tie loose around his collar, that grin of his held out to me like a gift. I lead him through to the sitting room but every surface, apart from the chair I had been sitting in, is covered in papers.

He says, 'I guess you opened the suitcase, then?'

'You knew I would.'

'And it's interesting?'

'Overwhelming, to be honest. There's so much stuff in there.'

'But you'll be able to do what your mother wanted? Knock it into shape?'

'I don't know. Maybe.'

I don't tell him that the aspect of the story that most interests me is what Mrs D. has implored me to set aside. 'Can I get you a drink?' I offer.

'Have you Guinness?'

'We've a whole bar full of whatever you want,' I say, inclining my head in the direction of the pub.

'A Guinness would be great, so. I'll go with you. I've always fancied pulling my own pint.'

I lead the way through to the bar. The shutters are closed, blocking out the evening light, so it's dark as winter night. My nostrils smart to the smell of stale alcohol and smoke. 'It smells pretty whiffy in here,' I say as I flick on the lights.

'It does, doesn't it? But never mind.'

I hand him a pint glass, point at the pumps. 'Let the first couple run off,' I say. 'What's in the pipes will be stale.' It's two weeks now since the funeral, the last time they were used.

'I can't get used to this place being closed.' Rory tilts the glass as the creamy black liquid pours in. 'Everybody misses it. Ryan's isn't half as good.'

'It won't be long before it's open again, I suppose.'

'Yes and no. I've heard from our friends in Düsseldorf.' He means Stefan and Hilde Zimmerman, the couple who have bought the place. 'They don't intend to open again until they've done major renovations. They have all sorts of changes planned.'

I uncap a bottle of fizzy orange for myself, pour it into a glass. Aware of his nearness, I move round to the customer side of the bar and sit on a high stool. 'Did they say when they'd be here?'

'Tuesday week.'

'Really? So soon?'

He looks up at me. 'Do you mind?'

'No. I'll just have to get organized a bit quicker than I thought, that's all.'

'You still plan on leaving as soon as they arrive?'

I nod.

'I thought you might hang around for a bit of a holiday.' He puts his pint on top of the counter to settle. 'It's been so long since you were home.'

He is echoing thoughts I've been having myself, thoughts that are taking me by surprise: that I don't really want to leave, that I just might stay a little longer. I think it's the documents: I'm afraid that if I take them away from here, they'll never divulge their secrets to me. I don't tell Rory any of this. Instead I say: 'I need to get back. I've already stayed longer than I intended.'

'Somebody pining for you over there?' He says it lightly but he's been waiting for an opportunity to ask.

'No significant other, if that's what you mean.'

'And you can send in your work by email, can't you?'

'Mmm.'

'Well, then . . .'

I shrug.

His Guinness is ready, a perfect ring of white topping a glassful of black. He holds it up for me to admire.

'Not bad,' I say. 'For a first attempt.'

'Cheers.'

I lift my drink to his and we clink glasses, our eyes meeting. The air between us becomes charged and we drink and swallow and put our glasses down with an unnatural awareness of every move.

Unsettled, I blurt out something I've come to realize in the past few days. 'We never had a hope, you know.'

'What do you mean?'

'You and me: we were doomed from the start. I know that now, from reading Mrs D.'s papers.'

'Because of the whole family thing?'

'It was all your great-uncle's fault.'

'It was? Excellent news! After all these years of believing that it was mine.'

I make a face at that, and he grins. 'Seriously,' he says. 'Which of the uncles?'

'Your great-uncle Dan. Your father's father's brother.'

'Never heard of him.'

'Really?'

'Don't think so.'

'That surprises me. Maeve and I heard so much about Barney.'

'Your mother's IRA uncle? The one who "died for Ireland"?'

'Exactly.'

'Everyone in Mucknamore has heard of him.'

'Well, he and Dan were friends. And comrades in the War of

Independence, apparently. They ended up in an English prison together.'

'Really? For what?'

'For drilling IRA soldiers. Well, also for playing the Sinn Féin trick of the time, carrying on as if the British courts had no jurisdiction over them. When you called, I was reading a newspaper cutting all about it.'

I go back into the sitting room to fetch the yellow clipping and bring it out. I lay it on the counter, careful not to tear the brittle paper, and begin to read.

> Unprecedented scenes of excitement accompanied the trial of two Mucknamore men, Bernard Parle and Dan O'Donovan, at the Wexford Assizes on Tuesday last. A large crowd of onlookers congregated outside the courthouse before the trial, and the District Inspector billeted 20 local RIC police to the building to keep order.
>
> The two prisoners were brought out and put in the dock and immediately began to speak amongst themselves. They also ignored the order for Hats Off. The police were forced to remove hats from the prisoners, leading to shouts and jeers from some among the assembled crowd and it took some time for the magistrate to bring the court to order.

'This was in May 1921,' I say. 'Sinn Féin had had their landslide win in the 1918 election and claimed this gave them a mandate to run the country. They set up their own parliament—' I stop myself, realizing that his grasp of history might be better than mine. 'Do you know all this already?'

'Kind of. I'd be a bit hazy on the details.'

'So was I until I reread one of Mrs D.'s history books. I don't know about you, but we learned nothing about the Civil War in school. Our history classes leaped straight from the glorious Rising of 1916 to the glories of having our very own theocracy.'

He laughs. 'I can't quite hear the nuns putting it quite like that.'

'That was what they meant, though.' I shudder ostentatiously.

'Never mind all that, go on with what you were saying.'

'Yeah, Sinn Féin. Because they won the vote by such a margin, they declared Ireland a Republic and set up their own government to run the country, ignoring the government that was already there.'

'And anyone who had voted for the other parties.'

'Exactly. The British, of course, were scathing and most people thought the whole thing a great joke. But they stopped laughing when the IRA – the army of the new Republic – got going.'

'Which is where the great-uncles come in?'

I nod.

'Right. Read on.'

The magistrate said he would bind them over in sum of £50 to be of good behaviour for twelve months, in default of which to go to jail for six months.

Magistrate: 'Do you intend to go to jail?'

O'Donovan: 'We do not recognize this court.'

Bernard Parle read out the following statement: 'We don't recognize your authority at all. The only authority we recognize is that of Dáil Éireann, elected by the free will of the Irish people. The British Government may dub it a crime to drill soldiers for the defence of Ireland but it is no crime in the eyes of the authority we recognize and to which we owe allegiance.'

At this, widespread applause broke out in the court. There were cries of 'Up the Rebels!' – 'Good on you, Dan!' – 'See you in six months, Barney!' Some members of the public began to sing 'The Soldier's Song'. The magistrate ordered the court to be cleared and an ugly conflict broke out as the police set to doing so with baton freely used. Many were injured in the melee.

'So they were jailed together?' Rory asks.

'Yeah. Two months later, in July, a truce was negotiated but they were kept in prison until the following December, when the Treaty was signed.'

'And after all that, the two of them fell out?'

'They took opposite sides in the war after the Treaty.'

'We talked about that, do you remember?' Rory asks. 'Back in college?'

'Did we?'

'Yes, don't you remember? My family voted for Fine Gael, yours for Fianna Fáil. And we wondered whether the bad feeling might go back to the Civil War.'

It makes me stupidly happy that he remembers something I've forgotten.

'But it never explained why they were still at loggerheads fifty years later,' he says. 'Other families were Fianna Fáilers and we weren't expected to shun them the way we avoided the demon Devereuxes. We thought something else must have happened.'

I nod. 'Something did. Lots of things did.'

He looks at me over his drink. 'Something to do with Nora, right?'

'Maybe.'

'Come on, Jo, tell me.'

I don't know what to tell. I'm just realizing that although Dan O'Donovan was never mentioned to me either, I grew up with him. We both did. He was always there, the secret behind our families' silence, like a shadow in the dark.

Rory says again, 'Tell me.'

'I will, but not yet. Not until I'm sure of what I know.'

He wrinkles his nose at me, decides not to push it. 'So long as I'm the first person you tell. I have a family interest in it too, remember.'

'I know you do, Rory, and I will tell you, I promise. It's just that I'm finding so much information, it's hard to sift out exactly what was going on.'

'You're loving this, aren't you.'

'I *am* intrigued.'

His expression becomes teasing.

'Don't,' I say, pointing a finger into his face. 'Don't say it.'

He says it, with a grin: 'Your mother was right.'

I reach across the counter and punch his arm, making him laugh louder. Then he slips from his stool and reaches into his briefcase. 'I brought something along tonight and I wasn't sure whether I should show you or not. Now I think I will.'

He places a large brown envelope on the bar counter between us. 'You can add them to the rest. Think of it as bringing the collection up to date.'

The flap is unsealed. I reach inside and bring out a sheaf of black-and-white photographs, all of the same person, in the same setting. A young woman with long, curly, dishevelled hair, lying naked on a tousled bed. Her lips are lightly parted and she is clearly, blissfully, post-coital. My face flushes red as I recognize her – me! – and my hand flies up over my mouth.

'Jesus, Rory.'

Again, he is laughing at me. 'What's the matter? Don't you like them?'

'Look at her. My God, just look at her.'

'She's gorgeous, isn't she?'

He is right, she is gorgeous. So young. So trusting. So unguarded. Me but not me. 'How can you say I haven't changed?' I say to him, staggered by her naivety.

'You haven't.'

I flick through the photographs, faster than I want because I am aware of his eyes on both of us, me and my young image. Each picture shows me in a different position: lying, sitting on the side of the bed, sheet folded strategically across my thigh in one shot, thrown emphatically aside in another. The feelings we had for each other when he took these pictures are flooding me.

'Do you still take photographs?' I ask, trying to settle myself, not to let them pull me in too far.

'I haven't for ages. Not in a long time.'

'That's a shame. You were good.'

'I had an exhibition in Dublin in '87. It went really well. But shortly after that, I stopped.'

'Why?'

'The usual reasons. Job. Marriage. Mortgage. Kids.'

Oh, yes. That.

I put the pictures back in their envelope. I'll look at them properly later. I am shaken. Once, I knew every inch of this man's skin, the taste of his sweat, his spit, his semen. The time we had together is there between us but everything that happened since is also there, crowding it out. I feel like I am swaying on top of a wall.

He is feeling it too. When he speaks again, his voice has lost its flippancy. 'Why don't you stay in Mucknamore, Jo?' he says, leaning across the counter towards me. 'Stay for a while. Work on your family papers and write whatever you're going to write. Have your baby here. Then see.'

'I can't do that.'

'Why not? One good reason.'

'Rory, I haven't even decided for sure whether I'm going to have this baby.'

'Oh.'

'And whether I do or don't, I'd need to be among friends.'

'You have friends here.'

'*Friend*,' I say. 'One friend. You.'

'I'd do whatever you needed.'

'Your wife would love that.'

He frowns.

I go on, repeating objections I have raised with myself: 'Anyway, where would I stay? I couldn't bear to stay at the Sea View or any of the B&Bs.'

I can already picture the long looks of their owners slanting after me as I come in and out. Intolerable.

'You could stay in our place. We have a spare room.'

Is he crazy? A flash of anger whips through me.

'OK, maybe not a great idea. Don't look at me like that, Jo. It's just that I'd say anything if I thought it would make you stay.' He stares into his drink. 'I don't want you to go.'

'You shouldn't say that, Rory.'

'I know. I know I shouldn't. But I hate the thought of you disappearing again. I'd like it if we could . . . if you . . .' He hesitates, takes a breath, plunges on. 'I want to tell you something. I lied to you that first day. I don't love living in Mucknamore. My family loves it here but it's killing me.'

'Too small?'

He nods. 'Too Mucknamore.'

My heart shudders. So he is still my Rory, I think. Silly, treacherous heart. 'I lied too,' I say.

'Did you? Don't you like San Francisco?'

'It's not that. I mean about everything being wonderful. Things aren't wonderful, they're a mess.'

He waits for me to go on, to explain. I try to decide how much I want to tell him. In the end I say: 'A while ago, I lost somebody.'

'A boyfriend?'

'No. But a dear friend. A special friend.' It incenses me that there is no title for what Richard was to me. Friend, yes. And brother and mentor and therapist and cook and minder . . . He was my lover, in every way but the sexual, and meant more to me than many husbands do to their widows. 'I loved him,' I say. 'He loved me.' Stupid, inadequate words. But it's OK. Rory is looking past the words into my face. He understands.

'So your mother dying now was a double blow?' he says.

'I suppose. Though I didn't think of it that way. For a long time, it's been one death after another.'

I check his face again but yes, it's still OK. No false sympathy. No narrow inquisitiveness. No inappropriate jokes. Just a clear face held open to me. 'Mrs D. now,' I say. 'Richard a while back.' A long while, longer than I want to admit. 'Before that, Auntie

Nora. Before her, Gran. And Daddy. And . . . you know . . . back then . . .'

Again, that frown. He doesn't want me to refer to that either. I could take this as another affront but I wore out my emotions on all that a long time ago. And I don't want us to lose the good feeling that's beginning to wrap around us. So I shrug, letting him off. 'I guess life is loss,' I say.

His hand lies on the bar counter between us. Small hairs curl round the edge of his shirt cuff. *Touch me*, I think as I'm talking. *Touch me like you used to touch me.* And just as I think the thought, he does it. He lifts his hand and runs the outer edge of his index finger along my cheek. 'Poor Jo,' he says.

Tears jump into the back of my throat and eyes. I want to take his hand and hold it there forever. 'Don't,' I say, pulling away. He takes his finger down. Its absence leaves a cleft.

How easily my traitor body rises to meet his but another part of me is appalled. He makes these moves as if he is not married at all, as if our not seeing each other for twenty years was some kind of accident. I try to fold myself back into place.

'Don't,' I say again, stronger this time.

'I'm sorry.'

We sit a small while longer, then he tilts back his stool, drains his glass. 'I should go,' he says.

Go on, I think. *Go to your wife and family.*

I nod.

'I might drop in again tomorrow evening, if that's OK.'

'Whatever,' I say. 'Suit yourself.'

After he's gone I return to the sitting room and slide the pictures of my eighteen-year-old self out of their envelope, stare again at this girl with her open, unlined face and body, her wild glittering eyes. Suddenly, I find I can't see the image any more: it is blurred and misted. I am crying. I have no energy to fight these tears and so I give in to them. The tears turn to sobs, the sort you don't want anybody else to hear, harsh and ugly, fading again in time to a sorrow that is quieter and somehow sadder. I cry, and cry again, in spurts, until I am drained dry.

After a long time, I pull myself, cramped and weary, from the chair. I follow Rory's suggestion and slot the envelope of pictures away in the suitcase with the rest of the papers, then I go upstairs, though it's only eight thirty, and settle myself into bed. I hug up tight under the sheet and blankets and give way to sorrow again. I cry myself into sleep and through the night I waken often and know that I am crying in my dreams.

7

They are unmaking Mrs D.'s house. I stand and watch the diggers as they trundle their mechanical dance around the building: forwards and backwards they go, all day long. Claws up, claws down. Buckets full, buckets empty. Huge drills puncture the walls and bricks that have supported each other for more than a hundred years are rent apart. On and on it goes, day after day. Inside, steel struts brace the structure they want to retain, stop the whole from collapsing.

I watch the work from the door of my shed, what was once one of Mrs D.'s outhouses, now cleared to accommodate me. A stretch of garden and a long lawn lie between me and the house, affording me just enough privacy to make this refuge tolerable. I spend most of my outdoor time around the other side, facing the sea, but every so often I come around, like this, to view the builders' progress.

Across the lawn Hilde and Stefan, the new owners, are also watching the work, their gaze open and fond. To them, these labourers are wonder-workers, making concrete the dream that sustained them through desk-bound years in Düsseldorf. A dream that last year became a goal when they came to stay in Mucknamore for the fourth year in a row and met my mother on their nightly visits to the pub and learned that she was thinking of selling. Now, arms entwined, they stand and stare, smiling at the work and each other.

One of the workmen in the distance sees me and waves across. He is a show-off who likes to go naked to the waist as he works, to roar along to songs on the radio that they play all day. His wave is really for the other men, not me. I don't return it.

They say I am mad, I know that, not just the builders but the whole village. Eyes lift skywards after I pass on the street or the beach. Behind my back, index fingers are circled around temples. I don't care. I can be mad if that is what they want: if it means I can live in my shed and forgo explanations. Living here was the only way I could bear to stay in Mucknamore. This shed, with its unplastered walls and primitive roof, is at least all mine.

Five black refuse sacks I filled with rubbish over the past two days. Bigger items – two broken bar stools, a rusted bottling machine, a punctured old sofa spewing yellow sponge filling – I dragged up to the big yellow skip hired by Hilde and Stefan. After I swept and mopped and dusted it out, Stefan helped me to carry some furniture across from the house. A single bed from my old bedroom, a small table I use as a desk, a wooden chair, a rug that I have placed by my bed to protect my feet. I have an oil lamp for light and an oil stove for cooking. Each morning, before the builders arrive, I draw water from an outside tap beside the house, lugging it across the garden in two enamel buckets. Calls of nature I answer on the sand dunes of the beach. It's rough living but the walls and the corrugated iron roof are sound. It's primitive, but I have as much as I need and something about it satisfies me. I feel like I'm being purged.

The kind weather makes it possible. Each morning, the sun comes up burning hot, as hot as it ever gets in SF. I leave the steel sliding door open during the day as I work; sometimes a small breeze lifts my papers so that letters or notes or newspaper cuttings have to be weighted down with stones but mostly it is calm and clear. And set to stay fair, according to Hilde: June, she tells me, is going to break all records.

Under Hilde's hands, Mrs Devereux's front-room shop is to become a substantial business, serving food as well as alcohol. Upstairs, what were family bedrooms – *our* bedrooms – are to be renovated to provide guest accommodation: six rooms – 'all en suite!' says Hilde – from which tourists will rise each morning and come downstairs for 'the Irish breakfast' – fried eggs and sausages and rashers of bacon.

She has supplied me with breathless details of her plans. Stone floors, wooden tables and stools, walls decorated with replicas of old advertisement boards: 'Guinness is Good For You'; 'For a Smoother Smoke – Smoke Sweet Afton'; 'Drink Lyons – the Quality Tea'. Tankards and bottles and musty old books scattered on high shelves, in calculated disarray. 'A real Irish pub,' she says, hugging herself. As the Zimmermans' ideas about Irish pubs were acquired in Europe, truly traditional features like outside toilets, men-only access or sawdust on the floor will not feature.

Hilde is a large woman, lavishly warm. My reaction to her plans is a great disappointment to her. 'Your dear, dear mother,' she says, bringing her face, a round melodrama of sadness, close to mine. 'What you must know is that we, Stefan and I, love this place as much as Máirín did.' Hilde gets everything wrong. She mispronounces my mother's name: Mayreen she says every time, instead of Mawreen. And my reservations about their schemes have nothing to do with Mrs D. I like Hilde but I cannot explain myself to her. I don't even try.

Every day at one o'clock, she comes to my door with a dinner tray held out before her. 'Hello, hello,' she calls, the same words each day, the same cheery tone. 'Are you there, Jo? I have brought for you a little food.' Hilde saw how I was at my mother's funeral, has spoken to my sister, has listened to the talk of the village, and her response is this kindness. Each day she comes with the tray, she eyes my accommodation with an exaggerated shudder. I live in a shed while she and her husband overthrow my old home: she is shocked at that. Shocked both at me – that anyone could choose to live like this but especially a woman in my pregnant condition – and at herself: she still can scarcely believe she allowed it. Her agreement was won only because it allowed her dream, Stefan's dream, to proceed. The house was legally theirs, I had no rights, but still she acts like I have done them a favour.

So I eat her food, all of it, although it is not to my taste – pot roasts, frankfurters, gravy. I even drink the accompanying glass of milk. To Hilde, Irish milk is something wonderful, and for a pregnant woman, essential sustenance.

Hilde knows I want to stay in Mucknamore until I finish what I am writing, though I haven't explained why. I have no reason why I cannot return to SF with the blue suitcase and do the work over there. No reason except I know it would never be done.

At first I slept badly here, my sleep perforated by noises of the night. The door has a big bolt and is secure but still I would jerk awake at certain sounds, heart pounding. Or I would turn over, thinking myself in my double bed in San Francisco, and wake against this mattress's narrow edge, with a sensation of being about to pitch out, the threat of the rough, unsanitary floor beneath me. All this has passed now. I have learned to turn in a smaller space, got used to the grimy ground, and the snaps and rustles of the outdoors now bother me no more than the night-time creaks and rattles of a house.

Sometimes I can't sleep and then I get up and turn on the lamp and work within its pool of light, cupped inside the dark. Silence is deeper at night, when the birds are asleep, and the work benefits from that.

I am content to be here, for now; I don't want to go back, not yet. I think of my empty apartment in San Francisco, its curtains standing open to foggy summer days and street-lit nights. I think of the agony letters I left lying beside my computer, unanswered, dust settling over them. I think of Deirdre and Gary and Susan and Jake and all the others who continue to meet in Benton's or Araby's or Café Crème without me. I find it hard to believe it's all still going on while I'm not there.

A replacement has been engaged to cover my column. 'She won't be the same,' Lauren, my editor, said when I telephoned, 'but she'll do us fine until you get back.' I was not to worry about work. I was to take all the time I needed. Lauren lost her mother two years ago; she thinks she understands. I trade on her sympathy to win myself this interlude.

It's all very temporary. As soon as the construction work on the house is done, the builders will turn their attention to terraces and gardens and my shed will go. Hilde tries to reassure me with terrible promises about what will happen then. The guest bedrooms will be done, she says, and I can join her and Stefan in the house. I will be most welcome, I must stay as long as I like. Her generosity frightens me, so I work hard, harder than I have ever worked in my life. Up in the morning with the sun to write out the previous day's findings. A break at nine for food, again at eleven for a run on the beach. Once, I was able to run for miles and I am taking this opportunity to do what I have been pledging to do for a long time and regain my lost fitness. After the run, it's back to my shed in time to wash and eat Hilde's lunch. The afternoon I spend writing until I can write no more. I make myself a light meal and after that, read something from the cache in the suitcase. Read and unravel.

And after nightfall, after the sun has disappeared in a flamboyance of oranges and reds that bodes well for the following day, Rory comes. He waits until then to visit knowing I won't see him earlier. He brings drinks, wine or beer for himself, orange juice or Coca-Cola for me. I look forward to his visits, I admit it. As the light seeps out of the day and I push my tired brain through another entry in Peg's diary or Nora's notebook, I listen for his footfall. As soon as he arrives, I fold away the papers and we go and sit on the rug I have already set down behind the shed. It's private there, we are high enough and far enough back from the edge to be cloistered from any passers-by on the beach below.

So we sit close for two or three hours each evening in velvet darkness and talk, our voices low, moths swooping in to knock themselves against the oil lantern set between us. We talk: we do not touch, except when he is leaving to go home, when he bends and places a swift, soft peck on my cheek. Each time, as I tilt forwards to receive this almost-kiss, I think about turning my head to allow his lips to meet mine. That would do it, I know: one gesture from me and the rest would follow. Yet he is glad that I don't. He loves his wife, his children. He is afraid of what sex with me would do to his feelings for them.

As for me, I don't have his belief in, his awe of, the sexual act. That he comes here every night is betrayal enough, surely? Yet I too hold back. Become Rory O'Donovan's other woman? Never. Unthinkable. So I don't turn my head. No.

After he is gone, I wash and brush my teeth by lantern light, turning my thoughts away from him and back to the doings of young Granny Peg and Nora and Barney and Dan and take them to sleep with me. And next day at my table, I read and write some more about them, piecing together what happened to me and to Rory and to some of the people who made us. It isn't always easy; often I worry that I'm getting it wrong or over-interpreting. I don't fully trust my own recollections any more than I believe everything I read in Gran's documents. Memories are like dreams: putting them into words makes them too solid. Even as I'm doing it, a part of me is thinking I shouldn't. But I do. I write. To my own surprise, I stay on in Mucknamore, in a crumbling, run-down shack of a shed, and I write.

11
Surge

Nora

. . . There goes Useless John, skulking up the road. Every evening at the same time: twenty minutes to seven. You could set your clock by his going out. Three miles up to Ryan's of Rathmeelin where he'll drink four bottles of stout and five whiskies – or more if somebody else is buying – then stumble the three miles back home in the dark.

And there's young Cissie Cummins, running up behind, to have a go at him. 'Hey, Useless,' she shouts. 'You're useless.'

Those Cumminses are always the same. She keeps a safe distance, mind you, in case he might turn and say something, frighten her out of her brazenness with some of his talk about Coolanagh . . .

. . . Coolanagh. The word hurts me too. Coolanagh and Dan. Dan and Coolanagh. Don't try to forget, Peg says. Remember all I want and write it down, like I used to do before. It's not what I remember that's the worst of it, I tell her. It's what I would be imagining if I let myself . . . Write that too, she says. Write it secret for no one to read but myself, later, if I want. That's what she does and it always helps her . . .

. . . Coolanagh. Lovers' Hollow. The December of the big fog. None of us ever saw one as bad. The way it clung to sea and land, day after day, shrouding the sky, pressing thick and white against our windows. People were shadows moving about in it and all the talk was fixed on it. Where had it come from? Would it never pass off? What were we to do about the herring? The shoals, long awaited, were in. A bay swarming full of fish we had, but every fisherman in the village grounded.

Six days of this, morning, noon and night, but on the seventh day, a change. Within an hour of daylight the air started to stir. Hopeful men got up and sat by their windows, watching the mist peel back and the sea reveal itself again, inch by slow inch. Once he saw Inisheen emerge, John Colfer knew it was over. He left his house and went down to the Hut – the little shed that protected his and four other small boats – and took out his craft. Dragged it out into the water, then clambered into it, his trousers wet to the knee. Off he set, his boat slicing through the patches of mist that floated still across the sea, like small fallen clouds.

Just as he was about to pull left of the island, out into the bay, a billow of haze laid across Lovers' Hollow shifted, revealing a shape on the sand. Colfer stared. Shreds of mist teased his eyes, made him question himself: Is it . . . ? No? Can it be . . . ? But even as he asked the questions, he knew. By the hammering of his heart in his chest, he knew.

He steered his boat across, as close as he could go without danger. Close enough to see that, yes, it was a person, jutting up out of the sand like a rock, looking like something sculpted, like a bust of himself. He recognized him, though the face was bulging blue and smeared in sand. Dan O'Donovan. 'It was his eyes that were the worst,' Colfer would say afterwards, telling his tale from his high stool in Ryan's. Wide open, Dan's eyes were, crusted over with a grainy glaze. 'One look at them eyes, and I knew I was dealing with a corpse. No living person could stand it.'

. . . For all his bar-stool blather, Colfer held his whist, then and since, on the question everyone wanted the answer to: how did Dan O'Donovan come to be out on Coolanagh sands that night? What would have brought him out there on one of the darkest, dreariest nights in living memory? Colfer's answer has never changed: three heavy-fingered taps to the side of his nose.

Everyone knows what he thinks, all the same. Since the day he found Dan, he's never since had a drink here in Parle's. He takes his few shillings – and his story – off up to Ryan's of Rathmeelin instead, a three-mile walk for him each evening, there and back.

It is admired, this reluctance of his to put words on his thought. 'Not so useless in that department, thank God,' Peg says, though it's my wish that he'd stop talking about Coolanagh altogether.

A killing or an accident? That's the question they really want to ask, but they don't really want an answer. All of them, those who think as Colfer does and those who believe us innocent, are half glad he can't be drawn. For the one thing, the only thing that everybody in Mucknamore is agreed on is that we've had enough talk.

It was talk that unhinged the whole country, throwing around words like 'betrayal' and 'honour' and 'loyalty' and 'principles'. Talk got us into such a state that our young men turned their guns on each other. So now another young man was dead – what was the use in asking how or why? Wouldn't an answer only lead to another question? Wasn't the country riddled with why? Why? Why? Why? Why? Why?

. . . John Colfer wasn't the only one shook by what went on at that time. But it was cruel to see what his queer mix of *scéal* and silence took from him. Every time he sold his half-story for another drink, he moved a fraction further from the truth, until the gap between what he said and what he could have said grew so wide that he fell right into it. He hasn't married and now he hardly will. The bit of a farm his mother left him lies neglected. His boat rots in the Hut from lack of use.

Now he walks the village drunk or fixed on drink. Sometimes he turns on the children who jeer him, frightens them about the dangers of Coolanagh sands, fills them with hints of how he once found a dead man out there.

Finding Dan the way he did, knowing what he knew, not being

able to do anything with the knowledge: that was what turned Colfer into Useless John.

My brother did that to people . . .

8

1922

A frosty night, black glistening starry white. A swollen moon dangling white over Carnagh railway station, above a tar barrel that crackled and spat its flame into the heavens. Below on the platform, clusters of people standing, waiting, their anticipation as tangible as their puffs of foggy-white breath. Anticipation barely dulled by the long delay they had put in, in cold that sliced through hats and scarves and overcoats, through skin to bone.

Twice already the shout had gone up: 'Here it is, it's coming.' Twice, the fife 'n' drum band boomed out the beginning of the heart-stirring 'The Soldier's Song'. Both times, false alerts. For a while after that they played through some old reliables but now they were taking a break, instruments hanging loose in their red-raw hands, saving themselves for the big moment. Which surely must be soon. Surely.

Peg Parle stamped her feet against the cold. It was pointless: she'd lost all feeling in them, was numb halfway up her calves but – *stamp, stamp, stamp* – the action allowed her to vent her worry about her mother. For if she was feeling the sting of the cold, how much worse must it be for Máire.

'Are you sure you're all right, Mammy?' she asked again.

'I'm grand, pet. Haven't I told you?'

But her pinched, white face went against the words.

As if to confirm this contradiction, a fit of coughing took a sudden hold of her, a fusillade of rasping explosions that took and shook her whole body, so that all she could do was turn her back and crouch over, try to contain its ferocity. Peg exchanged a look with her father, aware of the faces of the O'Donovans and other neighbours and friends behind them, faces that hid a question amid their concern, a question they wouldn't dare put words on. Her father, JJ, swore beneath his breath. Then: 'Why can the railway never get their blasted trains to run on time?' Peg had to turn from his vehemence. Nearly harder to take than her mother's condition was her father's intensity about it.

They both knew that whether the train was on time or late, whether the weather was warm or cold, whether she was feeling wretched or well, Máire Parle wasn't going to miss coming down here tonight. Earlier, when it became clear that they were in for a delay, JJ had tried to persuade her to sit in the trap at the back of the station until the train came in but she wouldn't hear of it. 'Our place tonight,' she'd insisted, 'is right here at the front of this platform.' So that was where she stood now, in full view, trying to haul herself out of her spasm.

She fumbled in her pocket for a handkerchief, held it over her mouth with shaky fingers, while scrabbling for the strength to stay standing. Peg saw it all and saw her succeed, the will of her mind overcoming the weakness of her body. In a short time she was once again standing tall, her spine locked straight and strong, her hand and smile out for whoever might cross over to offer congratulations and good wishes.

It was pride in her boy that helped her prevail. She – and Peg and JJ too, and the O'Donovans beside them – were delighted at the numbers who'd turned out tonight. It was a six-mile trek from Mucknamore to Carnagh station, yet every family seemed to have sent someone. Respectable people, too, not just the rowdies.

Nothing indicated how matters had changed in Ireland more than this show of support, Peg thought. Eight months before, when the two boys were convicted for their 'crime' of drilling Irish volunteer soldiers in Moran's field, more than a few in the village had turned their backs on them. Some stopped coming into Parle's shop, so many that JJ had worried for a time about the effect on business. But now, tonight, those selfsame people were here to celebrate the boys' release.

'None of them ever thought that boys the likes of Barney Parle or Dan O'Donovan could bring the British Empire to its knees,' Peg said to Nora, Dan's sister, when she saw the turnout.

'I suppose it's hard to blame them,' was Nora's answer. 'When we can hardly credit it ourselves.'

Nora was right: it was hard to believe, close on a miracle. A band of ordinary Irish boys, with a stash of rusty guns, had forced the greatest power on earth, the Great British Empire, into making a treaty with them. The wonder of that was what had brought so many out in the freezing cold.

A thud overhead broke into her thoughts: the red and white signal board thumping down.

'The signal! The signal!' shouted Sore-Toes Delaney.

From the cabin Mikey Lambert gave them the thumbs-up. The train had left Rosslannan station was what that meant; seven minutes now to wait. Horns and bugles were lifted, pressed to mouths. Drums began to roll. For the third time – the final time, they hoped – the band struck up 'The Soldier's Song':

Soldiers are we,

Whose lives are pledged to Ireland . . .

Third time lucky. They were on the fourth verse when the light of the train appeared under the bridge. The crowd went wild, jumping and cuffing the air, waving little tricolour flags and hats and handkerchiefs, banging kettles and tins with spoons. With a loud screech of brakes, the train belched to a stop, smoke and steam billowing. The crowd swarmed forwards and Peg couldn't see a thing. Another cheer went up at the far end of the platform, near the end of the train. 'They're up here,' someone called. 'Here's where they are.'

She felt somebody behind her taking a hold of her coat as she was jostled forward – Nora maybe? – but she couldn't even turn round to check, they were pressing that hard against her.

'Let the family through,' Jack Stafford called from up ahead. 'For the love of God, let Mrs Parle past, will ye?'

Peg saw Barney, being pushed down towards them. Their own boy: small as ever, a head shorter than most of those around him, but thinner and somehow cleaner than she remembered him. He was wearing the type of trench coat that now distinguished those linked to the IRA, belted tight. A smile had his face split in half. She watched him reach Máire and the two of them come together, both of a height, to take each other by the hands.

'Welcome home, son,' Máire whispered.

Barney put his bag down on the ground, grabbed his mother round the waist, lifted her up off her feet and spun her round in a wide, loose circle, so she all but kicked the people who had gathered to get close to him. 'Barney!' she cried, half delighted, half embarrassed, her hat knocked sideways on her head. Some of the onlookers smiled.

Barney smiled too. He was aware of the eyes riveted on him, Peg noted, and not averse to it. That was new: Barney was never much of a one for crowds. Was she mistaken, or had he been drinking? Well, what if he had? He was surely entitled, the night that was in it. Having set Máire down, he turned to JJ, put out his hand. 'Daddy,' he said, a boy's word, strange in the mouth of this new Barney. JJ took the hand in both of his and shook it mightily. 'You're welcome home, son, you're welcome,' he said, pumping his arm up and down for too long.

Peg's attention was pulled away by a commotion further along the platform: Dan being shoved down her way. Dan, handing that crooked grin of his out to everyone, right and left. Oh, but he looked good, dark hair glowing and skin blue-clean in the lamplight. A new hat on his head, his hand on it to keep it in place. He was loving it all, the scuffing and back-clapping and cheering. His parents were up beyond her, so he was going to have to pass her to get to them. Any minute now and he'd see her . . .

'Where's Peg got to?' she heard her mother ask, just at the moment that his eyes connected with hers. He grinned and passed her a discreet wink, a knowing signal that made her heart flutter up into her throat.

She bent her head to acknowledge the substance of the greeting while conveying, she hoped, that she did not approve of its unseemliness. 'Welcome home, Dan,' she said, her voice obeying her attempts to keep it calm but her foolish face glowing hot enough to light up the night.

'Peg?' her mother called again. 'Your brother is over here.'

Dan pressed on, to be claimed by his own family, and she turned to greet Barney but as she moved towards him, he was hoisted up and away from her, crying out as the ground went from under him. Some of the younger men were lifting him, and Dan, up onto their shoulders.

'Ah, lads, go easy,' Máire called.

'Three cheers for the Mucknamore men,' cried Sore-Toes Delaney, as they went up. 'Hip, hip . . .'

Three thunderous roars of approval answered. Somebody started to sing 'For They Are Jolly Good Fellows', and the band caught up and joined in. Then Slim Neal, the bandmaster, took charge and called for 'Step Together', the marching song of the Irish Volunteers. A long drum-roll then the thump of a martial air pounded out, with those who knew it chanting along:

Step together, be each rank
Dressed in line from flank to flank
Marching so that you may halt
'Mid the onset's fierce assault . . .

As they chanted, the band led the way to the station exit and the crowd fell into place behind them, bearing on high their two young men, living symbols of their district's patriotic pride. Flags waving, voices loud, they began the long march home.

'Where are you going, Peg?'

'Nora and I are going to walk back with the crowd.'

'Ah, pet, I can't let you do that. Didn't I tell you we'd need all hands in the shop tonight?'

'But I'll be back with everybody else, Mammy. Of course I'll help then.'

'We'll need you sooner, love. It's not only those who are here who'll be in. I'd say Tess and Pats are run off their feet as it is.'

'I'll have to tell Nora.'

'Be quick. Daddy said we need to hurry if we don't want to get stuck in here.'

Máire turned to follow her husband's stooped back. Peg didn't want to go but what could she do? Parents had to be obeyed.

'I'll come with you,' Nora said, when she told her.

'Are you sure? You don't have to.'

'I know that. I'd rather. It's a long old walk.'

But Peg knew she was only being kind, keeping her company: Nora was a great walker. They detached from the milling crowd and pushed up to the railway building where JJ was helping Máire up into the trap. He was handling her solicitously, as always, careful as if she was a newborn child. There was a time this used to mortify Peg, when she first came to realize how comical everybody thought it that JJ, an old man with a stooped back and frayed, white hair, still acted the ardent suitor with his wife. Look at the way he was tucking in the blankets around Máire now, staring into her face in full view of all, while she looked off into the distance, oblivious. Peg hoped Nora didn't notice. To cover up, she searched in her skirt pocket for the sugar lumps she'd put in there earlier and fed them to George.

JJ snorted when he saw what she was doing: 'You and that old pony.' Peg patted George's nose and then climbed aboard with Nora and shared out the rug between them.

Across from them, also sitting up and waiting to make a move, were Pat and Mrs Cullen. 'Congratulations to you all,' Pat shouted across, from behind his pipe. 'Brave boys, brave boys.'

Peg nudged Nora and whispered, 'That's not what he said when his Johnny wanted to join up.'

JJ lifted the reins and steered the trap to the outer flank of the crowd. Everybody was leaving now, all trying to squash at once through the narrow gate.

'Have those large bottles ready and waiting for us, Mr Parle,' Lama White shouted as they squeezed by. 'We won't be long after you.'

'We'll keep them warm for you,' JJ called back. 'Never fear.'

As the crowd parted to let them through, Peg saw Barney and Dan up ahead, swaying from side to side with the movement of the people under them. On top of their world, like two princes. She looked across at Nora. Was that tears gleaming her eyes? It was hard to tell in the dark.

'It's just . . .' Nora whispered, shaking her head. 'I never thought . . .'

Peg nodded. Nora didn't have to explain. Didn't Peg herself feel the selfsame emotion, a pride in their brothers so swollen that it had to overflow somehow. But Peg wouldn't, couldn't, dream of crying here, not with the eyes of four parishes on her. She reached over and squeezed her arm. It felt thin enough to snap. Peg was touched, as she always was, by her friend's frailty.

By the time they were level with the boys, Nora had herself under control. Their brothers looked like a pair of jockeys, balancing themselves on a huge multi-limbed beast. Barney punched the air as they passed. 'Up Mucknamore!' he called to them and the boys beneath him laughed. Dan lifted his hat to them with an exaggerated gallantry and gave Peg a long look that made her blush again and made Nora look at her, hard. JJ steered the trap out in front of the crowd, into the middle of the narrow road and the girls swung their legs around so they were facing backwards now. Some of the boys shouted after them: 'Have ye no legs on ye, girls?' 'Would you look at Lady Muck and friend.' Peg had answers for their jibes but swallowed them; she wouldn't lower herself to be shouting retorts at the likes of Sore-Toes Delaney or Jem Fortune. The gap between them and the jubilations opened wider and wider. Nora waved her little flag at the crowd as it receded. Then the trap turned a bend and they could see no more.

They settled down under their blanket. The cold was more noticeable, out on the open road. Above them, the stars gleamed and the moon played hide-and-seek between frosted tree-branches. For a time, they could hear the boom and blare of the band carrying across the still night but eventually it faded and the clink of George's harness and the trot-trot of his hooves became the noise of their journey.

Back in Mucknamore, those who hadn't gone down to the station had their front doors open, frost or no frost, the better to hear the procession arrive. Crowds had gathered at the crossroads and outside Mrs Tynan's sweetshop. Tricolour flags of green, white and orange hung from windows and gables and lampposts. It was like a different place, Peg thought, as the Parle trap swung round the bend and the village opened up to them. Somewhere busier and brighter and more exciting than old Mucknamore.

Lil Hayes, Máire's friend, was waving at them from her front door, so JJ reined up to let the women have a quick word. Lil skipped across the road, wiping her hands on the apron she was wearing over her overcoat. 'He's here, then?'

'He's here,' said Máire. 'He's in top form, Lil, and looking great, thank God. Not a sign of the jail on him.'

'Isn't that marvellous?'

'They're following on by foot, carrying him up on their shoulders if you don't mind.'

'Was there many down?'

'What a crowd. I never saw the likes of it.'

'Isn't it only right? Why wouldn't there be a crowd? Isn't it the best thing that's happened round here this long time?'

Máire smiled. 'We can't stop. We need to get back to the shop.'

'Don't be so busy now that you forget to enjoy it yourselves. It's your night more than anyone's, remember.'

'Will you not come down with us?'

'I won't, Máire, thanks all the same. Not tonight. You know how it is inside.' Lil inclined her head towards the house, where her bedridden mother-in-law kept someone, mostly Lil, at beck and call. 'If I could have got away, I'd have been at Carnagh station with the rest. No, tell Barney I send him my best regards and I'll see ye all tomorrow.'

She waved them off and George trotted them up the remaining few yards. A crowd of mostly young people had gathered outside their shop: girls sitting in a line on the garden wall, their hips close together for warmth; boys playing pitch-and-toss in the corner, near the light from the bar window. All turned as JJ pulled up, steered the trap to a halt.

'Are they here, Mrs Parle?' called Molly Redmond, a friend of Peg's, jumping down from the wall. 'Are they home?'

'All's well, Molly,' Máire said. 'They're following on. You won't have much longer to wait.'

From the boys' corner came a voice singing in a false tremolo: *O Danny Boy, O Danny Boy I love you so-o-o-o* . . .

Everybody laughed. Molly's fancy for Dan O'Donovan was well known in the village.

'You shut up, Martin Murphy,' was all she could think of to say.

Peg nudged Nora. 'I'm surprised Molly wasn't down at the station.'

'Her mother wouldn't let her.'

'That?' whispered Peg, 'Or she didn't want to be where others were going to be the centre of attention and not herself?'

Nora shrugged, as if she'd know nothing about anything like that, and Peg felt ashamed. She shouldn't be going on like that about Molly, their friend. It was uncalled for and if she wasn't careful she would give herself away to Nora.

'Come on, Peg,' Máire called. 'We've no time for chatter. The place inside is jam-packed.'

Peg seldom worked the pub. She was the local schoolteacher, after all, and to be handing up drinks to the fathers of the children she taught was a bit demeaning of her position. Except for nights like this, when all hands were needed. Inside the shop, the air was sticky with the smell of drink and smoke and high excitement, but everyone quieted to listen as Máire explained that both boys had arrived and both were looking well and happy and none the worse for their prison experiences. They were delighted with their welcome and proud to have done their bit for Ireland. Younger and fitter members of the welcoming committee were walking them home.

'And Mrs Parle and myself have been sent ahead in the meantime to line up the refreshment,' added JJ, his old features wrinkling up into a smile. He always referred to his wife in the third person, as if underlining the astonishing fact that she had married him. 'So our advice to ye now would be: to get your orders in while ye have a chance.'

They did, and Peg was quickly drawn into capping and serving up bottles of drink, running to and fro with money and change. As her mother had said, the place was packed to the walls and more and more kept arriving, so that before long they were spilling out through the open door onto the road. Those who had condemned Dan and Barney for the actions that led to their imprisonment were here, along with the rest. Some thought their turning up tonight hypocritical but Peg saw it differently. She believed that their better natures had been ignited by the boys' actions, that in almost every Irishman, even one who seemed to care only for land or money or where his next drink was coming from, a spark of patriotism burned. What was common to all here tonight was pride: pride that they lived in an unconquered, unconquerable nation. And it was her brother and his friend, her friend, who had sparked that. There would be no going back now, for any of them.

It was nearly an hour later when young Denis Mernagh stuck his head in the door and said they were almost there. Máire shushed the pub to quiet and, sure enough, the distant sound of the band was carrying across the still night fields.

. . . God save Ireland said the heroes

God save Ireland say we all . . .

Máire gave Peg a nod that said she could go watch their arrival.

Outside in the cold, she slipped over to stand beside Nora at the wall. The road was now lined with people on both sides, many waving tricolours. Mossie Whelan was holding up a large framed picture of the martyrs of 1916 and Mrs Whelan stood beside him bearing a framed copy of their Proclamation: *Irishmen and Irishwomen, In the Name of God and of the dead generations from which she received her old traditions of nationhood, Ireland, through us, summons her children to her flag and strikes for her freedom . . .*

Molly and Cat Hayes unfurled the banner they'd been working on for weeks: WELCOME HOME TO THE MUCKNAMORE PRISONERS in green writing decorated with harps and shamrocks. The other girls gathered round it, admiring the handiwork.

At last the torches flared into view, the band belting out the rhythms of the ballad, the two boys still on high. The waiting villagers elbowed each other to stretch up towards Barney and Dan, trying to be one of those who shook their hand. The procession snaked its way as far as the pub and there they halted and stood while the band finished out the song:

. . . whether on the scaffold high,

or the battlefield we die,

what matter when for Erin dear we fall . . .

With a loud *te-dum* the music ended and the two boys were set down onto the ground. Dan rubbed his haunches while Barney swayed and had difficulty standing straight. 'I feel like a sailor after a long trip,' he said. 'I've lost my land legs.'

'Nothing to do with the pints you had earlier, I suppose,' Dan said, and everybody laughed, as if the comment were the height of wit.

Peg pushed her way through the crowd to get up beside them.

'Here she is,' Barney said, as he saw her come through.

'The woman herself,' said Dan.

Peg smiled a shy smile but her thoughts were triumphant. Take that, Miss Molly, was what she was thinking.

She stepped between the two young men and took Barney's left arm and Dan's right. She linked herself to them not as Barney's sister, certainly not as Dan O'Donovan's sweetheart, but as president of Mucknamore Cumann na mBan, the women's auxiliary group. It was a position she inherited a year ago from her mother, when Máire's health began to fail her, and all through the Truce in the summer and into the Treaty negotiations, it had fallen to Peg to lead the work that kept the boys of Mucknamore IRA Company supported and motivated. She'd done her best and most would concede that she'd done a good job, as good as (some even said better than) her mother before her, whose reputation was known in three counties.

So she settled herself between the two returning heroes, her brother on her left, half an inch shorter than her, Dan on her right, a good half-foot higher, and her own head held up to Molly Redmond and anyone who might question her right to this place on this night. Cheeks flaming against the cold night air, she said: 'Before we go in, I'd just like to say a short ditty that I made up to honour this occasion tonight. It's called "The Boys Are Coming Home" and it goes like this:

Hear the rousing cheers around us
For the boys are coming home
Mothers, sisters, sweethearts greet them
The dear boys now coming home!
And Erin's bitter story
Of her fight so long and gory

Ends in sunburst of bright glory
For the boys are coming home!'

She took a breath and looked up and they started to clap. 'There's more,' she said. 'Go on, so,' shouted Big Jim Maher, and she started on verse two and then three and then the other seven verses. When it was over, the applause was loud and long and she waited it out. Then she took the arm of each of the two boys and turned, so that the three of them strutted, arm in arm, into the pub together. Just as she had dreamed it.

All Barney's mother wanted was for him to come inside to the kitchen for some food, partly because she wanted him to eat, but mainly because she wanted him to herself. But nobody else would hear of it. 'Time enough for food, Mrs Parle,' Big Jim said, and Barney seemed to agree, starting on one of the drinks pressed into his hand.

Peg's moment of triumph didn't last long: she was needed back behind the bar and had no time to talk to the boys as she ran from shelf to counter handing up bottles and taking money, fetching back used glasses and giving out change. Before long, every glass in the place was dirty again and they hadn't time to do more than rinse one off when needed. Many hadn't the patience to wait and began to drink direct from the bottle.

Busy though they were, Barney stayed out on the customer side of the counter throughout and none of them would have had it any other way. Peg loved to see him there, encircled by men so much taller, receiving their back-slaps and respect and congratulations. Neither he nor Dan was allowed to put a hand near his pocket, everyone who bought a round included them in it.

Each time Peg had to bring one of these drinks across to Dan, her heart and stomach would jump around inside her, like they were trying to swap places. As she lined up a new bottle beside the others, he would look up at her and either wink at her again, or make some remark on her appearance. First it was the way she'd done her hair. Then it was her dress. She had made a special effort and should have been pleased at the attention but there was something in his manner that she didn't like. At the station, she felt his wink was between the two of them, like he was sealing off a little space for them in the middle of the crowd. Here his gestures were public, nearly showy. She wished she could get him away, talk to him on her own.

When she was putting his fifth or sixth bottle of stout down in front of him, he caught hold of her wrist. 'Don't fly away again, you. Stop for a minute and talk to me.'

'Talk to you?' Couldn't he see she was run off her feet and that her parents were watching? 'We're a bit on the busy side, Dan, in case you hadn't noticed.'

'Well, just answer me this, then,' he said, loosening his fingers. 'Have you missed me?'

The other lads heard the question and sniggers rose behind faces that came in close, to see and listen.

'For the love of God, Dan.' She didn't know where to look.

'What do you mean, for the love of God? It's a simple question, isn't it? Have you missed me or haven't you?'

Seeing her discomfort, Sore-Toes jumped in. 'Don't mind him, Peg. He's had one too many.'

'Mind him?' She crowed a disdainful laugh. 'I'd as soon mind one of the little boys in school.'

'Well, you're always saying how fond you are of those children.' He leaned back on his stool, killed her with his slow grin. 'Does this mean there's hope for me yet?'

While the others were laughing at that, he slid her a look that nobody else saw, a look that said she didn't fool him, he saw right through to her fancy for him. Blushing, she pulled herself out of his grasp, picked up a cloth to cover her embarrassment and with a flick of it moved on to serve someone else. She could have thumped him. God, but he was full of himself.

It was a long night but it went in fast. At midnight, the singing started up again. Lama White set it off with 'The Bold Black-and-Tans', an old tune with new words, denouncing atrocities committed by those hated regiments. Ten verses long, and Lama knew every belligerent word of it. The band members who hadn't gone home played along to the tune and everyone else joined in by shouting out the last five words at the end of each verse: . . . *THE BOLD BLACK-AND-TANS!* On the final verse, with every one of the English soldiers gunned to death by the IRA, Lama dragged the words out slow, to indicate it was over: *And . . . that . . . was . . . the . . . last . . . of . . . THE . . . BOLD . . . BLACK . . . AND . . . TANS!* Everybody laughed, and clapped and cheered: 'Good man, Lama.' Then somebody called on Barney and he took the floor with a quieter tune, the emigrant's song of exile from County Wexford, 'Slaney Valley'.

At one o'clock, JJ sent Máire off to bed, insisting he and Peg could manage. At half-past one, Mossie Whelan got sick and had to be helped home. The crowd started to thin but those left were drinking with more determination, as if to make up for them. At two, JJ stopped serving. A select ten or so slowed their pace, knowing if they kept quiet, they'd be admitted to the back snug once the place was cleared. It was nearly three o'clock by the time that happened. JJ turned out the gas lamps, told Barney to lead them into the back: Dan and his father, who usually did his drinking at home; Lama White and Sore-Toes Delaney and a few of Parle's best regulars: the two Murphy brothers, John Mythen, Paddy Pender and Pat Spillane.

Barney was very drunk now, his jaw hanging slack. He tripped over the step on his way to the snug and would have fallen on his face only Sore-Toes caught him. Dan was holding up better. Only a loose glimmer in his eye that Peg didn't like told that he had drink taken. He made no attempt to catch her attention.

'I'll look after them now, Peg,' JJ said. 'You get yourself off to bed.'

'I don't mind, Daddy. I'll help. It's not like I have school tomorrow.' Peg was still on her Christmas break from teaching, the national schools not reopening until January 10th.

'No, no. I'll take it from here.'

He thought it unsuitable for her to see them any more advanced in their drunkenness and she had no option but to obey him. Slowly and reluctantly, she turned toward the front stairs. From the snug door, she called a general goodnight but they were all that much the worse for drink they hardly heard her. Only reliable old Sore-Toes had the manners to return the salute. Dan was leaning into Lama and Barney, telling them some story, and didn't even look up at her.

She took a candle from the shelf and pulled herself upstairs, hoping all the way up that something would call her back. A loud yelp sounded out – it could have been Lama – leading to a big guffaw of general laughter, then somebody banged the snug door shut. So that was it: she couldn't believe it had turned out this way. Nothing to show for the whole night, nothing – only a wink or two and a bit of back talk. Nothing real.

In her room, she undressed quickly in the cold and took the candle across to the dressing table. Using the key she kept on a chain around her neck, she unlocked the top right-hand drawer and took out the big shop ledger she used as a diary. Its comfort was the only thing that would soothe her this night, that would steady her enough to sleep. Hugging the hardback book close, she bent low and kept on rummaging. It took her some minutes, minutes that almost froze her bare feet to the linoleum floor before she found what she was looking for: Terence MacSwiney's memorial card.

For Peg, Mr Terence MacSwiney was one of the truest martyrs that Ireland's struggles had produced. In 1920, to protest against his imprisonment, he had gone on hunger strike. He was not the first IRA man to use this tactic, but it was with him that the British government decided not to concede to its pressure. After a fortnight, the eyes of the world turned to watch his defiant, determined end. Unfortunately for the authorities, they had greatly underestimated the time it takes for a resting human body to die of hunger. He lasted on, and on, and on: for seventy-four days in all.

Peg's memorial card showed him as he was near the end: gaunt, hollow-cheeked, pale. Underneath his picture was a sentence from one of his speeches, a thought Peg so admired that she had copied it out onto the fly-leaf page of her diary: *The contest on our side is not one of rivalry or vengeance, but of endurance; it is not those who can inflict the most but those that can suffer the most who will conquer.*

Back in bed, she read this quotation to herself once again and gazed into Terence MacSwiney's determined eyes. Moved, as she always was, she kissed his image with trembling lips, then slipped the card inside her nightdress. Drawing the blankets up around her shoulders, she set out candle, ink, nibs on the square piece of flat board she kept by her bed for the purpose and carefully picked up her pen and started to write. She surprised herself by not writing about Dan, as she had expected, but about Terence MacSwiney. *There is so much that is fine in that face, gaunt and thin as it is. The wasted flesh lets the character through clear and strong. He has the look of a saint about him. He was nobody special to start with, only an ordinary schoolteacher, like me. It was love of Ireland that made him singular. Seventy-four days of embracing hunger. Two hundred and twenty-two meals refused. What would that be like, to go to your Maker with love of country holding your arms open?*

She wrote her fill on that subject, then turned to Dan, and loosened by the earlier paragraphs, poured all her confusion onto the page. By the time she was finished, she felt better. It was foolish to think he'd have time to spend with her on this, his first night back. He was bound to feel it strange, being home again after so long an absence. Remember how she used to feel herself when she came home from Dublin during her teacher training? And he was tired. *And* he was drunk. The main thing was that he was here, home, again. She would see him the next morning at

Mass and soon again after that and once they were seeing each other regularly, they wouldn't be long getting back their old understanding.

Drained then, the back of her eyes sticky with exhaustion, she put the candle back on her bedside locker, her paraphernalia away on the floor under the bed. Downstairs, she could hear their muffled voices yet: still talking, still drinking. They would all have heads like kicked footballs tomorrow. 'Tomorrow,' she whispered to herself, blowing out the candle, slipping the MacSwiney card under her pillow. Then she rolled herself into a ball inside her blankets and let the promise of the coming day slip her into sleep.

She dreamt a raggedy dream that Terence MacSwiney came to her and stood before her with his hands pressed together, his wrists in chains. His shirt was open and showed his bones pressing against his skin. Behind him was a crowd of suffragette women all holding up chained skinny wrists like they were pleading with her. These women were well dressed and did not have as fine, as elevated a look as Mr MacSwiney. He was Irish which made it a more awful thing, when there were still old people living who had been young at the time of the Great Famine. The group of self-starved people moved towards her like an army, him in front, the women behind, one deliberate foot after another, arms up and imploring.

'What is it?' Peg asked Terence MacSwiney. 'What is it you want?'

'We want what we have always wanted,' he said, as if she knew what that was. She felt too that she did, if only she could reach on the knowledge . . .

'Wake up, Peg. Wake up.'

Light snapped her eyes open. A candle. Barney's face lit up behind it.

'You're wanted downstairs,' her brother whispered.

Sleep made her stupid. 'What? What is it?'

'Dan wants you.' She could smell alcohol on his insistent breath, alcohol and tobacco. 'He wants to talk to you.'

Dan!

'He's waiting outside. Will I tell him you'll be down? Peg? Are you awake?'

She was now. Dan wanted her. 'Yes, all right. I'm coming. Tell him I'm coming.'

Her brother left the room, his stockinged feet whispering across the linoleum floor. She lit her candle, checked the time: a quarter after five. Her parents would kill Barney if they knew what he was doing. They'd kill her worse. She slid from her bed, took up the clothes she folded onto a chair a while before, felt their cold touch against her warm skin. Dressed, and with boots in hand, she tiptoed out into the corridor, past her parents' room and down the stairs, careful to step over the squeaky second tread. Sleep clogged her head but a ray of excitement was cutting through the fug, sparking her into wakefulness.

It had been months since she'd done anything like this. Months. Life just hadn't been the same since he left. But now he was back. He was back and he was asking for her. With her heart high, she flew to meet him.

9

When Dan O'Donovan asked Barney to go upstairs to his sister's bedroom and get Peg to come down to him, for a minute Barney had stopped to wonder: how would his friend react if he had replied, 'I'll get Peg for you if you get Nora for me.' But of course he didn't. Even with the amount of drink he had on him, he couldn't speak out.

So now he lay in his single bed, only his smoking hand outside the blankets, his fingers freezing stiff around the cigarette. As he smoked, he tried to steady his head with the scenario he always thought of as his waking dream. It wasn't strictly a dream at all but one lived hour of his life, an hour that now seemed so unlikely he sometimes doubted whether it happened at all: the first time he ever spoke to her alone, to Nora.

The image wasn't coming. Maybe drink was the cause, although aside from a faint fuzz lining the inside of his skull, he felt clear-headed enough. As if he'd drunk himself sober. Earlier, he had got sick out the back – nobody saw him, thank God, or he'd have had to endure taunts about little fellows not being able to hold their liquor – and though he took more whiskey again after that, he couldn't make himself swallow. All the giddiness he felt earlier was gone, as was the longing that had set in later to lie down and succumb to sleep. Now he was in bed he found himself stubbornly awake.

So he lay there, trying to conjure up the memory that had kept him going through his prison months, but tonight it failed him. He kept trying to run the scene through his head, as he had so often before, but it was no good. The way she was with him tonight had frayed the dream. It was all unravelled and wouldn't ever be the same again. So he found himself instead conjuring up flights of future fancy. Tomorrow, he would go to her house and ask – no, tell her parents he wanted to talk with her. He would have it out with her about being so cold with him at the station, stiff as a cardinal. That weak, slithering handshake she gave him, that anxious look towards her father to see was he watching – was that any way to treat a man after not seeing him for eight long months? He hadn't expected her to fling her arms about him, but a bit of a smile wouldn't have told anybody anything, would it? Other girls were smiling away at him. A small squeeze from her hand, was that too much to expect?

And afterwards, when she could have been looking for a chance for a quiet few words, not one blessed thing from her. None of the soft, secret contacts they had enjoyed before he had gone away, that he had held so close all that time. The dogs in the street had given him a better welcome than she had. That was what he would tell her tomorrow, in front of her family if he had to.

Only he knew he'd do no such thing.

Nobody knew about Barney and Nora. In Mucknamore, all the young people kept their love affairs hidden for as long as possible. In Mucknamore, love was a joke, a fever of delusion requiring vigilance from those who were not ailing to stop it losing the run of itself. Jeering and mockery, that was what awaited Barney if his feelings became known. He wasn't able for that, not yet. Not ever, maybe. And Nora was even more set on keeping it quiet. It had to be a secret, that's what she said, since the very first time. Nobody else must know. Nobody. Not even Peg.

All through his prison stint, he had managed to keep her to himself. Which wasn't easy. When any of the lads asked whether he had a sweetheart at home, he had mumbled and smiled but never mentioned her name. It killed him to keep it in but keep it in he did. With Dan in the camp bed next to his, he had to.

He had done everything her way, but what good had it done him? Maybe he shouldn't have been so surprised by her carry-on tonight. Maybe he shouldn't have built himself up expecting any better. Wasn't this how it always was between them, every move forward followed by two steps back? No sooner did he think he'd made a bit of progress than she slipped away from him again. He never held it against her because he thought she had her reasons. He never thought of her as one of those girls who like to lead you on a dance, tease you onwards just for the fun of having your attentions only to brush you off when she felt like it.

Yet was that not what she had done? Was he a fool? Were his feelings making a fool out of him?

He *had* to see her alone, remind her of the way things were, get her back to how she used to be before.

Before. That first time, in the cemetery. She was fond then, though even then, she was trying not to be.

Last April it was, a month before his imprisonment. He had been playing a clandestine hurling match up in Jem Moran's field. The Tans were still on the loose then and all Gaelic games were forbidden by martial law. He was cycling back from the secret match, in high good humour, having scored the winning point for Mucknamore. Going by the cemetery he let go of the handlebars to freewheel down the hill there, when he thought he spied her red hair behind a gravestone as he flashed past. He squeezed his hands onto the brakes without thinking, pulled to a halt and dismounted. He was right: it was her. And she was alone.

He forced himself to climb the low wall and approach her, heart thumping against his ribs the whole way over. She was as bad. When she saw him coming, she jumped to her feet, blushing. Her hands folded across her chest and she clasped the book she had been reading in front of her like a shield. But she let him say his good evenings and answered him politely when he opened conversation with her. Talk came surprisingly easy between them and when, after a time, he suggested that he might show her the stream called the 'bloody river' that flowed up behind the cemetery, she let him lead her up there.

At the low stone wall behind the graveyard, he held out his hand to help her over but she ignored it and stepped across with ease. Just behind the wall was a ridge, then a small field and behind that, the brook where the water, bouncing and gurgling over the stones, seemed to run red.

She wasn't too impressed. 'I suppose it does look like watery blood . . . a bit,' she said.

He told her the story: that the water was said to have been stained by the blood of a persecuted priest in the time of the penal laws. Further up the field, at the top of the incline was an old Mass-rock where this priest used to say Mass because the English didn't allow Catholics to practise their religion. One Sunday morning, a troop of English soldiers surprised him in the middle of the sacrament. He ran from them, down the field, but they caught up with him at the stream and shot him.

'He fell into the river,' he told her, 'and ever since the water has run red, stained by his holy blood.'

He blessed himself and she copied the gesture, then she smiled at him and said, 'I think I heard a story like that about a river at home.'

He smiled back. 'Weren't there persecuted priests the length and breadth of Ireland?'

He bent down and cupped a handful of water. 'It's only the reflection of the stones, see? The water itself is clear.'

She dipped one hand – the other still held her book – making a cup of it. As she leaned towards the water, strands of hair that had escaped their pins fell forward about her face. Through the streaks of auburn, her skin glowed, blue-white, whiter than that of most redheads – than his own, for example – and not freckled. He had never seen anything as lovely. Her beauty seemed like something impossible to him, especially up this close. He could do nothing but stare at it.

Then she shook the water from her fingers, breaking the spell. 'I better go,' she said.

He stood as she did, stayed close. 'Can't we stay a small while yet?'

She hesitated.

'Please. Just another few minutes.' He reached out to touch her free hand, the one she had just held in the water. Her fingers were damp and cold. The creeping darkness gave him courage. With his heart thumping hard enough to burst out of his chest, he lifted her hand to his mouth and kissed it like a courtier. When she didn't take it away he kissed it a second time. Then he turned it over and kissed again, this time the lined valley of her palm, then the tips of her five fingers, each slowly in turn. The fingers stirred in his, then lay still.

What made him do that, he wondered; he never in his life imagined himself doing any such thing. But she was affected, he could feel that she was. As he was himself.

He kissed her palm again and the base of her wrist. This time she said, 'Please . . . Don't . . .' So he released her and she let her arm fall by her side.

Her other hand, the unkissed hand, still gripped her book. He bent to bring his face level with hers, trying to look into her averted eyes. A wave of tenderness like nothing he had ever felt before was sweeping him along. She was so small, so light, so fragile that he felt stretched to twice his real height.

'Nora,' he said, the word thick on lips that found it hard to speak. 'Look at me, Nora.'

She would not so much as peep at him and as he gazed down at her – yes, down, he who spent most of his life having to look up – it seemed to him that the smallest puff of wind could blow her away. He put his hands on her shoulders. Her hair was soft and smelt of something lovely. He said her name again, 'Nora,' and pulled her close, tucking her head under his chin. Her delicate frame put him in mind of chicken bones but she went in and out in all the right places. Feeling her shape beneath the fabric of her coat nearly floored him. He kept expecting her to cast him off but she didn't. She let him hold her.

She let him hold her, and after a time, he heard a thud, the sound of her book falling to the grass and he felt her small arms creep round his waist. He said nothing. In that moment, he had all he wanted. On and on they stood, as darkness swirled in and settled around the gravestones and a breeze rose from the sea to rustle the leaves of the trees above them.

So there it was: his waking dream. He had run it through in his head after all. He sat up in bed, took another cigarette from its pack and lit it off the previous one's red glow. (At least he had the consolation of unlimited fags, something he'd not had for eight long prison months.) His head was starting to hurt, as if it was clogged full of rattling pebbles. Whiskey was the culprit. He could down stout forever, but whiskey . . . He'd probably see no sleep at all.

Three more secret meetings after that. Three meetings, and in between lots of dodging and ducking but smiles and looks and, he had thought, an understanding. Then came his arrest for drilling and his imprisonment. He had wanted to write to her from prison, asked her before the trial if he could send her a few lines through Peg, but she wouldn't let him. So all he had was his memories.

Fair enough while he was imprisoned but memories wouldn't be enough to keep him going now, here, at home.

He wasn't so far gone that he really believed he'd follow through the things he planned now as he lay in bed. He knew he wouldn't really call to her house, speak to her in the open, announce his feelings. Even as he rehearsed his lines in his dream-drama – what he would say to her father as he met him at the door ('I love your daughter, Mr O'Donovan'); what he would say to her when she berated him for telling ('We've nothing to be ashamed of, Nora. I love you and I don't care who knows it') – even as he plotted his moves and her responses, he knew none of that would really happen.

But he would do something. He couldn't just leave it as it was now. He would talk to her, he vowed to himself, in a feverish exhalation of cigarette smoke. Somehow, he would.

10

In the dim light of the pantry, Peg could barely make Dan out. She started feeling around the shelf with her hand. 'Never mind the candle,' he said. 'Come on out.'

She hesitated.

'Come on. I can't talk to you here.'

'I'll need my coat.' She found it on the hook behind the door and drew the belt tight around her. Out the door they went, down the path, across the grass and down as far as the strand without saying a word. It was even colder than earlier, everything sharp silver where the moonlight fell. In the distance, the sea breakers looked like fluttering ribbons of lace. The frosty air on her face blew away the last cobwebs of sleep. She felt nothing now but pure excitement.

For all he had said about wanting to talk to her, he didn't speak until the ground had turned to sand under their feet and then all he said was: 'So here we are.'

He laughed, though, and in the sound she heard an echo of what she was feeling herself and then he put out his hand to her and she gave it. Somehow, without anything being said, things were coming right between them again. He had asked for her and here she was. Right now, she felt she would go anywhere with him. Anywhere. Never mind that such behaviour was unfitting for her, the schoolteacher, or that her mother or Father John would never forgive her if she were caught.

'Will we take a walk out the Causeway?' he asked.

She found herself blushing. 'All right.'

'You don't think it's too dark?' She could see the flash of his grin in the moonlight. That's the excuse she gave him last time, before he persuaded her.

'The moon could hardly be brighter,' she answered, deliberately misunderstanding.

'A darling moon.'

'A beauty.'

'So we'll step out that far, will we? If it's not too dark?' Another flash of his white teeth. He couldn't let it go, had to put her in her place.

'I didn't think you would be frightened of the dark, Dan.'

'Oh, no,' said he. '*I'm* not frightened.'

'Well, neither am I.'

'Good.' He pulled her closer, tucked her hand under his arm. 'Good. I'm glad to hear it.'

So they walked out the Causeway, just like in the old days, along the centre pathway through the dunes. The tide was in and on each side a bright strip of sand fell away into the black of the sea. 'While I was inside, I was forever thinking about this,' he said, waving his free hand out in a big circle. He meant the strand, the sea, the whole thing. Did he mean her too? She could hardly ask him that. Instead she said, 'What was it like in there?'

'Not too bad. All the lads looked out for each other and the Brits were easy enough on us. It was the higher-ups who got the grief, mostly. For the likes of us, the worst of it was the food.'

He was a bit slurred in his words and she realized the drink had a hold of him, which was hardly surprising. He must have downed ten large bottles while she was there and probably more after, or more likely went on to half-ones. He seemed sober but he must be far from it. She should disapprove but she couldn't care about anything like that now. If he hadn't drink taken, he would hardly have had the nerve to send Barney up after her the way he did.

Without discussing their destination, they found themselves back where they went before, on the Coolanagh side of the Causeway, at a spot near the edge of the dunes before the sand flattens out, where there was a dip, like a giant hand took a scoop out of the earth. Lovers' Hollow. A sheltered little spot, within which you were hidden from those passing on the Causeway, even by day.

They lay down there together and before long were kissing. His lips were cold on the outside, warm behind. She could taste the sour tang of stout on his mouth but underneath was the taste of himself, a taste she remembered now she had found it again. She reached for it, kissing him as hard as he kissed her. After a time he opened her coat and then his own, button by slow button, kissing her all the while. Under cover, he slipped his hand in under her cardigan, over the bodice of her dress. The hand was cold through the thin material. It was wrong what he was doing but she didn't stop him. His fingers started to trace circles where they shouldn't, round and round, stirring those feelings in her again. She heard herself moan under his lips and she pulled back. 'Go easy, Dan, for God's sake,' she whispered, nudging his hand away with her arm. Her voice sounded strange to her own ears, slurred like his, except she had no skinful taken.

'Ah, Peg, you're a great girl,' he said. She wanted him to say more. How great was she? How was she great?

'Do you not care for me, Peg?' he asked instead, trying to get past her restraining hand. She nodded against his shoulder, afraid to look at him. Wasn't that much obvious?

'Then what are you worried about?' he said, and he set to kissing and touching her again. 'No, Dan,' she said but it was almost a yes, and he knew it. She was dismayed by her weakness. This was as bad as the last time, when she did things with him that had her churning with embarrassment later. Things she wouldn't have believed herself capable of doing. In her room afterwards, or whenever she was on her own, she would flush up at the memory. One thing in particular that she did: whenever it came to her mind, she'd find herself letting out a long groan, waggling her head to try and empty it of the thought.

For months that had gone on. She swore she'd never be so

foolish, so immoral again. And now look at her, next door to the same situation. What in God's name was she thinking of?

'No,' she said, meaning it this time.

At first he didn't realize. He told her again that she was great and said she wasn't to be like that to him. Not with him after thinking of her night and day in prison.

'Were you?'

'Amn't I after telling you I was.'

But it was no good. 'No, Dan. No.' She pushed him away, pulled her clothes together.

He drew back from her and the soft, almost silly, expression on his face hardened. '"No",' he said, imitating her voice. '"No, Dan, no." Why is it "no" tonight, eh? You were willing enough before.'

She straightened out in shock when she heard him say that, as much at his tone as at the words. The derision in his voice.

'I'm only joking,' he rushed, when he saw how she took it. 'That came out all wrong.'

She stood up, buttoned her coat.

'For Christ's sake, woman. Don't make a meal out of it.'

Her fingers were shaking round the buttons. That he could speak to her like that, think of her like that ... *Not fair*, she screamed at him in her mind. Not fair. Not fair.

The walk back was terrible, no hand-holding this time and not a word spoken between them. His face was shut to her, tight as a fist, as if he were the one who had been wronged. By the time they were back where the Causeway meets the strand, her anger had turned to despair. She was softening, she would have liked them to make up. 'Are you vexed with me?' she asked.

'Vexed, is it?' He laughed, stiff-jawed, so it came out like a snort.

'Yes,' she said miserably.

'Go home to your bed, girl.' His mouth was sullen, beautiful, shut fast to her. He turned and walked away.

Dismissed, she turned in the opposite direction. She walked slowly, slackly, hoping he might call her back. When he didn't, she looked behind. He had stopped walking, was standing still halfway up the hill towards his place, his hands in his pockets, looking out at the sea, not at her. She ached to go back to him but something even stronger than her longing turned her around again, forced one foot in front of the other towards home.

She didn't understand how it all went so wrong. She could understand him trying it on, it was only what any fellow would do. But to be so cold to her after. He was a demon when crossed, she had seen that in him before. But did he have to be so hard-faced with her? He could hardly expect her to give him a free run, could he? What would he think of her if she did?

Next day was Sunday and they had to be up at nine for Mass. When Peg's eyes opened and searched out the clock and found it was beyond cight o'clock, her first thought was, no. No, no, she couldn't do it. She would have to say she was sick, or something. Her body, her head, her limbs, all were weighted to the bed. But even as she was thinking this way and groaning aloud and clinging to the warm hollow of her mattress and cocooning the blankets in around her, she knew she had to. It would be quite wrong of her to yield to this self-pity and tiredness, tiredness that was entirely due to going off gallivanting around the night, nothing but her own foolish fault. Oh, but it was so cold. The tip of her nose was icy. She lifted her head from the pillow to huff out some air, watched it vaporize before her face. Then suddenly, knowing that the longer she lay there, the harder it would get, she flung the bedclothes off.

It wouldn't feel so bad in an hour, she told herself, as she pushed herself out. One thing about the bitter chill that assaulted her bare skin through the flimsy fabric of her nightgown: it was refreshing, like a splash of cold water all over. She knelt as she did every morning, placed her face in her hands and began her prayers. *In the name of the Father, the Son and the Holy Ghost* . . . She said an Our Father and three Hail Marys, trying not to race through the words but to give them their meaning and offer them to God. Then she added a few improvised words. She never planned this prayer, just waited to see what popped into her head. This morning it was: 'Heavenly Father. Forgive me if I did wrong last night. I will try to do right today and all the days to come. Please, please, let him talk to me at Mass this morning. Amen.'

The ritual of prayer always made her feel better. She got up from her knees and in bare feet padded across the cold linoleum to open the curtains. Frost had made a pattern on the inside of her window. She rubbed a circle clear with a warm finger. Outside, the sky was only just light but it was going to be a bright morning. On the road, shadows hurried through the dark in warm coats and best hats: those who had been at early Mass returning to their homes. Mostly it was the older people who went early. Sometimes her own father went, if he had pressing work to do in the bottling store or on the shop books, but mostly they attended second Mass all together, as a family. Her mother liked them to do it that way, though Peg and Barney often questioned why. As soon as they got to the chapel, where men sat in the pews to the left of the centre aisle and women to the right, they would break up anyway.

Máire's attitude in this marked the Parles off from their neighbours. Most parents, with eight or ten or more children, had little time for such niceties, but the Parles were like a Protestant household, people said. Not just in their size – with their two parents and two children – but also in some of the mother's ways of going on.

Peg knew what it would mean to her mother to have the four of them setting out together this morning for the first time in months. She always held Sunday as special. Licensing laws meant that on a Sunday the pub closed until evening, allowing them all to sit down together to their dinner, without anyone having to jump up and go out serve a customer. And today, Peg remembered, was going to be even more special than most. They had kept the

Christmas goose for Barney's return. Last night, before they went down to Carnagh station, she and Máire prepared the bird. It stood now in the pantry, plucked, cleaned out and stuffed with Máire's best potato stuffing, wrapped in greaseproof paper. With it they would have carrots and peas and two kinds of potatoes, mashed and roast, and afterwards brandy pudding. Peg hugged herself: life was never all bad.

Down in the kitchen, Barney had the range well lit. He was sitting in beside it, as close as he could get to the heat, nursing a steaming cup, two hands wrapped around it. She laughed to see him, it was so obvious that his head was sore; she could nearly see the pain coming off it.

'Is that tea?' she asked him.

'Boiled water. I'm going to take Communion.'

She raised her eyebrows at him. 'With the amount of liquor you took into yourself last night? I'd say the holy bread will hop out of your mouth.' But she made it clear by the smile she gave him that she was only joking. She went over to the mirror by the window and began the daily chore of pinning up her hair. 'You're obviously paying for it, anyhow,' she said, pins in her mouth.

'I'm dying, so I am. Dying. Never, never again.'

'That's what they all say.' Peg was a Pioneer, a member of the Pioneer Total Abstinence Association of the Sacred Heart, and wore its pin on the lapel of her coat to announce to the world that she had pledged never to drink alcohol. To tell the truth, it wasn't much of a sacrifice for her; she'd never even been tempted. The smell of the stuff was bad enough, she could never imagine drinking it. And living in a pub, seeing what it did to those who did, would put you off for life.

'Hey, don't get carried away there, you, playing the saint,' her brother said. 'What time did you get in last night after?'

She nodded, sheepish. 'After six.' Barney was right, she was no saint. It was a bit embarrassing, him knowing now about her and Dan, but she didn't think he would use the information against either of them.

'Are you stepping out with him now?'

'I don't th— No. We . . . Em. I—' She stopped, miserable. Through the mirror she could see Barney looking hard at her across his teacup.

'Did he – are you all right?'

'I'm grand,' she said, blushing. 'We just argued, is all.'

'That fellow would argue with St Peter himself.'

Peg turned to him, surprised by his tone. 'I thought you and he were the best of friends.'

'We are. He's a good brave fighter and a good laugh always. But . . .' He hesitated.

'But?'

'Ah . . . nothing.'

'Come on now, Barney. You can't do that to me.'

'Do you like him?'

She turned back to the mirror, glad of somewhere to put her eyes. 'He's all right, I suppose.'

She'd love to ask if Dan ever said anything about her. Surely Barney would tell her if there was anything worth telling? But would he? He was a boy, after all.

Barney was frowning. 'I don't know if he's the kind of fellow you'd want your sister going with, that's all.'

'Why not? In what way?'

He shook his head, then grimaced when the gesture hurt. 'Oh, nothing, nothing. I'm sorry I said anything now.'

So am I, she thought furiously, ramming the last few pins into her hair. But she didn't want to fall out with him, not on his first day back. And what Barney thought was hardly the heart of the matter anyway.

'Never mind him,' she said. She poured herself a cup of water from the kettle and sat down in the fireside chair opposite him. 'What about you? How does it feel to be home?'

'Good, of course.'

'It's been awful quiet around here without you.'

He smiled, acknowledging the compliment lodged in the words. 'But all's well?'

'Grand. Not a bother.'

'Mammy looks thin,' he said.

Peg hesitated, then decided to tell him the truth. 'To be honest, she's not any better than she was before you left.'

'Worse, I'd say.'

'Maybe. Maybe worse. She's dropped a lot of her political work, handed it over to me. She's not able to keep everything going.'

Barney looked stricken, like he might cry. It was a peculiarity of her brother's that he felt life had been unjust to him, a sense of grievance Peg considered to be born of his lack of stature. All his life, Barney was small for his age and in manhood only stood five feet and four inches. It was far from the heaviest cross a person could be given to bear and he had many advantages to set against it: good health, good looks and a good brain; the relative prosperity of his family; good friends and neighbours. Most of the time he was happy enough with his lot but when life dealt him a blow, his hurt feelings attached to the little well of resentment that lurked within him, sometimes brimming it over so that it drowned his reason.

This tendency in him had beset their childhood together. Barney's favourite utterance as a boy was 'It's not fair . . .' Máire's explanation that life was never fair, that expecting it to be so was only setting yourself up for disappointment, did nothing to soothe him. Their mother was inclined to indulge Barney in a way that would have made Peg take up the 'it's not fair' cry herself if she hadn't understood, and also been inclined towards indulgence.

This overdeveloped sense of misfortune was her brother's only fault and the worst of it was its effect on himself.

She could see now that this news about their mother's illness stirred such feelings. They had never uttered the name of Máire's condition between them but he knew as well as she did what it was, and its implications for them all. They could become outcasts. People might stop coming to the shop, start avoiding them at Mass, turn the other way when they came walking down the road. It had happened to other families before. Still, it was right that he should know. Even though he was likely to feel sorry for himself for the shame that would be his through no fault of his own, even though she could see he was already thinking about the hazard of contracting it himself . . . For her, it would be good to have someone to talk to. Her father was pure hopeless and loyalty meant she could never go outside the family. So she brought her brother's attention back to where it should be, to Máire.

'She's still sparring away, though, illness or not. It's the Treaty now, how it's a complete betrayal of the Republic.'

'She's not on her own with that thought,' said Barney. 'In the prison camp, a lot of lads felt that way.'

'She's fairly on her own around here.'

'Well, wasn't she always?'

'That's true. If we were waiting for the people of Mucknamore, there would never have been a shot fired.'

'But they've swung round now, eh? I couldn't believe some of those I saw down at the station last night.' The thought cheered him. 'The things they were saying to me, I couldn't believe. You'd think they were all in it with us from the start.'

'I know. They'd make you laugh. Not an ounce of shame in them.' Peg got up and took the steaming kettle off its hook. Barney held out his cup for a top-up.

'So you think it could go the same way this time?' she asked, sitting back down when she'd refilled them both. 'That they'll swing round again to Mammy's way of thinking. Is that what you're saying?'

'I suppose. Maybe.'

'This seems a lot less straightforward. There's too much division.'

'Before we left the prison camp, you could see the arguments brewing up between the two sides.'

'Pro-Treaty versus anti-Treaty?'

Barney nodded. 'Michael Collins carried a lot onto the pro-side. If it was all right for the man who masterminded the guerrilla campaign, the most ruthless Republican of them all, it was all right by them.'

'You sound like you agree?'

'In a way. But I'm also inclined towards what de Valera says. To tell you the truth, I can't fully make up my mind. There's powerful arguments on both sides.'

'Yes!' cried Peg. It was a relief to hear somebody else say this after weeks of listening to her mother denounce the Treaty as pure poison. 'That's what I think.'

'The main thing is that we avoid a split.'

'Yes again! And, Barney, I think we will. Most people want unity above all else. We've never been more united than in these past—' She stopped as she heard footsteps approaching from the hall. 'Sssh! Here's Mammy.'

But it wasn't. It was JJ. He came in, stroking thin strands of white hair across his bald head. 'Would you bring your mother up a cup of water, Peg? She's going to take an extra few minutes in the bed.'

'Is she all right?'

'Just a bit tired, she says.'

Peg and Barney exchanged a glance.

'Is she going to Mass?' asked Barney.

'Of course she is.' He frowned at them. 'She's only lying abed for an extra few minutes. Why wouldn't she be tired, with the carry-on we had here last night?'

He took a cup down from the top cupboard, scratchy with irritation. They were not supposed to make any reference to Máire's weakness, no matter how vague.

'All right, Daddy,' said Peg, getting up. 'I'll bring it up to her now. You sit down here by the fire for a bit and have your own.'

At Mass, Father John used the first half of his sermon to make a call for ratification of the Treaty, without which, he said, they had no chance of a peaceful 1922. The second half he gave over to his dismay at the behaviour of the men and boys of the parish each Sunday after Mass, most especially the way they began to smoke as soon as they were out of the chapel. The Holy Host, he said, leaning over his pulpit to stare at particular offenders, could hardly have melted in their mouths and there they were for all to see, sucking on their cigarettes or pipes. This performance he considered very disrespectful to Almighty God. The least they could surely do was wait until they were behind their own front doors before lighting up. He spoke at length on this subject, so long that the Mass went on for over an hour.

On the way out of the church, Máire and Peg were put in the path of Mrs O'Donovan and Nora and the four of them stopped to talk. Ever since Barney and Dan were sent to prison, Máire had been trying to move her acquaintance with Mrs O'Donovan along, the two families now being linked, 'linked forever', she had said, by their boys' shared experiences. But Mrs O'Donovan didn't make it easy for her. A quiet woman, not inclined to small talk, she never settled into a conversation or encounter but always seemed to be nervously looking ahead to what was coming along next.

Máire began with the weather. 'It's a cold one,' she said.

'It is,' Mrs O'Donovan replied.

'Isn't it great to have the lads back?'

'Yes.'

'Are you doing anything special today with your boy?'

'No. Nothing special.' Mrs O'Donovan looked pained, her eyes flickering in their sockets, her weight on one leg as if she longed to be off. Nora, beside her, wore a similar expression.

Peg had noticed this before, how this edgy trait of Nora's was amplified whenever she was with any of her family. Some put this nervous quality in the female O'Donovans down to the man of the house, who was not popular. For a long time, rumours had been going around about what went on up in that farmhouse, rumours that John O'Donovan beat both wife and children, not a few slaps like any man might do, but serious. There was talk of one of the youngest children pelting down the lane one day, helter-skelter, tripping over the stones in bare feet, running from her father's temper. But as to which O'Donovan child it was, and who had seen her (or was it a him?), it was all very vague.

There was also speculation about why the O'Donovans sold up a place in Cork to come and settle in Mucknamore, where nobody knew them. All sorts of suggestions were made about that. Peg never knew whether to believe these rumours or not. She wouldn't put anything past Mr O'Donovan, a man who always seemed to be looking at people as if he were sizing up their faces for a punch. Dan had no time for his father, she knew that. They had terrible rows about his volunteering activities and once Mr O'Donovan had thrown him out of the house. Dan had spent that night in Barney's room and she had woken every few minutes, imagining him on the other side of the bedroom wall from her. Another time, she had tried to gently open Nora up about why she felt the need to keep everything, even the simplest thing, secret from her family, but Nora wouldn't be drawn.

Máire said the rumours were nothing but that, and should be disregarded until proven. There were people in Mucknamore who would believe anything bad about the O'Donovans just because they were not born and bred around here, she said. She had had a touch of that treatment herself from some when she first came to the village, and she was a Wexford woman who had only come from Forth Mountain, a mere ten miles away. The O'Donovans, being from Cork, were complete strangers. 'Foreigners,' as Miley Ffrench once put it.

Her mother was now trying to get Mrs O'Donovan going on the subject of Father John's sermon. 'Abuse of the pulpit, that's what I call it,' she said, in a fierce whisper, looking over her shoulder at the same time in case the priest, or any of the Holy Joes, might be near enough to hear her.

Mrs O'Donovan nodded, her eyes flitting towards the gates.

'You'd hardly expect him to say anything else, Mammy,' Peg said, trying to close the gap between the two women.

'It's his job to pray for peace, fair enough. But telling us it was "Ratification or Ruin"? That's pure politics. He has no right.'

A woman's voice called out from behind them: 'Who are you giving out about now, Máire Parle? God help him, whoever it is.' It was Lil, Máire's friend, and her daughter Cat.

Máire laughed, then looked over her other shoulder before whispering, 'Father John. I was just saying to Mrs O'Donovan, he's getting more political by the week. Someone should tell the Bishop.'

'From what I hear, the Bishop would agree with him,' Lil said.

'You're probably right. Peace, peace, peace, that's all they talk about.'

'I suppose it's what everybody wants to make sure of now.'

'But what kind of peace? That, surely, is the question.'

Dan had come out and was over by the church gate pillars with Barney and Lama and Sore-Toes. It was strange to see the four of them there together but not smoking. Father John's sermon seemed to be taking an effect, for now anyway.

Had he seen her? she wondered. She leaned into Mrs O'Donovan and Nora, smiling hard. Look at me, she was thinking. Look how nice I am to your family, how much they like me. See how lucky you'd be to have me. But when she glanced across his way again, he had his back to her, talking to Jem Fortune and it was Barney who was looking across with a very strange frown on his face.

'We had a so-called peace before 1916 but were the Irish people happy?' her mother was saying. 'No, they were not. That was what led to the Tan War in the first place. Have people forgotten that already? Peace at the wrong price won't last long.'

Mrs O'Donovan looked blank but Lil nodded. 'I was only saying to Billy last night, when the Treaty was announced, there was no sense of triumph in Ireland. Not a flag waved or a bonfire lit.'

'There you are. That says it all. People know in their hearts that these Articles of Agreement are nothing but a big let-down, however much they may try to make the best of it.'

Peg's mother was the only one still referring to 'Articles of Agreement' in that sarcastic way. Everybody else was now calling it the Treaty. But to Máire, who was always pedantic about such things, it wasn't a treaty until it was ratified by the Dáil. Her fervent hope was that that wouldn't happen, that more TDs, members of the Dáil, would vote against the Treaty than for it. Then they'd have to renegotiate the whole thing with the British, she said.

The main problem was the Oath, which would have to be taken by every public representative in the new Free State. Máire had read that bit out to Peg and JJ from the newspaper in scathing tones: 'I do solemnly swear true faith and allegiance to the Constitution of the Irish Free State . . . and that I will be faithful to HM King George V, his heirs and successors by law, in virtue of the common citizenship of Ireland with Great Britain . . .' The words made Peg's head spin but Máire had translated for her. 'Lloyd George sold us a dud,' she'd said. 'Nothing but Dominion Home Rule. The Welsh wizard outfoxed our boys and they gave away the Republic.'

The Treaty also fixed in place the border that cut the six northern counties from the rest of the country, but as it also agreed a Boundary Commission would be instigated to make adjustments to this border in accordance with the wishes of the inhabitants, that did not give Máire too much concern. Any such adjustment would take large parts of the Nationalist counties out of the rogue statelet called 'Northern Ireland' and topple it. On an island the size of Ireland, that border was a nonsense and would surely fall. No, never mind the North, said Máire; the real problem was that the Treaty denied them the Republic.

'When we were weak, we fought,' she said, now, outside the chapel. 'Before the Truce, Ireland was strong – in faith, in spirit, in men. And we had the English on the run for the first time in history. Yet we are going to accept now what we never accepted in centuries of weakness.'

'I never thought of it like that,' said Lil.

'And why? Because our fellows let Lloyd George outwit them. Holding up those two envelopes the way he did, saying take the Treaty for peace or else choose "immediate and terrible war"! That was so wrong. But our eejits fell for it.'

'You can't trust the English,' said Lil.

'What about justice? What about the dead generations who kept a vision in their hearts, who refused to barter? I tell you . . .'

When Peg heard her mother begin on the dead generations, she had had enough. She turned to Cat. Her friend's name was short for Cathleen but also given her because she was as languid as any feline. 'No sign of Lama this morning,' she whispered, pulling Nora across.

'He went to early Mass,' Cat whispered. 'They have a visitor calling to the house today, some uncle on his mother's side.'

'I can't imagine how he got himself out of the bed at that hour. He didn't leave our place until after three.'

'Was he in a bad way?'

'None of them were too sober, as you can imagine.'

Cat gave an indulgent smile at her boy's weakness. Nora looked less approving.

'Do you want to go for a walk after?' Cat asked.

'I can't,' Nora said. 'I have to help at home.'

'That's a pity. Molly is trying to organize the boys to go walking out to the island.'

'The boys? Which boys?' Peg asked.

'Lama. Dan. Maybe Barney might come?'

'Mmm. I'm not sure how we're fixed.'

'Ask.'

Her mother was still pontificating: '. . . they held the dream in their hearts and now we are going to throw it away . . .'

Peg touched her elbow. 'Mammy, am I able to go for a walk with the girls later?'

Máire pulled herself out of speechifying mode. 'You know we've a special dinner laid on for your brother, Peg.'

'Of course I remember that, Mammy. I meant afterwards.'

'Would you not rather stay home?'

Peg shrugged. 'I don't mind.'

'Stay home, so, the day that's in it.' She turned back to Lil.

Peg made a face to Cat and Nora.

'Not to worry,' Cat said. 'I'm not that keen on walking out so far anyway. If you two aren't going, I probably won't bother.'

That was even worse. That would leave Molly on her own with Dan. 'I have a better idea.' Peg interrupted Máire again. 'Mammy, can we have a few around for a card game instead then, later on? After tea, when you and Daddy are working.'

Now it was Máire's turn to make a face at Lil. 'What would you do with these youngsters?'

'Yerra, let them, where's the harm?'

'Barney would love it, Mammy,' coaxed Peg.

'I don't know. What do *you* think, Mrs O'Donovan?'

Mrs O'Donovan looked at Nora who had a face blank of any wanting.

After waiting long enough to realize she wasn't going to get an answer, Máire gave her consent. 'All right, so. But no more than six.'

'Ah, eight, Mammy, please. We have to have Molly too. And Sore-Toes.'

'That Delaney lad, God help him.'

'It wouldn't be nice to leave him out though, Mammy.'

'Oh, go on.'

Peg and Cat turned back to each other beaming. Nora was pleased too, Peg knew, though she wasn't showing it. 'Nora, will you tell Dan? Cat will tell Lama and Molly, won't you, Cat? Tell Molly nobody's bothered walking today, the day that's in it. Tell her to forget the walk.'

'I'll tell her,' Cat said. 'This will be much better.'

Peg agreed with her. 'It will, won't it? It will be just like old times.'

Back at home, as soon as they were inside their front door, Máire was at it again, giving out to JJ about Father John and his ratification speech and the feebleness of the people who were swinging in behind that way of thinking. She clattered the water bucket as she filled the kettle. She clattered the kettle as she settled it on the range and clattered the cups as she laid them on the table.

'Máire, Máire,' JJ said. 'There's no point in banging things about. The fact is, people don't want to go back to what we had before.'

He was right about that and who could blame them? Who'd want to return to waking to the crack of gunfire or the leaping blaze of buildings flaming up the night sky and wondering who was being tormented this time? Last spring, some families used to vacate their homes at sunset, to sleep out in barns or even in the open so as not to be in bed when the soldiers came swinging into Mucknamore in their lorries, banging on doors to be let in to turn the place over, letting off bullets or grenades, setting houses and farm buildings alight, shooting or bayoneting people in their nightshirts.

Máire took up the toasting fork and put a slice of bread on it.

'But that's not what you'd call the will of the people, John-Joe, is it? That's the fear of the people.'

'One reason or another, it makes no difference, does it? The Treaty is what they want.'

'That Treaty will do nothing for any of us.' She opened the door of the range, held the bread as close to the fire as she could.

'It's already let our boy out of prison.' JJ's quiet voice contrasted with her fervour. 'That's good enough for me.'

She swung round on him. 'He should never have been in there in the first place.'

'Máire, we all know we've been sold a pup. The question is, do we put it down now or do we rear it until it can use its teeth for us?'

'Bah! Michael Collins' argument.'

'Well, Mam,' said Barney from his armchair, 'Collins was the hardest man of the lot.'

JJ nodded. 'The Treaty gives us the freedom to win freedom,' he said. 'What's so terrible about that? We work within the Treaty for the time being, keeping our eye on getting our Republic down the road, when the time's right. Everything doesn't have to be done at once.'

'And what about our oaths? I suppose they mean nothing?'

'Look, I'm not interested in arguing it out. You could argue for days and never get to the bottom of it.'

'Meaning: you know the Collins argument doesn't stand up.'

'Máire, I've said my piece and I'll say no more. I never meant to speak at all. I'm tired of it, to tell you the truth, tired of it already. And so is everybody else.'

'Oh, everybody else,' Máire said, sneeringly.

'Well, who is your Republic for if the people don't want it?'

Peg was amazed to hear her father talk like this. Barney was staring at him, open-mouthed, and Máire too was taken aback to be challenged like this in her own home. JJ never engaged in political argument, considering it Máire's territory, though they all knew where he stood. The whole family – indeed the whole village – knew he would prefer if his wife were not leading meetings and marches and writing angry letters to the paper and bringing their children into law-breaking and agitation as soon as they were old enough. But he had let Máire have her way in this, as in everything. To hear him oppose her now was startling.

Máire looked around at the three of them, her face flushed up, maybe from his arguing with her, maybe from the fire. 'Does nobody in this house care for the principle of the thing?' she demanded.

'I see that the Republic's important, Mammy. But maybe—' Peg broke off when she saw her mother's face.

'Maybe . . . ?' Máire asked, sarcastic.

'Máire, leave the girl alone. She's entitled to her opinion.'

'No, Daddy, it's all right, that's not what I meant. I was only going to say, maybe we should wait and see what they say in the Dáil before getting upset. The ratification vote could go our way.'

'I hope you're right, girly,' said Máire. They all sat in silence for a few moments, watching the kettle boil. When the first slice of toast was done, Máire handed it to Barney, put another slice of bread on the fork.

'I can understand your father,' said Máire, after a while addressing Peg and Barney as if JJ wasn't there. 'That man even voted for the Irish Party in 1918, instead of Sinn Féin. I would expect *him* to be speaking up for this Treaty . . .'

JJ stared grimly at the kettle.

'But you youngsters . . . I tell you, if I was young again . . .'

The kettle boiled. Peg got up from her chair, made tea, put it on the heat to draw. Another slice of toast was done, JJ's. Barney passed him the butter.

'We have to stand together,' Máire said. 'Didn't we say all through the Truce time, Peg, that the English would probably deal us a dirty trick? Didn't we run those training camps for all the new recruits, so we'd be ready to resume hostilities if necessary? Well, now it is looking necessary.' Her flush was not from the fire. 'You took an oath when you joined Cumann na mBan, Peg, and you, Barney, when you joined the Irish Republican Army, and you can't take a second oath of allegiance to the Free State or the English King. Your allegiance is to the Republic. It's that simple.'

Peg could feel the force of her mother's logic and the purity of her ideals in every word.

'The Republic lives,' Máire said. 'It was brought into being by the Irish people in 1918. Nothing but the decision of the Irish people can dismantle it. But there are those now, those on our own side, who have decided to put it aside as if it is nothing. That's why it's up to the rest of us, who know what is right and true, to defend it.'

JJ stood up, his plate and cup in his hand. 'I'm going out to set the shop to rights.'

Máire looked up at him. 'We're not open until five.'

'I know. But I want it to be ready so I can take my ease after the dinner. The feast.' He smiled at her, trying to win her round. That was why he was going out to the shop too, Peg knew. He was giving Máire time to calm down, so they could get the day – this special day – back onto an even keel.

He waited a minute, hoping for a response. When she didn't succumb, he turned to Barney. 'Will you come out with me, son, and give me a hand?'

Barney looked up at him, his mouth full of toast. Peg could see he didn't want to help, that he wanted only to stay on sitting by the fire. And it was hard to blame him, his first morning back. But the look on her father's face turned her heart over. Go on, she urged her brother in her head. Go with him.

'I'll follow you out in a minute, Da. I fancy another slice of toast.'

'You go on out, Barney,' Peg said, knowing that if he didn't go now he wouldn't go at all. 'I'll bring the toast to you.'

He had no choice but to get up.

After the two men were gone, Máire waved Peg into the chair nearest her. 'We'll get going on the vegetables and the rest of the dinner in a few minutes,' she said, but first she wanted to make a list of those IRA and Cumann na mBan volunteers who were likely to stay sound. 'Forget the flag-waggers and the would-be warriors,' she said, taking a copybook and pencil down from the shelf. 'Think on those who were with us in the hard times.'

'Sore-Toes, Lama and those? You don't see any of them going over, surely?'

'It's hard to be certain,' Máire said. 'Go through them. I'd say you're right that the White boy is firm. And the Moran boys I'd nearly swear on. The three Fortunes. The Leacys. Jamsie Crean. Jack Kelly. The Connicks. And you think young Delaney?'

'Sore-Toes? Definitely.'

'It's just he's such an eejit sometimes. He could be talked into anything. Though I suppose,' Máire arched an eyebrow at her daughter, 'he listens to some more than others.'

Peg ignored that jibe.

'The O'Donovans?' Máire then said, lightly. 'Dan and his sister?' And Peg knew from her voice that this was the big question. The one her mother had been building up to.

'They're staunch.'

'You're sure?'

'I was only talking to Nora last night. As staunch as ourselves.'

'And her brother?'

'Of course, Mammy. You know he was the most fervent of all.'

'Lil tells me that he has already been heard saying what's good enough for Michael Collins is good enough for him. And John O'Donovan had been making ratification speeches all round the village since the day we heard the word Treaty.'

'Oh, *him*,' said Peg. 'The father was never with us, you know that. Poor Nora isn't even allowed to join Cumann na mBan and you know he nearly disowned Dan for joining up. We're not going to start judging men by their fathers, I hope.' If they did, where would she and Barney be? Wasn't JJ himself less than eager?

'Let's hope you're right,' said Máire. 'O'Donovan is a sharp lad, if not quite as sharp as he thinks he is.'

'He's an asset all right.' Peg couldn't keep her face from rising red.

'I just wish he'd be a bit more respectful,' Máire said, with a nod towards the door to the shop. Peg knew what she meant: Barney. This was an old refrain of Máire's. Barney had been captain of Mucknamore Company when Dan arrived to live in the village from Cork. By the time they were sent to prison, Dan had almost usurped the role from him. It was not, Peg believed, a conscious appropriation, more a consequence of the two men's natures. Dan was a born leader and had experience of combat in Cork that Wexford had never seen. The other boys instinctively knew this, and though he was a stranger they gave him a grudging regard. A different sort of regard than that they gave to Barney, which had more to do with the Parles' social position in the village than any innate soldiering or leadership qualities.

The other side of the coin, the side that Máire never wanted to see, was that Barney was inclined to be lazy. Dan had more 'go' in him than Barney would ever have and people responded to that.

'So long as he's faithful,' Peg said, pulling her mother back to the point. 'And I'm sure he is, he and Nora both.' She said it with confidence but she was shaken. What if her mother was right? What if he didn't care for the Republic any more? If that became the case, what would she have to offer him more than any other girl?

11

'The reason everybody in Wexford is getting so fired up is that you were so slow to get started,' said Dan. He slapped down a jack of hearts onto the Parles' card table and kept a tight eye on the play as he talked. 'Just when Wexford men woke up to the fact there was a war on, the Truce was called.'

The evening had begun well, the card game coming together as Peg had hoped and her hopes exceeded when he slipped into the chair beside hers. Cat and Lama hadn't yet arrived at that stage and he could have taken any of four other places around the table. So she was forgiven, it seemed, for the other night. He had passed her a nice smile as he sat and when the card game got going, his hand had grazed off hers more than once and she knew by the sardonic way he raised one eyebrow without looking at her that he intended it so.

At first, he had seemed more in line with her and Barney about Ireland too, talking about the need for unity and clear thinking. Hotheads should cool off, he said, a point on which she had agreed, until Lama spoke about the oath. 'If they'd only take out the oath and the English Governor-General, then the whole country would be with them,' Lama said. Dan had replied that that was just the kind of talk the country didn't need and she realized then that his definition of a hothead was anyone against the Treaty.

He was for it. Fully for it. He had said as much out straight. She couldn't believe it. And to make matters worse, he was also winning all the cards. The first two games were his and now another looked like it might go his way. Peg had nothing in her hand to stop him and unless somebody else had an unreckoned trump hidden away somewhere, this trick was his too.

After making his admission, it seemed he could talk of nothing else, all the while putting down the efforts made by Wexford in the late war. Wexford men were happy to dig a hole in the road, he said, or take letters out of Jimmy the Post's bag but they'd run a mile if anyone asked them to kill or be killed. Peg didn't know whether to take him up on this, or to let it go. The trouble was, Dan hadn't lived in Mucknamore long enough to know how the boys and girls around here had changed. Peg loved what the fight had done for them, that people were no longer judged by family or the number of acres they had but by worth – ability, idealism and readiness to work for Ireland. For the first time in their lives, boys like Sore-Toes and Lama – once only good for a drink and a good time – had something to fix their minds on. And they were rising to the challenge.

He didn't see any of this, all he saw was the absence of the gun in Wexford compared to Cork. Cork, Cork, Cork was all they heard from him.

It was all right, Sore-Toes had a trump. Only the two but that was good enough. Good man, Sore-Toes: that would show egotistical Corkmen what Wexford could do. As the cards were thrown in for the next deal, Peg decided she had to challenge his argument. 'We're not as bad as all that,' she said.

'No? Then why did HQ have to give the assassination of that district inspector in Wexford town to outsiders to do? The jibing Wexfordmen had to endure in the jail over that, I can tell you, I was glad I wasn't one.'

'God, will you ever let go of that? We've heard you tell it twenty times already and you're only home two days.'

'And I've not heard you answer it once.'

She took a breath, calmed her tone. 'I'm not saying more couldn't have been done – we can always do better – but even if we are not as active as fellows further west, we're every bit as keen.'

'Now, maybe. Now it's too late.'

'Wasn't Wexford one of the few counties outside Dublin that turned out for the Easter Rising in 1916?' she said.

He had no reply to that, of course.

She could go on. She could ask him where the Cork boys were then. She could go further back and remind him of all the 'Boys of Wexford' who died for Ireland in 1798. No county did better than Wexford in that rebellion, and well he knew it. But she let it go; she didn't want to be completely out with him. Instead she silently doled out the matchsticks that helped them keep the score while Molly shuffled the cards for her deal. Two to Sore-Toes representing ten points and one – five points each – to Molly, Barney, Nora and Dan. None for herself; she couldn't seem to get off the ground tonight. It was partly Dan's fault: his palaver was knocking her mind off her game.

Molly picked up the cards and started to shuffle them. She prided herself on being a fancy shuffler, fancy as any man. She could flick the cards, slice them, flip them over in the shape of a fan, string them out like an accordion and tonight she was in the mood for showing off all her skills.

Dan leaned across and touched her wrist. 'If you're not careful you'll knock the spots off them, Molly,' he said, in a voice that made Peg want to kill the pair of them.

And wasn't Miss Molly just delighted with herself? 'Now, now,' she said, smiling up at him. 'Where's your hurry, Dan? Haven't we all night?'

Another few manoeuvres to make the point that she wouldn't be rushed then she dealt. Six cards each and one turned over on top of the deck as trumps. Jack of spades this time.

'In the kingdom of the blind, the one-eyed jack is king,' Sore-Toes said, something he always said when a one-eyed jack turned up.

'Oh, shut up, Sore-Toes,' Molly said. 'Ignore that fellow there, Nora, and lead off.'

Nora led with a spade. Flick, flick went the cards, one from each person skimming onto the table. It was the early part of the game and they didn't have to concentrate too hard yet on flushing out trumps or keeping high men down. Peg tried to get into the game but then Dan started up again, unable to let the argument go. 'Just when you came to fancy the fight,' he said, 'the fight was over.'

'We're ready to fight again,' Peg said. 'And we'll put up a better fight next time.'

His eyes swung her way. 'Against who? The English are going to be gone, Peg. Wexford barracks will be full of Irishmen.'

'We have to stand together. We have to defend the Republic.'

He shook his head at her. 'Keep talking like that and you'll have every thick in the county running round with a gun. Is that what you want?'

'Did you hear,' Lama asked, in an obvious attempt to deflect them, 'that one of the Tans blew his nose in a tricolour in Wexford barracks the other day?'

'Is that true?' asked Molly.

'It's true, all right,' Dan said. 'Do you see what I mean, Peg? They're hopping mad. If the Treaty was nothing, why would they be so put out?'

'You've got to be joking,' said Peg, 'You know they thought they owned the place. Any concession to us at all is a concession too much for them.'

'It's no small concession.' The play started again, and Dan threw out his worst card, talking at her without looking her way. 'It's no small concession for every English soldier to be shifted out of their barracks and shipped home. Soon there won't be one of them left in Ireland outside of the North. We'll have our own army and our own government and our own judges and our own police. They're gone, Peg. It's over.'

Irritation grinded inside her. Why was she the only one at this table prepared to defend the Republic? Why wouldn't Barney talk up? Dan took no notice of her, but he'd listen to Barney, another boy, and one with credentials as good as his own. The same Barney was useless, like a wet dishcloth since he came home, not the brother she remembered at all. Look at him, slumped in the chair beside her, throwing out his cards as if any one was the same as another. She reached across the table to give him a puck in the arm. 'Tell him, you,' she said. 'Get him back into line, can you?'

Barney threw his eyes up. 'Who could tell the great Dan O'Donovan that he might be wrong?' he said.

'There's not one wrong word in anything I've said,' Dan insisted.

'Except that it makes no sense,' said Peg. 'You yourself said it was only the threat of war from Lloyd George that made Collins and the others accept the Treaty but now you say we should all be mighty delighted with the selfsame document. You can't have it both ways.'

'One thing is certain,' Barney said, drawn out of dreamland at last. 'If we're not careful, we're going to have a terrible split in the army and all around the country.'

'Surely,' said Lama, 'it would be better to go back to fighting the Brits, to hammer what we want out of them, rather than fighting ourselves.'

'If only Collins and his cronies had held out for a Republic,' Peg said, 'we'd have none of this trouble now.'

Dan snorted, an ugly sound. 'They were never going to get a Republic.'

'They should have come back to Mr de Valera before signing. They had no right to sign without referring back to him, no right in the world.'

'Don't mind that old *ráméish*,' Dan said. 'A Republic was never on the table and Dev knew that right well. That's why he stayed behind and sent Collins to negotiate instead of himself, so he'd have someone to point a finger at. Oh, the Long Fella thought he knew what he was doing but he lost out.'

'How can you, Dan? How can you say such things?' To speak like that of Mr de Valera, the noblest of all the noble statesmen who had emerged over the past troubled years? She could feel her face reddening to the roots of her hair. 'Mr de Valera would never have agreed to this Treaty, never. You know that—'

He held up a hand, cut her off. 'Forget going over and over the Treaty and what should and shouldn't have been done. What we have to do now is get on with making a country for ourselves. The people have had enough of killing and shooting. They want peace.'

'The people will go where they are led.'

Molly waved a card in each of their faces. 'Ah, would you give it a rest, the pair of you,' she said. 'We're supposed to be playing a game of cards, in case you hadn't noticed.'

Peg backed off into a bristly silence. He would listen to no one. Whatever he thought was a fact and anyone who thought different was a fool. Why was she surprised? It was just the way he was before he was imprisoned, only then they both thought the same. Then she believed he had respect for her but now she knew all he had admired was the sound of his own opinion coming back to him. And now he was flirting with Molly Redmond, mock-shaking his fist because she had topped his trump. Everything was going wrong, everything.

Another round was over. Nora did well this time, winning four tricks. The other two were Molly's. She took the matches from Peg and doled them out and, when finished, counted up each person's total. 'Nora's the high man now, with Dan,' she announced. 'Twenty-five each.'

'What about Sore-Toes?' Dan said. 'Sore-Toes has twenty.'

'And you have fifteen yourself, Molly,' said Peg. 'You're not far behind them.' Peg herself had nothing; not a single match before her.

Sore-Toes picked up the deck for his deal but Lama put his hand across to stop him while he eyeballed Dan.

'Myself, I don't think it will make much difference to the working man who gets the power,' said Lama. Lama was a Labour man and not too enamoured of the way that Wexford IRA were allowing themselves to be used to enforce rent decrees for landlords, in the name of law and order. Or the way Republican courts generally found for the employers in workers' disputes. 'But a Republic is what was fought for and a Republic is what we should have.'

'If it doesn't make much difference,' said Cat, leaning back in her chair, 'can we not just be quiet about it and let Sore-Toes take his deal?'

'Yes,' said Molly. 'We've had enough discussion of Ireland's woes for one night.'

'You're wrong, Lama,' said Dan, as if the two girls hadn't spoken. 'The ordinary man will have plenty of opportunities now, the way he's never had before. In the army. In the police. With our own government, Ireland will prosper at last.'

'But maybe we'd prosper better in a workers' republic.'

Dan cast his eyes towards the ceiling.

'Ah, come on, lads, and deal the cards, will you?' said Molly. 'You were all shouting at me to hurry up a minute ago.'

'Just a minute now, girl,' Dan threw her a smile from the side of his face to soften his words. 'This is important.' He turned back to the three boys, and spoke slow and clear, as if he was talking to children. 'It's down on our knees giving thanks we should be, instead of haggling about oaths and workers' republics. It's over, and the sooner everyone realizes it, the better.'

'It's not over until that Treaty is ratified by the Dáil,' said Barney.

'And when it's not ratified, they'll have to tear up their no-good Treaty and start again,' said Peg.

'They surely will, Peg,' said Sore-Toes, wanting to please her. 'I'd say they'll have to.'

Dan threw him a look that would scald a cat. 'Don't be a fool.'

'If you don't deal those cards, I'm going to do it for you,' said Molly.

Of them all, Nora was the only one who said nothing. Maybe that's why she was the one who won the rest of the cards.

12

For days, Barney waited and seethed, giving her every chance. Days in which he seemed to see her everywhere: at the card game in his house; at a meeting in the Sinn Féin hall; huddled into a corner of their kitchen with Peg; in the shop buying messages; cycling past the house on her bicycle. Everywhere, but never anywhere that he could get at her. And never any sign in her that she wanted him to.

Worse, there was a look in her eyes when she saw him watching her, in the second before she looked away, that was bothersome. Nearly frightening. That was what shook the trust that had taken him through eight months of prison: that look. He couldn't read it. Sometimes he thought it was irritation, that he annoyed her now. Other times, that it was something else . . . Injury, maybe . . . He couldn't read it.

She was never oblivious to him, he knew that. As she cycled past his house with her face forward, he knew she was aware that he might be inside, looking out at her. He could see it in the way she held her body on the bicycle, the cast of her arms, the way she pressed on, not turning her head. But that look when she was near him . . . Where did that come from?

On his eighth night back, a Sunday, there was a celebration, a ceilidh in the Sinn Féin hall in Wexford, organized by Cumann na mBan to welcome all the prisoners home. He set himself on seeing her there, planned how he would ask her to dance, all perfectly respectable, and how they would take it from there. But she didn't attend, much to Peg's surprise, for though her father had never allowed her to such events before the Truce, it was understood that he'd come round and she'd told Peg she was going.

That night, he slept a fitful sleep and the next morning, a Monday, he rose with the resolution that he would intercept her on her way to work. Rain was pattering against the roof, the frost blown away by grey, swollen Atlantic cloud. It was dark as night, the sort of morning that wouldn't brighten until eleven, if at all, but he wasn't going to change his plan. He got dressed all the way to coat and cap, went out and took his bicycle from the shed (just in case she should try to cycle away on him) and rode up to the main crossroads. There he stood in Miley Ffrench's gateway, half in the ditch so he was hidden from the road, hoping to take her by surprise.

As he stood waiting, Major Liddle from Derriestown House went by in his motor, lamps lit, engine chugging, tyres swishing through the rain. Up to Dublin, probably, on business. So long, Major, Barney thought. We'll see soon where our Treaty leaves you and your like. Last night at the card game, Lama had told a good story about the Major, how they had met on the road one day a few weeks ago and he had stopped him for a talk. 'Lamb of God, that imperialist land monopolist stopping to talk to *me*!' Lama had sniffed. 'He'd have been hard set to nod his head at me this time last year.'

It wasn't to pass the time of day that the Major wanted, of course. He brought Lama a sad story about his fences being broken through at night, his cattle let out, his land trampled. Admitting that he differed politically from the Volunteers, he assured Lama that he had the greatest respect for their bravery and their ideals. But, he said, there were always people on the fringes of a movement who were out for personal gain. Look at this matter of his fences. Greedy small farmers and men who never owned a spadeful of land were taking advantage of the Volunteers' brave fight to further their own interests. If such carry-on wasn't stopped, the whole movement would be degraded.

'He seemed to think I'd round up the offenders for him,' Lama said, eyes popping with indignation. 'But then, I suppose, why wouldn't he? There's some volunteers who would, they're so anxious to show the landlords and the big business boys that they can be relied on.' And he looked around the table as if to warn any of them who were thinking of becoming amiable to imperialist land monopolists to think again.

Under the wet ditch, Barney shivered. Everybody was so cantankerous these days, all he could say for sure was that he wasn't on the side of the landlords, who were all, or nearly all, on the side of the English, determined to keep the native Irish people in subjugation. Beyond that, was it worth getting so fired up about? Why couldn't they live and let live and not have to be jacking the other fellow around to their own point of view?

He lit himself a cigarette, pulled his coat collar up around the back of his neck. Marky Maloney passed on his bicycle, his lamp lighting up the gloom. The sun came up behind the clouds, bringing a dim, grey light that was hard to tell from gloom of night. He waited on, growing wetter and wetter.

Then, in the distance, he saw her. Unmistakable, the shape of her on her bicycle, even in her black mackintosh and hat. She looked like a tent on wheels but he couldn't smile; his heart was clattering too hard inside its cage of ribs. As she drew near, he stepped into the middle of the road. Head down to the rain, she didn't see him until she was almost upon him. So she was near enough for him to see the expressions that flashed across her face, one after another: shock first, then what looked like a sliver of fear (fear? of him?), then a set resolve.

She turned her handlebars as if to swerve and for a minute he thought that was what she was going to do, circle around him and cycle on past as if he wasn't there, but she thought the better of it. The bicycle slid on in the wet, then braked to a dead stop. 'It's no use,' she said, before he had a chance to say anything. She had one foot on the ground, one on the pedal, poised for departure. 'You're wasting your time.'

'I want to talk to you.'

'There's nothing to say.'

'You don't mean that.'

'I do.' She made as if to ride off but he took a hold of the bike's handlebars, curling his fists around the cold wet steel.

'Let go, Barney. Don't be stupid.'

'Is there another fellow, is that it? Did you meet someone else while I was inside?'

She shook her head and there it was again, that irritation. 'Well, then . . .' he said. 'Tell me.'

She looked over her shoulder at the empty road.

'Come in to the gate if you're afraid of being seen.'

Another shake of her head.

'Nora—'

'I have to go. You're making me late.'

'What's happened?'

'It was a mistake, that's all.'

His hands tightened on the bars. 'You can't say that to me.'

'Stop it,' she said. 'Stop being so dramatic.'

'Nora . . .' This time the word was a plea.

'I mean it, Barney.' Her voice was pleading too. 'I want you to leave it.'

'What do you mean?'

'Forget it. Put it away.'

'But, Nora, why?'

'Because you're mistaken, that's why.'

'What?'

'Mistaken in believing that there's some agreement between us,' she said. 'There isn't.'

'Since when?'

'Since ever.'

'You can't say that. You can tell me something else and I'll believe it. But I won't believe that.'

'You have to. It's what I am saying to you.'

He bent down to try and get her to look him in the eye. The

rain poured across her thin pale face, so thin and small that there was hardly room enough in it for her two big unreadable eyes. She tried again to steer the handlebars out of his grip. A drop of rain was dangling from the end of her nose.

'What's changed, Nora? Just tell me and I'll leave you alone.'

'Nothing's changed.'

'It was never anything?'

'No.'

'No,' he echoed, but in his mouth the word was only a whisper.

She sat back up on her saddle. 'If anything I did made you think different, I'm sorry.'

He was angry with her then, for the first time ever. 'That won't do. No, Nora, it won't. You can't just sit there and tell me that for no reason.'

'Not no reason. Every reason.'

Hope reared up in him. 'Do you mean your family, Nora? They'd come round, surely. It's not like—'

She shook her head, impatient. 'I mean the usual reason. That I . . . I have no feelings for you in that way, Barney.' She spoke with such finality that this time he lifted his hands off. 'I'm sorry. I'm sorry I made you think I had . . . I'm sorry.'

She pushed off onto her pedals and cycled away from him and he stood and watched her retreating back until the rain drew her in and folded her away like curtains closing across a stage. Still he stood there, watching. Watching nothing, while rain streamed unchecked down his face.

13

1995

What I always loved best about Rory and me together was how easily we talked. For me, that was the miracle of us: that tide of words that surged up and out of me whenever we were together. And it's still the same. That's what we do, night after still, warm night, sitting outside my shed, the stars above us, the sea before us, the dark all around us. Talk and talk . . .

'. . . But what about the niceties? Does nobody in Ireland have any visual sense?'

'You are hardly one to talk about the finer things of life, Dev. Have you looked around at where you're living right now?'

'That's different.'

'Why are you insisting on staying in this shed, anyway? Are you doing penance or something?'

'Where did you get that idea?'

'Are you?'

'I haven't examined why I'm here, Rory. I just did it on a whim.' I look behind at my shed. It feels like it chose me, not the other way round but that sounds too crazy to say. 'Maybe being here keeps it temporary? Maybe I'm afraid that if I stopped somewhere more acceptable, I'd never get going again.'

'I don't know how you do it,' he says. 'No kitchen. No TV. No *shower*.'

'It's surprising what you can get used to.'

'You seem to be feeling better here, anyway. You seem more . . .' He hesitates, stretching for a word that won't insult me.

'Intact?'

'Yeah. Yeah. Is that how you feel?'

'Maybe. I think I'd say safe.'

'Safe? From what?'

From me, I think. From what I have made of myself.

'It's a hiatus,' I say. 'It won't last but it seems to be what I need right now.'

'. . . S-U-E-D-apostrophe-E-N-I-M. Geddit?'

'No.'

'Sue D'Enim. Pseudonym.'

'Ouch!'

'I know. It was my editor's idea of wit. She was so chuffed with herself, I had to go with it.'

'What about the actual work? Do you enjoy that?'

'I did. Well, I'm not sure if "enjoy" is the right word. I found it riveting, all these problems arriving on my desk. I found it hilarious that I should be the one *anybody* would turn to for advice, never mind hundreds of people a month. And often, I found it overwhelming.'

'You're talking like it's past tense.'

'I think it might be. I somehow can't imagine myself going back to it.'

'What would you do instead?'

'Don't know. Maybe I might . . . write. Write properly.'

'Properly?'

'A novel. Maybe.'

'That would be terrific.'

'Would it?'

'It would if it's what you want to do.'

I nod, very slowly.

'But . . . ?'

'I do want to, have wanted to for . . . for a long time, a very long time . . .'

'But . . . ?'

'Wanting isn't necessarily enough.'

'No, I suppose it isn't.'

We digest this, then he says: 'You never talked about writing when we were younger.'

'Back then, it wasn't something I would even have let into my orbit.'

'Beyond the reach of little Jo Devereux from Mucknamore?'

'More than that: simply unimaginable. Writers were Yeats and Joyce and Synge. Extraordinary people. Dead. Male. From another realm. Teach English literature: that was what I thought I'd like to do. That was as close as somebody like me was allowed to get to writing.'

'You never did teach, though, did you?'

'No. As you know, I didn't finish my degree.'

He hesitates – we are tipping towards forbidden territory – but goes on: 'Never went back to college afterwards?'

'I thought about it. But no. I couldn't ever afford to stop working.'

A silence while we pretend we're not remembering.

'What about you?' I ask, my tone bright to distract us. 'Do you enjoy . . . soliciting?'

'Hey! Watch it.'

'Solicitors solicit, do they not?'

'People solicit me, actually.'

'You used to love taking pictures so much. I always thought you'd be a photographer.'

'There were hardly any openings here. Unless I worked for one of the newspapers or did the weddings and christenings circuit, I wasn't going to make a living at it. So my plan was: I'd "solicit", as you so delightfully put it, to pay the bills and take pictures in my spare time.'

'Tell me about your exhibition. You said it was in Dublin?'

'Yeah. In the Dublin Bay Arts Centre. Black-and-white stills of poor kids on special educational programmes in Dublin. "Velvet Shoestring", it was called. The *Irish Times* listed it as "Velvet G-String".'

I laugh.

'I swear to God. That's true . . .'

'You must bring the pictures down some night. I'd love to see them.'

'I haven't a clue where they are, up in the attic somewhere.'

'So what are you working on now?'

'I thought the exhibition would give me impetus but the opposite happened. When it was over, I found myself taking fewer and fewer pictures. Until eventually I stopped altogether.'

I know how that feels.

'I don't even take photos of the kids. It's been more than four years since I even picked up a camera.'

'That's terrible. You were good.'

'You have to say that.'

'I don't, you know.'

He shrugs. 'I tell myself it's because I don't have time . . .' He falters.

I wait. When he says no more, I venture, gently: 'That's not it, though?'

'No.'

'Courage?'

He looks up at me. 'You too?'

'Me too.'

'. . . I don't believe in this "new" Ireland I keep hearing about. The only thing I see that's any different is a bit more money swilling around.'

'Swilling. Now there's an objective term.'

'You know what I mean.'

'Come on, you must have seen improvements in twenty years. Remember what you left.'

'I do, very well, and it doesn't seem so different.'

'It feels a lot different if you're living here, I can tell you.'

'It's mostly superficial, though, isn't it? Like a skim of paint over a wall that's covered in cracks? You nearly see the flaws more clearly than before.'

'Do you really think we're so much worse than anywhere else? You're not going to tell me the States is perfect?'

'You're right, nowhere's perfect. I suppose it's not Ireland, really, it's me.' Me, here. The wrong mix of person and environment.

'Are you an American now? I mean, I know you have your green card, but is that how you think of yourself? A Californian? An American?'

'I don't really think of myself as anything. I don't believe in nationality, to be honest.'

'Since when is it a matter of belief? Nations exist, surely, whether Jo Devereux has decided she believes in them or not.'

'They didn't always exist.'

'When? When we lived in tribes?'

'Yeah. Or later, when people defined themselves in terms of religion, say.'

'What's better about that?'

'It's not that it's better, it just shows how it's all invented in our heads. We bring all this emotion to nationality, the flags and the anthems, and let ourselves be deluded into thinking that being Irish or American is something worth killing or dying for. That ferocious identification with an abstraction: it scares me. And I hate when people put me in that box marked "Irish".'

'So that's it. You're disowning the ould sod. You're ashamed of us.'

He is teasing. But that 'us' is exactly what I hate. 'That's *not* what I said. It's not about being Irish per se. I'd feel the same if I were French. Or Polynesian.'

'Interesting thought, that. You'd look great in a grass skirt.'

'What do you think being Irish says about you?'

'Oh, I don't know. Maybe because I've always lived here I've never thought about it like that. I am Irish. It's just one of the things I am. And I'm proud of my country.'

'Oooooh, you see. There's the difference. I don't even know what that sentence means. Like last year when the Irish football team were playing the World Cup and any time the fans were interviewed on TV they kept going on about being proud to be Irish. We saw them in the States and it just drove me crazy. I mean, what is that about: "I'm so proud to be Irish"? The Americans are the same. "Proud to be an American." What does it mean? What's to be proud of? You might as well be proud of having black hair or green eyes. Why don't we go to war with the blue-eyed people . . . ?'

Talk, talk, talk . . . So much to tell, so much yet to be told, including those subjects we keep dipping and swerving around. His marriage. His wife and children at home in his house while he spends night after night down here. What his family did to Barney. What my family did to Dan. And, of course, what we did to each other.

We'll get to it all in time, I believe, but for now we stay with easier topics. We have plenty to choose from, twenty years' worth of what we've thought and heard and seen and said and wanted and tasted and felt. And when we run out of that, I share some of the things I am finding in Mrs D.'s papers, things that happened when we were younger or before we were born.

We're not young now. We are easier on each other.

14

1966

Nine-year-old me sits at the kitchen table, with Maeve opposite. We've finished our soup and are waiting for the rashers and sausages, eggs and beans that our mother is preparing at the cooker. The kitchen is full of steam. Nobody talks but the silence is full of the sounds of cooking: sizzling meat, bubbling potatoes, clattering plates . . . Between us, at the top of the table, is the question mark that is our father's vacant chair.

We are in our Sunday best, though it is a Monday. In the afternoon, the whole family is to go to Enniscorthy, a town thirty miles or so away, for what Granny Peg calls the Golden Jubilee. Fifty years ago today, Irishmen took part in a Rising against British rule and that Rising started the war that won Irish freedom. Gran was involved in the Rising when she was young and is on the organizing committee for today. She is to get up on a stage in front of everyone and give the speech that she's been practising around the house for weeks. Whenever Gran talks about the Rising, I picture men in trench coats lifting up from the ground like the Virgin Mary ascending up to heaven, but not so high.

Across from me, Maeve is doing her best to land another kick on my shin. I have my legs pulled over to one side, afraid not so much of the pain from the kick as the mark her shoe might leave on my white tights. Such a mark would give Mammy the out her anger is longing for.

The kitchen door opens and it is Granny Peg. I perk up and sneer across at Maeve. She won't have a free run at me now.

'Something smells good,' Gran says, her voice all happy, but then she sees Mammy's face and the space where Daddy should be, and it changes. 'Ah no,' she says, 'don't tell me, not today . . .'

She moves across to the cooker. Mammy says nothing, just slaps six plates in a row along the counter. I send a mental message: *Come over here, Gran, over here*, but no. She whispers in Mammy's ear, but not quiet enough: 'Have you heard anything from him at all?'

'Nothing. Not a thing.' Mammy divides the food among the plates. 'I'm going to go in and collect him once we've eaten.'

'Yerra, let him rot there.'

'Don't you think I want to? But how can I? If he isn't with us today, it'll look so peculiar. We'll be the talk of the place.'

I listen to this exchange, waiting for a pause. When it comes, I call across: 'Hello, Gran!' and then notice, too late, the quiet lunge of my sister's leg. A leather toe cracks against my shin.

'*Yeow!*' I screech out loud. The two adults turn.

'What's the matter, pet?' Gran asks.

Maeve's eyes burn a warning into the side of my face. 'Nothing.'

Gran comes over anyway.

'I hope you two aren't fighting. What do I always tell you? Fighting . . . ?'

'. . . solves nothing,' Maeve and I both answer, in a sing-song voice together.

'That's right,' says Granny Peg. 'Fighting solves nothing. So,' she settles herself in between us, 'how is little Miss Tickles today?' She curls her finger at me in mock threat of a tickle-attack.

'Fine,' I gurgle. And I am, now. My heart hums with love of her.

'And Little Miss Manners?'

Maeve wrinkles her nose at her, pretending to object to this name. But we all know she likes it really.

'Listen, girls, come here till I tell ye,' Granny Peg says, in that confidential voice of hers that we love. 'Auntie Nora will be down in a minute and she's after going to great trouble to get ready. Wouldn't it be nice if we all told her how well she's looking?'

Auntie Nora's appearance is a great worry to Gran, who always has to coax her to wash her hair or have a bath or change her dirty clothes.

'So she's definitely going?' Mammy calls over, from the other side of the room, sharp.

'Now, Máirín, I told you, she has to go. There's no question of her not going.'

'Even though you'll be on the platform? Even though I'll have the children to mind as well?'

'I'm sorry, *a grá*, but it can't be helped. It would be all wrong to leave her at home today. You must see that.'

Mammy brings food over to us all then takes her place at the table. We feel the temper swelling against her skin. 'I don't know how I'll manage,' she says. 'You know what she's like when she's excited. She's been like a hen on a hot griddle for weeks.'

Gran lets the space where she should answer lie open.

Mammy tries again. 'How will I ever manage the three of them and probably on my own?'

'She has to be there, Máirín.' Gran's voice is quiet but certain. This is not like her. Usually she calms our mother, strokes her down from the heights of her anger with soft words and the right kind deeds. 'Nora did her bit for Ireland as much as any of them who'll be there today, more than most. You can't expect her to sit home alone on the day that's in it.'

Maeve sees a chance to step in: 'We'll be very good for you, Mammy.'

For a second, our mother parts the folds of her anger and lets out a smile. 'I know *you* will, love. It's not you I'm worried about.'

She turns back to her food and the unfairness of everything sweeps over her again, eats into her. Her eyes travel around the table looking for a target and land on a bowl of unfinished soup. My bowl. 'Who owns this?' She lifts the spoon so the soup slops back into the bowl from a height, looking straight at me.

My stomach curdles. Maeve perks up.

'Do I have to ask again?'

'It's mine.'

'How many times do you have to be told? Only take the amount you're going to eat. Don't I always tell you? If you don't want it, don't take it.'

'OK.'

'God above, isn't that reasonable? Isn't that fair enough? I can't stand good food going to waste. You'd better eat up that fry, every bit. You'd better clear that plate, young lady, do you hear me?'

She takes the bowl away. My sausages swell up on my plate. Gran sees my face, cuts them up small for me.

'And what about herself above?' She is picking on Gran now. 'Is she ever coming down at all this morning? How am I supposed to keep the food hot?'

'She won't be long,' Gran picks up Auntie Nora's plate. 'Here, I'll stick it under the grill for her. You have your own.'

Mammy settles into silence at the foot of the table, nursing her teacup, staring out at the grey sea. It's all right for her not to eat, but not for me. My sausages show pink where Gran has cut them; a pink that twists my stomach shut. What am I going to do? Mammy's anxiety is inside all of us now but at no relief to her.

The door opens and Auntie Nora comes in. She doesn't look like herself today: her hair is swelling out from her face in fat grey curls and a peacock brooch glitters on her new blouse. A tidemark of make-up wobbles along the fold of her double chins, spoiling the dressed-up effect, and her red lipstick has wandered outside the borders of her mouth. She looks like the sad clown I saw at the circus the last time it came to Wexford, a clown that featured in my dreams for months. The lipstick makes the non-stop motion of her mouth more conspicuous. Though Auntie Nora rarely speaks out loud, she talks a stream of soundless patter to herself all day long, every thought that goes through her head getting turned over in her mouth. Even when she falls into a nap in her chair, her lips keep moving and I often wonder if she keeps it up all night long in bed.

Gran smiles to see her, says: 'Nora, you look lovely.' Auntie Nora blushes, comes forward, shoves her big hips into the seat.

Gran gets up to fetch Auntie Nora's food. 'There you are now,' she says, putting it in front of her, 'and I'm just going to tie this tea towel round you so you don't get any mess on your nice blouse. Did you sleep all right with those curlers in? They've done a lovely job. Isn't Auntie Nora's hair lovely, children?'

A mumble from me. Maeve throws her eyes upwards.

Auntie Nora puts a hand up to her hair touching its surface softly, as if to make sure it's still there. Maeve sniggers.

'Auntie Nora *is* lovely,' I say, to please Gran. Maeve sniggers again.

Mammy cuts across everyone else, saying Maeve is to help Gran clean up and I am to get into the car. 'We're going to town to fetch your father.'

So I am to get away with not eating but this is even worse. I hate going into Larkin's after Daddy because he never wants to come out. But to say no to Mammy is unthinkable. We go outside to the car. It's a showery day and the ground is wet, though it's not raining now. I get in, stand in the middle, one foot either side of the little ridge between the two front seats, stretching my head up to graze the ceiling with my crown. It takes us thirty-five silent minutes into town by the back roads. Then it's down the Faythe, up Bride Street, across the back of the town and stop on the hill outside Larkin's. Same way as always.

'Go inside and tell your father I want him.'

'What if he won't come?'

'Make him come. Tell him we're not leaving until I speak to him.'

The handle on the pub door is high up. I have to stand on tiptoe to reach it. Inside, it smells like our own pub but different. I am surprised to see Daddy at the wrong side, the serving side, of the counter. Has he got mixed up, I wonder, about which pub he's in? He is leaning over a piece of paper, pointing something out to another man, something about a horse I think. 'Iron Jack,' the man says. 'Fifteen to two.'

Mrs Larkin is standing behind the counter too and it is she who notices me first. She nudges Daddy and points at me through her tea towel. Daddy lifts his head and the other men turn around to look. Daddy puts on the surprised face he always wears when he turns to see what everybody is staring at, and it's me. 'What are you doing here?'

'Mammy wants you.'

'Tell her I'll be home later.'

I move around his side of the counter, away from the others so he doesn't have to speak so loud.

'Mammy wants you.'

He shakes his head.

'She said she won't go away unless you come out and talk to her.'

'Is that a fact? She'll get to know the inside of that car right well, so.' He doesn't keep his voice down. He is looking at Mrs Larkin while he speaks, like he's talking to her, not me. I can feel the other men looking and feel that they are laughing, even though they're not. One of them says to me, 'Would you like a lemonade, love?'

What I would like is to sit down at the little table in the corner and have a Coca-Cola and a packet of crisps and a comic the way I did once before, but I can't. That time Mammy walloped me across the head, said that having a Coke like that was the worst of the many bad things I had done to her. So instead I say, 'No, thank you,' to the man and try to get closer to Daddy. I whisper to him. 'Please, Daddy. *Please*. She'll go mad.'

He makes his show-offy voice even louder. 'Tell your mammy to go ahead, I'll follow on home when I'm ready.'

Mrs Larkin sends me a look that says she'd like to help but what can she do. Daddy goes back to the talk about horses. 'Did yours come in, Francie?'

'Not at all, a dead loss, he's running still. But Nick had ten bob on Deuteronomy.'

'Did you hear that, Maisie? The drinks are on Nick.'

I go back out to the car. The door is open, waiting. 'He won't come,' I say.

She screams. 'Were you listening to me at all? Go back in there *now* and get him to come out or you'll get what's good for you.'

I go back in. Daddy looks up immediately this time, expecting me while pretending he isn't. 'Jesus, did you not hear what I told you?' he says. 'Is it Easter weekend or is it not? Am I to have no peace?'

'Ah now, Christy, go easy on the young one,' says the man who offered me the lemonade. 'It's not her fault.'

Mrs Larkin speaks up. 'Maybe you should go on ahead, Christy.'

'D'you think so, Maisie?'

'I do.'

'Are you sure?'

'I am.'

He nods his head, slowly. 'Maybe I will, so.'

There is laughter still in the men, just under their faces, like children in school holding it in. Daddy picks up his pint from the counter. It's more than half full but he lowers it down in one big swallow, then bangs his glass down.

'And what are you grinning at, Nick O'Leary?'

'Nothin', Christy.' The man called Nick has two teeth only, and both of them black. 'Nothin' at all.'

'I'm glad to hear it.'

Daddy takes a long time putting on his coat. The froth from his drink slides down the inside of the glass, settling into a slop at the bottom. The clock on the top shelf whirrs then chimes: one o'clock, *dee-dah-dee-dah*. He makes a great show of taking his ease, not letting anybody rush him. Then he puts on his hat, tucks his *Irish Press* under his arm. 'Goodbye, men. See you, Maisie.'

'See you, Christy.'

Out to the car we go. Mammy has what she wanted but she's not happy. Daddy gets into the passenger seat, looks off out the side window, trying to seal himself off into silence but she's not having that. 'That place must be the dirtiest hole in Wexford town,' she says.

Silence.

'If you must stay away from your family, you think you'd go somewhere with a bit of class, but oh no, you'd rather be with the dregs of Wexford town.'

Silence.

'Acting the big fella with a crowd of no-good townies. Have you no shame?'

Silence.

'For the love of God, answer me. Is there no shame in you for what you have done?'

'I'd be ashamed to behave as you are behaving now.'

'And how am I supposed to behave? Am I to say, "Welcome home, Christy"? "Thanks for coming home to your wife and family, Christy. Thanks for doing what every other man does every day of his life without thinking about it"?'

'What man would want to come home to the likes of this?'

Mammy starts to cry. 'Oh, the disgrace of it . . . That dirty townie tart—'

'That's enough now.' He says it twice. 'That's enough.'

'Near young enough to be your daughter . . .'

'Christ, Máirín, would you mind your mouth in front of the child.'

'Oh, the child, is it? It's little you care about the child or the other one either when you decide to take yourself off. On this day of all days, to be away from us. You *know* what this day means to our family.'

Daddy refuses to talk any more, no matter what she says now he won't answer her. On she goes anyway: how could he, that filthy place, no respect for himself or the rest of us, the talk of the village, the talk of the town, dragging us through the mud . . .

I know why Daddy isn't talking: it's because he only has bad things to say. Gran told me about it, how important it is to keep the bad words in. Our thoughts come from the same place we came from ourselves, Gran says, from the Good Lord above. We can't help what we think; it'd frighten the heart out of you some of the things that pop into your head, but as long as they stay in your head, no harm done. Spoken words are a different thing entirely. Spoken words you can control and the wrong ones let out don't fade away. They stay on, thickening the air we breathe. Bad deeds are even worse.

I sit in the back of the car, holding my breath, my fingers discreetly plugging my ears, trying to stop my mother's bad words from getting inside me.

As soon as we get home we have to leave again because Daddy has made us late. The others get into the car, Auntie Nora and Gran in the back beside the windows, Maeve in the middle, me sitting on Gran's knee. It's a squash. Daddy is driving now and it's Mammy's turn to be quiet and look away.

At the old cemetery, we all pile out again and walk up the little hill towards the Grave. Granny Peg's mother and father are both buried there and Granddad too. We will say a prayer for them but it's really Uncle Barney we're here for. Uncle Barney with his high cross all to himself, taller than the other cross even though that's for three people, taller than Daddy even.

Once we're arranged in a circle around the Grave, Gran makes a speech, the words heavy in her mouth: 'We offer this rosary for the repose of the souls of all our family and friends but especially for the soul of Barney Parle, who sacrificed his life for comrades and country.' Then she starts the prayer: 'Thou, O Lord, wilt open my lips . . .' and the rest of us do the responses.

Auntie Nora's lips move and her chins quiver but no sound comes out. My mother holds her rosary beads tight, like a weapon.

There's only time for one decade of the rosary at the Grave because we have to fit in the Plaque as well before going on to Enniscorthy. We drive two miles out the Rathmeelin road to Derriestown and out we get again, to stand in front of a square of marble on the pillar of a gate. It says:

Erected by the Mucknamore Active Service Unit, 3rd Batt., Irish Republican Army, to the memory of a gallant comrade. Lieutenant Barney Parle fell nearby in a glorious fight for Irish Freedom on the 10th January 1923. *Dílis do Dhia agus dÉirinn.*

It's starting to rain, little spatters falling on our heads and shoulders, but the grown-ups, in their silent prayer, don't take any notice. The Plaque done, we head back to the car and set off for Enniscorthy at last. Rain starts to fall in earnest and the wipers hum their criss-cross, criss-cross. The air in the car thickens, all our breaths heavy in it. I draw a picture of a stick girl on the foggy window. A triangle skirt and a triangle umbrella: it is raining for her too. Daddy wipes the front window with his handkerchief and swears.

We pass through Wexford, the traffic heavy along the quay. There is a commemoration in Wexford too but we are going on to Enniscorthy where the celebrations will be bigger and better. Enniscorthy was always at the heart of County Wexford's rebellion, Gran said, when she told us it was there we would go. She listed off a load of dates and battles the way she always does. The dates turn to wool in my ears but I like that word of hers that's always turning over in my mind: rebellion.

By the time we get to Enniscorthy, we are cramped and glad to get out. The rain has stopped but the paths are still wet and big drops fall from the trees and telegraph wires and the air tastes cool and clean. Flags flutter everywhere: rectangles of green, white and orange hanging from poles and trees and windows and strings of little triangles in all colours stretched across the streets. In the distance, we can hear the boom-boom of pipe-and-drum music.

People I don't know nod at us as we pass, or tip their caps, or come up to say hello. Men and women admire us: 'Aren't they lovely girls!' 'Isn't the little one the spit of her mammy?' I wonder how that can be when five minutes before somebody said I was the image of my daddy. Hands pat my head, smiles shine down at me, coins are pressed into my fist. Gran accepts and returns the smiles and chat on behalf of us all. Mammy and Daddy are stiff as two trees but they won't fight here in front of everybody, so we're all right.

I try not to look at Auntie Nora's bewildered face, her lips now gabbling around their soundless patter. Too many people, that's the problem: Auntie Nora hardly ever goes out or sees anyone but us. Gran sees her distress and takes her by the arm and talks to distract her, tells all of us about President de Valera, and how if he didn't have to be at the big celebration in Dublin he would be here with us in Enniscorthy, because Enniscorthy was one of the few places outside Dublin that rose in 1916. President de Valera always had a soft spot for Enniscorthy, Gran says.

Gran has a soft spot for President de Valera. Once, a long time ago, he slept in our house and afterwards she had the bed he slept in moved to her room. Dev's bed, she calls it, and she sleeps in it still. He wasn't president then – this happened the very first time Fianna Fáil went for an election. He was in our part of the country to canvass for votes and he stayed with us to acknowledge that our family had made the Ultimate Sacrifice, Gran said. When Fianna Fáil won that election Mr de Valera was ushered into Enniscorthy by fifty white horses. Gran will never forget it.

We are at the square now where she is to get up on the stage and make her speech so she hands Auntie Nora over to Mammy. A row of other old people are up on the platform already, looking like blackbirds on a wire in their dark hats and coats. The microphone is squeaking as a man shouts into it: 'Testing one . . . two . . . *squeeeak* . . . Testing one . . . *squeeak* . . . three . . .' At the other side of the square the band plays 'A Nation Once Again'.

Seats have been kept for us up near the front and we squeeze past those who are standing to get up to them. After a while, the music stops and a man steps out to speak. He talks for a long time about Easter 1916 and the Rising, about Ireland and England, about brave men and fine soldiers. He's boring. Another man gets up and goes on with more of the same. In the middle of his talk, he turns around to point out Gran and the other three old women in the row behind him. Without the brave girls of Cumann na mBan many a flying column would have collapsed, he says. When almost everybody deserted the soldiers those girls stood by them and the more dangerous the work, the more willing they were to do it. I stare at the old women in their black coats and hats, wonder if he's made a mistake.

Then Gran herself gets up and makes the speech we all know inside out, about how Ireland can never call herself free while her six northern counties remain part of the United Kingdom. She's just getting herself all worked up when – out of the blue – Auntie Nora gets to her feet and puts her hand up, like we do in school when we want to talk to the teacher.

Gran puts her hand over the microphone and leans past it. 'What is it, Nora?' Her voice sounds low without the microphone, as if she is whispering though she isn't.

Auntie Nora's fat cheeks are jumping and twitching like two small animals are having a fight inside her mouth and words whirr through her lips but none of us can hear what she is saying, even us who are closest to her. Her silence swells up around us. Mammy catches a hold of her coat, tries to pull her back down into her seat. Granny Peg, up on stage in front of everybody, doesn't know what to do. She looks across at the man who did the talking earlier, a question in her eyebrows, and he shrugs back. She looks again at Auntie Nora, who still holds her hand above her head but seems unable to do any more than that, caught in some struggle of her own.

After a minute, Gran decides she has to ignore her, turns back to the microphone. Just as she is about to resume, Auntie Nora finds her voice. Her out-loud speaking voice that I've hardly ever heard before. 'What about Dan?' she asks.

Now the silence jumps, crackles all around us. Gran's face turns cloudy. Daddy's head shrinks into his shoulders. Mammy's mouth falls open. 'Dear God, what is she trying to do to us?' she wails. Behind us, a buzz of talk begins.

Mammy tries to pull her down. 'Sit down, would you?' she hisses. 'Sit down, for God's sake.'

But no, Auntie Nora makes her stand. She tugs her coat out of Mammy's grip and turns around to face the audience behind us. She says it again. And then again.

'What about Dan?' she says. 'What about Dan?'

Peg

Dear Diary

Sometimes I wonder why I have Molly Redmond for a friend at all. She's good for a laugh, I know, and I like the way you can never be sure what she's going to do next and that she's afraid of no one. But the girl is so centred on herself, she's worse than a child. Tonight reminded me of how it used to be before Nora came to Mucknamore, when I used to depend on Molly and was forever feeling let down.

She called in after tea, supposedly to help me with folding the anti-Collins leaflets (Nora wasn't allowed to come and Cat pretended to Lil that she was here but really sneaked off somewhere with Lama). Wexford is to be 'honoured' with a visit from the great Mr Michael Collins in three weeks' time, part of a countrywide rally that's working on votes for the Provisional Government. Thousands of Wexford people are expected to turn out in St Peter's Square to hear him speak, a worrying number of them from Mucknamore. Plenty will only be going along for a gawk but of course the pro-Treatyites are going to claim everybody there as a solid supporter. A big crowd will look bad for us so we are working now on doing whatever we can to lower the turnout.

They are claiming that Collins is 'the man who won the war' against the British, as if everybody else did nothing. We've put together a leaflet that tells the truth about that, and gives some other home truths about our so-called Provisional Government. Namely that said government has no legal right to exist. The Dáil is the government of the Republic until people say otherwise in an election – the Treaty itself accepts that. But instead they have gone and appointed themselves to be in charge and are using every underhand trick they can think of to swing the election their way.

Chief of these is denying a vote to us, the younger women. The female TDs in the Dáil are urgently trying to pass a decree giving women the franchise on the same terms as men i.e. everybody over twenty-one, instead of the system we inherited from the British, where only women over thirty have a vote. This is in line with the Proclamation of the Irish Republic which addressed itself to Irishwomen as well as to Irishmen and guaranteed equal rights to *all* its citizens.

A women's deputation went to see Griffith about this and he answered them with all manner of invented objections, though the selfsame man happily supported the suffrage cause before the war, when the suffragettes were throwing axes at his political opponent, Mr Redmond. They're acting just like the English: all the English political parties used to run the suffrage question for all it was worth when it suited them, but as soon as they were in a position to advance that cause, then their cry was always: 'Oh, there is something more important before the nation.'

This is Griffith's answer to us now, though we all know the real reason is because he knows young women are against this Treaty. If the Voters' List were updated to include women under thirty (and all the young men who attained their majority since the last register was compiled two years ago, men like Barney and Lama and Sore-Toes) their precious Treaty would be voted down. We are the ones who did most in the fight against the British but we are to be given no vote in the country we helped bring about. THIS IS NOT A FAIR ELECTION: we have to make sure everybody knows it.

As I write all this I feel guilty, because the question is so important but I'm sorry to say that Molly and I got precious little work done on it tonight. As it turned out, we had the kitchen all to ourselves – Daddy and Barney were both working in the shop and Mammy had taken herself off to bed for an early night. We started off well enough but then Molly got us going on that game she's always playing with apples. She's pure mad to get herself a sweetheart, that girl. It makes me laugh the way she comes right out and says it. Most girls of twenty-two think the same way but there's not many who admit it the way Molly does.

She pulled one of the kitchen chairs out into the middle of the floor and made me put down my work and join in her game. The idea is to peel an apple trying to make one continuous strip out of the skin, then throw it over your shoulder and see if you can read a letter in the shape that falls. If you can, that's the initial of the boy you're going to marry. She made me go first, sitting me down in the chair, handing me the apple and the knife. I peeled until the skin broke, then threw it over my shoulder, chanting: 'Apple A, Apple B, tell me now, what name you see . . .'

Molly flew to where it landed on the floor and shrieked, 'It's a D, it's a D.'

I was glad Nora wasn't there to hear her say that. To tell the truth, I could see when I went across that it did look a bit like a D but I wasn't going to admit as much to Molly.

'I think it's more like a J,' I said, but she was hardly listening to me. All her attention was on her own turn. She took her place on the chair with such gravity you'd think it was a throne and it must have taken her a full ten minutes to peel the apple, she was that slow and that careful to remove as much of the skin as she could without breaking it. When it came to throwing it over her shoulder, she sat up straight and closed her eyes and paused for a long moment before solemnly casting it back. You'd swear it was her wedding itself, the go-on of her.

As soon as she had thrown it, she was over beside it. 'God!' she said with a sly look at me. 'Mine's a D as well.'

The little snip! I wasn't going to let her away with that. 'I don't know, Molly,' I said. 'It looks like a G to me.'

'Do you think so? G? Who do we know starts with G?'

'Gabriel Mooney,' I said, with as straight a face as I could muster, knowing what she'd think of poor fifty-year-old Gabriel who lives with his mammy and has a real squeaky voice.

'It's a man I'd like to marry, if you don't mind,' she said. 'Not a mincing old lady.'

'Hmmm. What about Gut Hayes? He's definitely a man,' I said, knowing she'd hardly think more of Gut, whose belly can hardly be got in the door of the pub. 'Maybe a bit too much man,' I said, unable to keep in the laughing.

'Ah, there's no good talking to you,' she said, starting to eat her apple. 'You don't take anything serious.'

We moved away from the table then, and the work, and settled into the fireside chairs. I threw the used apple skins in the fire and they sizzled in the flames and filled the room with a lovely scent. Then what did she do only take out a packet of cigarettes and a cigarette holder from her skirt pocket?

'What are you doing?' I said to her. 'You don't even smoke.'

'It looks like I do,' she said, fitting a cigarette into the holder and lighting it.

I looked over to the door that led to the shop, worried that Daddy might come in. 'I'll bet you wouldn't do this in your own house,' I said. 'Your mother would fleece you if she saw that in your gob.'

She blew a big mouthful of smoke in my direction, then burst into a cough.

'Give me a puff,' I said.

She did and it was horrible. While I was struggling with it, staying close to the fire to do it in case anyone came in and I had to throw it away quickly, she stood and started rolling up her skirt. She rolled it to her knees and then took the pins out of her hair and folded it over near her neck, trying to make it look short.

'Look,' she said. 'What do you think? Would I look good with a bob?' She took the cigarette holder back from me and waved it about with the other hand, trying to look like an American flapper.

'You wouldn't cut your lovely hair?' I said. Molly has great hair, dark brown and glossy.

'I wouldn't mind. I think it'd suit me short. Have you a hairband?'

I went to the sideboard and rummaged in a drawer until I found one. She put it on around her forehead, like a flapper's band, tucking her hair up and under to give the illusion of it being short. 'What do you think?'

It didn't work at all. She looked a silly mess and I could only laugh at her. 'It's your hair,' I said. 'It's sticking up all over the place.'

'Use your imagination, would you? Picture it.'

'You wouldn't really cut your hair, Molly? What would Father John say?' Father John was always going on about the immodesty of foreign feminine fashions. Nobody follows him too closely but if he were to see Molly now, knees and all showing . . . And he wouldn't be alone. 'What would your mam say and the other mothers?'

'Never mind the priests and the old women,' she said, admiring herself in the mirror. 'We have a new Ireland now and it's the young who'll run it. And clothes like these show the old folk we mean business. Anyway, Margie says bobs and short skirts are all the go in Liverpool, so I wouldn't say it will be too long before they take off here.'

Molly was still making faces in the mirror, acting the vamp. 'You'll get us an awful name, Molly, if you're serious.' By us I meant Cumann na mBan. 'You know we're having trouble enough keeping the village on our side,' I said. 'Those Cumann na Saoirse women are already going around the place giving off about the "wild women" of Cumann na mBan and there's a few too many willing to listen to them.'

She shrugged, careless as always of anything beyond herself.

Then she eyeballed me and asked what seemed to be an unrelated question. 'Are you back with Dan O'Donovan?'

'Em – I . . . We . . .'

'I'm only asking because I heard – I don't know if this is true, mind – but I heard that he's been out with that Miss Whitty.'

'What? Tell me. Quick!' I was too startled to cover my feelings as I usually try to do with her. 'Is it Agnes Whitty you mean? One of the Whittys from Rathmeelin?' This lady had already become known to me. She set up a branch of Cumann na Saoirse, the new pro-Treaty women's organization, and they have been actively trying to poach our unsteady members over. 'The one who was in the paper, saying Cumann na mBan women were "fanatical"?'

'The very one.'

I was horrified but I had to peel back. This was Molly I was talking to and there's something about Molly that you don't put yourself in the weak place with her.

'So what if he has?' I said. 'It's nothing to me.'

'Really?' She sat back down in the armchair opposite and leaned towards me. 'That's great that you feel like that,' she said. 'Because to tell you the truth, I wouldn't mind a go there myself.'

'What?'

'If he's nothing to you any more, then I'm going to take my chances with him, if you don't mind.'

What could I say? 'Why should I mind?' But of course I did. And she knew it too.

I picked up the poker and jabbed at the coals of the fire. 'Has he asked you?'

'No, he hasn't. Not yet. But we'll see now if we can nudge him in the right direction.'

'Oh, I'm sure you can, Molly. If anyone can, you can.'

She looked at me. 'You're sure you don't mind?'

'Didn't I say I don't?'

'You'd probably prefer to see him with me than with Agnes Whitty, anyway.'

We had a cup of tea together after that and I had to put up with her jabber for the rest of the evening. For much of the time, I hardly knew what she was saying, I was all inside my own head. But she didn't even notice.

The upshot of it all was that we got hardly any work done. I felt awful after she was gone but now, after writing it out, I'm clearer. It doesn't make any difference really because despite what she implied tonight, she never kept away from Dan before anyway. She was always available for a flirt if he wanted and if he did, thoughts of me wouldn't come into it with Miss Molly. No, Molly is not the problem. This Miss Whitty, though, whose politics lean in the same direction as his, I'll have to find out more about her.

Dear Diary

There was an awful row at Mucknamore Sinn Féin tonight. Mammy started it last week when she raised questions about the band. She was quoted in this week's paper, word for word. 'It was strange that the Sinn Féin band went willingly to Wexford for Michael Collins, without even putting the suggestion before the Executive, never mind the club membership. It was even stranger that they were now saying they were not going to attend for Mr de Valera's visit on Easter Monday. Here was the greatest honour being bestowed on Wexford, with Mr de Valera being here on Easter Monday, of all days, for the anniversary of the 1916 Proclamation. That the Mucknamore Sinn Féin band would refuse was certainly not a reflection of the feelings of their organization. Every member of the club had subscribed generously to the band and it was curious now to find it failing to support those who helped keep it up.'

All as if she didn't know at all that Dan was responsible for bringing the band to Wexford. Then she surpassed herself by claiming that the band had shown disrespect for Father John, as he had 'done so much for them, having kept some of the instruments at his house at considerable risk during the late war when they were in danger of being taken and broken up by the British military.' This when she knows full well that Father J. is every bit as up for Collins as Dan.

It's amusing right enough, but shouldn't we be trying harder to keep people on side? She's frustrated because our best efforts didn't manage to do much to scupper the Collins visit. We got a band of men and arms together and managed to stop the Waterford train between Carnagh and Bridgetown, where they ordered the driver out at gunpoint into a motorcar waiting outside the station that drove him some distance to prevent him from resuming his duties. Meanwhile the others set to tearing up the line, in case the authorities should organize a substitute driver. A few journalists and others abandoned the train and arranged to motor on to Wexford, but we were there before them, and had trees felled at strategic points along the road to hold them up. Similar actions were taken on the Dublin line and our actions must have had some effect on attendance but there wasn't much sign of it. St Peter's Square was packed full to hear Collins give a predictable speech, about birds in the hand and birds in the bush and the crowd going wild and throwing up handkerchiefs as if what he said was pure poetry.

So tonight Mammy called an EGM on the issue of the band, to condemn their action. Dan didn't attend and the executive demanded his presence at the next meeting of the club to give an explanation. They also condemned certain appointments that were being made in the county by the Provisional Government.

Lama remarked that the class which the Irish people had been for centuries trying to remove from power were all retaining control under this so-called Treaty. Mammy agreed and said this should be an eye-opener for those who were blinded by 'Articles of Agreement'. Others begged to differ and the upshot was half the room walked out.

15

1922

As soon as Peg came out of school, she saw him: sitting on the schoolyard wall facing the road, his back to her. He had his jacket off in the sunshine, his shirtsleeves rolled up. She spun round on her heel the second she saw him, to face the door she had just closed behind her. She had to lock up – making the school secure each afternoon was her duty, as Master Cole flew off home like a hare out of a trap each day as soon as three o'clock came – but she also had to take herself a minute to think. Was he waiting for her? He must be. What else would have him sitting there like that, at this time of the day? The key shook in her hand as she tried to fit it in the keyhole. Look at what he did to her, it was desperate. That his simple presence two hundred yards away could have such an effect . . . The key clicked in the lock and now she had nowhere she could go but forward, to see what he wanted. She put on what she hoped was an ordinary smile, as if it was no great surprise at all that he should turn up like this, as if he were nothing to her but an ordinary friend well met, as if there was no blush pumping through her face and forehead.

He stood and turned to the sound of her footsteps approaching, his jacket looped on one finger over his shoulder. 'Hello, you.' He was grinning, enjoying her confusion.

She fought for her voice to be normal. 'What has you down here? Is it thinking of going back to school you are?'

'Well, now,' he said, putting his head to one side as he pretended to consider it. 'Sitting in a little desk every day and you leaning over me telling me what to do. There's a thought.'

'I'd say it would be old Cole you'd have. You being a big boy.'

'In that case, I'll pass.'

Dark hairs coiled all along his bare forearms, she could see them from the edges of her eyes and something about them made her dizzy.

'Seriously,' she said. 'What has you here in the middle of the day?'

'I had to get away. The ould fella wanted me to fix some fencing in the upper field but I couldn't stay to it. Everything was telling me it was a day for a walk on the strand so I made my escape. And as I was walking down, I saw the children coming from school and I thought to myself, I'll go down to the schoolhouse and see does Peg want to come too.'

For a walk. In front of everybody. And down here to ask her, not caring who saw. Her insides warmed and she was smiling. 'They're expecting me at home.'

'But they'll manage without you for half an hour?'

Her mother wouldn't be pleased; only this morning she'd been spitting fire about Dan, but she could tell her that she took the opportunity to question him, to sort out where he stood. 'It *is* a lovely day.'

'And who knows when we'll get the next one?'

He started walking in the direction of the strand and she fell into step beside him. 'I won't be able to stay too long.'

In the ditch opposite Lambert's farm, some crocuses were peeping up purple and white and nearby were bunches of daffodils, tall beauties flourishing flamboyant yellow heads. This day had sneaked out from under a terrible stretch of frost and rain that had plagued them for weeks. Just when they had thought they couldn't take another day of winter, today had arrived, with a sunrise that burst bright on the world. Through the early hours the sun had climbed up and up, higher than Peg remembered it could climb, until, in a marvellous mid-morning moment, she felt what she hadn't felt in months: warmth! She rattled up the winter-grimed schoolhouse windows to let in the soft, fresh air and at break time happily went on yard duty and spent most of the half-hour staring up at the trees, at buds that were longing to puff open into new green leaf. Above, she could see the birds were feeling what she was feeling, the way they went spinning so fast, circling high, as close as they could get to the sun. The children felt it too, scurrying around the schoolyard, in and out of the glare and shade, laughing and screaming. When the time came for them to come in, she rang the bell reluctantly and afterwards was restless, longing to be back out.

It made the children skittish too and she had turned to the story of Maeve, Queen of Connacht, to settle them. As always a story worked, getting all quiet except the terrible threesome, Tom Dunne, Nancy Connick and Paddy Brady, a trio of dunces who could never settle to anything except playing with *marla*, which was what she let them do while she told the tale to the others. Peg enjoyed storytime herself and especially loved to tell the children the old legends about ancient Irish heroes and heroines. This passing on of the lore of old Ireland was her attempt to compensate for the school curriculum. The books that the headmaster, Mr Cole, taught from were full of British propaganda about Ireland and England being one nation and all the supposed benefits that being part of the Empire brought to the Irish. Once – a while back, admittedly, but still – she had heard Cole teaching the children that infamous recitation: 'I thank the goodness and the grace/Which on my birth has smiled/And made me in these Christian days/A happy English child . . .'

Peg was determined that her children would know the legends that were known to all the Irish before the coming of the English, legends that dated from a time when the country was ruled by bands of native warriors, each with their own *seanchaí*, or storyteller, from a time when the Irish people spoke only their own tongue and cherished these stories as the crucible of their heritage. In the same spirit, she also taught them some of the Irish words she taught in her Gaelic League classes – simple words and phrases like hello, *Dia dhuit* (literally 'God be with you'), and thank you, *go raibh maith agat* ('may good be yours') – and demonstrated to them how an awareness and love of God suffused the Irish language.

Mr Cole wasn't exactly hostile to this activity of hers – how could he object to the children being taught their native language and lore? – but he wasn't what you'd call encouraging either. As theirs was a one-roomed school, his big desk down beside the fire was only forty feet or so away from her own. So she liked to draw the children in close to her for storytime, so he didn't hear or question too much. This she did today, moving everybody except Tom, Paddy and Nancy into the front two rows and bringing her own chair down off the platform and up close to them.

She had promised them the last day that she'd tell them all about Queen Maeve, the fiery woman at the centre of the epic tale 'Táin Bó Cualainge'. 'Maeve was a great queen, daughter of the High King at Tara,' she began, in the intimate, coaxing voice she kept for storytelling, 'very rich and very beautiful. Her power over the men of Ireland was great indeed, for they all wanted to marry her and she was choosy. She always held that she would accept a man as husband only if he fulfilled three conditions: that he was without meanness, without fear and without jealousy.

'Many vied for her hand and over her long life she had four husbands: Conchobhar Mac Neasa, Tinne Mac Connrach, Eochaidh . . . Dála –' Peg stumbled a little over the unfamiliar Irish names – 'and Ailill . . . Mac Mata.' Not that it mattered to the children whether she got the pronunciation right or not, they wouldn't know either way. She loved the way they were looking at her now, their eyes and their faces open. Even Tom Dunne was looking up from his *marla*. Already, just four sentences in, they were ensnared.

She continued: 'It was during Maeve's time with this fourth and final husband that the most important event of her life happened, the battle for Bó Cualainge, the great Bull of Cooley. One night she lay arguing with her husband King Ailill over who had the most wealth. Wealth at that time in Ireland didn't mean money, it meant land and cattle, and she and her husband were well matched for both except that Ailill owned a magnificent white bull that gave him the winning of the argument. Maeve was raging and decided she wanted to get her hands on the Brown Bull of Cooley. This bull was the best in all Ireland, famous throughout the land. She marshalled her allies and called in Ailill's six brothers and put together an army.

'The journey to Cooley took a long time, and one night a seer appeared to Maeve and told her that the men of Ulster they were going to fight were all sick and weakened with labour pains.'

Peg looked around her young audience. 'Do you understand what labour pains are, children? In another part of this story – it's a very long story, you see, with lots of episodes in it – a curse had been put on these men for their bad treatment of a pregnant woman. For what they did they were made to feel the pain of birth all the time, day after day. As you can imagine, Maeve was delighted when the sorceress told her this but she soon found out it was not so simple because one man had been spared from this terrible curse. This young man was Cúchulainn, a name known far and wide across Ireland, a skilled warrior, champion of Ulster, ruthless and strong. The sorceress said that the bad news she had to give Maeve was that if she persisted in going to Ulster, Cúchulainn was going to defeat her army. Maeve was very angry to hear this and—'

The schoolroom door opened, stopping Peg mid-sentence. All the children's heads turned. The doorway was filled with Father John, his coat off in deference to the fine day, a big patronizing smile fixed in place above his white collar. He came in and bade her a good day and a good day to the children and how were they all today, making his way as he was talking down the narrow aisle between the desks to where Mr Cole was coming forward through the senior children to greet him. The two of them would now go and stand in front of the fire, Peg knew, to warm their self-satisfied posteriors, smoke a pipeful of tobacco each and put the wrongs of the world to right in their own minds. The priest often dropped in like this, supposedly on an inspection but really looking for company. Not the company of the sick and dying, mind you, but the only man in the village he considered his equal for a debate.

Mr Cole set the senior children a passage to copy out of their readers and led the priest across to the fire. Peg resumed her story, a bit self-consciously now, aware of the two men smoking and looking around and knowing that Father John would probably come over when he'd finished his pipe and start asking the children questions about what they'd been learning.

She went on: 'Cúchulainn agreed to fight man-to-man, in single combat, against any Connacht champion. And every one he met and every one he killed, until in the end there was only one remaining warrior, Ferdia, who happened also to be Cúchulainn's oldest friend and foster-brother. Cúchulainn didn't want to fight Ferdia and tried to dissuade him by reminding him of the days they had spent together as boys, training in arms, when both were subjects of the great female champion, Scathach. "We were heart companions," he said to Ferdia. "We were companions in the woods, we were fellows of the same bed, where we used to sleep the balmy sleep."' Peg loved the musicality of these lines that she had learned by heart and welcomed the chance to quote them.

'But Ferdia feared he might weaken under Cúchullain's pleas and responded with taunts against his one-time friend. And so the fight was fought. For three days it lasted, and each night the two young men dressed the other's wounds, so that they could each continue to battle the next day. On the fourth day, Ferdia wounded Cúchulainn badly in the chest and Cúchulainn flew into a rage and let loose his magic spear, the deadly GaeBolga, to slay his friend and brother.

'As Ferdia fell, Cúchulainn caught him and carried him to the riverbank, lamenting. He laid him down and then fell into a trance of sorrow and weakness. Overcome by despair, he abandoned the fight, and Maeve captured the precious bull and pulled her army out and . . .' Peg's voice faded as she saw Father John, smoke and discussion with Master Cole completed, coming up through the classroom towards her. She stopped where she was and stood to greet him.

'Good day, Miss Parle,' the priest boomed in his big public voice as he drew near to her chair. 'Hello, children.'

'Hello, Father,' the children chanted.

'So, Miss Parle, what are we working on today?'

'We're learning some of the ancient Irish legends, Father.'

'Are we now?' He turned to the class. 'So, who can tell me something about one of Miss Parle's ancient Irish legends?'

Katy Rowe's hand shot up first. Little Katy was bright as a military button, though being a Rowe, she'd be lucky if she got to stay on in school past the age of ten.

'Yes, Katy.' Father John was smiling at her enthusiasm.

'We were learning about Queen Maeve, Father.'

'Is that so? And who is Queen Maeve when she's at home?'

'She had four husbands, Father, and her army killed hundreds of bad men from Ulster. Hundreds of them she killed, so she did, 'cause she wanted this bull that they had, see . . . er . . . and . . . er . . .' Seeing Father John's raised eyebrows, his forehead folding into furrows, Katy stuttered to a stop.

It so happened that Father John was an Ulsterman himself, from the county of Monaghan. Fearing that he was getting cross because she hadn't explained the story well enough, Katie added, 'She was able to kill that many of them because they had labour pains, Father.'

The priest's eyebrows nearly disappeared under his thatch of grey hair.

'That's the pains you get when you're pushing out a baby,' Katy elaborated, helpfully.

Father John held up his hand, turned to Peg. 'What sort of a story is this to be telling to little children?'

'Katy got the wrong end . . . She . . . It's one of the oldest Irish legends, Father. It dates from the sixth century.'

'It's a pagan story, by the sound of it. I'm surprised at you, Miss Parle.'

'You have to hear it in its entirety, really, to understand it.'

'I'm thinking Bible stories would be a lot more elevating.'

'I didn't tell the children anything wrong, Father.' She had, in fact, withheld many shocking things about Maeve contained in the original tale: that the Queen had tried to win the great Bull of Cooley by offering its owner the 'friendship of her thighs', for example. That after she left her first husband he came to her home place in Tara and violated her while she bathed in the River Boyne. That it was her boast that she was never without one man in the shadow of another. But Peg knew she wouldn't get any credit from Father John by telling him that.

'You cannot go wrong with a Bible story, Miss Parle.'

'Yes, Father.'

He turned to the class. 'We'll forget about Queen Maeve, children. Let me see now, who can answer me this: who made the world?'

All the hands went up, Katy's first, waving furiously. Martin Dunne was nearly halfway up the aisle, waving his hand, calling, 'Father! Father!' It wasn't too often that Martin had an answer to anything.

'Well, Martin?'

'God made the world, Father.'

'Good man. Good man.' Father John put his hand in his pocket and took out one of the lemon sweets he kept for the children and fired it at Martin, who caught it with such delight you'd think it was one of the crown jewels.

'And who is God?'

This one was Katy's. 'God is a Spirit Infinitely Perfect,' she chanted in a sing-song voice, once Father John gave her the nod. 'God Always Was and Always Will Be, World Without End.'

A sweet came flying through the air at her and her hand shot up, fast as a cracking whip, to catch it. Instead of eating it straight away like Martin, she folded it away into her fist. She was happy now, content that Father John's disapproval had passed.

And so it went on, the priest asking the children the well-worn questions and the children restoring Peg's standing with their rote-learned grasp of their Catholic catechism. At the end, just before he left, Father John filled his two fists from his pockets and threw both handfuls of sweets up in the air for the children to catch. This was something he always did to conclude his visit and Peg hated it. He would laugh as he watched the children jumping and scrambling, elbowing and pushing each other, but when he was gone she was left to deal with the disappointment of those who were unsuccessful and had to calm the whole class out of its agitation.

Now, as she and Dan set out across the sand, she told him all about it. 'It took me a full half-hour and a blackboard full of sums to quiet them back down.'

He laughed. 'I'd love to have seen his face when the young one said that about pushing out babies.'

'You should have heard the helpful little voice on her. You could tell she thought a priest might not understand such things.'

'So does this mean you'll have to stop telling the Irish stories?'

'Indeed and it does not.'

He laughed again at her vehemence.

'Once the English are gone out of the country, all Irish schools will teach those stories,' she said. 'And our own native language too.'

'You're right there. Once we have our own Education Department they'll look after that.'

He had misunderstood her. Was it deliberate? She meant: once they had a Republic. He was implying that the Treaty had it all fixed up already.

Without discussing it, they took the gap between Lambert's farm and Dillon's to get to the strand, rather than going down to the Hole in the Wall, which would take them too near to her house. They made straight for the shoreline, where the sand was firm and rippled with small undulations. The tide was well out and still retreating. In the shallow sand-puddles left behind, gulls waded with slow, high-footed steps, admiring their reflections in the pools.

'Do you ever wonder about leaving here?' Dan asked. 'Think of heading off out there beyond the sea?'

'Not really.'

'I wonder what life is like over there.'

'Pretty much what it is here, I'd say.'

'I don't know about that.'

'If you go up to Forth Mountain on a day like this, you can see Wales,' said Peg. 'Did you ever do that?'

'I didn't. Maybe you'd like to take me up there sometime.'

She matched his tone. 'I might . . . if you're good.'

'Oh, good, is it. Good at what?'

He was the very devil of a man. He always bested her because he never minded going low.

'We went across once, when I was about thirteen,' she said. 'Mammy brought us on the ferry from Rosslare and we stayed in a boarding house.'

'What was it like?'

'The people talked funny. We took a coach into the mountains – their mountains are huge – but it rained all day and we could hardly see a thing.'

He nodded. 'When I said about being away, what I meant was for good.'

'Oh, emigration. No, I never considered that.'

'I suppose why would you.'

He was right, why would she? She was one of the lucky ones, with her good job and her nice home where she could live happily until the day when, please God, she'd have her own home and family.

'You only go if you've nothing much here, I suppose,' she said.

'I don't know about that. Sometimes people are pushed but

sometimes they're pulled on by the thoughts of something better.'

'Not if they're happy with their lot.'

'It wouldn't be hard to imagine better than what we have around here.'

'You sound like you're thinking of it yourself.'

If he were, would she go with him? He'd make something of himself wherever he was. Would he ask her?

'No,' he said. 'I might have considered it before. But the Treaty changes everything. There's hope for us all now. I'd rather stay here and be part of the new Ireland.'

'I don't want to get into an argument about the Treaty, but—'

'Good,' he said. 'Then don't.'

He bent to pick up a flat stone, and tossed it across the water so that it skimmed the surface once – twice – thrice – four times before sinking. How was it that boys could always do that, Peg wondered, and girls couldn't? It was a paltry skill, one that didn't need strength or any other masculine quality to succeed. It must just be that girls didn't bother with it. Because it was a boy's thing, boys became good at it. She wondered what it would be like to be a boy, to do what Dan did today with her, just decide that you wanted to spend time with somebody and turn up where they were. Imagine if she were to do it the other way round, call up to the O'Donovan farmhouse when she felt like seeing him. Just imagine.

After a while, he led the way towards the Causeway. She decided she'd better ask him the hard question now, get it out of the way. 'What's all this carry-on with the Mucknamore band?'

'Listen, I know your mother has me blamed for that but she's all wrong. The band members are ten men with minds of their own.'

'But you're not coming to the Sinn Féin meetings any more. And neither are they.' She kept her voice light.

'There's no point. There's only room for one opinion in Mucknamore Sinn Féin.'

'Mammy's.' She laughed and he – looking relieved, she thought – laughed along with her.

'That's right.'

'But if you want your opinion to get across to the other members, you can't go isolating yourself.'

He stopped. 'It's the other way round, Peg.'

'What do you mean?'

'It's ye who are isolating yourselves. You should be more careful, Peg. Your family has a lot of influence around here. There's no good hoping your mother will calm down but you – the schoolteacher – you could moderate the message going out to the village. More than half the hotheads around here don't know what they think and they are waiting for someone they respect to tell them.'

She frowned. Supposing he was right and her mother wrong? No. Mr de Valera represented an ideal. The ideal of the Republic. If that ideal was not worth fighting for, then what had they been at all these years?

'If ye had to go out and be shot yourselves, ye women might be a bit more careful what ye said.'

Well, that cut deep, that he should think so little of all she had done. 'That's hardly fair,' she said. 'While you were in jail, where nothing worse could happen to you, we were the ones who had the soldiers raiding the house, never knowing what time of the day or night they might show up and what they might find if they turned the house over well enough.'

And she had to balance her work for the movement with her schoolteaching and her duties at home. More than once, she had imagined what a relief it would be to go on the run with a band of others of like mind, to plan raids on barracks and ambushes, to have nothing only that to think about. And to receive the honour and glory given to those who go out and fight. But her role was more humble and she accepted that and tried to be cheerful and to rise to any task requested of her. Then to be told she was little better than a coward, stirring it up from the sidelines. That hurt. Oh, but I care more about him than I do about politics, she thought. I do. He is the thought that wakes with me on rising, that I take to bed with me each night. So why am I letting politics come between us?

She hung her head, not wanting him to see her confusion, and in doing so noticed that she had chalk-dust marks all across her skirt. She bent to brush them away and what did he do then only reach over as if to help her? Through the fabric of her skirt she could feel his hand, rubbing against her leg. Blood flooded her face, a blush so swift and so absolute that it was nearly sore against her skin and she pulled back from him. When she had composed herself enough to look up at him, she saw he knew exactly what he was doing. His mouth was stretched up on one side into that devilish half-grin of his.

'I'd better head back,' she said, still blushing.

'Ah, come on, walk on a bit. We'll take a rest further out.'

She knew what that meant. Lovers' Hollow.

'No, really. They'll be wondering at home.'

'Come on.'

She shook her head.

'All right, suit yourself.' He shrugged and she felt like a servant being dismissed. 'I'll stay on for a while, if you don't mind.'

'No, I don't mind,' she said. But she did. It would be much more gentlemanly of him to accompany her back.

'It's going to be a lovely night,' he said, maybe sensing her disappointment. 'I might call down to your house for you later.'

'Call to the house?' Her heart leapt but then she caught his expression. 'Oh, you mean, on the sly.'

'I'll throw a few stones up at your window. Around half twelve?'

'I don't know, Dan.'

'I'll bring a lamp. We could come back out here then with more time. And no one to bother us.'

'I don't know,' she said again.

'Don't make up your mind now. I'll drop down and you can see how you feel later.'

The walk back along the sandy Causeway path was awkward, feeling that he might be watching her from behind and also aware of the windows of her own house, knowing that if her mother was upstairs in her bedroom and looking out the window she could see them both. Her mind was knotted: respect was lacking in him, she had to face that. He was far too presuming, but he had called up to the school for her, that was a good thing . . . She walked mindlessly, snarled in thought, right to the end of the Causeway, then she spun herself around and quickly retraced her steps. If her mother *was* watching, she'd be wondering what on earth was going on. She hardly knew herself. She marched back towards him with determination, knowing what she had in mind but not letting herself think too closely about it.

He was still standing where she'd left him, looking out across Coolanagh sand, towards the island and the water in the distance.

'Don't call for me tonight,' she said when she finally reached him. 'I won't be coming out.'

Was that amusement glinting across his face? Never mind if it was. She carried on, said what she had to say. 'No. I don't want any more sneaking around. I don't see the need for it. I'll be at Johnny Fortune's American wake next Sunday night. If you want to call for me, you can come to the house then. Around eight o'clock would be perfect.'

He burst out laughing.

'That's funny, is it?' she said.

He just kept laughing and she could think of no other way to keep her dignity but to leave without saying any more. So that's what she did.

He called after her. 'Come back,' he said. 'Come back for a minute.'

'I'll see you Sunday,' she called over her shoulder and kept on her way.

She retraced her steps for the second time. Still divided, she at least had the satisfaction that he wasn't getting it all his own way. She had done the right thing, she knew it and was glad of it but she wasn't under any illusion that it was going to get her what she wanted.

16

1995

I wake in my shed, to the knowledge that it is Sunday: no building noise, all is quiet. Up at the house, the machines lie sullenly silent, abandoned since tools-down yesterday. I wake thinking I might run first thing today. Usually I get straight to work and save my run for when my brain begins to fug up, around mid-morning. Once I've been writing for a few hours, it feels good to lace on my running shoes and jog out into brightness. It refreshes me, clears my head and refills the well of words. By the time I have done my miles and had a cooling swim in the sea, come back and washed and eaten, I'm ready to sit back to my table for a long afternoon session.

Today, though, I think I might change my routine. Summer weekends are busy in Mucknamore, especially Sundays, when visitors arrive from early morning. I hated running through the crowds last Sunday, weaving my way between watching faces, then arriving down at the far end of the beach, beyond the curving cliff and finding other people there, walking or swimming, enjoying the solitude that is usually all mine.

It will be good, I tell myself as I unzip my sleeping bag, to be out in the earliest hours, while the sand and sea are empty and morning-clean. The best part of the day, Granny Peg always said. So that's what I do. I jog out slowly at first, across the grass verge behind my shed, through the spiky marram sea-grass, through the churning soft sand to the harder surface down near the water. After a few minutes, I pick up my pace. I feel good, know that I have plenty of energy to draw on. My first-trimester nausea has passed, taking with it the horrible fatigue and chronic reluctance to do anything. It feels good to be fit again. Five daily miles is my average distance now, as it was the last time I was fit: two and a half miles out along the beach and back again. It was tough at the beginning, struggling with breathlessness and sore muscles, but it didn't take me long to build back up; those earlier years were there, waiting for me to return.

The early sun flourishes a dappled path across the water. This ongoing heat wave makes me feel like I'm not in Mucknamore at all. Oh, we had days like these when I was a child, I know we did, when Mrs D. or Gran hung plastic buckets and beach-balls outside the shop and day-trippers came to visit, but such days were seldom. This part of Ireland might be dubbed 'the sunny south-east' because it is warmer and drier than the rest but, as Richard used to say, twice nothing is still nothing. To me, rain was always the spirit of this place, rain that could bear down on us at any time, winter or summer, in drops or sprays or showers or mists or slanting, angry strings. Its absence was always marvelled over ('Glory be to God, *another* lovely day!'), its inevitable return hovered behind every clear horizon.

Whenever I go to the little supermarket down the street for food, I hear locals talking about this summer, marvelling over the way each day keeps coming up bright and dry. The temperatures are perfect, rarely reaching the eighties and almost always accompanied by a seashore breeze, but I heard a woman the other day describe this fine spell as 'pure persecution'. They've never seen anything like it, they say, fanning their faces with newspapers, looking skywards.

I run until I come to the rock that tells me I've done my distance then turn to retrace my steps. My footprints are the only ones in the fresh sand. In this direction, the offshore breeze fans my face and I inhale it deep, lengthening my stride as I draw it down into my lungs. I'm going to have a baby, I catch myself thinking again. A baby. Day after day, the idea reverberates round my head, like my mind needs to catch up with what my body already knows. A baby? A baby. A baby! My feet beat the word into the sand as I run: *bay-bee*, *bay-bee*, *bay-bee* . . .

I have left the early stages of pregnancy behind, the breasts that hurt as I turned over in bed, the churning sickness that made mornings a misery. Food still doesn't taste as good as it should – I am told it won't until after the baby is born – but physically, I feel better than I have in years, better even than the last time I was alcohol-free and training daily. I don't remember this surging energy running all the way through me: into my face, my fingers; into the feet that whip my legs along through strong focused strides. Maybe it's second-trimester hormones or maybe the contrast with the first, gruesome three months. But I suspect that it's also, somehow, related to the writing.

By the time I'm finished my stretches and swim, visitors are starting to arrive. Some have come equipped as if for a battle, with cool-boxes of food and drink, stripy windbreakers and sun umbrellas, sunscreen lotions and books, games for the children. Others bring only their swimsuited selves and a towel. Back in my shed, I watch them while I wash and change and eat, but once I settle to work, I cease to notice them. I am gone, engrossed in the past that rises up through the page to claim me, so that when I glance up from the page, I am surprised to find them there: sprawled across the sand or bobbing about in the sea, calling to each other.

Hilde appears at my door with lunch and I am puzzled to see her. I rub my eyes to win myself a moment during which my everyday self can surface. I take the food from her, eat it in a trance, and immediately it is finished, take up my pen again.

In the afternoon, with the best of the day's work done, I am more distractable. A family walking by the edge of the water draws my eye from the page. A good-looking family: dark father, fair mother, matching son and daughter. The little girl, five years old or so, wears a pink-striped swimsuit. Her hair, longer and blonder than her mother's, streams behind her as she and her brother trot ahead of their parents. She carries two buckets and spades and can hardly see over them, running so determinedly that she looks as if she might tumble headfirst into the sand. The boy wears a baseball cap the exact blue of his swimming trunks. His fat little legs pump him along as quick as they can but not quick enough to keep up.

Ahead, the girl suddenly stops and bends to look at something. A pretty shell? A stranded sea creature? Buckets and spades slip from her fingers. She calls over her brother and the two small heads come together, crouching all their attention on it so that their steadily walking parents pass unheeded.

Father and mother are dressed alike, in blue jeans and white T-shirts. His hands scrunch in the pocket of his jeans, as if fisted; hers are folded under her breasts. Both bodies are bent to their walk, two question marks gliding across the sand towards the Causeway, a small but constant gap between them.

When they realize the children are not following them, the father turns and calls, his hand a cup around his mouth. The wind carries his shout up to me in my shed: 'Ella! Dara! Come on!' No response. He begins to walk back towards them, his calls growing louder and testier, until at last the children look up and acknowledge him. 'Come *on*,' he says. They pick up a bucket and spade each, rush to follow him. Behind him, his wife waits, arms still folded, smiling indulgence.

When they catch up, the man takes his daughter's hand, the woman, her son's, and the four of them turn onto the Causeway. Out towards the island they walk, breaking in and out of their foursome like a dance. I watch until they are specks too small to see and when I can no longer see them I watch and wait for their return.

And that night, Rory comes to see me and tells me that he was thinking of me as he walked on the beach, past my shed, with his family. 'I knew you'd be at your desk,' he says. 'I kept thinking about you up here, looking down, watching us.'

I let him tell me this, though I don't know what I'm supposed to do with it. For a while we sit marooned in one of our silences. To distract us, I talk to him about the memories of my father that I am writing about now. I describe for him pictures that I can never shake out of my head, pictures I have only imagined but that are as sharp in my mind as any real memory: Daddy stepping off the boat in Fishguard, his suitcase in one hand and Mrs Larkin in the other, both of them all a-quiver at what they have done.

From that small image, it all unfolds. The pair of them on the train to Birmingham, sitting side by side, holding hands maybe, gazing out at the new sights churning past: rows of back windows of back-street houses in backward towns, all bigger than Ireland's capital. Nuclear-power stacks. Factory pipes pumping arrogant smoke into the sky. My father, taking it all in, gusty with confidence about what he had done, what he and his new woman are going to do.

Then the actuality of finding themselves in 1960s England. I tell Rory: 'It would have come as such a shock to him to be looked upon as just another Paddy. At home, he was so used to being the big fellow who didn't mind coming down a level.'

Rory moves in the dark, sits up to take another bottle of beer from the sand where he has burrowed them to keep cool. Usually we use my oil lantern for light but tonight Rory has brought along one of those big scented garden candles that keep stinging and biting creatures at bay. It tinges the night with the tang of lemon.

He takes a long draught from his fresh beer bottle, lies back down and waits. I go on, tell him more, things I have never told anybody else. When we were last together, thoughts of Daddy were still too raw.

'They only lasted a year. After that, he lived alone in some Birmingham bedsit.' I picture that too, though I never saw it: one room high over a busy road, traffic snarling below.

I pull some grass out of the ground I sit on, make a little pile, pull some more. I don't tell him how I see my father sitting in a sleeveless vest, smoking and drinking tea at a Formica table, one toe peeping through a hole in his sock. A black bin-liner full of fish-and-chip wrappings. An aluminium sink and a two-ring counter-top cooker. Copies of the *Wexford Weekly* and other Irish newspapers growing in a pile beside his armchair. Sometimes, the amount of details in my imaginings frightens me. I'm afraid of sinking into a place where I cannot tell what is real and what I have made happen in my head.

'What became of her, the woman he went with?' he asks.

'We never heard another word about her. Maybe she got tired of him when he wasn't Mr Devereux of the National Bank any more.'

'What was he over there?'

'He never got himself a proper job, as far as I can make out.'

'I only have a vague memory of him,' Rory says. 'He was nothing more than a face to me.'

'I know so much more now than I knew then, especially about being Irish in England. There is so much I'd ask him now, if I could.'

'If he was still alive?'

I sigh, knowing the truth. 'It would take an even bigger miracle than bringing him back from the dead, I think. I don't think we'd be able to talk much, even now.'

'I know what you mean.'

'Do you?'

'Completely. When my own father was dying, I wanted more than anything to tell him I loved him. One evening near the end I was left alone with him in the hospital. He was on a breathing apparatus and I sat in silence beside him, thinking: I'm going to say it, I'll say it on the way out, during my goodbye, so that I'll be gone before either of us has time to get embarrassed. But I couldn't.

When the moment came, all I got out of me was, "Take care." "Take care", for Christ's sake!'

I laugh. 'And my English friends think the Irish are so unbuttoned.'

He lies back down, hands behind his head, his elbows two arrows facing away from each other into the dark. 'We are, though. Compared to the English.'

'Are we?'

He turns his head at the challenge in my voice.

I say, 'You know I don't believe in generalizations like that.'

'But there is a difference between the Irish and the English,' he says. 'You said so yourself, that you felt it, living in England. That your father felt it.'

That is true. I have felt the difference and so have countless others but that's only one story. There is another: all the people I met in England who are more like me than many of the people I met here.

'And what about this child you're expecting?' he asks. 'How will you feel about it growing up American?'

'I'll feel fine,' I say, surprised. This is the first time since the night in the pub that he has referred to afterwards.

'Will you, though? Wait and see when it happens.'

I don't see why it should bother me at all but perhaps he – being a parent already – knows something I don't. Generally in these night-time talks of ours, I have the advantage: Rory can't reach into the places I have been the way I can unreel his life in my head. Parenthood is the one area where he has gone ahead.

We lie in silence again for a while. I am feeling it strong tonight, the awareness of each other that's always there, lying just underneath. Our memory of how we used to be: young, lusty, careless. Together.

He sits up, looks at me. 'Gimme a kiss,' he says, lightly, like it's a joke.

'Feck off.' I match his tone.

'Don't be such a miser. It wouldn't kill you, one little kiss.'

'There's no such thing.'

He starts to sing, Bogie style: '*You must remember this, a kiss is just a kiss . . .*'

I don't laugh. 'Stop it, Rory. Stop pushing this over onto me. You're the one who's married, remember?'

He flinches.

'We shouldn't even be here, like this, each night. It's—'

'OK, OK, forget it. Sorry I spoke.' He lies back down.

I close my eyes, trying to steady myself. Behind the whoosh of the sea are other sounds: car doors banging, voices calling, somebody heading out into the night. With Mrs D.'s pub closed, they have to drive up to Rathmeelin for a drink.

After a while he speaks into the dark: 'So . . . never?'

'No.'

'You've gone right off me?'

'That's it.'

He knows it's not true. 'But we were good together, weren't we? You will admit that much.'

'Ancient history, Rory.'

'I know that, I know. But important. It's OK to admit it, Jo. I'm not going to jump you if you show a moment's feeling.'

He is right: I wouldn't be so rigid if I wasn't vulnerable to him. I do want him, I do. Sometimes I fear that he is the real reason I came back to Mucknamore, the reason I stayed on after Hilde and Stefan arrived, the reason I didn't rent a cottage down the coast where I could have just as well done what I do here, day by day. Just to keep him in my sights. To return to the scene of our separation.

My grass pile is growing into a mound. I keep plucking away, adding to it. When he realizes I'm not going to answer, he says: 'After you cut us short, did you never wonder—'

'*I* cut us short? *Me?*'

'Come on, Jo, you gave me no chance.'

I stare at him, boggle-eyed.

He says: 'You took me completely by surprise and I didn't know how to react. One mistake and bang, you were gone, and I never saw you or heard from you again.'

'You could have found me if you wanted to. Maeve knew where I was.'

'You left the country, for God's sake. You made it clear you didn't want to be found.'

'It was up to you.'

'Maybe it was. But then . . . Everything was different then. I was so young. It was all too much for me.'

That was the truth. That was what I knew then, what I found so hard to take. It was all too much for *me* too but I hadn't the choice to opt out. If I could have, would I? Would my love have let me? Old questions that once revolved round and round until my whole self was spinning.

'It doesn't matter now, does it?' I say.

'We thought we were Romeo and Juliet, thought it was all so romantic.' He smiles. 'We forgot that *Romeo and Juliet* is a tragedy.'

'I hate thinking about the young me. She was such an idiot.'

'She was wonderful.'

'Don't.'

'She was. You are.'

'I mean it, Rory. *Don't.*'

He drops his head, starts to pick at the label of his beer bottle. 'What are you trying to say, Jo, that we're just *friends* now? Is that why you think I come up here each night, putting my marriage under strain . . .'

'Then don't come, Rory. Don't come. I don't want—'

'You do want, you know you do. And you know I'll come. Don't say what you don't mean.'

That takes me aback. That's my line.

'We know each other, Jo. Nobody knows me like you.'

Nobody? Not even her? 'Oh, Rory. We're different people now.'

'Not inside.'

'Yes, inside. Inside and out, every way. I am not that eighteen-year-old girl.'

'I still see her in you.'

'What do you want, Rory? What do you want from me when you say things like that?'

'You know what I want.' His voice is low.

'Then why? Why do you want that?'

'Why?' The question surprises him. 'For all the . . . usual reasons.'

'What, seven-year itch? Wife doesn't understand you? Midlife crisis?'

'You don't have to play the cynic all the time, Jo. Is it so hard for you to believe that I . . . want to be with you?'

I laugh, I can't help it. A laugh hoarse with grievance. Even I hate the sound of it.

'You don't know . . .' he says. 'You don't know how coming up here each evening is keeping me sane.' He reaches across, stops my hands from plucking grass, holds them in each of his. His palms are cold from the beer bottle, so cold they feel wet. 'Ever since you've come back, I feel like we are playing out a part. All these things you are finding out about our families, all this history before we came into the story. It's like we have unfinished business, like we have to play it out . . .' He hesitates, shakes his head. 'Does that sound crazy?'

'No,' I whisper.

'See,' he says. 'You understand. I couldn't explain something like that to *anybody* else.' Another veiled reference to her. After a small silence, he goes on: '"Wife doesn't understand you . . ." You fire it off like it's a joke and I know what a cliché it is but let me tell you, it's no joke when a marriage is going awry and there's nothing clichéd about how it feels. I'm not saying I'm blameless in it, I know I'm not, and I know she feels every bit as bad as I do. We haven't been good for a long time. There: that's the first time I've said it out loud to anyone.' He takes a long swig of beer. 'We haven't. So when your mother approached me last year about looking after her will, and it meant I was going to see *you* again, I felt like a small light had been switched on for me. I didn't think you'd come back here so I used to imagine going across to California to you. I spent hours envisaging it, what I'd say, how you'd be . . . I fixed on it, held onto it, it got me through. Seeing you, I thought, would sort me, take me out of the terrible paralysis that seemed to be squeezing me dead. I'd know what to do next. And now you're here. And I—'

He has looked into my face and what he sees there makes him falter: writhing anger. I pull my knees into my chest, wrap my arms around my legs to try and hold it down.

'You talk about unfinished business, Rory,' I say, winnowing out words that won't say too much. 'You talk as if we mislaid something and now we can reclaim it. I could never, ever see it that way. For me, that time . . . what happened . . . it was a cleft. I can no more take up where I left off than I could go back to being a toddler.'

'That's not what I meant.' He untangles my fingers from their grasp around my legs, takes my hands in his again. 'Look at me, Jo. Please. I know I let you down before. But now . . . Now we're here and we're together. I'm not saying our feelings are the same as then, or that there aren't complications. But the feelings are there, you know they are. Can't we just concentrate on what might come next?'

It's a good speech but it fails to touch me. Again I pull my hands out of his. He is talking about us, but I'm thinking about two other people. Two little children lying in bed. Their mother downstairs, contorted with loss. Their daddy gone. Gone out, off, away from them.

17
1967

My birthday, ten years old. For the first year that I can remember, my mother doesn't bake a birthday cake. When I come home from school, in the place of my favourite home-made chocolate sponge is a square shop-bought fruit cake. She has slathered some icing across the top as a disguise and stuck in ten candles but I recognize it: O'Connor's Fruit Cake, which we eat often, with the chewy raisins and the plastic red cherries like little clown's noses cut in half.

She is sitting at the table between Auntie Nora and Gran, half-smoked cigarettes squashed into zigzags in the ashtray in front of her. I know why she hasn't baked, she hasn't the heart for it. That's her excuse for everything these days. Some mornings she hasn't the heart to get out of bed. When she is up, she doesn't bustle and boss in the old way but stays hunched over the ashtray or folded tight into a chair, staring into the fire, her eyes a world away. Everybody is kind to her. Gran and Eileen cover her hours in the shop. She has flu, the men in the pub, the women in the grocery, are told.

Yesterday Granny Peg told her that people are beginning to suspect. 'You'll have to put your face out there,' she whispered, glancing across at me doing my homework by the fire to see am I listening. I keep my eyes on my books.

'Otherwise, what's the point in trying to get him back before anyone's any the wiser?' Gran says. 'You might as well write it up on the walls for all to see.'

She tries: plucks up a face, plasters on a smile, takes it out to the shop. Later I'm out there myself getting milk and Mrs Cummins is in the grocery, telling her how great it is to see her about again. 'Flu, was it?'

Mammy agreed that it was.

'It must have been a bad dose,' says Mrs Cummins, eyes like flecks of bone. 'To have you missing Mass.'

A terrible dose, Mammy agrees, changing the subject by holding up a small red notebook. 'You'll want those –' she points to the groceries on the counter – 'in here, I suppose?'

Mrs Cummins nods, slapped back into place by her debt.

In the shop she keeps up a front but in the house, with us, her gloom is thick and sour and dumped over us.

'That's a lovely cake,' I say to her now, coming into the kitchen and sitting down beside them and my birthday offering. 'Thanks.'

She rolls her eyes. 'Why did I ever bother baking a proper one for her before? She doesn't even know the difference.'

I cannot win. To punish her, I say: 'Will Daddy be home for my party?'

'No, your daddy's away.' Her voice acts normal but I see the chip of alarm she flicks across the table at Granny Peg, though it lasts only a second.

Can she really believe that I have not noticed days of red eyes and snuffly noses and cloudy whispers steaming out under the kitchen door when she and Gran close themselves off over cups of tea?

I make my voice clean of knowing, ask: 'Will he be here later on?'

'No.'

'When, then?'

'Ask no questions,' she says, 'and you'll be told no lies.'

'Tell me,' Gran puts in, 'you didn't happen to see my scissors, did you? I've been looking for them all day.'

If they were not so busy covering up, they would see through my questions. Why should I suddenly expect Daddy to be at a party of mine? He never was before. My party is unlikely to attract him; always a slack affair, not really a party at all. Just Coke with my dinner instead of milk and an overdose of sweets from the shop afterwards. Then Mammy lighting the candles on the cake and Gran shouldering her and Auntie Nora through 'Happy Birthday to You' and 'For She's A Jolly Good Fellow'. Just the four of us, nobody else. Same as last year, and the year before.

I never bring anybody from my school to the house. Nobody wants to come, and anyway, to bring someone here and let them see how we live: it would be like handing bullets to your own firing squad. What if Mrs D. flared into one of her rages? What if Auntie Nora took off her underwear like she did the other day? It stopped me in the hallway, her panty girdle and skin-coloured stockings bent right and left across the floor like a pair of fractured legs and underpants open to the world, showing a stain. Yellow water oozed across the tiles and I knew what had happened just by looking at them. She had wet herself again and then walked away from her accident, pretending it hadn't happened.

I wanted to slink off too, but I was afraid for Auntie Nora in case it might not be Gran who found her leavings. So I got the rubber gloves and picked up the hateful underclothes and dumped them in the wash. I wiped the mess with a cloth that I put into the bin when I'd finished. I made it like it never was and didn't tell anybody about it, not Maeve, not Gran. To share those stained pants with anyone would have made me sick.

I hate our life. I miss Daddy. No matter how hard I listen at doors I cannot find out where he is or why Mammy thinks he's not coming back. I miss him but I don't blame him for going. I know what drove him away.

I am walking out the Causeway behind three other girls. Two are from Mucknamore – Mary Cummins and Sally Rowe – and the other is Louise Farthington, home on holidays from England. Louise is eleven and the rest of us are only ten. This, among other attractions, makes her the desirable one, the one we all want.

Our hands are full. Louise and Mary and Sally each carry a long stick but they have made me carry a heavy stone. A rock. This is my punishment, though I'm not sure exactly what I am being punished for. I just do what I am ordered to do. These girls are my new friends. My *friends*. Louise is English. Though her mother is from Mucknamore and her father from Donegal, she was born and lives in London. Her skin seems softer and whiter than ours, her hair glossier, her accent shinier. She calls her mother Mummy and makes ordinary things sound fancy with her way of saying them: caah for car, ba-naw-naw for banana; hat and tomato with the 't's clipped tight. Louise's school has uniforms and bells, assemblies and school dinners, a PE hall and a headmistress, just like the schools in the *Mandy* and *Bunty* comics we all read. Everything about her is dazzling.

Mary won't admit this. She and Sally jeer at Louise's way of talking. 'Very lah-dee-dah,' Mary says, trying to put her down, but still she wants her and has taken her away from me. Louise was mine first. Her grandmother is Mrs Redmond, my mother's friend, and she was happy to play with me until Mary and Sally came along. Now the three of them have me under orders to stay back, ten paces or so behind them, carrying this stone. Louise's long dark plait swings against her spine as she walks, making my heart ache.

We are on our way out to Coolanagh. The sticks are for poking, the stone for sinking. This has been our craze since Louise invited Mary and Sally out to play with us three days ago: investigating the sinking sands. Our experiments are teaching us the character of the place: that the sands are erratic; that a heavy stone will sink in a certain spot one day but stay on the surface there the next. Each day we talk about going out further and testing more, but in fact we cling close to the Causeway. We are not as brave as we pretend.

I hold the stone as if it's a baby, cradled in one arm supported by the other. My muscles ache from its weight so I have to keep changing arms. Up ahead I can hear Mary explaining my inadequacies to Louise in words that are really aimed at me: 'just not good enough', 'giving her too many chances . . .' Foul glances are torpedoed back at me, over their shoulders. The day before yesterday the problem was the way I walked ('the state of her, like Quasi-bloody-modo'). Yesterday, it was something I said. ('No, we won't tell you what it was. You can just think back and work it out for yourself.') I spent all day thinking but couldn't come up with anything.

It seems especially unjust that they are mean to me here, when it was my idea to go out to Coolanagh in the first place. It was I who told them the stories about the place, stories Gran told me. About a bad man who met his deserved end out there, confessing to all his sins as he went down. About a woman who was too fearful to go to the aid of someone in trouble out there, and never had a lucky day after. About the special *liugh* that people are supposed to send up if they go astray out there, a particular shout for the purpose, high-pitched and staccato, that everybody recognizes, so that anyone passing on the Causeway might know the meaning of it and come and help. About the ghosts of such screams that can be heard echoing through the night, when the wind blows a certain way.

Coolanagh belonged to me while I was telling them those stories. Now it is theirs, the backdrop to my torment. Halfway out the Causeway, the three of them stop, turn to face me, noses held high.

'Can't you keep up?' says Mary. 'Why are you so slow?'

'It's heavy,' I say.

'It's heavy,' she mimics. 'Of course it's heavy. It's a rock, isn't it?'

'She doesn't want to keep up with us,' says Sally. 'She thinks she's too good for the likes of us.'

'You're right, Sal. She thinks she's better than us but we know the truth, don't we?'

I protest. 'You were the ones who told me to stay behind y—'

'The Devereuxes think they're something but everybody knows what they really are.'

'Except her.'

'She's so stupid she doesn't even know that.'

I look across at Louise, who is appalled and fascinated, both.

'But we all know, don't we, Mary?' Sally looks across to Mary for approval.

'You don't know the half of it, Sal,' Mary says.

Sally bites her lip. Mary always does this, has to be the best of the bunch.

'I do so,' Sally says.

'I bet you don't.'

'What? What don't I know?'

'I can't say,' Mary says, pointing her eyes at me.

'Never mind her.'

Mary shakes her head, sorrow saturated. 'No, I can't, Sal. Sorry. You're too young.'

Louise's eyes shine wide with curiosity. Something real lies under the jibes, it seems. 'Tell me, then,' she murmurs. 'I'm older than Sally.'

'I might tell you sometime,' says Mary, smug with the power of knowledge.

'Why not now?'

'You'd never talk to her again, that's why. Isn't that right, Jo? We shouldn't even talk to you, should we, never mind let you hang around with us?'

The phrases she is using sound second-hand, not her own. They are adult words, I think, and she is repeating them. *The Devereuxs think they're something . . . Everyone knows what you really are . . .*

What is she talking about? What does she know? Is there any way I can get her to tell me?

A few days later, they have tired of Coolanagh and Mary suggests we should go further, out as far as Inisheen to examine the stream that trickles off the island into the sand. Fairies are supposed to live in this stream under the rocks. Tiny fairies, impossible to see unless you get down close enough and are really lucky.

We walk all the way out, a long way. I am wary of them now and I don't believe in the picture we make, four friends walking out to Inisheen together, but still I'm glad to be seen with them. On the island, Mary leads the way to the stream, and we lie beside it staring into the water. Mary lifts a rock and Sally shouts out, 'They're there. Look.'

'Oh my God, Sally,' cries Mary, excitement jumping from her. 'You're right. Can you see them, Jo?'

Of course I can't. Is she serious? Fairies don't seem like Mary's kind of thing but her face is all puffed up with delight.

Louise stays where she is, lying on her back, her eyes closed to the sun. Mary calls her. 'Look, Louise, look. We're after finding them.'

'That's super,' says Louise, but she doesn't move.

Mary whispers in my ear. 'Are you able to see them? Look closer. Look now or you might never get the chance again.'

I stare. I see stones and silt and plants swaying in the water. She points, at what seems to me like tiny blobs of black. Dirt maybe. Or some tiny form of water slug?

'I can't believe I'm actually seeing fairies,' she says. 'Can you, Sal?'

'I can't believe it either. I never thought I'd see the day.'

Mary calls Louise again. 'Janey Louise, would you get up off your bum and come and have a look?'

'It's all right. I don't need to see them.'

'But it's beyond all, isn't it, Jo?'

I decide to join in. 'It is, Louise, honestly. It's unbelievable. You can see them, clear as anything.'

Louise says, 'Oh, Mary, give it a rest. You don't really believe in fairies. You're just trying to trick Jo.'

Mary looks at her through slitted eyes and I feel a sinking in my gut. Why did I pretend? Why, why, why?

'Or perhaps you do?' Louise says with a laugh. 'Perhaps you think they're leprechauns?'

Now it's Mary's turn to be stung but nobody is allowed to put her down. She takes a step back to stand between me and Sally and says: 'We don't want any English bitch coming over here to laugh about leprechauns, do we, girls?'

Louise sits up, shocked. A word like that would never be allowed to cross her lips. Mary decides to hurl another bad word at her. 'Why don't you fuck off back to England with yourself? We don't need any English lah-dee-dahs here.'

I look at Louise, her eyes swelling wet with offence and hurt, and I am glad. I have no pity. She did nothing to help me: she only told about Mary and the fairies because she didn't want to get up, not because she cared about me. Now it is her turn to suffer and I rejoice.

It doesn't last. Next day, I'm in the wringer again. Louise cries too easily and is too likely to tell. Louise's mother would not stand for anybody giving her girl a bad time. She would bring it into the open, tackle Mary's and Sally's parents, get them punished. I, on the other hand, am safe. I take what they dole out and wrap it up inside myself.

Louise goes back to England and the other two stop calling for me. I feel myself dimming in their eyes. And in my own: even bullying me isn't interesting enough to hold them. All that summer I feel something leaving me, draining out of me like water down a plughole.

Back in school in September, Mary tells everybody that I believe in fairies. I have never been popular but now the others sense a new weakness and round in. Mary leads the pack, guides the moves. Water is poured into my schoolbag, ink onto my hair. My books are scribbled on with indelible marker. I am held down behind the bicycle shed and the boys are lined up to look at my knickers.

Now each evening, I am first out of school, like a hare out of a trap as soon as Mr Walsh says we can go, but a hare who must appear to dawdle. The five-minute walk home is torture to me, with what feels like the rest of the school walking behind me, firing jeers and occasional pebbles. Aching to run, I glue slow, indifferent steps to the ground. I bite the inside of my lower lip as I walk along, a habit I have taken to. My teeth gnaw on the soft pink flesh until salty blood runs to the back of my throat. I swallow it down.

Sometimes adults pass us on the road, see what's happening, and I smile at them, as if it is a game. They are unconvinced but nobody does anything to help me. Mammy is glad Mary and Sally have stopped calling for me. The Cumminses were never 'in the book', she says, her phrase for respectable. 'You were right to drop them,' she says. 'Why would you want to be going around with the likes of Mary Cummins?'

I think about telling Granny Peg, but tell her what? I have no bruises to show, no war-wounds to flaunt, and anyway Gran's days are full of trouble already, balancing Mammy and Auntie Nora. She knows I am not popular and she says it's because I'm too brainy, that the other children are jealous. She gives me a saying: 'Sticks and stones may break my bones but words will never hurt me.' It doesn't sound right to me but I try it anyway, hurling it at the girls in school one day, when they are calling me names. They laugh it right back to me.

So I don't tell Gran, or anyone else, the things they do to me. A bunch of spiteful girls is all they are. I am shamed to silence by how much they can hurt me.

Maeve comes home for half-term. 'What's wrong with Mammy?' she asks, making new again what I am getting used to: the scrunched-up eyes and jagged face, the lying in bed with the sheet pulled over her head like she's a corpse, the cigarettes half-smoked then crushed into little elbow-shapes, piling high in the ashtray.

'Daddy's gone,' I say, 'and she's broken-hearted.' It's Gran's word I use but it's not the right one. Mammy's sorrow is not pure: it skulks around the house, waiting to pounce. It has claws.

'Gone?' Maeve says. 'What do you mean? Gone where?'

'Nobody is saying.'

It feels good to have someone to tell. I know that once Maeve is back a while, we will be squabbling again but today, the first days of her holidays, we are almost friends.

'I don't think he's coming back,' I say.

Maeve says we have to know. We should be told. So we go to Granny Peg and Maeve tells her what I have said.

'Not at all,' Gran says. 'Whatever gave you a notion like that? Of course he'll be back.'

'Are you sure, Gran? It's been so long.'

'You know your daddy. Doesn't he always turn back up like—' She stops herself saying it. Like a bad penny.

'So he'll definitely be back?'

'I'm sure of it.'

'When, Gran?'

'Soon.'

Arriving in school one morning, I realize Mary Cummins knows. She keeps looking back over her shoulder at me, knowledge packed behind a pair of stretched lips. I sit on my own in my double desk, gnawing my inner lip, cutting through the healed-over scab with my teeth, reaching for the raw, familiar wound underneath.

I miss him badly now. Each morning I get up on my own, breakfast alone in the quiet kitchen, looking out at the grey sky pressing down on the grey sea. I wish he would come back for a while. He could go away again, if that was what he wanted, but I wish he would just check in with us. I pine for the glow of the outside world he used to bring to the house. Mammy is too much for me, for us all, without him.

At break, Mary bears down on me with a gang of cronies behind her. Eyes swimming in their heads with excitement, they form a circle around me. I am backed up against a wall, hugging my ribs, awaiting my fate.

'Her da's after leaving home,' Mary tells the others, as if they didn't know. 'Gone off with a fancy woman from the town.'

I make my face blank to the sneers and staring wonder.

'Have you nothing to say for yourself? That's a mortal sin he's committed. He'll go to hell.'

'You can hardly blame him, though, Mary,' says Sally. 'Who'd want to see *that* ugly mug sitting across from them at the table every day?'

Everybody laughs.

Silence is my only defence. If I don't speak, my voice can't tremble. If I don't shout, my face doesn't turn red. If I don't put words on my feelings, my eyes don't fill up.

Mary starts to sing, a song with the words changed, just for me. *Where's your daddy gone?* And the others join in, in a laugh-along routine they must have planned, maybe even practised. I stand silent, without an answer for them or the question they chorus.

Little Jack Breen comes home for his holidays from Birmingham and tells everybody that he met Daddy over there, that he sees him often in the Irish club. He is living with Mrs Larkin except she calls herself Mrs Devereux now and the two of them live off the money she got from the sale of her pub. Living the life of Riley, according to Little Jack, going to race meetings and hotels and dinner-dances, out on the town every night of the week.

All the customers find a way of letting Mammy and Gran know that they know.

*

I am outside the front of the house collecting the milk when Bartie comes along with the post and gives it to me to bring in. In between the brown window-envelopes, one that is pale blue sticks out. The head of the English queen is on its stamp. I pull it up to the top, insides already churning, even before I recognize his writing.

Like a thief I look around to see if anyone is watching me. I go round the back of the house where I can't be seen. I think about hiding it, steaming it open later like I have read about in books. I consider this for a long time, but in the end I am afraid. I slip it back into the middle of the pile, set out to find Mammy.

She is upstairs, making beds. 'Post,' I say, handing it over as if it were a normal bundle. I stay and watch as she files through them. She stops when she comes to it and flushes up from neck to forehead, then looks at me, hard. She knows I know. I shrink from the slap that's certain now she's seen through me. The slightest thing these days nudges her to rage. Shoes abandoned in the living room: Slap. Clothes not laid out on Saturday for Sunday Mass: Slap, slap. Spat-out toothpaste not rinsed off the wash-hand basin: Slap, slap, slap.

I point at the unmade bed. 'Will I give you a hand?' I ask, wiping my face clean of anything but the willingness to straighten sheets and blankets.

'Since when did you turn into Little Miss Helpful?'

I cower but the blow doesn't come. She folds backwards so she's sitting on the bed, shrivelled into herself.

'For the love of God, what are you trying to do to me?' she says, shaky fingers clutching the blue envelope. 'Are you trying to send me over?'

I shake my head.

She stares at me out of splintered eyes. 'Jesus, you're pure useless. Get out.'

Later, when she has gone into town to the cash-and-carry, a trip that always takes hours, I search for the letter. It's not in the desk in the living room where important papers are kept. Not in the kitchen drawer with the bills and notes and parish newsletters. Not in the little side locker beside her bed. I have to go to more secret places. Her underwear drawer. No. Beneath the account books in the sideboard where I once found a book of mine she had taken and hidden as a punishment. No. Under the mattress. Yes.

Under the mattress, out of its jagged envelope, lying flat and open. One sheet only, writing on one side. Blue ink.

I take it to the bathroom, lock the door, sit on the lid of the toilet seat. For a minute I am blind, unable to see. Blackness floods in through my eyes, turning me cold all over. I shiver and my vision rights; I can read again.

It has no address or telephone number at the top. It says:

Dear Máirín

You're to stop sending people after me because it will do no good. How you found out where I was, I don't know, but we can get lost again if that's what we have to do, go to Coventry or London or some place where there will be no tracking us down. We'll change our names if necessary.

What I'm saying to you is, sending people to see me will not change my mind and only wastes your money.

You must know by now that I took nothing with me. Everything I left behind is yours, for you and the girls. I hope some day you'll tell them I did that.

This is for the best, Máirín. You mightn't think so now but I'd say you will come to see it that way eventually.

Yours sincerely

Christy Devereux

I read it and read it and read it again, until I have drained the words, until I can suck no more from them. Then I slip it, letter and envelope, back under the mattress just as I found them.

The knowledge of the letter follows me around through my days and nights, summoning me to look again. The next day, while

Mammy is in the shop I take a chance and scurry up to her room, slide my hand into the slit beneath the soft mattress again. It is back inside its envelope, telling me that she too had had it out for another look. I read it again and find I know it, word by word, off by heart.

Next time I return, it's gone. My hand pats and rummages and feels around but comes out empty. For weeks afterwards I search the house whenever I can, trying to find its new hiding place. If Mammy moved it because she suspected my investigations, she gives no sign.

I search and search but turn up nothing. It is as if it never arrived, except for the words I have branded in my head.

18

1922

'Will the lads make a guard of honour and lead Mr de Valera's car all the way between Wexford and Enniscorthy?' Máire asked.

The question stopped Peg in the act of laying the kitchen table. 'No,' she said, knives and forks pointing upwards in her hands. 'No, Mammy. We won't have time for them to walk all that way.'

Máire folded her lips and Peg was stung by the disapproval. Three weeks ago, Máire handed over to Peg her part in organizing the great day because she just wasn't able for it. It was frustration at her weakness that was making her critical, Peg knew, and she strained for patience with her. 'The Enniscorthy meeting opens at three, Mammy,' she explained. 'By the time Miss MacSwiney and the others say their bit, it will be nearly four before Mr de Valera gets to speak. They have to be in Wexford for five so there's not time enough to walk it.'

'But you'll escort them into the town, surely?'

'Ah, Mammy, of course we will. They'll motor as far as Ferry-carraig where the troops will be waiting to lead them through.'

And after the public meeting in Wexford there would be a reception in the Talbot Hotel, and it was there that she, and two other girls, would make their presentations.

Máire turned back to her frying pan, and leaned into the press as she stood by the cooker, turning meat. Always now if she was standing, she had to rest against some surface to steady herself – a hand on the table, a hip against the chair. And she moved slowly about the place, as if weighing up each step before putting her foot down. These changes had advanced so gradually that Peg hardly noticed them, until something reminded her of her old bustle, the way she used to come swinging through a door with five times more force than was needed.

A lot of her mother's strength went into trying to hide her weakness, in ways that turned Peg's heart over. She tried to catch Barney's eye behind their mother's back, but he had his face dug into the newspaper so she went back to setting the cutlery.

'It'll be a great occasion,' Máire said, trying to make amends. 'I might make it in myself.'

'Are you serious, Mammy?'

'What do you mean, am I serious?'

'I never thought for a minute you'd not come along.'

Her mother frowned. 'I'll do my best.'

'You have to come, Mammy. Every Republican this side of Enniscorthy will be there.'

'All right, all right,' she said, short with her again. 'I'll do my best, I said. Don't pick me up till I fall.'

Every time Peg thought of herself handing that statue to Mr de Valera, she felt dizzy. To think of him taking her hand in his, probably addressing a few words to her. Whatever would she say back? How would she answer him without blushing?

'It will be so strange to see him in the flesh,' she said.

'He has a powerful presence all right,' said Máire from the cooker. 'And Miss MacSwiney too. They say she's a great speaker.'

Barney lifted his head. 'They say she'd talk the hind leg off a donkey. Two and a half hours she went on for during the Dáil debate on the Treaty. Two and a half hours!'

'I know, but worth listening to, wasn't she?' Peg said. 'All that stuff about blades of grass and dragon's teeth . . .'

Máire picked up the quote, word perfect: '"If they exterminate the men, women and children of this generation, then the blades of grass, dyed with their blood, will rise, like the dragon's teeth of old, into armed men, and the fight will begin again in the next . . ."'

'Strong stuff, Barney,' Peg said. 'You have to admit it.'

But of course he wouldn't. None of the men liked Miss

MacSwiney; she frightened the life out of them. And Barney, once again, was in a disagreeable mood. 'Will the dinner be long, Mam?' he asked, drumming his fingers on the table. 'I'm in an awful hurry.'

Peg said, 'Aren't you always in a hurry these days?'

She wouldn't mind if it was movement work he was going to but it was only an old game of hurling, not even a match, just a friendly. Her mother crossed the room and put his plate of food on the table, pinching his cheek as she passed, like he was still a child.

Peg laid the potatoes in front of him. 'Surely they'll not start the match without the great Barney Parle?'

He stuck his tongue out at her.

'Don't start, you two,' said Máire. 'Leave the chap alone, Peg, and run out to your daddy. Tell him his dinner is on the table.'

'Do you want me to take over the shop?' It was Saturday, a day that had a different routine to weekdays. Peg had no school, and both Pats and Tess had a half day, with one or the other of them coming in late afternoon till closing time.

'It seems quiet enough,' Máire said. 'I'd say we're safe to leave the door open.' They did that sometimes when it was quiet: the customers tapped on the counter with a coin if they had a need. Máire liked to get everybody fed at the same time, so the food didn't spoil, but she didn't approve of them eating behind the counter like some publicans.

The dinner was fried pork chops, one of JJ's favourites, and he came in rubbing his hands. 'Looks good and smells better,' he said, taking his seat at the top of the table. Máire brought over the rest of the plates.

'Are there many in?' she asked, settling into her seat.

'A few,' said JJ. 'But they all have a drink in front of them.'

Barney was steadily advancing through his meal, his first chop shorn to the bone already. He and JJ had two, and the women one. Máire's own plate held the smallest helping but Peg knew she wouldn't finish even that.

'So,' said Peg to Barney, 'are we expecting many on the sidelines today to cheer on the heroes of the hurling field?'

He ignored her, carried on working through his plate of food, barely stopping to swallow. His cup of water sat beside him untouched.

'I think some girls are mad,' said Peg, 'to stand for an hour and a half on the side of a hurling pitch on a day like this.'

'If you had an eye for one of them,' said her father, 'I'd say you'd be out quick enough, same as the rest.'

'Not if Pádraic Pearse himself was playing.'

'Where is the game?' Máire wanted to know.

'Creel,' Barney said, his mouth full of meat.

'You'll be going on the bike, so. Did you get that brake fixed?'

'It's all right.'

She frowned. 'Is it fixed, is what I asked.'

'I'll manage all right for now.'

'You didn't manage too well when you hit that hole on Rathmeelin hill last time, did you? Weren't you lucky not to break a limb? Daddy, tell him.'

'Your mother's right, son. You need the brakes to be in order.'

'I'll fix it later. I've no time now.'

'What has to happen to you before you get sense? What do you have to be inviting accidents into your life for?'

'I'll fix it later, Mammy. Honest I will.' He gave her one of his smiles, humouring her. 'Honest.'

Close under her chiding of them these days was an anxiety like gone-off milk under a film of cream. They all sensed it but none of them wanted to poke through to it.

Barney pushed back his chair.

'Are you not waiting for a cup of tea?' Máire said.

'I haven't the time.' Already he was at the door.

'What hour of the day or night will you be back?'

'Around six. Bye.' And he was gone, leaving a space behind him.

The golden days of Barney's return from prison have faded for Peg. Tarnished, even. Dan had made a comment once about Barney not being much of a leader and at the time she had defended her brother like a lioness, but afterwards she had confessed to her diary her agreement. What she had expected after he came home from prison, his reputation enhanced, was that he would escalate his involvement. Instead, the opposite had happened: if he was easygoing before, he was positively indolent now. Yesterday evening he had let her down again. She had asked him to let Sore-Toes and Lama and the other boys know about a meet in the snug to plan their village's travel arrangements for the de Valera visit. Not only did he forget to inform half of those she'd instructed, he also failed to turn up himself. It just wasn't good enough. Not as things grew hotter by the day.

And, at the back of it all, Dan. Dan, Dan, Dan. This morning, Molly had called in to the shop with a message from him. This had surprised her – why send Molly, of all people, with his messages? – but she overlooked that when she heard what he had to say. 'He told me to tell you he was definitely going to Johnny Fortune's American wake tomorrow night,' said Molly.

Seeing Molly trying hard not to look glum made her feel that this must be good news. It was good news, wasn't it? He wasn't calling for her but he would see her there. In the afternoon, after her committee meeting, she was going to town to buy that new pin for her blouse she'd been admiring for weeks, and this evening she would take a lemon from the grocery and squeeze it into the rinse water when she washed her hair. She was going to look her very best for that wake and be on her best behaviour too, sweet and pleasant and attentive. She would show him, she thought as she pushed the last mound of food onto her fork, that she could hold to her convictions while allowing him his.

Finished, she stood to gather the side plates and pile the potato peelings and the dirty cutlery. She needed to leave – her meeting started at two thirty – but she didn't like to take off too quickly after Barney's sweep-out. Time was when her mother used to be the one always off somewhere in a hurry.

'Are you finished, Mammy?'

'I am.'

JJ looked up. 'Ah, Máire, eat another bit, for pity's sake.' But she shook her head.

Peg scraped her plate, stacked it with the rest, carried them over to the board. She put the kettle on the fire. It had boiled earlier and only needed a minute back on the heat. As she stood waiting for it, she felt herself wilt in the heat of the fire and realized she was tired. Between teaching in school, helping out at home and her Cumann na mBan work, she never seemed to have a minute these days. Steam and water came hissing through the spout of the kettle and she lifted it off, made the tea.

'Good girl yourself,' said her father, as she put down the pot.

'I need to go as well, Mammy,' she said.

'You've no time for tea either?'

'I'm sorry, I have to be in town by half-past two. But I'll be back in time to give you a hand with the supper.'

She replaced the butter and salt in the pantry, put the dirty delph in the basin, poured boiling water into it.

'Leave it, so,' her mother said. 'I'll do them myself.'

'Are you sure?'

Her mother made a face. 'You have to go is what you said.'

That wasn't fair. How was it allowed for Barney to trot off to a hurling match without a word said about it? Or, for that matter, for him to neglect the troops, as Mammy surely must know? No, she'd rather give him a lecture about his bicycle brakes than face up to the truth about him, while Peg was always the one to get the lash of her tongue.

'Go on, then, if you're going,' said Máire, standing up quickly, too quickly, and bringing on one of her coughing attacks, the sound of which racking immediately turned Peg's anger into something else. She stood, unsure whether to cross over to help or whether she'd rather it ignored.

God, but this was a long one. Would it never stop?

Máire scrabbled at the fabric of her dress trying to reach into her pocket – for the flask she kept there that was small enough to spit into without making a fuss, perhaps, or for her handkerchief – but before she could get what she wanted, a spout of blood burst from her mouth. She put her hand up to try to hold it.

'Mammy!' Peg cried, rushing to catch her. She steered her towards the armchair, snatching a tea towel off the chair at the same time and pushing it into her mother's trembling fingers.

Her father stood, helpless.

'Get water, Daddy.'

He turned to do it while Peg held her mother's shaking frame. The eruption had eased the cough and the worst of the shock was subsiding. The scarlet stain screamed out of the grey towel. Máire tried to fold the fabric so it couldn't be seen.

As soon as her control returned, she pulled away from Peg. 'I'm . . . all . . . right,' she said, her breath struggling through the words. She tried to smile, unaware of the blood that smeared her teeth. Peg wanted to turn away from the sight, wanted to cry, but had no intention of allowing herself to do either.

'We'd better get you up to bed,' she said.

'Your . . . meeting . . .'

'Never mind the meeting.' Peg took the glass of water from JJ, held it to Máire's shuddering lips.

'Can you stand, Mammy? Can you walk up the stairs?'

Slowly, carefully, using the arms of the chair to lift herself, Máire moved to put weight on her feet but her strength failed her and she dropped back into the chair with a sigh of disgust. From the shop came the sound of a sharp rap-rap-rap on wood, followed by a yell: 'Anyone at home?' In the agitation, they had forgotten all about the customers.

JJ stood transfixed, like he'd forgotten how to move his legs, and Peg saw that it was up to her to take charge. 'Daddy, go out and serve whoever needs serving, and see who you can send for the doctor.'

Máire tried to protest. 'No . . . doctor . . . no . . .'

'We're getting the doctor, Mammy, and that's that.' She turned back to her father. 'As soon as they're looked after, come back in here to me. I'll need your help to carry her upstairs.'

Máire opened her mouth to object again. JJ dithered, to see what she'd say.

'Quick, Daddy,' said Peg. 'Go on. What are you waiting for? Go.'

So there they were, catapulted into the next stage of Máire's illness. It wasn't that she hadn't coughed up blood before, they all knew she had. Each morning broke with the sound of her raucous, distinctive cough. They knew she had been losing weight and that she'd been struggling for months with a continuous tiredness of mind and body.

What was changed now was the secrecy. The moment had come when even JJ was going to have to admit the truth of what was happening. After months of circling around it, of never saying it aloud (they might as well say it now: TB. Tuberculosis. Consumption. Phthisis. The white plague . . .), of each of them making small advances and retreats from the edge of all that it might mean, the illness had now reared up and insisted they face it.

After getting the patient up to bed, and admitting Dr Lavin, and listening to his diagnosis and administering his prescription, and seeing Máire off to sleep, Peg and JJ – and later, after he came home from his match to be told the news, Barney too – did what they felt had to be done in the face of death: they kept life going. Peg, her Cumann na mBan meeting now unfeasible, cleaned the kitchen and, while she was at it, gave the back pantry a good going over. JJ was struck by his children's two white faces, so similar today despite their different colouring, the shock seeming to have bleached the colour from Peg's dark hair and darkened Barney's red crop. He was struck too by the irony of their chastened awe and felt tempted to make the kind of speak-out against their activities that he never bothered to make anymore – to point out that the death they were brushing against now was the very same death they were playing with when they made merry about Dying For Ireland. Perhaps now, once they saw what was ahead for their mother above in that bed, they might amend their ways.

But he said nothing. He tended the customers and when Pats came in spent an hour with Barney in the bottling store, filling bottles of stout from the big vat, stocking up for the weekend rush. And Barney, as well as helping his father by putting the caps on the bottles and sticking on the labels, also, finally, fixed the brakes of his bicycle. All the things Máire would have had to nag them to do if she was in the whole of her health were done without complaint.

Máire's eyes flicked open. She had been dreaming of her Aunt Hannah, her father's sister, who, years and years ago, lived in her house at home on the mountain. She had been dreaming of hanging out clothes in the back yard with Auntie Hannah, of picking the pegs out of the basket and handing them up to her, as she used to do, and now, for one moment, she was confused at the darkened room she found herself in, unsure of where she was. To her left, a candle burned. Turning her head towards its light, she found her daughter, Peg, sitting on a chair beside her, sewing, a basket of mending beside her. Then it all flooded back: she was at the end of her life, not the beginning.

When Peg saw her move, she stopped her work. 'You're awake, Mammy. How are you feeling?'

'All right. Better for the sleep.'

'Are you hungry? I've made some soup.'

Soup? The thought of it turned her stomach. It had been months since she knew what hunger was. It was the way with her always now, to be neither hungry nor full.

'Maybe in a while.'

The blinds were pulled but she could see it was dark outside too. 'What time is it?'

'Nearly nine.'

'I've slept for hours.'

Peg nodded. 'Are you sure I can't get you something? You really should eat.'

'Is Barney home?'

'He is. Do you want him?'

'No. No, just wondering.'

The way you always wondered, even when they were great strapping lads of twenty-two. Soon, she wouldn't be here to wonder. She knew it, was not fooled by the evasions of Dr Lavin this afternoon. The black knowledge that she was going to die reared up in her and she gagged on it. *Sweet Jesus.* She clutched the two sides of her bed like she was adrift on a raft. *Mother of God, help me.* My life is over, over. Over and it feels like it hardly started. Over. She couldn't believe it. *God above in Heaven, help me.* She began to pray to herself, inside her head: a God our Father, a Hail Mary, another one. She fixed on the familiar words, using them to drive other thoughts away. It worked, her panic subsided enough for her to lie there without screaming.

Something was niggling at her, something small. Then she remembered, and was glad of the distraction: 'I'm sorry,' she said to Peg. 'For the way I was with you earlier.'

'Don't be silly.'

'No, I am. It's foolish anger that gets me that way sometimes.' Anger at my sickness, anger at God, anger at everyone who's well, everyone who doesn't yet know what it's like to wake in the morning and inhale death with their waking breath.

'No one could blame you, Mammy.'

She was a good girl, Peg, the one they'd all rely on now, the one who'd look after the other two when . . . It was wrong of her to get irritated with her the way she did, for no good reason. Maybe that was the way a mother always felt about a daughter: a bond that looked smooth on the surface but was all edged underneath. She wasn't sure, as her own mother died the day she was born, died in the having of her. What she did know was that her feelings for Barney had always been easier, even these days when he was acting the complete scoundrel as far as Ireland was concerned, and treating her as though her condition was a personal insult to himself.

Yet a daughter was someone you could talk to and she was gripped with the need to talk. While she still could.

'I hated this place when I came here first, I never told you that, did I? When we came home here after our honeymoon in Killarney, every customer in the place was lined up along the counter to have a look at me. I was only eighteen and I found it terrible hard. Only eighteen, younger than you are now. That's why they were so curious, your father being so much older.'

It had always stayed with her, the way their male eyes had all harboured the same low thought, their curiosity like another person following her around. 'They could be as ignorant-rude as they liked but I was not allowed to give offence, or let on what I really thought of any of them. You know how it is, you've grown up with it, but I had never set foot in a pub in my life.'

'It must have been hard, all right.'

'I had to learn everything. But I did learn. I kept my side of the bargain.'

'Bargain?'

'A match is a bargain, isn't it?'

'I suppose.' Peg looked pained, making the face she used to make as a girl when Máire fed her a dose of cod-liver oil. Young ones and their romantic notions. The girl was surely old enough to know that her mother and father were hardly a pair of turtle doves. She must surely have worked out that JJ was an old man when he picked an eighteen-year-old wife to marry. Had Peg never spared a thought to wonder what that had been like for her?

What sort of a face would she make if Máire was to tell her that she had spent the first months of her marriage making lists in her head of all the things she hated about him, this old man who up to then had been nothing to her but her father's old friend? A long list it was too: the pink scalp that beamed through the combed-across streaks of his papery hair; the explosion of red veins across his nose and cheeks; the long, yellowing teeth, his breath blowing hot and stale between them; the fuzz of grey hair like moss across his chest; the bulge in his long-johns like a small animal curled up between his legs; his toenails, thick and tough as bone . . .

What if she was to tell her that for years she was haunted by an image of the pair of them – her father and her husband-to-be – shaking hands over their deal? If she told her that JJ himself knew he had done her wrong? That as she was passed to him at the altar, he wasn't able to look her in the face? No, and not for the rest of the wedding ceremony either. Not once, for the full length of the day, was he able to raise his eyes any higher than her eighteen-year-old neck.

If she told her that a year into their marriage, she went to a priest in town about it?

'Does your husband mistreat you?' the priest had asked.

'No, Father.'

'Is he perhaps too fond of the drink?'

'No, Father.'

'A gambler?'

'No, Father.'

'Have you any complaint against the man?'

I can't bear him to touch me, Father. I can't bear the touch of him.

But how could you say the like of that to a priest?

What if she were to tell her daughter that once she became pregnant (with her, Peg), she had turned her back on him, that she only allowed him the run of her once again after that, when she wanted a second child?

And what, oh what, if she was to tell her daughter of the flirtation she ran herself into with Billy Ffrench, one of the customers, a fascination that nearly ruined them all, only Lil Hayes pulled her back from the brink? Young Billy, wiry as a whippet. Nothing special to look at, with a face that looked like nothing as much as a skin-shrouded skull, but very tall, with a certain strange presence. And young. Young.

One day she found herself wondering what it would be like to have someone like him kissing you, putting his hands on you, and once the thought had been allowed, she couldn't rid herself of it. After a while, she didn't even bother to try; it gave her solace. After another while, she found that she was going over to him whenever he was in the shop, leaning into the counter to have a laugh and a joke with him. Harmless, she told herself. She was just being agreeable the way JJ explained you had to be with the customers. But she knew Billy was coming into the shop more often and that whenever he did, his eyes would skim the counter up and down to see if she was there, an echo of the way she scanned the place herself whenever she came through from the house.

Soon they were the butt of talk, and trouble so distressed her husband that she wasn't able to look at him straight. But still, she went on. She made a fool of herself for the bold Billy and he let her. Until word of the carry-on got back to his father.

The night Mr Ffrench heard what was going on he beat Billy with the leg of a kitchen chair. Beat him until every part of his body except his face and hands was bruised black. Beat him, then refused to let him go 'next, nigh or near Parle's' until he had sorted things out. Within a week, he had him engaged to a girl from Baldwinstown.

It was Lil who told her what happened, not Billy himself. Lil was kind about it, in her straightforward way, kinder than any other woman in the village, young or old, would have been, but blunt. Told her straight out that she had been foolish, that everybody was talking about her: every man in the pub, every woman in the grocery and others too who never came near the place. Maybe the priest. Maybe even her own father, above on the little farm towards the mountain. It was altogether possible that word had stretched that far.

Nothing had happened between them, she told Lil that. 'Even bigger fool you, then,' was Lil's reply, in a consoling voice that took the bite out of her strong words. She was telling the truth, nothing had happened, nothing more than their hands touching for a second too long when she'd be giving him back his change. For that, she had thrown away her reputation because once there was talk, people always thought the worst.

It was as if that conversation with Lil tore a film from her eyes; everything afterwards looked different. Her admirer did what his daddy told him to do, got engaged then married and never came near her with a sincere word again. She saw that he had little real feeling for her, that the thrill for him had been in having a woman, a good-looking woman and a married woman at that, making it obvious that she had a fancy for him. He had loved not her, but the digs in the ribs, the winks and nudges of the other men.

It was the lowest point for her, lower even than her engagement, or the black hours of her wedding night. She took to her knees. Weeks and months she spent praying, asking God to show her how to live, how to make amends, how to do right. And, in time, her prayers were answered. She came to understand her flirtation for what it was, a foolishness born out of resentment for her situation. Weakness might have made her consent to this marriage her father forced on her but now she came to believe that the way to show strength was not by resistance but acceptance.

She didn't stop sleeping with her back to her husband but in every other way she struggled to accept her lot. Rearing two children, looking after the house and doing her share in the shop would be enough for most women to be going along with but she also started to take an active part in the movement that was shaking up the country, her generation's response to the ancient problem of English rule in Ireland.

Máire looked over at Peg, her head bent over her mending. 'He let me do what I needed to do,' she told her. 'That was the best thing about your father. He didn't push his will on me. On you children either.'

Peg nodded without looking up and when Máire waited, wondering whether she was listening to her at all, she lifted her head and nodded again. Go on, her eyes seemed to say. You need to talk. Go on: talk.

'He hated it when I joined Sinn Féin. He didn't mind the work for the Gaelic League so much. Teaching Irish-language classes was one thing but canvassing for the new political party, that was quite another, he being Irish Party himself. As for encouraging Barney to go raiding the farmhouses for guns, or training you into Cumann na mBan work – well, you know yourself how he hated that. But he let me off. Only one time, when I took money out of the leather purse under the floorboards unknown to him, to buy Barney his rifle, did he lose his temper with me. And he was justified in that. It was wrong of me but I had to do it; I knew our boy had to have a good gun if the others were to look up to him as they should.'

It was JJ's shame at what had been done to her at eighteen that made him acquiescent, that was another thing she didn't say to Peg. Neither did she explain, for this she did not fully understand herself, how the work she did for Ireland restored her self-respect after that misguided business with Billy Ffrench. This time, she didn't care when people talked. This time, she knew in her heart that she was working for something honourable, whatever others might think. The movement for Ireland's freedom repaid her tenfold for the work she put into it. It gave her back her pride in herself.

Those years as the impossible unfolded and became reality and the English were put on the wrong foot were the best years of her life. On the day that Barney was sent to an English jail with Dan O'Donovan, she came back to Mucknamore from Wexford town and went on her knees to God. With the sound of the tin-drummers and the shouts of the rioters ringing in her ears ('Up the rebels!' 'Good on you, Dan!' 'See you in six months, Barney!'), with a bruise on her chin from where she had caught a flying police baton but with her heart exultant, she had made straight for the chapel. There she knelt and gave thanks to God that her struggle to accept her marriage and her lot had not been in vain.

But now, a year on, she felt that maybe, it had. For what she never foresaw when Barney was dragged off to prison in handcuffs that day, was that he might need more than ever to be kept on the right track after he came out. Half of County Wexford might think him a hero but she was his mother and she knew the truth: he wasn't nearly clear enough about how this Treaty was a betrayal. Peg had a much better grasp of the principles.

'I need you to speak to Barney,' she said. 'His thoughts are everywhere but where they should be.'

'So you *have* noticed, Mammy. I didn't like to say.'

'I think he might be suffering for love.'

'Love? Really?' Peg looked at her over her darning, eyes popping.

'Maybe I'm wrong but I believe he has a fancy for Nora O'Donovan.'

Had Peg really not noticed? Too caught up in her own fascination for the brother, maybe.

'I did think one time, last year, that there might be something there,' Peg said, of her brother and Nora. 'I asked her outright at the time.'

'And . . . ?'

'She said she doesn't think about boys in that way.'

'Did you believe her?'

'I don't know. Her father is very strict, I do know that much, but he can hardly expect her to stay single forever. She won't say a word against him, though. She's very private about things like that.'

Máire could see Peg was turning over the idea of Nora and Barney in her mind, and liking it. But she cursed the day they arrived in the village, setting hearts a-flutter. Oh, she could see why her children were impressed: all that family had good looks. The girl Nora was like something in a picture and as for her brother, with his sharp ways and jaunty talk . . . what young girl wouldn't be dazzled? But Máire noticed what Peg's less mature eye missed: how young Mr O'Donovan liked to play up to all the girls, for the wonder of watching his charm do its trick. How he was inclined to make little of those who hadn't his brains or advantages: she had seen him have a go at poor Sore-Toes Delaney more than once, flattening him with a fancy phrase. He was the kind who'd use a rock to smash a fly when all that was needed was to swat it away.

He was also the kind who'd take advantage of a young girl with a soft heart. She knew that Peg believed her trots out the Causeway with him were a secret, and no doubt thought her mother too old to know what went on between a boy and a girl in Lover's Hollow. So far Máire had said nothing, trusting the thing would resolve itself as the girl came to see him for what he was. Forbidding him to her daughter would only make the hanker worse.

Even when he had been on their side, Máire had been wary of Dan. He never gave Barney the respect that was due to him as the senior boy of the neighbourhood, just came in and took over and was always too fond of publicity about himself. So she, for one, was unsurprised now to find him joining the so-called National Army.

'Do you not, Mammy? Why not?'

'Those O'Donovans are too cocky altogether.'

'Ah no. You couldn't say that of Nora. Dan, maybe. But not Nora.'

The foolish girl blushed every time she said his name. But at least she recognized his arrogance.

'Oh, him!' Máire decided to use the opportunity. 'Is it true he's going to join the Green and Tans?' That was the name true Republicans had put on the new army.

'I had it out with him. We might change his mind yet.'

'I wouldn't count on it. He seems just the type to do a turncoat. Well, much good it will do him.'

'I think . . . I don't . . .' She was blushing even harder. 'I'd like to think . . . that we could agree to differ, Mammy. They *are* our friends.'

Máire pulled herself up in the bed, holding her breathing steady against a cough she could feel forming deep inside. 'I want to see this Treaty defeated,' she said, as soon as she was sure of her wind. She said it loud and clear into the darkening room so Peg could not misunderstand her. The words got through. Peg stopped in the act of biting a thread to look at her, her eyes full of what was not being said: *Before I die.* But why keep it unspoken? It was too important. 'I want to leave something worth leaving behind me.'

'Ah, Mammy. Don't.'

'We'll say no more. But I can count on you? To keep up the struggle and the work? To fight for the Republic, no matter what?'

Peg leaned across to her, fervent. 'You know you can, Mammy. Of course you can. Of course.'

Peg

Dear Diary

Things are certainly hotting up now. Our boys have seized a number of buildings in Dublin. The Kildare Street Club is one, where the Unionist gentlemen used to enjoy their brandy and smoke their cigars. Where once there was a concierge type in a top hat outside the door, now the place is guarded by a pair of Dublin Brigade republicans with rifles. John Mythen told Nora that some of the boys play handball in one of the reading rooms.

More importantly, they've captured the Four Courts. What was the very hub of the English legal system in Ireland is now the headquarters of the Irish Republican Army. It's like a re-run of 1916, only instead of Pádraic Pearse reading out the Proclamation of the Irish Republic, Liam Mellows (whose mother is a Wexfordwoman) read out the conditions under which those inside the Four Courts would be prepared to hold discussions with those inside the Dáil. This is the clearest indication yet that those who have taken an Oath of Allegiance to the Republic intend to keep it.

On the political side, Mr de Valera has been travelling the country, winning many over, making them understand that the issue of this election is the same issue that has been before Ireland for seven hundred years: the issue of the English in Ireland. In the war against the English, those who had least to spare stinted themselves to purchase Republican bonds. Labourers, domestic servants, even those in need gave money, whatever they could, with the intention that it be used to defend and maintain the Irish Republic. Now these loans are being used to buy arms, armoured cars and munitions *from* the English, in order to crush those who still believe in the Republic. Mr de Valera is giving it to them straight.

And he's not afraid of saying the worst. Yesterday in Carrick-on-Suir he spoke of how the fight for freedom would go on, even if the Treaty is accepted. That it would lead to Irish people having to fight the Irish soldiers of an Irish government set up by Irishmen. The press and the priests are criticizing him for saying this but they don't understand. He knows the horror of such a scene and believes that to state the truth of what will happen is our best means of preventing it.

All the preparations for his coming visit to Wexford are in place. The New Ross O'Hanrahan Pipers' Band, the best band in the county, will be there to play. Supper is arranged for the Talbot and it is there, after the dinner, that we will give him our gifts. Martha Connick will give him an illuminated address of Celtic design and in addition, as a particular gift from the women, Theresa Kearney will present a gold signet ring, but it is my offering that is the nicest, I think: a miniature of the Bullring Piker, the statue that dominates the Bullring in Wexford town, our commemoration of Wexford's rising against the English in 1798. He'll surely like it. It's a fine cast, in bronze, that well captures the piker's determination, his foot forever forward, his pike forever aloft.

It's said that Michael Collins was offhand in his acceptance of Cumann na Saoirse's gift when he visited Wexford three weeks ago. Agnes Whitty was involved there, so it's hard not to crow. It could hardly have been the present itself – a case of Irish-made pipes – that displeased him. No, it's that Cumann na Saoirse are too genteel to impress a man like him. Whatever treachery Collins might have got himself involved in with the Treaty, he knows who was who in the fight against the English. He knows the women of Cumann na mBan are the women you can depend on.

And Mr de Valera knows it too. He has written an Easter

Proclamation, an echo of Pearse's, addressed to us, the young men and women of Ireland. 'Yours is the faith that moves mountains,' he wrote, 'the faith that confounds misgivings, the faith and love that begot the enterprise of 1916 . . . Ireland is yours for the taking. Take it.'

19

1995

I know all about TB; it was one constituent in Richard's cocktail of killers. The bacillus is inhaled from the coughing or sneezing of an infected person and lodges itself in the alveoli of the lungs. Its presence alerts the immune system and white blood cells rally to fight the infection but, encased within a waxy cell wall that surrounds it like a thick rind, the bacillus manages to resist, so that equal numbers of bacteria survive as are killed. This is the latent phase and it can go on for years, even decades. An internal war rages but the body feels nothing, like a coastline that seems to withstand the sea.

Then, for some reason – pregnancy, HIV, hunger, stress, age – or for no obvious reason at all, the balance tips and the bacteria begin to win, slowly but steadily replicating until each white blood cell is so full that it bursts. The alveoli fill, the walls of the lung become inflamed, begin to bleed easily and now the creature is in the blood, able to swim to every organ system: kidneys, intestines, ovaries, skin, brain, heart. Hippocrates dubbed it the 'Captain of the Three Men of Death'.

Today is Friday. I've been standing outside my shed for almost an hour, watching the tide come in. I think it's approaching its highest point now: the waves are lapping tight around Inisheen and the wide expanse of sand that borders either side of the Causeway at low tide has narrowed to a strip. Perhaps it has already turned? From here it's impossible to tell the moment when its seemingly unstoppable advance goes into retreat. What would happen, I wonder, if some day the mechanism that turns the tide faltered, if the water just kept on coming? We trust the ocean to do what it does, what it has always done, just like we trust the sun to rise and set and the seasons to take their turn one after the other, but what if one day the workings of the world failed us?

I sigh. I don't want to be here like this, staring out to sea, thinking strange and useless thoughts. I want to be in my shed, at my table, working on my writing. But my writing has rejected me. So I stare a while longer and think longingly of how it used to be – only days ago but another time from now – when the words flowed through me as if they came from somewhere else, when all I had to do was turn up and catch them with my pen. Now memories hurt me in the remembering and the events of the past resist me, twist out from under my control. For hours, I sit immobile, rearranging papers, staring at an empty page, holding my pen. Or else I stand like this in front of the ocean, feeling that the endless movement of the waves has a lesson for me if I could only work out what it might be.

'It's so hard,' I said to Rory, last night. 'It's killing me.'

'Nothing worth doing is easy,' he said.

He thinks I have been working too long without a break. 'You should take a day off and come out with me. A bit of relaxation would do you good.'

I tell him I cannot afford the time and in a way this is true. I have already taken time away from the desk to go into town, to do research in Wexford library. The weeks are ticking away and I want to finish as much as I can before I have to leave Mucknamore.

Selection: that is the nub of my problem. I have ideas about my family's past, and about the links between what happened to them and to me. But the task of deciding what is relevant has ground me down. And I have strange feelings about meeting the younger Gran and Auntie Nora. I keep wondering how they would feel about me rummaging through their histories. Every so often Gran writes in her diary that she would die – 'just die' – if anyone were to read what she writes. Does this dread extend to her granddaughter reading her words after her death? I don't know. I am not being self-serving, I honestly don't.

While I was in Wexford, I thought about seeing a doctor but didn't. I could go now, while I'm not getting any work done anyway but again I don't. I can't seem to do anything except hang around my shed, waiting. I want to be here, no further than a run away, when the writing returns. That's how I imagine it happening, the flow turning back on as suddenly as it switched off. I want to be available to it.

I am afraid. If the writing lets me down, I'll start caring too much about Rory. I don't fully understand this connection but I know it exists. In the evenings now, when dusk is approaching, I have nothing to do but wait for his arrival. I lay out the rug we will sit on and then, as his time approaches, I go down to the edge of the dunes and hide in the long spiky grasses to watch him walking down the beach towards me. Once he draws near, I scurry back so that he finds me sitting on the rug, calmly reading my book. I don't want him to realize that I look out for him just for the pleasure of looking, of watching him swing his sauntering way towards me. It reminds me too much of the girl I used to be. I, of all people, should know that once admitted, such feelings don't go away. They grow and swell until they take over, demand resolution. What I might do frightens me.

'You need stimulation,' he says to me. 'Contrast. A bit of fun.' But I don't go with him as he wants. I tell him I cannot afford the time though it doesn't escape him that a day spent staring and scolding my brain produces no more work than a day spent off, enjoying myself with him.

I don't believe that my block is due to overwork. I believe the writing is trying to tell me something. But what? What?

Tuesday. Another day, another struggle. After two hours of moving papers from one pile into another, I decide to take my notebook to Kehoe's Kafé. Maybe getting into new surroundings will help? Aside from daily visits to the shop and runs on the beach, this is my first public outing in Mucknamore. I walk up through the dunes, then along a path that takes me to the place where steps are cut into the short cliff face. I climb the fourteen steps, coming out at the newer end of the village. A path to my left leads along the cliff top to Rory's house but I ignore that and cross the road, to where the café sits between a fried-food takeaway and a provisions store.

I peer through the slatted blinds. It seems surprisingly full and I hesitate. A woman comes out of the shop next door, looking at me curiously. We nod hello and I have nowhere to go but in. I'm greeted by a haze of smoke and tables full of workmen in heavy boots tucking into plates of fried food. A chalkboard announces the 'House Special: All Day Breakfast' that they're eating: two sausages, two rashers, fried egg, black and white pudding, all for £4.99 including tea and toast. Everyone in the cafe has turned round for a look. I do not recognize anybody. The workmen are not Hilde and Stefan's but from one of the holiday-home developments in progress all over Mucknamore. Locals hate these estates of identical houses that lie empty nine months of the year and keep driving property values up.

I take a seat at the only vacant table, near the wall. Smoke sullies the air, thick and noxious. A triangular No Smoking sign adorns my table but in a room so small, with the tables so close together, it is meaningless. I think of my local coffee house in San Francisco, cool and airy Café Crème on the corner of my block. I taste in my mind my regular breakfast order: double decaff, skinny latte and low-fat blueberry muffin. For the first time since I came back to Ireland, I feel homesick.

A waitress with black hair pulled into a bunch on the crown of her head comes across. 'Hello, there. What can I get you?'

She speaks casually, trying to disguise that she knows just who I am and all about me. I order a white coffee and Danish pastry.

There are only six tables besides mine and five are occupied. Beside me, six men in work boots sit and say nothing to each other, smoking furiously, thinking their thoughts. At another table by the door, four of their colleagues are having an argument about money, something about some fucker who didn't fuckin' pay what they were all fuckin' due . . . Despite the swearing and the angry tone, the emotion feels manufactured. In the far corner, two young women whisper, their chins almost meeting across the table. The fairer one has a problem, man trouble, I would guess. Beside them a little boy bangs his spoon on the table of his high chair and wails. The dark-haired girl beside him – his mother, presumably – hands him a chocolate button from the pack she holds in her hand, without looking. His clumsy sucking pushes the chocolate in and out through his lips but he is oblivious to the mess he is making over his face and hands, oblivious to everything but his pure, chocolate pleasure.

I know by looking at them that these women are from the council estate out the Wexford road. Across from them, two older women share confidences too but in every other way they are different: older, browner, richer. These are women who play golf and bridge, who do yoga or Pilates, who drive SUVs. It's not just their clothes that distinguish them from each other, or their hair, or their jewellery. It is the lives they have lived, clearly written in their faces and bodies. In my San Francisco world, people who smoke and swear, who wear rough and dirty clothes, who put their cigarette butts out in the remains of their fried eggs as the man beside me is now doing, are kept at a further distance from those who don't.

My coffee arrives, and my pastry, sticky from a heat-up in a microwave. The coffee is instant and tastes like reheated tea. I swallow as much as I can bear, put my payment on the table and leave. As the door clangs behind me, I know I will be talked about. For hours afterwards, the pastry sits, greasy in my stomach.

Thursday. After an hour of pain at my desk, I lace on my running shoes. I don't feel like running but I go because I don't know what else to do. I run out earlier in the day than I would if I were working. The air feels fresher at this time, like a spray of fine water on my face. Later, when the sun commandeers the sky, I know that everything will haze over and slow down.

I run beside the water's edge until I come to the curve in the coastline, then I move up the beach, closer to the small cliff, so I cannot be seen from above. Rory's house is set on top, a big modern house with peaked dormer windows set into the roof, with large windows and French doors overlooking the sea. An 'executive home', not what I would have expected from him. Her choice, perhaps? I imagine her looking out from her window, like a queen in her castle, and seeing me, running past. That is why I hug the cliff.

If she is queen of the castle, what am I? Nothing. Women like me don't appear in fairy tales. Not unless I was to become the wicked stepmother. But that is not going to happen. That is not what I want. No.

I am glad when I get beyond the curve that takes me out of the house's line of sight. I run in despair, wretched that my writing still won't come. I run hard until I reach the rock that tells me I have done my customary two and a half miles but I don't turn as usual. There is another mile or two before the beach peters out and I run on, push myself faster than usual, stretching for something. I run until the beach turns shingly. Up ahead I can see where it becomes too narrow and rocky to pass. I turn then, retrace my steps, pulling back the pace, settling into a gentler rhythm. My breathing is even and I feel like I could run through any limitation.

From this end of the beach, Inisheen and the Causeway look tiny, like miniature models of themselves. What age was I when Gran first brought me out to the Causeway to point out Coolanagh sands? The height of her hip, whatever age that was. I can still feel the damp of her swimming costume against my cheek as I leaned my face against her. Beneath the fabric was her soft old flesh and underneath again her tough hipbone.

We stood on the Causeway and she pointed across Coolanagh

and I knew from her voice that this was significant though I didn't know why.

'Look across now at that sand,' she said to me, 'and tell me what you see.'

Auntie Nora was with us. When she heard what Gran said, she walked away from us, across to the other side of the Causeway. Gran looked back at her but, unusually, didn't follow. So I pulled in closer, gripped tighter. Gran's palm was rough, like the skin on a rock but hers was the hand I most loved to hold.

'Do you not notice anything strange about what you're seeing?' said Gran. 'Come on now, pet. Look a little harder.'

I stretched my eyes for her.

'Can't you make out that double row of sand-hills near the edge and that long, straight dip running in between?'

All I could see was a lumpy blanket of sand that flattened out the further away it stretched. The tide was way, way out.

'I wish we could walk across to it,' she said. 'If we could walk the length of it, you'd feel what I'm saying to you.'

But we couldn't walk across Coolanagh sands. Young as I was, I already knew that.

'What would you say if I told you that what you're looking at is the rooftops of a sunken city?'

I turned my face up to hers, tried to read her.

'Yes, a sunken city. Under that line of dunes near the edge are the houses, that's why the bumps are so regular, all in a row. And across there . . . that dip behind them –' she pulled my hand up, pointed my finger – 'that lies above the long main street below.'

She began to talk in her story voice. '*Fadó, fadó* – a long time ago – a city stood on that spot there that I'm showing to you now. A fine city it was, with its own charter to prove it; one of the largest seaports in all of Ireland. Not big but so rich that it used to send not one but two Members of Parliament to the government in London. I'm talking hundreds of years ago now, not long after the English first came to Ireland.

'What the poor people who lived in this city didn't know was that their town was built on sinking sand. From the first day those buildings went up, the sands were sucking at them – slowly, slowly drawing them down. So slowly that at first they didn't notice, but day by day it went on, until they came to know what was happening and to realize that they'd all have to leave. So they did. But still the city kept on sinking, until nothing was left of it above the ground only those bumps and hollows in the sand that you see before you.'

At that, Auntie Nora, who was listening behind us, made an explosive sound, something like the harrumph of a horse. She started to walk away, back along the Causeway towards home. Let her go, the inside of my head pleaded to Gran but already we were turning after her. 'It's all right, Nora,' Gran called. 'Wait.'

But she wouldn't. We broke into a run, my arm pulled along. When we caught up with her, Gran let go of my hand to stop her going any further. 'Nora, Nora, don't be going on.'

Auntie Nora pulled out of her grasp and ran on again. Gran called after her back: 'Where's the harm in telling a bit of an old yarn, Nora?' but this time she let her go. We followed a distance behind.

'Don't worry,' Gran whispered to me. 'She'll be all right in a while.'

I wasn't worried – I was used to Auntie Nora being strange – but I was curious. 'She didn't like you talking about Coolanagh,' I said.

Gran looked at me hard, then we walked the rest of the distance back in silence. And we never went out that way together again.

The adult me jogs on, along the beach, bringing the Causeway closer, and when I reach the point at which it joins the beach, I still don't want to stop. My mind is honed sharp the way it can only be by a long run. I am a brain, a body, a pair of legs, nothing more but all of that. I turn out to run along the Causeway, something I almost never do. Too many people walk here later in the day and I get pushed up against them passing on the narrow, foot-worn path. I run with my eyes alert to the unevenness of the surface underfoot as the pathway climbs and dips between the marram grasses, over the dunes. I feel like I am on the high deck of a ship that's sailing through an ocean of sand.

To my left is Coolanagh, flat and innocuous-looking behind its barbed-wire fencing. While I was in Wexford library I researched all I could learn about quicksand and found that almost everything Gran told me about Coolanagh was wrong: quicksand does not suck, it is not bottomless, it does not have a life of its own. It is a phenomenon, not a substance; any sand can become 'quick' given the right circumstances. Here in Mucknamore, the circumstances are a stream flowing off Inisheen onto Coolanagh strand, the stream in which I once pretended to see fairies to please Mary Cummins. Underlying the sand is a layer of rock that slows drainage, so that the sand grains are held in a permanent liquid suspension.

The books are divided on the dangers of such places. Some say it is impossible for humans to sink, no matter how deep the quicksand, because the density of human body mass is less than that of any sand–water suspension. People die, these authorities claim, through panic that makes them wriggle and writhe, pulling them face down into suffocation. Others hold that a human body falling into deep quicksand behaves as it would in deep water, plunging below the surface then rising back up again, but because quicksand is of higher density, this down-and-back-up motion takes longer. Fatally long, with the lungs running out of breath before the body re-emerges from the depths.

On the tidal sands of Coolanagh, there's a third possibility: the sea. A victim who survived an initial immersion in sand, who succeeded in resisting the urge to struggle, would remain stuck until the arrival of help or the return of the next incoming tide, whichever came soonest.

As I run, my steps tracking and reinforcing the uneven pathway forged by other feet, I look out across Coolanagh and I wonder: which was it for Dan?

Friday. Yesterday's exertions have tired me: I ran to Inisheen, all around it and all the way back, more than twice my usual circuit. I stay in bed late, sleeping an exhausted sleep; even the juddering, drilling noises of the house building fail to keep me in consciousness. As I cannot write, there seems no point in getting up so for hours I drift in and out of sleep, too warm as the day goes on. I am stiff as I turn in my bed, the front of my thighs the sorest, like knotted elastic.

It's after twelve when I rise. I eat, then bring the rug outside into the shade beside the shed and there I sleep some more. I feel shut down, like I'm a shop whose keeper has turned the sign and gone away.

Maybe I'm tired not just by the run but by the baby. My body is not only my own now, she is nurturing herself from me. I am supposed to keep my energies for her. A small niggle rises in me at this takeover, at being imprisoned by a jailor that I am harbouring. According to my baby book, she can squint now and frown and make a grimace but these are simple responses, undirected. I am nothing to her, not yet, nothing more than the realm in which she swims.

Sunday. After ten captive days, I am released. I am not in the shed but out running again when the key clicks open in my mind. Something Nora said.

Yesterday I spent a long time going through parts of Nora's notebooks that defeated me before. Her writing is much harder work than Peg's. Lots of her notebooks are a jumble of confusion, full of words that lie flat on the page, unconnected to each other or to any clear meaning. As if she wrote not to communicate but just for the sake of moving her pen, moving her mind. In these sections, her handwriting is often difficult, jerking into tight angles and sometimes ignoring margins and lines. But I furrowed through it, copying out phrases that struck me, searching for something. In the doing of that, certain passages opened up, and I found meanings there that I never suspected.

Now as I run, one of those disconnected phrases comes rising in my mind. Did it say what I now think it said, I wonder, or am I imposing a meaning? I cannot wait to finish my run, to check. Back in my shed, before I even wash, I take out the notebook and find the paragraph. My heart recognizes its significance as I read and starts to drum-drum-drum. This pumping pulse of excitement makes me go back and read the words again, this time with every sense keen and quivering. Yes, there it is. In two sentences. Two little strings of words that say nothing and everything.

Realizing the significance of my find, I hurry to my table and begin to write furiously. I write not only what I think I have just discovered but all the connections and associated details that are now surging through me. My mind flings up thought after thought and I race after them with my pen.

The day speeds past. When Rory comes on his nightly visit, I send him away. It is dark by then, too dark to write any more, but I don't want to sever my link.

'I can't see you tonight.'

'What? Why?'

I feel as though I've jumped off a cliff and have to concentrate on flapping my arms to keep myself airborne. Conversation with another person, even with Rory, even about what I have come to know, would bring me crashing down.

'I'm sorry. I'll explain the next time. Please. Go.'

He goes, annoyed, but even his feelings don't touch me. I have to be alone, I know it. Even using the words to ask him to leave pained me.

Next day, I am steadier but still I know that finding that passage in Nora's notebook changed everything. I had been trying to write the story straight, to outline and explain, draw conclusions, elucidate lessons learned: the Sue D'Enim school of writing, hard and clear and certain of its standpoint. It wasn't working. Nora is leading me to a new place. What she revealed can never be contained within my well-wrought structure. I have to get out of the way. I must trust the words that arrive and place themselves on the page, trust that the writing knows, better than I do, what it all means.

20

1922

Jig music jumped and skittered out the open windows and doors of Fortune's farmhouse, the whine and bounce of Dandy Rowe's accordion chased along by a couple of fiddles. It bounced down the lane to meet Peg as she made her way towards the party, its lilt enticing her on. The faint breeze playing on her face and hands felt so sweet after two days in a sickroom, a kind of balm. Something was going to happen tonight with Dan: she could feel it in the stilly quality of the fading light, in the carpet of yellow crocuses that blazed along the base of the ditch, their hearts yawning open. She felt their nearness. 'Glory be to God,' she murmured, making the sign of the cross on herself and kissing her thumbnail. Then she skipped on to meet her evening.

A crowd had gathered already around Fortune's front door. Their parlour, one of the biggest in the neighbourhood though it was, was not big enough to hold all who had come. After greeting those she knew well, Peg went on into the house, passing through the kitchen, where Mrs Fortune sat weeping and wailing, surrounded by female relations and friends. Johnny was his mother's favourite – everyone knew it – but even allowing for that Mrs Fortune's distress over his going was considered excessive. For weeks now, she had been cracking into tears in front of anyone and everyone and nobody knew what to be saying to her.

Tomorrow, Johnny would be gone. He would take the train to Cork, then to Cobh, where he would board a ship, leaving behind this farmhouse and a future as flat and firm as a future could be, to switch to a new life, unimaginably different. Mrs Fortune would probably never see him again but he had to go, even she knew that. The farm would pass to Jem, the eldest. Pat, the second son, was already at the seminary in St Peter's but the priesthood held no attractions for Johnny. Mucknamore had nothing to offer him, nothing now, and nothing that might ever call him back.

Hard to imagine little Johnny in big, bad New York. It was said that the winters there would freeze your blood to ice. That the tenements were worse crowded than the worst of Dublin's, with the Irish huddled together close as rats in a nest. That in the noise and rush, the poorest get trampled to death. Not that Johnny would be reduced to that level. Mary, his sister, who left four years ago, had sent across his passage money and had a job and a bed lined up for him. With that kind of assistance, Johnny could make something of himself over there. But given the choice, Johnny would stay put, they all knew that. Johnny wasn't one of those who were driven to get out, get up, get on. A few acres and his own girl and he'd be happy for life. All of which made the letting go of him harder.

And so, an emigration wake, to honour their sorrow. A big ham in the centre of the kitchen table. Around it, slices of white and brown soda bread spread with yellow butter and stacked into towers on plates. On a side table set up for the occasion batches of square scones dotted with sultanas, soft as sponges, and the crumbly wheaten buns that were Johnny's favourite, and slices of warm seedy cake spicing the air so that everyone who passed commented on it. Dishes of butter and blackberry jam occupying the spaces between the plates. Also flowing was a plentiful supply of snuff and tobacco and, of course, drink. Stout and whiskey for most of the men and some of the women. For the other females, the children and the Pioneers, bottles of minerals and cups of tea.

Peg passed through into the parlour. The big table was pushed to the side and all the chairs of the house arranged in a circle around the room. Dandy sat on a high stool in the corner, his squeezebox held high on his chest like a trophy, with Sore-Toes and Johnjo Gregg on two upturned crates at his feet, their bows bouncing across their fiddles. The dancers kept their movements small so as not to kick the onlookers or land on their toes. Among those dancing the set, Peg immediately noticed, was Dan. Dan, who by his own admission had a pair of left feet, who never once could be coaxed to dance with *her*, was up there with a girl. With Miss Agnes Whitty.

Nothing untoward was passing between them. He was attempting to follow her directions for the dance and both were laughing as he exaggerated his blunders for her amusement. That was all but in that moment, before either of them even knew she was there, Peg had the measure of it. She knew now what sort of night she could expect, knew her plans and hopes were all undone, knew her regret at not having got into town for her new pin was needless, her effort of shining and polishing herself was misspent. Quick as that, it all turned around, and she had to admit to herself that he had gone off her. That, truth to tell, she'd known it for weeks.

Oh, but Agnes Whitty, of all people. Was this what it seemed to be: a direct slap at herself? Dear God, why had she come? Where was Nora? She needed Nora.

No sign of her but she spied Molly at the far side of the room and she skirted around the edge of the crowd towards her. When she saw her coming, Molly gave her a little wave, and as soon as Peg recognized the zeal on her friend's face, she wanted to turn back, but back to where? She allowed her arm to be pulled, endured the secret wet hiss of Molly's questions in her ear. Had she seen? What was he playing at? Who was the girl?

Peg waved her hand to dismiss it all, trying furiously to remember how much she had said to Molly the evening before. 'Dan and I are over this a long while now.' She stretched her mouth wide into what she hoped was a smile.

'Oh, really?' said Molly.

'Yes. We never went back the same way after he was inside.'

'So what was he doing sending you messages, then?'

'I don't know. Pulling the wool over your eyes, maybe?'

Molly looked indignant at this attempt to turn the tables. 'You looked fairly surprised when you saw him with Her Nibs.'

'Surprised?' said Peg. 'Not at all. She might do for a bit of dancing but he'll find she and her like are not much use when it comes to the fight.'

'A crowd of milksops,' laughed Molly. 'All the Cumann na Saoirse girls are the same.'

Peg had pulled her smile so wide she didn't know what to do with it. 'Is Nora about?' she asked.

'She's not. I haven't seen her anyhow. But tell me—'

'Did you see Mrs Fortune on the way in? Isn't she in an awful state?'

Molly set upon that subject, as Peg hoped she would. 'Oh, Lord, the poor woman. I was in the kitchen earlier. She's broken-hearted, broken-hearted. I don't think she'll ever get over it.'

'Miss Parle!' A booming voice behind interrupted them and Peg felt her back being slapped. 'A cure for sore eyes to see you. We knew our humble festivities were lacking but now our evening is complete.'

It was Jem Fortune, Johnny's brother. Jem would *plamás* the teeth off a saw. Enjoyable to play along with, you'd never take him serious.

'He said the same to me earlier,' said Molly.

'Ladies, ladies. Didn't be getting particular on me. What's this I see? An empty fist, Miss Parle? Have those strawboy brothers of mine been neglecting you?'

This was Jem's way of asking her would she like a drink. 'I've only just got here, Jem. Have you a lemon soda?'

'Don't budge one inch from where you're standing. It will be with you before you knew you wanted it.'

The music stopped for a few minutes to allow the musicians to take refreshment. Agnes and Dan retreated to the side but Peg could see them out of the side of her eye. Agnes, flushed with exercise and triumph, kept throwing looks over and one or two reached their mark. Dan never looked her way once. Jem came back with the drink as Dandy stretched out the squeezebox to begin again.

'Would you do me the honour of stepping it out?' Jem asked her. So she did, playing at smiling and laughing all the time, as if she was having a great time.

She kept it up through the evening, as other boys asked her for a dance, or while talking with the girls. Later on, hours into the night, after they'd danced till their feet were sore, and had a feast of food, then danced again, they started to slow the evening down. Patsy Cogley took out his French fiddle and played the plaintive old tunes by Carolan and Rose Mooney and other Irish harpers that were usually a favourite with Peg. Tonight, though, the melancholy pull of bow across string was like salt in a sore to her.

At one point she looked across and saw another girl from the town sitting in his place, talking to Agnes Whitty. Peg thought about it for a minute or two, then got up and went out to look for him. As she entered the kitchen, she saw him coming in through the back door and walked across his way so he'd come flat up against her. Her heart was smacking hard against her insides.

'Well, Peg,' he said when they were face to face.

'Dan.' She smiled to let him know she had forgiven their last argument.

'Are you not listening to Cogley?' He wagged his head in towards the parlour. 'I thought you loved that banshee music.'

'It's too sad for the night that's in it. With Johnny going so far away from us.'

'Ah, yes. Johnny.' His eyes closed in, seemed to pierce through her skin and inspect her desolation. Her traitor skin began to flush.

'I've known Johnny all my life,' she said. 'We went to the national school together. No one would expect you to feel it the same.'

He ignored this jibe at his outsider status. 'Is Barney not coming down tonight?'

'He's working. He'll be along soon, I'd say.'

A pause. How had she slid back into bickering with him when that was the last thing she wanted?

'What about Nora?' she asked. 'I was expecting her to be here before me.'

'Nora's not coming.'

'She told me she was.'

'Well, she's not.'

And that was it. He turned away from her then without so much as a goodbye and headed back into the parlour. Back into Agnes Whitty.

At three in the morning they were all still there, Peg hanging on, determined not to leave before the other two. The night was young, Jem Fortune kept saying, every time another group rose to take their leave, keen to keep as many as he could. He needn't have worried. Many of them looked like they would be there till dawn or after. Some, like Barney, had come along late, after the pub closed, and were only now getting into their swing. Others were too drunk to know where their homes were. Young Johnny had passed out in the corner and some wag had put his mother's hat, the one with the peacock feather, on his head. He'd be sick as anything tomorrow for his travels but maybe that was as well.

The dancing and performance was finished and they were onto the sing-song. Dan – whose singing was no better than his dancing – was giving a recitation: 'Dangerous Dan McGrew'. It was his party piece and Peg had heard it many times but it was new to some of the others here. He did it well, speaking loud in some parts, softer in others, sometimes going fast, sometimes slow, pulling them in with his words like a fisherman with a reel. At the end of each verse they joined in the last line and the laughs and yelps increased as it went on. By the time he was finished, laughter had spread all round.

'B'God,' said old Nick Cummins, wiping his eye, 'that was better than a play.'

Agnes's face was creased with pride as she joined in the applause, nearly clapping the hands off herself, looking up into his face all the while.

Then it was back to singing. Lama took the floor with 'Kelly the Boy from Killane', a favourite always with Forth and Bargy people as it mentioned their own area.

Goodly news, goodly news do I bring, youth of Forth
Goodly news shall you hear, Bargy men
For the boys march at morn, from the south to the north
Led by Kelly, the Boy from Killane.

Lama had a voice like an old jackdaw but to his own ears he sounded just fine. *Enniscorthy's in flames,* he crowed, *and old Wexford is won*, the veins standing out in his high, balding forehead as he reached higher and louder. By the time he'd finished, he had moved himself close to tears.

'Good man, good man.'

'Up Wexford.'

'Let's have another Wexford one. What about "The Boys of Wexford"? Come on, Denis.'

That song was known to be Denis Mernagh's and he began it suddenly from where he stood, one elbow angled against the shelf.

We are the boys of Wexford
Who fought with heart and hand
To burst in twain, the galling chain
And free our native land . . .

After the applause died, Peg called on Sore-Toes. 'We could do with a bit of light relief. Give us one of your Percy French's, Sore-Toes. That one about the motor car?'

She smiled across at him and to her horror saw that he was looking back at her with pity. He *knew*. She had done everything right all night, talking, singing, dancing and smiling, smiling, smiling until the back of her throat was sore from it, but still Sore-Toes knew. And if Sore-Toes – a semi-eejit who didn't know what was going on half the time – knew, that must mean everybody else did too. Tomorrow would she and Dan and Agnes Whitty be all the talk?

She should never have said anything about him to anyone. For so long, she had kept the thing quiet, then when he came back from prison, after all that waiting, she had to say something. He became too big for her to keep inside herself. So she told Nora more than she should and also told some things, not as much, to Cat and even (God help her, what had she been thinking of?) a bit to Molly, knowing full well that if Molly knew, half the country knew. All for the small pleasure of talking about him, of having his name in her mouth.

Now she'd pay for it. Now they'd all be asking her what happened. Or not asking, talking about it among themselves. The older women were probably sharpening up their snide comments already, looking forward to the amusement they'd have on the morrow. How would she stand it?

She was so tangled in thought that she barely heard what Sore-Toes was singing, aware only that it wasn't a Percy French. Slowly, though, the atmosphere of the room began to penetrate, drawing her out of the gnarls of her mind, so that she saw faces all around the room tightened with shock. Open whites of eyes stared at Sore-Toes who carried his song through with gusto, his fine tenor voice loud and clear:

. . . 'Tis traitors vile who damn our Isle,
And prolong the tyrant's sway
They played the dirty Saxon game
They're still playing it to-day . . .

These were new words to an old tune, indicting those who supported the Treaty. Such songs had been doing the rounds, whispered between one anti-Treaty person and another but not – not until now – sung out in the face of the pro-Treaty people in Mucknamore. All the Fortunes were strongly anti-Treaty and the sympathies of most people in the room leaned the same way. But not, everyone knew, those of Dan O'Donovan and Agnes Whitty. Which was why everyone was looking at the two of them to see how they were taking it.

Dan was sitting forward in his seat, his thick black eyebrows pulled together into a V. Miss Whitty looked like a turkey, Peg thought, her face red-swollen with indignation, looking at Dan to see how to react.

. . . For filthy English lucre
They've sold their race and sod . . .

At this Dan jumped up. 'Come outside and fucking say that,' he shouted across the song. Sore-Toes kept on singing to the end of the verse:

. . . They've played the role that Judas played
When he betrayed his God.

Finished, he closed his mouth and folded his hands across his chest. Peg couldn't believe it of Sore-Toes. Strong stuff; strong because there was truth in it. Nobody had clapped for the end of the song. The tick of the clock on the parlour mantelshelf could be heard, the room was gone that quiet. Dan repeated his demand: 'I said, come outside and say that.'

'Ah, now, Dan old pal, take it easy there,' Jem Fortune said.

'It's only a song, Dan,' Barney said.

A few other voices joined in the persuasion, telling him to calm himself, that no offence was intended but others, those who'd quite welcome a fight to finish off the evening's entertainment, said nothing. Sore-Toes's eyes were locked onto Dan's and not a sign of apology on him. Peg stared at him, amazed. Usually Sore-Toes didn't know what to think, never mind what to do, without someone to tell him.

Agnes Whitty whispered something in Dan's ear but he shook her away. 'I'm not letting any fucker call me a traitor,' he shouted and he jumped out of his seat at Sore-Toes and made a go at him. It was a drunken, half-hearted effort and easy for the other men to hold him back.

'Let him go, lads,' cried Sore-Toes, putting up his fists. 'Let him go and let's have it out.'

Dan pulled himself free of the hands gripping his clothes. 'Twenty to one, is it?' he asked, looking into the faces gathered around him. He swivelled round to face Sore-Toes again. 'When there was English soldiers to be fought, you weren't so quick off the mark.'

The room was already on Sore-Toes's side and this remark of Dan's finished off any bit of sympathy for him.

Barney said, 'Steady on there, Dan.'

But Dan was beyond calming, by Barney or anyone else. 'That's it, back-clap each other,' he sneered. 'That's about all ye're good for around here.'

He pulled out of their restraining hands and blundered across the room away from them. At the door, he turned around. 'Ye're a crowd of fuckin eejits, so ye are.' In his anger, his Cork accent was very strong. 'It's ye that are the traitors and ye haven't even the wit to see it.'

It seemed to Peg that he stared right at her as he spoke. She felt the insult to herself and to everybody else but none of it made any difference. All she would do, if she were let, was try to console him. Hold him and kiss him and stroke him down until he was happy again and seeing sense. Where she should have anger, she had only the pain of her unwanted love.

She knew he was not as defiant as he sounded. She knew how joining the movement made him accepted around here and how he liked that. He didn't want to be an outsider but he had made an outsider of himself now, and knowing it, he stalked out of the room, leaving the door swinging open behind him. Every piece of her yearned to go after him but instead it was Agnes Whitty who got up and click-clicked across the room after him in her hard-nosed boots.

They left behind a second of pure silence, then Jem Fortune, with a face and a voice as deadpan as each other, said: 'Who's been eating his porridge?'

Sore-Toes guffawed. Guilty laughter spread around the room. So . . . there was no love lost for Dan among these people, her people. That was something she hadn't noticed before. Impressed by him, she thought everybody felt the same. Not so, it turned out. It wasn't only the politics, she could see that much. For some, it was probably no more than the fact that he was from County Cork, an outsider with a funny accent and a different way of looking at life, but not everybody was that closed-minded. It was that he didn't bother with the few soft words that made all the difference to people. He was a big man, too sure of himself, and he made smaller people feel their size.

Now she saw it, she knew it had always been that way. It was like looking at two pictures of the same scene, similar but different. Yesterday she saw people looking up to Dan, as a fighting man, as a man who made things happen. Today she could see how that regard was tinged with hostility. Nobody had it in for him exactly, but nobody, not one person, not Barney, not even herself, was sorry to see him challenged.

In the unity of the room Peg felt something close in around her, and she gave way to it, let it enfold her like a prickly blanket on a cold night, comforting and irritating, both at once. Suddenly she felt deathly tired, weariness pouring through her limbs, thick and sticky. She thought of her bedroom, her bed with its white coverlet, her pillow soft and warm.

Molly Redmond said, 'I think it's time we called it a night.'

Peg was delighted. 'I'll go with you, Molly.'

But Jem Fortune wouldn't let them go, wouldn't let anyone go. 'No, no, no,' he said. 'The night's young, only a pup. You can't be going home yet, not until we get this bad taste out of our mouths. Sore-Toes, give us an encore there. Something a bit lighter this time. Something that won't drive any more guests down the road.'

Sore-Toes started on 'Are You Right There, Michael?', Percy French's song about the West Clare railway. So Peg sat put for a while longer, thinking. She would pretend they fell out over Ireland.

Sore-Toes's performance, by bringing that question out in the open, made it easier for her. Maybe he even did it on purpose? He'd love to play her Sir Galahad, she knew that. But he'd hardly have the wit to work it out, would he?

From across the room, he smiled at her through his song and she didn't know whether she should smile back or not. She hoped he wouldn't start mooning over her again, like he used to before Dan came on the scene. But for now she was just grateful that he'd given people something else to be talking about tomorrow besides her broken love affair.

Love affair: was it ever even that? Or was it nothing more than Dan wanting from her what she had once been foolish enough to give him? The thought heaved up from her depths, dark and sticky. Was that it? The lowest thing a man can want from a woman, was that all he had ever wanted of her?

A new emotion began to harden in her, behind the tears that were behind her eyes. She wasn't sure, she couldn't examine it properly here, not with everyone still half-looking at her, not with trying to sing along with the silly chorus of Sore Toes's silly song – 'Are you right there, Michael, are you right?' – but she was very much afraid that it might be hate.

21

1969

I turn twelve and leave Mucknamore for the first time, to go to secondary school, boarding school, in Wexford town. It's a convent school and the routine is rigid, every hour accounted for with prayers, meals, classes, study, exercise or pastimes, but I am glad to be here. The nuns are strict and expect what they call 'the highest standards of behaviour'. With two exceptions – Sister Therese, who is very young, more like one of the girls than one of the nuns, and Sister Ancilla (Silly Anne), who has no authority even over herself – any one of them can silence us with a look. If we do something wrong, they tower over us in their stiff black habits, immediately shrinking us into apologies.

Our day begins with the dormitory bell and Sister Elizabeth roaring a thundering chant at us, the same words every morning: 'Good morning, girls . . . Seven o'clock . . . Mass at half-past . . . Praised be Jesus.' Then she brings a font of holy water round from cubicle to cubicle, thrusting it through our curtains with a Latin blessing. We have to be up before she arrives at our cubicle in order to dip our fingers in the font, make the sign of the cross, answer her with an 'Amen'. All the way round she harangues us: 'Up now, girls, please . . . Take off your night clothes and wash yourselves properly . . .'

Deirdre Mernagh says Lizzie only wants us to take our night-dresses off so she can have a gawp as she goes round with the holy water. Lezzy Lizzie, Deirdre calls her. Deirdre is always saying things like that. Somehow, she seems to like me. I overheard her describe me to Monica Rowe, another girl, as her friend.

Once we are washed and dressed, we have to strip our beds: blankets, sheets and under sheets must all come off and be folded across our chairs to air our mattresses. Then it's downstairs for Mass with mantillas clipped onto our hair and prayer books in our hands. The priest comes down to us from the local boys' school and the nuns play altar boy to him, passing his vestments and cruets, his ciborium and chalice, fussing over his needs. Mass takes anything up to an hour and every few weeks one of the girls, overcome with hunger or boredom, falls into a faint.

After breakfast, we, the boarders and nuns, are joined by day girls and lay teachers for school. The lay teachers are not so strict, but the nuns are said to be better teachers. 'They've nothing else to be thinking about, that's why,' says Deirdre, rolling her eyes. 'No family, no boyfriends, no sex. Imagine.'

Deirdre loves saying the word sex. And 'fuck' or 'ride' or 'bollox': any word she's not supposed to say. I am learning other words from her too, words that are not taboo but that I never heard in Mucknamore. I now describe girls I like as 'dead-on' or 'the business'. Those who are boring are 'drips'. Good things are 'desh' or 'deadly'; bad things are 'woeful'. These words come from the town via the day girls, but Deirdre picks them up and makes them her own. Because they are town words, to us they seem glamorous.

We like to think we have more in common with the girls from town. As Deirdre puts it, we might be from the country but we're not culchies. She comes from Oulart, a village in the north of Wexford that sounds even worse than Mucknamore but she laughs at its awfulness. Her father is an 'alco', she says, and her mother worn to nothing trying to cope with him. Deirdre does what she can to help but is afraid to give her mother advice anymore, ever since the day she told her she should leave him and her mother cracked apart, saying she would have left long ago if it hadn't been for her, Deirdre, and the other children. Frantic her mother became that day, Dee says, clawing at her wrist, saying, 'Tell me I did right, tell me I did right.'

Straight out, she tells me all this. I listen, nod my head, laugh when she laughs, pass her my box of tissues when she begins to cry. Under my sympathy is wonder at how she lets it all spill out. I want to give her something back. At night I plan how I will share some Mucknamore story with her but in the light of day I can never get one past my teeth.

Dee never stays down for long. She turns her family into a joke, laughing at her father's drunkenness and her mother's attempts to cover up. Mr and Mrs Mernagh, she calls them, when she is telling these tales. I begin to refer to my mother in a similar way – Mrs Devereux, Mrs D. – and it feels good to open that space between us.

I have other friends beside Deirdre: Monica Rowe and Mary Stafford and Breda Hayes. Friends! Friends who know nothing about Mucknamore, about hero uncles, absent fathers, mad aunts or old, unbearable mothers. I shove my difference down deep under my skin and – miraculously – they don't smell it out. They believe in this manufactured, ordinary me.

I am happy in the convent, though sometimes my eyes grow tired of tracking other faces, checking what they want of me. Occasionally I have to lock myself in the toilet or go to one of the secret places I have hunted down – behind the grotto in the corner of the grounds, at the bottom of the slope beyond the far end of the hockey pitch, under the stairs on the way up to study – to sit tight and empty my mind for a while, breathe deep and hard until I am able to breeze out wearing the same broad smile I brought in.

Terms pass, my life parcelled out between school and home. During the long summer break, I go away to the Gaeltacht, in the west of Ireland, with my friends. Mucknamore becomes bearable because there is always back-to-school to look forward to.

I have breasts now and hips that elbow out beneath the red sash that knots around my gymslip. My legs have sprouted and it feels good to be tall, to look down on younger girls. Deirdre and Monica and I skip hockey games by going to Fanny-Jo (Sister Frances

Joseph) and asking for aspirin. Fanny-Jo is enthralled by periods. 'Your monthlies, is it?' she whispers, when you turn up at her door, clutching your forehead or your abdomen. 'You poor dear,' she will say, guiding you to the high, hard bed, never seeming to notice that it's only been a week since you were there before.

It is widespread among the nuns, this fascination with bodies and the secret things they do. Soupy – Mother Superior – takes over one of our Home Economics periods to give us the Talk, an event that older girls have warned us about since we joined the school. She stands in front of the blackboard with her face set around her duty, to tell us all about wombs and babies. She draws a picture of our insides on the blackboard with neon-pink chalk: womb and tubes and ovaries. Embarrassment twitches around the classroom as she talks. She tells us what can happen after a bath, when you are drying yourself. It's not a sin, she says, to feel yourself as you towel yourself dry, but to linger over such a feeling would be a grave sin indeed. Some girls are weaker than others in such matters, more subject to immoral impulses. Each girl listening will know where she falls, her own conscience will tell her whether she is vulnerable.

Soupy's eyes flick around the classroom as she talks. I try hard to meet them but my gaze keeps sliding away from her words. If we examine our consciences and decide that we are in danger, she suggests precautions: wear a vest when having a bath; sleep with hands outside the blankets at night; avoid love stories in books and magazines. I feel Deirdre's shoe pressing against mine.

Afterwards, when she has finished and gone from the classroom, we crack into laughter. 'I hope you always wear your vest,' we joke with each other, in shaky voices. 'Where were *your* hands last night?' Underneath the jokes, we are looking at each other in new ways, wondering who does what. We mock the nuns, but we are just as bad, twisted inside our own silence that dresses itself up as laughter.

*

It is evening, recreation time, the half-hour between study and bedtime that is one of the few unstructured times in our day. Clumps of brown-uniformed girls are scattered around the hall. In one corner, a record player spins out Elvis Presley and eight pairs of girls jive through 'Blue Suede Shoes'. At the games table, the Doyle sisters are once again beating all challengers at chess. The rest of us hang around, just talk.

Deirdre and Monica and I are slumped over a radiator, talking. Usually we are among those fighting around the record player, queuing to take off the show-band music favoured by the girls Deirdre calls culchies, and replace it with the latest 45 by Marc Bolan or David Bowie, or LP by Bob Dylan or the Rolling Stones. We deride the dum-de-dum music by Big Tom or Red Hurley – bogman shite, Deirdre calls it – and the foxtrots, waltzes and jives of the culchie girls. When we dance, we dance alone, letting our bodies go with the beat of the music. Headbangers, they call us as they line up with their country-music discs for their go at the turntable but their insults have no sting. We feel superior to them, a new experience for me.

Music is a seal on friendship. Under my pillow I keep a small radio so I can listen to the pirate station Radio Luxembourg after lights out. Deirdre, her bed just three cells down from mine, listens to the same programme and we communicate by sneezing when we like a song, coughing when we don't. Sometimes I cough even when I like something, if I think Deirdre might jeer. I cough at 'I Think I Love You' by David Cassidy and 'Rock On' by David Essex, even though both songs reach something in me. Singers like David Cassidy and Donny Osmond and David Essex – fancied by most of the other girls – are dismissed by Deirdre and Monica and me. Too clean, too nice, more like girls than boys.

We look for something else in our pin-ups and I find it in Marc Bolan. He is beautiful, with his slush-brown eyes and long curling dark hair but it is not just his beauty that makes me shiver when I look into his picture. Something else swims in the liquid brown of his eyes, something I acknowledge but cannot name. In my posters it is under control; I can use him as I want. In real life, I know it would be the other way around.

I haven't told Deirdre or Monica about Rory. I could never gossip about him, giggle over him, drop him into our talk. Instead, I concoct crushes on good-looking boys from St Peter's College. One in particular I swoon over, a boy called John Foley. It is true that the set of this boy's jaw sends my heart fluttering down into the pit of my body. That before we go out walking, I belt myself into my gabardine coat and adjust my beret with the thought that we might see him on the way and he might look at me. That at night I do deals with God: Get John Foley to talk to me and I will give up the bedtime probing of my body that I have recently embarked on, the secret fingering that had me looking forward guiltily to lights-out.

I have become a cauldron of sensation and John Foley and his jutting jawline is part of that. But neither he, nor Marc Bolan, nor the churning explosions I barter with God, have anything to do with Rory O'Donovan. He is in boarding school too, half a country away in Gormanston, County Meath. It is two months, three weeks and four days since I last saw him, the last Sunday in August when we traded our usual glances through Mass, and it will be nearly another two months before I see him again at Christmas. Sometimes I consider telling Deirdre about him but I know I won't. To speak of him to her, to anyone, would be to fracture something.

Tonight is November 1st, All Souls night, and we are thrilling each other with ghost stories. I stand with my two friends at the window, hugging the heater, our faces and the lit hall behind us reflected back by the black outside. It is Monica's turn to tell her tale but she is distracted when the rec. room door opens and Sister Martha, the parlour nun, comes in. Sister Martha is the height of most first-year girls but many times wider and rounder. She scoots across the hall through clumps of girls towards our window.

'She's coming for one of us,' Monica says and it turns out it's me.

'Jo Devereux, you're to come to the parlour.'

'What's wrong, Sister?'

'You have a phone call from home. Come quick now and don't be wasting your father's money.'

The last time somebody got called to the parlour for a phone call, it was news of a dead relative. Granny Peg? I hurry down the corridor, my loafer shoes clicking loud on the polished green linoleum, Sister Martha scuttling behind, failing to keep up.

In the parlour Maeve is already on the phone, called down from choir practice. She pops her eyes wide at me as the phone spills a long string of squeaks into her ear. Nobody is dead, anyway; I can tell that much from her face.

'OK, Mammy,' she says, after a little while. 'Jo's here now. I'll put her on.'

She pulls another unreadable face, hands me the receiver.

'Hello,' I say.

'Siobhán.' It is Mrs D., clipped and businesslike. 'I'm ringing because we've a bit of news here. Eileen is getting married.'

'Oh.'

'The thing is, she wants you to be bridesmaid.'

'Me?'

'Yes. The wedding is in three weeks' time. I've told Mother Superior and she's given permission for you both to come out for it. And I'll be in next Saturday afternoon to take you off for a few hours, so we can go down town and buy you a dress.'

'All right.'

'So I'll pick the two of you up on Saturday around twelve o'clock.'

'All right.'

'I'll see you then, so. Bye now.'

'Wait . . . Who is Eileen marrying?' As I ask the question,

Maeve's head sinks into her shoulders, like she's ducking something that's been thrown.

'Séamus Power,' Mrs D. says, after a pause.

'Séamus Power?' Does she mean the same Séamus Power who is first cousin to the O'Donovans?

'That's what I said,' she snaps.

'Gosh.'

'I know . . . I know. What can we do only make the best of it?' The words sound weary, like she has used them before on herself and others. 'I don't know what she was thinking of . . . After all we've done for her.'

'It's happening very fast, isn't it? A wedding in three weeks?'

A yell punctures my ear. 'What are you saying, you foolish girl? Did anybody hear you say that? Did any of the nuns hear that?'

I look at Maeve, at Sister Martha at the far end of the room, smiling at us. 'No.'

'Keep your mouth closed about this, for God's sake. Say nothing, do you hear me? Nothing to anybody, especially Geraldine Kehoe.' Geraldine Kehoe is a girl in the year above me, from Rathmeelin. 'There'll be talk enough without us advertising the thing.'

'All right. Sorry.'

Maeve shakes her head at me as I put down the receiver. 'God Almighty,' she says. 'Do you do it on purpose or are you just plain thick?'

'Oh, shut up.'

'Can you believe it?' Maeve says. 'Of all the men in County Wexford, Eileen had to pick Séamus Power. What a wedding we'll have, us on one side of the room, dozens of O'Donovans on the other and the bride's family stuck in the middle.'

'Do you think they'll go?'

'Of course. You know the Powers and the O'Donovans: they're like that.' She holds up her middle and index fingers, fixed together. 'Mammy said they're definitely going.'

‘What about Auntie Nora? Will she go?’

‘Oh my God! That never struck me.’

‘She’ll have to be invited,’ I say. ‘She’s connected both ways.’

‘Why don’t you ask Mammy about it on Saturday? That should make for a jolly afternoon.’

I make a face at her and we part. As I am walking back to the hall, the bell rings and the corridor suddenly swarms with faces heading towards the refectory for bedtime orange and biscuits. I decide to slip away, to head up to the dormitory for a few precious minutes alone. The loose knot of fright brought on by the ghost stories has gone, unravelled by a fiercer feeling. A feeling I want to have and hold, to take with me to bed, where I can hug it close. Hope. A delicious, finger-crossing, heart-piercing hope.

He is there. As soon as I walk into the church, I know. I know even before I see him, on the aisle-end of a pew, almost halfway up. He faces the back door through which we, the bridal procession, have just entered. Turned round in his seat by the pounding organ announcing the coming of the bride.

So many times I have sat, rooted to one of these seats, a spectator. Now it is his turn to watch. I smile as I step up the aisle behind the bride, not at him but generally, like an actress beaming for the press. Eileen is the chief exhibit in this spectacle but I too am on display, and I look good in my long blue dress, my face scrubbed and polished and made up, my hair scooped into a floral headdress; as good as I have ever looked. As we approach his seat, I slide him a look and let it rest on him for a second before sweeping past.

Up at the altar, I perform my bridesmaid duties as required: prettily. With my hair up, cool air teases the back of my neck. I imagine his eyes resting on the pale skin there and I shiver. The awareness that he is behind me is branded into my every move.

Afterwards, in the hotel, most of the men ignore the sherry reception and line up at the bar instead, three-deep, shouting for pints of stout and large whiskies. The women take the sherry, and sit in sets around the reception area, little stemmed glasses pinched between their fingers. Between swallows, their lips twist sideways to one another with comments on the ceremony, on the cracks in Séamus's whispered vows, or the finery of Eileen's dress.

It is the women who keep the closest eye for any clash between the two families, but in this they are disappointed. We are in the corner nearest the door, the O'Donovans occupy the furthest end of the room and between us lies a gulf of hotel carpet that nobody intends to cross. I sit in Mrs D.'s female circle, with Maeve and Granny Peg and Mrs Redmond, who played the organ and sang in church. Auntie Nora, to everybody's relief, has stayed at home. Also in our group are Mrs O'Neill, Eileen's mother, and her sister, Mrs Maher. They sit with us out of respect due to Eileen's employers.

I drink Coca-Cola, bottle after bottle of it put down in front of me by one person or another, while the hotel delays the meal to increase the profit at the bar. The sweet fizz adds to the excitement already popping inside me. From where I sit I can see him at the far end of the room, in a circle of men that mirrors ours: with his older brothers and his uncles. I see him trying to join in when they burst into laughter, or slap his back, or spout asides into his ear. Sometimes his crooked smiles look more like frowns. I watch him without seeming to, not looking too close or too often. I have to be careful.

On our table the glasses of sherry sit, barely sipped. Mrs D., as she tells everyone, would prefer a cup of tea any day. She feels awkward here, with all these people she half-knows. At home, in the house and the shop, she is the boss. Here she is exposed: a woman without a husband, a deserted wife.

Her friend, Mrs Redmond, admires my dress, addressing her remarks to Mrs D. 'That's a gorgeous shade of blue she's wearing, Máirín. You have her lovely.'

'Ah, now,' says Mrs D.

'And what about Eileen's dress?' says Gran, mindful of Mrs O'Neill beside her. 'I never saw any dress as nice.'

Mrs Redmond slants a look across at Eileen, who is talking to the priest. 'It's very fancy all right. Was it made or bought?' she asks, knowing well that the rushed wedding hardly left time to have a dress made.

'Bought,' says Mrs O'Neill.

'In town, I suppose?'

'Some place in Dublin, I believe.'

'Dublin?' Mrs Redmond's eyebrows disappear up under her perm. 'Is that right? Imagine that.'

'I knew as soon as I saw it that it hadn't been got around here,' says Mrs D. 'No local dressmaker ever produced the likes of that.'

Mrs D. and Mrs Redmond are scandalized by the dress. Excessively expensive for someone like Eileen, they think, and in the face of her shame, nothing short of brazen. This is what they said in our house last night. Now, in front of Eileen's mother and aunt, they let the set of their faces speak.

Mrs O'Neill's cheeks are pink. 'I felt myself there was no need for it,' she says. 'But . . .'

'Girls like to go all out for their weddings these days,' says kindly Gran. 'And why not? Aren't you only married the once?'

'Thank God for small mercies.' Mrs Maher takes the bite out of the talk by making everybody laugh but above her half-smile a pair of narrowed eyes have hooked into Mrs D.

'Ah, now, Mrs Maher,' says Gran. 'Don't go putting off the young ones.'

'That's right, don't.' Mrs Redmond touches Maeve on the leg. 'This girl has probably got her eye on the bouquet later. Have you, Maeve? Will you be jumping for the bouquet?'

Maeve smiles at her. 'I haven't thought about it.'

'She's way too young for any of that, Mary,' says Mrs D. 'She has her studies to finish first.'

'Of course she has. I'm only joking with her. And how is the study going, Maeve?'

'All right, thanks.'

'Maeve is hoping to get into Carysfort College,' Mrs D. explains to Mrs O'Neill and Mrs Maher. 'To be a national schoolteacher.'

'Oh. Like her grandmother,' returns Mrs Maher, and the words are drenched with significance. Whatever the shot is, it finds its target. Mrs D. pulls back in her chair, jerked away from her pride in Maeve.

'Oh, yes,' says Mrs Maher, thumping her glass down on the table and addressing Mrs D. directly. 'I was one of your mammy's pupils, many moons ago.'

Whatever it is that she's saying doesn't bother Gran. 'You're going a long way back there, Margaret.'

'You never forget a good teacher.' Mrs Maher gives Gran a smile that says her argument is not with her. 'And at my age,' she says, swivelling her eyes back round to Mrs D., 'you remember things that went on years ago better than what happened yesterday.'

A prickly quiet settles around this pronouncement.

Protected by the audience, I dare to play innocent. 'You never told us you used to be a teacher, Gran.'

'It was a long time ago, lovey. Before I was married.'

'Maybe Maeve will be lucky,' says Mrs Redmond, twisting the conversation back to the present. 'Maybe she'll get a job back in Mucknamore when she qualifies.'

'Wouldn't that be great?' says Mrs D. 'That would be just too good to be true.'

'Give Father Pat a dance later on, Maeve,' says Mrs Redmond, 'and he might look after you when the time comes.'

Again Maeve smiles, as if Mrs Redmond's blather and the possibility of coming back here is pleasing to her, as if the snarls in the conversation never happened. Is it possible that her smile is real? Or is her face like my own, a lid that seals away true thoughts? I imagine their faces if I were to do what I long to do: walk away from this cryptic baiting, grab Rory O'Donovan by the hand and run out the door with him. But I know I will do no such thing. I am impotent, snared in the mesh of family expectations and my own weakness.

The day draws on. I buy cigarettes and sneak up to the ladies' room to smoke. Deirdre has taught me how to inhale, drawing a fraction of smoke back through my nose. It's a neat technique that we both consider to be sophisticated, but I need practice. The ladies' room is empty, with a partition in front of the door that allows me plenty of time to drop the evidence down the plughole if someone comes in.

I like smoking in front of the mirror. 'Let's face it,' I say out loud to my reflection, 'I need a cigarette, the day I'm having.' I say this in a drawl, rolling the words out along my tongue, savouring myself as the kind of person who says things like that. I watch myself smoke. Everybody does it differently: it is a stamp, like your signature or your way of walking. It can look sophisticated or sad, cool or anxious. I practise Deirdre's new method, feeling the nicotine jolt my brain. Inside me, a vein of frustration throbs.

I go back downstairs, endure the day bleeding on. I dance with Séamus, with each of Eileen's brothers and with every other male who feels he has a duty to take out the bridesmaid. When not dancing, I sit quiet in Mrs D.'s corner, peeping across. How can anything happen here under the drilling eyes of our families? I feel my hopes for the day splinter and die.

Towards the end of the night, on my final visit upstairs to the ladies', I let down my hair. My scalp is aching from having it pulled so tight, for so long. I can never make up my mind whether I like my hair or hate its spring of red fuzz. I take my comb from my little bridesmaid's bag and run it through, unsnarling the knots. When I am finished, I lean across the basin, rest my scorching cheek against the glass. Tears swell behind my lids but I push them back. Later, in bed, I will cry. Not now. Not here.

The door creaks open and I jump back, as if I have been doing something wrong. As I turn on the tap to pretend to be washing my hands, Mrs D.'s face appears around the partition. 'There you are,' she says. 'We were thinking of sending out a search party.'

The soap revolves around my clean palms.

'You've been gone so long Eileen's gone up to her room without you. It's one of the bridesmaid's duties, you know, to help the bride change into her going-away outfit.'

'I didn't know it was that time. I'll go up to her now.'

'Forget it, it's too late now. I sent Maeve instead. What were you doing up here for so long?'

'Nothing, really.'

'You took your hair down.'

'It was giving me a headache.'

'It's not half as smart down.'

'It doesn't matter now, though, does it? It's nearly all over.'

'Thank God. As soon as the going-away bit is done, we can get on home.' She sinks down onto the red-velvet chair in the corner, unstraps one of her shoes, kicks it off. 'My feet are killing me,' she says. 'On fire.'

She crosses her knees, brings her ankle up and takes her foot in her hands. It's misshapen, rutted with bumps and blemishes that are visible even through the sheath of skin-coloured nylon. I loathe that foot, I realize, loathe the cracked skin, the protruding bunion, the slug-like toes, the moist feel and the stale smell that doesn't reach me here, on the far side of the room, but that I know surrounds it. And I detest the other foot too, sitting there still encased in its shoe, its flesh bulging beyond the straps. And the ankles above the feet, so puffed up with their pain, and the two shins, snaked by jutting varicose veins, and the knees like a pair of angry knots in an ancient tree and . . . and . . . And . . . ? All of it, I suddenly know. Yes, all. Every piece and part of her fills me with distaste.

Swinging my revulsion away before it shows, I carry my wet

hands towards the towel machine in the corner. The exposed section of towel is soiled, already used. I tug at the loop, trying to pull down a clean piece, but the machine grunts and cranks tighter, refusing to dispense. As I yank, I feel something rip underneath my skin. Why do I care if she finds out about my smoking? About Rory? About anything? Why should I care about her disapproval? She disapproves anyway. Always has, always will.

'I'm going on down,' I say, my hands still damp.

She looks up, surprised by something in my voice, squints hard at me through her glasses, sensing something in me but not knowing what it is. How could she when I don't know myself?

Outside on the corridor, as I am approaching the stairs, I see Mrs O'Donovan and her daughter May heading up. His mother, his sister. As soon as they notice me, they avert their eyes, turn in towards each other so they can pass without acknowledging me. I want to stop them, explain that I am different, that I don't know about the family row or care, but we pass in the usual way. They will walk into the Ladies Room just as Mrs D. is washing her hands or walking out. I imagine them stopping a moment in surprise, before swinging away from each other.

Let them at it: I am going to find him.

And then I look down to the bottom of the stairs and find that it's going to be easy, so easy. Because he has come looking for me. There he is, standing just inside the front entrance, waving up at me. The lobby is empty apart from the receptionist with her head bent, behind the reception desk. Something quivers inside my chest and I begin to hurry, almost run, down the stairs. He takes a second to smile then he walks out the door. I slither out after him.

Outside, night has fallen and a dark breeze is deliciously cool on my cheeks. My ears are pounding with the echo of the Mooney's bass drum. He leads the way: down the road, around the corner to the back of the hotel, where we stop, between two cars. The *boom-te-boom* of the wedding band reaches us, muffled, playing 'Little Arrows'.

We are shy with one another. He asks me whether I smoke, offers me a cigarette, lights a match for us, making a cup of his hand against the breeze. I dip my face into the flame, shake back my hair on the way up. I inhale nicotine deep, feel my light-headedness. He begins a conversation: about his uncles, how they had started drinking before the wedding Mass that morning, how many pints each had, who's holding up the best. He has had a few himself, he says.

'What's it like?'

'Fairly disgusting, to tell you the truth. But you get used to it.'

He calls me Dev, short for Devereux but also a nod at my family's political preferences and at our disdain for such things: he has no more time for Fine Gael than I have for Fianna Fáil.

'Is that why they don't talk?' he asks, meaning our families. 'Politics?'

'I think there's a bit more to it than that. Something that happened in the old days, some dirty deed your family did on us,' I say, smiling.

'I heard it was the other way around.' He is smiling too. For the first time, I look fully at him. My eyes are wholly open to him but it's OK. I don't feel unsafe. When he speaks again, his voice is husky. 'I had to fight to come here today.'

'What do you mean?'

'They didn't want me to come, said Séamus would understand with me being away in school. I had to feed them a story about not wanting to miss the family occasion and really wanting the day out.'

'So what was your real reason?' I want to hear him say it.

'I heard you were going to be here.'

I let out a breath I didn't know I was holding and with it the small, deep-down fear that I had not acknowledged to myself, that our connection might exist only in my mind, might only be a yearning of my own. A reasonable fear, but I had been right not to admit it.

I lean across and kiss the lips I have touched so often with my eyes. I find them gentle, softer than they look. It is a light kiss I give him, our mouths barely touching and when I pull my head back, we are both smiling. He takes the cigarette from my fingers, drops it onto the ground with his own, and grinds both under his shiny black toe. The long, unsmoked tubes split, spilling their tobacco guts over the ground. He pulls me close and this time our kiss is firmer. As our mouths tighten on each other, our bodies follow, burying deeper, until we are pressed full length against each other.

We kiss for a long time. Afterwards, we keep our heads close, our breaths mingling. He whispers, 'If our mammies could see us now,' and we laugh a murmuring laugh, both of us, together. For that moment, our foolish families – like the rest of the world – are nothing.

We talk then, our first real talk. I tell him about the convent, what the nuns are like, Deirdre and the trouble she sometimes leads me into. He tells me all about a vicious priest who has it in for him. Then we kiss again. This time his hands move across my dress, the tight blue dress bought with him in mind. I knot my legs against his and through our clothes I feel it, hard and unmistakable, delightful and alarming. I pull my mouth away.

'I better go back,' I gasp. 'They'll be wondering where I am.'

'Never mind them.'

We kiss some more but anxiety bears down on me now. If anyone was to see us . . . If Maeve came looking for me . . .

'Really. I'd better go.'

'All right.'

I step away from him. Cold night air slides in between us. I feel like something has been cut.

'Aren't you coming back in?' I say to him.

'Better let you go ahead. In case anyone sees.'

'Oh . . . Yes. Of course.'

I walk away, backwards, still looking at him. I'm photographing the moment. I know I will rerun it in my head a thousand times.

'Tell the nuns I was asking for them,' he calls after me.

I smile. 'Yeah. Give my love to the priests.'

I turn and hurry towards the hotel, wondering what I will hope for now. For so long, all I have dreamt about is talking to him, kissing him. Now my dream has come true, I'll have to change it.

At the corner, I look back one last time. He bows, pretends to lift a hat from his head in a flourish. He is still smiling, a smile wide as the sea. I take this smile and his silly gesture and pack them away inside me. Then I turn and climb the steps into the hotel to face our relatives.

22

1922

'It's hard for you, Nora. Don't think I don't see that it's hard. But sooner or later, if you are determined to keep up your involvement, then they'll come to know. All I'm saying is that sooner will be easier, for them as well as yourself.'

'Ah, Peg.'

'Really and truly. You're twenty-two years old, Nora, not a child. You're entitled to your own mind.'

'Sssh. Keep your voice down. Your mammy will hear.'

Peg and Nora were locked together in the grocery. The shop was closed for the night, the blind pulled down and Nora sneaked in under cover of darkness. All of this was necessary now, because John O'Donovan, Nora's father, was now – like his eldest son – avidly pro-Treaty and not a man to take disagreement lightly, especially from one of his own.

Peg knew that Máire, or JJ or Barney for that matter, would not dream of betraying her, but Nora, overly apprehensive, didn't want any of them knowing she was there. She was always that way. In the pre-Truce days, when Dan – the old Dan, the loyal Dan – had gone public about his volunteer involvement, it led to the most dramatic fights in the O'Donovan house, the sort of hostility gentle Nora could not bear. Her dedication to Ireland's freedom was true and earnest but she had hidden herself in the shadows of Dan's rebellion, let herself be carried along within it. Now Dan was no longer of the same mind and she was going to have to make a stand for herself or give up altogether.

Nora's father wasn't shy about announcing where he stood. All his pre-Truce arguments with Dan were now forgotten, 'as if they never happened', according to Nora. As far as Mr O'Donovan was concerned, the new army that Dan had joined was going to put a stop to what he called the 'disorder' and 'anarchy' of the past few years. It was only his personal interest that he was thinking of, Peg believed, his fear that instability would affect farm incomes. He was not alone in this, plenty were adopting the pro-Treaty side out of self-interest.

Mrs O'Donovan was so delighted to see her husband and son getting on again that she fell in with everything they said. And as none of the younger children was old enough to understand or care, poor Nora had no one on her side. She had to endure almost daily the galling habit her father had developed of reciting the latest statement of Arthur Griffith or Michael Collins like it was the word of God. Or, worse, quoting her brother at her, until some days she thought she'd explode into argument and shock the life out of him with her own thoughts on the same matters.

Which was what she should do, Peg thought.

But she didn't. Tonight, if they wondered when she got home what kept her, she would say she was working late, what she usually said whenever she called into Parle's. It wasn't quite a lie – she was working, though not at her job in Furlong's department store as they would presume. Instead, she laboured for the cause she held dear, helping Peg to collate election leaflets.

'You're entitled,' Peg repeated.

'"Honour thy father and thy mother",' Nora said. 'Isn't that what the priests say?'

Peg cast her eyes up to the ceiling. 'Oh, the priests. The priests say more than their prayers these days.' The hierarchy had recently spoken out again, condemning the actions of the anti-Treaty soldiers and urging the people to support the provisional government, until the outcome of the election was decided. She reached into a cardboard box and pulled out two bunches of leaflets. 'Here,' she said, handing them to Nora. 'Put those two together.'

It was a bit late in the day for handing out leaflets – the election was the following Thursday – but they had had to wait for new, replacement material to come through from Dublin. Their old bills had called for an anti-Treaty vote, argued that the issue of this election was the old issue – the English in Ireland – and urged the people to vote for the Republic. Then Collins and de Valera – in a last-minute attempt to avert division – had agreed an electoral pact. Both pro- and anti- candidates were to put themselves forward as Sinn Féin nominees, forming a coalition panel of candidates for the election and forming a coalition government afterwards.

This was a good development for the anti-Treaty side and so new leaflets had been rushed through by Dublin. The intention was that this second leaflet should replace the first, but Máire suggested – and Peg agreed – that they might as well distribute both together. This was what she gave Nora to work on now, joining the two bills together, folding them into bags for delivery. Over the next few nights, she and Molly and the other girls of Cumann na mBan would give one into every house within a four-mile radius. The boys had also been put on election duty, to go round the same houses with their guns on show and give people a little 'persuasion' in doing the right thing on voting day.

They worked in silence for a while, just the sound of folding paper between them, then Nora surprised Peg by bringing the conversation back to her father. 'Daddy says the pact is biased towards Republicans.'

'He's not the only one saying that. But such people never say anything about the dirty dealings of the other side. What about the voting register, that leaves the likes of you and me and Barney with no vote? And what about the Constitution not being published? They're asking people to go out to vote on a document that most of them won't even have seen. They—'

'I'm not arguing with you, Peg,' Nora interrupted. 'I know all that is wrong. As wrong as anything.'

Peg snapped her mouth shut. Of course Nora knew as well as she did the injustice of it all. The poor girl was gripping the folded leaflet so tight, eight of her knuckles jutted out white. She was feeling the strain. It wasn't easy for her to confide about her family as she had earlier. 'Would you not just talk to them, Nora?' she said, gently.

Nora shook her head. 'You don't understand what they're like.'

'I know it's easier for me, Nora,' she said, sifting out her words. 'Our own father has never been too keen on our activities but –' she hurried on as she saw Nora about to speak – 'we've never had to face Daddy down because we've had Mammy there to do it for us. But still I think you're going to have to face it. Don't misunderstand me, Nora. I know that's not easily done. We're girls, for God's sake, trained from the minute we're born to do what we're told. It's not easy to go against all that. But I also know that doing what is right – no, don't look so stony-faced – doing what is right has a habit of making the unexpected happen. Look at what we have gained so far. We can gain much, much more if we only hold onto our courage.'

Peg paused to let Nora respond but now, it seemed, she had nothing to say. Had she convinced her? 'The old have had it all their own way in Ireland for too long, Nora. That's why this country was so low for decades – all the young people emigrating or else being bullied by the older people into submission. But that is changing now. We've changed it, our generation. And we can change a lot more, if we hold onto what we know to be right.'

'So I should go home tonight and just tell him what I think?' Nora looked at Peg as if the suggestion was that she should dance naked with the devil down the village street. 'Is that what you're saying to me, Peg?'

'Knowing that there will be a storm, but knowing too that once they've finished huffing and puffing, you can get on with doing the work you want to do for Ireland. Yes, Nora, I think if I were you I'd just do it.'

Nora let out a bitter laugh that hurt her friend to hear. 'Maybe if I were you, Peg, I might do the same.'

'What do you mean?'

'We're not all the same in this world, however much we might wish it. You can lift that bag of sugar over there with ease. I couldn't if I tried for a week.'

She turned her eyes on Peg, two big jewels of green in a tiny skull. It seemed to Peg that an accusation lurked in those eyes, as if Nora considered her a dunce. 'Your family look at you and they see Peg,' she said, her face pulled tight as the skin on a kettle drum. 'Mine look at me and they see another O'Donovan, who does and says what O'Donovans are meant to do.'

'Don't think only of your family. What about your country? What about Barney?'

'What about him?'

Peg pulled back, she'd said too much. She pointed to a cardboard box in the corner of the counter. 'Pass me over that box, will you?'

'Peg . . . ?' Nora was looking at her with a shrivelled face.

Should she tell her? 'Nora, you know. Surely you must know.'

'Do I?' She brought her hands together, fingers twisting each other crooked. 'I suppose I do.'

Peg reached past her for the box, opened it, took out another sheaf of papers. She wasn't going to pry. Nora could tell or not, whichever she wanted.

After a while she asked, 'Do you think others know?'

'I've never heard anyone else say anything. Nobody else knows the two of you like I do.'

Nora nodded, chewed her thumbnail.

'Nora, have you any time for him at all? I only ask because, to tell you the truth, he has it bad for you, so bad. If he's wasting his time, you should tell him. Really you should because . . . Oh, Nora, I'm sorry, stop. Don't cry.'

Nora burst into shuddering tears. 'Peg, I don't know . . . I just don't – I don't—'

'Oh, don't cry, Nora. Don't. I'm so sorry.'

'It's not you . . . You're right. Everything . . . you say . . . is right.'

'Oh, dear Nora.' Shocked, Peg put her arm around her. 'Here. Take this.' She pressed her handkerchief into her friend's trembling fingers. Nora let her face fall forward into it, buried small sobs into its folds. All the while, Peg kept her arm in place.

When she recovered a little, Nora said in a voice washed empty, 'You're right. I'm a coward.'

'That's *not* what I said.'

'That's what it amounts to . . . And you're right, you're right.'

No, it was Nora who was right. Who could say what she, Peg, would be like if she grew up in Nora's house? Bolstering her friend was what she should be doing, not encouraging her tendency to self-blame, not making her feel worse than she felt already.

'Look, Nora, forget what I said. Only you know what's right for you.'

'Me? Stupid, useless me.'

Then she started to hit herself, to punch herself on the forehead, hard.

'Nora!'

She broke into a flurry of blows, beating herself around the head with both hands.

Peg was truly shocked now. 'Nora! Stop that. Stop it right this minute.' She caught hold of Nora's wrists, stopped her hands. For a moment, there was resistance, then her arms went limp. She looked back at Peg with a face as blank as the sun, a face that turned a gnarling fear in the pit of Peg's stomach. Fear made her bluster: 'Stop that nonsense, Nora. Lord God, I never saw the like . . .'

Nora was crying again, quiet tears rolling down frozen cheeks. 'Don't shout,' she said, in a dead voice. 'Don't shout, please. You'll have them out after us.'

Peg let her arms go. 'Then stop crying. And stop talking about yourself like that. Come on, Nora, blow your nose. Dry the tears.'

Nora did as she was told.

'There, that's better.' Peg's soothing was aimed at them both.

She was shaken. She never knew the strength of feeling Nora kept hidden behind her pale quiet face. She would be more careful about what she said in future. 'Look, Nora, what I was trying to say is . . . No, don't interrupt. What I want to say is this: don't listen to anybody else, not your family and not me either. Examine your own conscience, then you'll know what to do.'

Nora shook her head, patted her eyes with the puckered handkerchief. 'It sounds so simple when you say it, Peg.'

'Underneath it all, under the confusion and the pressure from all sides, it really is that simple.'

'Is it, Peg? Is it really?'

Peg

Dear Diary

So we lost, thanks mostly to the traitorous acts of Mr Michael Collins, who with only days to go, reneged on the pact he signed with Mr de Valera. We brought the Republic within sights but the old-timers and the respectables, the farmers and the shoneens, the gombeen men and the merchants got in behind Mr Collins and voted it away. 239,193 votes to the pro-Treaty candidates, 247,226 to Labour, Farmers and Independents between them. 133,864 to us.

Mammy got up out of bed to go to the polling booth. We didn't even try to stop her because we knew we'd have no hope and she managed fine. She got excited at being out and about with people coming over to her and making a fuss: all enquiries about her health were brushed aside and she concentrated on the politics, getting herself rightly worked up and agitated, especially about the failure to publish the Constitution until the morning of the election. 'A thundering disgrace,' she called it, sounding just like her old self.

As for the actions of Michael Collins, reneging on the pact at the last minute: she was fit to be tied whenever she thought of it. As usual she was right in what she said, even if she expressed herself a bit strongly. Collins's carry-on *was* disgraceful. It's clear what consorting with the English has done to that man's morals. Look at how they only published the Constitution this morning, the very morning of the election. Once we saw it we knew why. The English had the writing of it, with every nail of the Treaty driven home. It left no possibility of a coalition government, which was no doubt why Collins backed away from the agreement.

Tonight, in bed, Mammy was still going on about the result, her anger mostly directed at Mr White, Lama's father, who seemingly made a remark to Daddy that the result expressed a wish for compromise among the ordinary people, a concern about social and economic matters. That was why the Farmers' Party and Labour did so well, he held, because people wanted the fighting put aside and for the new government to concentrate on things 'that mattered', like jobs and land reform and housing. Daddy had passed this on to Mammy, hoping, I think, that she might take some notice of that point of view (it being, to some degree, his own).

If that's what he hoped, he must have been sorely disappointed. All the reminiscences and stories of the past that she's been occupied with of late were forgotten as she ranted and railed against the Whites ('a crowd of Bolshevists sheltering under the name of Republicans', she called them). Then on to all the self-seeking people who put their own welfare above the noble cause of nation ('Who were the Farmers' Party anyway, only a string of Orangemen and Freemasons?'). And then back to denouncing the Provisional Government and her outrage that people in general were now taking up their label for anti-Treaty soldiers: 'Irregulars'. This was a scandal, she said, when these were mostly the men who brought the government into being in the first place, while most of those joining the new 'National' Army had never seen a day's service in their lives.

At first I feared she might strain herself if she got too worked up but after a while I came to feel it did her good to fume and think of something besides her own poor health. To see her so excited and alive again nearly made me hope . . . But no, that is silly. We know there is no hope.

If the register had been updated to include young women, we could have won it, that's what fills me with anger. Well, they needn't think that it ends there. I don't know what we do next but we won't be lying under this injustice, of that they can be sure . . .

Dear Diary

I was supposed to be going to Ring College in the Gaeltacht for an Irish course. All the arrangements are made, I've paid my money and Father John is agreeable and has sponsored me. He won't be too pleased when he hears what I'm going to do instead. This afternoon I leave for Enniscorthy where our troops are preparing for war against the Free Staters. Outright war has come to Wexford.

Since Mick Collins took two 18-pounder guns from Winston Churchill under orders from Lloyd George and used them to blast apart the defences of the brave men holding the Four Courts in Dublin for the Republic, the rest of the country has been waiting to act. Some on the government's own side were sickened by this betrayal and unwilling to shoot at old friends but such men of honour are not wanted by our so-called 'National' Army and have been rounded up and arrested.

All Dublin is said to be a shambles, the heart, liver and lights torn out of the city. After days of bombing and shooting, Sackville Street lies destroyed, a pile of rubble from one end to the other. They blasted the Four Courts to high heaven and scraps of its books and documents and records were carried for miles like leaves on a storm wind. And our boys have taken a fearful hammering. The fighting is dirty. We are outgunned with English weapons and recruited men by the hundreds, men who were nowhere to be seen when it was the English we were fighting but who are all for it now there's a salary going and free uniform and boots.

'Official IRA' they have painted on their lorries and armoured cars. Meanwhile, we are nothing but 'Irregulars'. Mammy is right: it is beyond belief.

So there's an end for any hopes of unity. We can forget any notion now of being able to work together. They've declared war and war they shall have, and though they may have might on their side, we have right. They'll not find our country lads as easy to defeat. Down here it is they who are outnumbered, by at least four to one.

In Wexford, all the main towns – Gorey, New Ross, Wexford town and Ferns – are held by us. Only Enniscorthy is not ours, not yet, so it must be taken. Barney has gone ahead, so have Sore-Toes and Lama and Molly and I'll be leaving myself as soon as Daddy gets back from the station. I can stay there as long as I wish as we started our school holidays yesterday. I haven't told Father John of my intentions – I wasn't in the mood for one of his little talks and would prefer to face that music when I get back. Even if school was still on, I would be going. This thing is bigger than any one of us.

Mammy is delighted to see us off, only wishing she could join us herself. When Barney told her what was planned, and of the concerns we had about leaving her, she waved them away. 'Go. Go with God's blessing and my own,' was what she said to us both. 'Go save Ireland.' Daddy too is being better than brave about it all.

At the back of Barney's thoughts as well as my own is Dan. He hasn't said anything to me but I know he finds it as hard to believe as myself that Dan will actually turn out for the army and turn an English-sponsored gun on us, his old comrades and friends. I can't see it. Surely now he'll cross over, now that he can see what true treachery looks like in action. I only pray to God that he will.

I hear George's hoofs pulling into the yard. Daddy is back. It is time for me to go. I will lock you up now, dear diary, and my next entry will be when I come back from Enniscorthy. I should have plenty to report by then.

(4 pm)
Dear Diary

The best-laid plans . . . Here I am still in Mucknamore having taken you back out of the drawer in which I so carefully locked you away. I was about to leave my bedroom, giving it a last go over, making sure there was nothing untoward if Mammy or anybody else should decide to pop in while I was gone, when next thing I heard a call from Tessie downstairs. 'Peg, are you up there?'

'Yes.'

'Someone to see you.'

I went out of the bedroom and hung down over the banisters to see who it was and there stood Nora, her eyes like two big lamps shining up at me. 'Come on up,' I said to her and she took the stairs two by two, most unlike her, bursting to tell me her story. I've never seen her so agitated.

All day long she had been stuck behind the counter in Furlong's, listening to the hearsay being carried into the office from customers visiting the store. Furlong's had no shortage of customers, it being a Saturday, and no shortage of rumours about the goings-on in Enniscorthy: the fighting had started with an all-out attack launched on the courthouse where our boys are; the fighting had started with the Republicans besieging the Castle where the Staters are lodged; the fighting had not started yet but wouldn't be long now.

It was torture for poor Nora, listening to all this, not knowing what was true, what was false. Then through the window of her office she saw that Mrs Redmond was in, Molly's mother, and that she was deep in conversation with Miss Ellen Bolger at the millinery counter, whose sympathies are in the right place. So she made an excuse and under pretext of making notes about the gloves and umbrellas at the next counter managed to listen to their conversation and to hear that Molly had gone up to Enniscorthy to get involved. Mrs Redmond was upset, hadn't wanted her to go, but Molly had been insistent. As Nora listened to this, something in her just clicked.

'I knew this was the moment,' she said. 'That if I didn't go to Enniscorthy like Molly I would regret it for the rest of my living days.'

So she went back to her office for her coat and hat and went to find Mr Carr. She found him in men's footwear and told him she had to leave and when he asked why, she told him out straight. And he said to her, that's not a reason I'd allow any of my girls to leave work. And she, brave as can be, said it was as good a reason as she could think of, the future of Ireland. And he says, if you leave now, you needn't bother coming back. And she didn't have to even think, not even for a second. 'I'm sorry you should say that,' she told him, 'but I'm afraid I have to go.' And she went.

'I went,' she said to me in my bedroom, amazed at herself. 'I just went.' At this she burst out laughing and I joined her. It was the kind of laughing you do after you've come round from jumping out of your skin and find out it was only someone shouting boo.

'So I'm going with you,' she said. 'But first I have to go up home and get my things.'

'What will you tell them?'

'I don't know yet. As little as possible, maybe. I'll see when I'm up there.'

I was afraid for her when I heard her say that. 'Come ahead now instead and say nothing. I'll lend you clothes and whatever else you might need. Face them when you come back.'

But she wouldn't hear of it. On up she went and she's been gone nearly an hour now. I hope to God they haven't talked her out of it.

23

1973

Mrs D. is late. By the time her car pulls into the convent car park, I am the last girl waiting by the recreation-room window.

The nuns have started to let us go home at weekends. Not every weekend, but twice a month we can leave after study on Saturday morning and stay out until eight o'clock on Sunday evening. It is optional, this home visit, and does not suit everybody. I'd rather stay in school and I'm pretty certain Mrs D. would prefer that too, but she'd never leave me here like some parents do: what would the nuns think of that? So every second Saturday she arrives to ferry me home and I play my part, lining up with the other girls at the window, calling out, 'There's me,' when I see the blue Ford swing in through the gates, marching down to her with my weekend bag slung over my shoulder, as if Mucknamore is my idea of a good time.

Today, she is not hunched over the steering wheel in her usual way, but out of the car and walking up and down beside it, her footsteps scrunching the gravel, her face split by a nervy smile.

'Sorry I'm late,' she says, as I approach. 'Maeve is getting in on the half-two train, so there was no point in coming earlier. We'd only have been sitting in the car, waiting.' Just the two of us in that small space putting in half an hour: intolerable thought.

Maeve has left the convent now, gone to Dublin to teacher-training college. I had forgotten she was coming home this weekend but surely it is not this that has Mrs D. beaming like a bride?

'By the way,' she says, getting back into the car. 'We have a surprise at home.'

'Oh, yeah?'

I walk around the car, open the passenger door, throw in my bag. Every cell in me resists her mood.

'Don't fall over yourself asking me what it is, anyway.'

'What is it?'

'I'm not going to tell you,' she says. 'It wouldn't be a surprise if I told you, would it? But you could show a bit of interest.'

What can I do with this nonsense but ignore it? She flicks her eyes heavenwards and her sigh is full of reproach. Not even two minutes together and here we are: irked.

We sit into the small car, me in the front seat beside her, her perfume heavy in the closed space of the car. She turns the ignition and reverses jerkily, making the engine snarl and the medal of St Christopher, patron saint of motorists or safety or something like that, swing wildly on its chain hanging from the mirror. It takes us only moments to drive down to the station. She parks and before getting out of the car, takes off her driving shoes and puts on a pair with slightly higher heels. Is she under the illusion that this improves her appearance? Doesn't she realize that, dumpy high shoes or dumpy low, she looks just what she is: old and old-fashioned? Martha Moran's mother, when she collected Martha today, was wearing gypsy pants and a cheesecloth shirt but Mrs D., who is twenty years older than some of the girls' mothers, wears a variation of the same clothes she has worn all my life, knee-length skirt (tweed in winter, cotton in summer), sensible blouse or sweater, skin-coloured stockings. An outfit that surely was never fashionable? Surely?

I move into the back seat, leaving the front free for my sister, take my transistor radio out of my bag, turn it on. BBC Radio 1. It's the golden oldie hour and they're playing Dusty Springfield's 'Son of a Preacher Man'. I adore this song. The lyrics and Dusty's ardent tones perfectly capture my fervid feelings for Rory O'Donovan. I lie down on the car seat, turn up the volume, holler along with the words. The song ends just as the train pulls in, puffing and snorting like a giant animal. As my mother and sister return to the car, I sit up and turn off the radio before I'm told.

They are full of talk about Mrs D.'s surprise. 'At least tell me, is it good or bad?' Maeve is pleading as they sit in.

'Oh, good,' Mrs D. says, as if her smirking didn't already answer that. 'Definitely good.'

Back home, she leads us into the house like a tour guide then stops us outside the kitchen door. 'Are you ready?' she whispers and when Maeve nods, she reaches in front of us to flourish the door open. Our surprise sits at the kitchen table: Daddy.

Daddy, drinking tea.

Daddy, with long straggles of hair tickling his shirt collar and two big sideburns. Looking up at us through a squint that is also new.

'Hello, girls,' he says.

He doesn't get up, carries on nursing his mug of tea. Clinging to it like a raft.

'What are you standing there for?' says Mrs D. 'Go on in and say hello to your father.'

We sit in chairs opposite him. Maeve says: 'Hello, Daddy.'

I can't say anything. It's too sudden. The man I remember is still in England and this person in front of me is someone else.

'My God, you've grown,' he says, to both of us.

'I'm nearly eighteen,' Maeve tells him. 'And Jo is fifteen.'

'My God,' he says again. 'Imagine that. You're a real pair of young ladies.'

He takes a mouthful of tea, peers over the rim of his cup with two hunted eyes. I notice how old his shirt is, the thin blue stripe is faded at the collar, the cuffs are frayed. He is not the man he was. My head rattles full of things I can't ask.

Later, Gran tells me what she knows, 'which is not a whole lot'. He turned up on Wednesday evening without a by-your-leave and got a welcome from Mrs D. as good as the prodigal son's. Had his feet back under the table by supper time and now goes around the place like he was never away at all. 'Been good for business, mind you,' she says. 'Every man and woman in the parish has been in for a look.'

Later that day, Mrs D. sends me out to the shop to get some cooked ham for tea. I have to walk through the bar to get to the grocery and for this ordeal I always let my hair fall forward to shield my face. I hate this small journey: twenty-two steps of torture if certain customers are in, those who see me as a target. They jeer my name ('Shove on your knickers . . .') or my clothes ('Nice blouse,' they'll say, their eyes poking through it) or my hair ('You'd think the Parles would be able to afford a hairbrush . . .'). If I respond, they'll mock my voice or my words. Any part of me is open to their taunts.

They are farm labourers, mostly, or fishermen or tradesmen. Lower on Mucknamore's social pecking order than me, the daughter of the public house, whose father wore a white collar to work, whose mother was a nurse before she married, who attends boarding school and is intended for university. But the advantages are not all mine: they are grown men, I am a teenage girl. Their family histories hold no mysterious, shameful secrets. And they are our patrons. My shyness is a chink through which they can funnel their feelings about our family: their awareness of our dubious past, their scandalized delight at my father's defection, their resentment of the money they spend here, the very money that funds our social advantage.

I'm not supposed to take their teasing so seriously, I know that. I'm supposed to mock them back, like Maeve does, pretend it's a game, that there is no loathing on either side. I wish I could. Even better would be to be like Daddy: indifferent.

He is seated on the high stool behind the counter, his arms folded and his eyelids drooping over their talk, in just the old way. While I'm waiting for Eileen to cut the meat, I stand where the customers can't see me, on the grocery side of the divide, listening. Easy chat slides across the counter and back in a way that hasn't happened since he left. Man-to-man talk, about last Sunday's hurling match.

The bell rings and Pat Rowe comes, stopping in the doorway when he sees Daddy behind the counter. Even if you didn't know that word must be well and truly out by now, you could tell that he's putting on a show.

'Well, well,' he says. 'Boys, oh, boys. Look who's back in town.'

He comes up to the counter, shaking his head. The other customers sit to attention, hopeful of a bit of excitement: Mr Rowe is known for his direct talk. 'Well, well,' he says again. 'Christy Devereux, back in the saddle.' He is talking, as he does, like he is in a cowboy film. 'And there was the world thinking you were gone for good.'

'Ah, now,' says Daddy. 'We all know what thought did.' This is an old joke. What thought did: stuck a feather in the ground and thought he'd grow a hen; peed in his pants and thought it was raining.

Mr Rowe won't be diverted. 'So where have you been, stranger?'

'Ask no questions, Pat, and you'll be told no lies.' Daddy holds up a big glass. 'A pint of the black stuff, is that still the order?'

Mr Rowe nods, unsure what to say next. 'Birmingham, was it?'

'Birmingham,' nods Daddy, his eyes narrowing above the word, a warning to back off. And it works. Something in him – What is it? What? – stops Mr Rowe's advance.

'Did you see Mulcahy's tackle?' John Buttle asks from the lower end of the bar.

'Tackle, how are you,' says Daddy. 'It was nothing but a dirty foul.'

Talk of the match resumes. Mr Rowe pulls up a stool, pays for his pint and lets his jibing go.

Gran is right. Daddy has slipped back into his life as if it were an old jumper he found and decided to start wearing again. His armchair is pulled out of its resting-place in the corner, his boots slump in their old place inside the back door, tripping everybody up. While Mammy is in the garden and Gran gone for her walk, I go upstairs. In the bathroom, his razor and toothbrush have reclaimed their spot. The only change is that he is exiled from the bedroom he used to share with Mrs D.

In the spare room, I find his comb on the dressing table and the faint tang of Old Spice, his aftershave, in the air. Under a pillow are his pyjamas and a book: *The Honey Badger*. On the cover a woman with gold skin holds a sheet in one hand to cover her pubic bone. Her eyes are turned away but two pneumatic golden breasts stare hard at me. It looks like the kind of book that has dirty bits, something that would get passed around in school with giggles and page numbers. It gives me a strange feeling to find it here, in my father's bed. I open the wardrobe: two pairs of trousers, one hanging over the other beside a small row of scruffy shirts and jumpers. One shiny suit. And down at the bottom, his red canvas travel bag, empty and flat, like a deflated balloon.

Sunday morning over breakfast, Mrs D. announces that we'll be having lunch in the dining room today for a change. It's a celebration, we all know, though she doesn't say so. After Mass, while Daddy looks after the shop, she and Gran and Maeve jiggle pots and pans in the kitchen. I stay in the sitting room, avoiding them, stretched on my front across the rug in front of the fire, reading book four of *Poldark*, a ten-volume Cornish romance that has been sweeping me out of my life for weeks. Auntie Nora too ignores the cooking fuss. These days, what's happening on TV seems more real to her than the events in our house. She has not commented on Daddy's return any more than she seemed to miss him while he was gone. Gran has turned on her favourite programme, *The Addams Family*, and aside from one thumb rapidly revolving around the other when Gomez kisses Morticia's extended arm, she is relaxed. We share the same room but inhabit separate worlds.

Smells of roasting meat and bubbling vegetables fill the house. Close to serving-up time, Mrs D. interrupts my reading.

'Siobhán, make some gravy. I'll be back in a minute to serve up.'

In the kitchen, Gran is mashing potatoes in the big pot. A roast leg of lamb sits in the serving dish, its bone sticking up like the handle of a club. I mix Bisto powder with water in a cup, stirring it to get the lumps out, and when it's smooth, I add it to the meat juices. Mrs D. comes back. She has taken off her apron, brushed her hair, put on make-up.

Gran's face creases when she sees this. 'Lipstick now, is it?' I'm so shocked I stop stirring. I have never heard Gran criticize Mrs D. before.

'And a daub of lipstick is a sin, I suppose?' Mrs D. puts on a pair of oven gloves that make her look like a boxer, picks up the meat dish and sweeps it off to the dining room.

When she's gone, I sidle across to Gran.

'What is it, lovey?'

'Are you not glad that Daddy is back?'

'As I've been told, it's nothing to do with me.'

I pull close to her, searching out her softness. 'Please, Gran.'

She looks at me and shrugs. 'Your daddy disappears off with himself then turns up four years later as if he only went out to bring in the milk. He just—' She breaks off.

'But it's good he's back, isn't it?'

'What would happen in the world if we all did a bunk when we felt like it?' A shard of envy spikes through her words and I am shocked. Gran is drawn to the notion of 'doing a bunk'? For the first time, I think about Gran's life from the inside, how it might feel to her.

'If you bring two children into the world,' she says, 'you do your duty by them.'

But if it was so wrong for him to go away, why is she not happier that he's back? 'Gran, can you not just forgive him?' I'm thinking of all the times she forgives Mrs D. I'm thinking if we can forgive him, why can't she?

'Oh, Jo, don't give me the hard face. It's only that I'm afraid for ye, that's all.'

'Afraid for us?'

Under her pounding, the potatoes turn to mash.

'You think he might go off again? Is that what you mean?'

She looks up at me through glasses that have steamed over and when she speaks she doesn't answer my question. 'I'll say one thing to you now, and listen to me, because this is one of the best bits of advice you'll ever get: don't interfere in life. Let the Lord above look after what's to happen and stay out of matters as much as you can.'

What is she talking about?

'I mean it,' she says. 'You can think you're doing good and right and end up with things all wrong.'

'What do you mean, Gran? I don't understand.' What has that to do with Mrs D. and Daddy and all that's going on?

She sighs. 'I suppose you don't. But think about it all the same.'

That's it. She's said as much as she's going to say. She turns off the cooker, points towards the bubbling gravy pot. 'Now get that into the sauce boat, like a good girl. We better get this food shifted before they come out after us.'

Now, writing down the words you said, Gran, I think I know what you meant. I think you believed that you never should have arranged for your daughter to marry Christy Devereux.

It was in 1953, when your daughter was thirty years old, that you began the earnest search for a husband. Her young life had been devoted to making something of herself, knowing she needed all the status she could muster. She became a nurse in Wexford hospital and was tipped to become a ward sister, but by the time she was thirty she no longer cared about all that. She was tired of night-shifts and bedpans and anyway, it was all useless to her if she remained single. Being good, working hard, getting on, she had done it all with a view to attracting a husband. As a spinster, ward sister or not, she was nothing, and she knew it.

It dawned slowly on you, Gran, the fact that nobody was going to marry her. She was a good-looking girl, a qualified nurse, the only child of a family with a public house behind them: she should have been flooded with offers, but she wasn't. You railed against the weak boys from one place or another who showed interest but only for a while, who shrank from her sooner or later because of what they were told. Against the locals who took newcomers aside and hinted that they'd be better off not getting involved. Surely, you thought to yourself, there was *some* family out there broader in mind than the rest, able to get beyond the small talk.

But by the time she was thirty, you could deny it no longer: none of it was her fault, but the consequences were hers to bear all the same. The guilt you felt . . .

You decided that since it was you, the older generation, who had brought the stigma on the girl, it was up to you to mend matters. And while you were thinking this way, who should you meet in Wexford one day but the widow Devereux, an old Cumann na mBan girl, now a good Fianna Fáil woman, who had a son she wished to marry into money. For the sake of this boy, the widow had worked two jobs since her husband's death in 1938: as housekeeper in the mornings; serving in the public house on her street corner by night. Jobs that allowed her to be home when her son Christy came from school in the afternoons, so she could have his dinner on the table, and supervise his homework while still keeping enough coins and notes in her red money-tin. Out of her industry, she was able to give her boy an education. She got him past the primary certificate into St Peter's College and people were starting to give him the same respect they gave to the sons of farmers and small merchants. Her plans didn't stop there: her intention was that he should go to the university.

Except the boy didn't cooperate. First he said he didn't want to go. Then he failed the scholarship. And not even the widow's sacrifices could support him at university without that. He could still have looked for a good job, an office position in Wexford or even further afield, but instead he became a shop assistant in Doyle's hardware, selling nails and the like to the tradesmen of the town. She was livid with him and frantic that he should correct his error before it was too late. Sometimes she blamed herself. She told you so, Gran, that day when you met her in the Main Street. She had spoiled him, given him everything, and now he understood the value of nothing. What was she to do with him?

Back home in Mucknamore, you started thinking. Being married into a pub would be a great deal better for that young man than serving in a hardware shop. And you might, just might, be able to swing him an office job in the new building society that was opening in the town. A lot of Fianna Fáil people were involved in that enterprise and Fianna Fáil people were behoven to look after each other when it came to jobs and positions, after the way they had been treated by the Free State. The widow had done her bit for Ireland in her day, as had her dead husband – it was the scandalous treatment he had received in a Free State jail that had killed him. The boy deserved your help.

You wrote some letters and in time you were able to call to the little house in Hill Street with a proposal.

The boy resisted at first, blustered and blew, and never admitted then or since, to his mother or to you, that a part of him relished the plan. He knew that with a pub in the country and a job in the town, he could be a very fine fellow (might even, maybe, in time, be able to buy himself a motor car). The girl was older than him – thirty to his twenty-one – but he couldn't claim she was bad looking. She wasn't grey or fat or wrinkled and she seemed biddable enough. And – unforeseen inducement – Mucknamore was far enough from Wexford town for him to put distance between himself and his mother, who for some time had been a burden to him with her plans and ambitions.

So he did it. And when it didn't work out you blamed him but you also blamed yourself. Was that what you were referring to that day in the kitchen, the first Sunday after he came back to us? How you thought you'd done a good thing finding your girl a husband but learned in the outcome that you hadn't? Or were you thinking further back, to the days that began the trouble, to the things you did that made your poor girl so unmarriageable in the first place?

24

1922

On the outskirts of Enniscorthy town, Peg and Nora dismounted, leaned their bicycles against the wall of a shop. After their journey – a twenty-three-mile cycle in July sunshine – all they could think of was a drink, something blessedly liquid. Peg took the two steps up into the shop with a jump, Nora walking more circumspectly behind her. Their eyes took time to adjust to the darkness inside the small premises, so small that a third customer wouldn't get in beyond the door frame. Flies buzzed, loud and insolent above shelves that were half bare. Behind the counter an enormously fat middle-aged man sat, leaning over one of his newspapers, ignoring them.

'Em . . . Good evening,' Peg said. 'Are you open?'

He lingered on his reading material a long moment before dragging his eyes up to look at them. Then he let another long moment elapse before he answered. 'I am if you're paying,' he said, his eyes travelling over their Cumann na mBan uniforms.

'Of course we're paying. We only want two lemon sodas.'

He leaned behind, tipping back his stool and stretching towards the shelf, trying to reach. The orangeade bottles were within his grasp but not the lemon soda. With sighs and wheezes he lifted himself down and turned to face the shelf. Leaning heavily on the stool, he bent from his hips, turning his vast, shop-coated rump up towards them. Peg widened her eyes at Nora and they both folded their lips to stifle rising giggles.

Straightening up, the shopkeeper held the two bottles aloft between his fingers. 'You're part of the shenanigans going on above, I suppose?' he said.

Peg nodded. He could see their uniforms; he knew what side they were on. Slowly he drew the corks from the bottles, all the while looking at them from between creased eyes.

'I had your lot in here this morning, commandeering. Eggs, potatoes, butter, bread.'

'Soldiers must eat,' said Peg.

'Commandeering, m'foot. Stealing by another name.'

Peg said, 'If they were genuine Republicans, you'll have been given a receipt.'

'A Republican receipt won't feed seven children.'

Peg felt like saying that if the rest of his family were the size of him they could live off themselves for a year. That he should be proud to do a small thing like that for his country. That many people with a lot less to give than him had given a lot more. But she knew his type too well, she wouldn't waste her breath. 'How much do we owe you?' she said instead.

Back outside, they crossed to the riverbank to drink their minerals. 'Wouldn't they drive you up the wall?' Peg said, after they'd drawn the first long, delicious draughts down their throats. 'The way they don't see past their few greasy pence? We should have tried to find McDaid's.' McDaid's was a shop they were told was friendly.

'Don't mind him,' said Nora. 'Just wait till we win them back the Republic. Then their old talk will turn.'

Peg smiled at her. It was the first time she had ever heard her friend say something like that. Nora was full of surprises today, in a state of high excitement ever since they left Mucknamore, whooping up at the birds in the trees, freewheeling her bike down the hills with her legs sticking out each side.

'So who's going in with the empties?' Peg asked, when they'd finished.

Nora looked at her, wide-eyed. She hadn't changed that much.

'I'm only joking, give it here.'

The shop man was stuck in his paper again.

'I'm bringing back your bottles,' she said, placing them on the little counter.

'Do you know what I'm wondering?' he said. 'I'm wondering how two well-brought-up girls like yourselves have got yourselves tied up with them rowdy boys above. Do you know the type you're dealing with at all, I wonder?'

He held the tuppence he owed her aloft between two fingers, like a priest holding up the Communion host. When Peg reached for it he pulled back his hand, swallowing it into his palm. 'As low a crowd of corner boys as Enniscorthy ever produced, demanding salutes and God knows what else from respectable people.'

'They're the cream of the country,' Peg said, and as soon as she'd said it, she was sorry. She'd never get a money-grabbing huckster like him to understand, not if she talked to him for a twelvemonth.

'The cream of the country, is it, and they wrecking the same country from end to end? Do you even know what you're fighting for?'

'For the Republic, of course. For the future. For the coming generations.'

'To grow up in a country that hasn't a bridge or railway or decent building left intact. A country ground to its knees by a war that nobody wants. The coming generations are not likely to thank you, I'd say.'

'You can keep your old tuppence,' Peg said, getting out.

She found Nora talking to two young men in trench coats with guns slung over their shoulders and it took her a minute to work out that one of them was Sore-Toes. The other fellow she didn't know, a tall, thin chap with a helmet of tight curls. Sore-Toes saw her and nodded over and the other two turned her way.

Nora looked worried when she saw her face. 'What's the matter?' she said. 'What has you bothered?'

'That ould fellow in there. You wouldn't believe the way he went on at me.'

'Did he now?' said the stranger, putting his hand to the strap of his rifle. 'Do you want me to go in and have a little chat with him?'

'Oh, Lord!' said Sore-Toes, fidgeting on his feet at the thought.

The stranger nodded. 'We can't have it said that we stood idly by while the women of the Republic were insulted.'

'Don't be soft, the pair of you,' said Peg.

'Are you sure?' said the stranger.

'Would you stop your nonsense. He just annoyed me, that's all.'

'If you're sure,' said Sore-Toes, now that the chance of it was past.

'Stop, I said. It would be more in your line now to introduce me to your friend.'

'Denis Heffernan,' said the stranger himself, lifting his cap to her and a second time to Nora. He gave Sore-Toes a puck with his elbow. 'Where's your manners, Delaney?'

'Oh,' said Sore-Toes. 'Sorry. Miss Peg Parle and Miss Nora O'Donovan.'

'Two fair and fatigueless fighters for Ireland, I gather.'

'We do our bit,' said Peg.

An awkward silence followed the introductions. To fill it Peg said, 'Is it true we've taken over the Portsmouth Arms?'

'Aren't we on our way there now ourselves? You should see who can you get staying there. Give us the *rothars* and we'll wheel them up for you.'

He took the bars of Peg's bicycle and jerked his head towards Nora's. 'Hey! Delaney!'

Sore-Toes resentfully took Nora's bicycle. Peg fell into step beside the new boy, leaving Nora and Sore-Toes to come together. He seemed all right, this boy, a little bit full of himself maybe but it was nice to be meeting new people instead of the same old faces from Mucknamore. She was surprised it wasn't Nora who'd pulled his interest. Nora looked even lovelier than usual this evening, her eyes all lit up. But lucky, it wasn't every fellow who liked his girls petite and quiet.

'So tell us what's been happening,' Peg said, as they began to walk towards the bridge. 'There's that many rumours about we don't know what to believe.'

Heffernan filled her in. The armies had been co-existing in the town for some days, each remaining in their own quarters, with only occasional shots being fired by one or the other. An uneasy tension hung over them all as they waited to hear the news from Dublin and to receive their orders. Yesterday morning, a column of Staters had marched out of their quarters to take over Enniscorthy Castle.

'Mr Roche and his family who live there were none too impressed. But not even he could argue with a battalion of National Army rifles. As we speak, they're moving more troops in there and—'

'They've set up a machine gun,' Sore-Toes shouted from behind. 'On the roof.'

'Hey!' Heffernan said, throwing a look back over his shoulder. 'Who's telling this yarn?' He turned back to Peg. 'He's right,' he said. 'They have a machine gun looking down on us now from the Castle roof but we've not been hanging about ourselves. The courthouse has been fortified and tomorrow we're going to take over a photographer's place beside it and a couple of other adjacent houses. And at the moment we've a troop clearing out St Mary's.'

'St Mary's?'

'The Protestant church.'

Peg laughed. 'No! You're codding?'

'I'm not. The church has a fine belfry. With the Staters up in the world on the roof of their castle, we needed to climb up there to meet them.'

'And the Proddie church is the only other building in the town that's high enough.' Sore-Toes laughed his peculiar gurgling laugh.

'Have you been up there, Sore-Toes?' Nora asked.

'No, but—'

'Sore-Toes?' laughed Heffernan. 'Sore-Toes! Is that what you call him? He told me his name was Martin.'

Sore-Toes's whole face and neck turned red. Just then, a sound like thunder approached from behind, rescuing him. Two military motors appeared and rumbled past, each packed with men, flags fluttering from all sides of the vehicles.

'They're Tippmen,' Sore-Toes said, bringing up his hand in a salute. Peg and Nora followed suit, touching their fingertips to their temples.

'Reinforcements are pouring in,' said Heffernan. 'We've at least fifty men from Tipperary already. More Dublin boys are on the way too.'

Sore-Toes was leaning on the handlebars of the bicycle to look after the disappearing lorries, his mouth hanging open around his too-big tongue. You could drive a coach and four through that mouth, Peg thought.

'We'd better move on,' Heffernan said.

As they got into the heart of the town, they found people standing at their doors to watch the activity. Peg felt self-conscious walking past in her uniform, her first-aid knapsack on her back, flanked by the two boys with rifles. They were like actors on a stage, she felt, all eyes turned their way, with a scrutiny so silent that she could hear the tick of the bicycle wheels circling.

The hotel was protected by a wooden barrier held together with barbed wire and fortified with sandbags. But the two volunteers standing guard of the door knew Denis and let the four of them climb in over the restraint.

Inside, soldiers swarmed all round, their activity contrasting with the luxury of their surroundings. Tables and chairs had been upended, piled high behind the windows. The dining room was now a store for ammunition, grenades and other explosives. The bar had been sealed off. At the reception desk, two officers Peg had never seen before pored over a map of the town, one making lines on it with a pencil. Denis Heffernan lifted Peg's bicycle up over his head and led them through as if he had lived in the place all his life. Sore-Toes copied him and they carried the two vehicles through to the back door and the yard outside. 'They'll be safe there,' said Heffernan.

'Where are the girls?' Peg asked. 'Have you seen Molly, Sore-Toes?'

'She was in the basement earlier,' he said.

'That's where most of the women are holed up,' said Heffernan.

Down there too, activity was humming, women in groups performing various tasks: washing and drying dishes, making bread, mopping the floor, wiping down shelves and tables. In a side room off the kitchen, a group was cutting up bandages and making first-aid dressing packs.

They found Molly in a corner of the kitchen, blacking a cooker. 'Ah, girls, it's great to see you. D'you want some dinner? What's left is going to the pigs.' She upended a big pot to show them the remains of a stew. 'They ate well, but I could heat this up for you. Do you fancy?'

They declined.

'I'm surprised to see yourself here, Nora,' Molly said, with her usual directness.

'I had to come,' Nora said.

'It's great you came, that's what I mean. Isn't it amazing? I have to keep pinching myself, so I do. Cat is coming up too. She sent a message with Jim Healy that she'll be up in the morning.'

A soldier came in and slapped a heavy brown cardboard box on one of the long tables. 'Wait till you see what we got you,' he said.

Molly slit the box open with a knife. It was packed from base to brim with sausage meat, separate pounds wrapped in greaseproof paper. She picked out one pack, held it up for the others to see. The volunteer slapped his hand down on the top of another box. 'Rashers of bacon,' he said. Another slap on another box: 'Black pudding.'

'Where have you been?' Molly asked.

'Buttle's meat factory. Provisions for the Irish Republican Army, I told the supervisor. He wasn't too inclined to do his patriotic duty until I made him acquainted with Betsy here.' He tapped the barrel of his revolver.

'We'll have a feast and a half in the morning,' Molly said. 'We'll get up early and make brown bread for it. You'll help, girls, won't ye?'

'Of course we will,' Peg said. 'Isn't that what we're here for?'

'If you're not busy now, you could take over the last tea round. Mary-Ann Maloney said she'd do it with me, but to tell the truth, we could both do with a bit of a break. We've been hard at one thing or another since the forenoon.'

She showed them where the cups were kept and told them to put the milk and sugar directly into the big teapots. 'They'll have to take what they get and be glad to get it,' she said. 'We've too many to serve to keep to the niceties.' When everybody was finished, the cups had to be collected, washed and dried and replaced in the cupboard for the morning.

'Leave it to us, Molly,' Peg said. 'You've done your bit for the day.'

They made the tea as instructed and carried it up. Peg took charge of the big teapot with the two handles. Nora followed behind with a tray of cups stacked two high. Everyone was delighted to see them. 'Here comes the tea,' the shout went up. 'Good girls.' They saw Barney in a corner with a group and he came over but there was no time to talk; everybody wanted refreshment. First the tea ran out, then cups, then tea again. It took five journeys to the kitchen before all were catered for.

Collecting the cups was an altogether more relaxed task, with time for a bit of banter, meeting up with old acquaintances, being introduced to new, so many new people they couldn't possibly remember them all. When the crowd around them thinned out a bit, Barney slipped across again, he and Nora both flushing red just at being near to each other.

'Is there any bit of news?' Peg asked, trying to cover their embarrassment.

'Nothing much,' said Barney. 'Still just preparation work.'

'But we're definitely going to make a strike?'

'Definitely. But not tonight. We need the church back first. The vicar sent a representation to Fleming, asking if he could do Sunday services as normal, then we could have it back.'

'That's gas,' Nora said, flicking a little smile at him.

'Isn't it just? A Protestant minister bowing the knee to the likes of us.'

'I never thought I'd see such a thing,' said Peg.

'Anyhow, we obliged him,' said Barney. 'The lads made good the defences and have vacated the church until noon tomorrow so the Protestant prayers can be said.'

'I think it's a generous gesture,' said Peg. 'It shows our finer instincts have not been blunted.'

'It might be more of a military motive,' Barney said. 'Reinforcements are still coming in. The more we have the better, before we make our move.'

'So it'll be tomorrow, you think?'

'That's what everyone's saying. Tomorrow afternoon, probably.'

Sore-Toes bounded over to them, like an over-keen hound. 'I've got a room for ye, girls.'

'Did you? Thanks,' said Peg. 'That's great.'

'It's number twenty-seven. On the second floor. Ye'd want to be taking it now to keep it.'

'We've cups to collect yet, Sore-Toes. Is there a key you could give us?'

'The key for it can't be found, which was how I got it. I'm after putting a few sandbags on the beds but if ye don't stake your claim, somebody else will take it over.'

Peg frowned. 'Is that the way it is? We don't want to be putting any men out of their beds. Nora and I can bed down anywhere.'

'No,' he said. 'It's yours.'

'But it's the men need their sleep, more than us. If there's action tomorrow they'll want their wits about them.'

'No. It's for you,' he said, in the tone of a stubborn two-year-old.

While this one-sided conversation was going on, Nora and Barney had drawn together. Now Nora, a blush flashing across her face, whispered in Peg's ear to ask if she'd mind if they went for a walk after they'd finished. Barney stood apart, pretending not to listen.

'Go on ahead,' Peg said. 'I can finish off here.'

'Are you sure?'

'Mind yourselves, though. Don't go putting yourselves in the way of any stray bullets.'

Sore-Toes piled some empty cups onto her tray. 'So, will I go up and mind it for you? Until you're ready?'

'Really, Sore-Toes, there's no need to go to all this trouble . . .'

'Where's the trouble? There's no trouble.' Specks of saliva spattered out of his mouth on each 'b'.

'All right, so. Go on.'

It was three-quarters of an hour later before she got upstairs but he was still standing guard outside the door and when he saw her coming, his face spilled into his slack, sloppy smile and he threw the door open as proud as a bridegroom on honeymoon night. Two twin beds under each window. Neat brown bedspreads. A sink with running water.

'It's lovely,' she said, feeling a compliment was called for.

'Ye'll need to put that dressing table against the door to keep it closed. Otherwise they'll be coming in on top of you all night.'

'We'll be grand.'

'You're at the back here, so even if there is shooting . . .'

'I don't think there will be, not tonight. Where are you sleeping yourself?'

'Downstairs.'

'On the floor, I suppose?'

He shrugged.

'I meant what I said, Sore-Toes, there's no need—'

He waggled his hand at her, that big wet smile allowing her no more objections. She shrugged. 'All right, so. If you're sure. Thanks again.'

She turned to go in, her hand on the door handle when he said her name – 'Peg' – in a voice that made her fear he was going to make some sort of declaration.

'Goodnight, so,' she said again, and went to close the door behind her.

'Wait,' he said. 'Wait a minute. I—'

'Yoo-hoo!' came a voice. It was Molly, bustling along the corridor, waving a key at them. 'Yoo-hoo! Look! I got one too!'

Peg was never so glad to see Molly in all her life.

'Have ye heard the news?' she asked out of a hot face.

'No,' said Peg. 'What news? Tell us.'

'There's pure uproar below. Fleming is on the rampage. Pat Simmons and his lot got into the store and started passing bottles of stout around after Fleming gave strict orders that no drink was to be touched. Carty caught them and raised the roof.'

'Carty did right,' Peg said. 'It's a war we're here for, not a night out.'

'Marky Field and Pat Murphy have been put on guard duty outside the store.'

'No harm meant,' said Sore-Toes, his smile showing where his sympathies lay. 'Haven't they had a long old day of it?'

'Yerra, Sore-Toes, don't be talking daft,' said Peg. 'If they start drinking, discipline will go out the window.'

'That's what Carty said,' Molly nodded.

'If they could keep it to a bottle or two, maybe it would be all right. But you know what they're like.'

Sore-Toes said, 'That's right, of course, when I think about it. Of course that's right.'

Peg decided to take the chance to make her exit. 'I don't know about you two,' she said, 'but I'm exhausted. I'm off to bed now. Goodnight to you both.'

Closing the door, she caught sight of Molly's surprise at her abruptness. Inside, she leaned her forehead against the inside of the door and could hear their voices in the corridor.

Molly said, 'What's wrong with her? Is she all right?'

'I don't know,' said Sore-Toes.

'Where are you going?'

'Duty calls.'

'Does it now? No sign of it calling you a minute ago, before I came along.'

'I was only showing Peg her room.'

'Of course you were.' Molly's tone was facetious and from the other side of the door, Peg could feel Sore-Toes's confusion. After a long silence, he said, 'I'd better go.'

Molly burst out laughing. 'Goodnight, Sore-Toes,' she said, as his footsteps retreated. 'Don't go getting yourself shot now.'

As far as Peg could hear, only one set of steps moved away. She imagined Molly outside the door, looking after Sore-Toes's disappearing back, mulling over possibilities. She moved away from the door and, sure enough, a moment later heard a knock-knock and Molly stuck her head in. 'Did I interrupt something there?'

'What's that supposed to mean? Of course you didn't.'

'You left in a mighty hurry.'

'I'm just tired, is all. It was a long cycle we had today.'

'You don't look that tired.'

Peg wasn't going to answer that.

'Maybe yourself and Mr Delaney are becoming more than friends?'

'Molly, don't be doting.'

'I suppose he's no great shakes. But it would do you good to be with someone else, even if you weren't that pushed. Get you over Mr D.O.D.'

'Oh, I'm well over that, believe me.'

'If you are, why not give poor Sore-Toes a look-in?'

'I'm only going to say it to you once more, so open your ears, girl. *Not a chance.*'

Molly rolled her eyes. 'He has it bad for you. You must know that. Everyone knows that.'

'Listen, Molly, I'm awful tired . . . We'll see you in the morning, Nora and I, in the kitchen. About half-six, isn't it?'

'Between half-six and seven.'

'Grand. We'll be there.' Peg sat down on the bed.

'Speaking of Nora, where is she?'

Did the girl never give up nosing? 'I'm not sure.'

'Oh?'

'There's no "Oh?" about it. She off doing some job.'

'Is she? What job?'

'Molly, will you give it a rest? I don't know, I said. She didn't tell me what job. Are you going to go or do I have to throw you out?'

'You *are* throwing me out, grumpy-drawers. All right, I'm gone. Goodnight.'

25

On the Wednesday morning, Barney woke with the dawn. He was stiff and sore from sleeping on hard ground, pains up his lower back into his neck and arms, but he felt no distress. The beat of his blood was humming, happiness – no, joy – throbbing through him.

He was lying at Nora's feet, her boots beside his face, as she took what sleep she could on the hard chair he'd found for her the evening before. Her sleeping face above him leaned to one side, her cheek resting on a first-aid pack rolled into a rough pillow, her mouth slightly open, a sliver of wet visible on her bottom lip. Tendrils of hair escaped their clips and curled loose. A trench coat – his coat – was a blanket wrapped around her waist.

Just to look at her sleeping face there beside him . . . He could hardly credit it . . .

And in forty minutes' time, he would be working on a job, a secret mission, with no less a man than Ernie O'Malley, an O/C fresh from the battles in Dublin, come south to organize the Wexford contingent.

At last, Barney felt like he imagined a proper soldier should feel, part of a real army, fighting a real campaign, with manoeuvres and maps and plans, not the road-trenching and bridge-blowing that they had been calling war up to this.

From his worm-eye position, he surveyed the room. All over the floor, bodies lay asleep, angled into every kind of attitude and position, some even piled on top of others. Coats and jackets served as blankets, any bit of rolled-up fabric could be a pillow. Even girls slept on the hard floor though most had been given chairs or cushions.

Since Monday, they had spent their nights and much of their days in this storehouse on the river, the property of a Mr Yates. For the past three nights, the two armies had been sniping at each other from a fair distance without anything in the way of progress. The only casualty was a young fellow hit by a bullet ricocheting off the hotel wall. Since Monday also, Peg and Nora had been off kitchen duty, allocated to communications and despatch. The Republicans had seven different posts around the town, all needing to be kept in communication with each other. It was dangerous work, cycling through the bullet-ridden streets, but the more dangerous it was, the more willing they seemed to do it. Both girls, trained in first aid, were also on standby for casualty duty. He was proud of the pair of them – not a word of complaint about discomfort, though food was scarce and roughly served and sleep a luxury, taken in snatches, fully dressed and booted. Last night it was after two before the shooting quieted enough for sleep.

Nora had helped him to see the true nobility of their cause. She was as gentle as a girl could be but in her own way as dedicated as his mother and sister and he found a half-hour of her soft talk more persuasive than a lifetime's lectures from them. So here they were, the soldier and the auxiliary, fighting side by side for the same dearly held beliefs. He had told her how he admired her bravery, especially after Dan's defection. He had told her everything, everything, in snatched whispers, surrounded by others, the noise of sniper-shots clacking all around them. Things he never thought he'd reveal to a living soul. And she was entrusting him the same way.

It was an unexpected side-effect of the fight, this open expression of their feelings. In Mucknamore, it would have taken them months – years, maybe – to get to where they were with each other now. Away from the watchful eyes of parents and elders, with bullets firing, the usual reservations had melted.

Everybody knew about him and Nora now. She had pushed the worry of that away, he knew, shoved it forward into the future, and he had promised her he would protect her in whatever ordeal she might be facing when she went back to Mucknamore. She'd brushed off the offer – 'What can you do?' she'd said, turning her gooseberry-green eyes on him – and he hadn't been able to say what he had in mind, which was that he could marry her and be done with it. It was too soon to say it, he was afraid he'd frighten her, but that was what he wanted. If they had that, there was nothing her family could do to them. That was what he had to make her see.

It was a wonder she could sleep like that on that wooden chair. He pushed himself up on one elbow to get a better look at her. Her breathing was heavy, almost but not quite a snore. For comfort, she had loosened the top two buttons of her blouse and he could see a white V of skin at her neck. He followed the line of it down her clothed body. Her figure was neat and soft and tantalizing. Sleep made it look like it was on offer to him, relaxed in a way she would never be when her waking self was in control.

He checked the clock: quarter-past five. Time to go. He stood, and, with a quick look around to make sure all were asleep, bent and tucked the trench coat up around her shoulders; he would manage without it. He dropped a small kiss onto her forehead and she moved in her sleep.

'Oh— Is it – Barney . . . ?'

'It's morning,' he whispered. 'I have to go.'

He kissed her again and she reached her arms up around his neck and, still half-asleep, kissed him full on the lips with the kind of kiss she'd never given him before. The kind of kiss that made him want to stay. But they were surrounded by others, some already waking, and besides, he had to get to this job. She would be impressed when he told her about it afterwards. He detached her hands from behind his neck, placed one kiss on each bracelet of wrinkles round her wrists and tucked her arms back under his coat. Before he was done, she was asleep again.

The light was lifting. He picked up his rifle and his canvas ammunition sling and in stockinged feet picked his way between the bodies to the back exit. The door squeaked as he opened it. That's another few awake, he thought, pushing it closed behind him. Down the lane and around the corner. No firing to disturb the morning quiet yet. He sat on a doorstep to put on his boots, attached the ammo sling to his waist, checked his supply. These first minutes of the summer day were beyond lovely, bright and definite as a coin new-minted, and he stopped for a second to breathe in the sweet dewy morning air. He felt the life within himself expand to meet the day.

He set off again. Turning into the next empty street, he saw two fellows up ahead: Lama and a chap called Denis Heffernan. They were headed where he was going – it was Heffernan who put the job their way. He ran to catch up and jumped in between them, slapping each of them both on the back. 'We're on, so?'

'As on as we'll ever be, boy,' said Heffernan.

Lama just nodded but Barney could see excitement rising off him like steam off boiling water. Frank Carty had got a tip-off that the enemy had secretly occupied the post office, planning to ambush Republicans from there. Their intention was that the surprise would be the other way round: instead of them being ambushed, Ernie O'Malley was to lead them in an attack on the building, putting a brake on the army's plans before they even had a chance to get them going.

So eleven men met at the corner of Friary Place. Ernie O'Malley and another Dublin-man, Paddy O'Brien; Paddy Fleming, head of the Third Eastern Division, and Frank Carty, adjutant; five Enniscorthy volunteers, Denis Heffernan, Dick Sullivan, Thomas Roche, Michael Kirwan, Andrew Redmond; and Barney Parle and Charles (Lama) White, the Mucknamore men. Good men, true men, one and all. Rifles to the ready, and a plentiful supply of ammunition and grenades.

O'Malley – a wiry redhead, terse and intense – outlined the plan.

They would rush the narrow lane leading to the back of the post office, smash the glass in the windows and through the holes throw in a series of hand grenades.

'Bit rough, isn't it?' Heffernan whispered, out of the side of his mouth to Barney. 'Lobbing grenades into a room full of sleeping men?'

'He's the boss,' Barney replied.

O'Malley burned with the sort of single-mindedness usually seen in missionary priests, but wars aren't won by the fainthearted. And the aim was to win, wasn't it?

Down the hill they trooped, directing their rifles right and left as they went but encountering no trouble. Turning the corner, they passed a pub that commanded a view of the lane but none of them took any notice of that. (And why would they? It stood as shuttered and silent as the other buildings around it.) They trod past it and down the lane, fast and quiet as they could be in their boots, towards the red-brick post office that faced them at the end. The windows were barred but O'Malley managed to shatter the glass with the butt of his rifle and Fleming, Carty and Sullivan copied him. *Smash! Smash! Smash!* O'Malley took the catch off the first grenade, lobbed it in. Then a second one. Everyone stopped: they heard the pop of bursting cases and they pulled back, leaned away from the building, hands over their heads to the blast. But the blast didn't come. In its place, silence lengthened until it became obvious that it wasn't going to shatter.

'Fuck it!' said Fleming. 'Don't tell me. More faulty ammo.'

The attention of all eleven men was on the red-brick building with the smashed windows. So they didn't hear the window of the public house behind them sliding open, nor see the barrels of three guns nudging out. The crack of rifle fire behind them came as a complete surprise. Denis Heffernan fell instantly to the ground, folding like a concertina. Another series of cracks and Paddy O'Brien staggered and sprawled forward, his collar shooting red. Michael Kirwan shouted, 'I'm hit. Jesus, I'm hit.'

O'Malley turned and emptied his revolver in the direction of the fire. Tom Roche and Barney copied him, while at the same time trying to move towards safety. The others had scattered, as fast as their love of life could carry them. Kirwan too, despite his wound, was running.

Fleming and Carty, the two nearest the wounded O'Brien, lifted and carried him between them, hauling him back along the lane behind the protective fire of O'Malley, Roche and Barney Parle. Roche took a graze in the face, cried out but carried on, retreating backwards, firing all the way. Somehow they succeeded in getting the injured man around the corner without being gunned down. Barney and O'Malley took cover in a shallow gateway in the wall near where Denis Heffernan had fallen.

The shooting ceased. Barney could hear Heffernan trying to say an Act of Contrition. 'O . . . my God . . .' Slowly he spoke, haltingly, the sound draining from his voice. 'I am . . . am heartily . . . sorry . . .'

'It must be a habit with him,' O'Malley said, 'to be able to say it like that when he is dying.'

Barney stared at the young man on the ground, struggling with his last prayer. He wanted to turn his eyes away from the sight but they were riveted onto the contorted body. 'Is he? Dying?'

'I'm afraid he is.'

Heffernan never got to finish his prayer: he let out a small shuddering gurgle and his voice stuttered to a stop. O'Malley hesitated, but as no more shots came, he went out into the lane. Barney followed. O'Malley put his fingers on the wrist pulse.

'Nothing,' he said, and he dropped the arm, in a careless way that made Barney flinch. Why be squeamish about it? Heffernan didn't know what was done to him now, but still . . .

A thread of blood leaked from the corner of the dead boy's mouth.

'Did you know him?' O'Malley asked.

'I only met him a few days ago. He was the friend of a friend.'

Barney was shaken all the same, ringing with a sense of disbelief. He couldn't believe this was happening. But it was: now they had to pick him up. O'Malley took the legs so Barney took him under the arms, the weight of him on his chest. The head fell to the side, the neck at an impossible angle but they proceeded, back down the lane, hugging the side of the wall as they went, nervous in case of more shots. None come.

O'Malley's talk was all about Paddy O'Brien. The two of them had fought side by side against the Tans, he explained to Barney between breaths, and had been together in the Four Courts in Dublin since last April. When the Four Courts was attacked, O'Brien was one of the worst injured but he was determined to get back into the fight. As soon as he could walk he had joined them in Enniscorthy, his head bandaged to hold it together. He was unfit for service, really. 'But . . .' puffed O'Malley, 'his eagerness to help . . . was greater than his strength . . . His weak and wounded body . . . was made to . . . obey.'

It was clear to Barney that this was what Ernie O'Malley admired, the same sort of never-say-die courage for which he was himself renowned.

Around the corner, they laid Denis Heffernan's dead body on the path. Sullivan had notified first aid and said they were on their way with stretchers. Paddy Fleming came up to them on the street outside with Dick Sullivan. 'The post office wasn't occupied at all,' he said. 'We were set up.'

'Fuckers,' said Sullivan. 'Dirty fuckers.'

Michael Kirwan half lay, half sat against a wall, a hand supporting his wounded side, face bunched with pain. O'Brien was bleeding badly from the chest. O'Malley went over to him. 'Paddy, are you all right?'

He got no reply.

'I think he's been shot in the lung,' Fleming whispered. 'Best not to talk to him.'

The lull in the shooting brought spectators onto the street, already carrying the rumour that there had been a fatality.

'Oh my God, it's true.'

'Who's dead?'

'Who is it?'

'It's Denis Heffernan.'

'Ah, *no*, not young Denis . . .'

In seconds, it seemed, the crowd grew. Even the children were out, staring round their mothers' legs. There was a ring around the dead body, a circle people didn't dare to cross. They stood, awkward with shock, all their looks fixed on the same spot, as if there was nothing else in this world to look at but poor Denis Heffernan, lying there on the pavement, his face open and pale as water, turned up to the sky. Barney took off his own jacket, put it over the dead face, wanting to shield him from the probing eyes. *This isn't a show*, he thought, wondering whether to let a crack of his rifle into the air to scatter them all like so many crows.

Then he heard the bell of the ambulance and it came flying around the corner and the doctor and the Cumann na mBan girls with their medical armbands were jumping down, organizing stretchers and first aid, bristling with duty.

But what was that other noise, like a terrible wailing? The crowd parted as if it was Noah's Red Sea to allow a woman of late middle age – hair half put up, clothes half put on – to come running through, shrieking. She fell to the ground beside the dead young man, threw Barney's jacket off his face. The crowd stood still, very still, some of the heads moving in gentle shakes from side to side.

Mrs Heffernan lifted her son's dead head onto her lap and held it there. Her words were indistinct but the sounds she made were unmistakable. She held his head and rocked it back and forwards, rocked it on her lap just as she once used to rock his little, baby self.

Peg

Dear Diary

It's Wednesday, very late. I'm sitting in the ladies' room of the Portsmouth Arms, locked into one of the water closets with a candle, the only place around here that it's possible to be alone. I can't think right after meeting Dan. He's thrown me into a heap, as he always does. I need to set my thoughts down to steady them.

But before I get to Dan O'Donovan, let me first write these glorious words: The Republic lives! Enniscorthy's fight is over and the 'National' Army defeated!

It didn't take us long in the end. We had a shambles of a morning during which we received a number of injuries and lost one man – that boy Denis Heffernan that Nora and I met with Sore-Toes the other day. After that, Mr O'Malley got decisive. He gave orders to collect all the petrol and explosives we could get our hands on, planning to blow in the yard-gate of the Castle, the army's stronghold, then fire the building.

A deputation of priests, hearing of the plans for this attack, went to see him and asked him to withdraw from the town so that further bloodshed might be prevented. Mr O'Malley said he couldn't do that, that he was here as a soldier and was going to storm the castle soon. If they really wanted to prevent bloodshed, it would be better to interview the garrison and tell them to surrender. He'd arrange a ceasefire for an hour, he said. The news went around the town in no time and the people piled onto the streets. After the hour was up, an army soldier carrying a white flag was led blindfold to our HQ, asking to arrange terms of surrender. And that was that.

We've won. The Republic has won.

I am pleased, of course I am, delighted, though I can't stop thinking about Denis Heffernan. I don't know why I feel so bad about him, I hardly knew the chap. My feeling is that it should never have happened. A lie to pull our men into a sneaky ambush: that's not soldiering.

Watching the green-uniformed soldiers surrender was very satisfactory, hearing them swear they would never again be disloyal to the Republic. It was decided to permit those who had fought in the War of Independence to keep their arms, on condition they took an oath swearing they would not use them again against us. I know this was done from the best of motives but I'm between two minds about it, as are others. We could have done with those guns is one thing but also, can we trust them? They broke their first oath, why do we think they'll keep this one?

We have nowhere to house prisoners, so all we could do was march them out of town. Within a few hours they were back, the green uniforms turning up on the streets and in the pubs. They were greeted magnanimously: our lads are not men to be haughty about victory, especially against old comrades. Again I can see the sentiment is admirable, but is it wise?

That's how we came to meet Dan. Nora and I were walking up through the town, talking about going back home to Mucknamore to face into our ordinary lives. I can't imagine how I'll settle back down but if it's bad for me, it's a far sight worse for poor Nora. The past few days have been like a place apart for us all but for none more than her. How she'll face her family, she doesn't know. She is nothing short of petrified. That we've won will only make her father worse, she thinks. The thoughts of a Republican victory will sicken him and the thoughts that she was part of it . . . fighting against her own brother . . . Uproar, that's what she's facing. And now that everybody knows about herself and Barney, she's terrified he'll get wind of that too.

I tried to console her as we walked out the river-walk that Enniscorthy people call the Prom. Right to the very end we walked, then all the way back, and afterwards we sat on the grass, reluctant to go back to Mr Yates's. These fighting days have really brought her out of herself. She's much freer than she used to be, as if the work here, or maybe being with Barney, has released her from some tightness in herself. But there are still things she finds it hard to talk about, especially about her family. In another person, this unwillingness to speak would be offensive but with Nora, it's something you understand. There's no lack of trust in it, just a discomfort with disclosure. You have to respect her privacy. And admire her loyalty.

We sat for ages. Lack of sleep had caught up with us and we were too tired to move. The sun took a long time about setting and even after it went down, the sky held onto the light, reluctant to let go of the day. For a time we remained there, murmuring into the dusk, but then darkness settled in for real and we knew we had to go. Reluctantly we lifted our weary bones from the riverside, made our way back into the town.

As we were turning into Slaney Street, at the top of the hill we saw two men arm in arm, one wearing the green uniform of the National Army, the other the trench coat of the Volunteers. The first dark, the other red; the one tall, the other a head shorter. Simultaneously, we both realized who it had to be: our two brothers, arm in arm, their free hands holding their porter bottles. Leaning into each other and singing: *Soldiers are we, whose lives are pledged to Ireland . . .*

Dan looked down and saw us and stopped his singing. He began to drag Barney down the hill towards us, laughing, nearly knocking him over, he took it so fast. 'There's the girls,' he said and – foolish! foolish! – I felt my heart take an excited tumble as they rushed towards us.

'Look at the state of you,' I said to Barney when they righted themselves. I ignored the other fellow.

'Ah, Peg,' Barney said, half wheedling me and half annoyed. 'Don't be like that . . .'

'Barney, you're drunk.'

'G'way out of that. A few drinks, is all . . . a few drinks with my friend here . . .'

'Friend now, is it?' You'd think he'd never heard what Dan O'Donovan has been going around saying about us.

''Tis a good thing, surely?' says Barney. 'Men who were shooting at each other earlier today are now able to enjoy a drink together. That's a grand thing. Don't you think so, Nora?'

Nora didn't answer.

Dan had a look of drink taken, loose lips, eyes too heavy-lidded and moist, though you'd need to know him well to see it. Barney was visibly stocious, barely able to keep himself standing. He was looking at Nora with his feelings all over his soft, silly face.

'What separates us is nothing . . . nothing compared to what unites us. It's Ireland we both love. Isn't that right, Dan?'

'Sure, Barney. That's it. Good old Ireland.' I could have slapped him, and my fool of a brother too, who hadn't even the wit to see that he was being laughed at.

Then what did Dan do only lean across and whisper in my ear, so the others couldn't hear: 'It's grand to see you. You're looking good.'

My traitor heart twisted inside me.

Out loud to everybody else, he said: 'I think the four of us should go for a bit of a walk, to sober up this fellow.' He elbowed Barney in the chest. 'What do you say, girls?'

My insides took another nosedive. 'No,' I cried, almost shouting, so the three of them looked at me in surprise.

'No,' I said again, more controlled this time.

'The Prom by the river is lit all the way to the end,' Dan said. 'It makes a nice walk.'

Barely lit, as Nora and I knew, having only just come back up from down there. Full of shadows and trees along the way. And part of me was tempted, I admit it as I always admit the truth to you, my dear diary, but – thank God! – I had the wit to resist. I knew now that he had it in him to be with me under some tree down the Prom tonight and back with Agnes Whitty and the National Army tomorrow.

'No,' I said a third time. 'We're not going anywhere with you. We wouldn't be caught dead with you two, the condition you're in.'

I looked over at Nora and was pleased to see her nodding her head in agreement. I thought she might have been keen to step out with Barney, but I should have had faith in her good sense – what decent girl would want to be caught near either of them? Only an eejit like myself would even consider it.

'And what about Ireland?' I said to my brother.

'Ah, now, Peg.' He stopped, fumbled around his sodden head for words. 'Ireland is . . . Ireland will be . . .'

'I mean it,' I said. 'Go to your bed. We've a long way home to find tomorrow, and we've work yet to be done. I shouldn't need to remind you, Barney.'

Enniscorthy's battle might be won but there was Wexford town and the other towns still to be freed. And the Provisional Government weren't going to take defeat lying down. Barney shouldn't – none of us should – be there, on the side of a hill, consorting with the enemy. 'Come on, Nora.'

We walked away from them, up the hilly street, not looking back. Not once, not even when we heard Dan make one of his remarks. What he said was indistinguishable but I know it was something facetious by the tone of voice in which it was said and by the way Barney let out a guilty laugh and then tried to swallow it.

26

1974

Unleashed, that is how I think of myself. Like I am letting out a breath that I have been holding since I was born. I am in Dublin, in university (Dublin! University!). This is where I live now, where I will live for the next four years (except holidays). Mucknamore is now (almost) my past. I have to hold myself back from wallowing down on the soft grass, from throwing my books and papers in the air, from shouting out loud.

Instead, I walk circumspectly down to the lake that is the centrepiece at University College Dublin, a sunken concrete tub, square like a swimming pool but brown-grey, not blue. Leaves, papers, bottles, rusty tin cans, too-white plastic cups and other, less identifiable rubbish collects in its corners and lurk among the murk at the bottom. Hundreds of extinguished cigarette butts line the sides. It's hardly picturesque, but still the students are drawn to it: they amble around the wide flat steps that form the perimeter, or loll on nearby benches. Couples lay down coats to lie on the grassy verge, limbs twisted around each other.

Underpinning my delight is the knowledge that Rory O'Donovan is here too, walking around this very campus somewhere. Early this morning, I saw him, standing outside Lecture Theatre M, a crowd around him. He looks good: long, straight, black hair looped behind his ears. A long military coat, down to his ankles, complete with epaulettes on the shoulders. Black jeans and black poloneck jumper underneath. Compared to most of the other guys in their woolly jumpers and duffel coats, he is . . . oh, incomparable. For a while I watched him like I used to watch him at Mass when we were children, then I slipped away leaving him to his new friends. It won't be long, I know. We'll find each other soon.

He seems to have met a lot of people already. I am the only person from my old school in my faculty. Deirdre is doing science, Monica has gone to Trinity College, others are doing secretarial courses, or teacher training or are going to be nurses or doctors or vets. But I will get to know people, I know I will, interesting, intelligent, amusing people. Everything is here for me, for the taking.

The convent, which once felt like a release to me, had become a prison in my last two years there. Those days divided up by bells, with nuns watching us always, with Mass in the morning and prayers in the evening and people everywhere, always, became more and more unbearable. Deirdre was expelled in fifth year for sneaking out over the wall to go to a dance, though she was allowed back as a day girl to do her Leaving Cert. I toiled on, growing ever more amazed at the ability of so many girls to put up with it, to be good girls. I pretended to be one of them but I was aimed at the Leaving Cert. and escape. It came just in time.

Books got me through: reading and knowing that there were other lives, other ways to live, waiting for me when I got out. It was no way to live – waiting, waiting for life to begin – but now it has. My moment is here. October sunshine skims the square of flat, still lakewater, burnishing it to brass and my heart swells with the beauty of the day. Rapture cracks through my skin and my walk turns into a skip down the concrete path. Inside the red folder is my timetable, a reading list and four pages of close-written notes from my first lecture. Professor Augustine Martin on 'Anglo-Irish Literature: The Irish Literary Revival 1893 to 1916'. Augustine: even his name is something better than I am used to. I walk on, my red folder clasped to my chest.

Behind me, a shout roars out. 'Oi, O'Donovan, get back here.'

A stampede of feet and leaping yells comes hurtling my way. I turn to see him, Him, running towards me, his coat (that military coat) crooked across one arm. He runs a smoker's run, to the tune of gaspy breaths, and behind a group of guys running after him are gaining ground. When he sees me ahead, his face cracks into a smile. 'Well . . . well . . . If . . . it isn't . . . Dev,' he pants. I expect him to run past but instead, he grabs me from behind and swings me out in front of him like a shield. Into my ear he whispers, 'Sorry about this.'

Out loud to the others he says, 'Stop right there . . . or . . . the lady gets it.'

I try to pull away from him. 'Rory. For God's sake! Are you insane?'

His grip tightens on my arms. The idiocy of the warning has confused his pursuers. They turn to a tall guy with arms so long they almost reach his knees. He moves forward. 'You'll have to do better than that, O'Donovan.'

'I mean it. One . . . more step . . . and in she goes.'

'Hey! Leave me out of your boy games.'

He pulls me closer still, so the length of his body behind me lines mine. His hair tickles my face; it smells of stale smoke. And of him.

Long-Arms advances cagily and Rory bends me over, towards the water, as a response. I kick backwards at him and connect with his shin. 'Ow!' His voice is wounded.

'Let her go!' insists Long-Arms.

Kick or no kick, Rory is resolute. 'Lay off your yes-men and I'll think about it.'

His opponent looks behind, gives a toss of his head, says, 'All right, lads, you can leave him to me.'

Objections murmur up but the group disbands, most moving away. One or two stay behind to watch, hopeful of action.

'Now,' he says. 'Let her go.'

'Yeah. As soon as you clear off the same way your stooges went.'

'I'm not going anywhere, pal. You owe me and I always get what I'm owed.' He advances.

'I told you,' says Rory. 'One more move and in she goes.'

'Look, you can fuck her in for all I care. I just want what's mine.'

'Stop this, both of you. You're being ridiculous!' I twist my mouth down towards Rory's hand, my teeth close around flesh and bone as I bite, hard. A yelp of pain loosens his grip a fraction, enough for me to slip away. I am pulling free when I feel a hand, his hand, between my shoulder blades. I have one perching, teetering moment of disbelief – he's *pushed* me? I'm going to *fall*? – then I teeter forward, hands clawing the air.

I hear Long-Arms shout – 'For fuck's sake, O'Donovan' – as cold, clammy water slams up to meet me. As I break the surface, my nose fills. Gasping, spluttering I find my feet, stand up. The water is shallow, halfway up my thighs. Water streams from my eyes, my hair, my clothes. Water and rivulets of rage.

'What . . . Why . . . Why did you *do* that?'

Around the lake, people are looking, pointing and laughing, delighted with the action. Rory's face is a pouch of mixed feelings: surprise at himself, stifled laughter, contrition. And something else entirely. I feel his eyes on my breasts, a look that plucks me out of my own body, so that I see what he sees: my wet top clinging and my hands up squeezing water out of my long red hair. I am Woman in Water. Venus among the waves. Miss Wet T-shirt.

Long-Arms extends a hand to me, an offer of help. Rory sees this, crouches and proffers his hand too, and it is his I take, his palm warm and dry against my own. He tries to pull me up but my grip is loosened by slippery water.

'I can't,' I say.

He bends closer and says, 'Give me your other hand too.' So I do. He leans forward onto his toes, penitent, keen to help. Leans too far. A sudden yank on both hands, as hard and strong as I can make it. His weight slips. 'Nooooo!' he cries. With a splash, he's in.

'Yes!' I cry.

'Well done!' Long-Arms cries.

Before Rory has righted himself in the water, I am hauling myself out. Trying to ignore the growing audience around the lake, I retrieve my folder and walk away from them all, my knees turned out, cowboy-style, my jeans dragging between my legs, my socks squelching inside my boots. I press my way through a tunnel of laughing faces.

I haven't gone far when I hear him behind me, calling. 'Hey! Dev! Wait.'

It's the name that stops me, his name for me and all it holds in it. I look back. He is clambering after me in wet clothes, insouciant of the nudging crowd, not ignoring them as I was, not even seeing them, his eyes fastened on me.

'Wait,' he shouts. 'Please. Wait.'

I wait.

When he reaches me, he is puffed out again. 'Pax,' he pants, index and middle finger crossed and raised to me, like we're a pair of schoolyard children.

'Pax?' I throw my eyes skywards. '*Pax?*'

'Ah, come on. We're evens now.'

'We are *not*.'

'We're not?'

'No, we are *not*. Why did you do that to me?'

'I'm sorry.'

'What the hell were you thinking of?'

'I don't know. Nothing. I wasn't thinking, was I?' His eyes are beginning to crinkle.

'What about that other guy?'

'He's gone. I gave him what he wanted.'

'Pity you didn't do that in the first place.' My voice is still cross but my anger is fading, overwhelmed by other feelings. 'What did he want?'

'A magazine.'

'A *magazine*?'

'Mmmm. *Furry Freak*. This month's issue, precious stuff.'

'I ended up in the lake over goddamn *Furry Freak* magazine?'

He nods, and releases his laughter.

I find I'm laughing too. 'You're ridiculous, you know that?'

He nods again.

'You read – no, you *steal* – ridiculous magazines. You do ridiculous things. You even *look* ridiculous.' His hair is dry-black on top but wet-black at the ends, as if dye is growing out. His wool jumper is leaking runnels of water down his legs and around his feet.

'You look wonderful,' he says. 'Goddamn gorgeous.'

The words stop the laughter bubbling in my throat.

Then he is bending down and scooping me up. God, what now?

'Come on. You can't walk in those wet jeans. I'm bringing you home to dry.'

He lifts me like I weigh nothing, settles me into place: my knees looped over one arm, the rest of me curled tight into his chest. His wet sweater soaks my cheek but underneath is the heat and smell of his skin.

After a few minutes of carrying me, his breathing becomes alarming.

'You don't have to carry me. Put me down.'

'No . . . Least I . . . can . . . do . . .'

'Rory, I mean it. You can hardly breathe. Put me down.'

'. . . Nearly . . . there.'

'Where?'

'Car . . . park. Don't talk . . .'

He has a car? He has indeed. He deposits me at the passenger door of a VW Beetle, grey and ancient. When he's regained his breath he asks, 'Do you like it? My sister gave me an advance on my grant.'

'You're on a grant?'

'Every farmer in the country gets a grant. Creative form-filling.' He opens the door for me. 'Hop in.'

I sit in onto the leather seat with a squelch.

'If you spent your grant on a car, what are you going to live on?'

'The old man has given me some money and I've got myself a job. Barman at the Arrow.'

'All in two days?'

'Not bad, eh?'

We drive out of Belfield, down the dual carriageway to Donnybrook, but instead of turning right for my flat in Sandymount, he goes left, towards Ranelagh.

'I live the other way.'

'Do you want to go home? I was going to bring you to my place.'

'Oh.'

'Is that all right? There's a launderette beside me. They'll dry the clothes for us.'

His flat is wonderful: two rooms and a bathroom all to himself. Like most students, I am sharing. Deirdre and I have rented a cramped bedsit with a kitchen in the corner behind a counter. It's decorated in a flowery wallpaper and swirly carpet combination that makes us feel seasick but I love it because Mrs D. had wanted me to live in a university hostel run by nuns. The idea of Deirdre and me loose in Dublin with no supervision filled her with horror but Maeve and Granny Peg came in on my side and she had to give in. Rory's flat is in a different league: smooth beige walls and floors, a suite of furniture that matches, a breakfast bar, a dining table for four. On one of the walls, he has put up a poster of 'Che' Guevara, on the others two Salvador Dali prints.

'This is lovely,' I say.

'I spent all summer planning the sort of place I wanted. I've everything in place now. Well, almost everything.'

He sends me a significant look that makes me shiver.

'Come on. We'd better get you out of those clothes.'

Everything he says has two meanings but he doesn't seem to notice.

He plays the gentleman then: shows me how to use the shower; presents me with his dressing gown, soap, shampoo, towels. I undress. The water is strong and hot and I stay under its comfort for a long time, its prickles re-awakening my chill-numbed skin. Afterwards, I wrap myself in his robe and find his smell wafting up to my nostrils every time I move my arms.

When I come out of the bathroom, he is sitting at the counter, wearing only a towel. Hair black and silky as a pelt covers his chest and weaves down his legs to the bare feet resting on the bar of the stool. He has a curl of black hair on each big toe. On the counter, a cup of tea is waiting for me, steaming.

'You can put your clothes into that bag over there,' he says. 'I'll bring them down to the launderette when I've had my shower.'

While he is showering, I sip my tea, look at his books. Stephen King. Leon Uris. James Michener. *Catch-22. Zen and the Art of Motorcycle Maintenance. Lord of the Rings.* Boys' books. On another shelf, beside a large professional-looking camera, are some photography books: some instructional – *The Guide to Freelance Photography* – others full of pictures. I flick through them for a while then I notice a brown manila folder with a black-and-white picture peeping out. I open it and lay the pictures I find out on the counter. At first they look abstract, a series of unusual shapes taken from different angles, then I realize I am looking at close-ups of animal body parts: a cow's udder, a horse's nostril, a sheep's tail, a pig's eye. I sit up on the stool to look closely. They are strange, these fragments of bodies, almost alien.

The bathroom door clicks and he comes back out. Dressed. Fully dressed: jeans and a white T-shirt and even socks.

'Oh, God, those pictures,' he says, when he sees them laid out.

'You took them?'

'Guilty as charged.' He is blushing, just a little.

'No, they're good. Different.'

He shakes his head. 'They didn't work. But I think I'm on to something. I need to keep working it out.'

Uncombed knots of wet hair hang down his back, spattering a line of wet across his T-shirt. He sits beside me on the second high stool, close enough to touch. I smell on him the sharp soap that has also washed me.

'So,' he says with a smile, 'if our mammies could see us now.'

What he said to me at the wedding. My heart leaps to the words and then – somehow – we are leaning into each other and kissing and I am off my stool and he is off his and we are wrapped around each other and I am straining towards him and one of his hands has slipped inside his dressing gown onto my bare body and is gliding across my skin.

He pushes the robe from my shoulders so it slithers to the floor. The buckle of his belt is digging into my belly, and the prod of his swelling underneath it. I am naked against him. Inside me, lust rears. I lean into him, wanting to swallow him up. I want to do everything with him, everything, anything. This is it, at last. What I have been waiting for.

Next morning, I arrive back to my new flat, lips swollen, thighs aching. Deirdre looks up from the table where she has been writing, takes one look at me and lets out a shriek. 'Ah, no,' she says. 'Not you. No, no, no.'

I glance in the little mirror that hangs over the table. Is it so obvious what I have been doing? In the dappled glass, I see my face, split in two by a smile.

'I don't believe it,' Deirdre wails. 'It's not fair.'

I have won a competition I didn't even enter. All through our last year in the convent, Deirdre moaned loud and long about her virginity. Leaving home launched her campaign to rid herself of her seventeen-year-old hymen, her tag of shame. She has a bet with Monica: whoever gets rid first is to be paid a tenner by the other.

'So come on, tell me all. I presume it was the mysterious Mr O'Donovan.'

Deirdre knows a little about Rory now. She cannot understand that we allowed ourselves to be kept apart. Dee would knock aside barriers like boarding schools and summer colleges and vigilant families. She would slip him a note or arrange to 'bump' into him or call to his house by night and throw stones up at his window. She is scornful of my weakness and even more of his. Is he a man or a mouse? Does he really like me at all?

I don't mind her thinking this way. It keeps her from realizing how much I care. I'm not sure why – Deirdre is obsessional about her own crushes – but I'd rather she didn't know that through all the months and years of not being with him, my feelings haven't lessened at all but hardened and brightened inside me, like crystal.

Over cups of instant coffee, I tell her what I am happy for her to know, about the lakeside incident and going back to his place.

'You did it, didn't you?' she says. 'You went all the way?'

I nod. I can't switch off my smile.

'Oh my God. Come on, tell me: what's it like? Did the earth move? Was there blood?'

'Dee!'

'I hope you were careful.'

That turns my insides over. All the way home in the bus, I have been quashing that thought.

'Did he use a condom?' she asks.

'Jesus, Dee, you're unbelievable.'

'Did he?'

'He doesn't like them,' I say. I have no idea whether this is true or not.

'I wouldn't say he's too fond of squally babies either,' Deirdre says. 'You'd want to get yourself down to one of those new clinics for the pill.'

'Clinics?'

'One of the new family-planning clinics. That's what they call them but they're not just for marrieds. You don't even have to be engaged. All you need is your money and your health and they'll sign you up for a prescription there and then.'

'How do you know so much about it?'

'I've looked into it. I intend going down there myself to get kitted out. I'll go with you.'

'But, Dee, you don't even have a boyfriend.'

'That, my dear friend, is a very temporary state of affairs.' She laughs at my face. 'I mean it,' she says. 'I'll bring you down. They're supposed to be really nice.'

'I don't know, Dee . . .'

'You're not labouring under some thick notion that nice girls don't, I hope. You're going. That's it.'

In the afternoon, she skips her zoology practical so we can go together and she is right: it *is* easy: no judgements or disapproval, all so matter-of-fact that my embarrassment feels silly. It takes just twenty minutes to fill out some forms and see a doctor and then we're back outside with six foil-packs of pills each. Six little packs of permission.

At the top of the steps, Deirdre already has hers out of the bag. She selects a pack, pops open Tuesday's bubble. 'Bless us O Lord and these Thy gifts,' she says, stretching out her tongue and receiving the tiny tablet like it's a Communion host. She gulps it down with a grin. 'Amen.'

I open my packet and copy her. The pill is small and hard and sweet on my tongue, covered with a smooth coating that makes it slide down easily.

I get myself a job as a lounge-girl, in the pub where Rory works. Three nights a week I bring trays full of drinks to customers too lazy to go to the bar. The hourly rate is poor, a pittance really, but if I smile and flirt I get good tips, especially towards the end of the night as alcohol loosens the punters' grip on their wallets. I dodge the men's compliments and the occasional pinch; ignore them when they try to look down my white blouse or up my black skirt as I bend forward with the heavy trays; find lines to spar away their slurred come-ons.

From behind the counter, Rory sends me looks that I hold and post back to him: promises of later. We are a couple now: Jo and Rory, Rory and Jo. After the pub doors are bolted and the counters and tables wiped down, we sit with the rest of the staff and have a complimentary night-cap or two. Then we walk home, usually to his place because although it is further away, it is more private. Hand-in-hand we walk, through empty streets where only the late-night chip shops or taxi ranks are awake, our heads blurry with alcohol. The wet tarmacadam is lined with little suns, reflections from the streetlights above, and the loud silence of the streets makes us feel like we are the last people on earth.

I love these walks, weaving from side to side of the pavement, stopping every so often for long deep kisses, not drunk but a long way from sober. Cider is my drink, sweet and fizzy. A bottle or two of Stag cider unclicks something inside me, dizzies me with possibilities. I have always known why men wanted to buy drinks for women; now I understand why women let them.

Back in Rory's bedroom, we astonish each other all over again and afterwards fall asleep, spent, our limbs knotted. Next morning, we wake in our bed salted with sex and begin again.

He takes pictures of me, of my fingers spread wide or rolled into a fist; of the sole of my foot; of one crooked toe and its painted toenail; of my collarbone and the hollow above it; of my elbows over my face; of one breast, first in profile then face on; of my pubic hair, zoomed so close that crinkles of hair fill the entire frame of the print and the pores of the skin beneath are visible. I am always surprised when the pictures come back: they are never what I expect.

Whatever part of me he wants to photograph, I make available to him. He does full-body shots too, usually naked, often after sex. These are my favourites, though I can see that the fragmented ones are more interesting. Even when I'm taken in full, I don't recognize myself in the final picture. With my wild hair and turbulent eyes, I look like somebody else, somebody who knows more than I know.

Soon we're spending every night together but still we haven't had our fill: our days are spent on the soft chairs outside the Student Union shop, burrowed beneath his army coat, hands under each other's clothes, fingertips on fire. We become known as the couple who are always at it. Everybody notices us, Deirdre says, her voice oscillating between censure and jealousy. Enfolded in our haze of love and lust, we never notice them.

My clothes begin to mutate. The coloured V-neck jumpers Mrs D. bought me stay in my wardrobe while I wear grey sweaters or black polo necks hunted down in the Dandelion weekend market. My jeans fray and blanch to fit my new colour scheme of black or white or shades of grey. My skirts turn black, shrink up to well above my knees. Clompy boots weigh down my feet. I think about cutting my hair, short and sharp, but Rory asks me not to. He loves it long, he says. During sex, he twists his fingers in its curls, buries his face in it, uses it to hold back my head when he wants to stare into my eyes.

Mrs D. hates my new image. I go home to visit and when I get off the train she takes a step backwards from the black net tights that climb from my Doc Martin boots all the way up under my short, tight skirt. I knew she would detest this outfit but I wore it anyway. A small mutiny, pathetically small, but I have to try hard not to be nervous.

'Is that a skirt you have on you at all?' she asks, when we get into the car. 'Or are you wearing a black handkerchief by mistake?'

At home, she uses this same line three times – to Gran, to Eileen, to Mrs Keating in the shop – as if it is the height of wit. I hold in my temper, say nothing, but I have changed. Before I might have taken off the offensive clothes; now I pep-talk myself in the mirror, think of Deirdre and what she would do, of Rory and what he would tell me to say. Mrs D. does not realize that she and I have endured so far only because I have been switched to mute. Now I find myself drilling words in my mind, flexing and stretching them for combat.

When I get up next morning, it is the tightness of my faded jeans that brings her eyelids down in exaggerated dismay. 'Where in the name of God did you get those yokes? Where are the nice skirts we got for you when you were going to Dublin?'

I shrug.

'You must have had to jump off the bed to get into those,' she snorts, and turns to Gran, who is drinking tea beside her. 'Mammy, will you talk sense to her. She's losing the run of herself entirely.'

'They're a bit tight, all right,' Gran says.

'They're made to be like that, Gran,' I say, bending my knees to show her that they're quite comfortable.

'You have the figure for them anyway,' she says.

'Oh, thanks very much, Mammy,' Mrs D. says. 'Encourage her, why don't you?' She turns back to me. 'If you insist on wearing such things, you'll have to keep them to the house.'

'There's nothing wrong with stretch jeans,' I say. 'Everybody's wearing them.'

'What wardrobe have you planned for tomorrow? You wouldn't think of going to Mass in anything like that, or what you had on you yesterday, I hope.'

Ah yes, Mass. The clothes will be nothing to this. I take a deep breath and splurt it out: 'I don't go to Mass any more.'

'What!' Mrs D.'s face flashes red. 'What do you mean?'

'I don't believe any more.'

Gran puts down her cup. Fashion she can go along with but this is something different altogether.

'What has got into you?' squeaks Mrs D. 'Is this what I'm spending all that money on your education for? So you can come home with this kind of rubbish?'

'I don't *believe*.'

'As long as you're staying in this house, you'll go to Mass. I don't want to hear another word about it.' She thrusts herself out of her chair, out of the room, slamming the door.

I sit down beside Gran. She says: 'Is it the truth, Jo? Have your really lost your religion?'

'That's not how I think of it, Gran.'

'You don't believe any more, you said.'

'No.'

She looks stricken.

'It's not something to worry about, Gran. Some people do and others don't.'

She shakes her head. 'You'll come back to it,' she says. 'Father Matt was talking about this a while ago, how the young people sometimes leave for a while. But they come back.'

I say, as kindly as I can, 'Maybe, Gran, but I don't think so.'

'I don't want you to say that, Jo.' Her voice sounds strange. 'Some day not too far off, I'll be meeting my Maker. It would make it hard for me to go . . . if I thought I'd never see you . . . hereafter . . .'

If I wind up in hell, she means. 'Oh, Gran . . .'

'And for yourself . . . You'll make life very hard on yourself, Jo, if you don't have God. When you make your mistakes, you'll have nowhere to turn.'

I shrug.

'It's very few of us who don't go some way astray in this life. If you haven't got God, in those times, you'll feel like you have nothing.'

'You don't make mistakes, Gran. You do everything right, always.'

'I was young myself once. I remember what it's like not to know what end of yourself is up.'

I look into the hot coals. I'm young and I'm doing fine. Fine. Without Gran, without Mrs D., without God. I have all I want in Rory.

'I'd say myself you'll come back, wouldn't you?' she says.

'Maybe,' I say, my face hot. 'Who knows? Maybe.'

'I'd say you will. I'm sure of it.'

Back in Dublin, I get a phone call from Maeve. What am I doing to poor Mammy, telling her the truth about all sorts of things? Can't I do what everybody else does and tell a few lies? Do I think that she, Maeve, goes to Mass every Sunday? Is there any need to broadcast the matter? I endure her lecture without putting the phone down but I am not listening to her.

I start to miss lectures, because I am too tired to get up, worn out by pub work and late-night drinking and sex. I skip seminars and tutorials because no class can compete with the thrill of time spent wrapped around my love. I skip meals and appointments and duties.

I fall out with Mrs D. 'Do you intend ever coming home for a weekend again?'

I fall out with my tutors. 'You can't expect to pass your exams if you don't come to tutorials.'

I fall out with Deirdre. 'For God's sake, Jo. You'll have no friends left!'

I put all of me into him. All.

Peg

Dear Diary

The days of our triumph are over already. As soon as news reached Dublin that we had the main towns occupied, a 'National' Army column was dispatched. It arrived in Co. Wexford in the early hours of the morning of July 8th: a convoy of 22 lorries bearing 230 men and 16 officers. First they took Blessington, then Gorey, then Ferns and at about 3pm in the afternoon, they entered Enniscorthy, advancing in two lines, one via Nunnery Road, the other via Wafer Street to come together in Market Square. Our lads got out, what else could they do, when the enemy was protected by more artillery and hardware than has ever been seen in Ireland before – five armour-plated cars, two Lancias, more than 150 rifles and four Lewis guns. And an open 'bird cage' into which they rounded up their captives for all to look on and jeer.

And jeer they did. In each town along the way, the streets were thronged, with town and country people both. All out to greet the soldiers with wild cheering and waving of hats and handkerchiefs, thinking – poor fools – that might had somehow become right. The press is full of stories about these flag-waggers. Not a mention, naturally, of those who stayed home with their heads in their hands, unable to believe what we've come to.

The press is also following orders on how we are to be described: 'Irregulars', not Republicans; our soldiers are 'bands of men', not an army; our engagements are 'incidents', our battles are 'attacks on property or people'.

On Sunday July 9th, the column moved on to Wexford, again

cheered in by rejoicing crowds. They took more than 100 of our boys prisoners, but plenty escaped and before evacuating, they made sure to do as much damage as they could – setting fire to the courthouse and barracks and any other buildings that might be used to house soldiers, felling trees and digging trenches in the roads and bridges, to hamper progress as much as possible.

So it's back on the run for Barney and the boys. The flying columns that won the Tan War for us are forming as I write. We beat the British once with such tactics, and can surely beat them again, even if they have Irishmen sent out this time to do their dirty work.

And dirty it will be, with twenty of their men to each one of ours and every weapon and luxury that an army can have at their supply (money no object, when you've the Bank of England behind you!) while we'll have to make do with neither barracks nor base. This will leave us very unpopular as we'll have no option but to requisition goods and provisions from the shops.

But we must not despair. The real challenge for us now is to carry the truth to the people in the face of falsification and censorship. The people must be woken from their slumber. We know they voted for peace and, knowing all they have suffered, we can understand why. But the fact is, the Republic exists and no one had the right to destroy it or vote it away. That is the message that we must get across.

Dear Diary

Nora came down to our place for a few minutes this evening. It was so good to see her. This was her first time out of the house since we came back from Enniscorthy, a full four weeks ago now. They say she's locked in her bedroom, let out only to help with cooking or washing.

She sneaked up to us, coming up the back way from the strand and tapping on the back door. Mammy was in the kitchen and tried to get her to come in but Nora wouldn't, asking if I could come outside to her instead. Her mother had sent her to the priest's house for a Mass card and she was under orders to go straight there and straight back. You could see she had frightened herself by disobeying this injunction: all the time she was here, her eyes were darting about the place, ready for the off.

But she looked better than the last time I saw her, on our way back to Mucknamore from Enniscorthy. She was sick with dread that day, physically sick. At the end of our journey, a twenty-three mile cycle, her face was the colour of candle wax. As for the sight of her disappearing up the road after she left me outside my place, with her head bowed to the wind, her back bent in half over the handlebars . . . it near broke my heart.

Her disappointment when she heard Barney was away with the boys was deep. She was counting on him giving her comfort and I thought how nice it must be to have your own boy you could lean on like that. That whatever their troubles, at least they have that in each other. Then I caught myself on, remembered all that I have myself, and the awful things that Nora endures up at home, things I can only be guessing about.

'Has it been terrible?' I asked her and she said it wasn't great but she hoped the worst was over. I'm afraid to think about what that might mean. She talked a bit about all the things we did in Enniscorthy. I asked her if she had any regrets and she said no, she'd do it all over again. It was strange the way she talked about it, as if her life is already over and Enniscorthy was the high point, everything before leading up to it, everything after a downfall. She sounded like an old lady looking back on her childhood; you'd think it all happened years ago, not two weeks ago.

Her job is gone, for definite. Everyone in Wexford knows why she left Furlong's that day and since the Staters reclaimed the towns, Republicans are next door to dirt in the eyes of the business community. So no job and no prospects of one. It's desperate to think of her confined to the house, with nothing to do but assist her mother. She's far too bright for that. I was lucky myself that the call to fight came during the school holidays or I too could have been facing unemployment. Father John grows ever less delighted with my activities but it's easy enough to avoid him during the holidays.

We said nothing about Dan and the ferocious things he has been doing and saying. He is firmly back in the enemy camp and even Barney is sickened by his duplicity. On Wednesday, he made a speech that's quoted in all the papers, saying the country will not be 'held to ransom by a crowd of blackguards masquerading as soldiers'. So much for drunken *ráméish* about friendship.

With all the fretting she did about being caught, the few snatched minutes she had were hardly worth her while, though she said as she was leaving that she felt the better for it. We have worked out a way of keeping in touch. Going to the church to pray is the one thing her family won't disallow so we will leave notes for each other under a loose stone around the back of the chapel. I said I'd get a letter to Barney if she wants to write and leave it there. This should, I hope, prove some sort of comfort to her.

Dear Diary

Mucknamore was honoured today with a visit from a 'National' Army car. A great lump of a Lancia military motor, driven by Mr Dan O'Donovan. He came sweeping down the village street at around eleven o'clock, driving alone at first. He's got himself a promotion, Nora told me the last meeting we had, and is to appear in a photograph in the *Wexford Weekly* next week alongside the big-wigs from Dublin, newly appointed Brigadier-Generals and the like.

When the Lancia arrived in the village, and people saw who was driving it, they trooped out onto the road like a herd of cattle to have a gawk. Even some of our own customers got off their stools and went out. Your man sat off in the motor, taking in the compliments, letting the children climb all over the seats. After basking in the attention for a while, he drove on up towards his own place and we saw no more of him until the afternoon when we heard the sound of the engine roaring down the road again. As he passed our place, he let a loud honk on the motor-horn. The nerve of him. Mammy and I went upstairs to look out of the window in her room – standing back a bit from that window, you have a prime view of the road but you can't be seen from outside. We nearly fainted with surprise when we saw who he had in the passenger seat beside him: Nora! She looked tiny in the big front seat and trying to make herself look smaller, shrinking down into the leather with her hand on her hat to keep it from blowing off. Every line on her face spoke of her humiliation – the poor girl.

Her brother had his 'National' Army uniform on and a sneer of a smile that spoke of what he was doing. Off down the road he drove, then he must have turned at the cross because in less than no time he was back, parading past our place again, blaring on his motor-horn once more, delighted to be playing the big fellow and rubbing our noses in it, as well as Nora's. Up and down he went – fifty times if he did it once – until he made sure everybody in the village saw and heard him.

We went back downstairs after a while and tried to ignore the commotion that attended his passing. Everybody loved the show and could hardly contain their glee at the insult to us. We gave none of them the satisfaction of letting on that we noticed.

Dear Diary

The picture was in the paper today, 'Lieutenant' O'Donovan sitting up on the motor, the same motor he drove out here last week, leaning on the fan of leather that folds up like a squeezebox at the back. He stares straight into the camera, his peaked military cap at an angle but the face beneath it as blank as the opening into a cave.

They all have the same look on them, the six army men in this photograph, with their self-appointed titles (Dan O'Donovan a lieutenant, Martin Hayes a brigadier!!!), their strutting heads and polished guns. They think they awe us with their shiny boots and their up-to-the-minute weapons but it's the opposite. Their finery is English-bought and for all their swaggering, you can see the knowledge of that in their eyes. They know their own perfidy and they have to live with it. Give me a battered trench coat any day, for the heart that beats beneath it.

Dear Diary

The boys captured a barracks tonight, in Donore. We've been planning the strike for a week and Barney and the boys set off from here after tea aiming to get there around nine. It was after midnight before we got word. I was counting the day's takings with Daddy – Mammy having gone off to bed – when the knock came to the bar window. Daddy and I looked at each other and, putting the cash away in the strong box, he gave me the nod to answer it. We had been working quietly together all evening without mentioning Barney's absence or the worry on both our minds. I slid open the big bolt on the door and there stood Sore-Toes, all excited, the way he gets, as if his tongue is too big for his mouth. I suppose they sent him to carry the news because he'd be no great loss if he were caught.

'What are you doing out here?' I said to him, sweeping him in before he was seen. 'Would you not go round the back?'

I knew by the look of him though that things had gone well. 'Success?'

'Defin-I-tely,' he replied, pronouncing the 'I' in the middle as 'eye', one of his little sayings.

'Come on in, lad,' Daddy said from inside. He made the offer of a drink which, needless to say, Sore-Toes didn't refuse and we sat to hear how it went. Like clockwork, apparently. Barney opened the attack just after dark, firing at the two sentries on the bridge. These were two sensible men who lost no time in retreating inside the post. That brought the number inside to about fifteen, Joe Latimer commanding. They had a Lewis gun which they used to reply to our offensive and we focused our attack on that. Before too long, we had it silenced.

More of our lads were arriving all the time, word having got out. Before long, we had over thirty, Sore-Toes said. By firing from four points, they soon gained access to the yard and from there it was an easy matter to lob Mills bombs into the building. All the time, the enemy were only sniping back half-heartedly while they waited for reinforcements from Wexford but Ballymolane Company did the needy for us there, keeping the soldiers in Wexford barracks occupied and unavailable. As soon as the Donore boys realized they were on their own, and not going to be rescued, they didn't take too long about surrendering. The white flag went up on the roof and that was that.

Barney took the surrender and complimented Latimer on the good fight he had put up. The whole procedure took only two hours with no casualties either side. We captured the Lewis gun, which is faulty now but not beyond repair, some rifles and a fine haul of ammunition. Unfortunately, though, we had to release the men we took. Not having a place to hold prisoners of war, we had no option. Nothing hampers our work more than this inability to hold prisoners. All those men are now free to fight another day but if they take any of our lads, it's inside with them to be interred indefinitely without trial. Oh yes, Mr Michael Collins and his followers have learned their English lessons well.

All the same, it was a sound evening's work. We'll sleep well on it tonight.

Dear Diary

The 'National' Army sent a massive contingent today to clear Dunore, led by none other than Dan O'Donovan. We were apprised of their intentions in advance, about half an hour before they arrived. Our boys gave consideration to staying put and fighting it out but we knew we'd be outgunned and outnumbered and so decided to get out in advance. We cleared it of as much ammunition as we could and Barney, Pat Connors and Roller were still at it when the Staters arrived with a contingent twenty strong. Barney started shooting like mad while trying to get away and somehow made it over a high wall. He ran like hell until he came to a brake of bushes and hid there, surprised that they were not following him. But they were not.

Pat and Roller got caught. They didn't even put up a fight. All of this was sensible tactics as there was no point in causing unnecessary bloodshed. They've been taken prisoner and are in Wexford gaol.

So Dunore is in Free State hands again but only for the moment. The soldiers they have put in place are very jumpy after our last encounter with them. They know they haven't seen the end of us. Several times a night, a mobile patrol is sent out from Wexford to provide back-up in case we decide to make a return call. As far as we can make out, the fools do it on the hour, every two hours. So punctual you could set your clock by them, according to Lama White's information. Can they really be that stupid? Barney has sent a message that Molly and I are to go up there and find out. If we find Lama is right, we won't be long about setting up a welcoming committee for them. Let's see how Mr O'Donovan likes that.

Dear Diary

Michael Collins is dead! Shot in an ambush! I have to admit I was drawn to my knees by the news. He was once such an inspiration to us and it would be inhuman, never mind unchristian, not to mourn his passing. Oh, but it is hard to read of the pomp and circumstance of the funeral – soldiers in green uniforms marching with arms reversed, bands playing the 'Dead March' – without thinking of how the dead on our side are buried in silence with only their families to mourn. As it is hard to hear those who once glorified the ambush as a tactic of war now talking like the English and deriding it as murder. And it is hard knowing Collins was brought to Glasnevin cemetery on one of the gun-carriages he borrowed from the British to attack the Four Courts. Yes, it's hard not to be bitter.

Richard Mulcahy is who they have put in Collins's place as 'Commander-in-Chief'. The walls in Dublin are already carrying the slogan: 'Move Over Mick, Make Room For Dick'. Mulcahy is no match for Michael Collins – few men are – so that is probably good news for us. Who could have foreseen a fortnight ago that both Collins and Arthur Griffith would be dead? The two men most responsible for the Treaty, both gone.

Can it be true, what people are saying, that this turn of events means God is on the anti-Treaty side?

27

1975

'I've something to tell you.'

He puts down his dessert spoon to look at me. 'No,' he says.

How can he tell from what I have said? Is it in my voice or my face that he reads it?

It is my birthday tomorrow, my eighteenth. I am officially an adult at last and tonight, at the Granada, a candlelit Dublin restaurant, Rory and I have been celebrating, with linen napkins and a bottle of wine, with soup followed by steak and now with plates of Black Forest gateau. Rory's treat, from his bar wages, and a fine treat for two impoverished students. Or it would be, if only . . .

'Yes,' I say. 'I'm afraid so. Yes.'

'Jesus. Fuck! I don't believe it. Fuck!'

'That's what did it, all right.'

He lashes a that's-not-funny look across the table at me. 'But I thought you were on the pill,' he says.

'Apparently, the pill is only ninety-nine point nine per cent effective. I – exceptional as ever – am one of the point one per cent.'

Why am I talking in this strange, flippant way?

'Jesus!' he says again. 'Fuck!'

'Will you stop saying that?'

'What do you expect me to say?' He pushes away his plate.

'Maybe something like, "Don't worry, we'll be OK"?'

'Just give me a minute, Jo. You've had time to think about this. I am really shocked. I just don't believe it. Jesus!'

Anybody would think he didn't know the facts of life. But how can I blame him? To me too it seems impossible that our molten nights have anything to do with this cold, daytime reality. And I have had the connection pounded into me all my female life.

'You seem so calm,' he says.

'I am *anything* but calm.'

'Have you thought about what you want to do?'

I shake my head. 'I only found out for certain this afternoon.'

'That's not an answer.'

'What about you?' I hand the question back to him. 'What do you think we should do?'

'I asked first.'

'Well . . . None of the options exactly thrill me . . .' I say, holding him off, trying to see what he is not saying.

'No . . . ?'

He wants me to have an abortion. It's in the set of his mouth, in the narrowing, still shocked eyes. He wants me to take it away, rewind the tape, make it like it never was. He won't say so, though. He just sits there, looking at me like I've suddenly become the opposition.

So I say it for him. 'I suppose the old boat to England is the best of a bad lot.'

He doesn't bother to hide his relief. 'Are you sure?'

'I'm sure.'

And maybe I am. Me, a mother? Eighteen years old, convent-educated, as immature as eighteen can be, with a degree to finish, a world to see, a self to find. A mother, me? How?

This is what I tell myself, and what I tell myself is true, but underneath I know another truth: that I would do it. I would follow my love into marriage and parenthood if he was willing. If he would come away with me – because the one thing I could never, *ever* do is bring this news home to Mrs D. – we could leave our families and their stupid quarrel behind and start over, somewhere else. The two of us. Then the three of us. Make our own family.

But such a thought doesn't seem to cross his mind.

And he's probably right. What he wants is what I too have thought, during fearful, sleepless nights, might be best: best for him, for me, for the baby-not-to-be, because what sort of life would it (she? he?) have with two impoverished teenage parents, reluctantly, prematurely bound?

I look at his face again and see what's going to happen. We are going to have an abortion. *I'm sorry*, I find myself thinking, addressing the living thing inside me. *So sorry. It's his fault, not mine. Please don't blame me.* How stupid: as if it will make any difference to it (him? her?) whose fault it is.

Rory reaches for my hand. 'What else can we do?' His fingers are bony.

'Nothing,' I say.

'Nothing,' he repeats, taking my word and setting it in certainty.

I say it again, his way: 'Nothing.'

Decision made. The boat it is.

Decision made, the tears come. What shakes me – what makes me get up from the table and hurry out to the ladies' room, to spurt my tears into a fistful of toilet tissue, to scowl at my crying face in the mirror and wrap my arms around my head – is not just the knowledge of what I – we – are about to do. It is grief for something else that has died. Our love is insufficient, it is not what I thought.

Next day is Saturday, my birthday. I travel down to Mucknamore by train to spend a night with my family.

At the station, I get into my mother's car, feeling I must emit clues like a stench. She looks me over in the usual way, seeing nothing but a version of me that she detests. Her mouth creases against the good intentions she brought with her down to the station. It's my birthday, she intended to be nice to me but my clothes (skirt short and tight, Doc Marten boots), my eye make-up (black and heavy) and my hair (pulled high into a knot at my crown) just won't let her.

'Did anybody we know see you on the train?'

I shrug the question back at her.

'You'd better stay inside tonight. I don't think Mucknamore is ready for this latest get-up.'

Back at the house, a cake with eighteen candles and 'Happy Birthday Siobhán' across the top waits for me and an envelope of money beside it. Granny Peg is there too at the birthday table and Auntie Nora. It's my birthday, my eighteenth. I try to care, try to be grateful.

Gran asks, 'Are you all right, Jo?'

'I'm all right. Just a bit tired.'

'Overdoing the celebrations, I suppose.' Grinning at me, her lovely old-lady grin that's really a caring question. For a moment, I wonder what would happen if I told her. Only a moment. In a little while, it will all be gone. My tender breasts will return to normal, my morning nausea will dissolve. Why on earth should I tell? After the meal, Mrs D. goes out to the bar to tackle the Saturday-night rush with Eileen, and Auntie Nora heads for the sitting room and the television. She has her timetable worked out for the night. *Starsky and Hutch. Our Great Nation. The Late Late Show.* Gran is left with the washing-up and I volunteer to help, brushing away her protests about it being my birthday. We chat about college, my courses. She wheedles out of me that I have a boyfriend. 'Is he kind to you?' she asks.

I tell her he is.

'Good,' she says. 'Good. That's what counts. The rest of it means nothing.'

She wipes down the sink with her cloth. Could I tell her? I wonder again. Could I?

'Auntie Nora seems in good form,' I say.

'They have a new doctor above and he's put her on different tablets. He said they'd suit her better and I think they do.'

'She seems more alert.'

'Definitely. The other pills used to knock her out of it altogether.'

'When did she get these ones?' Gran likes us to care about Auntie Nora, to ask.

'A few months back. It took her a while to settle onto them, mind. When she started taking them first, she began the night-walking again, like she used to do years ago. She had your mother and myself shattered from broken sleep.'

Gran tilts the basin as she talks and the plughole glugs down the sudsy water. Lifting the draining-board, she wipes down the sink underneath, then the counter-top, then the taps. 'It brought us right back, I can tell you. She used to be a divil for that at one time, the night-walking. She couldn't be kept in the bed.'

'I don't remember that.'

'No, it was a long time ago. Anyway, your mammy and I put up with it for two weeks this time, until the three of us were near killing each other and it couldn't go on. I brought her back to the doctor and he fixed her up a stronger dose. Since then, we haven't had much bother.'

'That's great,' I say, because I think that's what she wants to hear. But is it?

'I don't know. Sometimes I wonder whether half her problems are caused by the side effects from those old pills or the thing itself.' She folds the dishcloth over the tap, sighs. 'But we can't manage her without them, that's the truth of it.'

I put the last plate in the cupboard. Our chore is done. She steps away from me, towards the sitting room. 'Are you coming to watch telly?' she asks.

She would like me to, I know. It would brighten her night to have company in a fireside chair beside her and Auntie Nora, sharing *The Late Late Show* with them, having a cup of tea at the ads. But I can't endure Gay Byrne's smug patter tonight, or Gran's patient explanations to Auntie Nora about what's happening on the screen. Not tonight.

'I will later,' I say, hanging up my tea towel. 'But I think I'll take a walk first. It's a lovely evening.'

On the beach cool air fans my hot cheeks. The sun dips towards the western horizon throwing long shadows. No tourists yet, it's too early in the season. I walk by the edge of the water, the soles of my sandals clinging to the sand, each step lifting with a small, wet smack. White-winged commotions of seabirds flap up, up and away as I approach, settle again further down the sands, like flurries of snow. I plough on, ignoring their fuss.

At the Head, an outpost of rock crooks towards the sea like a long bony finger, barring my way. I turn around, follow my own footprints back to where I started. By the time I reach the Hole in the Wall, darkness has seeped across the sky and along the sea. I am warm and more than a little tired after being up all last night wrangling with Rory. I should go home but instead I look up to the sky and find what I hope to find: a moon, dull-yellow and not full, but there and rising. It will light my way. I turn left, away from the village, out the Causeway.

The tide is in and the waves rush past me in a hurry to get to the shore. I lengthen my stride, walk purposefully up and down the dips in the Causeway path, as if I have somewhere to go. About halfway out, the barbed-wire fencing and warning signs that mark off Coolanagh sands begin: 'WARNING!' they shout. 'DANGER! The Sands on this side of the Causeway are Unstable and Unsafe. Stay on the Path.' I pass them, unheeding. All the way out to Inisheen I go, then I climb the shelf of rock that takes me onto the outer path of the island. The moon is now full-bellied white to light my way.

I walk all the way up to the top of the cliffs. When I reach the plateau at the most southerly edge, I stop and sit, breathing hard from the climb, which is more arduous than it seems. I stay on the path, clear of the edge. Outlines are sharper on this side of the island and more frightening: crags and slabs of granite jut out into the ocean and down below the cliffs the water boils and bursts against the rocks. It wouldn't be safe to cross to the edge in the dark and even if I did I wouldn't be able to see, but I can hear it pounding and exploding into spray. I sit, let the noises of the ocean and the night settle around me. I am not afraid. I know the trick is to close your eyes, not to peer into the dark, imagining what might be there, but to rely on your other senses. I let my ears and nose and skin tell me I am safe.

Once I was afraid of the dark. Once I believed in night monsters, ugly men-beasts with horns and stiletto claws who were willing to bide their time. Under my bed, and in my wardrobe, and behind my closed curtains, they used to lurk, taunting me with silence. Sometimes, not often, I dredged up the courage to place my feet on the carpet, inches from where one of them might be lying and bend to look under the bed. Or to tiptoe across the room and yank open the cupboard door. Whenever I did, all I found was the space they left behind.

Challenging their existence was my only power but mostly I wasn't strong enough to use it. Mostly, I lay rigid with terror in the bed, crossing myself, praying to God, to Jesus, to the Blessed Virgin Mary, not to let them get me. I would make myself say the Rosary, the longest, most tedious prayer, from start to finish and if I got lost among the Hail Marys, if my concentration slipped, I would make myself go back to the beginning and start all over again.

Lining the bottom of my fear was shame. I knew how Maeve – happily asleep in the bedroom next door – would jeer me if she knew. Monsters! I knew they weren't real but that made them more powerful, not less. And now? Now I pride myself on sitting alone and unafraid on Inisheen in the dark but I know the truth. I am still frightened of figments.

'This is a fine time of the night to be coming in.'

Mrs D. is not asleep though it's 2.43 a.m. unless the clock is wrong. She's been sitting in the fireside chair and waiting through all these hours, chasing thoughts that have stirred her to high temper and the disgust that's now spilling out her eyes. Sex, is what's there. Her daughter, out God knows where, doing God knows what with God knows who. Loathsome.

And if she is wrong about this particular night, she is not wrong in general. I *have* been having sex and it has led where she always feared it would. Inside me is her worst imagining, alive and growing. Maybe that is why, tonight, I know I won't let her tantrum pass.

'I'm eighteen now,' I say. 'I can come home any time I want.'

'Not while you're in my house.'

'When Maeve was eighteen, she used to come home this late.'

'You can leave your sister out of this. I always knew where Maeve was. Maeve could be trusted.'

'Good old St Maeve!'

'That's enough now. Your sister has nothing to do with this.'

'Except that what was OK for her is not OK for me.'

'If you're trying to imply favouritism, young lady . . .'

'I'm not implying, I'm *saying*. Favouritism, bias, unfairness, call it what you like. That's what it is. That's what it always is.'

'You'll find anything you want in life if you go looking for it, Siobhán. But if you weren't always and only thinking of yourself, you'd see that—'

'I don't see why I can't stay out late if I want, that's all. What do you think happens when I'm in Dublin?'

'I don't want to even *think* about what you get up to in Dublin.'

'Why? Are you jealous?'

'What sort of nonsense is that?' A bitter red stain tracks up from her throat.

This is the shape our rows always take. We argue about small things – my clothes, my timekeeping, my study, my music, my reading – until I make a small interjection, some comment she doesn't want to understand that lets her see I have my own version of what goes on between us. Then, when the barb strikes and she fumbles around its meaning, I feel sorry for her (because, as Granny Peg is always pointing out, she has had a hard life, full of bad things done to her . . .) and I am afraid (I'm not quite sure of what: of her withdrawing her love? Of the weight of the guilt if I went *too* far?) and I retreat.

Knocking my corners off, she calls it, when she snaps or slaps. She is the opposite of those mothers who compensate for their own hardships by striving to give their children what they never had. She wants me and Maeve to sink into the same small, stifling hole she's settled in herself. I am being shrunk to fit, I realize tonight. To fit a space I don't even want to occupy.

'What is that silly comment supposed to mean?' she says, nostrils flaring, face ablaze.

Usually, I would begin my disengagement around this point, but not tonight. 'I might as well tell you one of the things I "get up to",' I say. 'I'm going out with Rory O'Donovan.'

'Rory who?'

'You know who I mean. Rory, John O'Donovan's son.'

'No!'

'Oh yes, I—' But I don't have time to say any more. Her hand, clenched into a fist, swipes towards me. I duck to avoid it but it's too late: her knuckles catch the upper part of my cheek, just under the eye. I hear the crunch of bone on bone, then a wave of shock jounces through my face, ringing pain.

She has punched me. Not just one of her slaps, a punch. A punch in the face. Now an acid rage sears through my centre, flares into my head in flashing, hot thoughts. *I'll box her back, I swear it. Box her face. She is smaller than me and old and I can punch harder . . . I can . . .*

I want to brand all that she knows and does not know into her body with bruises.

. . . I will do it. It would give me pleasure. I can do it . . . I can. I will . . .

But I can't. I don't. No sound comes out except tears gurgling in my throat.

She has shocked herself. Her hand, her punching hand, is covering her mouth and guilty words, bloated to bluster, leak through her fingers. 'What have you made me do? Dear God . . . What . . .'

I hold my swelling jaw with both hands. I want to tell her the rest, tell her the worst, but I can't. Even now, I still can't.

The door opens. We start and turn, like illicit lovers. Granny Peg in her dressing gown, her grey hair down.

'Máirín! Jo! I thought I heard . . . Good God, what's the matter? What's happening here?'

Mrs D. tucks her fists under her arms and when I see her face as she turns to Gran, my fury chills, congeals to something that will last, I feel, forever. I allow words to shape what my body has held close for so long: *She doesn't love.* Then I think, I can say that if I want. So I speak, to the side of her face, softly, as if I have just discovered it: 'You hate me.'

My mother's eyes swivel back to me.

'Jo!' cries Granny Peg.

I ignore her.

'You do, don't you? But you know what, Mrs D.?' I linger on the name that distances her from me, my first time to say it to her face. 'You know what? It's all right. You can let it out now. Because I hate you too.' In that moment, it is almost true.

'Jo!' Granny Peg's eyes are as widely round as her glasses. 'Jo, stop it. Stop. What are you saying?'

I take down my hand to reveal my face, not knowing what it looks like but thinking such pain must surely show. It does: shock cracks in Gran. She turns to Mrs D., back to me. She is a question, divided between us.

'Ask her what she's been doing!' my mother babbles. 'Go on! Ask her!'

Gran looks back to me, full of fear. Poor, poor Gran, who doesn't deserve any of this.

Mrs D. shouts, 'No, she has nothing to say for herself now, has she? Oh, no. She's too ashamed to say it, and well she might be. Let me, then, be the one to tell you: she's only gone and taken up with young O'Donovan.'

'O'Donovan. You mean . . . ?'

'Yes. Yes! Him! Yes!'

'Oh, Jo. No.'

'She picked it . . .' Hysteria cracks in Mrs D. now. 'She picked the thing that would hurt me most . . . Went out of her way to do this to me . . .'

'Now, Máirín, stop that. Stop. Of course she didn't. These things happen. Jo doesn't know . . .' She shoots her a look, a warning: *Don't say too much.*

Mrs D. starts to cry then, fingers splayed across her face.

'No, no, Máirín pet, don't cry.' Gran wraps her arms around her. 'Come here. Don't cry.'

I walk away and leave them to each other and to their precious, protected secret.

III
Crest

Nora

. . . Dan was like Daddy, that's what we never saw, not till afterwards. He ended up being what he started off hating. It's a way boys often go.

As a little chap, he was lovely. A right softy, if you can believe it. A milky-white neck on him, slender as a swan's as he bent over his dinner. And a nature to match. Then. It was being a boy that ruined him, that's my belief. Our eldest boy and all that went with that – the second-biggest dinner and the second-softest chair and the right to the biggest and the best once Daddy was out of the house. All his needs covered by the rest of us: 'Make your brother's bed.' 'Pick up your brother's dirty washing.' 'Don't touch that, it belongs to your brother.'

Making too much of him was what sent him astray. It did no one any favours, not us, not him.

We had only eleven months between us, me and Dan. Each year, for a small while in December, the same age. I'd get all excited as that time drew near and get on to him over it: 'I'm going to be the same age as you. I'm going to be as old as you.' And he'd get cross explaining why I was wrong. Each Christmas we used to eat our Christmas oranges together. It was a tradition. We'd take the morning over it, him starting the ritual by sinking his thumbnail in and peeling one circle of skin back from the flesh. Then we'd put the fruit aside, leaving it lie on the side table between us, inhaling the orange tang in the air around it until we could stand it no longer, when it would be my turn to make a start on mine. And then we'd put them aside again.

That's how we'd go, him first, me second, peel by slow peel, until both oranges were naked. By that time, we'd be nearly in a frenzy dying for the sweet, sour taste of it. You'd think we'd be disappointed in the eating of it, with a build-up like that, but we never were.

But then came Christmas 1918, our first year in Wexford. When I got up that morning, early as always, he was gone out of the house, off with the boys somewhere, to concoct one of their plots. Yes, on Christmas morning! Mammy was raging with him but when he came back she said nothing and neither did I. I watched him offer his airy explanations and go across to where his presents lay unopened. On top of the wrapped parcels I had left his orange. I watched him pick it up from where it sat. Watched him throw it up into the air and catch it in the hand that threw it. Watched him stick it into his pocket, never looking at me once.

No wonder there's some who think he got what was coming to him . . .

28

1995

The air in my shed is thick and stuffy, like a hand over my face. I'm coated in the dream that just spat me out: somebody – a woman whose voice I knew but could not place – was in the newly renovated house, calling across to me from one of the upstairs windows. 'Come,' she entreated, her voice both cry and whisper. 'You know why you are here. So come on over.'

'In a minute,' I said. I wanted her to stop but at the same time I knew she was right: what she wanted me for was what I had come back to do, was why I had insisted on staying here, on site.

'When?' she said. 'You don't mean it. You're not coming.' Then she leaped from the window and hurtled through the air towards me, so fast I couldn't see her face. Through the night and in through my window she flew, frightening me out of sleep.

'Noooo!' I screamed as I jerked upright in bed, heart thrumming.

I'm still in my terror for a second or two longer, then I come to. A dream, that's all. I look around: nobody else is here, only me and my heated hallucinations. My shed's whitewashed walls, my few belongings, the broken furniture at the end, Mrs D.'s suitcase: all are here, wearing their night-time look, less distinct, less separate from the world and each other than in daylight. If I can see like this, there must be a moon outside. I stare, settling myself with the actuality of things. They are here, I am awake, it's OK.

Through the shed window, I can see the new version of the house, its outer shell complete except for doors and windows. The remodelling has been extensive: our old house hunched in that space but this new construction, not even finished, is already preening itself.

Only a dream, I tell myself again but, for some reason, it has left me feeling obligated. I swing my legs out, slip my feet into their shoes. I have to visit the house.

Outside the shed, the night air is still and warm: no need for a jumper or jacket. Under the light of a three-quarter moon, my white T-shirt glows and the push of my belly underneath mimics the lunar bulge. My body's rate of change has accelerated, I feel like I'm expanding day on day. I am changing fast but not as spectacularly as the little life inside me. She is about a foot long now and already she has fingernails and skin, a nose and eyes, lips and ears. She has a heart and a stomach and kidneys and tiny ovaries containing all the eggs she'll ever need to have a baby herself. Two days ago, I felt the first strange shudder of her movement, a quiver that was in me and of me. They have come often since then, little seismic flutters that make me smile. Tonight I placed Rory's hand there, to feel.

'Isn't it amazing?'

'Amazing,' he said, the intimacy of the act – the first time in twenty years that I have asked him to touch me – spiked with the knowledge that he has felt such movements in another belly, twice before. Not that we mentioned that. Since the night we almost quarrelled, we've given up such talk. He has stopped pushing me towards sex, which should have eased the tension between us, but hasn't. While he kept pressing for more, I held the line, but now he's stopped, I can feel my own need hardening.

I shuffle through the night, up the garden path, past the machines that crouch in the dark like beasts, through what will be the back door. In the hall, the stairs are naked timber, blobbed with cement. I climb the wooden steps, my shoes too loud in the night. Holding the banister, I get cement powder under my nails and I tighten my fist against its chalkiness.

Upstairs, stars peep through the open slats of the roof. This is not the house I lived in. Throughout this floor, concrete squares have elbowed out our unsymmetrical rooms: eight squares, six doubles, two singles, each with a smaller square attached around the outer walls, to be fitted out as shower rooms. I go to where Mrs D.'s room used to be. When Daddy died, he was laid out just here, beneath this window. Mrs D. had him moved back in for the wake. I hated to see him where he hadn't been for years, knowing it was all for show, but still I haunted that room, kneeling and pretending to pray while I waited for other mourners to finish and go.

Alone with him, I would run my fingertips over his dead face and hands, searching out places that looked soft: the swell of his cheek, the pout of his lips. All unyielding; even his eyeballs under their lids were hard, like marbles. I never touched him while others were there, praying beside me. Then I would only look. His mouth was not quite closed, a tiny crack of black showing between the pink. I would look so hard that I'd think this gap was opening, that his lips were about to part, pop open into a surprised O.

I remember that the room was cold: there was no central heating in Mucknamore then and anyway, you don't heat a room that holds a corpse. I remember the smell of wax from the candles on either side of the bed and the taste at the back of my throat as I stared at what was left of him, my first taste of death. I remember the look of Maeve, her eyes hollowed out by shock, and Mrs D., sitting on a chair opposite, watching me watching him.

I shiver and back out of the room. Down the corridor, my own bedroom has also had its corners knocked into place, the little alcove where I kept my toys gone, the walls shorter than they used to be, squared off from each other. It smells of new plaster and wood, empty and open, not a trace of me in it. Nothing is the same except the sea outside the window, still where it always was. I cross to the open rectangle, look out at the same old picture, milky in the moonlight, listen to the familiar lullaby of the turning waves. I rest my elbows on the brand-new concrete windowsill and lean out and look.

29
1975

Breasts tender as bruises. Nausea squirming in the pit of me like a nest of snakes. And tears, rivers and rivers of tears. Hormones, I tell myself, mopping up. Just hormones. Once I have done the deed, they will disappear with the rest.

Deirdre thinks it is breaking up with Rory that makes me cry. I have not seen him for three days. I am home, snuffling around the flat in my dressing gown, or sobbing under my blanket. What happened? Deirdre wants to know. Are we finished? Can't we make up? Why won't I tell her?

I want to tell but I can't. The word curdles in my throat: I cannot get it up and out. I know I am (relatively) lucky, to have England next door. To have a safe, legal option to flinging myself down stairs with fingers crossed. To all the whispered things you hear that women do. Gallons of gin and a scalding bath. Wire coat-hangers. Knitting needles. I am lucky, I won't die of it.

If I could just get it organized.

I spend Monday hovering for hours outside the clinic where I got my ineffectual pills, walking towards the door and walking away, like I am dancing a grim minuet. I can't go in. Every time I imagine myself telling the helpful person in the white coat what I want, I balk.

On Tuesday I follow around a young woman I have seen before handing out leaflets about Women's Right to Choose. Beneath her alarming hair (green), she looks kind, the sort of person who will listen, who will not judge. I track her in the restaurant, the bar, the students' union. I even follow her into her social-science lecture, sitting behind her for an hour of social policy, rehearsing the choice of words I will whisper to her when class is over. I'll be direct. ('I need an abortion. I thought you might know where I could arrange one.') No, I'll spare my blushes by lying. ('My friend is pregnant and she has asked me to ask you how she'd go about getting an abortion in England.') No, she'll see through that. I'll simply throw myself on her compassion. ('I'm pregnant. Help me, please.')

When the lecture is over I follow her out the door. A guy comes across to talk to her and I am not brave enough to intrude myself between them. I let her melt away into the crowd.

I turn desperate then. If I cannot even say the word, how am I to do the deed?

In the end, after another night of tossing and sobbing, I blurt it to Deirdre at coffee break. 'Oh, no,' she says, just what he said when I told him. 'Jesus, I should have thought of that. I'm so stupid.'

I shrug.

'What are you going to do?'

'England.'

'Oh, Lord. You poor thing. Is he going with you?'

I shook my head, a snap from side to side. 'I don't want him to.'

'Why not?'

I have no tidy answer to that. Deirdre stirs her coffee, probing my closed face. 'Is this what you want or what he wants?'

'Both.'

'Poor Jo.' She puts her hand on mine. 'Look, if you've made up your mind to do this, you have to just go and do it. You can't be condemning yourself all the way.'

I look away from her towards the open squares that cut us off from the kitchen. All around us, crockery clatters, spoons tinkle and voices talk. Happy talk, from laughing student faces, talk about essays or relationships or plans for tonight or the weekend.

'What about money?' she asks. 'It costs a lot of money, doesn't it? And you'll have to get a boat and stay over there for a few nights.'

'He has money, he's said he'll pay.'

She nods, approving. 'The least he can do.'

I sip some of my coffee. It's tepid and bitter.

'Do you want me to come with you?' asks Deirdre.

I put down the coffee cup. 'Oh, Dee, would you?'

'Of course I would. Of course, if you want me to.'

A wave of gratitude and relief breaks inside me. Everything flows out of me then. I tell her my trouble with the clinic and the Right to Choose girl and my worry that I won't even be able to make it happen because I don't know how.

'What about an English telephone directory?' she says. 'They stock them in libraries, don't they?'

'Would they carry addresses for places like that?'

'I'd say they would.' She squeezes my hand under hers. 'If not, we'll find a way. This doesn't have to be as hard as you're making it, you know.'

'What do you mean?'

'You're doing what you have to do. Don't let the bastards tell you anything else.'

'I know. It's just I never thought—'

'I know, no one ever does. But you're a good person, Jo. Don't believe anyone who tries to make you think anything else.'

Deirdre takes me over. She hauls me off to the library, finds a London business directory, places it in front of me, opens the front pages under the letter A.

'You'll hardly find it there,' I say. 'Wouldn't it be under Clinics or something?'

She upends the book and pushes it across to me. There it is, between Abattoirs and Abrasive Materials, two matter-of-fact words on a page: Abortion Advice. We write down the names of all the clinics in the listing and their telephone numbers then take the bus into town, to the public telephone boxes in the post office with their heavy, sound-proof doors. I squeeze in, line my £5 worth of fifty-pence pieces on the shelf, dial the first number on my list and am quickly through to a matter-of-fact English voice. Certainly, she can give me information. Have I done a pregnancy test? What stage of pregnancy am I at? Am I certain that abortion is the option I want to take? In that case, as I am from Ireland, they can fit me in to do everything within twenty-four hours: counsel me in the morning, perform the procedure in the afternoon and I can leave the next day. I must, however, spend the night in England; that is a legal requirement. Would I like to book an appointment?

Clunk, clunk goes my money, dropping into the telephone box. I give her a false name for her appointment book: Siobhán Devoy. The soothing voice drones on. Would I like details of bed-and-breakfast accommodation near the clinic, details of local transport? Have I any more questions? No? In that case, they are looking forward to seeing me on Saturday the 24th.

'It's all arranged,' I say to Dee, coming out. 'Saturday week.'

'There, that was easy, wasn't it?'

It was. Almost too easy.

Starfield Women's Clinic. A double-fronted suburban house, the garden concreted to a car park. Inside, the reception area: pale pink walls with pink-and-white candy-stripe trimmings and white woodwork. A smiling girl behind the desk. As soon as she speaks, I recognize her as the girl I spoke to on the phone: her tone of professional helpfulness is unmistakable. Would I like to take a seat in the waiting room? Certainly, my friend can wait with me but I must go in to see the doctor on my own.

The clinic is full of women, every age and type and size. They eye Dee and me as we come in, careful not to stare. Everybody has somebody with them, except one older woman, at least forty, in the corner beside two vacant seats. She is well dressed, her face painted and powdered. She looks up from her *Good Housekeeping* magazine, smiles at us as we take the seats beside her, says,

'Hello.' Deirdre returns her greeting for us both while I lower my eyes. What I want now is quiet, no words from Deirdre and certainly not from a stranger imagining we have something in common.

I pick up a magazine myself, hide behind it to watch her. She is obviously well-to-do. Among the rings on her hand is a wedding ring. I wonder why a woman like her . . .

I am called from the door. 'Miss Devoy.'

A raised eyebrow from Deirdre for my alias. She squeezes my arm: 'Good luck, Jo.'

The doctor is a young Asian woman smiling at me from behind a desk. I say yes to her explanations, her queries, her advice: yes, yes and yes. Her red lips purse and swell in and out around her words. I resent her choice of lipstick colour – scarlet – thinking it tactless, which I know is silly. Everything seems false, like it's not happening at all.

When I come back to the waiting room, more people have come in. Dee is grimacing, mouthing something at me behind her magazine, her eyes swivelling towards the opposite corner. Following their direction, I look and find I am staring into a face I know. A face from home. The mouth is open, the eyes are solid balls of dismay. It is Mary Rowe: Monica's younger sister. Mary Rowe and her boyfriend beside her, holding her hand. Blood surges into my own face, hot and sore and my heart begins to thump as if I am running, not standing shock-still in a doorway. Our stares lock onto each other, the room between us flooding with shame.

I turn from her at the precise moment that she rotates her eyes away from me, back to her magazine, and I fold into the chair beside Deirdre. I want to cry. After a time, the receptionist calls her name – her real name – and she and her boyfriend get up. I don't look at them and I don't suppose they look at me. We are unknown to each other, made invisible by a cloak of dishonour.

*

'I'm not going back.'

Deirdre stops her toast on its way to her mouth. 'What do you mean?'

'I'm not going back to Ireland.'

'Yeah, let's stay forever.'

'I mean it, Dee. I've been thinking about it ever since we arrived. I've made up my mind.'

London. Already I love it. Its size is what makes it great. Coming in on the train the day before, I couldn't believe how big it was. I sat staring out the window as we whipped through mile after mile of semis and terraces, through endless back views of endless backstreets. On and on it went and still on, until it began to feel like somebody's big, mad joke. Then we stepped out into Paddington Station and immediately I knew I was in a new country and I wished that Deirdre and I were what we looked: two young visitors with backpacks, here for the sights. The sights. A group of boys our age jostling each other off the pavement, their dark skins and the whites of their eyes shining. A black woman at least six and a half foot tall, hugely beautiful in red and yellow. Another brace of boys around the entrance to a park, gravity-defying hair like cockatoo plumage, chains and spikes jangling. Awesome buildings, taller than trees and wider than fields, not just the touristy places, the palaces and churches, but the day-to-day buildings, the banks and offices and shops just sitting in splendour at the side of the street, thinking nothing of themselves.

I love it all but I especially love the people sliding past each other, unseeing, locked in the shell of their own thoughts. You could never do that in Mucknamore or even in Dublin. Here, I marvel, you can be no one right in the middle of everyone. And the thought begins to surface: could I stay?

Everything is different, except the language, and even that is not really the same. In the pub at lunchtime I ask the barman for a white lemonade and he hands me a Wagon-Wheel biscuit. Three times I have to repeat myself, blushing redder each time, before he hears what I am saying. Deirdre bends in two laughing and afterwards, at the clinic, tells the story to one of the nurses – an Irish girl from Carlow called Mary – to make her laugh too.

Mary tells us that in England, there's no such thing as red lemonade. She tells us she had great trouble making herself understood when she came over here first. The English think we talk like those stage-Irish people on TV and in the films, she says. We all sound the same to them, whether we're from Wexford or Dublin, Cork or Donegal. Mary has lost a lot of the Carlow from her own way of talking. She speaks slow and quiet, separating out her words; speaking not for herself but for the person who's listening to her.

She's a nice girl and a good nurse. As she takes my pulse and blood pressure, only a shade at the very back of her eyes shows her awareness of what I'm doing. She is sorry for me, I know, for all the women here in the clinic. I know – even as she gently leads me into theatre, even as she offers me her hand to hold while the anaesthetic takes affect – that later on I will resent this pity.

Afterwards, when it is over and I wake up, she is there again, offering me tea, but I don't want to talk to her or to Deirdre or to anyone now. I ignore the look that passes between them when I refuse the tea, turn over in my bed to face the wall, my back to them and the rest of the ward, the rest of the world. I feel scoured. What was there is gone, leaving nothing behind but a pain between my legs and a flow of blood. I wrap my arms around my empty body.

After a time Mary comes over and taps me on the shoulder. I have to get up. 'No,' I say. 'I can't.' I am giddy with absence. I feel like a blow-up doll with an air-leak and I know if I try to stand up, my legs will fold beneath me.

'That's the anaesthetic,' Mary says. 'You have to help it wear off.' She gets Deirdre to walk me up and down the stairs.

While all this is going on, underneath I am thinking about

staying, the idea hardening inside me while I am caught up with everything else. But it's not until next morning over breakfast that I finally get the idea up and out. 'I'm not going back.'

This is unfair to Dee, I know that. She has been good enough to come over to London with me and now I'm going to leave her to go back alone. And she will have to find somebody else to share our flat. She tries to change my mind. I haven't got a job. I haven't got anywhere to live. What about my degree? My family? Rory?

'Rory and I are finished.'

'You don't mean that.'

'I do,' I say, and I do. If I go back, Rory and I will be together again but only for a while. I will blame him, we will fight, sooner or later we will finish. Sooner is better, I think. As for Mrs D., I haven't spoken to her since the night I left Mucknamore. It's unthinkable that I should go back to living off her money, under her charge. Granny and Maeve cannot help me either, they are all caught in the same tangle of lies. I am supposed to take the hit so they can all go on pretending that life is other than it is.

Deirdre thinks I am being overdramatic. The whole point of having an abortion, she says, is so you can step back into your life as if nothing happened. She says I'm overtired, a bit depressed maybe. It's natural, after what I've been through. Come to think of it, she should have expected something like this. This is no time for making big decisions. I should go home, see how I feel, and if I'm the same in a few weeks, I can come back.

It makes sense what she is saying but it terrifies me. If I go back I know I will never escape again. While she is speaking my feelings are banking up inside against her words and for the first time in our friendship, she doesn't sway me.

After breakfast, we pack up our weekend bags and I go with her to Paddington. Up to the last moment, she doesn't believe I'm not going with her. At the platform, I give her a hug, thank her for everything.

'You really mean it? You're staying?'

I nod, more nervous than I'm admitting.

'But what will you do? You've no job, nowhere to live, no money.'

'I'll be all right,' I say.

'Here,' she says, unzipping the front pocket of her backpack. She presses something into my hand.

My fingers close around some notes and coins. I feel tears pressing against the back of my eyes.

'I owe you,' I say.

She smiles, shakes her head. 'It's not much. I wish it was more.'

'I don't just mean the money.'

We look at each other, awkward with feeling. The train growls behind us, anxious to leave. 'You'd better go.'

'Yeah.' She turns, strides down towards the second-class compartments. She hasn't said goodbye.

'Dee!'

Her head turns round to me and I see she is crying. For me?

'Don't tell anybody where I am,' I call after her. 'If Maeve or my mother ask, just play dumb. Don't mention England.'

She frowns, walks back. 'You'll let me know where you are when you get set up, won't you?'

'Sure.'

She looks at me hard through wet lashes. 'Jo? I mean it. I want an address and phone number as soon as you have one. You're not to disappear on me, d'you hear?'

'I won't. Honestly.'

'And you never know, you might change your mind, come back to Ireland after a while?'

'You'd really better go.'

I watch until her red backpack climbs on board, then I turn to go. Walking away I hear her voice behind calling my name. 'Jo!'

I turn back. Her head is sticking out the window. 'Up the Irish!' she shouts after me.

I laugh, lift my hand in one last wave. The train revs up and begins its shunt and before it has even pulled out, I've stepped away into the swarming crowd.

30
1922

The back road over the mountain to Dunore was the one they had decided to take. It was longer and harder going than the other two routes but it was the most isolated. It also took them closest to the town around teatime, a time when Peg felt the soldiers might be less inclined to be on the prowl.

They walked in pairs: Peg and Barney ahead, Lama and Sore-Toes behind. Lama hadn't wanted Sore-Toes to come but Barney had insisted, partly to annoy Lama was Peg's impression, though why he should want to do that, she didn't know. He was in low humour, annoyed with Nora for not finding some way to get out to see him. As if the poor girl had the saying of it.

Walking was far from comfortable for Peg. She had a canvas sling of ammunition around her waist and a bomb held in place by strips of an old torn sheet tight against her skin. A belt held a pair of guns strapped down along her two sides, digging into her flesh. But the discomfort was like crown and robes to her, a mark of her pride. It was a joy to be doing such work for Ireland. The stuffy worlds of home and school, with their rules and duties, were far away today. Today was about comradeship and adventure and she was going to allow nothing to be annoying or vexatious, including her brother.

Since last week and the passing of the Emergency Powers, to be caught walking the roads in possession of a gun or ammunition was as good as walking into Wexford gaol and giving yourself up. Anyone convicted of possessing firearms (or ammunition or explosives), or of making any attack on 'the National Forces', or of destroying property, private or public – in short, anyone who believed in the Republic and was prepared to do anything to defend it – would be dealt with most severely, anything from a spell in prison without trial to execution by firing squad.

In short, they were right back under the same martial law they had suffered under His Majesty's Government, only this time it was Irish men putting their heels on their necks.

It had been Peg's suggestion that she should be used to carry the bomb to Dunore: if they were to be stopped by the army on their way to or from the job – a high possibility – she was the only one the soldiers wouldn't search. Barney had resisted the idea at first, said he was unwilling to involve her in danger, but she would have none of that. She was in as much danger any day of the week in their own house, she said, whenever the Nationals came calling to raid the place, considering all the despatches and incriminating items she held there. Barney argued it was quite possible the army's morals had degraded to the level of doing a close search on a female, but she'd insisted that she had a better chance of evasion than any of the men. Which she had. If they didn't want to use her, then they might as well call off the Dunore operation altogether, she said. 'And wouldn't that be an awful pity, not to use that nice bomb you boys got from the munitions raid, it being just the perfect size and type for the job?'

She persisted until he gave in, though she knew he wasn't happy about it. He didn't know whether it was seemly for the column to use a girl that way, whether it was being done in other places. And he would have preferred if the suggestion had come from him, or one of the other men. Bother to that. The men had had it all their own way for too long in Ireland. A new day was dawning now: anyone who believed in the 1916 proclamation had to believe in the equality of the sexes. She was proud that Ireland was the first nation to proclaim the equal rights of women and men. The distinction between the sexes and the subjection of one to the other was a foreign institution, another inequity foisted on the Irish by the English (and, curiously, the only iniquity completely accepted, indeed some might even say cherished, by Irish men).

Now things were going back to the way they were in more equal, pre-English days.

Over the weapons she had put her larger undergarments, an extra vest and cardigan for disguise and on top of all, her mother's old coat. This was too big for Peg normally but with her added bulk, almost too tight to close around the middle. Looking at herself, she had a premonition of how her body might look twenty years hence.

'I'm like Ten-Ton Tessie,' she'd said to Molly, who'd helped her dress.

'It's not that obvious, not really,' Molly had said. 'Just walk easy, else you might blow up.'

So they walked careful and steady. For miles they didn't meet a thing on the road. The day was colder than yesterday, with showers of rain, and clouds that raised a little and seemed to promise a clearance only to lower themselves and spill over again. The rainfall of the past week had had a terrible effect on the roads and in places they found themselves near ankle deep in mud. At Hayestown they heard the clop-clop and crunch of a donkey and cart coming up behind them, a farmer with a load of beet. He raised his cap without looking as he passed, his wheels throwing up dirt behind. They watched him pull ahead, the cart swaying left and right like the rump of some exotic beast, getting smaller and smaller as it pulled away, disappearing into what was ahead, giving her a strange sense of significance.

Once he was gone, they had many more miles of nobody and nothing. They walked mostly in silence, Barney not seeming to want to talk. He walked with steady deliberation, something weighing down his steps. Nora, more than likely. Why couldn't he lighten himself on that? All that was asked of him was a bit of patience, you'd think the girl was dead and in her grave, the way he carried on. God made them and God matched them, the pair of them so intense.

A spattering of rain was beginning to fall when Barney unexpectedly stopped. He looked behind, then looked at Peg.

'What is it?' she asked.

He looked back again. 'Hold on there a minute.' He turned and walked back, past Sore-Toes and Lama, his eyes fixed on some point beyond. They caught up with her. 'What's up?' Lama asked. All she could give them was a shrug.

Barney walked back about five hundred yards, then started talking to the ditch. He said, 'Come out.'

Nothing happened.

'Come out, I said. I know you're there.'

Nothing.

'This is your last chance. Come out or I'll shoot you out.'

The ditch moved and Bronco Fortune emerged, brushing off a line of burrs that had attached themselves to his sleeve.

'Well, well, well,' said Barney.

Tall, gangly Bronco looked down at the older smaller man, his O/C, and his face was sheepish. 'I want to come with you,' he said.

'I can see that,' said Barney.

Peg had the feeling he was trying not to smile.

'Send him home, Parle,' Lama called over. 'He's only a babby. He hasn't the brains he was born with.'

Peg had heard plenty from the column about Bronco's exploits. Like the day they were in retreat from a troop of Staters, when Bronco decided to take pot shots towards them. One of his bullets went so close to the side of Barney's head that his ear felt it sizzle past. The shooting was nothing but a waste of ammunition, as they were well out of range. All he succeeded in doing was drawing attention to them so that he and Barney and three others had to slide into a dyke of water and crawl like worms along, every moment fearing a shout of 'Halt' from above or a plug in the back.

He got himself a right bawling out afterwards but the gun to Bronco was like a mirror to a pretty girl: he loved the image of himself that it reflected. Now Barney was trying to insist that he should go home but Bronco was pleading to be allowed to take part in the action.

'He'll let him come,' said Lama to the other two, as they listened to the argument. 'Watch.'

'Sure and why not?' said Peg. 'The lad is only eager to do his bit. We'd all be the same.'

Barney walked back to them, Bronco gambolling along behind like a puppy dog wanting to be brought for a walk. 'What do ye think, lads? Will we let him come?'

'No,' said Lama.

'Show of hands,' said Barney. 'All those who say yes, hands up.'

Peg raised her hand and, as soon as she did, Sore-Toes did the same.

'And all who say no,' said Barney.

Lama raised a lone hand.

He turned to Bronco. 'You're in luck, lad.'

'Yes!' said Bronco, cuffing the air.

'But the gun has to stay behind.'

That brought him back down again. 'What? Why?'

'It's the same for us all.' Barney held his hands out, his fingers spread. 'The only artillery we have is what Peg is carrying. We're going into Free State territory now, near the town. It's not like hanging around the villages.'

'But . . .'

'Hide it there in the ditch and you can come back for it in a day or two, when the heat's off.'

'It could get damp in a ditch.'

'Your choice – dump it or else away off with you.'

Bronco went back across to the ditch he'd climbed out of, looking like a mother forced to abandon her child. Peg even thought she saw his lips moving in a goodbye.

'For Christ's sake, lad,' Barney barked. 'Come on.'

'Yes, sir!' said Bronco, giving him a salute. 'Sorry, sir!' He fell into line with Lama and Sore-Toes and left with a last, lingering look back. They resumed their journey.

Nobody had come along during the contretemps and they saw nobody for miles. Peg had never seen the roads as empty. Was it the war that had them this way? In a way, she'd like somebody out to see them, a witness to their mission. Stupid thought: she was getting as bad as Bronco.

They were on their second last mile when they heard the rumble of a lorry in the distance, sounding like it might be coming their way. Sore-Toes looked back first. 'Oh, Lord! It's them.'

'It's all right,' said Barney. 'Stay calm. We knew this would likely happen.'

'We're only walking, remember,' said Lama. 'Not breaking any law.'

Peg glanced back. 'It's definitely them,' she said. 'This is it.'

As the vehicle pulled close, they kept their eyes ahead. The lorry pulled in close beside them, revving. When they didn't look back it pulled ahead and drew itself crossways up ahead, blocking their way. The engine stopped and a soldier jumped down.

Dan O'Donovan.

'These are mine,' Peg heard him say to the other soldiers in the car and he stood by the vehicle, waiting, his legs planted in a firm triangle, his hand on his revolver.

He looked fine, there was no denying it, six foot two of manhood in its prime, all shiny boots and buttons, the very picture of a soldier. She felt ashamed of her dilapidated coat and if she was shabby, the four boys beside her were next door to tramps. One look at the contrast between them and him told the story of this war's injustices.

The other officer stayed behind the wheel, a man she didn't know. In the back, a third soldier petted a Labrador puppy.

'So,' said Dan, as they approached, dragging the word out. 'We're a little far from home, aren't we?'

Silence.

'What brings us to this vicinity?'

Barney gave him the prepared line. 'We're visiting,' he said.

'Of course you are. And the person who's to be honoured by this visit?'

'An aunt of mine who lives in Ferrycarraig. Mrs Roche.'

'Looking forward to seeing half of Mucknamore village, is she?' This with a nod towards Sore-Toes and Lama.

'She's a hospitable woman.'

This is witless talk, thought Peg. 'Going for a walk is not a crime, Dan,' she said.

He turned to her. 'You know well I could take you all in for questioning.'

His eyes travelled down her body and she could feel a blush rise in her cheeks. He was staring hard at where the bomb was pressed between flesh and fabric. She looked down, found that what he was looking at was a streak of whitewash down one side of the coat, which she got one night painting wall slogans. 'We're whitewashing the sheds at home,' she said, then realized he hadn't asked the question.

'Is that a fact? I must come around and see them,' he said. 'To admire your handiwork.'

He was right, of course. If he were to come, he'd find the shed walls as flaky and unkempt as ever.

Oh, this petty taunting: it was hateful. She was flooded with a longing to say so. If they were alone, she would say to him: all right, Dan, we are enemies now. All right, let it be so. But let us, please, have respect for one another. Let us not have smallness between us. If the others weren't there, listening, that is what she would say.

He threw her another look like something you'd fling at a yapping dog, then turned his attention to the boys. 'Hands up,' he said.

Six arms were raised. Sore-Toes started smiling like a clown, because the attention had switched from Peg. If he wasn't able to keep better control of his face, he'd give them away. Dan ran his hands down the torsos of the men who used to be his friends – *pat, pat, pat* – in the most mechanical way, like he'd no expectation of finding anything. Then his eyes returned, slowly, carefully, pointedly, to her. His face was quizzical as he let his look travel down to the centre of her again as if he could see right through her mother's coat.

How could she ever have thought it would fool anyone and especially him, with his eye for the female form?

'New overcoat?' he asked.

She shook her head. 'It's Mammy's.'

'I was thinking it wasn't your style. And what has you wearing your mother's coat?'

'I don't need a reason, do I?'

She was done for. He was going to search her. He was well capable of it, the conventions wouldn't matter to him. One touch of his hands and he would know it wasn't flesh he was feeling through her garments but solid steel.

'Open it,' he said.

She began to undo the coat buttons. For some reason, that day on the Causeway came to her mind, the day he'd bent to wipe the chalk-dust marks off her skirt, and another flood of blood surged to her skin and with it the realization that whatever it was they had had for one another was now gone, spoiled forever. In that moment she knew again, but only fully knew for the first time, their estrangement. He and she were enemies. This full and final knowledge cracking in her made her want to bend over and close her arms across her chest. She was splitting inside. This must be what people meant when they talked about hearts breaking, she thought. She'd believed she'd understood that phrase but she hadn't, not until now when she recognized just how precisely it described the feeling. Heart. Breaking.

Forbidden now from loving him, what felt like an irrevocable thought gripped her: I will never love another. You were the only one for me. (Was it a premonition, that thought? A foreknowledge of her future? Or did she decide that it was so, and so it was?) The tragedy of it all pulled her eyes up to his. Search me if you like, she thought, knowing the thought showed on her. Search me, do your worst, do whatever you want, because it makes no difference now to me. I am bereft anyway.

He stared at her. He was going to do it. As the moment grew and grew between them, she saw him decide that he would. She saw him change his mind. Then change it back again. And again make a reverse. Indecision danced forward and back in him until, finally, he dropped their mutual gaze.

He turned to the others, gave them all a peremptory shake of his head. 'Go on,' he said. 'But ye'll stay out of trouble if you know what's good for ye.'

At Dunore, the sunset was dripping liquid oranges and golds and the rain-filled potholes all along the bridge glowed full of its light, as if they were broken fragments of the sky that had fallen to earth. Peg went behind a copse of wet bushes to divest herself of her load. By now, her flesh was screaming. The indentations the weapons made in her flesh were pink weals turning red, so deep that she felt no immediate relief on untying the straps and belts that held them in place. She placed the bomb carefully on the grass so she could put herself to rights, her cupped hands aware of the heat of her own body on it.

She brought her booty over to where the boys were gathered on the bridge, smoking. Lama and Sore-Toes took a gun each to the sounds of complaints from Bronco. 'That's not fair.'

'You're lucky to be here at all, lad,' Peg said to him. 'Remember that and respect your officers.'

She handed the bomb – which seemed by now to her overheated mind to be throbbing, as if it had a pulse – to her brother and they all took their places on the bridge, looking down on the flat road below. The sun was gone now, leaving a fading shadow of pinks and golds behind on the point where it dipped the horizon. A wet star came out to shine. Then two. Soon there were dozens, and then too many to count. If they didn't come on quick, it would be dark.

A moment later they heard it, faint and distant but unmistakable: the engine-sound of the military motor, *chugga, chugga, chugga.* They stiffened themselves, each making eye contact with all. Barney leaned across the bridge. Peg could see the twitch of that little muscle of his that always flickered beneath his temple when he was nervous. Sore-Toes and Lama pointed their double-barrelled guns down to where the car would pass.

'Like taking sweets off babbies,' Lama whispered. 'Nearly too easy.'

Maybe but maybe not. It would all be down to timing.

The chug of the lorry drew nearer. Nearer it came and with it the sound of voices: the soldiers were singing, yes, singing. 'A Nation Once Again', a song they had no right to sing. They took the bend that brought them into view. There were five of them, two in the front, three in the back.

No sign of Dan. A flood of relief swept through Peg, not entirely surprising her: would she never learn?

The car approached, oblivious, closer and closer until it was almost under the bridge. Barney lobbed down the grenade. It fell with a clean arc and seemed, as far as Peg could see in the dusk, to land right in the middle of the vehicle.

'Bull's eye!' hissed Lama. 'Bull's fuckin' eye.'

The soldiers had time for a moment's surprise. In the dimness it seemed to Peg that they took the moment to look down at the bomb then up to see where it had come from before the explosion erupted, blasting them beyond thought. The lorry veered off course. One body was flung clear. He might have had some chance of survival if he had stayed where he was and played dead but instead he picked himself up from the road and ran. Barney and Lama turned their guns on him, *clack-clack-clack*, and one or more of their bullets did its job: he crumpled onto the ground.

The vehicle, thrown off its steer, hit a wall. The driver had fallen sideways over his companion in the front seat, and both were apparently dead. The two in the back were also unmoving. Barney sliced the air sideways with his palm, his signal to the others to cease fire.

They stopped. The air drained of sound, became eerily empty. Above gulls cawed, casually, as if nothing had happened.

Peg was horrified but at the same time exultant. *I am alive*, she thought. They are dead now but I am alive. She could feel her blood moving. She could feel her skin and her fingernails and her scalp as if she'd never felt them before. Everything that she normally took as nothing was glowing bright in her, she was like something charged. The men on either side – her brother, their friends – were all looking to her and to each other, all bonded by the same wild and fearful and exhilarated awe. Now I understand, she thought. For the first time, I *know*.

Her brother shook his head at her. 'You shouldn't have been here for this.'

'Don't say that.'

'You shouldn't.'

He meant well but he was misguided, suffering from an outdated code of chivalry. The call to blood and dirt and sacrifice and glory was in her human heart as well as his. This was her world too, she wanted it just as he did. 'Well, it's too late now,' she said, not wanting to argue with him but knowing that if he had the power to take this moment from her, she would fight him for it, claw it back from him with nails and teeth.

'Come on,' he said. 'Strap those guns back on under your coat. And lads, scarper. We'd all want to be getting ourselves gone out of here.'

At the Dunore outpost, a quarter of a mile off, the Free State soldiers had heard the explosion and were already jumping into their lorries, guns unlocked and ready, minds leaping with intentions of what they would do if what they heard meant what they thought. Three minutes was all it took them to reach the bridge but they were too late. Only their five dead comrades remained at the scene. The killers were gone, swallowed by the rising tide of night.

Peg

Dear Diary

Dan O'Donovan was in the paper, and the outrageous speech he made at the Dunore inquest was quoted in full. 'When the British forces were installed here, it was hard to find man or woman in Wexford with pluck enough to fight the foreign intruder. To my knowledge, no British soldier was fired upon around here during the whole of the Anglo-Irish war and I do not think I am wrong in stating that the present occasion is the first on which a soldier was killed in Wexford since 1798. The Truce begot a lot of warriors and those now attacking the National Army are just emerging from the burrows where the British terror drove them.

'Hysterical young females are among the most active adherents to the Irregular cause because hitherto it has been safe to be so. They disfigure walls with lying propaganda and they are active carriers of documents, arms and ammunition. Some have been known to accompany men on expeditions of murder, concealing arms in their clothes until required and taking them back when used, relying for safety on the chivalry of those whose deaths they are out to execute.

'This ambush was a contemptible attack. Those who did these foul deeds may call themselves warriors but I would call them murderers.'

Jesus, Mary and Holy St Joseph, the superiority of that.

He is not alone in vilifying us. Outrage and recrimination are being hurled at us from all sides. As Mammy says, people haven't the brains they were born with. Can't they see it is one and the same cause as has been fought in this country since 1916, a cause they all claim to support? Can't they see it's one and the same tactics?

Father John condemned the action from the altar yesterday morning. Sunday after Sunday now, his sermon is nothing but a tirade of political abuse. It's getting very awkward in school and I dread having to deal with him. Mostly I avoid him and I've come to notice lately that the reason I'm so successful is that he is avoiding me too. He's no keener to have a conversation about the matter than I am. For all his huffery and puffery when he's protected by his pulpit, he's no braveheart when he has to speak one to one.

What he, and all the others who find it so easy to condemn, fail to realize is that we fully understand the horror of these killings. None understand it better than us, the ones risking our necks. Soldiers go into battle knowing they may die. It's what they are trained for. War *is* terrible but we cannot afford to let ourselves shy away from it.

Dear Diary

The raid we'd been waiting for since the Dunore action came last night. At eleven o'clock they arrived, two lorryloads of them, but no Dan O'Donovan, thank God. They started beating down the doors with their rifle butts. As well as ourselves, every man drinking in the pub was hauled out onto the road while they went through our goods and belongings. Even Mammy was brought out of her sickbed, shivering, into the night cold (but of course defiant). When I saw her there, like that, I could have run them through with a bayonet myself. I said nothing for the whole entire time, let Daddy do the talking for us because I was afraid of what would come out of my mouth.

They gave the place an awful going-over, everything out of the cupboards and drawers again, though I'd only just got them back to rights after the last time. The locks on the bureau are busted and they butted in some of the wood panelling in the parlour. To fix it will cost a fortune. They even took the Sacred Heart down from the wall, the soldier blessing himself as he removed it. Another brave warrior took it upon himself to break some of the crockery in the kitchen. Black-and-Tans were gentlemen compared to some of these boyos.

Bad and all as the wreckage is (it will take us days to get the place to rights) what worries me more is how close they came to finding my stash, including this diary. I had it in the usual place which I've always thought of as foolproof but they spent so long going through that particular corner of that particular room, it was as if they had a tip-off. So I've made the decision that tomorrow I will put some of the stuff into Molly's safekeeping for a while and find a new place, even sounder than where I keep you at the moment.

Barney is having a night home here for a change, which we're counting on being safe enough, please God, after last night's raid, as they'll hardly come again so soon. And it's a cold one, unseasonably bitter again. The poor chap was in dire need of a bit of comfort: after a wash, a shave and a feed, he put on fresh clothes and felt like a new man. He's sleeping now, on the settle bed in the bottling store. Nora managed a small while with him and has promised more tomorrow so he went to sleep happy.

Dear Diary

More reprisals for Dunore. 'Lieutenant' O'Donovan arrived out from Wexford with a party that proceeded to set fire to a row of cottages on the Wexford road. The Whites own one of those cottages. A short few months ago, he was happy to take a drink with Lama – does friendship mean so little to him? I can pardon him for backing the Treaty, others have done so who still manage to retain their honour, but that he can be so zealous in putting down those who were once his friends, that to me is unforgivable.

Lucky the worst of the blaze was put out before too much

damage was done. White's place is the worst affected. Lama says his parents have a legal cause for action against the government, that no parliament has given them the powers they are exercising. He thinks we should also make a claim but Mammy says no, she'd rather be homeless than ask them for compensation. I told Lama to hold fast, that he would only be wasting time and energy and that his best redress would come when we broke these tyrants as we broke their English friends.

Meanwhile, all classes of blackguards are taking advantage of the situation, even worse than before. We've got used to robbers holding up banks and post offices under the name of the IRA but for several weeks lately, a band of armed thieves has been terrorizing the Kilmannon district, calling to houses late at night with masked faces and demanding money at gunpoint, claiming to be Republican soldiers. We had a fair idea who the culprits might be but it took time to be sure. Saturday night, the lads went after them and made an arrest. They were brought before a Republican court set up in the Sinn Féin Hall and found guilty and on Sunday morning, the lads tied them to the front of Cleariestown chapel gates and put a label on each of them saying: 'Robbers Beware! The IRA is on your track! Leave the Country within 24 hours!' They also put a placard beside them, detailing the affair and setting down their names and addresses.

After the Mass was over, anyone who wanted had their chance to tell them what they thought of their dishonourable conduct. Then they were run out of Mucknamore, told to leave County Wexford and never come back. It was all that could be done, seeing as we don't have prisons in which to punish criminals.

Dear Diary

Disaster. Disaster. Disaster. I didn't go to Redmond's outfarm last night as Mammy was feeling poorly and I didn't like to leave her alone. Molly and Cat went up and a friend of Molly's, a Miss Kathleen O'Brien. I don't think Molly even asked Nora, presuming she'd be unavailable. They were all together, with Barney and Sore-Toes and Lama and eight other men, when Joe Breen came running in from cycling over the fields to warn them he had heard the Stater troops were headed out there after them. That very moment, they began to hear the rumble of the lorries and all hastened to make an escape. Some were lucky but not all. Not Barney. Nor poor Sore-Toes either. And Molly and Miss O'Brien who were slow-moving across the fields were also captured.

Dan O'Donovan led the raid, loving every bit of it, especially capturing Barney. He was striding around, snapping out orders, the boys say, and his men took great pleasure in wrecking the place, putting holes in the walls of the old house, turning over and wrecking whatever they touched. Also captured along with them were sixteen rifles, seven revolvers, twelve hand grenades, hundreds of rounds of rifle ammunition, two mines, a bag of gelignite and a quantity of wires, cables and electric batteries.

But what is worse, what is truly terrible for us all, is that Dan located Molly's papers, every last despatch and list in her possession. The two large sackloads of stuff I gave to her a few weeks ago were found, hidden under a stack of hay. I cannot believe her carelessness, hiding them all in the one place. Why did she not separate it out and keep it in different stashes as we have all been trained to do? Near everything was in those sacks. A record of all our activities from January up to the end of last month. The names of all our forces throughout South Wexford, our strength and equipment, places of parade etc. And all the correspondence on the bank raids, the amounts taken and how distributed. In short, our entire scheme of operations and plans. I'd never have handed them across if I thought she'd be so careless.

So my poor brother is back in prison again, he and Sore-Toes both. Cat was lucky, she and Lama running 'like hell' she said as soon as Joe gave the warning. They got as far as Moran's, then hid in the dug-out. Lama and the rest of the column are now lying real low but it will be hard for them to stay out of trouble after this.

It was hard enough to think of the poor devils facing a life on the run as the winter took its hold but now, thanks to Miss Molly, the enemy knows every active man in our area, every safe house and source of supply. It must have been a spy who gave her away – it's said they knew just where to go to find the papers. This means she'd probably been blabbing.

I really am vexed with her while at the same time sorry for her too. She'll feel terrible about it. But never once, in all the times we were raided, did the enemy ever find anything in *this* house. Can you imagine what would happen if this diary I am writing ever fell into anyone's hands? You have to be careful.

Molly wasn't careful enough, that much is clear. And now we'll all pay the price.

31

1977

Montgomery's is a company based in Hillingdon, North London, that sells paper products – serviettes, kitchen towels and dispensered toilet rolls to hotels and restaurants and garages. I get a job there as a sales clerk. I am a voice at the end of a phone-line, the person customers get to shout at when their paper rolls don't arrive or are the wrong size or colour. I take the insults that spill into my ear, the accusations of incompetence, hand them apologies and politeness in return. I don't care whether they get their product on time, or at all. I expect the planning department or distribution to bungle, although I always pretend to surprise. If you cared about the worst and hoped for the best, you couldn't do my job. It's fine for me.

I live nearby, in a dark, dank basement flat. Its single window – in the bathroom – faces the garden, making the upper quarter of the opaque glass glow green. Mrs Fairbairn, my landlady, resents her dependence on paying tenants. Aside from visiting us once a week for her money, she does her best to pretend we're not here. Her dog Bruno thumps his tail on my ceiling all through the hours that I am there.

But I am not often there. A crowd from work has hooked me into a whirl of drinking and dancing. Our time in Montgomery's is the dead part of our day: when we clock in we are thinking of tea break, then we are aimed at lunch, then at half-past five when work is over and life, real life, can begin. It usually begins in the Rose and Crown when we snuggle into the soft seats and light up our insides with alcohol while darkness presses up against the window.

I take pleasure in these new friends of mine, Mark and Sandra,

Joe and Frank, Sadie, Kim and Natalie. All you need to join their group is a willingness to tease each other and belittle our bosses. A bit of a laugh, as Joe calls it. Where's the harm? That's how each evening starts. By the end of the night, the mood has changed as secrets come surfing out on the alcohol. Sandra cries about how she always wanted children and now it's too late. Frank confesses to a bullying father, Natalie to the family stresses brought on by a Down's syndrome brother. I share too, telling them about the convent and the village and other things that are ordinary in Ireland but exotic to them. They don't know I'm only handing over the bits that don't matter.

On weekend nights, we usually follow our drinking bouts with a nightclub, an Eden of wet kisses and grinding hips. As I writhe to the music, all sorts of delicious sensations rise inside me, filling me up. I meet men, lots of them. No one like Rory but I know now that Rory was not what I thought. I expect nothing of these encounters but desire. Their desire, not mine. Admiration is what I am after, and I collect it from any source, even from those who are too eager. That's the way I prefer to keep them, keen and slightly beneath me, taking what they offer, then flitting on to the next.

The key to it all is vodka, clicking me open and surprising me with what pops out. I always watch for the moment of intoxication when the sober world gets shrugged off like a dull outfit and a new, daring me emerges dressed in flashes and sparkles. It usually comes about halfway through my fourth drink, sometimes earlier. Occasionally – if I've had too much to drink too many nights in a row – I can slide right past it. As resplendent me emerges, I feel as if the whole world is contained in whatever warm and noisy place I am in. I am suffused with love – there is no other word for it – for my drinking friends and myself.

That perfect moment is what I drink for. That, and the licence alcohol gives me to be bad. Whenever I start to sing or shout or flirt or laugh too loud, Natalie teases me: 'So you are Irish, after all.' As if they ever thought of me as anything else. One of the guys in the office even calls me that: 'Hey, Oirish!' he says, by way of hello.

My real name is also different here. Jo Deveroh, I am called now, the 'x' that Wexford people always sound made silent. 'Dever-ex?' they shrieked, when I first introduced myself. 'Dever-ex!' They laughed so hard that I have learned to say it their way.

I am the outsider and so my way is not just different, it is wrong. Lots of things about me are wrong but nothing more than this, my way of talking. I have never been garrulous but now, when sober, I speak only when I must. I slow my words, enunciate more clearly, try to master the dreaded 'th's. I learn to swallow Irish jokes, knowing from where they arise: every foreigner lacks fluency, feels awkward as they grapple with new ways but because the English don't think of Ireland as another country, they interpret our lack of fluency, our different way with the language, as stupidity.

It makes me long, sometimes, for the ease of the familiar. On the tube or the bus or walking down the street, my ear picks up the soft, hissy 't's or thudding 'th's of another Irish person. Sometimes, we get talking, our Irishness enough to connect us. We tell each other what part of the country we're from, a distinction that is lost on the English. We talk about how long we've been over and whether we want to go back. There are only two answers to that. People either yearn to return or, like me, they'd never even consider it. Exile or escape.

Coincidences crop up so often when I meet these strangers – shared times or places or mutual acquaintances – that when they don't I feel cheated. Though I laugh at Londoners who expect me to know everyone from Ireland, I find myself doing the same. The place seems very small from over here.

Mostly, I am glad to be here, feeling awkward. It keeps me attentive, stretches me. And not everybody here thinks Ireland inferior. Katherine in marketing, though born and bred in Bolton, considers herself Irish because she spent every childhood summer with her grandparents in Donegal. She has an Irish, not a British, passport, she tells me, and not just because it is cheaper. 'It's because I *feel* Irish.'

What does it *feel* like, I want to ask, but I can't disappoint her eyes that have grown shiny damp just thinking about it, her look that assumes I'll be delighted.

Everybody has an opinion on Ireland and the Irish over here but none that makes any sense to me. The newspapers talk about 'Northern Ireland' like it's a dark, inexplicable place, doomed by sectarianism. The fighting Irish, irrational and truculent, dark and violent, caught in a fanatically religious quagmire of their own making: who could be expected to understand them? Who could possibly make them see reason? Their own country's part in the North's creation, their government's part in its continuing troubles, doesn't come into it.

One late November evening, I return from the ladies' toilet to the drinks table and know from the hasty way that conversation is picked up that I was being talked about. Later I ask Natalie what they'd been saying.

'We were talking about the bombs.'

She means the IRA bombs that have been going off all over England. The most recent, the third one this year, killed twenty-one people and injured hundreds in Birmingham. London and Guildford have also suffered. The Guildford bomb went off in a pub too and that is what my friends were talking about while I was gone: imagining if one should explode there, then, in the Rose and Crown. A conversation they felt they couldn't have in front of me.

I try to explain to Natalie that I am from Wexford, as far away from the North as it is possible to get in Ireland. That I have no sympathy with the IRA. That I don't care whether Ireland unites or not. I do not tell her how English assumptions of superiority annoy me or how her country's ignorance of its own history makes me angry but it doesn't matter: they have put me in the Irish camp anyway. Irish is what I am whether I claim it or not.

Dear Jo

I got your address and telephone number from Deirdre Mernagh. Don't be cross with her – I bullied it out of her by telling her there was a crisis at home (there isn't). I was going to ring but I thought it might be better to write first.

I hope you're keeping well. Deirdre tells me things have worked out for you over there. That's good anyway, although it's a pity about your degree. I heard a bit about what went on the night you left but I don't really understand why you left so suddenly, or why we haven't heard from you. Mammy is very upset about it all but I suppose you know that. Don't worry, I'm not taking sides. It's just that she would love to hear from you. Maybe you might think about coming home at Christmas? Whatever happened, it shouldn't be allowed to drag on. The longer you go without talking, the harder it will get.

Granny Peg is not that well. She took a bit of a turn a few weeks ago and has been told she has a heart condition. She's on tablets and is supposed to give up the fags but you know yourself how likely that is. Auntie Nora is herself, no change.

I am still working in the school in Terenure. I teach fifth class this year, they're a nice group so I'm having a fairly easy time of it. Also, I have met a nice fella. He's called Donal and he's an accountant. I've been going with him for six months and I suppose you could say it's getting serious. He goes to England a lot on business so you never know, I might go with him sometime and meet up with you.

Don't lose touch altogether, Jo. I'll give you a ring in a while.

Love

Maeve

I am promoted in work to customer services manager. Mr Green, my manager, tells me my prospects are excellent, if I play my cards right. Work hard is his recommendation, but more important, be seen to be keen. Take an exam by night: the subject doesn't matter, the piece of paper is the thing. They're on the lookout for career girls, one of the higher ups says they have to improve their 'gender quota'. He says this with a sneer that holds the words out, away from him.

My new job often keeps me late in the office but as soon as I can, I join the crowd in the pub. They thought my new status might affect our drinking dynamic but I was determined that it would not. When the drink is flowing, I tell them things I'm not supposed to tell.

I am never home. I let dishes accumulate in my sink until fur grows on the debris on the plates. Papers and magazines pile up around my bed. My clothes never go back to the wardrobe, are laundered as I need them. Some days I have to turn my knickers inside out because I have none clean and no time to get to a shop before work. Underwear, tights, food, shampoo: all are bought at the last minute. I am always short, of time and money.

Suddenly, unexpectedly, I meet Jack. Jack Ward. From the minute I meet him, I like him. I allow him close, then back away from him in a push-pull dance that keeps him keen. Jack is easy, so easy. He's good-looking and clever but what I love about him is his openness. He has none of Rory's flamboyance but he is good for me. He lets me be.

For the first time in my life, I don't try to impress, don't do what I think will win his admiration. I carry on drinking as I have always done and in his company I am raucous – shouting and singing and swearing – but none of it fazes him. He smiles through everything, goes home when he feels like going, stays and sings along if that's his mood. Jack takes pleasure in everything – walks in the park, Sunday mornings with the newspapers, nights out to the cinema and theatre – but the me he likes best is the one who comes out when we're home in his bed and three-quarters way down a bottle of red wine. He is uncomplicated in bed, easy to delight.

Jack is not like my other friends. He rarely meets us straight after work though he easily could, his job being just one tube station from the Rose and Crown. But Jack likes to shower his working day away, to change his clothes and have something to eat before he goes out, instead of making do with crisps and salted nuts until closing time like us. He rarely comes clubbing with us either, though he loves to dance. He prefers it when it's just the two of us, he says. He says this without rancour, without the least pressure on me. It annoys me that he is so agreeable. He has such confidence in himself, in me. He is not being careful enough, he is asking for trouble.

Still, I move into his flat when he asks me. It's a two-bedroom flat, brighter and more expensive than mine. We have a moving-in-together party and people buy us things like sauce bowls and matching towels. I buy an apron and a recipe book and spend Monday and Tuesday evenings cooking for us, a housewifely turnabout that amuses Jack. He comes up behind me while I am cooking, puts a glass of wine into my hand, slides his arm around me under my apron. We go to the launderette together and sit watching my underwear and shirts revolving around his.

Sundays, Mondays and most Tuesdays are his but the other nights still belong to the pub. He comes with me less and less often. When I come home late at night, he turns to me in the dark and we make love, his body hot against my cold skin. I act drunker than I am, to make him chuckle into the dark. Next morning when my head is thumping with pain and I am groaning, 'Never again,' he still chuckles, still indulgent. He makes me tea and puts his hand on my forehead while I wonder whether I love him.

Maeve comes across to London to spend a weekend with me, to show off Donal, her new fiancé. For the first couple of hours I'm pleased to see her but before long, she's getting on my nerves. The four of us go out to dinner to celebrate. She sits enfolded inside Fiancé's arm, glancing down at her ring when she thinks nobody's watching. When the waiter comes, they order off the menu for each other.

'It's more interesting,' says Maeve when I ask why anyone would want to do that. 'It's nice to be surprised.'

'And anyway we know what each other likes,' says Fiancé. They cannot stop showering each other with smiles. While they're not looking, I make a vomiting gesture to Jack.

He and Donal talk about work, suss out each other's place on the career pecking order, while Maeve fills me in on 'the news' from 'home'. During a silence, she leans across her plate of mussels to Jack. 'Have you ever been to Ireland before, Jack?'

'No.'

'You'll love it. You'll have to get Jo to take you to the west. It's much more scenic over there. The west is what people think of when they think of Ireland, like the Highlands in Scotland.'

Jack looks at me. 'I'm not sure if—'

I cut in: 'We've no plans to go to Ireland, Maeve.'

'But Jack will surely come to the wedding. We'd love him to come.'

'On his own? I don't think he'd fancy that. Would you, Jack?'

'Jo,' says Maeve. 'You didn't mean what you said about not coming. You have to—'

'Maeve, I told you.' I had too, in the bedroom before we came out.

'But—'

'No buts. I'm sorry. I won't be coming. Please accept that.'

Fiancé Donal says: 'Maeve was hoping you'd be her bridesmaid, Jo.'

'I'm sorry,' I say again. I don't attempt an explanation, it would be pointless and only extend the discussion. Instead I lift the champagne bottle to pour us all a refill but find I am the only one whose glass is empty. Replacing the bottle in the ice bucket, I catch a long look sloping between Maeve and Jack and – horrified – I realize that he has discussed me with my sister. Rage makes me tremble. I have to get up and go out to the ladies', to sit on the toilet seat, trying to grasp hold of my anger, to push it back down where I can contain it. What have they discussed? How can they have ended up on the same side? I cannot believe this of Jack.

After that, the night is a disaster. I get drunk and pick snarling arguments with them both, about everything. Fabulous Fiancé looks on, dismayed. We leave the restaurant early. Back in the flat, the two men scoot off to bed and Maeve starts one of her lectures: I am so unwelcoming, so rude to Donal, so selfish. As for Mammy and Granny Peg, I have broken their hearts. The wedding is the perfect opportunity to put all this behind us and here I am, throwing it back in their faces.

'What's it like to be perfect, Maeve?' I ask her. 'Does it never get tiring?'

Feeling something on my face, I put up my hand. I stare at my damp fingers in surprise. I am crying. But I never cry any more, not since the abortion.

'Now look what you've done,' I accuse. 'Why can't you all just leave me alone?'

Months pass, turn into a year, then two and more. I get to know Jack's family, the mother and sister who both think he's wonderful. They are kind, if a little puzzled by me. I am not what they hoped for him. But if I make him happy . . . Jack only laughs. We do not need family; we have our friends. And each other. We spend Christmas away, one year in Scotland, the next in southern Italy, a third in New York.

Maeve gets married. Her old friend Anita Shiels does bridesmaid. I receive a slice of wedding cake in the post, and some photographs: an older Mrs D., heavier but somehow also more frail, trying to look composed; Gran and Auntie Nora just the same, Auntie Nora somewhere off in her head, Gran gently holding her arm. They seem like people I saw in a movie once, or on TV, in a show that was axed but went on running anyway, though nobody was watching. I push the pictures to the back of a drawer, so that I don't destroy them.

Maeve begins to telephone me regularly, to give me unasked for news of Mucknamore, but at least she has stopped nagging me to go back.

I still have my nights out with the Montgomery's crowd. The group gets smaller as time goes on and people break away. The hard core is Natalie, Frank, Sally and me. We believe we are connected to each other but our real bond is to booze and it's tightening all the time. Sometimes now I have blackouts. I don't tell Jack about this. I don't tell anybody, even Sal or Natalie, though we love to rehash the shocking or silly things drink makes us do. Everything that happens during an alcohol-induced blackout is irretrievable, I read in a book I borrowed from the library. It cannot be revived by any of the methods that recover lost memories, like truth drugs or hypnosis. Something about that frightens me.

I do magazine quizzes that all tell me what I already know: I should cut down or give up. I resolve to give up drinking doubles, drinking so often, drinking before six but can never make any of these resolutions stick. What the hell, becomes my most used phrase as I tilt back another illicit glass.

At work, I begin to miss targets and deadlines. I gargle with Listerine in the morning, suck peppermints and chew gum all day, spray Gold Spot into my mouth before going out for the evening, but still I reek. People sniff me out and I hate them for it.

At home, silence is piling up around our apartment like snow muffling a storm. I begin to lie, something I have never done. I don't know why. Jack of all people can handle the truth but I never come home late now without a story prepared. He hates lies but pretends to believe mine. Sometimes, when I am drunk, I insult him, trying to goad him to a reaction, and he looks at me as if I'm a crazy intruder and he's wondering how I got in. When I sober up, I get frightened and try to blot out whatever I've done with sex. We fuck furiously, long sessions that leave me physically drained but dissatisfied. I am losing the ability to tell pleasure from pain.

32

1922

To Peg Parle from Barney Parle:

The Gaol
Wexford

27th October 1922

Dear Peg,

Thanks for your welcome letter. To answer your questions: 1. There are between forty and fifty of us here in the gaol. 2. During the day we're allowed out of our cells and confined to a large dayroom. 3. We pass the time as you might imagine, reading, playing cards, sparring. Our exercise is one hour walking round and round the yard. I'd give anything for a game of football but that's not allowed.

One of our officers in charge is Dan O'Donovan. A Lieutenant now, as I'm sure you've heard, and he likes that a lot, I can tell you. Takes his duties very seriously. He's getting himself a name as a right hard man. Lucky, I don't have much to do with him. The odd time when he is in to do a check our eyes cross but we act as if we never knew each other. Neither of us knows what other way to do it.

Thanks for the offers of help. We know you are 'always there' and thank God we do know it. The only thing you can do for me is the one thing I ask of you all the time, to be a comfort to Nora. She doesn't have your strength. I have written to her as you know but I'm not like you with the letters – my words never seem to say it right.

My poor Nora, we had such great plans. Only God above knows when or if they'll happen.

Hoping, anyhow, that you're in the best of health. I'll write again when I get the chance.

Yours sincerely

Your affec Bro

Barney

To Peg Parle from Molly Redmond:

Kilmainham Jail

1.11.1922

Dear Peg,

Well, my dear, you will have heard by now that they got me and how. So here I am in Kilmainham, where the 1916 leaders were brought to die. Could we ever have believed then that Irish men would stoop so low?

I am one in a ward of nine and each of us takes turns doing orderly for the room. The girls in single cells also take their turn, serving food, washing-up etc. We have one bathroom to our floor and we share this amicably for personal use or washing clothes, but are forced to hang our washing over banisters or on improvised lines across the corridors to dry, an embarrassment in front of our male warders.

To keep our hands and minds busy, we study Irish, knit or sew and read. We have to be indoors by nine and have lights out at ten. A bit of a candle sometimes finds its way into our possession but when lit it has to be kept under the bed with the readers or card players squatting on the floor to enjoy its beams. If the least glimmer is seen outside the sentry roars in: 'Put out that light' and if this order is not followed, he fires his gun in our direction. On one such occasion, his bullet came in the window, leaving its mark on the wall opposite.

Friday night is the soldiers' pay night and we are usually treated to a musical watch. We too often sing in the dark to each other and sometimes we hear our men across the way doing the same. If one of us asks ourselves the question, why am I here, the answer comes then: because they are.

What did you think of the Bishops and their pastoral letter against us? None of us gave into it, of course, and we haven't been allowed to attend Mass or Holy Communion since. The girls in here now use the old adage that once was the highest compliment – 'May you be the mother of a bishop' – as a insult. Well, so be it. God hears our prayers one way or the other. If Cromwell and the Penal laws didn't succeed in breaking the faith of the Irish rebel, the Bishops of Ireland won't either.

I hope this letter reaches you. We have been told we will be able to get out a stack of letters by a laundry van in a day or so. There's little point in writing otherwise – half our communications never get out and the other half are so censored they might as well not be sent.

Give my love to all and tell them to remember the poor convict in their prayers and to write to me. Even a few censored lines would make all the difference to . . .

Your affectionate friend,
Molly

The Barracks
Newbridge

4th November 1922

Dear Sister,

This letter comes to you from Newbridge, where we are put up in the old British Cavalry Barracks. We were transferred two days ago, brought up by train. Conditions are not bad, about twenty men to each room, and we all have a bed and enough blankets. Food, unfortunately, is not too plentiful. The Dublin boys are well away, able to get food parcels from home. They don't share with Wexfordmen but we fill up with the cuts of bread and cold porridge they don't want.

We spent a long day on the train the day we were brought up, locked into one of those old-fashioned closed carriages with nothing to eat but tinned fish and you know how I love that. It was dark when we got to Dublin and after a long wait we set off again. They didn't tell us where we were going. A rumour went round that we were being brought to St Helena. Instead we stopped at a wayside station about an hour from

Dublin. From there they marched us towards a searchlight that scanned the skies and fields until we came to this place.

We were left standing for hours outside a group of low, dark wooden huts in the freezing cold while they checked us in, six prisoners at a time. It was early morning before I was escorted through. I was shown my mattress and fell gratefully into it.

Since then, it hasn't been too bad. Sore-Toes is here as well and Larry Crean, Joe Duggan, Paddy Doyle, Thomas Keogh and the Redmond brothers from town. Other 'yellow-bellies' too that you wouldn't know so well. All are in good form. Sore-Toes sends his regards.

Tell Daddy never to believe the slanderous stories that are used against us (I know you and Mammy wouldn't) and tell them both to pray for us. I have written to them too but saying less than I say to you. Take care of yourself too, Peg. We know the risks you take for us. It is only now that we have our backs to the wall and everybody against us, that we appreciate you girls of C. na mBan as the fine comrades you are. Without you the fight would have died long ago. God bless the work.

Your affectionate bro,

Barney

Peg

Dear Diary

I had a horrible dream last night. I dreamt I was out with the boys, part of the column, with a gun in my hand looking for Dan O'Donovan. I saw him ahead of me and ran after him. He was faster than me and I would never have caught up with him but suddenly as he ran down a long, narrow passage he came upon this ten-foot-high hedge and he could go no further. I had him and he knew it. So he turned around to me and started trying to persuade.

'Now, Peg . . .' he started, in the same smarmy voice he used to me that night with Barney in Enniscorthy. 'Let's be sensible . . .'

But I let him say no more, I shot him straight on and he grabbed his front where the bullet went in and slowly folded to thc ground until he was lying, flat on his face, dead. I went over to him and knelt down beside him to turn him over and when I did, I got the shock of my life for I saw it wasn't Dan at all I had killed, but Barney. And I woke up shouting out, 'No, no, no . . .'

Well, I couldn't get back to sleep for the rest of the night. Of course it was only a dream but it left a horrible black feeling pressing down on me, a feeling that has stayed with me all day.

This evening I went up to Mammy's room for a chat. She was in bed early, having a rest, and I sat down on the side of the bed. She wasn't looking the best and I decided not to burden her with my worries but she sensed my mood and wheedled it all out of me the way she does. I told her about the dream and the heavy feelings I am carrying around with me.

'Such feelings are only natural,' she said, 'considering all that's going on. What you mustn't do is let the worries turn you away from the work.'

'No, no, the work is no burden, Mammy,' I said, surprised at her misunderstanding. Yes, I had been up the last four mornings before dawn, painting slogans on walls: CALL OFF THE MURDER GANGS. DON'T TORTURE OUR PRISONERS. THE IRISH REPUBLIC LIVES. Yes, as things get hotter, I've never been busier and with Molly gone and Nora a near prisoner in her house, it nearly all falls onto me. But I don't mind. It's an honour to work for Ireland.

'Work isn't just typing notices about informers or calling meetings, Peg,' Mammy said. 'It's coping with feelings the like of what you're having. Not letting such feelings deflect you.' She took my hand and I felt bad, because I knew she was thinking how much she'd like to still be up to such work.

She went on, explaining that holding up my hands in horror and giving up now would be the easy thing to do. 'You're missing your brother, that's part of the problem,' she said. 'You have to take too much on yourself while he's away in prison. But we mustn't let him down.'

Again she didn't say it but I knew she was thinking of herself, of how hard it was for her not knowing when she might see him next or how she might be by then.

I hadn't thought about it in that way but she's right; I do miss Barney, and Nora too. She's only up the road but she might as well be in England itself for all I get to see of her. And though I know those who think like us were always a minority, that Boland and Pearse and Tone and Emmet and many more, all the way back, were always in the minority, still it can be hard to hold fast when press and pulpit and people unite against you as strong as they are right now.

As well, there's all the terrible things that you read every day in the paper, the killings and maimings, the reprisals and counter-reprisals, the executions, official and unofficial. Sometimes it feels like one whole half of the country has a gun pointed at the other half. And then there's the North. The things being done to Nationalists beyond that border are criminal. Pure wicked.

But I suppose Mammy is right, it was never going to be easy. Thank God that at least I have her to turn to. Whenever I am wavering she is there to set me straight.

Dear Diary

As I was walking home from school today I came upon Father John at the end of the school lane. He suggested he walk home a bit of the way with me and as I had little choice, I agreed. I had a fair idea what was coming but he took the long way round in getting to it, asking me first about Mammy's health and how was Daddy and any word of Barney and how was the teaching going and would the children be ready for the parish concert by the night. All very proper and almost pleasant, if it wasn't for the fact that we both knew he hadn't joined me just for a chat.

He started the subject by referring to the Rathmeelin robbers and asked me if I didn't think they should have been reported to the authorities.

'It was the people troubled by the blackguards who made the choice, Father,' I said. 'They went to those they thought best able to help them.'

'You'll agree, maybe, that they were at fault in that.'

'I wouldn't be sure, Father.'

'You wouldn't be sure. Tell me, Peg, don't we have a police force who could take up for them?'

'I don't think they put much pass on the new police, Father.'

I had gone too far. His eyebrows came down into that false furrow he puts on when he wants you to know he's cross with you. 'You are aware of the statement of our bishops on these matters.'

'Ye-es.'

'You know that it is a sin to take on the work of the government, to set up our own policing and armies and so on. You must know that.'

I let my silence speak.

'You know what you must do?'

I looked down at my shoes, dusty from the bad condition of the road.

'Peg, your job as a national-school teacher brings responsibility with it.'

'I know my responsibilities, Father. I've always taken them serious.' I knew he could have no complaint about my work for since September I've made sure to be over-and-above diligent.

'I'm not referring to your school duties, Peg. As I think you well know. Those are not the responsibilities I meant.'

'You mean politics,' I said.

He came to a halt on the road. 'It's gone beyond politics, Peg. You heard the words of their Lordships the bishops read off the altar.'

To deuce with their Lordships the bishops, I felt like saying. The same bishops have deprived Republicans of the Sacraments. The men out there fighting – devout Catholics almost to a man – now go into danger without absolution of their sins and know that if they fall in action or are captured or executed, they might be refused the Last Rites.

'Am I not as entitled as the next person to what I believe, Father?' I said to him, quiet and polite as I could make it. 'And believing as I do, am I not to work for what I believe to be right?'

He dropped his eyes and started fiddling with his cuffs, embarrassed. He can't take straight talk. I could have said a lot more only I was afraid of where I might take us.

After a while he said: 'We must not be proud, Peg. Pride is a great sin. We must listen to those who know most about these matters. Follow the guidance of your bishops and you won't go far wrong.'

It was pointless trying to explain anything to him. I nodded my head towards the house instead, in an attempt to change the subject. 'Will you come inside, Father?'

'It was my intention to go in and see JJ. Is there a need for me to do that, d'you think?'

'You mean . . . about what we've been saying?'

'Yes.'

Was this his way of asking me whether I intend to give up my work? He stood like he was waiting for an answer but I wasn't going to lie outright to him, so I just stood there too. I killed a man, Father, that's what I was thinking as I stood there, looking into his comfortable chins. I've done more, seen more than you in your safety ever will.

After a long while he sighed. 'I'll leave it for today,' he said. 'Tell your mammy I sent a blessing.'

'I will, Father. Thank you, Father.'

'You think hard about what I said and be sensible, like the good girl you are.' And with that, he took himself off.

For God's sake! To think I once was afraid of him. I told Mammy all about it afterwards and she only laughed. 'Don't mind Father John,' she said. 'All he wants is the quiet life.'

Dear Diary

Barney is home! Escaped from jail! He turned up tonight while Mammy and I were on our knees in the kitchen saying the rosary. I nearly died of fright when the two faces – himself and Sore-Toes – popped up at the window. Mammy was nearly crying to see him. Since the Staters executed those four prisoners the other day we've been so worried.

It's so awful what they did, I still can't believe it. Four men taken out and murdered without trial, without word or warning, their relatives not even informed. How they found out their loved one was dead was they received a telegram saying: REMAINS OF ______ HAVE BEEN COFFINED AND

BURIED IN CONSECRATED GROUND. SIGNED: GOVERNMENT, SAORSTAT EIREANN.

It is meant as a warning: nobody on our side is safe, that is what they're trying to tell us. Nobody. Not even – or maybe especially not – the ordinary boys. Their hope of quashing us is misguided but thank God, thank God that Barney's out of it now.

They escaped through a tunnel, with six others from various parts of the country, and then had to walk the whole way back, it being too dangerous to take lifts – a distance of a hundred and fifty miles across hills and fields. Ten days of non-stop marching they had, poor things. They only encountered Army boys once along the way, near Arklow so at least they were in luck there.

They are both well, though they've lost weight from the long trek and from lack of food. They had to change outside because their clothes were hopping with fleas and stinking from repeated wettings. Worse than the fleas, he says, is a rash that makes him itch all over. They both have it, God love them. They're downstairs now, in the usual place, putting in the night here. Probably not the safest but what could we do? We could hardly send the poor devils off into the dark.

Barney will go nowhere, anyway, until he sees Nora. He's like a hen on a hot griddle at the thought of having to wait until the morning. I've written her a note and took it down to put it under the stone in the dark – nothing less would do him. Hopefully, she'll be down in the morning. He's that bad he'd nearly go up there after her.

33
1980

Jack is withdrawing his love. I can feel it pulling away, like the tide going out, leaving me beached. Nothing is said, especially not by me. I lie in bed beside him pretending to sleep, not touching, my head blistered with thoughts. I eat breakfast on a stool opposite him, the *Guardian* divided between us. I watch television from a separate armchair, the couch we used to share staring back at us from across the room.

By the time he asks me to leave I expect it, but still, it seems sudden. It doesn't seem right that we can pass through all the stages and arrive at the end without even a decent quarrel. And I am frightened; I don't want to be on my own again. So I humiliate myself, beg him to reconsider, make promises we both know I can't keep, even though inside I have already said goodbye, even though I know breaking up is right for me as much as him. Jack always does the right thing.

So we go until the evening he comes home and firmly tells me I have to leave. I am to be gone by the end of the month. The end of the month. His face is set against me, the craggy lines shutting me out.

'We haven't tried hard enough,' I say. 'We haven't talked. We should talk.'

He shakes his head. 'Too late,' he says. Two words only, as if they are rationed.

I gabble: 'I'll stop drinking, Jack . . . I know that's the problem . . . If that's what you want . . .'

Again, that shake of his head.

I put myself on his mercy. 'I have nowhere to go.'

He spreads his hands wide, as if he is the one who is helpless.

I am starting to cry. 'I gave up everything for you, you bastard. Where the hell am I supposed to go?'

'I'm sorry, Jo.' He doesn't sound it or look it but underneath my blustering tears, I know he is. His sorrow is an axe, slicing me off.

I move in with Natalie who owns a flat in Camden Town and has a box bedroom she never bothered to fill after her last flatmate moved out. The decor is dire and I keep promising myself I will paint the walls and the cheap melamine furniture but I can't seem to get round to it. I'm too busy, home only in time to cry myself to sleep.

I have started to cry a lot, especially after a few drinks. I tell everybody who will listen that Jack has broken my heart. This half-truth sustains me, gives me permission to wallow in my sorrows, to try to drown them. Natalie and I drink now in the pub near the flat instead of the Rose and Crown. It's handier. We can just walk home instead of having to negotiate the tube after closing time. Anyway, the old gang has broken up. People have moved on, to relationships, marriages, mortgages. Natalie and I bicker, like an old married couple. She is small-minded, about money and motives, and not very bright. Often I wonder how I ended up with her. I miss Deirdre and resolve again that I will write to her, a letter that I will finish, all the way to the end of a page or even two, and put in an envelope, and actually send.

Natalie is also a nag. She ticks me off for not keeping to the housework rota she drew up. Though I want to oblige her in this, I keep finding the effort of it beyond me. When we're not out drinking, I sit in a corner of the couch, or on top of my duvet, staring at nothing, locked inside a struggle. Not moving but with every coil in my brain contorted and every muscle under strain.

*

People think when you're slipping you don't know, but you do. You're the first to know. For a long time before anyone raises a whispered note of concern or passes a comment across a sea of laughs from others, you've been telling yourself what's wrong, and how to put it right. Giving yourself sensible advice that you can't seem to take.

I never drink at home but I'm not stupid enough to believe that matters. I know what I am. I know I have to stop. And I try, I do try, and sometimes I succeed. But even when I'm not succeeding, when I appear to others to be unabashedly drinking, internally I'm straining with effort. Every day starts with good intentions pressed into place but somehow, by evening or sometimes earlier, I am once again pouring drink down my throat.

I am a limp drunk, occasionally boisterous but mostly weepy and full of self-pity. I can't stand her, this interloper who intrudes into my evening, wet-eyed every time, yet still I feed her. Whisky now, Scotch (never Irish) on the rocks. One night I wake in bed beside a stranger and have no memory of how I got there. The skin on my chest and back stings and when I investigate I find I am covered in scratches.

My boss calls me in. I have used up all my leave, paid and unpaid, and my sick days, certified and uncertified. I am late three mornings out of five. If I don't improve my performance, he has no choice but to let me go. So what, I say to myself after this rebuke, it's not like I like this low-grade, beneath-me job. But I have no qualifications and so no hope of a better one. It's a dilemma. Unsure how to solve it, I take to the pub with Natalie.

At some stage in the evening, she goes home but I go on to a club. Somebody puts me into a taxi at the end of the night. Staggering up the steps to our front door, I trip and burst my lip. Next morning, I arrive late to work again. I am shuddering a coffee cup to my broken mouth when the boss calls me to his office, makes me sign a form. My final warning.

'Do yourself a favour,' he says. 'Get a grip.'

He is right, I know he is right. That's what I need to do: get a grip. I need to stop.

I stop.

I'm in Natalie's kitchen, crouching on the floor, stuck. Unable to move. Darkness is fondling the windowpane, which means it's late but I have no idea how long I have sat here like this, immobile. In my right hand I hold the kettle, full of cold water, but I have no memory of filling it. My arm hurts from holding on but I can't let it go. My hand, my arm, everything is jammed. My body has wound down, like a clockwork toy, while my mind has gone into overspin, spewing up thought after self-lacerating thought.

I am captive, paralysed by the parade of taunts that come swooping in, cascading one over the other to flay out at recoiling, cowering, me. Then, somebody speaks to me from behind, over near the door.

Do it, she says.

Fear creeps along my skin. I know that voice and I know she can't be here. Did I imagine it? It doesn't seem so, it sounds like she is in the room behind me, her voice real and solid as a voice can be. *Do it*, she says again.

On the table above me is the bread knife, with its row of shiny, sharp-toothed smiles all along the blade. It doesn't hurt: slash, slash the serrated edge once, twice, across the skin, faster than thought. Two burning flashes, then the thoughts fade to silky black whispers . . . It doesn't even hurt, that's what they say.

Just do it.

My hand jerks and opens. Cold water splashing over my jeans breaks the spell. I can move again, though not quickly, not easily. I leave the kettle on the floor where it has fallen, the lid where it has rolled away, the water gliding along the brown lino. On my hands and knees, I crawl away. In the bedroom, I close the door behind me, lean against it. The thudding of my heart is echoed all over my body. Even my toes and fingertips throb. I am so frightened.

I have to go, that is what I realize. If I don't get away, her voice will move in, come to live with me. She will feel entitled, invited by default. I have to go and I have to go now before Natalie comes back, before I am back into the everyday world where thoughts like these slip down under the surface and pretend they're not there.

I find the backpack I brought from Jack's place and begin to fill it. It takes a huge effort, deciding what to bring. I would prefer to just walk out the door with only the clothes I am wearing but I cannot afford that, I am going to need everything that is mine. Into the bag they go, clothes, records, books, anything I can fit. When I am packed, I sit down at the kitchen table to write Natalie a note. I'm trying to find words when the key turns in the door. She is home early, but not – I read by the slackness of her jaw – too early to have had a few drinks.

'Whatever are you doing?' Her wide, inebriated eyes take in my rucksack, the other bags, my duvet and pillows rolled into a black sack. 'What's going on?'

I put down the pen. 'I have to go.'

'Go? What are you talking about? Go where?'

'I have to . . .' My voice has the shakes. 'I—'

'What about money for bills, for rent while I find someone else? Were you going without paying?'

'Natalie—' Aghast, I realize I can't speak. If I do, I'll break.

'Where are you going?'

I shrug.

'Jo, this is stupid.'

I cannot look at her drunken face, her swollen, fluid eyes. I crumple up the sheet of paper I have been writing on.

Something conveys itself to her and she changes tack. 'You're a bit down,' she says. 'Are you? Is that it?'

I pick up my bags.

'You could have told me, you know. You should have. Sneaking off like this . . .'

The doorbell rings.

'Taxi,' I say.

'You can send it away. We'll call it again in the morning. We'll sort something out then.'

I shunt my backpack up onto my shoulder; hug the big plastic bag to my chest so I can barely see over it.

She doesn't get it. She thinks that some day we'll look back on this, analyse it over a drink. She hasn't a clue, about anything.

I turn away and she follows, picking up my other bag and walking behind me like a porter. Outside the hall door, it's raining. I hand a bag to the driver, take the other from Natalie. Bending my head to the weather, I run down the steps. She follows me out to the gate, hugs me, her skin hot against my cheek. Drips slink down the shiny black rump of the cab. The engine grumbles impatiently. I pull out of her grasp.

'Ring me.' Her shout reaches over my shoulder as I climb into the back of the taxi. 'Ring me soon.'

I slump into the seat, dizzy with relief. I'm getting used to leaving, getting to recognize its imperative: shut down; face forward.

The driver asks, 'Where to, love?'

'Heathrow Airport,' I say.

The taxi pulls away from the kerb and I turn to look back, just for a second, but I can't see anything. Already, Natalie and her flat have blurred into rain and disappeared.

34

1922

'Slap your eyes on that one. What d'you think of that?'

'Fuck-ing hell.'

It was a dirty picture. Jem Fortune had a supply of them – God alone knew where from, he wasn't telling. When not amusing himself with them, he liked to give himself a secondary thrill from passing them around. And the freedom fighters of Mucknamore Active Service Unit, bored out of their brains sitting in an outhouse full of nothing but the smell of old straw, were even more than normally willing to give such matters their attention.

Seven of the column were there, in a rickety shed that once sheltered cattle but was now falling into disrepair: Barney and Sore-Toes, Roller and Lama, Jem and young Bronco and Jamsie Crean, all enduring a miserable, wet afternoon that was turning into a dark, drawn-out night. Rain fell like a curtain in front of the open shed door. Every so often a gust of wind whipped the downpour indoors, so a wet semicircular patch guarded the entrance to the building. They were trapped.

Jamsie held one picture in his hand, Jem the other, their eyes riveted onto them, their chins slack. 'Oh, man,' said Lama, coming over to stick his head between them. 'Oh, man.'

'A baggage, if ever there was one,' said Jem Fortune, proud to be the owner of the image. 'I think you'll agree, gentlemen?'

Lama plucked one of the pictures out of Fortune's hand, passed it on to Barney. 'Take a look at this, Parle,' he said. 'She'll put hairs on your chest.'

The girl was in a state of undress, lying back on a sofa with her vest up to her neck and bloomers pushed low down on her hips, showing some personal hair. Her dids were round and plump with nipples big as saucers and the way she had her arms folded underneath pushed them up and out at him. The bold-as-brass look on her face was as disturbing as her display of herself.

He tried to stop looking. If he was alone she would have all his attention but he was made uncomfortable by the presence of the others. He passed her on and sat back down on the upturned bucket he'd been using as a seat.

They had been brought to this place, eight miles from Mucknamore, by a suspected spy, a man called Browne. Tomorrow – it would have been today if the weather hadn't put a stop to it – Barney and Lama intended to dress up in Free State Army uniforms they had confiscated and hidden in old sacking in the back of the barn and pay him a visit, make him an offer of money for information about their own whereabouts. If he fell for the inducement, they'd have the proof they need. Their own information had it that said Mr Browne pointed the way for the last military round-up. Twenty-two men got picked up in that – including their own Leary brothers, all three, and Jack Kelly and Gut Hayes – along with rifles, revolvers and ammunition.

They were lucky the army didn't decide to do round-ups more often, it was their best tactic. Early as dawn they would come out from Wexford, assembling in bands of twenty or so, then moving systematically through the area, townland by townland, to search all suspect houses and hiding points. Regular round-ups could clear an area of Republicans in a matter of days but lucky the Free State Army in Wexford were lazy, as half-hearted about this as they were about everything else.

What the column would do to Browne when they found him guilty had yet to be resolved. Jem Fortune said he should be shot. 'May the gates of hell never screech for want of grease while there's marrow in the bones of a traitor,' he had said earlier, waving his revolver in the air. Others were less histrionic. It was Barney's opinion that they should be merciful – punish the man, yes, but not shoot him. No agreement had been reached on the matter when Jem Fortune pulled out his pictures, the subject of which now seemed to exercise him a great deal more than vengeance on the informer.

Another photograph was placed in Barney's hand. 'Perhaps,' said Jem, 'you are more of an arse man, my friend?'

The second picture was even more shocking. The same girl taken from the back, bent forward from the waist with her bloomers pulled down to the top of her legs, just below the large white globes of her rear end. Her legs were a little apart, showing the shadow between them. His breath stiffened in the back of his throat. He wanted to stop looking, he wanted to never stop looking. She gazed over her shoulder out of the picture at him, her long hair loose and hanging down.

'What do you think of that, Barney me boy?' said Lama. 'Fancy running into that on a dark night, would you?'

'Give us a look,' said Crean, snatching her away.

In the dim light, they huddled close to see. Cackling whoops of laughs were passed around. 'Jaysus. Look at that.'

'What I wouldn't like to give her.'

'In your dreams, Delaney. What would a one like her want with a thick like you?'

The jeers were forced, a matter of making any noise rather than admit to the cramped urges the pictures stirred. Their laughter was lined with fear: fear of the sin of looking, but under that and stronger, fear of their own need.

Jem and Jamsie Crean retired to the back of the shed with their pictures and nobody was under any illusions about what they were doing back there. Barney sat on, as was his custom now, alone, watching the grey light outside fade to darker grey. They had no lantern. The faces of the men around him blurred to moving shades, then disappeared altogether as day become evening. Then, almost immediately, it was night. A night black as tar. Nothing but the palpitating rain, falling, falling. No more ogling now for Jem and the boys. No more anything, except empty conversation into the damp darkness, for anyone who could be bothered. They were sick of talking to each other: anything any of them had to say had long ago been said.

For Barney, there was nothing to do and fourteen hours of night to do it – it would be near eight o'clock in the morning before they saw daylight again. He got up off his upturned bucket, stiff and cramped, the damp of the rain in his bones. In the dim light, he felt his way across the straw, moving as far as he could from the others to the far corner of the shed. He settled himself there, heaping some straw under his head to make a pillow, huddling down into his coat.

He took out his last cigarette, which he had been hoarding, and lit it. Fortune's pictures had unsettled him. He found himself thinking about what had brought him here, to this place, to playing the part of soldier: what he saw in Nora O'Donovan's eyes when she looked at him now. All the women were bloodthirsty, even gentle Nora, their ferocity strengthened by the fact that they so rarely saw action. He would never forget the glitter in Peg's eyes that night on the bridge in Donore – his mother he was used to, but this was something else. It was all too much for him. Sometimes he felt like the world was drowning in human blood. Their own country's troubles were trifling compared to what other parts had seen – the Great War, the revolutions in Russia, the goings on in Africa and China and every part of the world. All those men killing and being killed because of the light in some girl's eye. It was madness. And in his own case doubly so, because he wasn't even seeing his girl enough to enjoy her admiration. He thought he was going to be the star of the show but really he was playing the fool.

The rain spattered on, relentless. Even his thoughts felt pallid and unconvincing, like his brain had been bleached. He squashed his cigarette butt out on the ground beside him, careful – with all the straw around – to ensure that it was extinguished. Then, hours earlier than usual, hours earlier than was good for him, he gave himself over to the squirms and spaces of the night.

*

He woke to find the rain had stopped and he pushed himself up off his bed of straw, stepping over the bodies of his comrades still slumped in sleep. His bones were sore. Outside, the air tasted new and clean. He stretched, breathed in deep. The heaviest of the clouds had parted, allowing a gleam through the grey, and the grass was plump with rainwater. He breathed deep again, felt the air fresh on his face. They'd get their man today, then he had to get home for a night or two.

He walked up the roadway that skirted the field, to stretch his legs. He hadn't gone far when he saw Doyle's daughter on her bicycle, a pail over each handlebar, and he turned back. 'Breakfast is on the way,' he called into the shed.

Jem Fortune was out the door in an instant. He let a loud wolf whistle at the girl as she drew near. She dismounted from her bicycle and he moved to help her with the buckets and did his best to engage her in conversation. She was having none of it. A surly lump of a girl she was, with none of the hero-worship for freedom fighters that they liked to read in female eyes. And no time at all for Jem's brand of talk.

At the shed, she handed them two loaves of bread wrapped in a tea towel and a copy of the *Wexford Weekly*. 'Mammy said you might like a read of that?'

'Thank your mother for us,' said Jem. 'And thank her too for sending the vision of your fair self to open the morning for us.'

She threw him a look that would wither a bush.

'If you can, bring the buckets back down to the house when you're finished,' she said. 'If not, I'll collect them later.'

She turned away to pick up her bike.

'You look even better from this side,' Jem shouted after her, his gaze pasted onto her rump.

After breakfast, it was down to the business of the day. Barney sent Sore-Toes and Bronco to the hideout to retrieve the army uniforms. They were found to be dishevelled from their time in the ditch so the column set to scraping the worst of the dirt off and brushing them down with damp leaves. If they were not smart looking, they wouldn't convince. While doing this work, they argued again about shooting the spy if he was guilty.

'I think what we should do is put a good fine on him,' said Barney. 'And send him out of the county, as we did with the Kilmannon robbers. Let's not sink to the level of the Nationals.'

'Robbing is one thing,' said Lama. 'Informing is something else entirely.'

'I'm in agreement with that,' said Jem Fortune.

Barney combed his head for words. Even if it was Browne who gave them away – and that was what he expected – who was going to do this execution that they all claimed to want so bad? Not Jem Fortune, surely, who was known to have swallowed his lit cigarette the one and only time he saw action, at the Ardnacree ambush. Not Sore-Toes Delaney, who kept to the back of the firing in any encounter. Maybe Lama might have it in him, but what if he didn't? What if he funked it? Or worse, did it and never got over it?

'It's one thing to take a man out in an ambush,' he said, 'quite another to shoot him at close range.'

'But if he's a spy . . .'

'I won't be doing it, anyway.'

'What's wrong, Parle?' jeered Lama. 'Not up to it?'

'I don't see the need for it.'

'It makes sure Browne never gets the chance to inform again. It frightens others who might be tempted to do the same.'

'Sending him out of the county won't send the same message,' said Jem.

'What do HQ say?' asked Sore-Toes.

'Oh, HQ. Sometimes I wonder if they even know we're here.'

The argument lapsed into spiny silence. They finished brushing the uniforms and laid them out to dry. Barney picked up the paper that the farmer's girl left behind. When Jem Fortune blasted the left ear off him with one of his wolf whistles, he took no notice, thinking it was the girl come back for the dishes. He was stuck in an article about a lecture Father John gave at a meeting in town, disparaging the immodest style of dress now worn by female folk. All that was going on in the country, and this was what the man chose to lecture people about: that was what he was thinking when he was jolted by a nudge in the ribs. Jem said, 'Your visitor, Parle, I do believe.'

He looked up and across in the direction of Jem's nod.

Was it . . . ? It *was*. Nora. Nora, alone, standing behind the far gate as if she dared not come any farther.

His heart jumped, jerking him to his feet. Ignoring the jeers that were starting up behind him, he crossed the field to her, breathless. This was a surprise. And, Lord, the force of his feelings! Was it like this for everyone? Lama showed no sign of being cuffed in the stomach whenever he set eyes on Cat Hayes. But then neither did he, Barney, let on. Did everybody feel this way and go around pretending they didn't?

When she saw him coming across the field, she pulled back behind the hedge, away from the inquisitive eyes behind him. He climbed over the gate and landed with a jump beside her but she was off, already walking down the lane, not giving him a chance to get near her, to kiss her hello as he would have liked.

'Are you all right, Nora?' he asked when he caught up.

She shook her head, like she was shaking out a dirty rag.

'It's great you've come,' he said. Something had happened. That shut face again, tight as a tomb. He pulled her into a gateway. How different it was, he thought as he kissed her, what he felt doing this and the sensations brought on by those pictures last night. That was his body getting the better of him, leaving him full of disgust after, disgust at himself and at the trollop in the picture. This was entirely different, even if it did bring on the same stirring down below. The shocking beauty of her, fresh all over again – every single time, it knocked him over. The bones under the white skin of her neck were so fragile. He put his lips on the skin there and held the kiss. Dear God, the softness of her. And her glorious smell . . .

It was some moments before he noticed she was not responding. There was no reaching toward him today, no acquiescence even. She was gone, leaving him only the shell of her lovely face, her perfect body. He stopped kissing her. He took a step backwards. 'What is it, Nora?' he said, but she just shook her head again.

He felt himself getting irritated: they didn't have the time for this, not when they only got to see each other once in a blue moon. She was stricken with some grief or fear, he could see that much. But why wouldn't she share it?

Peg had told him of this inclination of Nora's, lately, to retreat into silence. A quiet as cold as the grave was how Peg, with her liking for the dramatic, had put it. She said she could talk to Nora for whole minutes without being heard. Call for her attention, even wave her hands in front of her face. Then, after a while, Nora would surface, like a swimmer coming up from under water, looking around with pure puzzlement. Well, Barney couldn't be doing with that; they didn't have the time for it.

'What's wrong, Nora? You have to tell me.'

No answer.

'I'll help you, whatever it is. Why don't you stay here for the night, forget about going back.'

'Oh, Barney, don't talk daft.'

'It's not so daft. What tie do any of them have on us if we don't allow it? We could go wherever we want, you and I. We could survive the way men on the run survive until we got ourselves away from here.'

'And the cause?'

He shrugged.

'Ireland needs all her men now,' she said. 'Especially men like you.'

'Oh, Ireland.'

She looked at him, shocked, took a step backwards. He could

see that she was pulling back inside herself, as if she shrank from her own skin. It wasn't fair of her. One word from him that she didn't like and she turned prickly as a pear. 'It's all for you, Nora, do you not know that? I'd walk from it tomorrow if you gave the word.'

Again, that shake of the head. Yet she had come to him, come all the way out here, eight miles on her bicycle with, no doubt, the threat of her family questioning her whereabouts when she got back. What was the point if they weren't going to speak truly to each other? 'All I want is you,' he said. '*All*.' Maybe a man wasn't supposed to say a thing like that but there, it was said. No sign of it melting her, though. 'Come over here to me, sweetheart. Tell me what's wrong.'

Even as he was saying the words, he knew it was useless. She had gone down inside herself, down to some place where no words of his could haul her back.

35

1995

'If it weren't for the warning signs and the barbed-wire fence, you'd never know, would you?'

Rory is bent over a camera lens, looking out across Coolanagh. He has lived beside this place all his life, apart from his college years in Dublin, but he knows almost nothing about it. Neither did I while I lived here, not until I did my research in Wexford library. Two nights ago I told him that Dan died out here, and my suspicions about how it happened. His immediate reaction was that he wanted to come and take pictures. Take possession of it, he said.

So here we are, out together in daylight in Mucknamore for the first time ever. As we walked out the Causeway to get here, I felt so exposed, the windows of the village stuck in our backs, though it was so early and most people were still asleep. Rory didn't seem to care. Out here I can relax: we are beyond view in a hollow that dips down behind the dunes, facing Coolanagh rather than the village so I can freely stand near him. Lovers' Hollow, Gran used to call it, though I haven't said that to Rory.

'You'd expect that there'd be some sign but it looks no different to the sand on the other side,' he says, drawing me back.

'I think maybe it's darker in colour? There?' I point over his shoulder, my bump gently nudging his back, sending shots of sensation all round my body. 'Where the stream comes off the island?'

'Hmmm . . . Maybe.'

'That's what causes all the trouble: that stream. That's what saturates the sand and makes it unstable.'

While he surveys the scene and plans his pictures, I take the cloth from the basket we brought and spread it beside the rug.

'Another perfect day,' I say, taking out the food and utensils we have brought for our picnic. Each morning we wake and there it is again: the sun. Nobody can believe it.

He smiles. 'I've never seen a summer like it. You're lucky you didn't come here last year, when it rained nearly every day and we had the central heating on all through the summer. You'd never have survived in that shed of yours last year.'

'That's hard to imagine when it's like this.'

Rory slings his camera over his shoulder and lifts the top rope of barbed wire to slide through. 'What are you going out there for?' I ask. 'Be careful.'

'I won't go far. I just want to get a close-up of that grass.'

It's only ordinary marram grass but I know he sees something in it that I don't. While I lay out the food – sandwiches, fruit, cheese, chocolate – on plastic plates, and set the cups and the knives and forks like a wife, I watch him squat to direct his viewfinder at the pointy tips. Sturdy thighs strain against denim as he bends, rapt, every cell focused on his subject. He zooms his lens in. *Click. Whirr.*

It was seeing me so intent on my writing, he said, that brought him back to photography. He bought himself a new digital camera but has got no further with it than loading the software onto his computer. Instead he is drawn back to his old camera.

Whirr. Click. The film reaches the end of its roll and the camera hums through a rewind. Rory slips back through the barbed-wire fence. He puts the camera in its case, rolls the case in a towel to protect it from the sand, and joins me on the rug, stretching his legs to their full, long length. I'm aware of those legs, their closeness to mine, the bulk of the body that tops them but he seems blithe, pouring himself a juice and starting on some sandwiches. To cover up, I ask him about something else entirely: 'Did you ever hear a story about a sunken city being down there, under Coolanagh?'

'Mmmm,' he says, chewing. 'The city swallowed by sand.'

'You did? Then it wasn't a story of Granny Peg's?'

'No. Though I can't remember where I heard it. I've a feeling it might have been told to us in school.'

'What exactly did you hear?'

'That the sands rose like a wave and covered a city that used to be here. That the city is down there under the sand, like some sort of cross between Atlantis and Pompeii.' He laughs. 'I think they told us . . . or maybe I heard from somebody else . . . that they tell the same story over at Bannow.'

'Bannow Bay, that's right, that's what I read in the library. Except at Bannow there's evidence that it really happened.'

'Surely Ms Sceptic doesn't believe in devouring sands?'

'No. I mean it wasn't just a legend. There was a city there.'

'A city? At *Bannow*?'

'According to this book, for nearly four hundred years, from the twelfth to the sixteenth century, Bannow was one of the finest corporation towns in Ireland. A thriving seaport that was so significant it sent not one but two MPs to the Parliament in London.'

He looks disbelieving. 'And it just disappeared?'

'Over the years, the bay silted up. By the sixteenth century, it wasn't navigable any more and it went into decline.'

Rory asks: 'Have you ever been to Bannow? There's hardly a village there – a couple of houses, a shop, that's all. And no castle or ruins. If it had been that significant, would there not be some surviving trace?'

'You would think so. Seems not, though.'

He shakes his head. 'There are Norman castle ruins from that time all over this part of Wexford.'

'I know. But in Bannow, it's as if that city never was. That's what the book says.'

'Are you sure that book of yours is right?'

'There's plenty of other evidence, once you go looking. Old maps and documents. Valuation returns prepared under Oliver

Cromwell that list all the streets and the names of all the people who lived there in the 1600s.'

He shakes his head, conceding the argument. 'Amazing.'

'And Gran's story is evidence of a sort, isn't it?'

He reaches for another sandwich and we are silent for a time, the small noises of chewing and swallowing the background to our thoughts. The story told most often about Bannow Bay now is that it is where the English first landed in Ireland. In 1169, Dermot McMurrough, the King of Leinster, was having trouble defending his kingdom from other Irish chieftains and he became a vassal of the Anglo-Norman king, Henry II, in order to recruit some Norman military might. He travelled across the Irish Sea and lured a fleet of mercenary soldiers to Ireland with promises of land, bringing them into Ireland through Bannow Bay. For this, he became one of the most reviled men in Irish history, blamed for the whole sorry story of what came afterwards. A nonsense, because at that time 'England' and 'Ireland' as we know them didn't even exist, but stories have a life of their own.

Rory sits up, brushes crumbs off his T-shirt. 'Jo, I want to ask you about something completely different.'

I turn towards him, alerted by something in his voice.

'I wanted to ask you about' – he points to my bump – 'about . . . the father.'

I'm taken aback. 'The father of this child?'

He nods.

'Why? I told you before, he was nobody. A one-night stand.'

'Does he even know that you're pregnant?'

'He wouldn't want to.'

'How can you be so sure? How come you get to make that decision for him?'

I don't want to talk about this. Now that I am used to, happy about, the idea of the baby, it pains me to think of how she came about. That drunken coupling. That split condom. That guy's anxiety to be rid of me, almost shouldering me out of his apartment. Then that time of wild panic while I realized what I had done to myself. All the broken moments that had brought me here, to Mucknamore this summer.

'Rory, let it go. You don't know anything about it.'

'I know plenty about it,' he says. 'Who would know better than me?'

'Ah. So *that's* it.'

'You never gave *me* a thought either, did you, any more than you do him?'

'Rory—'

'How *I* felt didn't come into it for you.'

'That's rubbish. You made it perfectly clear how you felt.'

'There you are, you see. Wrong then, so possibly wrong about this other guy now. Poor schmuck, whoever he is.'

'You made it obvious that . . .'

'I didn't, Jo. I did *not*. We barely discussed it, then – snap! – you were gone.'

Why are we talking about this now? It's just too long ago. 'If you want to know,' I say, hoping to mollify him, 'I thought about little else but you during those first months in London.' Lying in that grotty bedsit bed day and night under the blankets because I didn't have enough money to plug in the electric heater. Lying and weeping and wondering what might happen if I telephoned him, if I asked him to come over. 'Maybe I should have had more faith,' I say.

'You should, Jo,' he says vehemently 'You really should.'

But I was my mother's daughter. I knew how it felt to ask for what a person cannot give. If I didn't ask, he couldn't let me down.

Is that how it was? Which is true, this new story, or my earlier version of events?

'Why are you asking me about this now?' I ask him.

He hesitates.

'Go on.'

'I . . . I suppose I've been thinking . . . about what might happen if I left my marriage.'

That silences me.

'And I don't like what I see, the way fathers get shut out when they . . . when a marriage breaks up.'

I laugh at that, a small laugh that I don't like but can't help. He doesn't rise to it.

'Jo, I don't want you to think . . . I haven't decided anything . . .' he says. As if I asked him. As if I had ever said that was what I want. 'If I didn't have kids, I think . . . But maybe not . . . I don't want to hurt Orla either.'

'It must hurt her that you come up here, night after night.'

'It didn't at first.'

'Really? She didn't mind? Did she not know anything about . . . about our history?'

'Of course she did.'

'And it didn't bother her that you visited?' This seems amazing to me. No married woman I know would be so sanguine about an old flame.

'She thought you needed a friend.'

'Ugh!'

'Well, it did seem that way, Jo. She knew – everybody knew – that you and your mother were estranged. So when you turned up at the funeral . . . And then, when you moved into your shed and locked yourself away, like a hermit . . .'

'Oh, great, she felt sorry for me.'

'And I suppose, if I'm to be honest, I played on that a bit.'

'And now?'

'Last night, when I told her I was coming out here with you today, she asked me not to.' His voice is pained.

'But you're here.'

'I'm here.' He shakes his head, as if he is trying to deny it. 'They call this place Lovers' Hollow. Did you know that?'

'Oh, Rory.'

Out on Coolanagh strand, the seabirds splash in and out of sand-puddles, each one a small mirror holding and feeling and reflecting the depth of the sunlit sky.

'It's not just about you,' he says, after a time. 'We – Orla and I – we haven't been right for a long time.'

'Arguments?'

'No. That's not how it goes with us. Our relationship was always different to yours and mine. Never as . . .' He hesitates, reaches for the right word.

'Intense?' I suggest.

He shrugs. 'Yes, less intense. Less passionate. And less troubled, which was what I wanted, then . . . after you. We had good times together. She was attractive, clever, good at everything. Everybody liked her. Likes her. She was . . . she is a good person.'

'But?'

'Jo, I'm so confused. Our marriage is not what it was, but how could it be, after fourteen years? I don't know what I want. One minute I have fantasies about leaving my job, leaving everything, running away with you to the States and becoming a photographer. Starting everything over and getting it right this time. But then . . .'

'You think of your kids.'

'I think of my kids. And Orla. She doesn't deserve this.'

God, he makes me sick. We both do, with our clichéd lines and our clichéd feelings. But still I ask: 'How much does she know about the way you're thinking?'

'More than I tell her.'

Another gust of laughter spurts out of me. Then I find I can't stop, giggles flooding up and out from I don't know where.

'Jesus, Jo. Stop it.'

I try but I can't. I laugh and laugh.

'Christ!'

'I'm . . . sorry . . . Sorry . . .' I make a stern effort, squash the gurgles that are pushing up into my throat. Breathe deep. Focus. When I've got control, I say: 'I'm sorry for laughing. It's just that sometimes it all seems too ridiculous. All that wasted emotion. All for what?'

He takes me by the shoulders, kisses me on the mouth. A severe kiss, full of hard feelings, and something in me leaps to it. We kiss and kiss and on we kiss, no other part of our bodies moving but our searching, accusing mouths. Oh, what a kiss. On it goes, my half-open mouth pressing all that I want to say onto his lips: you know me . . . you *know* me . . . I shouldn't have let you go . . . I want you . . . I want you but I'm afraid . . . I'm afraid to let myself love you again . . . of what might become of me . . . I want you . . . but you are not mine . . . not mine . . .

Not mine.

I stop.

He stops.

We look into each other's face, ribs rising and falling over short pants of breath.

'Be mine,' he says, echoing my thoughts just like he used to. 'You be mine and I'll be yours again, just for one day.'

One day, in a vacuum, sealed off from his marriage and everything else. I love the idea, I love the words in his mouth and the way he says them to me. But I don't believe in it. I begin to pull away.

'Please, Jo,' he says, gripping my arms, holding on to me. 'Give me something.'

That emotion in his voice, in the clutch of his hands – how can I know whether to trust it, to trust the way I thrill to it?

'I can't, Rory.'

'Why? Why not? Don't pretend we have nothing between us. I felt that kiss.'

'It's not that. You know I have –'

He raises his eyebrows.

'– feelings—'

'Feelings!' His upper lip curls. 'Steady on there, Jo. Take it easy, don't go overboard . . .'

'What do you expect me to say?'

'You know what I'd *like* you to say.'

'Look at me, Rory. Just look.' I wave my hand down the front of my body. 'I'm six months pregnant by a man who meant nothing to me. Less than nothing. I don't want to be careless, not with you. I'd have to be . . . I'd want *both* of us to be sure.'

'OK,' he says.

'What do you mean, OK?'

'I *am* sure,' he says. 'Forget what I said earlier, I am sure.'

'Oh, come on.'

'I do. I'm sure, I fully want to, just like you said.'

'What you want is for us to have sex and then to see what happens next. That's not what I meant.'

This time I succeed in pulling away.

'Woman, you are driving me crazy. You say you don't want to be careless, I assure you I am anything but careless. You say you want me to be sure, I tell you I am sure. But nothing is enough.'

He stuffs his fists into his pockets, as if he is afraid he might use them. 'What about you, Jo? Do you have any idea what *you* want, or are you happy just to keep on playing this little game of "will we, won't we"? Because I tell you, I can't stand much more of it.'

My heart is still thudding from our kiss. It would be so easy to give in but what I have told him is true. I cannot be light, not with a six-month-old baby inside me and not with him, of all men. Also, it bothers me that he is so ready to cheat. One conversation about how bad he feels and then, Bam!, never mind, let's do it anyway.

When we're together, he makes me feel as if we are the love story and she is the one on the outside but I know that's not how it is. I know they share their own story that excludes me.

But . . . still, still my heart thuds . . .

'I want us to go away and cool off,' I say. 'I want us to think about what we expect from each other, and why, and where it might take us. Then you come back and tell me and I'll do the same. And then, maybe . . .'

'Jesus, Jo! "Maybe"?'

'Or,' I say, putting a finger to his lips, 'maybe not.'

Peg

Dear Diary

What a miserable Christmas Day we had yesterday. I keep comparing this year with last, when Dan and Barney came home. The bonfires, the songs and celebrations, the vote on the Treaty yet to be taken. We could do anything, was what we thought then. Hadn't we already achieved the impossible?

This year, we are living in the Free State, beholden again to the English Crown. Christmas is Barney absent from the table and all of us making the best of it. It's Mammy trying to let on she's not as sick as she is. It's Dan estranged from us and Nora isolated. How could we have imagined any of this last Christmas?

But the good fight goes on. Mammy gave us a small speech as we sat down at the Christmas table: 'If Kevin Barry's mother could keep her eyes fixed on the tabernacle while the hangman's rope was round her boy's neck, and if Terence MacSwiney's sister could endure his agony as he starved himself to death in Brixton jail, and if Cathal Brugha's wife is instilling into her children the "No Surrender" policy their father lived and died by, then surely to God we can put up with not having Barney to Christmas dinner.' All of which sounded good and true and inspiring until you thought about it and realized that she might not see another Christmas.

As it turned out, we could probably have taken the chance of having Barney here yesterday. We would have, only a rumour went round that the Army were going to use Christmas Day to do a big round-up all over. So the lads broke up into small groups and while we were eating our meal he was not a million miles away eating dinner in a friendly hay-barn. In the event, nothing happened. It was probably a rumour started by the Army to ruin Christmas for us. Even the Germans and Allies were able to acknowledge the spirit of Christmas across the trenches. But not the Free State National Army, no.

And to cap it all, Nora never got down to see me. She said she'd do her best to sneak out on Stephen's Day, that she'd need a break after being locked up with her family all over the Christmas. Dan is due home and she will have to put up with her people fawning over him and he gibing at her about our side. Is it any wonder she hasn't been herself lately? I think the strain of it all is too much for her, she's not coping well. All day long I waited, but no show.

Dear Diary

Still no sign of Nora and it's very awkward for me to call up her way. I thought about it and I'd manage her mother easy enough and maybe even her father. But then I thought to myself: Dan. Dan is up there, home for the Christmas. And that I just can't face.

Dear Diary

I took my courage in hand and went up to O'Donovan's and now I wish I'd gone sooner. It was pure cowardice kept me away, nothing else. When I didn't see Nora at Mass on Sunday, I knew something was wrong. She must be sick, was what I thought. So heart rattling, up I went.

Mrs O'Donovan came to the back door when she saw me crossing the yard and I knew by her face I was not going to be invited in.

'I've come to ask after Nora, Mrs O'Donovan,' I said, as if there was no national question between us.

'Indeed?'

'I was worried she might be sick.'

'She isn't.'

'Can I see her for a minute?'

'No.'

'Please. I won't keep her long.'

'She's not here. She's gone away.'

'Away?'

'Away, yes. Now would you mind? There's work to be done.'

'When will she be back?'

'Listen, child, would you go away with yourself now and let me get on.'

'Will you not tell me?'

She carried on brushing the floor, trying to act like I wasn't there but when it became clear I wasn't going to budge, she couldn't keep it up. 'Nora's got herself a fancy job in Dublin. She left two days ago.'

'But she never said goodbye. And she never mentioned anything about a job to me . . .'

'Now you listen to me, Peg Parle. We've had as much trouble as we can take from your family. You think about what you're saying there. Go home and think about it.'

'What do you mean?'

'Think about it, is what I said. Then maybe you'll keep your opinions to yourself.'

'But—'

'I don't want to see either of you near any of our family again, you or your brother. You should be ashamed to come near this house. Now get yourself gone before her father comes back. If he sees you here, I can tell you, he won't be as light on you.'

There was nothing I could do but go. Since I have come home I can't stop thinking about what she said and I have the most awful feeling about it. If what I'm thinking is right, would Nora have told me? That is what I ask myself. If it was me, would I tell her?

Please God, I'm wrong. Please God, there's another explanation entirely. My poor friend. She could have told me, whatever it was. I wouldn't have thought less of her. Never. Not for anything.

Dear Diary

This morning I was feeding the hens when two cold hands came round my face, covering my eyes. I knew straight away who it was.

'Barney,' I said, delighted.

'We're below in Colonel Taylor's, so near I said I'd have to come home.'

I bombarded the poor fellow with questions. 'Are the boys around here now? You look thinner, have you been eating all right? Did ye get my despatch about the barracks job? Have ye a plan for it? Are you hungry?'

He laughed. 'Which do you want me to answer first?'

'All, all. Oh, Barney, it's great that you're here. Christmas was awful miserable. And Mammy—'

'Is bad.'

'Bad, yes. But she'll perk up now. She'll perk up now. You can't stay long, I suppose?'

'No. I need a wash and some clean clothes. What I'm wearing is stuck to me and the itch is back.'

I threw the last of the meal in a heap in the middle of the yard. The fowl clucked, beating each other off.

'Come on inside,' I said to him, wiping my hands on my apron. 'I'll put on the kettle. How does a feed of rashers and eggs sound?'

I was shocked by the look of him though I didn't let on. It was only three weeks since I had seen him but he had grown even thinner than before and filthy and bearded again. 'Have a wash of your face and hands there in the barrel before I bring you up to Mammy,' I said, 'or she'll think you're the devil himself come to visit.'

While he was washing I put on water to boil for a proper

soak in the tub and got food from the shop. Then I brought him up to Mammy. 'Ah, son,' was all she said when she saw who it was. Two thin arms came up from the blankets as he went to her and they held each other in a way neither would have done six months ago. When they parted after a long closeness, we both sat on the bed, one of us on either side of her, while she asked him questions that came slow out of her soreness, about the talk we were hearing that surrender might be imminent. He tried to fob her off, to talk of other things, but not a chance. In case her embrace of him might make him think she'd gone soft, she dragged herself up in the bed and gave us one of her speeches.

'At a moment's notice . . . this country produced . . . the finest politicians and soldiers, drawn from all walks of life. Six years ago they were nothing but they . . . they came to command the admiration of the world. Why?' Her finger poked the counterpane. 'Why? Because they stood on the side of right . . . that's why. They had a principle . . . Now, the talk is of giving up that principle . . . or of watering it down but . . . principles . . . can't be watered down.'

He agreed with her, of course; you might as well argue with a goat on the charge. When she got tired, we took our leave, Barney promising he'd come back after he'd eaten. Downstairs, he was very quiet. After a long while of saying nothing, he asked me straight if it was only a matter of time. I told him the truth, that it was.

'And what way is Daddy about it?'

'Still pretending it's not happening.'

He let his head fall into his hands.

'What are we at, Peg?' He gave a sigh I didn't want to understand. 'What are we at, at all? What difference will any of it make in the end?'

'Don't say things like that. If you lose faith, we're surely doomed.'

He sighed again and shook his head and I knew nothing I

might say would do. So I left him to his thoughts. Something in him had changed. It was like he had been to another country and there was no point in trying to describe it to me because I'd never be able to picture it.

After a time, he asked me to go up to O'Donovan's and see if I could fetch Nora. He was dead set on it so I had to tell him that Nora was nowhere to be found and that I could get no news of her from anyone. I didn't like to repeat or even hint at what people were saying.

'Gone away to Dublin?' he said. 'No, surely not. She'd surely never do that without saying goodbye to us.'

'That's what I said. But she is gone, Barney. I've been up there, asking after her.'

'And . . . ?'

'They told me nothing, just that she's gone, no more than that. If there was anything to tell, it's not me who would be told it, you know that.'

He looked that confused, I felt sorry for him.

'You'll be wishing you hadn't come home at all next,' I said.

He shook his head but he was far away in his thoughts.

Afterwards, when he was leaving, I told him I'd see if I could talk to young Martin, Nora's little brother. He might give away some information. 'I'll get a message to you tomorrow at the Colonel's,' I promised, 'one way or the other.'

Dear Diary

This morning Sore-Toes arrived with a letter for me from Barney, marked 'private and confidential', which he was told to put directly into my hands and no other. I was never more surprised in my life than I am after reading this letter. Barney has lost the will to fight (not that it was ever that strong in him). I wish he were here. I know Mammy and I would get him back on track if we had the time for a proper talk. Or Nora, if she were here.

I said nothing to Mammy about it. She's in fine fettle this morning. Four lorryloads of Army boys went honking up through the village in the direction of Colonel Taylor's a while ago, making sure to slow down going past here and hoot their horns at us so we'd know they were there. When she heard them, she just laughed her most disdainful laugh. 'Go on out of that,' she shouted after them (it's been months since she had a shout in her). 'You might hoot at the women but our boys will give you something to hoot about.'

If she knew how Barney was thinking, it would kill her.

Derriestown

9th January 1923

Dear Peg,

This letter is for your eyes only. Destroy it when you've read it. You'll see why.

I hope you'll soon have news of Nora for me. You know as well as I do that something must be up. We'll get to the bottom of it, never fear.

But what I also wanted to write to you about, Peg, is the talk we had today. I want you to face the truth, that it's all up with us. It can only be a matter of time before surrender is called. I know this is not something you want to hear and I didn't go through it with you today because our time was so short, but that's the truth of it, believe me.

I hate to say this to you of all people, after all the work you've done to keep us going, not to mention the food, the clothes, the tobacco and all the rest of it. When everybody else deserted us, you girls stood by us and faced danger as hard as we did. Don't think we don't know it. Don't think it will ever be forgotten. But the truth of the matter is we are going through several kinds of hell with this fight. Continuing on is nothing but a waste of blood.

When we were fighting Black-and-Tans it didn't matter that we were outnumbered, for they could hardly tell one of us from the other. We had the advantage of surprise, the ability to melt back into the countryside without them ever able to find us. All that is changed. The Enemy now knows every man jack of us. They know what we're planning to do before we know ourselves. They have all our areas overran and there's so many of them that killing a few of their side does not count. They can easily be replaced. Not so us. We're completely outnumbered.

Then there's the lack of money. Our arms are a joke, we have hardly any ammunition. Joe Sills asks HQ constantly for supplies but we get nothing. They're stony broke and anything they manage to requisition gets sent down Cork and Kerry way, never to us. Three of the lads who escaped an ambush last week had to leave their boots behind and have been going barefoot since.

Now I can't talk the truth like that around here. All the talk among these boys is as strong as ever for the Republic. They think if we destroy a railway line without anybody getting captured that we've won a major battle. They think if they're brave enough and stubborn enough that it will all come good in the end. And they are so brave and good-humoured that I can't argue with them.

But I know it won't come good in the end and I know that it won't be long now until it's all over and – I have to tell you the truth, Peg, I have to tell it to someone for it's driving me mad keeping it to myself – I'm glad, so I am. Surrender can't come soon enough for me.

What exactly will happen me then, I'm not sure. Prison maybe for a while but maybe not, or not for too long anyway. Then Nora and I will get a nice little house together and get married. That's all I think about now. It's not a lot to ask, is it? Other people seem to manage it without great difficulty. I will find her, wherever she is, if you haven't found her first, and tell her that whatever has happened, she shouldn't have run away from us. I will persuade her that the time for secrets is over and show her there's no need to be afraid. There is nothing anybody can do to her, not when I'm there to mind her.

Her family won't like it, of course, but if we have to, we'll go somewhere else. I would give up the pub, a lot more than that I'd give up. I will work at anything and if there's no work in Ireland, then I'll take us to England or maybe even to America. We won't need much. We'll manage.

It was good to see you today, Peg, to see you so well and full of hope. It did my heart good. You're a great survivor. Look after Mammy and Daddy during the coming weeks. What they would do without you, God alone knows.

Like I said, tear this or burn it when you're finished reading. You can imagine the trouble if it fell into the wrong hands (which is anybody's but your own). God bless you and keep you safe.

Your brother

Barney

36

1995

I am at my desk, writing, lost in work, when a voice from the door interrupts me. 'Jo Devereux, sometimes I think you're mad.'

Irritation coils in my belly. I don't want to stop work, certainly not to listen to my sister's views on my living arrangements. Yes, it is Maeve, standing at the door of my shed, neat and slim in linen shorts and Ralph Lauren polo shirt, her key ring looped over one finger, her eyes tracking round my shed. I follow them with dismay. Living here, day after day, centred on my work, I no longer even notice the dilapidation but for a moment the haze of the customary drops and I see what my sister sees. Flaking walls, dirty floors, unmade bed, debris piled in the corners.

'What are you doing here?' I ask.

'Lovely welcome, I must say. Can I come in?'

I get up from my chair, conscious of my shape and that I never did get round to telling her. Her eyes fall on my body, then swoop in on my abdomen. Her forehead furrows and she swings her look upwards to my face. 'Are you—?'

'Yes.'

She is stunned, her face so very shocked that I can't help laughing and the balance that always tugs between us tips back in my favour. 'Oh my God!' she gasps. 'I don't believe it. Oh my God!'

'Let's go round the back,' I say, conscious of the builders at work on the house. 'That's the nicest place to sit.'

I take my rug from the end of the rumpled bed and lead her to the grassy patch where Rory and I sit each night. It's private here, between the shed and edge of the small cliff. 'You should have let Hilde know you were coming,' I say, keeping up my unruffled hostess act. 'I'd have arranged to meet you somewhere a bit more comfortable.'

She pulls herself out of her astonishment to complain. 'I've been expecting to hear from you. You've been down here now for eight weeks and not so much as a phone call. But,' she breathes, 'never mind all that . . . What about this . . . ?' She leans across as if to touch me, changes her mind and just waves her hand in front of my belly. 'Look at you. My God.'

I sit on the rug and wave at her to do likewise. 'Would you like something?' I remember to ask when I'm down. 'A drink? I only have orange juice.'

'Orange juice would be nice.' She puts a hand on my arm. 'Don't get up. I'll get it. Where is it?'

'Just inside the door, in the corner. It's the coolest spot.'

She comes back with two paper cups. 'That's one mountain of paper you've got in there on the table.'

'I know. It keeps growing on me.'

'Am I allowed read it?'

I shake my head. 'Not yet.'

'When?'

'Soon. I have to type it up and it needs a lot of tidying.'

I change the subject by tasting the juice and wrinkling my nose at her. 'Sorry the juice is warm. No fridge, obviously.'

'It's fine,' she says, sipping it. Then she looks me face-on. 'I thought I was beyond being shocked by you, Jo, but you've done it again. Why didn't you tell me?'

'I didn't tell anybody.'

'The father?'

'Especially the father.'

She dips her head down to her plastic cup, trying to stop the criticism rearing up inside her. She is thin, I notice, too thin; her hipbones jut against her trousers.

'What about you?' I ask her.

'Fine. Fine.'

'Are you sure?'

Her face creases. 'Up and down, I suppose.' Then she points her head across at the house. 'Two shocks in a row. I couldn't get over the house . . . It's so different, isn't it?'

'Unrecognizable.'

'I wish it could have been kept as it was, at least for a while. I hate it being gone. It would have been nice to get used to Mammy being gone first, before we had to deal with that.'

'Are you finding it hard?'

She nods, head down. 'I still can't believe I'll never see her again. I think of things I want to tell her, then I remember she's not here to tell. And it hits me all over again.'

'Time helps,' I say.

'Is it helping you?'

'I'm not mourning her like you,' I say.

'I know you weren't close, but she was your mother.'

I try again. 'I do know the feeling you're talking about and how awful it is. Time really does help.'

'Your friend Richard.'

My turn to nod. But I'm glad she remembers.

'Well, then, I wish time would just hurry on and pass.' She shakes her head, pulls herself away from thoughts that do no good. 'But tell me, what have you been doing with yourself since?'

'You saw that heap of papers in there. I've been reading and writing, mostly. Lying low.'

'Is there anything of interest in those papers of Mammy's? Are they all rubbish?'

'Oh, no, they're not rubbish,' I say.

'Tell me.'

'I think you better wait until I've put it together.'

She is intrigued. 'What on earth have you found?'

'All sorts of things, I think.'

'Deep dark secrets?' she grins.

'Yes, as a matter of fact.'

'Things Mammy didn't tell us?'

'You're forgetting, Maeve, Mrs D. never told me anything.'

That stops her smile. 'Oh, no, Jo, you're going to write it all, aren't you? The bad and the good.'

I nod.

'But what about the bits that Mammy said she didn't want aired?'

I shrug.

'Jo!'

Above us a gull screams, slides across the air towards the sea. How much did Mrs D. know, that is the question. In her letter, she said she didn't read Nora's 'scribblings' or all of Gran's diaries. I have read everything, every word, more than once, some many times, and still I'm not certain. Sometimes I see one thing in Nora's notes, sometimes another. On one reading more, on another less, but never enough. Maybe I'm like Mrs D., twisting what I read to make it fit but I don't think so. The way that Peg and Nora's words shrink from what they say even as they say it: that's what speaks loudest to me across the years.

'You have to tell me,' my sister says. 'It's not your story to do what you like with, it belongs to us all.'

'Hey, calm down. I will tell you.'

She looks sceptical.

'I will, Maeve, I promise. I just want to be sure myself first. Let me get it straight on paper.'

'Are you going to publish this?'

'I might try.'

She looks frightened by the thought. 'You can't publish anything Mammy wouldn't want said.'

'Does it matter? It can't hurt her now.'

'Of course it matters. We can't do something she wouldn't have wanted.'

'I've told you: if she really didn't want it, all she had to do was censor the papers.'

'Maybe she wanted you – us – to know, but not the world.'

I shake my head, though I know quite well that is possible.

Maeve takes off her sunglasses, squints at me in the sunshine. 'Jo, for your own sake, as well as Mammy's, you need to be clear about your motives,' she says. 'If you publish something she wouldn't like just to settle some score, you'll be sorry later on.'

I don't think that's what I'm doing. I think I want to tell my family's story because, contrary to what my sister thinks, I don't believe it 'belongs' to us. Because the world needs to hear all the stories and hear them whole. Because if I don't tell, nobody will. I shrug. 'Which of us is ever clear about our motives?'

She blinks harder at me. I see her trying to calm herself, trying to find tactful, persuasive words to convince me. Just at that moment, my baby ripples inside me, then settles, like she is snuggling down. I put my hand to where I feel her and Maeve notes the movement and smiles. 'Where are you going to have it?'

'I don't know.'

'What does your doctor say?'

'I haven't seen a doctor.'

'What? You're . . . how many months pregnant?'

'About six.'

'Six months pregnant and you haven't seen a doctor?'

I close my eyes, take a breath, wait for the onslaught.

'That's just downright irresponsible.'

This is why I haven't told her, because she would think it gave her rights. 'I'm sorry, Jo, but that's what it is.'

'Correct me if I'm wrong, Maeve, but I thought this was my pregnancy?'

'When you're pregnant, Jo, you have more than yourself to consider.'

'Yeah, well, I don't happen to think pregnancy is an illness. And I don't see why I need some doctor I've never met before to tell me I'm fine. I know I'm fine.'

'But at your age especially . . .'

'Is this why you came, Maeve? To deliver a series of lectures?'

'Oh, God.' She sighs, heavily. 'How do you do this to me, Jo? Coming down in the car, I swore I wasn't going to criticize no matter what I found. But I never ever expected to find . . . this.'

She's right, she can't help it any more than I can. Here we are, thirty-eight and forty years old, and as testy with each other as ever. We'll always be the same. The best time we ever had together was when she visited me in San Francisco, when we were on my territory, but here she'll always take liberties. Somehow, though, it doesn't matter as much as it used to. I try to appease her. 'As a matter of fact, I am going to see a doctor soon. Just as soon as I make up my mind where I'm going to have her.'

'I'm glad,' she says, trying to match my conciliatory tone. 'Make it soon, Jo.'

'I will, I will.'

I lie back, close my eyes to the sun. We sit quiet, still edgy but both keen to hold our moment of peace. After a while, Maeve speaks again: 'You said "her". You think it's a girl?'

'Maybe. That's how I find myself thinking, of "she", of "her".'

'So you don't know for sure?'

'No, how could I? But right from the start, I don't know why, I've had the feeling that it's going to be a girl.'

'She,' 'her': I told Maeve that's how I think of you. It's not strictly true. That *is* the pronoun I use when talking to others, to Hilde or Rory, but most of the time I'm – we're – not with others. Most of the time we're alone, and then the word I use is 'you'.

You are changing me, making more of me: swelling my breasts and my girth, expanding my heart and my lungs, ripening and plumping my genitals, filling and darkening my nipples, increasing the volume of my blood. You have splashed my skin with colour, drawn a bold line of brown down my belly.

Greased and furry, somersaulting and thumb-sucking inside me, getting firmer in the world, you rely on me. Though soon you will be what they call viable, able to at least breathe and eat on your own, still I can see how you will draw on me, body, heart and soul, for the rest of my days. But I don't think I mind. You've unpicked the me I used to be. I am going to join the band of mothers, those people who let themselves fade in the light of their offspring, a group of people I have always slightly disdained. Now I have disdain for that earlier, unknowing me.

Peg

Dear Diary

Was it only this morning that I got that letter from Barney, and that I wrote the above about Mammy jeering the Army? That entry reads to me now like it was written by someone else. I was someone else then. From this day forward I'll be a new person, a smaller person, trying to live the same life.

Barney is dead, may the Lord have mercy on his soul. My brother Barney is dead. Dead. No matter how often I say it and write it I can't get myself to believe it.

Sore-Toes it was who brought the news to me and he was that upset he was hardly able to get out of him what he had come to say. When it dawned on me what he was getting at, I let out a big scream of No. 'No, Sore-Toes. No. You've made a mistake. You're not right.' But at the same time as I was denying what he said, I was starting to cry, admitting with my tears that I knew it was no mistake, that it was true.

I'm crying again now as I write this. Harsh out-loud crying that tears at my throat and gets on my own nerves to hear.

Barney is dead. We always knew it could happen but I've learned this morning the wide ocean of difference between imagining something and the real living of it. Barney is dead and they're saying it was Dan O'Donovan who fired the shot that killed him.

God help us all. How are we supposed to bear it?

IV
Drift

Peg

Dear Diary

It was I who had to tell them, Daddy first. He was in the bottling store and when he saw me come in, and the state of me, with tears running down my face, he stood up from his work and waited. I didn't know how to say it so I just blurted it out. 'Barney's dead,' I said. 'Shot in an ambush.' For a long, long moment he said nothing, just stood there holding onto a bottle like a child asked to mind something without knowing why. Then he said: 'I knew. I knew it would end in this.'

He got straight down onto his knees and started to pray. I stood looking at him, wishing he'd stop because I felt I couldn't just go and leave him to it but I thought we should be telling Mammy. When he finished he got up and said, 'Have you told your mother?' and asked me to do the deed, saying he wouldn't be able. I didn't know if I'd be able myself.

She was out the back, coat and hat and scarf on, sitting on the bench she set up years ago under the apple tree, facing the sea. It was starting to drizzle. She heard me coming and when I got close she spoke without opening her eyes. 'I know you're going to tell me it's starting to rain and to come in,' she said. 'And I will in a minute when it starts in earnest but it's so good to feel the wind in my face.'

'I've bad news to tell you, Mammy,' I said. She opened her eyes and I told her. She took it so brave, not a word or a sound out of her. After a while she said, 'Leave me alone now, Peg, for a bit.' I said to her to come inside, that the rain was getting heavier but again she told me to go and in such a way that I felt

I could do nothing else. There she sat under the tree while the weather worsened and turned to a downpour. I went out again and begged her to come inside but she wouldn't. Daddy tried then but she refused him too.

Next, the military called to give us the news but when they saw we knew already they didn't stay long. They've brought him to the barracks as they have to do a post-mortem. There will be an inquest to determine exactly what happened.

Then the word was out. Once people heard what had happened they started to flood to the house. One after one they went out to Mammy, offering their sympathies and trying to get her inside out of the rain. Father John came and at least didn't give me any of his spiel against the Republic but just offered comfort and prayers and asked about arrangements. I sent him out to Mammy thinking he could make her come in but no. I was really worried by then because the rain hadn't stopped and it would be bad for anybody to be outside that long in it, but for her . . .

Lord, it was hard to watch her.

Sore-Toes left the column to come by again, at no little danger to himself. He says all the boys are broken-hearted. They are all talking of how brave Barney was, saying he died so the rest of them might escape to fight again. He told me that it is true about Dan. It *was* Dan who fired the shot that killed him. He was trying so hard to be a comfort, the poor chap, that I found it hard to get rid of him. So he was there in the kitchen, along with a crowd of neighbours, when Mammy walked in, her hair streaming around her face. 'It is a glorious thing that has happened today,' she said. 'The name of Barney Parle will go down with that of Pearse and Emmet and Tone. Greater love hath no man.'

Her hair was plastered wet into her head and I dried it as best I could with a towel. Finally, after a long time and the helpful persuasion of Lil Hayes, I got her into bed. She was shivering like a kitten. Dr Martin came over and gave her a sleeping draught. How we'll get her through the next few days, I just don't know. I'm so tired. There's the wake to arrange and then the funeral and nobody to help me. Daddy's distraught and it makes him worse to see Mammy the way she is. If only Nora was here.

Nora. Dear God, what will it do to her when she finds out?

Dear Diary

They didn't want us to wake Barney at home. The doctor at the hospital suggested he should be brought straight to the chapel with the lid on the coffin and to our surprise Daddy recommended the same but Mammy wouldn't hear of it. Her boy would be waked in his own home, she insisted. As usual, her will won the day.

The ambulance brought him out from the morgue and the attendants were good enough to carry him up to his old bedroom for us, on the stretcher. We had the room all ready for him, clean sheets on the bed, a candle lit at each side of the bedhead, a statue of Our Lady on the bedside table with a font of holy water. The two men carried him onto the bed for us, keeping the white sheet that covered him, face and body, in place. After they had gone (with ten bob in their pockets for their trouble) we stood over him, Mammy and me, and found we weren't able to go on. She looked at me, I looked at her, we both looked at the sheet between us, the lumps and bumps rising under it that we knew was Barney's nose and chin and chest and feet. I don't know what she was thinking but to me it seemed impossible that I could ever peel it back and confront the remains of my brother.

Then we heard a step on the stairs.

'Quick,' Mammy said. 'That's Lil. She'll think we're a right pair of cowards.'

She pulled back the sheet and as soon as she did, I understood

Daddy's motives in wanting to have Barney coffined straight away. He had been trying to spare us because he, when he went in to identify the body, had seen what death had done to our boy. His face was all twisted, the eyes bulging, showing too much yellowing-white. His jaw was knocked out of line with his cheekbones. But it was his mouth that was the worst of it, all curled up in one corner into a leer. What would put such a face on him and he on his way out of life? He looked like a man possessed by badness. We could do nothing but stand and stare at him.

That's how Lil found us, stiff solid unable to move, all sorts of dreadful thoughts flying through our heads. She took one look at us then started barking orders, telling us what to do and how to do it. Pull that sheet off entirely. Strip off those clothes. Get hot water and soap and a couple of cloths. We fell to obeying her and while we carried out the tasks, she kept up a long string of talk. It was a disgrace that he was left like that. Why had no one closed the eyes, straightened the jaw? She had seen many a dead person in her day but never one left that way. It was too late now, he'd have to do. In any other mouth her talk would have sounded like disrespect but from her it was a strange sort of comfort. With her matter-of-fact words, she brought us back down, made us see that it was nothing but a turn of the eye, a twist of the mouth. No more than that. We began to see our Barney again.

He was wearing the clothes he had on him that day, the clothes I gave him. We opened the jacket and found the jumper and shirt stuck together with blood. We took them off and everything else too, stripped him back to the skin. I could feel myself turning redder and hotter as we took off the last of the clothes and came to his naked person. Mortified I was, in front of Mammy and Lil, though they didn't make much of it. Nobody looked at me, all eyes were on the job and I suppose they had bigger things on their minds than my foolish embarrassment.

An attempt had been made to dress his stomach wound in the hospital but it was still a raw and bloody sight.

Once he was cleaned off as best we could, we dressed him. We had the best of underclothing for him and the lads had done us proud getting together as good a Republican uniform as they could muster. A proper pair of army britches. A Sam Browne belt. A tall and shiny pair of boots. How Lil cursed those boots for the difficulty of pulling them on over the stiffness of his feet and legs.

He's above there now lying on his back, his dead hands clasped around a rosary beads, a couple of candles lighting either side of him. For all our efforts, he still looks tormented, like someone you'd be afraid of. 'Keep the light dim,' Lil said to me on the way out when Mammy was hanging back and not listening. 'A clear look at him could put the heart crossways in anyone with a weakness.'

Dear Diary

The military gave us a bag yesterday, with the things they took from Barney's pockets. Mammy asked me this morning would I go through it, that she wasn't able herself. I'm glad she did, for what was in it, only every note and letter ever sent to him by Nora, rolled up in string? I don't think Mammy would have been able to stop herself reading those letters if they fell into her hands, so it was good for Nora that they didn't. I was curious myself but of course I didn't give in to such a low feeling. I've put them away where they won't be found by anyone else and will return them to her when I see her. Whenever that will be. Maybe she'll turn up for the funeral? Or maybe she doesn't even know he is dead? That's the worst to think of.

As well as her letters the bag contained: a half-empty packet of cigarettes, a blue pencil, two safety pins, a spool of wire, a scapular, a holy medal and, a curious thing, a stone so smooth it nearly looked polished. I didn't know what to do with any of these, so I put them back in the bag and put it above in his room. We'll have a lot more of his things to sort out afterwards and time enough for all that.

Sore-Toes was our first visitor this morning. He came to the back door before daybreak, knowing we'd be up all night. He asked for me and when I went out he said he had something for me. In his arms he cradled a canvas bag like it was a baby. When I asked him what was in it, he opened it to me much as a mother might allow you to peep under a blanket at her child. It was a gun, a Webley. The minute I saw it, I knew what it was. 'Barney's,' I said.

'I thought you might like to have it.'

'It was a good thought, Sore-Toes. Thank you.'

He took it out of the bag and handed it to me and I held it, the weight of its butt heavy in my palm. With two hands, I raised it, pointed it at the ditch, fondled the trigger with my index finger. What would it be like to take aim with this and fire to kill? I wondered. Who would I use it on?

When Barney joined the volunteers, back in '17, before Daddy ever knew he was involved, he kept this gun under a loose floorboard in his bedroom. As I stood there, pointing his gun at the wall, I tried to call up his face the way I remembered it that night and I couldn't. I could recall the bright, bursting expression he had on him but not the face itself. I reached for it in my mind – the arrangement of his nose and eyes and mouth, the real look of him – but they were no longer there, wiped out by the image of that leering corpse above. Only dead a day and already his physical features were gone from me.

'It's not loaded,' I heard Sore-Toes say, and his voice sounded a long way off. I dropped my arm. The tears that are only barely held down in me were welling up again.

I was grateful to him for bringing me the gun, knowing how short they are of arms at this time, but he brushed away the thanks. 'One rifle will hardly be missed,' he said but I knew better.

Outside the family, nobody cared about Barney more than Sore-Toes. That makes him dear to us in these dark days. After he'd eaten, he helped us transport the coffin across to the chapel. Barney will lie there today, giving those who have not paid their respects in the house an opportunity to see him and pray for him. He lies on a catafalque in front of the altar. Two of the boys stand to attention in front of him with their arms reversed. They are taking turns at it so he won't be left unattended between now and the funeral at eleven o'clock tomorrow morning. And a ring of armed men surrounds the village on all roads in case the Staters get any ideas about calling by.

Dear Diary

We've just got rid of the last of them from after the funeral – Lama and Andy White were last to go as usual. I thought they'd never shift.

Never in my life have I felt as tired but still I can't sleep. Everything that has been said to me today about Barney is buzzing around in my head as if the words themselves were living things. And murmuring away underneath are all the words that are not being said at all. Nobody mentions Dan O'Donovan though we all spent the morning wondering whether he would show up.

It was one of the largest funerals Mucknamore had ever seen. We're not the only ones spinning from the shock of how my brother died. Many you wouldn't expect to be there at all turned out to honour him. We held our heads high, didn't let our sorrow overcome us, even when Father John made that speech. Who'd have thought he'd turn up so forgiving? It's true what he said, some things are bigger than a man himself.

The burial was the worst, desperate altogether. It was I who let the volley off over the grave, using his own gun, three shots of promise and warning. I didn't flinch from the task, kept my eyes open as I let the fire and didn't screw up my face to one side as I have seen others do. It's the sounds of the day that keep echoing around my head. The three loud cracks of the Webley followed by the cry Mammy let out of her as the coffin went into the ground. The thud of the first sods of clay hitting the wood. The sea-chant of the prayers, breaking in a holy wave across the headstones, down to meet the sound of the sea itself. It twists my heart to replay these sounds through my head but I can't stop myself.

I was so proud of Mammy. It's hard enough to keep control of yourself when you're in the whole of your health but when you're feeling weak and ill, it must be near impossible. It's her pride in Barney that keeps her going. I never told her about the letter he wrote me and I've hidden it away in a safe place. She'll never see it, or hear a word of it, from me.

Mr and Mrs O'Donovan were at the church, standing at the back with their younger children, but no Dan, thank God. And of course no Nora. People say to each other (not to us) that it was brave of the O'Donovans to come, given the circumstances. Behind their fists, they talk about the two who couldn't be there, the two who had most reason: Barney's sweetheart and his old comrade and friend. The poorly kept secret of Nora and Barney's love affair is known to all now, common knowledge, passed around like a parcel nobody wants.

We know well enough what they are saying, behind their commiserations: they're recalling what happened to James Tracey and Nellie Shiels two years ago, when the Shiels boys tarred-and-feathered James's private parts and Nelly was sent away to England to an aunt. They're saying that it is not unusual for the menfolk of a family to set upon a young man, if he's thought to be interfering with a girl of theirs. That it's not unknown for such a young man to have the life near beaten out of him.

Was such a motive in Dan O'Donovan's mind when he shot and killed my brother? That is the question on everybody's lips when they are speaking to anybody but us. Only Dan himself knows the answer to that and Dan is the only one not talking.

Dear Diary

We had the inquest today and it was worse than the funeral, listening to their soldiers, their lawyers and, especially, that doctor with his horrible, detached, medical voice giving details of what took Barney out of this life – 'a large wound in the front of the abdomen with a knuckle bowel protruding. Death caused by laceration of the bowel and kidneys, haemorrhage and shock.' Another sound to add to the torture in my head.

And Dan O'Donovan in the witness box, never looking at us once. What he said was nearly worse than the doctor's evidence. Our solicitor, Mr Nolan, submitted that there was no evidence of how Barney was shot. Surely some of the soldiers must have seen him fall or come out of the outhouse but Dan said that in the melee, with both sides firing for upward of ten minutes, it would have been hard to distinguish any particular man getting shot.

Believable enough. Where he lost me was when he was asked what answer Barney gave him when the troops had the house surrounded and he knocked on the door of the stable to take the surrender. According to him, Barney said 'Wait until we put on our clothes'. I don't believe that, not for one minute.

Sore-Toes and all the boys say that what he said was 'Surrender we never will'. And that the Staters started shooting first. And that Dan was seen to take aim at Barney as he was racing towards the wall, Barney having hung back to keep up a defensive fire that allowed others to escape.

I'm so confused. I want to believe the story that makes our boy a hero, of course, but I can't be like Mammy and just believe what I want to believe. On the other hand, I'm disinclined to believe Dan O'Donovan's version of events, though he sounded so sincere, when he spoke of Barney being his neighbour and good friend. He said he assured Barney that it was himself who was in charge and that if they came out, he would see to it that they were protected. That wouldn't have been much assurance to Barney but that isn't the same thing as saying he didn't mean it – or didn't even say it, as some of the lads are claiming.

In the end, the jury pronounced themselves satisfied that Barney had been shot by National Troops 'in the course of their duty'. Poor Daddy was so frustrated by this – he is as convinced as anyone that Dan did it – that he stood and made a speech, saying he considered it a 'poor specimen of a national army when it was a case of fifty to one'. He said his wife had seen the troops going past the house and there was more than fourteen of them, for sure.

Then Capt. Kennedy rose and in a manner as superior as any English commandant made a public spectacle of Daddy, not caring an ounce for his obvious grief. 'Do the Republicans claim the sole right to carry on?' he intoned. 'Are we to go to war as they wish? Are we to send out three or four? That is all bunkum, my friend. If they had surrendered that morning, as they said they would, there would not have been one shot fired. If they had simply come out when they were asked, nobody would have been killed.' Oh, God, is that the truth of it? You could see the jury thought so. Thoughts hammer through my head, tumbling one over the other, but don't take me any closer to knowing.

The verdict came as no surprise. A Free State court with a Free State judge and the Free State Army giving the evidence were hardly going to bring a jury round to convicting one of their own for murder. And in any case, if Dan is a murderer, then so are we. So am I. That is the truth that won't let me go.

This is a just punishment for what I did, what Barney did, at Donore. An eye for an eye.

Now we are supposed to keep the thing going, tit for tat. Plan another raid or ambush. Go after Dan himself. Oh, dear diary, dear Barney, I don't think I can, not now. I'm too frightened of where it will take us, if we make another family feel like we feel this day.

Weakness, Mammy calls this. Understandable weakness but to be transcended. She says Barney died because he didn't keep the faith. She only said that once, up in the bedroom last night. He was wavering again, she said, and she put Nora at the back of it – if he had kept strong, this wouldn't have happened. I didn't really understand what she meant and I nearly told her about the letter he sent me but something held me back. This morning, I'm glad I didn't because she's back where she was, full of the official line, that his death is a glorious thing. It keeps her stronger, that story, than the other one.

And it gives me some consolation too, to think of it so. So I am writing a ballad – something to keep Barney's memory alive. The new Free State would like to make it as if men like Barney Parle never lived. Whatever the rights and wrongs of our beliefs, whatever remorse I carry, I cannot allow that.

For Freedom's Sake
By Peg Parle

The soldiers searched the countryside for many a weary day,
Seeking out concealed positions where the freedom fighters lay.
Around a Big House stable one morning they did creep
To ambush brave Republicans while they were still asleep.

The stern command: 'Surrender' rang out o'er Derriestown:
'Surrender, Barney Parle, to the Free State and the Crown'
But Barney grabbed his rifle and his comrades did the same
Jumped up to fight for freedom and for dear old Ireland's name.

With that a crack of muskets broke, a terrifying sound
Of gun and bomb explosions that went echoing all round.
Brave Barney called out loud and clear above the piteous roar,
To rally on his comrades as he'd so often done before:

'Prepare yourselves m'gallant lads, m'true born Irish boys
To make a dash for freedom and for Holy Ireland's cause.'
Then he shouted at the Staters (and made his comrades thrill):
'To traitor threats and bombs and guns, Surrender We Never Will.'

So they made their dash for freedom at the dawning of the day
Through flames and blasts and rifle shots so cruelly flung their way
Barney held the firing line, while his comrades scaled the wall
They escaped but he fell murdered by a Free State cannon ball.

Sleep on, sleep on, brave Barney Parle, we weep that you are gone
But know that on your life and death God's wondrous blessing
  shone
And on your soul the angels still bestow their precious smile
Though you've left and gone ahead of us, it's only for a while.

You fought your fight for freedom's sake, like all brave Irish men
You fought your Holy country's cause. God Rest Your Soul. Amen.
A cross now marks the hallowed spot where your wounded body
  lies
Fear Not: We never will forget the cause for which you died.

SURRENDER WE NEVER WILL!

37
1983

Grace Jones purrs her hymn to her 'Jamaican Guy' from two massive wall-mounted speakers, pained vocals underwritten by a pounding bass drum. At the head of the exercise class, an instructor faces the group and leads them through jumps and bends and stretches, shouting her commands to be heard above the music: '. . . and reach, two, three, four . . .' At her bidding, nineteen people arch their arms over their heads and bounce into a waist stretch. She lifts her left knee, they lift theirs; she moves right, they all shift in the same direction, swinging their arms just as she does, half a second behind her in synchronized unison, like one multi-limbed organism.

She is fit, this Lycra-clad instructor: strong, supple and lean. She can run six miles in under forty minutes, bend from her waist to touch her nose to her knee with palms flat on the floor. She can bench-press 88 pounds, leg-press 110. While instructing her classes, she stretches further, jumps higher, lasts longer than those following her instructions, though this is the third class she has given in four hours.

Sometimes, the control she has over these people's movements bewilders her. She imagines herself doing something silly or lewd – pretending to pick her nose or rub herself between her legs – just to see if they might copy her. She never does, though; it would slight what they do together and she loves what they do: the giving over of their bodies to the music, letting the beat drive them, push them further and faster, faster and further until every muscle is primed. When it goes well, it's a high like no other, and tonight is a good night. This group is one of her most advanced, well trained, fit, responsive: she can push them hard. As the apex of the class approaches, as the faces contort with effort and the smell of sweat rises in the room and the ceiling-to-floor mirrors fog over from breath and perspiration, her shouts grow more excited: 'Yes . . . and just eight more: . . . eight . . . seven . . . push harder, that's it . . . and five . . . four . . . three . . . two . . . one . . . And again . . . ten . . . nine . . .'

A good class.

When it is over, after she has cooled them all down with slow stretching and breathing exercises, a short line of people forms, waiting to ask her questions or share their diet or exercise dilemmas. Her friend Richard also waits, but over by the window doing extra hamstring stretches, as she works through the line, advising, counselling, consoling or deflecting.

When the last of them has gone, he comes across, pecks her on the mouth. 'Terrific, as always.' His grey vest is streaked with sweat. 'Just what I needed.'

'Oh?' She returns the kiss. 'Stressed out *again*?'

He shudders, theatrically, and she motions for him to turn round. She puts her hands on his shoulders, under the towel, just at the base of his neck. 'Let me see.' Her fingers slide over his damp skin, her thumbs kneading the bunched muscle underneath. 'Work? Or Gary again?'

He lets a long, low groan, part physical delight in her ministrations, part frustration. 'You won't believe what the bitch has done to me now.'

'Richard!' She nips his flesh between her fingers.

'Ow! That hurt.'

'Then don't talk about Gary like that.'

'Wait till you hear, though. On Sunday—'

'Tell you what, hon . . .' She gives him a final manipulation of the trapezius and releases him. 'Save it for dinner. Then you can give me the full treatment.' Richard's stories are always part performance, and she enjoys the entertainment. 'Hit those showers,' she says, 'and see you down at reception in twenty?'

This engagement for dinner after her Wednesday class has become a fixture in both their diaries. She sees Richard on other nights too, and with other people, but Wednesday's tête-à-tête has become the bedrock of their friendship. There's no one in this city she'd rather spend time with. It was Richard who encouraged her career in fitness. When she started teaching aerobics classes part-time in a local hall she wanted to be more than just another Jane Fonda clone. As she experimented with new moves and methods, Richard urged her on. Whenever she hit on something uniquely her own, he loved it. 'Don't be afraid, Squirrel,' he used to say. 'You're great at this; go for it.'

So she did. She shunned the pure dance music used by other instructors in favour of songs with slow beats that allowed muscles and joints to be put through a fuller range of movement: Talking Heads, Marvyn Gaye, Grace Jones . . . She devised routines that took the body from its highest attainable point – leaping through the air – to lying prone on the floor and back up again, all in a series of controlled moves that worked the main muscle groups. To an onlooker, her class might look less strenuous than the more usual fast-stepping, high-impact workouts but those who did the routine knew just how tough – and effective – it was.

Richard was right. The more experimental she became, the more the punters loved it. She quickly got slots in the top gyms in the city and people began to book for her class in advance, sometimes even weeks ahead. Instead of taking one of the full-time jobs she was offered by the gyms, she set up her own company, Rí Rá. 'In Ireland,' her publicity material read, 'a *rí rá* is a rollicking and raucous good time. That's just what you're guaranteed with a Rí Rá (pronounced Ree Raw) Workout. A pulse-pounding, dance-based aerobic routine set to an eclectic musical mix – everything from Classical to Celtic Rock – that will challenge every muscle in your body. In Ireland a *rí rá* sometimes turns into an outright *ruaille buaille.* What's that? Why don't you come along and find out . . . ?'

It felt hypocritical to play on her Irishness this way, after years of renouncing the place, but Richard convinced her. 'You *are* Irish,' he said, 'and if for some misbegotten reason the Irish are suddenly cool, then you might as well take advantage.' She knows that some people consider what she does to be superficial, or worse. Her friend, the defiantly large Susan, has put all the arguments to her. Susan is scathing about what she calls body fascism and carries every one of her 180 pounds with pride, a testament to her resolution to 'take up space'. Susan does not approve of exercise classes, considers exercise instructors to be implicated, 'up to their necks', in a system that uses ideals of female beauty as a weapon in the war against women. Susan's arguments sway her but she knows too, to her core, that exercise saved her. She won't let herself deny that truth.

Often now, she sees both sides of an argument; sometimes more than two. This used to worry her until she read Walt Whitman's 'Song of Myself': 'Do I contradict myself? / Very well then I contradict myself / (I am large, I contain multitudes.)' She had the lines written up in large letters and framed, to hang on her wall.

She has men in her life, this woman. Lovers aplenty. Generally she loves them serially, one after another, but sometimes they overlap. Monogamy no longer seems to her like the only, or even the best, way to live. With so many people in her life she is rarely lonely and if she, just sometimes, finds herself marooned in a moment of yearning, she is able to extricate herself. To catch herself on, as her grandmother would say. She no longer believes in 'the One'.

She, of course, is me. I like her, this creation of mine, though I don't quite believe in her. Living in San Francisco has changed me: I am not the person I was when I arrived. If I had stayed where I was, or gone somewhere else, I would be different again. Knowing this makes me feel strange. Conditional.

*

Richard and I sit at our table in Mani's, drinking love bombs: alcohol-free cocktails of passion-fruit juice, wheatgerm and ginseng. We are both dry, one of the many things we have in common. This makes us mildly self-conscious – since its lawless, boomtown beginnings, San Francisco has been a hard-drinking town – but it's just beginning to be cool to be clean. Health is a burgeoning business and sober clubs are opening up.

Over the menus, Richard is making a tale out of his complaints against Gary. On Sunday afternoon, after an argument about Richard's staying out all night after a trip to the Glory Holes, his favourite bathhouse, Gary flounced out of their apartment and hasn't been seen since. The word on the gay grapevine is that at least one of those absent nights was spent with Reno Lewis, who just happens to be an old flame of Richard's. '*Reno Lewis*,' wails Richard, dropping his face into his hands. Under the dramatics, I know his dismay is real.

Real but misplaced, it seems to me. For weeks, months, I have listened to Richard bemoaning Gary's predilection for monogamy as if it were a vice.

'So what's the problem?' I ask. 'I thought this was what you wanted.'

'Reno Lewis,' he groans. 'Reno Lewis.'

'I'm confused,' I say. 'Just who are you jealous of here?'

'I'm not jealous. You know I don't do jealous.'

Is he serious or treating me to his particular brand of heavy irony? Even after three years of friendship, I sometimes can't tell. 'You're doing a good impression,' I say.

'Come on, Squirrel, keep to your script. You're my buddy. You're supposed to pat my hand, tell me I've been wronged.'

'I can't, you contrary old queen. For months Gary has wanted you to be a couple and you insisted on your inalienable rights to visit the Glory Holes whenever you fancied. Now he's playing things your way and you're outraged.'

'Ouch!' he winces.

'Why are you doing this? You two are so great together. What's with the death wish?'

'And ouch again! Enough, Cruella.'

Our waiter comes over, a new guy, dark hair in a pony tail, whiter than white teeth, very young. Richard and I exchange a look that says: nice, very nice. Richard has taught me how to admire men, how to look at them frankly, without fear. It helps when they are younger, as this one is. He takes our order and departs, the strings of his apron tied into a heart shape over his butt.

Richard sees me look and nudges me. 'Eyes off, Squirrel, he's mine.'

I groan out loud; he can always tell. 'Aren't there any straight men left in this town?'

Richard laughs. I'll get no sympathy on that score, I know. And he's right, it is he who is in the minority, even here in San Francisco. I turn back to our conversation about Gary. 'You know, Richard, you can't have everything.'

'I don't want everything, O Heartless One. I only want . . .' He stops.

'Go on.'

He looks over his shoulder. 'Is this an X-rated restaurant?'

I laugh. 'Come on, Richard, be serious. What is it that you want?'

'I *am* being serious. At least half the time –' he lowers his voice – 'I am the horniest man alive and all I want, all I think I'll ever want, is filthy, glorious, anonymous sex.'

'And the other half?'

'The other half, I want what Gary and you and the rest of the goddamn world seems to think I *should* want: side-by-side TV dinners and hand-in-hand trips to the stores. Romance and undying love with one wonderful man.'

'So-o-o-o, all you need is to find someone who understands all that and loves you anyway. Somebody who lets you be both.'

'That's *all*, huh?'

'But, Richard, you have that. With Gary. At least, you had, if you haven't blown it.'

He fiddles with his napkin.

'Your problem isn't that you want everything. It's that while you are doing one thing, you're longing for the other.'

He picks up another napkin, stuffs one into each ear.

'I'm right, and you know it. While you're at home with Gary, you're wondering what's going on down the baths. After a few nights in the Glory Holes, you're thinking: what am I doing here when I could be home with that great guy of mine?'

He takes the napkins down. 'While I'm at the Glory Holes, honey, thinking is about the only thing I'm *not* doing.'

I giggle. 'But I'm not altogether wrong, am I?'

'You're just telling me back what I already told you. I'm a condemned man. This isn't a phase, it's the story of my life.'

He looks so miserable that I laugh. 'Come on, aren't you the guy who told me that happiness is a decision?'

'Oh, that. I never believed that, I was only trying to cheer you up. You and I know better than that. Come on, could you ever be happy in Mucksville? Could I, in Telport?' Richard comes from a small town in the Midwest. For him, indeed for many of the people we know, home is a four-letter word.

'But we're not in Mucknamore or Telport any more,' I say. 'We're here, in one of the best towns in the world. Especially for you.' I reach across and touch his hand. 'Look, Richard, I just have to say one more thing, so you can't fool yourself that you don't know. If Gary wasn't scared of you leaving him, he would never have gone near this Reno Lewis person. Gary is man enough to let you go prowling if that's what you need to do, once he can trust you to come home to him after you're done.'

He chews a piece of bread roll, but he is listening. 'To stick to one person for the rest of my life: it makes me gag with panic to think about it,' he says.

'And when you think of being alone?'

'See? A condemned man.'

Our waiter friend comes across with our food. Richard throws him such heavy looks that the poor boy breaks into a blush.

'New to town?' Richard asks.

'Yeah.'

'Just arrived from . . . ?'

'Minnesota.'

'Well, Minnesota, we'll have to show you around a little. What time do you get off?'

The boy looks uncertain. 'Eleven.'

'Great.'

'Em, I'm not sure . . .'

'Oh, I'm sorry. Pardon me if you've got better plans.'

'No, it's not . . . It's just . . .'

'Tell him, Squirrel. Tell him I don't bite.'

'He doesn't bite,' I say, flatly. The boy looks at me, then at Richard.

'Relax, Minnesota. This is a friendly town. I'll just take you around, introduce you to a few people.'

'OK.' He flashes his perfect smile. 'Yeah . . . why not?'

He goes off to attend to someone else. Richard is jubilant. 'Take that, pal Gary,' he says, discreetly punching the air.

Coffee arrives via another waiter and I tell him my news. 'I got a letter from Ireland today.'

'No! Not from the indomitable Mom?'

'From her representative, Sister Maeve. She's coming over here for a visit.'

'This, I deduce from the droop of your chin, is not a good thing?'

'Oh, Richard, you know what she's like. She only wants to come here so she can have a good snoop around my life, check me out.'

'That's what big sisters do, I guess.'

'She's bringing Donal with her.'

His eyebrows lift into a question.

'Her husband. A hollow man, a suit.'

'Poor Squirrel. How long will they be here?'

'Two weeks,' I wail. 'What will I do with them for fourteen whole days and nights?'

'I'll help you.'

'Oh . . . OK. Thanks.'

He notices my hesitation. 'Unless I'm one of the things in your life that you don't want her snooping around.'

'Don't be silly, Richard. It's not you, it's them.'

He shakes his head. 'She's a big girl.'

'Yeah, my big critical sister.'

'If she wants to be critical, you can't stop her. Let her be critical.'

I make a face. 'Come on, it's not that simple and you know it. What if it was your mother coming to see you?'

He shudders. 'That's not too likely, praise be. She can't come because she hasn't told any of her cronies I live here. She's afraid they'll put two and two together and work out why I'm not married.' He takes my hand. 'Just be yourself, Squirrel. Stand tall.'

'I can imagine what she'll say about teaching aerobics.' I stick my nose up and imitate my sister's voice at its pickiest: '"I'm sure it's fun, Jo, but it's hardly a *proper* job, now is it?"'

'Let her come, let her think what she wants, then let her go home again. That's all you have to do.'

Richard is the only person who understands why I left Mucknamore and never went back. Why I won't get in touch with my mother or grandmother if they won't contact me. I have told him everything. He lifts my fingers, brushes them with a kiss. 'You know you're fabulous, darling. If the Mucksville contingent can't see it, that's their loss.'

'Thank you.' I whisper. Then, lighter: 'You're right, I *am* fabulous.'

'You are. Too, too fabulous.' He looks over my shoulder. 'But now,' he says, 'it would appear that dessert is approaching.'

I follow his eyes. Our waiter is crossing to our table, white apron gone. 'I got off early,' he says, sliding into the chair opposite me, his skin glowing with youth and promise.

I get up, leave my half of the check on the table. 'Be nice,' I whisper into Richard's ear as I kiss him goodnight. 'He's sweet.'

He answers me with a horrible leer.

'Night, night,' I say, to them both. 'Be good.'

'Honey, you know I'm the best.' His chuckle follows me out into the foggy evening.

San Francisco is my city. I knew that from the moment I arrived, from my very first morning walking through Golden Gate Park, entranced by the smell of eucalyptus and sunny November skies. It was a Sunday, I remember, and the park was full of people but it was big enough to hold us all. On my way in, I passed a circle of hippyish-looking men drinking cider around a set of bongo drums and a guitar. One of them lifted his can to me as I walked past. 'You have a good one,' he said, smiling, and I found myself smiling back. I couldn't help myself, he seemed so amiable. They all did, though there were eleven of them and only one of me. It was impossible to imagine passing a group of homeless men in London or Dublin and feeling so unthreatened but with these men I was safe. I could feel it.

I love it here: that was the mantra humming round my head as I walked, this place born out of gold and silver, built on a core of wild spending and carousing. This city that was never a small town, but wild and lawless, gaudy and greedy, diverse and world famous, right from the start.

All the way down to the far end of the park I walked, then I crossed the highway to Ocean Beach, wanting to put my feet in the Pacific. The sand was pale cream and the icy water, indifferent to the sunny sky, was a shock. Still, I was charmed. I held my feet in its freezing grip, thinking about how it also touched the coasts of China and Japan, how, though I might still be on the western edge of a continent, here I was facing east.

In those early days I walked everywhere, getting to know my new place. The first year was difficult, chopping and hopping from job to dead-end job, apartment to dreary apartment, trapped inside a void left behind by alcohol's absence. For sanity's sake, I walked and walked – later, jogged – all around the city, up and down the unfeasible hills, through streets where music drummed out from under psychedelic blinds, in parks where grey-haired people went roller skating, on beaches where meditators worshipped the morning sun. I revelled in the sunshine and also in the fogs that billowed in from the ocean as if huffed through the Golden Gate by an unseen mouth. I came to love these fogs that shrouded me in a blanket of anonymity as I went, that ensured I never took the sun for granted. All the while, the city was unfolding itself to me.

I even came to love its faulty underpinnings: San Andreas and Hayward, San Gregorio, Greenville and Calaveras and the earth shudders they threw up, always hinting towards the long-anticipated 'Big One' that might come at any time and topple our city down on top of us. Or trigger a tsunami out in the ocean, a tidal wave that would swell as it swept in from the bay, rising taller than the skyscrapers it broke against, smashing them to smithereens and sweeping away the bits in its flow, like so many pebbles. It was frightening to ponder it, especially downtown among the office towers, frightening and thrilling. According to Richard, the risk of earthquake has us all permanently turned on. With catastrophe ever imminent, better try whatever you fancy now or else die wondering. I don't fully buy the theory – I can't imagine Richard reining in his excesses wherever he lived – but I've come to believe that it is good for me, for us all, to live so, within the full, daily knowledge of our vulnerability.

I hadn't been here long when I first heard the expression 'only in San Francisco . . .' It came to be widely used afterwards – 'only in Hollywood', people would say, or 'only in Europe' – and usually used disparagingly but I heard it first applied to the town I was beginning to own and I took it as a tribute. So many things could, and did, happen only in San Francisco. This city had given the world Beats and Hippies, Free Love and Flower Power, Multi-culturalism and Gay Pride . . . Only in San Francisco, it seemed – still seems – to me, do civic institutions extend American can-do culture into realms beyond the financial.

It was on nights out with Richard that I first cracked open my inhibitions without alcohol. His frankness about matters sexual made me see how I had always stood at the border of my own desires, hesitating, playing safe, nursing my sexual disappointment while berating myself or my lover de jour. By example, Richard taught me to own my full self. By joking, he led me past fear and shame. 'Forget what your mother told you about sex,' he said. 'Apply what she told you about olives instead.' Mrs D. never had anything to say to me about either but I took the point: sex is an acquired taste and it takes several tries to know which particular flavours you enjoy. There are techniques and responses to learn, social as well as sexual skills to acquire. Richard showed me the way.

But it was the night he turned up at my house with his face disfigured by a gay bashing – for yes, even in San Francisco there are bigots – that turned our fondness into something more. When I found him standing on my doorstep, pretending like he didn't care, and brought him in to sit on my sofa and held him hard while he tried to stop his bruised face from creasing into tears, that was when I knew I loved him. With my new, San Franciscan, way of loving.

Susan I met later and she forced herself on me. I was browsing in a bookshop when she came peering over the top of my book, two enormous brown eyes in a wide, shiny black face. 'You don't want that,' she said.

'Excuse me?'

'That.' She pointed at the book I had in my hand: *Woman's*

Words, Woman's Worlds. 'You don't want it. It's just another whitey whine.'

I pulled back from this intrusion but she didn't seem to notice. 'Trust me. This is the one you want.' She held out another book to me. *This Bridge Called My Back*, it was called. *Writings By Radical Women of Color*.

I looked up at her. 'No,' I said. 'I don't think so.'

'Where are you from?'

'Ireland,' I said, instantly regretting that I had answered. I decided to be rude and turned my back.

'I knew it,' she said, coming round to my front. 'I said so to myself when I saw you. But I'm reckoning on you being the right kind of Irish. That's why I'm saying to you that this here is the one you want.' Again she shoved the book towards me and resisted as I tried to push it back. When I wouldn't take it from her hands, she carried it across to the checkout. 'The lady will take this,' she said, pointing across at me.

Now I was outraged. I worked in a bar back then, a down-at-heel place where the tips were poor and given out once a week, with our pay packs. That day I had less than $5 in my purse and if I bought that book, I wouldn't eat again until payday.

Susan saw my expression, opened her purse. 'Here.' She handed twenty dollars to the assistant.

'No,' I protested, crossing over. 'Stop.'

'I'm making you do this, honey,' Susan said, taking her change. 'So don't waste no time feeling bad. But I do have a condition. You've got to call me when you've read it and tell me your opinion.' She was writing down her number for me on the paper wrapping.

'Whether I like it or not?'

'Why, sure.' She looked at me appraisingly. 'But you'll like it,' she said, slowly nodding her head. 'Yeah, I'm getting the feeling I know just what you like.'

I caught the hint in her voice, enough to make me wonder if

she meant what I later learned she did. By the time I knew for sure, I didn't recoïl from the notion as I would have on that first day. By then, I knew Susan well enough to be glad that, if she had been mistaken in that, she was proven right about the book. And about lots of other things too.

It was a great book, just what I needed to read at that time. I had always held that any sensible woman had to be a feminist, and living in more than one place had taught me that each culture has its own particular ways of keeping its women under. Now, just as I was getting used to the idea of a pan-national, trans-historical sisterhood, the essays in this book – by Afro-, Asian-, Latin- and Native-American women – complicated that idea. Frustrated by their experiences of female exclusion in their communities and racial exclusion in the women's movement, these writers asked: 'How can we – this time – not have our bodies thrown over a river of tormented history to bridge the gap?' The essays were eloquent, passionate and thought-provoking and made me see how I benefited from having white skin. For the first time in my life, I saw myself as a person of relative privilege.

When I telephoned – or called, as I was learning to say – to tell Susan so, she squealed with delight. 'I knew it,' she cried, her voice an even deeper shade of chocolate over the telephone. 'I knew you were the right type of Irish.'

I said, 'I don't know what you mean by that.'

'Your people come in two kinds, honey: those who pretend like there never was an attitude that said "No Blacks, No Irish". Those ones like to put as much distance as they can between their black brothers and sisters and their own white, lily-livered asses. Then there's the ones who've learned somethin' more from their own persecution than how to do the same thing to others.'

'Solidarity versus self-interest.'

'I guess.'

'It's not a matter of wholly signing up for one or the other, is it? Surely everybody is always negotiating those two positions.'

'Hmmm. The way I see it, if you're not actively working *for* the struggle, then you're against us.'

She made me quail right from the start. I've never had the courage for Susan's kind of stern, clear anger: all my emotions are mixed. But we talked for a long time on the telephone and at the end of the call she asked if I would like to come with her on Monday night to Joni's, a woman-only health spa on Polk that hosted CR sessions three times a week.

CR?

What, I had never heard of Consciousness-Raising? I was going to *love* it. They were a great group of women and they talked about everything, *everything*, exploring how their personal dilemmas were politically rooted. There used to be hundreds of such spaces all over this town but in recent years, she didn't know why, they were closing down, little lights going out.

The spa was in what looked like an old factory building. There was no elevator and we walked up three flights of rickety wooden stairs to be met at the top by a dainty Latina woman, about forty years old, wearing a buttonhole that said: *Cunt Power!* She hugged Susan for a long time then they both turned to me and she said, 'Welcome, Jo,' and kissed my cheek. 'Susan has been telling me all about you.'

Her lips were dry, powdery, and she smelled of something herbal.

The same smell permeated the lemon-and-lavender-striped corridor they steered me through. 'Susan tells me you liked *Bridge*,' Dolores said, taking my arm.

'Yes.'

'I'm so glad. It's a really seminal book, I think.'

'Shouldn't that be "ovumnal", sweetheart?' Susan called from behind us.

'Hey, that's a great word,' smiled Dolores over our shoulders. 'Ovumnal. I love that.' She turned back to me. 'Have you ever done a naked consciousness-raising before, Jo?'

'Naked?'

'Oh, sorry,' said Susan, breaking into peals of laughter behind us. 'Did I not mention naked?'

'Please do not mind her, Jo.' Dolores's arm locked mine, propelled me onwards. 'It is all very non-threatening. Very gentle and supportive. The idea is we present ourselves to each other in all our vulnerability. Also that we take off our inhibitions with our clothes.'

In the spa room, three women were already in the jacuzzi pool. 'This is Gloria,' said Dolores. 'And Zoe. And Arlene. Women, this is Jo.'

'Hi, Jo,' the three responded, together.

Gloria was fortyish and black, Zoe was my age, white with dreadlocked hair, and Arlene, also white, was much older than the rest. That was all I had time to notice as Dolores led us through to the dressing room. I was busy appearing nonchalant. In the time it took me to hang my jacket on the hook and unzip my bag, Susan had her clothes off and was parading around the dressing room, her towel trailing from her fingers. I was drawn out of my own self-consciousness by the vast expanse of her body. Furrows of fat cascaded from beneath the bowls of her breasts. Her girth was frightening, each thigh the size of an average waist. She seemed like a parody of a fat woman, the sort you see in cartoons, as if her feet were too small to support her and she was going to topple over. Half hideous and half magnificent, she postured around the room, and I couldn't make up my mind whether the magnificence was accentuated or diluted by her defiance.

Meanwhile I slinked out of my clothes and let her lead the way back to the pool. Behind them, I held my head up and managed not to use my hands to cover myself. I wasn't normally prudish but something about the artificiality of the situation, the weighing of our nakedness with meaning, made me want to grab the nearest towel and run. I tried to pull my eyes away from the enormous wobbling black half-moons of Susan's ass.

One after each other, we slid into the pool. Everyone else's breasts were held above the water line so I did the same. The water bubbled against my skin and the underlying drone of the pump was soothing but my thighs clutched the smooth plastic of the seat and refused to relax. Dolores opened the session by introducing and welcoming me, then outlining – as she did each time – the rules of the coming conversation. We must suspend judgement. We must listen with respect, seeking to understand rather than persuade. We must speak freely and with sincerity of what has personal heart and meaning. The topic for today would be our experiences with the medical profession.

'Before we get started,' said Arlene. 'I just thought y'all might like to know that I did it.'

'Way hey, girl!' cackled Susan. 'And did you find what you went looking for?'

'Tell us everything, Arlene,' said Dolores. 'Everything. Did you buy the hand mirror?'

'Uh-huh.'

'And you took it to your bedroom?'

'Bathroom.'

'Ran a bath?'

'Mmm.'

'Lit candles?'

'Yes.'

'Good,' said Dolores. 'Candles are good. Low, gentle light.'

'Arlene is – or looks like we can finally say *was* – a masturbation virgin,' Susan explained to me.

'Oh,' I said.

Arlene reclaimed the conversation, told how she had also bought – she quivered at her daring – some female erotica. And then she did it . . . felt her . . . touched herself . . . down there . . .

'Not "down there", Arlene,' said Dolores. 'Come on now.'

'Touched my . . . vagina,' Arlene whispered.

Dolores clapped her hands. 'Well done, Arlene.' Gloria and Zoe joined in.

Susan was unimpressed. 'Can you be a bit more specific?' she asked, melting Arlene's expression of triumph. 'It wasn't your "vagina" you were aiming at, was it?'

Furrows erupted on Arlene's forehead. She began to bite her lower lip.

'Christ, girl! Ain't you ever going to say cunt?' said Susan.

'I don't want to say it, I told you.'

'Now, Arlene, we've discussed this,' said Dolores. 'We have to embrace all the words. We have to reclaim our bodies, especially our sexual organs, from patriarchal disfigurement. We have to own ourselves and love ourselves.'

'Well, I can't help it,' Arlene said. 'I just hate that word.'

Dolores reached across, put a hand on her shoulder. 'You've been conditioned to hate it, remember? Remember last week, when we talked about the word "country"?'

Arlene nodded.

'You don't hate that word, do you?'

She shook her head.

'It's only a collection of letters, Arlene. If you hate it, what you're feeling is men's hatred for women. You have to break that in yourself.'

'I used to be the same, Arlene,' said Zoe. 'But now I'm totally able to say any of 'em. Cunt! Pussy! Vagina!'

'Labia!' said Gloria, cupping handfuls of water and throwing them in the air. 'Vulva!'

'Men have plenty of names for their genitalia, Arlene,' Dolores said. 'And none of them is vague.'

'Too right,' said Susan. 'No fear of *them* mixing up their prick and their balls. "Down there", Arlene? I mean, Jesus! It's the 1980s.'

'Hold on,' said Zoe. 'She did say "vagina".'

'Don't any of you want,' whispered Arlene, pulling herself up into the dignity of her years, 'to hear what *happened*?'

Dolores was contrite. 'Of course we do. Come on, everybody, this is Arlene's time to talk.'

'But, honey,' said Susan, 'until she starts naming names, we can't even be sure what she's saying. What did you go a-rubbing, Arlene?'

Arlene looked like she might cry.

'It's OK, Arlene,' said Gloria. 'You take your time. You'll say it in a minute, won't you? When you're ready?'

But she didn't. Dolores made an attempt to steer the conversation towards the topic of the day, asking if anybody had any stories about patronizing doctors or female-phobic medical technology. The talk veered off to the problems Gloria was having with her daughter, Sam. Sam was trying to own her own sexuality, Gloria said, but was hurting from being called a slut by her friends, girlfriends as well as boys. As far as Gloria could see, sex was still just a performance for the boys. Zoe agreed with that, said it was a high-wire act for girls, impossible to negotiate without falling off. Arlene wondered whether it might all have been easier after all in the old days, when everybody knew where they stood, and Dolores cut in before Susan could tell Arlene what she thought of that.

Afterwards, I found myself beside Arlene in the dressing room while Susan and Dolores were showering. She said: 'This is your first time here, isn't it?'

I nodded.

'I hope you weren't offended by that talk earlier.'

'No.' I shook my head. 'No, I wasn't offended.'

'It's hard at the beginning. After my first time, I was so shocked I stayed away for weeks but something made me come back.'

I dried between my toes.

'I'm still a bit overwhelmed, as you've probably gathered,' she went on. 'I sometimes have to fight myself not to put my hands over my ears.'

I nodded with what I hoped was empathy.

'Can I ask you something, dear?'

'Sure,' I said, my heart sinking.

'Is Susan,' she whispered, 'saying that "cunt" is the word for "clitoris" and "pussy" is slang for "vagina"? Is that what she means?'

'That's how it sounded.'

'And is that right?'

'I don't know,' I shrug. 'I never thought about it before. I'm a bit vague about it too.'

'I'm so glad.' She smiled. 'I always feel like it's just me.'

'Definitely not,' I said, smiling back. 'Just don't report me to Susan.'

'She's formidable, isn't she? But kind too, very kind. I've seen that in her. That's why I persist. I know they are right and I'm just a foolish old woman.' She zips open her bag, starts to put on her underwear beneath her towel. 'But you know, I wish they hadn't gone on about the words again. They didn't give me a chance to tell them how grateful I feel.'

'Grateful?'

'To have found it.' She beams a smile so beatific you'd think it was God she'd found. 'After sixty-three years of being ignored, there it was. And still . . . still in good working order.'

We are both smiling now.

'I knew it must be *something*, from the way you young people are always going on. But, oh my! I was quite shocked.'

'1923,' I find myself saying.

'I beg your pardon?'

'You were born in 1923.'

'Why, that's right, dear. How did you know?'

'You're the same age as my mother.'

'Is that so? You should bring her along next time.'

'Oh, no,' I say and the way she looks at me tells me I've been over-vehement. 'I can't. She lives in Ireland.'

'That's a pity. But maybe she's more advanced than me?'

'Oh, no,' I say again. 'Not at all. She's Irish.'

'Then you should bring her along, when she comes across to visit you. You should tell her what happens here. Tell her about me: sixty-three years old and . . .' She drops her voice to a whisper: 'I can't get enough of myself.'

Richard loved that story but he didn't like much else about the group. Whenever I ever tried to get him to acknowledge the links between gays and women, he would ostentatiously yawn. 'Don't be a bore, Squirrel,' he would say. 'You're getting far too political. It doesn't suit you.'

This is ironic, because in the group I am considered not political enough. Susan, in particular, thinks me hopeless: I wear short skirts, I defuzz my armpits, I teach *aerobics*, for pity's sake. She wrinkles her nose at all this, implies that she would probably find it unacceptable in anybody else. Mostly I ignore this unasked-for indulgence – Susan needs her convictions, I am glad to have lost mine – but sometimes it's annoying.

Like when she starts on Richard. 'He's a woman-hater,' she says. 'Can't you see that?'

'He doesn't hate me. And I am a woman, am I not?'

For all that I have learned from Susan and the group, for all their insistence on the naming of body parts and sexual oppressions, I am disappointed that the way we talk about sex feels like dressed-up silence. So many of us came to the group and to feminism because of feelings about sex – because we wanted sex we couldn't have or didn't want the sex we got; because we were afraid we liked it too much or too little; because only feminism told us that desire was firstly for ourselves. Yet whenever our talk strays into the territory of the erotic, it always keeps to the same safe path. We allow complaints, or disappointments or angers about sex, especially male sexual shortcomings. Our advances are prescribed: masturbation and homosexuality are celebrated but other traditional taboos – voyeurism, bondage, fetishism, promiscuity, porn – are as shameful to us as to any Reaganite backlasher.

All we have done, it seems to me, is taken one sexual coin and flipped it over, so that heterosex is never good and lesbian sex never bad. I think often about breaking this with my own truth. Once I tried to make an offering but I wasn't understood and my courage failed me. It makes me all the more admiring of Richard's hard-won honesty.

To him I say: 'Susan says I'm a fag hag.'

'At least she didn't say fruit fly.'

'She says gay men despise women.'

'That's her idea of a chat-up line, Squirrel. She thinks you find it seductive.'

Now it is him who is being annoying. 'No, she doesn't. She knows I'm straight.'

I don't tell him that she thinks I shouldn't be. For Susan, lesbianism is a political choice as well as a sexual preference. Men fragment female unity, she says, and heterosex always puts men first. I take the point but I can't – don't want – to take it any further. Fantasies about sexy women are one thing but I shrink from real breasts, smooth faces, soft skin. Men are so easily pleased but a woman, I'm sure, would find me wanting.

So I call my sexual orientation straight and refuse to choose between Susan and Richard. In my new, busy life I want them both and all the people they bring with them and the other friends I am making in work and other places and the dear companionship of the city itself, its parks full of the rolling beat of bongos, its head shops selling drug paraphernalia, its kaleidoscopic street murals, its pride marches and street demos, the blue theatre of its bay. Still now, three years on, walking across Golden Gate Bridge at sundown thrills me: watching it show off its glowing, pink-white buildings undulating against the hills down to the sea. I know as I walk that I am on the 'Bridge of Sighs', the 'Golden Leap', the best-known suicide site in the Western world, where more than a thousand named people have jumped to their deaths. I know that countless more have jumped unseen, at night or through fog, into the strong current that runs oceanward beneath, the sharks feeding there and beyond. But still, for me, the tourist cliché of this city viewed from the bridge, or this bridge viewed from the city, is a wonderful thing.

But now my sister is coming here to see it all. Why do I feel that once she does, it will all look different – lesser – to me?

38

1923

Mucknamore
28th March 1923

Dear Molly,

Thanks for your letter and I'm glad to hear things are not too bad for you in Kilmainham.

You'll probably have heard that Lama is O/C of the column now. When he took over he made a speech saying any man who felt unable to stand the heat was at liberty to go home anytime. Most stayed put but operations like Dunore are no longer attempted: it is felt they are futile, when every Free State soldier taken out can be replaced by ten or a hundred more. The aim now is to make government of the country impossible. We're disrupting the railway and destroying as many public buildings as we can. Private Property is a target too, especially the 'big houses' owned by Unionists, as you can imagine, with Lama in charge.

All the talk here has been of the executions. We were so shocked. I know that more than fifty Republicans have already been killed by firing squad in other parts but it is so different when it comes to your own home place. I was talking to Kitty Frayne in town the other day and she was telling me how she and Mrs Sinnott were getting the tea-shop ready to open when they heard the barrage of rifle-fire resounding out from the jail, closely followed by four single revolver shots at short intervals. You could hear it all across the town, she said.

Mrs Sinnott sent her up to find out what she could and as she got to the jail gate, a soldier was pinning up the death notice. 'By order of the Government of the Irish Free State, the following men were executed by firing squad on this day March 13th 1923: James Parle, of Clover Valley,

Taghmon; John Creane of Clonerane, Taghmon; Patrick Hogan of William St Wexford.' The soldier had spatters of mud on his boots, she said, and he was whistling as he hammered in the notice. 'I'm Forever Blowing Bubbles' was the tune. She will never forget it.

We organized a crowd that night to gather around the jail to recite the rosary and afterwards we marched on to St Peter's Square, where we held a protest meeting against these executions. The Staters broke us up, of course, firing shots over the heads of the crowd. But they won't find us as easy as all that to scatter. What their actions are doing is bringing more and more people onto our side. People are sickened by them, sickened to the core. So we soldier on! A reprisal has been planned. I'll keep you posted.

I am happy you enjoyed Mammy's pamphlet about Barney. It was Mr Connolly, the printer, who said we should put on it that it was written 'by a comrade' – he said it would sell better if people thought it was by one of the boys. Maybe he was right because it has sold very well – he is going to be doing a second printing. Mammy is delighted.

Write again soon and let me know how you are getting on. I suppose it must be hard in the jail but it must be nice too, to have the company of the other girls.

Yours truly,

Peg

Dear Molly,

This is the letter I wish I could write instead of the one I sent you. I am tired and sick and lonely. I miss you and I miss Barney but mostly I miss Nora. I would give anything to see her or even to be able to write to her and ask her what she makes of it all. I could tell Nora the truth, instead of the half-truths I have to feed you and Mammy and everyone else around me.

I could tell her how Mammy squashes any scruples with her certainty, and how I fear that can't be good for her. I could tell her how a decade of years has settled on poor Daddy's shoulders since Barney was killed and bewilderment taken over his eyes. How each of us in this house lives with the fragility in the other two, making us too careful of one another, and so separate in our sorrow. We are like a family of exiles in America, lamenting all the fine things we have lost, things we took for granted when we had them. Yearning to go back, and knowing we never can, which only makes the yearning worse.

Nora would understand if I told her how I am sickened by Lama White's attitudinizing and firing of houses. That I am frightened by somebody who thinks the finer a property is, the more extensive its artworks and libraries, the more priceless and irreplaceable its treasures, the more pleasure is to be got from destroying it. When I expressed a regret at the burning of Sir Thomas Esmonde's home, a house that had stood on that spot since the 1300s, Lama was outraged. 'Immoral wealth,' he called it. 'Built on the sweat and starvation of the native Irish.' I know he is right about that but still. Still . . . Nora would know what I mean.

As she would know without having to be told – for how can I tell what I don't understand myself? – how low I felt when four Free State officers were shot dead as a reprisal for the executions.

I could explain to her all the opposing opinions I carry inside me that seem to be ripping me open sometimes. The certain knowledge that the Republican ideal is noble and virtuous while the Free State grows more ignoble and savage and grasping by the day fighting all the time against the queer guilt I have.

If Nora was home, she'd have been there when our boys arrived – masked – to her house by night and ordered out her parents and the younger children, before sprinkling the house with petrol and setting it alight. Would she be glad or outraged by this action? It's all so confusing, I can't even tell. For I, who couldn't regret what they had done, given what Dan O'Donovan has been doing to us, was still glad when prompt action by some neighbours saved the house, with only slight damage to the front parlour.

What I do know is that even if Nora didn't see it like me, she would understand. Unlike everyone else around here, she wouldn't blunder in on top of me with her own opinions, trying to flatten mine.

I am lonely – that's what I would write to Nora. If I only knew where to write.

North Dublin Union
May 21st 1923

Dear Peg,

You'll have noticed the change of address above. So much has happened since I last wrote, I hardly know where to start.

I have to say that we felt not altogether unfortunate to be in Kilmainham prison for Easter weekend, as you can imagine. The seventh anniversary of the 1916 Rising felt like a good day to take again our Oath of Allegiance to the Republic and to be in the place where those brave men were executed. Now, two weeks later, what a contrast!

It began when we were told that we were to be moved from Kilmainham to North Dublin Union, a former workhouse, and we were none too keen on this idea, as Kilmainham with its noble associations suited us far better. Also Mrs O'Callaghan and Miss MacSwiney were still on their hunger strike (nineteen days by then) and we were very anxious about them.

At about three o'clock on the Monday word came that we were to be moved that night. A meeting of the prisoners was immediately summonsed and it was unanimous: it was unthinkable that we would leave the hunger strikers alone in the empty jail, at the mercy of such cruel tricks as were played on Miss Costello (remember what I told you in my last letter – it got worse after that if you can believe it). So we sent our decision to the governor: no prisoner would consent to leave until the hunger strikers were released.

Next thing, the news came that stretcher bearers had come in. We had a moment of joyous triumph followed quickly by the shock of dismay: Mrs O'Callaghan was released but not Miss MacSwiney. This was appalling news. We knew that Miss MacSwiney was no less dangerously ill than Mrs O'Callaghan. They had been on hunger strike the same number of days, arrested in similar circumstances. It suggested malice against Miss

MacSwiney that, for all we knew, might intend her death. So we were more determined than ever: we would not be moved until that poor suffering woman was released.

Our best strategic position seemed to be the top gallery, as it is caged in with iron bars running around the horseshoe-shaped building, and an iron bridge joining its opposite sides. So we took our places and waited. Our officers gave us our instructions: we were to resist but not attack; we were not to come to one another's rescue; no missiles to be thrown; above all, for the sake of the patient in her cell, no one was to cry out. Then we knelt and said the rosary. We had fastened the doors of our cells and the great well-like place was in darkness, except for one lit window beside a gateway, behind which figures of soldiers and wardresses hurried to and fro. We waited and sang some of Miss MacSwiney's favourite songs.

Suddenly the gate opened and the men rushed in, across the compound and up the stairs. The attack was violent but unorganized. Brigid O'Mullane and Rita Farrelly, the first seized, were crushed and bruised between men dragging them down and men pressing up the stairs. Our Commandant, Mrs Gordon, was next. It was hard not to go to her rescue as she clung to the iron bars, the men beating her hands with their clenched fists again and again. When that failed to make her loose her hold, they struck her twice in the chest, then one took her head and beat it against the iron bars. I think she was unconscious after that. I saw her dragged by the soldiers down the stairs.

The men became determined, they had many methods. Some twisted the girls' arms, some bent back their thumbs. Some were kicked by a particular CID man who was fond of using his feet. One was disabled by a blow on the ankle with a revolver. Annie McKeown, one of the smallest and youngest, was pulled downstairs and kicked (perhaps accidentally) in the head. One girl had her finger bitten, Lena O'Doherty was struck on the mouth, one man thrust a finger down Moira Broderick's throat. Lily Dunn and May O'Toole, who have been ill, fainted. They do not know where they were struck.

My own turn came. After I had been dragged from the railings, a great hand closed on my face, blinding and stifling me, and thrust me back down to the ground, among trampling feet. After that I remember being carried by two or three men and flung down in the surgery to be searched. Mrs Wilson and Mrs Gordon were there, their faces bleeding. One of the women searchers was screaming at them like a drunkard on a Saturday night; she struck Mrs Gordon in the face. They removed watches, fountain pens and brooches, kicking Peg Flanagan and beating Kathleen O'Farrell on the head with her shoe. The orders not to hit back were well obeyed.

The wardresses were bringing us cups of water and they were crying and some of the soldiers too looked wretched. But the prison doctor – and a few other soldiers – looked on, smiling, smoking cigarettes. The doctor seemed to have come along for the entertainment, he did nothing to help any of the injured girls.

After another long struggle, we were thrown into the lorries, one by one, and driven away. The whole thing took five hours.

Peg, you have to let the world know of this disgrace. I don't know whether word has reached the newspapers or not, we're so much more isolated here than we were in Kilmainham. Please also tell the world that Republican women are housed in a place that is filthy and freezing, with no privacy or facilities for washing or bathing. The sentries can (and do) look into our wards on the ground floor. We've asked to have the lower window panes frosted or painted but no, so we have to hang clothes over them to get in or out of bed. We're experiencing every kind of discomfort: hunger, cold and dirt. And, though only a few yards from one of the populous districts of Dublin, cut off from everything.

We have had no news since of Miss MacSwiney. And we hear rumour of peace moves outside but never see a paper. Please fill me in on everything you know when you write. And tell Cat I haven't heard from her this long time and she's not to forget me. Nora too. Not a single word from her in months. The person who gives you this letter will tell you how to get mail through to me untampered.

Please also tell your mammy and daddy I was asking for them and that I keep Barney in my prayers. I was thinking of you and the family at Easter time.

Write soon, won't you?

Your friend

Molly

Mucknamore

17 August 1923

Dear Molly,

Thanks for your letter. What do you think of the ceasefire? I don't know what to make of it. I agree with Mr de Valera that further sacrifice would be in vain but I don't understand what's going to happen next. Neither side has conceded any ground on the issues, yet it's over. What was worthy of bloodshed now is not. That doesn't make any sense, does it? I am glad anyway they didn't make us give up our arms. The few bits we have left went into a safe dump and I suppose we can add to it as time goes on.

Areas never before visited now swarm with troops. And now we have this new Public Order Bill. Ceasefire or not, they don't intend to soften. Flogging as a punishment for arson or robbery!

I don't suppose the ceasefire makes it any more likely that you or the others will be let out. The authorities fear released prisoners will go at once to their weapon dumps and start the fight again. But they can't get away with it, it is against any notion of democracy to incarcerate thousands of people without trial or prospect of release.

You'll have heard that young Bronco Fortune died in prison? Despite our campaign, they wouldn't release him. His remains were brought back to Wexford last week and buried in Ballymore cemetery before a huge crowd. Mrs Fortune is in no doubt but that it was the treatment he got in that Free State jail that killed him.

And now we are having an election, run by a State that we say we don't believe in, yet we are to field candidates. And we're supposed to think it all right because they won't take their seats if they win. I will support it, of course, and do what is asked of me, but I don't know what to make of it all. What do you think? At least this time women under thirty will have their vote. I'm doing up a bulletin to distribute, house to house.

Your friend,

Peg

Dear Voter

We were told the Treaty would bring peace. If so, what sort of a thing is War?

We were told it would bring freedom. What sort of a thing is Slavery?

We were told it would bring prosperity. What sort of a thing is Economic Starvation?

We were told it would bring ordered conditions. What sort of a thing is Chaos?

They said the Treaty would fill Irish pockets. But it has filled only Irish Prisons and Irish Graves.

On behalf of the British king and commons, the Irish 'Free State' government has, in fourteen months, murdered, executed, tortured and imprisoned more Irishmen than the British themselves did during all the years of the Terror (1916–1922). If the British Government is going to go on fighting us and destroying us as she has been doing since June 28th 1922, we prefer that she should use English troops – as she does in the North of the country – and not our own misguided creatures.

By your return to Republican Allegiance, you can re-establish unity, assuring us of peace and providing the basis upon which we may together build a prosperous and happy national life.

Then we shall all share in what shall be the final victory over England.

Come back to us.

Vote for those who will yet Save the Nation from this Treaty.

Oulart
Co. Wexford.
29th September 1923

Dear Miss Parle,

You don't know me. I am writing on behalf of a friend of yours, Miss Nora O'Donovan. I am sorry to be the bearer of bad news. Miss O'Donovan has asked me to tell you that the reason you haven't heard from her is because she is in the asylum in Enniscorthy. She has been there since May of this year, put in by the Holy Sisters of Mary where she was held before.

I had a small stay in the asylum myself, caused by having a bad time when my mother died. I am better now and out in the world again but your friend remains enclosed.

She is in good health and manages all right most of the time but it can be hard. She is inclined to be a loner and that is not allowed in the asylum, not unless you are sent into confinement and that's too much solitude even for them that likes their own company.

She also asked me to say that she has written to you many times, from the asylum and also from the Holy Sister's home. It was her firm belief that you never got those letters. We know the asylum holds on to letters if they do not want them sent.

I believe a visit from you would cheer her greatly.

I hope the contents of this letter have not proved too much of a shock. Write to me at the address above if you want more information.

Yours sincerely,

Mary Clooney

39
1995

Rory comes with me to Enniscorthy, takes a day off to drive me there. I could have taken a cab but when he heard what I intended to do, he insisted on coming along. That big building up on the hill always fascinated him, he said, he'd love a look inside. And after all, Nora was his aunt too. We are both intrigued by poor Nora and all we did not know.

'It's hard to believe that she used to be good-looking,' I say, aware of his nearness in the car. 'Peg is always talking in her diaries about how pretty she was. It doesn't show in the photographs.'

'I hardly ever saw her. I only remember her as an old woman.'

'She looked terrible by then. She had been through so much, it showed in her.'

He slows the car as we approach Wexford town, and in changing gear his hand brushes against my thigh. Since the day we spent together in Lovers' Hollow, he's been touching me like this: on the arm, the hands, the hair. And I am letting him. Why, after all that I've said? He still visits me every night and whatever drives him to come also compels me to receive him. I don't know what we're doing but I have given up trying to figure it out. It won't last, I know, this postponement. The time is coming when we must either tilt forward or retreat but I am not urging that time on as I would have before. I like it here on the unknowing edge.

Writing has done this for me too. All the looking back into my own life has made me realize how absent I was for so much of it. That when things were happening to me I was off inside my thoughts, working out what was coming next, or what had gone wrong before. Writing down my thoughts and my feelings has separated me from them. I am not my mind, that's what I've come to realize. Putting old incidents from my life into words has made me more aware of the deeper life that runs beneath the thoughts, as I live it. When I'm like that, mindful of the moment I'm in, not hurrying forward or harking back, the straight line of time, the line that used to seem to be moving me ever faster from birth to death, opens out like a flower and I glimpse infinity. That's when I feel it: bliss. Yes, bliss! Yes, me!

That deeper me is watching now as I let myself go, let my feelings slide me along, let myself grow heady. It's so *physical*, the attraction I feel for Rory: whatever it is that makes one body vibrate to another, we have it. Always had. Parts of me that I thought numbed forever, lost to my youth, are thawing. He is not the only reason I feel so good these days – writing, pregnancy, exercise, they all play their part in what I'm beginning to think of as my recovery – but this quivering, physical delight that runs through me all the way down my limbs and into my fingers and toes: that's him.

Each night now, he fills my sleep. Him and tiny babies, that's all I seem to dream about these days, as if my subconscious mind is funnelling in. Such dreams! Two nights ago it was that the baby was born and I was running along the beach with her snug in a sling against my chest. I looked down to smile at her and found the sling was empty. She was gone. Panicked, I retraced my sand footprints, but no matter how hard I looked I couldn't find her. I have dreamt of breaking her leg while changing her clothes, of dropping her on her head, of her floating out to sea. Once I dreamt she slipped down behind the skirting board in my San Francisco apartment: I was calling everybody in a frenzy, all unknowing that all the time she was there, at my feet, crying for me but with cries too tiny to be heard.

We drive for three-quarters of an hour, until we are a mile or so from Enniscorthy town and the building comes into view, a massive neo-Gothic red-brick construction, resplendent with wings and towers and turrets, set on a small hill outside the town. The size of the building is staggering and always draws comments from visitors. 'What is it?' they ask, as they pass by on the train, or in their cars, cowed by its hulking presence, awed by the more than two hundred front windows which glower down at the road and railway below.

In the convent, we used to joke about this place, like we joked about everything that was shameful. We'd circle our fingers round our temples or turn our eyeballs inwards towards our noses. Today, the stigma is supposed to have gone. People talk about mental illness now, not lunacy. Walls have been knocked down, gates opened, people released into the community but it's still a place apart, moated by green fields and trees, the nearest house a distance away.

The car swings in through the gates and purrs up the short avenue. Up close, the building is tamed: we approach from the side, the avenue curling round to the front door, so the scale of its vast dimensions is lost. Up close, it's the smaller details that catch your attention: the weeds cracking through the tarmacadam, the shutters blacking out so many windows, the paint flaking off pillars near the door. Two men sit at the entrance, one beside each pillar, so still they might be statues. One of them is shrivelled with age, perhaps old enough to have been in here with Nora. Only their eyes move as they watch us park, get out of the car, approach.

Their staring makes me wonder how we look to them. Like a couple, I suppose: a man and his pregnant wife. I am acutely aware of my belly, thrust forward, and I have a strange longing to take Rory's arm and lean against him, to be supported and helped through what is to come. I resist and walk midway between the two men, a gap of air between the two of us. The younger man says, 'Good morning,' as we approach but in a blank way that makes me wonder whether I imagined it. 'Hello,' Rory and I say together, our voices too loud.

Inside, after a wait in reception, we are welcomed by Miss Bell, the administrator, who shows us the cupboard where the hospital records are stored and allocates to us an empty room – the big building is full of empty rooms – with a desk and two chairs. She apologizes for the confused nature of the files. Nobody, she is sorry to say, knows what is where. A work-experience girl once tried to get them into order but she never finished the task and that fortnight, some eight years ago now, was the last time anybody touched these papers. Miss Bell wishes they were more ordered, she wishes she could be of more help, she wishes us the very best of luck in our search.

The cupboard smells of dust and over-boiled cabbage, stale and unpleasant. We soon find that Miss Bell was wrong, that only the files from the 1960s onwards were poorly kept, sheaves of loose papers escaping their binders. Nora was admitted further back, when records were painstakingly transcribed into big hard-backed registers titled Wexford District Lunatic Asylum for the Insane. We know that Nora was admitted sometime in 1923, so we start looking for the admissions register for that year. It is Rory who finds the one we want – a heavy buff-coloured book – and he hands it over to me like a prize. I receive it with equal solemnity and, blowing dust off its edges, lay it down on the desk. The spine cracks as I open it. Rory moves across beside me and we both lean into its words.

Each person's name and details carefully line up with those above and below. Rory is standing too close to me but I let him, liking the nearness of him, liking that we are doing this together. We each run a finger down the careful column of names and find her easily: May 19th 1923: Miss Nora O'Donovan, Mucknamore. I am unprepared for the feelings that rush through me when I see her name: the hairs on the back of my neck stand to attention and something inside me, in the pit of me, starts to tremble. Each word that describes her shines on the page, clear and cold and distinct as a star, a bright burning echo of a flame that burned long ago.

Patient No:	1496.
Name:	Nora O'Donovan
Address:	Mucknamore, Co. Wexford.
Age:	20 years.
Marital Status:	Single.
Religion:	Roman Catholic.
Education:	Reads and writes.
Previous Occupation:	Home Duties.
Category of Insanity:	Puerperal Mania
Cause of Insanity:	Childbirth

CASEBOOK

May 19th 1923

Admitted from the Holy Sisters of Mary Convent, New Ross, where she gave birth two weeks ago. She had a troublesome labour with forceps delivery leading to a severe puerperal rupture. This rupture extends to the rectum and has turned septic.

Patient resisted coming to asylum having to be dragged up the front steps kicking and struggling wildly. The Convent reported that she seemed all right in mind when she was first admitted there, being quiet and obedient and willing to work in the laundry. Since she gave birth, however, the nuns were unable to control her. Won't sleep or eat, weeps and wails through the night, disturbing others. Threatened to kill one nun, also to do away with herself.

Patient placed in D ward and given a bath. Her wound was cleaned and a poultice applied. She submitted quietly to the bath and other attentions and afterwards took some warm milk.

30g Veronal administered.

May 20th 1923

Patient slept the night and seemed in better spirits this morning. She is a well-spoken and well-educated young woman, and at first seemingly very rational. Says she is not insane, that the convent put her here because they could not cure her birth-wound or help her cope with the pain. It was pain that kept her awake at night, crying out loud, and nobody would do anything to help her.

Her family had placed her with the Holy Sisters of Mary when they learned of her condition. When asked if they would be willing to take her back should she be discharged, patient became agitated. She began to cry and shout at me – that she shouldn't be here at all, that we have no right to keep her, that she would not stay, that she didn't care what happened or where she might have to go, she would not stay here. She exhausted herself with crying and abusing and I left her to the care of attendants.

She is not so sound in mind as she appears at first.

June 25th 1923

Patient tried to escape today. Left by front gate somehow unobserved but brought back by two local labourers. Very excited and threatening on her return. Said she had plenty of help outside if she wanted to call on it and that we were as bad as the nuns and we had no authority to keep her here.

June 26th 1923

Very cheeky and resistive today. Long interview with her this morning which started well but degenerated. She refuses to work saying she doesn't see why she should be expected to work for nothing. Also complains that she never has a minute alone the whole day long with attendants and patients coming and going. She can't sleep at night with the noise in the dormitory and the heat and the smell. She became very excited and restless and refused to stay in bed, throwing her arms about, pacing up and down and shouting in a loud voice. 30g Veronal administered.

August 10th 1923

Patient has latterly built herself a sort of shelter in the field beside the avenue hedge from sticks and old sacking. She sits in this little hut most of the day, talking to herself or feverishly writing. She suffers from delusions of a persecutory nature, saying that those who accuse her of wrongdoing are lying. She is a good girl and the bad things that happened to her were not her fault. God sees all and God would forgive all.

She abuses us as she sits there in her little hut, saying she should never have been brought here, that the food 'is not fit for a dog' and many other complaints.

Attendant Lizzie Cloake gives her paper for her writings and when it runs out she harasses Lizzie and the other attendants, or other workers, or even doctors, anyone who might be able to procure pen and ink for her. The writing is gibberish, neither rhyme nor reason to it. As it is not harmful to herself or others, the behaviour is permitted. She is less inclined to abuse the attendants or other patients once she has her pen and paper.

August 24th 1923

Since last note the patient has conducted herself well, being quieter and generally obedient though still refusing to work. Spends her days in her outside hut, writing and talking to herself, coming in only to sleep and for meals. While waiting for the meals she paces up and down the corridor, refusing to talk to anybody.

September 12th 1923

Attendants today tried to get patient to give up her hut as the weather grows colder and more wet, but she resisted.

September 24th 1923
The patient is now confined to divisions. It is too cold for her to spend all day outdoors. Also she was becoming very untidy and collecting a large store of rubbish in her 'hut'. She has taken her confinement very badly, becoming troublesome again.

September 25th 1923
Patient caused a disturbance at breakfast when she accused another patient, Frances Sills, of putting a dead cockroach in her porridge and attendant Lizzie Cloake of laughing and turning a blind eye. Then at dinnertime she put an earthworm onto Mrs Sills' dinner plate and a struggle ensued, with them hitting and scratching each other. The other patients became very excited, cheering one or the other on. Patient would not let go of Mrs Sills' hair and had to be forcibly restrained by attendants and removed from the dining room.

The incident led to a great deal of unwelcome excitement with some patients becoming greatly distressed. It was mid-afternoon before order was restored. Patient placed in seclusion overnight.

September 27th 1923
Patient out of seclusion today. She emerged quiet and withdrawn. Interview attempted but she refused to speak when spoken to.

October 1st 1923
Patient's behaviour has improved, though still not communicating. She is withdrawn and passive, ignoring all around her. Still refusing to work but less troublesome than before.

40

1923

Visitors, Dr Kennedy told Peg, were generally received in the day room by the friend or relative they had come to see, but in this case he would wish to be present when Peg and Nora met for the first time. 'Her behaviour is unpredictable,' he said, referring to the big brown casebook on the desk in front of him as he talked. 'You can never be sure with her.'

He began to read to himself from the heavy book, frowning at the words as if they held a personal insult. His pen-stand held a careful row of identical pens, shiny and sharp, and beside it a pile of clean sheets of paper, edge to edge. The brass cover of his inkwell shone like a mirror. At the window a fly trapped between the blind and the pane was thudding itself wildly off the glass. He didn't seem to hear it.

Peg wished he'd give her a better idea of what to expect from Nora. She wished he would tell her what was in that book that made him look so affronted. She wished he'd have better manners. 'Doctor, are you able to tell me what's wrong with her?'

He answered her without taking his eyes from the book. 'Miss O'Donovan suffers from a form of mania.'

She tried again. 'But can you explain to me what that means, Doctor? In Nora's case?'

This time he looked up. 'I'm sorry, Miss Parle. I could only have a more detailed discussion with a member of the inmate's immediate family.'

'I'm only wondering what happened to her. It was such a surprise to us.'

'She showed no signs of her weakness before?'

'No,' said Peg, thinking of that night in the grocery, when

she saw passions in Nora she never imagined existed. 'Not at all.'

He picked up his pen, made a note in the casebook, the scratch of his nib loud in the solemn room.

'So can you?' Peg asked, when it looked like he wasn't going to speak again.

'I beg your pardon?'

'Can you tell me what's the matter with her, how she came to be here, whether she's going to be all right?'

'Haven't I just said, Miss Parle, that such a discussion was possible only with direct family?'

'Nora was my best friend, Doctor. She was engaged to marry my brother only . . . only he died. We are very close to one another, closer than many sisters.'

'Nonetheless . . .'

'I want to help her and so do my parents. We're all so fond of Nora.'

'No doubt, Miss Parle. I do not doubt you. But you will appreciate the nature of our work here. It would be most unorthodox to discuss such matters with anybody who turned up wanting to know.' He frowned at her over his spectacles. 'The asylum must be sensitive to the need for confidentiality.'

'Have her family been informed that she's here?'

'Of course. Most certainly. By the Holy Sisters as well as ourselves.'

'But she's had no visitors up until now?'

He hesitated, realizing the point to which she has been steering him.

'She hasn't, has she? As soon as I heard where she was I came, Doctor, but they won't. You see? It's those who care for Nora who must look out for her now.'

'You know them, the O'Donovan family?'

'I do.'

'Her father is a farmer, I have been told, of some substance. Is this correct?'

'They have about thirty acres.'

'Good land?'

'Good land. In Mucknamore, on the south coast.'

'I see.' His lips pursed. He made another note, this time on a separate piece of paper. Peg wondered whether perhaps Mr O'Donovan might be not paying for Nora's upkeep. It was a common complaint of the asylum, that some of those who could well afford to pay didn't bother. The governors were always writing in the paper about it.

He looked up from his writing. 'Is it elsewhere in the family, do you know? Do any relatives suffer from insanity?'

'I don't know, Doctor. The O'Donovans are not from Wexford. They moved here from Cork some years ago.'

'Usually in cases of this kind, there is an hereditary factor.'

'I don't know anything about that.'

'You told them you were coming here today?'

'No. No, I didn't.'

'Your reason, please?'

'They don't want to know, Doctor. They sent Nora away and now they don't want to admit that this is where she has ended up.'

He took off his spectacles, rubbed the inner corners of his eyes with finger and thumb. Two red pressure marks stained each side of his nose. He asked: 'Would your friendship extend towards ensuring that her keep was paid for while she was here?'

'Oh . . . I . . .' Then she saw his face. 'Certainly, Doctor. That would only be right.'

He let another long silence lapse, so long she began to wonder would he ever speak again. When her discomfort was becoming intense, he finally spoke. 'Very well, Miss Parle . . . As you obviously care greatly for your friend and, as you rightly point out, you are the person who has made the effort to visit her and enquire after her health, I will make an exception.'

He clasped his hands together on top of the open casebook, papery white hands with blue veins raised to tracks along the skin.

'What you need to understand, Miss Parle, is that insanity is a dissolution, a regression to a lower nature. In this respect, your friend is a classic case. For years, she goes about her business, a seemingly respectable young girl, until the underlying insanity manifests itself and her true nature is revealed.'

He circled one thumb around the other, paused a moment. 'You know, I presume, the chain of events that led to her committal here?'

Did he mean what she thought he meant? Peg opened her mouth but shut it again, unsure of what to say. She could feel herself starting to blush. The doctor, also embarrassed, hemmed a small cough. 'You are aware of the circumstances that brought her first to the Holy Sisters of Mary?'

Peg bowed her head.

'This, as I say, is a classic example of female insanity. You will pardon me if I speak frankly. It is essential to your understanding of the case. In your friend's case, after her gestation and delivery, the balance of her circulation was greatly disturbed.'

Oh, dear God, thought Peg, not knowing where to put her eyes. Does he have to talk about *that*?

'This made her liable to disorder from the application of any exciting cause. If something as simple as a cold affecting the head, a violent noise or the want of sleep distresses a puerperal patient before her milk comes in and there is any underlying weakness there, such an impetus is readily converted to the head and may produce either hysteria or insanity.'

Peg stared at him, he had lost her completely.

'Insanity of lactation is only one such disorder that may affect a woman. We suspect that this is the cause of your friend's condition but we cannot be sure. Ovarian madness is also a possibility. We have given her the general diagnosis of puerperal mania.'

He looked at her as if he expected her to say something.

'Are you saying, Doctor, that women are more inclined to insanity than men?'

'Oh, yes. Yes, indeed. The female reproductive organs are frequently the seat of disease or abnormal function. And men, even when predisposed to insanity through heredity or other factors, have superior powers of resistance that can overcome their latent tendencies.'

'But I thought there were more men in the asylum than women.'

His looked at her, his eyes opening wide behind his glasses, lips pursing. Why had she gone and said that? Now he thought she was being picky with him. 'Maybe there are other reasons for that, Doctor?'

'Indeed. These things are never as simple as they seem.'

His eyes still held her, unsure of her.

'How is Nora now, Doctor?'

He looked down at the big casebook in front of him. 'She has improved somewhat. When she was admitted here by the Holy Sisters, she had forsaken all vestiges of self-control and become a prisoner of her passions. Here, she has learned to exercise self-restraint. For some time now, we have witnessed an improvement in this regard. However, we would not consider her cured. No. Far from it, indeed. She does no work, for example. She does not mix with the other patients. She is subject to delusions –' here he glanced again at the case notes – 'yes, delusions of persecution.'

It wasn't fair, Peg thought, what happened to Nora being written up like that. Turning her into a package wrapped up in words. And why should she work for the asylum for nothing, anyway? Or mix with a crowd of lunatics?

'Is she well enough to go home, Doctor?'

'Miss Parle, I do not think you understand what I am explaining to you. Miss O'Donovan is far from well. At the moment, she is moving from acute mania to a more chronic stage that looks like it may settle into one of the many forms of melancholia. I think it unlikely that we shall witness any real improvement for some time. Perhaps never.'

'But maybe at home . . . ?'

He shook his head. 'I'm sorry, I could not recommend such a course of action.'

'I can't believe it, I really can't. Nora was as sane as myself the last time I saw her.'

'It may have appeared so to the untrained eye, Miss Parle, but I assure you, insanity does not occur in people who are of sound mental faculties. It does not, like smallpox for example, attack indifferently the weak and the strong. It will only raise itself in those whose mental constitution was originally defective. Your friend's immorality . . . and her insanity were both symptoms of an underlying flaw. Now do you understand?'

The door crashed open. Even though Nora's arrival was expected, they both jumped. 'My goodness,' Dr Kennedy said, crinkling his forehead.

Nora was standing in the door frame, holding on to the handle, looking as if she might fly off again. She was breathless, her chest rising and falling. A sheen of sweat glowed on her forehead. An attendant came running up behind, panting. 'I'm sorry, Doctor. I couldn't stop her . . .'

The doctor nodded, dismissing her. He said to Nora: 'Come in, Miss O'Donovan,' he said. 'You have a visitor.'

Peg could see he was annoyed with Nora for bursting open the door. It made her want to laugh. Lunatics of every order paced the place and the doctor fretted over people coming into a room without knocking. You'd think sanity was a matter of manners, of keeping your desk tidy and your record books straight.

Nora was still transfixed in the doorway, staring at Peg. It was as if everything that had happened since they last saw each other flooded the space between them. The gap between what she was and what she had become paralysed her. Peg took a step towards her but Dr Kennedy stopped her: 'No, Miss Parle, please.'

To Nora, he repeated his order: 'Come in, I said.'

Peg longed to meet her halfway but under the doctor's eye she waited, as bidden. Waited and watched her friend walk towards her, walking as she never walked before, like it hurt her to make contact with the ground. So it was true, she had lost her sanity. Oh God, dear God, would she be able to get it back?

When Nora reached Peg, she slumped down. For a moment Peg thought she had fainted, then realized she was kneeling. She reached for Peg's hand, for both her hands, and Peg gave them to her, tried to help her back up onto her feet. Nora wouldn't let her. Instead, she brought Peg's hands to her lips and kissed them. 'Thank you,' she said, into Peg's skirts, trying not to let the doctor hear her. 'Thank you, thank you . . .'

'Oh my God,' Peg replied. 'Don't do that, Nora. Please. Don't be doing that.'

41

1983

It's September when my sister comes to stay. The wind blows from the north and the light of the city is so clear that Maeve says she feels her eyes go ping whenever she looks out at the shimmery bay. Both she and Donal love San Francisco and are awed by my loft apartment with its grey industrial carpet, its steel racks and track lighting. Relying on Richard, I decide my tactic will be to play up my difference. So I put them sleeping on a futon, feed them sushi and noodles, sneer at instant coffee and steak and chips and other things I remember from home, and am pleased when I see I have hit the mark. It's petty but I can't help it. I want Maeve to be impressed. I want her to see that there is more than one way to be.

I take them to do all the touristy things I never do: ferries to Alcatraz and Sausalito, sunbathing on China Beach, overeating in Fisherman's Wharf, snapping Golden Gate Bridge from Marian Green. Richard takes us on a voyeuristic tour of Folsom Street and the Castro. And at Donal's request, after a book-buying session in City Lights, we go on to an Irish bar so he can have 'a decent pint of Guinness'.

Another night, I take them to Ice, one of the new cafe-bars in the Castro. While Donal is ordering drinks, a leering queen gives him the eye. 'Don't look now,' I smirk, 'but I think you've made a conquest.' He turns and rebounds in horror off the dissolute, painted face that blows him a kiss. 'Jaysus,' he says. 'That isn't a woman, is it?'

'Loosen up, darling,' Maeve says, annoyed by his lack of cool.

Maeve decides she'd like to do one of my classes. She has been doing aerobics herself, she says, twice a week in her local hall in

Rathfarnam. I take her to Blues, the premier gym, confident that the best Dublin has to offer will not compete. In our leotards I see my body is better than hers now, firmer. She still has bigger breasts and face-wise there's no contest, but the comparison doesn't sting in the old way. She's wrong here. It's not just her clothes and hair but something in her: the difference between somebody who has lived away from home and somebody who hasn't.

All the way through the class she beams at me, and when we're finished I don't have to ask if she enjoyed it. 'It's really different to what they do in Ireland,' she says, her face flushed. 'Fantastic.'

Fantastic is her word for everything San Franciscan, though she's surprised I don't know more Irish people. She and Donal get excited when they see the Irish flag hanging from St Patrick's. They buy copies of the *Irish Herald*. They ask me about the St Patrick's Day parade. The eighties have been economically tough in Ireland and the Irish are pouring into the States again. There are fifty thousand Irish-Americans in San Francisco, Maeve tells me, and on our trips around the city, she always finds one of them to talk to.

I move away from these encounters. I don't like the way most of the Irish behave over here, clustering together in their bars or parishes, creating little Irelands for themselves. I don't like that our contribution to American culture is green beer and Irish bars. And I don't like what is thought of as Irish politics. Since ten Republican prisoners in Northern Ireland starved themselves to death two years ago in an attempt to win political status, a growing Irish lobby has been challenging the traditional British-American perspective of the 'Troubles'. Supporters prop up bars all around the Bay area, singing IRA songs and thinking themselves on the cutting edge of the Cause as they drop money for guns and bombs into a fund-raising box.

I steer clear of all this. I hate when another Irish person hears my accent and tries to claim me. My community is those who think like me, not those who happen to have been born on the same small island.

Or in the same small house. I have found people who love me, really love me, not like Maeve, in spite of what I am, but willingly, wholeheartedly. As I put it recently in a magazine article that I am thinking of trying to sell, the first that I have written that is not about fitness, friends are the new family. But how can I tell that to my sister?

To my surprise, Maeve and Richard get on well. He and Gary take us to Troopers, a bisexual club with an indulgent attitude to extra-dancing activities. The four of us spend the night on the dance floor while Donal minds the drinks. As we walk home afterwards, fog swirling white around the streetlights, I link Richard and Gary, let Maeve and Donal walk on ahead. 'She's fab,' Richard says.

'Mutual admiration all round,' I say. 'She thinks you two are great too.'

'You gave her a lousy billing,' Gary says.

'She seems different here.'

Richard jerks me a look and I squeeze his arm. 'OK, OK, maybe I see her different here.'

'And Hubby coped with Troopers.'

'I'd say Maeve spoke to him before we went out.'

'I'll never forget his face when Mona gave him the treatment,' says Gary. Mona is a butch friend of Gary's who likes to shock: tonight she was wearing nothing but straps around bare breasts under her leather jacket, so she could show off her new nipple-ring. She had honed in on Donal for the night, refusing to let him avoid her.

Richard says: 'I reckon Hubby would be quite a goer if you could crack the frozen exterior.'

'Yeah. Anyone *that* hung up has got to be repressing like mad,' smiles Gary. Gary is a psychologist.

Richard nudges him. 'Hey, maybe we should see if we can unleash his inner slut.'

'Richard!' I say. 'Don't even think about it.'

They come back to my apartment for coffee. Donal goes to bed but Maeve stays up, sitting on the chair opposite Richard and Gary, talking about San Francisco's gay culture. I keep the kitchen hatch open, half listening as I fix coffee. Maeve's feet are curled under her in the chair and her opinions are coming out harder now she's relaxing. As I listen, I decide I prefer her ill at ease. It keeps that damned certainty of hers at bay.

As I put the coffee down in front of them, Gary is telling her that, for the past years, five thousand gays *a week* have moved to the Bay area, the greatest influx of immigrants since the gold rush. 'Freedom,' he says. 'As prized as any precious metal.'

'Tell me,' Maeve says, with the air of someone breaking a taboo, 'why do gays all dress the same and act the same?'

'Do they?' I try to catch her eye as I hand her coffee, stop her in the track I fear she may be about to lay.

'It seems that way to me, like there's a uniform of clothes and—'

'Biker gear for the leathermen,' I say with a laugh, trying to head her off. 'And crotch-clutching Levi's, flannel shirts and work boots for the rest.' Now everybody is laughing because that is what both Richard and Gary are wearing. 'The same thing happens in my women's group.'

Richard groans. 'Oh, no, not the politico-dykes. Not at this hour of the night.'

'It does seem to go that way, though,' I say, thinking of Susan. 'One minute a woman starts making connections between male power and the events of her own life: next thing, she's getting her hair chopped and buying dungarees.'

Maeve nods, sagely, and though I don't believe we're on the same side, I go on. 'I have wondered about that sometimes, why so many people swap one set of codes and rules for another? Especially people who've been so bruised by rules.'

Gary smiles at me. 'Not everyone is brave enough to go it alone, hon.'

'It's not just clothes, though, is it?' Maeve says. 'It's the way they go on.'

Richard's eyes narrow. 'And how do "they" go on?'

'You know what I mean. I'm not being bad, I just don't understand why you have to be so obsessed with sex all the time. So out of proportion about it.'

'Whoah there, lady,' Gary says, gently. 'Don't you think you're generalizing a little?'

'What about the keys and hankies and all of that?'

Gay cruising gear. I told her about this the other day, when she asked me about the bandanas she noticed hanging from rear pockets. When nobody says anything, she goes on. 'And the thought of those places where you don't even see the person you're having sex with.' She shivers. 'I'm sorry, it gives me the creeps. I can't help it.'

'It's the Roman Catholic in you,' Richard says, and I wonder does my sister hear the steel in the words. 'You need deprogramming.'

Maeve shakes her head, her mouth tightening over her coffee cup. 'Personally, I think it's a male thing. Men are afraid of intimacy.'

How can she say that, having met Mona? I wish she could have been here for the last Freedom Day parade and seen the Dykes on Bykes or the Ladies Against Women, carrying their signs saying 'Recriminalize Hanky Panky' and 'Suffering not Suffrage', or the leatherwomen strapped and handcuffed to each other in all kinds of bizarre positions, showing the world something truer and braver than Susan's brand of one-fits-all, earnest lesbianism. But Maeve would probably have missed the point. Like so many straights, she doesn't want to learn from the lessons that gay people are bringing us from the sexual front line.

I yearn for her to shut up before she says something even worse. The other night she was quizzing me about 'the gay cancer' and looked completely dubious when I argued that there wasn't any such thing, that AIDS also afflicted drug addicts and blood-transfusion recipients and Haitian refugees and others. I wondered whether she was one of those who held that AIDS was a punishment for licentiousness; if so, she was afraid to admit it but tonight she is fired with judgement. I feel tainted by her ignorance. But why? She is not me.

'Are you sure it's not you who's afraid?' Richard asks her.

'Of course I'm not. I'm—'

'Afraid of sex, I mean. Proper sex: the low-down, dirty variety.' He runs a look down the length of her body and back up. 'Have you *ever* had it really good, honey? I mean *really* good?'

My sister blushes and I feel sorry for her but she asked for it.

'Richard is right, Maeve,' I say. 'Sex is sex, intimacy is intimacy. It's perfectly possible to have one without the other.'

Richard and I have shared a bed, spent nights together on my couch wrapped around each other while we watch TV. I've told him things I haven't told some beloved lovers.

'But the two together,' insists my sister. 'That's best of all.'

'Best for what?' pounces Richard. 'Best for who?'

She shrugs, her face red and set, defeated by our unity but unconvinced. Gary, kind Gary, tries to ease the tension. 'You know, Maeve, I don't think you're acknowledging the reality of being gay. After years of trying to be what the straight world tells you to be, don't you think it's natural that some of us act like kids let loose in a candy store when we're allowed to be who we truly are for the first time?'

'Maybe,' Maeve says, doubtfully.

'All that guilt and self-alienation has to find an outlet,' Gary says.

'Oh, puh-leaze,' says Richard. 'Spare us the psychobabble. It's just sex, that's all. We're just doing frankly what straights keep furtive.'

Gary ignores him. 'And, Jo, you talk about people swapping one set of rules for another, but there's one important difference: you can be gay and opt out of the scene if you want, lots of people do. Gays won't batter you or kill you for failing to conform.'

When she's leaving, Maeve packs copies of the *Chronicle* and *Fitness World* and *Zoe* that have articles of mine. 'They'll want to see them at home,' she says. 'They'll be delighted to know you've done so well for yourself.'

I lean on her suitcase, while she tries to fasten the clasps.

'Mammy will be delighted.'

When I make no response, she says: 'Have you any message you want me to pass on?'

'Did she send one to me?'

She sighs, shakes her head. 'There's a pair of you in it, you know.'

I make a face at that.

'Look, Jo, I know she wasn't the easiest of mothers but I find it hard to imagine what she could possibly have said or done to you that you could cut her off completely like this.'

'Maeve, don't—'

'To just walk away like that, and never go back . . .'

Maybe I should tell her: I left to have an abortion, Maeve. And I never went back because, well, because I couldn't, *couldn't* go back and pretend to Mrs D. and you and everyone else that the biggest thing in my life had never happened. And telling you the truth wasn't an option, you all made sure of that. Yes, *all.* It wasn't just Mrs D. with her obsessional hiding from life's truths. It was you and Gran too, the way you went along with it all.

So I came away and I stayed away. Me, and hundreds of thousands of others. Nobody in Ireland wants to look too closely at why so many leave: whether it's really about jobs, or whether we feared we would suffocate under its warped certainties, its sanctimonious lies. Those who can stand living there don't want to know the truth about those who can't, they don't like what it says about them. At Christmas, I'm told, they make a great show of welcoming the emigrants 'home', Dublin airport doing itself up with *Céad Mile Fáilte* signs – 'A Hundred Thousand Welcomes' (as long as you're gone again in the new year). Maeve would like me to be one of those. If only I would go home now and again, write them the odd letter, make the occasional phone call to them, then they could all pretend everything was fine.

Sorry, folks, no deal.

'Was it that she broke up your relationship with Rory O'Donovan? Was that it?'

I make my face a blank.

She tries again. 'I don't know what went on that night you left, Jo, and maybe Mammy did say or do something so terrible that you just can't forgive her. But what I can't understand . . . what I really can't understand is how you wrote the rest of us off as well. Granny Peg, Auntie Nora, and yes, me too. I often feel if I didn't contact you, I'd never hear from you again.'

'Maeve, leave it. Please. Let's not ruin everything on your last day. We've had such a good time.'

She sighs again, folds the magazines away in her suitcase. 'We have had a good time, haven't we?'

'We really have,' I say, surprised.

42
1923

'No, Peg!' Máire pulled herself up on her pillow. 'Holy Mother of God, what are you thinking of? To even *ask* such a thing!'

Hold on, Peg orders herself in her mind. You knew she wouldn't say yes straight off. Take your time, best words out. 'Mammy, it's not right, is it, that she should be left to rot in that place? That she should have to bear it alone?'

'I know it's hard on the girl, I'm not saying it isn't. But don't you think we've had enough trouble ourselves?'

This was the first word Peg ever heard her mother say that was anywhere close to self-pity. She was having one of her weak mornings: unable to get out of bed. The good days were becoming fewer, the bad days getting worse. The blood in her sputum had changed in colour from a dark, venous red to bright crimson. She had passed from the world of the healthy to the separate, shunned world of the tubercular.

Peg sometimes felt she was locked up in that world with her. The house had to be swept and disinfected daily and kept well ventilated. Her eating and drinking vessels and cutlery had to be kept apart, her utensils and bedclothes cleaned separately from everyone else's. They had lost custom in the shop and nobody ever came to visit her any more, except loyal Lil Hayes. After all Máire had done for the community, and the country, she was forgotten now, left to her disease.

'You better get started on that porridge before it gets cold,' she said now. 'It's made of milk, the way you like it.'

Máire picked up her spoon, sliced through the thin skin that coated the surface of the porridge, mixed it round in the milk, releasing steam. Peg could see the effort of will it took for her to lift the spoon, open her mouth, swallow the food. After a couple of mouthfuls, she paused. 'Even supposing,' she held her spoon aloft. 'Even supposing we were to do such a thing—'

'Yes?' Peg felt her head spin. It was what she wanted but the thoughts of it made her dizzy.

'Could we not set her up in Dublin or somewhere?'

'That wouldn't work. The asylum would only let her go to us if we were to take charge of her care. Anyway, she wouldn't be able to look after herself in Dublin, Mammy. She's not what she was.'

Máire made a face. 'Another person to look after, that's all you need.'

'I don't think it would be like that always,' said Peg. 'I don't believe that old doctor. She'd get better in herself if she were out, I'm sure of it. The asylum might be the right place for some, but not for her. If she were . . .' Peg paused: this was the tricky bit. 'If she were to be reunited with her child . . .'

Her mother put the spoon down. 'Dear God in heaven! That's not what she wants, is it?'

'It is.'

'Are you sure?'

'She's told me. You can talk to her same as ever, you know. She's troubled but she's no fool.'

'You haven't encouraged her in this madness, I hope?'

'Is it madness, Mammy?'

Máire sighed, put the spoon in the bowl with the half-eaten porridge, pushed it away. 'Will that do?'

'Mammy, you haven't even had half. Can you not do a bit better?'

'I'm sorry, *a grá*. Not this morning. Maybe later on.'

Peg took it from her, put it over on the dresser. Guilt pricked her: it was encouraging her mother to eat she should be, not arguing with her and springing surprises that would put anybody off their food.

'Come back over here, Peg, and sit on the bed where I can see your face,' Máire said. 'Good girl, that's it. That's better.'

She took a breath. Peg could see her reaching for the strength to talk through all she wanted to express. 'I don't want to say no to you, Peg. I know you are trying to do right and that's what I've always taught you to do . . . But think about it. Really think about it.'

When Peg said nothing, Máire went on. 'Think about the O'Donovans. They'll go mad, so they will, and they'd be within their rights. There's already what was done to . . . what happened . . . between us. Do we want to start an unholy row that might lead the Lord knows where?' She stopped, reached again for breath, holding up her hand to stop Peg saying anything. 'No . . . wait . . .'

The rise and fall of her chest hurt Peg to watch but she knew better than to suggest they might leave it, talk about it later. If Máire had something to say, she would be heard.

'Then . . . What about Nora herself?' she asked, strength marshalled. 'Do you think she could settle in here, could be happy in herself, knowing that her mammy and daddy were a small walk away and so upset? Knowing what the whole place would be thinking and saying about her? Is it fair to do that to her after all she's been through?'

Peg let her head fall. Her mother was raising the very questions that most worried herself when she considered her plan. 'I'm sorry, Peg,' Máire said, in a voice that declared the argument over. 'I know what good friends you were but if her family won't help her, we can't. It wouldn't be right to go against her family.'

She broke into the coughing fit she'd been staving off and her face took on the unmistakable mask of her disease. On the peak of her cheeks two bright red spots, like paint, appeared as if dabbed on. Her eyes turned glassy and perspiration broke across her forehead. Peg handed her the bowl, stood by while she coughed and spat. Once, not long ago, she used to find this nearly too distressing a job to do; now she was so accustomed to it, her attention often wandered off.

She understood what her mother was saying. But the feel of Nora's lips scorching into her hands . . .

After Máire recovered, Peg covered the bowl with its special clip-on top and put it outside the door. She walked across to the window where the pale morning sun fell onto her arms. Gently she asked, 'Mammy, why should we bother about the O'Donovans? If they object, what do we care?'

It was not something they discussed, Peg and her mother, Barney's death and Dan's part in it. The subject was too raw, even now, months on. What could be said that wouldn't widen the wound? Each morning still, Peg tumbled out of the comfort of sleep into the heavy weight of consciousness. *How could he?* was still the question that drove her out of her bed as soon as her eyes fell open and that stayed with her all through the business of the day. Her mother felt it the same way, she knew, maybe even worse. Neither of them had the slightest doubt but that he did it. You only had to look at him since to see the guilt in him.

Her mother didn't answer. So then she said the other thing, what she had held back, hoping she wouldn't have to say. 'After all, Mammy, it *is* Barney's baby.'

Her mother puts her hands over her ears. 'Holy God, child! Hush!'

'It's Holy God's own truth I'm saying.' She sensed a weakness, pressed on. 'Are we going to let Barney's child be brought up by some strangers from God knows where? Or leave her – yes, her, she is a little girl – leave her to grow up in an orphanage?'

'Stop that talk: we all know what happens. There's no need for that kind of talk.'

Peg looked out the window. She was getting to know the view from this room as well as she knew her own on the other side of the house: the village street below and then the flat fields all the way to the far-off hummock of Forth Mountain. For years, she never came in here. It was private, cut off to her and Barney, Mammy and Daddy's room with its grown-up secrets. Now she's in and out of it twenty times a day. Now her father sleeps in a settle bed in the corner or sometimes, if he's very tired, in the spare room next door with his door open – like Peg's – so they can hear Máire if she calls. Now everything in this room has been swallowed up by the paraphernalia of sickness: medicines and peppermint drops on the bed table beside her and facecloths and handkerchiefs to cool her down or mop her up. And, on her bad days, bed-bottles and a good fire going all day. The window open for ventilation, no matter how cold. Porridge and soups and beef tea.

'Oh, Peg, I don't know . . . All my life I've done what I thought was right and I have to say that it hasn't got me very far. And now I'm dying—'

'Ah, Mammy!'

'It's the truth, isn't it, God's own truth, like you said. If that's what we are to have here this morning, then let's have that said, along with the rest. I can't say it to your father, you know that, so let me say it to you.'

Peg went back over to the bed, sat beside her. 'It's only a matter of time for me,' Máire continued. 'So here I am. I've lost one child and I'm leaving the other behind with an ageing father and an ailing business. If I thought what you wanted was the right thing, I'd say go ahead, and the O'Donovans and all the tattlers of the village could go to the devil. But is it, Peg? Is it?'

Peg hung her head. How could she know the answer to that? 'I can't read the future, Mammy. All I know was that leaving her there might make everyone feel easier but I can't believe it would be right.'

Máire lay back. The clock ticked loud in the room, reminding

Peg to get up and wind it. When she was finished, she sat back down in the bedside chair. After another period of silence, Máire spoke. 'The child could have been adopted already by somebody else. Have you thought of that?'

'She hasn't.'

'You went checking?'

'I've checked.'

Another silence. Then: 'But Peg . . . Martin Delaney?'

'Sore-Toes will do it. I know it's not many men would but—'

'That's not what I meant. I know he'll do it, the poor eejit would jump off the Causeway onto Coolanagh sands if you asked it of him.' She smiled a dead smile. 'No, it's you I'm thinking of.'

'I'll be all right.'

'No.' She turned in the bed to take hold of Peg's wrist. 'You're not listening to me, girl.'

'I am, Mammy, and I understand what you're saying. It's not like I haven't thought it through. I know what it means and I'm happy to go ahead.'

'How can you know? You can't know what a marriage is like until you're in it. And think of this: supposing Nora *doesn't* get better? Supposing she's a hopeless case and she ends up back inside? You'll be left tied to . . .'

She let the sentence trail, worn out maybe, or maybe just afraid to put a word on the man who might become her son-in-law.

'The child has to have a father and a mother,' Peg said. 'They won't give her to us otherwise. Sore-Toes is the only man who'd do it.'

'Oh, Peg . . .' She lay back, weary.

'Don't worry Sore-Toes, but what about Daddy?'

Máire closed her eyes. 'You don't need to worry about that,' she said, her voice fading into her exhaustion. 'You can leave your daddy to me.'

*

Enniscorthy Lunatic Asylum

CASEBOOK

October 24th 1923

Patient Discharged. Not Improved.

43
1995

I let myself in by the side door as instructed by Hilde and find myself stopping in the door frame, transfixed by change. The door is hinged and it swings shut behind me with a slap that nudges me inside. Still I stand, bath towel cradled to my chest, looking at what has happened to our old home.

The hallway is all new, a section of it cornered off by a tall mahogany desk where staying guests will sign the register, collect their keys. Down the corridor stretches a row of open doorways, like empty picture-frames. 'Well, look at you,' I say aloud. The blank, empty rooms echo my voice back to me: 'yoo-oo-oo.'

It seems vast, this premises, as I walk through room after empty room, across floor after bare wooden floor. The square-footage of the house has been doubled but it feels four times as big: the old strangely angled walls knocked down and re-erected somewhere more logical, the redundant nooks knocked into place. All the walls are naked, plaster-grey. The entire back wall of the building, along the dining room, bar and lounge, is glass, overlooking the sea. From here, I can see my little shed. Its days are numbered: now that the buildings are almost finished, attention will switch to the terraces and the gardens. Soon it will be time to go.

I am here for a bath, a long soak in piping water. This is my first time inside the house in daylight, the first time I have seen it since the roof went on. I wait for a feeling to hit me, nostalgia or regret, but it's like a blank canvas that has nothing to do with me.

My sandals leave footprints in the powdery dust as I walk up the stairs. Tubings of wire protrude from walls and ceilings, awaiting light fittings. Only the bathrooms are completely finished, tiled and plumbed. When Hilde came by my shed with lunch today, she found me sitting in my swimsuit at my desk. Yesterday, the small offshore breeze dissolved and the air grew thick and humid. I sat with sweat dribbling from beneath my breasts down my bulging abdomen, hating the heat. (Yes, another change you've wrought in me . . .) Hilde laughed. 'Poor Jo, always the pregnant women find it difficult, the warm weather.' It was then she offered me the bath. Usually I say no to Hilde's offers, but after weeks of washing from a red plastic basin I couldn't resist.

I find the bathroom at the top of the stairs. She has left out towels for me, and toiletries: soap and shampoo, conditioner and bath oil, perfume and talcum powder. Kindness in a collection of bottles.

The room is stuffy. I open one of the windows a little, at the top, but no air comes in. Down on the beach, a mother calls her daughter out of the sea. 'Tríona, come in now,' she shrieks. 'I won't call you again.' But she does: 'Tríona! Come in, I said. Trí-í-í-íon-a!'

I turn on the taps and a gush of water drowns her out. Hilde's bath oil smells sweet, like pear juice. Under the torrent from the taps, it bubbles up, a froth of scent. I stand into the water while it's filling and my reflection appears in a big bath-end mirror. It's the first time I've seen myself in months. I am a new me, brown face and arms and legs and in between, the big belly, white and round like a giant mushroom. Underneath is my pubic hair, dark and close.

I turn sideways to inspect myself. I am a miracle of engineering, my front cantilevered out from an improbably flat backside. My breasts, swollen and heavy like overripe fruit, are marbled with veins. With my fingertip I trace one of the blue coils.

I slide down in the water, supporting my bump as I go. Heat and scent prickle my skin and draw from me a long, slow, sigh. I fill the bath until the water is level with my scalp line then turn off the taps and lie still in the soft water, so different from the salt sea. Lying quiet, enjoying the cosseting, I notice a sputtering at the pit of my stomach (me, not you) and realize that it's been there all day, ever since Hilde suggested this bath, lighting up my insides. I recognize the feeling, an old sensation, from long ago: excitement. Anticipation. I'm not sure whether I want it or not but there it is, flickering away, regardless.

I find I can't lie still under it and so I sit up, take the sponge and begin to soap my distended body.

He comes up the path as always at dusk. It falls earlier now each evening, making our nights together longer. We sit on the rug outside, watching the light leak from a heavy, purple-clouded sky. Tonight, the sea is grey and flat as a floor. Inisheen seems much closer than usual.

'A sign of rain,' Rory says, when I remark on it.

'I remember,' I say, reciting the old weather forecast: 'Inisheen far is fine; Inisheen near is rain.'

'And when you can't see it at all, it's raining already.'

'It's been so long since we had rain, I find it hard to imagine.'

The word 'it' comes out of my mouth long and drawn, with the 't' soft at the end, so it sounds almost like 'sh'. My accent is slipping, I hear it myself. My vowels are shortening and flattening, going back to what they were. Sometimes I find myself saying things I haven't said for years: 'Go on out of that'; 'You're having me on?'; 'Thank God.'

Rory has brought red wine tonight instead of the usual beer. He tries to persuade me to join him, stopping in the middle of twisting the corkscrew to curve his eyes up to meet mine. I shake my head to the wine but smile his long slow significant smile back at him.

(Why now? Why 'yes' tonight after all the months of 'no'? I do not know. I cannot care . . .)

He reads the smile. He knows too. His excitement mingles with mine, doubles it up. The cork slides from the bottleneck with a faint, quiet pop. I pour myself a juice and we lift and clink our glasses together. The air is calm, eerily calm, thick and hard to breathe. The low cloud weighs down on my head and, for a moment, I feel something like fear but I know it's only atmospheric pressure, pressing on my brain.

I tell him, 'Your hair is getting long.'

'Orla hates it.' He imitates her voice: 'Get a haircut, would you?'

I shake my head. I don't like him doing that, mimicking her. 'I always liked it long,' I say.

'I know.'

I decide to dispense with the preliminaries and touch his wrist with the flat of my hand. 'Do you still want to fuck?'

He flinches. 'Jesus, Jo.'

'What? Do you?

'You know I do.'

'Why?'

'We've been through this before.'

'If you can't even say why . . .'

He tilts his head to the side, trying to think. In the end he says: 'If you're there, if you're near me, *that's* how I want you. I can't help it. It's biological. But—'

'You always talk as if there's only the two of us.'

'When I'm with you, that's how I feel.'

'But most of the time, you're not with me.'

'Do you want me to be?'

I drop my hand. I don't know what to say to that. If he were free, maybe . . . maybe . . . we could begin again . . . But he's not.

'I seem to have made such a mess of my life, Jo, and I think it was because we went wrong, you and me. You ask me now why I want to . . . be with you . . . to make love . . .'

'Fuck,' I say. It's a good plain word. I like it used in its proper sense.

'OK, if you insist on reducing it to that: why I want us to fuck. For the same reason that I find myself spending night after night with you instead of doing the things I did before you came.' He spreads his fingers wide, as if he's helpless: 'You were my first love, Jo. Part of me never got over you.'

I have stopped breathing.

He goes on: 'The way we broke up . . . I . . . For a long time I was bitter at you for running away. I used to fantasize about finding out where you'd gone and rehearse over in my head the crushing things I'd say to you when I found you. It took me a long, long time before I could begin to see it any other way. Then I started blaming myself instead of you. I would go back over and over our last night in my head, wondering which particular thing I had said was the one that failed you.'

'It wasn't your fault,' I say.

'I know that now. I did get around to absolving both of us: we were so young, so inadequate to the situation. Neither of us was to blame, I decided, it was just life. Well, now life has brought us back together. You're here and I can't pretend you're not. I am not over you, Jo. Twenty years on and I still feel . . . I want back some of what was taken from us. I know I have no right but—'

I interrupt him with a kiss. A long kiss, deep and breathless, and by the end of it his hands are up under my T-shirt, palming across clammy skin. I pull away. I want this to be slow and deliberate, nothing pushy or clumsy, not yet anyway. I kneel up and pull my T-shirt over my head and fold it, as if we have all the time in the world. My bra is for pregnancy, more harness than lingerie, but I sit back on my heels all the same so he can get a good look at what thirty-eight and pregnant looks like. My eyes hold his, trying to pin him to the moment, to what we are doing. (What are we doing?) It seems a point of honour to reveal myself and I want the same from him.

He understands. Kneeling up, he unbuttons his shirt, slips it off his shoulders. I stand, take off my shorts and wait. He copies me. So we go, item for item, the garments getting smaller and smaller until we are both naked. Only then do I move back into his arms.

His body is changed too, though not as much as mine: his belly is soft and his pecs have drooped. Above his hips swell two handles of flesh. He is softer but his penis, standing to attention in the candlelight, is just the same.

We are naked, here, outside my outhouse, in full view if anyone should decide to climb up the small cliff-face, or come in around to the back of the house and shed. But no one will. He kisses me. We are quiet, as always: we never spoke during the act. He traces a tingling line from the hollow at the base of my throat to loop around my right breast, then gives the same attention to the other side, until both hands are centred on my nipples, tightening taut as desire ripples out around my body. I hear myself moan. His smell is invading my nostrils, unchanged: I would know him by this if we met in total darkness.

He lies down, pulls me on top: the perfect position for a seven-month pregnant woman, uses his hand on me. He knows more than he used to know. I shiver and the thought swirls away, melts into overrunning sensation. He wants entry but it's too soon. I pull away, kiss his chest both sides, then trace a path of kisses down the centre, through his chest hair and down, to where the flesh softens over his belly. I press my ear against his skin, listen to the mysterious inner murmurs of his body. His hands are everywhere on me. I keep going, down to the warm, smooth flesh that jerks when touched.

In time, I sit up again and move to guide him inside me. A sudden shiver of wind tears the air but I ignore it. I sit astride him, riding the root of him but that won't be enough on its own, I know. So I take his hand and place it where I need it and sensation twists in me and takes me over. Large, separate drops of rain start to ping against my bare skin, their cold caress adding to my mounting pleasure. I am getting close, so close. I bear down and squeeze tight and, yes, I am there. Heart and muscles and tissue and blood pounding, pounding, pounding. There, there, there.

I slump against him.

It takes me a long time to come back into myself. He is still with me, hard inside me. He sits me back up, takes hold of my hips and writhes beneath me: his turn now, his rhythm. Another gust of rain-logged wind slaps the back of my neck, then it is falling heavily, in sheets, all over the rug and the wine and our clothes and the sleeping bag, drenching everything but we don't care. I throw my head back to feel the drops on my face as we go on and on, believing we'll go on forever. His breath rises and rises and at the top, just before he lets go, catches in the back of his throat. Beloved, long-lost sound.

But then we are back in the world and jumping to our feet to pick up things, pick up everything, quick as we can, and run for shelter. The rain is now pelting down, stabbing our bare skins, plastering our hair flat on our crowns. Inside the shed I turn on the oil lantern to find a towel. I am shivering. Water streams in runnels down my cheeks. Above us, the rain hammers down on corrugated iron, hurting our ears. We look at each other and laugh.

'Is this place waterproof?' Rory yells above the din.

'I don't know,' I shout back. 'It hasn't rained before. I hope so.'

I hold out a towel to him and he catches my hand, pulls me in close. I feel his lips on my wet scalp.

'How are you going to get home in this?' My shed feels like a boat, tipping and rolling on an open sea.

'Maybe I'll stay,' he murmurs into my hair.

'I can't put you up in the guest room.'

He looks across in the direction of my small bed. 'Would it take two?'

'Two and a half, you mean,' I say, my hand moving to my bump. 'I doubt it.'

'Let's try.'

I get in first and he squeezes in behind me, my back to his front, his hand settled on the base of my big belly. We are sealed in tight, like two sheets of paper in an envelope. We are damp and chilled but beneath our wet skin is warm blood.

I turn the lantern off and darkness tucks in around us. Above, the rain pounds on the roof, like it wants to be let in. The noise is deafening, but somehow, almost immediately, we plummet into sleep.

A while later, I waken. One part of me feels like I've been asleep a long time but I suspect not. Beside my ear, Rory lets out a small snore on each breath.

So . . . we did it. In the end, after all the pushing and parrying, it just happened.

And I don't regret it. No, no, I don't. His arm lies heavy across me, strangling my waist, and his body is too close, too hot. I slide from beneath his hold. His breathing changes as he feels my absence through his sleep, then he shifts and spreads himself out across the mattress and his slow, noisy inhalation and exhalation intensifies. Only then do I notice the quiet in the shed. The rain has stopped.

My shoes are not where I usually leave them, beside the bed. I have to cross the dirty floor in bare feet to the table where I find what I'm looking for: my torch. Putting my hand over the lamp, I turn it on so my fingers glow transparent pink. I look across. He hasn't budged so I release the glow and use it to retrieve shoes and clothes. I dress in a dry pair of jeans and warm jumper, then go to sit at my desk. I want to write about what we have done.

I write quickly, lightly, without stopping to think or amend. As I have written, so it was. Physically pleasing, more pleasing than before, when we were young. I don't think he knows it but tonight was my first climax with Rory. When we were young together, I used to pretend, so grateful to be with him that I felt no lack. I no longer love like that.

So how *do* I love? What now?

I imagine myself writing to Sue D'Enim, as I often do when I find myself lost or confused. *Dear Sue, Tonight I slept with my first love, the only real love I ever had, who is married to somebody else* . . . How would she answer me?

Granny Peg's stacked diaries tower over my writing hand. On top of them are Auntie Nora's notebooks and all those loose pages of hers that I struggled to organize into chronological order. Rory has taken pictures of these and of some of the other papers, shot two or three reels of film of their letters to each other. He has also taken a series of me, sitting here like this, writing about them, and the other day brought me outside the shed to hold up an old photograph that was taken on Gran's wedding day in the exact same spot. He stood me carefully just where Gran had stood, the little slit in the wall near the roof showing in just the same place over my head.

That photograph of her is out of its file now, lying on the desk where he left it. I take it up. It is old and cracked and somebody has torn a small piece off its bottom right-hand corner. *Wedding Day, November 4th 1923*, is written on the back in Gran's beautiful writing, the kind of handwriting that is both legible and ornate, the kind nobody does any more. Gran looks out at me, her eyes unreadable, and I feel something give in my chest. It's a physical feeling: a kind of pop-crack-melt. I put down my pen, go across to the bed and shake him awake. 'Rory, get up. Rory!'

He is a long way down. I shake him harder until he feels me, until I cannot be ignored. He groans, tries to roll over. Another shake. 'What?' he grunts. 'What do you want?'

'You have to get up. You have to go home.'

'Don't be silly,' he says, eyes shut fast.

I shine the torch full in his face and it creases with annoyance. 'Hey! Stop! What are you doing?' His hand shoots out from under the duvet, pushes the torch aside. 'Stop.'

'Get *up*.'

He rubs his eyes. 'What's happening?' His voice is exasperated. 'What's the matter?'

I retrieve his clothes, dump them on top of him in the bed. 'Put these on. You need to go.'

'Why? Why do I need to go?'

'It's not right that you stay here.'

'I don't understand,' he says.

'Come on, get up.'

I shine the light on him again, searching his face. Wrinkles crag his forehead and fan out from round his sleep-starved eyes and I want to smooth them out with my thumbs. He puts his arm up across his face against the light. 'Will you put that thing away?'

'Come on.'

I cross back to my desk to wait for him to do it. My torch makes a spotlight on Gran's picture, on the four young people dressed up for the day: bride and groom, bridesmaid and best man, two pairs carefully posed in front of the pebble-dashed wall. Bride and groom in front, the groom in military uniform, of course. A rifle resting across his knee. His face angled sideways, his mouth open as if he is answering the quip of some off-stage joker. Even in the black-and-white print, you can see his face is unused to being so scrubbed.

Behind me, Rory sighs heavily and my bed creaks under the weight of him getting out. I hear him search out his clothes, the rustles of him dressing.

The bridesmaid also looks away, but in the other direction, locked inside the casing of her thoughts. Both she and the bride wear costumes in the faux-traditional Irish style fashionable among nationalists of the time: over-the-shoulder capes held in place by Tara brooches. Their heads are bare, their hair tied into chignons at the base of their necks, the bodices of their dresses embroidered with intricate Celtic designs, like those that illuminate the ancient manuscripts held in Trinity College. Only the bride looks straight at the camera, her gaze serious but steady.

He is behind me now, standing over me. He touches the back of my neck. 'It's OK, Jo.' His fingers are cold already.

'Is it?' I whisper.

'Yes. I—'

'Please,' I plead, cutting him off. 'Don't say anything now. Just go.'

44

1986

'So I like fucking strangers. Call me old-fashioned.'

I've heard Richard use this quip before. He still wants to be Mr Entertainment but he hasn't the energy to think up new lines. He hasn't the energy to do anything much, which is why he is lying here in a hospital bed. George, one of his nurses, is holding his wrist and Frank, another patient, sits on the bed beside his. It's for them that he has delivered his line, though it's addressed to me, and they respond with the requisite laughter. In the AIDS ward, good humour is an imperative.

I put his *GQ* and *Esquire* onto his bedside locker and lean low to kiss his forehead. His rash is inflamed, a flash of red blazing up his neck and face from beneath his white linen pyjama top. 'You're wearing that look again,' he says. 'You really *must* try to be more tactful.'

His nurse, George, releases his wrist, makes a mark on his chart and hangs it back on the bed. 'Make him rest,' he says to me, on his way out of the ward.

George and the other nurses know me well. I spend long hours here: because of my schedule I can visit at odd times, when Gary and other friends are at work. I bring in good soups and salads, the ones I know he likes. I coax him to sleep, chide him out of self-pity, ensure he takes his medication. Often, I sit silently beside him while he sleeps: more like a wife than a friend.

Today he doesn't want to rest: he has something to tell me. 'Marcus was in yesterday after you left.'

Marcus is a friend and another PWA, as they are coming to be called. Person With AIDS. 'How's he doing?' I ask.

'He brought me a present. I kept it to show you. It's in the top drawer.'

I open the bedside locker, take it out. It's a book, a Bible. 'Oh-oh,' I say.

'I *know*.'

'He meant well, I suppose.'

'Meant well, shit.'

'Come on, Richard, it's not like you to be so tetchy.'

'Tetchy.' He giggles. 'Tetchy.' It's been a long while since my vocabulary tickled him. 'I'm *tetchy*, my dear, because I was looking forward to a real conversation with somebody who knows what this damn thing feels like. Instead, he brings me this born-again booby present and an evening of sermons.'

He's not joking, he's offended. Deeply.

'What did you say to him?'

'I sent him packing.'

'Poor Marcus.'

'He deserved it.'

'But, Richard, if it gives him comfort . . .'

'Comfort? Hasn't he registered that the Bible-brigade has us all down as damned, whether we believe their hooey or not?'

'Do me a favour,' he says when I don't respond. 'Put it in the bin.'

I'm surprised at his vehemence. Marcus isn't even that close a friend. I look at him to make sure he means it then drop the Bible into the wastepaper basket and go over to sit beside him.

'He actually asked me to repent. Can you believe it? The guy used to be queen of the pleasure dome and now he's turned into one of those freaks who hawk God from door to door, trying to sell Him.' He shudders. 'I mean, how insulting is that? Do they really think any God capable of creating this foul and fabulous world is going to be flattered at being marketed like a household gizmo?'

I don't know whether to laugh or pat his hand, so I do both.

'Come on, cut the guy a break. Whatever gets him through the night, and all that?'

He lies back, feeling better for his outburst, closes his eyes. Under the rash, his skin is colourless as water. We've seen two close friends go already, Joe and Lucien, and others we loved a little less. Richard knows what this disease's cocktail of assaults can do. Will do. He has faced what's ahead and has no patience with those who console themselves with what he believes to be fantasies.

'The Afterlife . . .' He shudders, theatrically. 'Ugh.'

'Come on, I don't believe in it either but I can see the attraction.'

He opens one eye. 'Honey, you'd be miserable there. We both would. With the God squad in charge of the guest list? And the entertainment? Can you imagine? We'd hate every minute of it, believe me.'

Thanks to a visa amnesty I am no longer an 'alien'. Instead of teaching aerobics to the public for cash, I now franchise my routines to teams of instructors. Now, thousands of people do a Rí Rá workout each week, in gyms and halls and studios all across the Bay area and beyond. I even have a small slice of fame through my exercise video and the features I contribute to newspapers and magazines, not just on fitness now but on all sorts of 'issues'. I am moving from facilitating health and exercise to writing about it. The *Chronicle* has approached me about doing a column. So has *Fitness World*.

I make a good living: I have an agent and an assistant, a bank account and health insurance, a payment just put down on a two-bedroom apartment in the Haight. I eat at Mani's, buy my clothes at Mary Coles, drive a European car, a Saab. All things that might catch me occasionally with surprise or even pride if I were free to think, if my friend did not have this disease that is going to kill him. Instead I find I'm going about like an aged English lady who lost her beau in the Great War, or an American who was a flapper in the 1920s and hungered in the Depression, forever looking back in awe. Oh, that younger me! The way I went about my youthful business all unknowing! The way I had nothing to worry me but my mind's mindless worries!

The breach came the night I called to his apartment to hear the results of his test. As soon as he opened the door, there was my answer, in his eyes, in his face, in the stoop of his shoulders: positive. It was what we had been waiting for, we did not expect good news – how could we, with his night sweats and his weight loss and his history? – but still I looked at him and said those stupid words we always seem to say at moments of crisis: 'No. I don't believe it.' As if he were not a promiscuous gay man, as if we knew nothing about AIDS and its predilections.

I held him hard, there in the doorway, held him for far too long, like I'd never be able to let him go. Then we went inside and waited together for Gary, who came home steely, well prepared. I made dinner in the little white kitchen while they had their words and when the meal was prepared, they made me stay and eat with them. Over the food we talked ourselves out of disbelief so that by the time coffee came round, Richard was able to look at the man he loved, for once not joking, and say with true, discerning knowledge: 'We're all going to die.'

AIDS punched a hole in our liberation theories. No wonder some thought initially that it was a CIA conspiracy to obliterate the community. Who could believe in a disease that targeted only gay men? Those were the days before we realized it was practices not populations that nurtured the virus. Now we know, and now the people who were the front rank of my sexual avant-garde are floundering around the Castro, open-eyed with horror. You bump into somebody you haven't seen for a while and feel a flood of relief that he is still alive, followed by a wave of dread that he might tell you he has it. So many are afflicted that those still testing negative are beginning to suffer survivor's guilt.

The Castro men have become like women, Susan says, now that

their pleasure comes edged with danger. Women have always known what it is like to live with worms in the bud: unwanted pregnancy, sexual violence, fatal childbirth . . . That, she says, is why women are responding so generously to their brothers' cause, though the same brothers were so dismissive or even hostile to them in the Castro's heyday.

Susan is one such, applying her formidable skills and energies to the crisis, organizing fund-raisers and aggressively lobbying for political and medical attention. Her indignation is voluble: men like Richard are dying not just because they have a medical condition but because Ronald Reagan's administration doesn't give a god-damn about a disease that, in the main, kills gays. This homophobia that keeps the government from investing in medical research, that keeps our B-movie cowboy president from being able even to *say* the word AIDS: that is what is killing people, every bit as surely as the virus. And it isn't just AIDS, she storms. You can see the work of the Republican vandals everywhere: in her project for recovering drug addicts, now failing her clients because of axed funds. In the growing army of the homeless people on the streets, shouting half-crazed at their phantom enemies, or hustling for money or food or some other, nameless need that isn't so easily granted.

The surprise is that, through all this, she and Richard have reached a tentative liking. At a time when he felt he was losing everything – his job, his insurance, his good-time friends – Susan turned up regularly to visit and wouldn't be jibed away. When he is hospitalized, she shares visits with me and Gary and helps with the practicals. Richard accepts services from her, as from me, that he won't take from Gary: grumbling at our 'fussing' but acquiescent. Something in him makes him recoil from such solicitude in a lover. We all know that nicety will have to go with time, that he will have to learn to accept his dependence, but for now we indulge him.

The other night, the three of us sat around him, Susan sprawled across the end of his hospital bed, while Gary spoke of how lesbians are ahead of gay men in so many ways, especially in their sense of cooperation and interdependence. Lots of men are now getting this message, he said, beginning to look anew at ideas of love and intimacy, beginning to make different choices. 'The party is over,' he said. 'The "Me generation" has been replaced by the "We generation".' Susan was visibly delighted with this, keen to believe that AIDS might have some redemptive meaning beyond the horrors, but Richard would have none of it.

'Oh, my,' he protested, 'it's the 1950s again. Except now it's gays peddling myths and getting "married" for all the wrong reasons.'

The Faggot Mystique, he called it, and even Susan had to laugh.

He is out, taking pleasure from things that he wouldn't have noticed before, making me stop to look at a garden crowded with primroses and orange California poppies, or a baby crawling across the grass. Everything is dear because soon he won't be able to see them; the virus is chomping at his retinas. Already the light in his left eye is almost gone. He leans on me, so frail I feel no burden.

Back in again, another pneumonia. This afternoon, he is sleeping or perhaps lying still with his eyes closed. His breaths are short and shallow, like little sniffs. Beads of sweat form periodically and crawl like insects down his forehead until I wipe them away. I sit in the chair near the window, reading. Everybody is quiet today. Bill and George, two nurses, are talking to Patrick in the corner bed, acting out for him some bureaucratic drama with hospital administration, trying to cheer him up: he got results yesterday and the news is the worst.

Steps approaching from the hall make us all look up: something new has arrived. Steps in an AIDS ward are usually tentative, not this stamping tread. Richard opens one eye when he hears the footfalls. 'She's here,' he says and he begins to haul himself up his pillow. The doorway of the ward fills with a large middle-aged woman in red pant-suit. Only North America could have produced her. Richard's mother. He finally got round to telling her two months ago; now she has finally got round to coming to see him.

Mothers are moving in their droves to San Francisco, to care for dying sons who have been left alone. Gary's friend Lucien's mother left a disapproving husband and a job in some upstate New York town to move west. She lived in his apartment until he died, both of them broke, managing to survive only through the kindnesses of friends who kept them supplied with gifts of food and money. Richard's is a different type of mother: if I had never heard a word about her, I would know this from the way she holds herself in the threshold of the door, taking in the scene, rigid with umbrage. Her eyes come to rest on George and Bill engaged in their camp pantomime with Patrick.

Hurling her eyes heavenwards, she alights on her son's bed. 'This is unbelievable, Richard. Beyond belief.'

'Hello, Mother.'

'Who is responsible, that's what I'd like to know.'

'Mother dearest, what are you talking about?'

She puts her handbag down on the bed. Distress contorts her face. 'Can we close this curtain?' she says.

'Sure. But first let me introduce you to Jo, one of my very best friends.'

I get up from my chair near the window, hold out my hand. She barely takes it, then lets it drop. 'Is she one too?' she asks Richard.

'Excuse me?'

'I think you know what I mean.'

'Jesus, Mom!'

'Well, Richard, you're the one who said it's no big deal. If it's no big deal, then what's the problem with asking?' Her double chin is half the size of her face, a cushion on which the rest of her face – her pursed mouth, the hard line of her jaw – reclines.

'Shall I close the curtain for you, Mrs Burke?' I enquire, pulling it across before she has time to answer. I toss Richard a sympathetic face but he doesn't see me. He is terrified, like an animal on its way to the abattoir. I take my seat a discreet distance away and sit, in case he needs me.

Inside the cubicle, Mrs Burke whispers loudly. 'What are those people doing here?'

'Who?'

'I must say, they are the last people I expected to see here.'

'Who, Mom? Who?' Richard's voice is lined with pain. I don't know if he is playing dumb or whether she genuinely has him confused. I know that it's George she objects to and Bill: the two nurses who are so obviously gay. 'It's a disgrace. They're the last people who should be here. They did this to you.'

Light dawns for Richard. He raises his voice, addresses us outside the curtain. 'Ladies and gentlemen,' he says. 'My mother.'

'There's no need to get fresh, young man.' She scrapes the curtain open again and steps out. 'I don't want you here,' she says to George. 'Or you,' to Bill.

Their faces freeze.

'You needn't stand there smirking. I'm going to see what can be done. I am his mother, you know.'

She walks out.

'Oh, God,' Richard groans. 'Why did I ring her? Squirrel, get in here.'

I go to him, try not to laugh at his crumpled expression. 'Poor Richard.'

'What did I tell you? See, mine wins.'

He means our mother competition. I try to imagine Mrs D. here and find I can't. I don't know how she'd be: lost, I think. I think.

I take a tissue and wipe his forehead. 'I'm not able for this, Squirrel. She didn't even say hello.'

'She's upset. She'll come round.'

'What's she trying to do down there?'

'Shhh, Richard, it's OK. Nobody's going to pay her much attention. They're going to realize she's upset.'

He groans. 'You have the right idea, Squirrel. Cut off. Don't look back. I should never have rung her. Why did I? Why?'

Dear Jo

Surprise! I hope you haven't fainted away with amazement to see this letter arrive on your mat. I ran into your sister in Dublin last week and she wrote down your address for me. I'd often wondered where you got to but didn't know how to go about tracking you down – there wasn't much point in ringing your mother, I knew that much. So it was great to meet Maeve. She had the little one with her, she's lovely. I'm an aunt myself, four times over. 'Auntie Deirdre': I still can't get used to it, even though my eldest niece is twelve. Every time one of them calls me that, I have to give myself a little prod to remind myself they mean me.

Anyway, what's the crack? Maeve says you have it made out there. Things are the same as ever here. I finally finished my PhD and I've got a job offer from an agricultural research centre. It's a good job, and good jobs are pretty scarce in Ireland these days, as you may or may not know, but the way I feel is that I've had enough of microscopes and white coats and root nodules for a while. I want to take a year off and see a bit of the world before I sign my life away.

My mother is having kittens – after all those years of impoverished studenthood to turn down a good permanent and pensionable job! Her plan after I finished my BSc was that I should do a teaching Dip. Mine was a Master's and a PhD. I won, but not without major ructions. Now I've gone and done this to her. I'll never earn a crust, she says, after all her investment.

I have to say I do feel a bit guilty. As you know, it wasn't easy for her to scrape the money together to send me to college in the first place, not with what Daddy left in the pot after he'd finished in the pub. But (BIG BUT . . .) it's my life and the way I see it is, once I start working, that's going to be it until retirement (or maybe maternity leave, but the way the love life is going retirement looks closer . . .). Mammy doesn't understand where I'm coming from at all, no matter how much I try to explain.

All this is of course a roundabout way of inviting myself over to you for a visit. I'd love to see you and 'Sin City' too. Is it true they have orgies in the streets over there? If so, I might stay on for a bit.

Anyway, one way or the other, write to me, Jo. I'm dying to hear what you're up to. I've enclosed a couple of pictures so that if I do come, you'll recognize me when I get off the plane!

Love
Your old pal
Dee

She stays in my spare room for two months, until she gets a job in the Silver Tassie, and a place of her own in the Mission. Before long, she has amassed a crowd of party-loving people and is always asking me out. Sometimes I go along but they're a hard-drinking crowd and my orange juice or mineral water keeps me separate. It amazed Deirdre that I don't drink any more. She recalled for me our days in UCD, when we used to boast about getting drunk on 27 pence, the price of two ciders.

'What made you quit?' she wanted to know.

'Aerobics. Alcohol really interferes with your fitness level. I gave up smoking back then too.'

'You don't even take a glass of wine with a meal?'

'No.'

She turned a wide-eyed look on me.

'Really, I can't be bothered any more,' I shrugged. 'It just doesn't interest me.'

She made it obvious that she didn't buy this and I teased her, told her not to be so Irish. I couldn't tell her the truth. 'Alcoholic' is a word I have never spoken aloud and I certainly couldn't say it to Dee. To her, it spells her father, her nemesis, who still makes her spit hate when she's had too much to drink herself. It is not a word for people like me. Or her.

She shies away too from Richard and Gary and their world of other unspeakable words: lymphadenopathy, mycobacterium, pneumocystis, Kaposi's sarcoma. I don't blame her, I am tired of it all myself. In a dark corner of my mind I often find myself wishing it were already over. Because I want to spare him what lies ahead? Yes, but I also wish it for me. I don't want to do this any more.

Peg

Dear Diary

We were hardly out of the beds this morning when Mrs O'Donovan called. From the sand on her boots I could tell she had come the back way up the strand. Wariness had her hunched over, her black shawl drawn in around her and a look on her face that said she'd rather be anywhere else in the world than at our back door.

'How is she?' was her first question and I told her Nora was not too bad and invited her in to see for herself. It felt strange dealing with Mrs O'Donovan like this, especially after the last time we faced each other, when the boot was on the other foot. I determined to treat her better than she had treated me but I would not fall over myself either.

All the same I felt a need to warn her before she opened the kitchen door. 'You'll find her quiet in herself,' I said.

'She was always a quiet girl.'

'Not like this.'

Nora was in the fireside chair that used to be mine, before all the changes to our household (I now sit – when I get a chance to sit – in the chair that was Barney's). The chair was in the middle of the floor, sideways onto the fire, looking like a raft adrift in the middle of the pale linoleum. She had a blanket across her knees and beside her, on a small table, a blank copybook and a pen. I had provided this: after talking to the doctor about the way she used to scribble away for days I thought it might be some comfort to her. She's certainly not able to do much in the line of talking, so writing her feelings down might help, I thought, knowing how it always helps myself. So far, however, she hasn't even picked up the pen.

Indeed, since she arrived, she has done nothing. Nothing but sit silent in this armchair, either turned towards the fire to look into the flames, or in the opposite direction to look out the window at the back yard and the sea beyond. She will come to the table when bidden or do any small chore she is asked to do. Otherwise she sits, still and silent.

As I expected, she did not get up or even turn her head when her mother came in. 'Your mother has come to see you, Nora,' I said and she turned her eyes away, towards the window.

Mrs O'Donovan squeezed herself into the chair opposite. After a small glance at me, she licked her lips and said, 'Well, Nora.' I marvelled at how still Nora could hold herself, not even the movement of her breath in her chest to be seen.

'You're looking well anyway,' her mother said.

When again she received neither gesture nor reply, she looked across at me, her face asking for my help. I went over and knelt in front of Nora, tried to look into her face. 'Nora, are you not going to talk to your mammy?'

Nothing. Her eyes remained stubbornly on the window, her face pale and set. I stood up and shook my head at Mrs O'Donovan. She frowned. 'Maybe if you were to leave us on our own?'

I wasn't a bit keen to do this. For a start, I knew it would make no difference whether I was there or not, that Nora would not speak to her one way or the other. I was also reluctant to abandon her to any member of her family, or indeed to anybody. On the other hand, how could I refuse to leave her with her own mother?

I looked to Nora for help. If she objected, wild horses wouldn't drag me from that room but she gave me nothing to go on, not a flicker. Reluctantly, I moved towards the door. Go easy on her, I wanted to say, but of course I couldn't say such a thing. 'I'll be outside if you want me,' I said instead.

I stood right outside the door, leaning my forehead against it, but I could hear nothing. I knew Mrs O'Donovan would be disappointed. (Aren't we disappointed ourselves? My hope is that once the baby comes, things will improve. If all goes well, we should have it next week.) The sound of a voice raised came through the door: 'Answer me, won't you?'

I went back in. Mrs O'Donovan was standing over Nora like she was a badly behaved child. 'Surely to God you'll speak to me, Nora, after I'm coming down to see you? Surely you won't let me go without a word?'

Underneath Nora's bright hair, her face was pale, washed out as a bleached rag. I knew what a mine of stubbornness lay under that weary surface, that Mrs O'Donovan could stay there for ten years but Nora would neither look at her nor talk to her. So I drew the older woman away, walked her towards the door. 'Don't upset yourself, Mrs O'Donovan,' I said. 'Nora talks to no one at the moment. It's part of her trouble.'

She looked at me, like a bewildered animal. 'What should I do?'

'Give her time.'

'I can't come again.'

So we were still forbidden territory. 'Let's see how we get on,' I said. 'Everything should get easier with time.'

I didn't like to refer direct to Nora's father and his ways, or to Dan either. She drew her shawl tighter in around herself and looked so miserable I felt sorry for her.

'I'm sure Nora is grateful you came. Aren't you, Nora?' I didn't really expect an answer and I didn't get one.

'Grateful, is it?' said Mrs O'Donovan. 'Grateful, by God.'

She turned to go and noticed for the first time the big black perambulator that I had brought down from the attic the day before. This is the pram that wheeled me about myself, as a child. And Barney too. It's old-fashioned and a bit battered, but clean and well polished since the work I put into it and well up to the job. Mrs O'Donovan looked at it like it was a weapon. Without warning, her head dropped into her shawl and she started to cry. I didn't know where to look.

'May God forgive her is all I can say.' The shoulders under the shawl were shaking. 'May God forgive you, Nora.'

Nora just carried on staring out the window.

Dear Diary

Today Nora has started to write in the copybook I bought her, scribbling furiously. The doctor in the asylum told me about this, it's pure gibberish she writes, he said. It was my first time to see her at it and the concentration she brings to the task is ferocious, her whole self gathered up in the physical act of writing. Her face looked clearer as she wrote, more like the old Nora.

All through the day she kept this up in fits and starts. While we were having our meals she kept the notebook on her lap the whole time and afterwards when we were sitting round the fire with Mammy and Daddy, she sat on top of it. Later when Mammy and Daddy had gone off – one to bed, the other to work – I spoke to her about the way she keeps hiding the book. 'You don't have to worry that anybody will read what you write, Nora,' I said. 'Nobody in this house would go near it.' She didn't reply and didn't change her behaviour either, keeping the book close, bringing it with her whenever she went out of the room and upstairs with her at bedtime, no doubt to sleep with it under the pillow.

It does no harm but I wish she had more trust in me. I, of all people, would never read somebody else's private writing. I know how I'd feel if somebody read mine.

Dear Diary

Mass this morning. She didn't want to go, and who could blame her? I had explained all to her last night, that we have to face them down from the first, that if we stayed away today it would be even harder next week and then we'd never be able to go at all. But she acted like she had forgotten all I said. When I went in to call her, she made as if she didn't know I was there.

I had a jug of hot water with me and I poured it into the basin and then spoke firmly to her, so there could be no mistake. 'Nora,' I said, 'I'm only going to say this once and after that you can make up your own mind. I think you should go to Mass and not be hiding up here like a criminal. We need God on our side, Nora. If we can't even face a trip to Mass, what will He think of us? I'm going to leave you now. If you come down dressed I'll know you're coming, if you stay up here, that's grand. Nobody will say a cross word to you, I promise. I'll just go ahead with Mammy and we'll see you when we get back.'

I went down, praying she'd find it in herself to do the right thing. And she did. I was finishing off the drying when she came in, her hat and coat on, ready to go. It was hard for her walking down that road, hard for myself too, but she just closed herself off the way she does and greeted nobody. Mammy and I did as we'd planned, smiled and said hello to the staring face of whoever we met along the way, the same smile and hello we'd give if Nora was not with us, then moved on quickly before they had time to act on their curiosity. It was easier than it would have been one time – between those who won't talk to us because of the war just gone, and those who are afraid to approach us because of Mammy's illness, we don't have as many making chat as we would have had once.

We made it into the chapel without any scene arising and sat in our usual place. The O'Donovans were not yet there and we sat there waiting for them, knowing well that everybody else around us was doing the same. With only a minute to go, they arrived. I knew they had come in without turning around by the change in atmosphere in the crowd. I could feel the attention of everybody in that chapel flying between us to them and back again. Mrs O'Donovan and the little ones sat in the same spot as always, three seats behind us, the perfect spot from which to see us, without us seeing her. The father and the other boys stayed at the back the way they always do.

As soon as Father John came out onto the altar it was obvious someone had notified him about what was going on, because his eyes went flickering about the place, obviously on the hunt. When they alighted on Nora, he gave her – and me and Mammy as well – such a look. He held it on us for ages and I have to say I didn't think it was very Christian behaviour, standing up there like that with his eyes going through us like two bullets for all to see.

Once the Mass was over, we got out as fast as we could without seeming to rush. In the yard, we were headed off by Lil Hayes who came over, and in front of everyone stopped us. 'I'm glad to see you back home among friends, Nora,' she said, in a big, loud voice.

I was so embarrassed and not a bit grateful for the attention, though of course it was a generous gesture. Lil walked back home with us, giving everybody we passed a look of defiance as if to dare them to say a word to us. The walk from the chapel never felt as long and once we got back inside our front door, we all fell apart.

Lil started us off, doing an imitation of Mrs Sinnott's face. 'What's this I see before me, a piece of dirt?' she said, wrinkling up her nose. 'My old fella has an eye for every woman, young or old, this side of Waterford so it's grand for me to have someone else to criticize.'

She made us laugh and we all relaxed and started saying, 'Did you see the face of this one,' or 'What about the go-on of that one,' and nothing seemed so bad any more. Nora didn't join in, just sat quiet among us, but her forehead was clear and though I can't say I saw her smile, it felt to me like she felt a bit better too.

Dear Diary

I got up early so I could tend to Nora before setting out for school. When I went into her room I found her awake, sitting up in bed with her coat around her shoulders, writing in the notebook again. She looked up as I came in, closed the book over. 'I've told you, Nora,' I said. 'Nobody will read what you write. You don't have to worry about that.'

She didn't answer me, of course. She held the pen in her hand like an arrow, so tight that the skin of her knuckles stretched white.

'Did you sleep all right?'

No answer.

'Nora, I have to go to school this morning. You'll have to mind yourself until I get home. Mammy's not getting up today but Tess will be here in a while. She'll get you anything you need.'

Nothing.

She lowered her pen onto the cover of her book, drew a small open circle that spiralled into another slightly bigger. Round and round her pen went until the ink ran dry and the nib was scraping the paper. I said, 'Come down for your breakfast whenever you want. There will be tea on the brew. Tess will get the dinner around one. I'll see if I can get a chance to run up here during the day but I might not. I take the Feis singers for a practice at break time on a Monday.'

The scratching of the pen was annoying me. I took it out of her hand, put it down on the bedside table beside the candle. She didn't respond, her finger and thumb stayed open around the air where the pen had been.

'You'll be all right, Nora, won't you?'

'I was always a respectable girl,' she said, out of nowhere and I nearly jumped out of my skin, the sound of her voice was so unexpected. Her eyes were properly on me for the first time since she came home, open wide, the same look in them as I once saw in a little tinker child who plucked hold of my sleeve one day in town outside the Mechanics' Institute and pleaded with me. 'Please, miss,' he said, over and over. 'Please.' I gave him a copper. What Nora wanted from me now was not so easy to work out.

'We know that, Nora. Don't be troubling yourself about things like that.'

'A sin is a sin, says the Lord.'

'Don't be torturing yourself about what's done and gone.'

'The sin was not mine alone but I was left alone to face it.'

I felt hot and ashamed when she said that, I who had encouraged Barney to keep on fighting. How had I never thought of it from Nora's point of view before? Of course that's how it must feel to her.

'Oh, Nora, that wasn't his intention, I promise you that. He was going to give up the fight, so he could go and find you and set up with you. I have a letter, a letter he sent to me the day before he died. I'll find it for you when I come home from school, show you what he said.'

She shook her head at me, blanking off her face again.

'I'd find it for you now only I have to go,' I said. 'There'll be a roomful of children wild as chimpanzees in a zoological garden if I don't get into school quick. First thing this evening, all right?'

She was pulling back, way back.

'I'll see if I can put off the singers and try and get home at lunchtime, would that be better?'

Her fists were clenched and on her face a film of sweat had appeared, like mist. For the first time I saw what an effort it costs her to keep her shell of stillness intact.

I couldn't go and leave her like that, I just couldn't.

'Oh, all right,' I said. 'I'll get it for you now. Wait till you see what he said. He was going to give it all up for you, Nora. To get married to you was all he wanted, all he cared about. Wait a second till I get it from my room. It will make you feel better to read that, won't it, Nora? Of course it will.'

I found the letter and gave it to her and stayed with her another half hour, making me twenty minutes late leaving the house. As I raced down the road, planning my excuses, I met Jem Fortune, who said the priest was looking for me.

'What do you mean?' I asked.

'What I'm saying. Father John is standing at the school gate, asking everyone if they've seen you.'

That put the heart crossways in me and as I rounded the turn in the road I could see him, his face as black as his clerical robes.

'This is a grand time to be strolling into school, Miss Parle.'

'I'm sorry, Father. We had a bit of a situation at home this morning . . .'

'Did you indeed? And did your "situation" have anything to do with Nora O'Donovan by any chance?'

I just nodded then, knowing whatever I said would make no matter.

'I would have been up to your house yesterday,' he said, 'only I had to talk to the O'Donovan family. They are broken-hearted, as you can imagine, by what you have done to them. I'm beginning to believe you're a bit unhinged yourself. Is it trying to punish them you are?'

I couldn't hold my tongue on that one. 'Of course not, Father. I . . .'

'The girl's family believe, as I do myself, that she has to go back. The asylum is the place for such cases.'

'No one was caring for her, Father. I saw how it was in there.'

He softened a bit then, told me that he understood my intentions were charitable but that I was misguided. Then he asked me about the baby, said outright that Mrs O'Donovan had told him we intended to bring her back and asked if it was so. I nearly died of embarrassment to hear a priest talk of such things but I told him he was right. He shook his head so hard I thought it was going to come off its neck.

'Don't do this, Peg,' he said.

'It's done, Father. We've been told we can have her.'

'I never heard the like of this in all my born days. I'm very sorry to see you behaving so out of character. All I can think is that the upheavals of the country over the past years have turned your head.'

He had to get that dig in, of course.

'What I have to tell you now, young lady, is that if you insist on doing this, we won't be able to keep you at the school.'

It was stupid of me but I hadn't expected that.

'We'll have to look for a new mistress.'

'If that's how you feel, Father.'

He let a small laugh out of him.

'Don't give me that tone, miss. You couldn't seriously think that you could stay on after bringing the evidence of immorality to grow up in your house? You are the mistress in a Catholic school, in case you have forgotten.'

I bowed my head. 'When do you want me to leave?'

'We might as well make it now.'

No chance even to say goodbye to the children. 'Very well, Father.'

I turned to go.

'Stop,' he said. 'I have another question for you. Is there a pair of you in it?'

'I don't know what you mean, Father.'

'I'm referring to your wedding.'

I looked at him still not understanding.

'The unseemly hurry of it.'

My face started to flame when I realized what he was insinuating. Even the roots of my hair were blushing. 'No, Father,' I said, meek as anything, running off before it was out of my mouth what I thought of him and his smallness.

As soon as I was out of his sight, I slowed my walk to a crawl and diverted down the strand, while I turned over in my head what I should say to them at home. The thought of telling Mammy especially . . . It had been her own dream as a girl to teach, only her father had matched her in marriage instead. The day I got my teaching certificate was nearly as proud a day for her as the day Barney joined the volunteers. Now she has no Barney and I'm no longer a teacher. No other school will hire me after being let go like this. It's hard not to think that this is all my fault for insisting on bringing Nora back, but it's hard too to see how I could have done any of it any different.

45
1989

Richard dies on the evening of October 17th 1989, a date known to every San Franciscan, and when he dies I am not there. Gary has called me. Susan has called me. I know his time is getting close. I know I have not seen him for weeks. I know, I know . . .

I am at home in my apartment, alone, doing not much, certainly nothing that can't wait. Sitting at the kitchen table making notes for a magazine feature titled, somewhat ironically, 'Urgency Addiction: Why You're Not As Busy As You Think'. It is a perfect October afternoon, blue and balmy. I have an orange juice – freshly pulped from my new juicer – before me. I am wearing my favourite, most comfortable T-shirt, my best and fastest pen is between my finger and thumb, filling my page with words and phrases I know are just what my editor wants. All is as it should be, except for the awareness of my failure underlying every thought and feeling and act.

I haven't been to the hospital for weeks. Weeks. In August, the disease started in on his brain. For the longest time before that he had seemed to us too fragile to last. Just skin on a shrunken skeleton, everything that made him Richard, including his sense of humour, gone. He was just a sick man, full of sickness's self-pity. And after that came the dementia.

I push on with my work. 'The stress addict has the same troublesome dependence as any other addict,' I write. 'Just because your mood-altering drug of choice is the physiological responses of your own body doesn't mean you are safe. Surging epinephrine or glucocorticoids won't get you in trouble with the law or leave you bankrupt, but like any addictive substances they trigger side effects that can wreak havoc with your health and happiness . . .'

Though I am getting proficient at this writing, learning just the right tone of certitude, part of me despises it, especially magazine-land's breezy conviction that life is eminently fixable, just a matter of tweaking the right buttons. I won't be able to do this forever, I say to myself, not for the first time. As I write, the table begins to vibrate beneath my notebook and I feel – or is it hear? – a subterranean growl, like a deeply buried tummy rumble. The windows rattle, making me look up. Quake. I set to sit the tremor out, as I always do, but then the earth growls and everything is wobbling, violently. The floor jerks and screams rise from the street outside, flying in through my open window. This is not the usual, could it be the long awaited 'Big One'?

So, I think, it may not just be Richard. We may all go together.

The thought leaves me strangely comforted. At the same time, facts I have heard or read about old concrete, new concrete, stress levels, earthquake procedures are flashing through me, each more useless than the last. There is a low-roaring snarl underfoot then the world bucks. Books come crashing down off my shelves. A second newsflash from my mind asserts that I don't, in fact, want to die and for the first time since I came to San Francisco, I go to stand in the doorway. The steel L-shape shelving unit that lines one corner of my living room is flapping back and forth violently, trying to tear apart. Crockery is falling, smashing against tiles and more books tumbling down in heaps. Oddly, my television, atop another shelving unit, doesn't budge.

It goes on for what seems like a long time, though it can only really be seconds, then the world slowly settles to stillness. I wait. Yes, it is still.

It seems to be over.

It seems I am to live.

Now I have a good excuse for not being at the hospital. Crossing the city becomes an impossibility, I give up even pretending that I might go. I stay home, listening to the news reports come in on my battery operated radio. The upper deck of Bay Bridge has collapsed onto the lower, squashing hundreds of cars. A building has collapsed here, a gas-main has flared into fire there. Of the inhabited areas, the reclaimed land in the Marina district and parts of the inner Mission are worst hit. Liquification, they call it, when earthquake dissolves reclaimed soil, so that it temporarily acts like a thick, viscous fluid. Like quicksand. Those with power still up get to see it all on TV – history's first real-time disaster movie – available on three major networks, thanks to the World Series football game that was in progress when it struck.

Sixty-seven San Franciscans die that day from being in the wrong place, at the flashpoints of the quake. In the weeks that follow, the whole city is in mourning, which feels fitting for Richard. But I, I am not good at grief. I cannot cry and I don't want to. I go about my days, aghast. Stunned by what it is to know that he is dead. Dead. His mouth was covered in ulcers and his body, inside and out, in excruciating KS lesions. He was blind in one eye, only barely sighted in the other. He couldn't hold his own coffee cup, his own medicine, his own shit. A time ago, I heard him writhing through the night, pleading with no one: 'Please . . . *please* . . .' And it got worse after that. Dementia. That last day I arrived at the hospital and he screamed at me from the bed about stealing his food, I looked at his face disfigured by KS and rage and thought: you are *not* Richard.

But who, then, was he, this crazed stranger in Richard's bed and body?

I couldn't bear it. By the end, Susan was going into the hospital more often than me. There: *that* is how loathsome I am.

Death was a release. That's what I tell others, at the funeral. Not Richard's mother's Episcopalian cremation but afterwards, at the memorial we hold for ourselves and all his friends. Mozart's Requiem and Judy singing 'Somewhere Over the Rainbow'. Gary reading Thom Gunn and Oscar Wilde and me reading my own poem: ('. . . We thought the laughter would roll on and on / But we were young and we were wrong'). The horror of scanning the room, seeing those who were going to die next and all the other missing faces, those gone already. And afterwards, everybody talking about Richard's enthusiasm for life, his humour, his irrepressibility.

He would never have let us away with it, I find myself thinking, even as I cling to the compliments. Death was a release, that's what I tell all those people who so kindly try to comfort me, and it's true but it's no consolation. Really, I am outraged, *outraged* by his loss.

Sometimes I dream about him, dreams where he is fleshed out again, his old self. He is usually silent but once I dreamed that I answered my buzzer and his voice said, 'Hello.'

When I opened the door, there he was, standing on my step, looking sheepish. 'Hi! I'm back!'

'But you're dead,' I said to him. He turned his eyes away from me, evasive. 'Richard, you're supposed to be dead.'

'I went to Ireland.'

'No, you didn't. You died. I was at your funeral. You were cremated.'

'Hmmm,' he said, ambivalently, smiling a maddening, unanswerable smile.

Everyone tries to be kind. Susan goes into motherly mode and I have to pull out of her grasp. Maeve sends a surprisingly thoughtful letter. Deirdre too tries to help but she's at a loss; Richard was sick before she arrived out here and she never knew him well. She is getting impatient with me, can't understand why I'm taking it so hard.

I don't fully understand myself. He was my friend and I loved him and I miss him. But why do I feel like it is my own life that has ended?

What Gary finds hardest is that he wasn't there for the end. He rang Richard's mother in Telport to let her know and she thanked him by arriving and making him leave so that it was she, not Gary, who saw Richard out of this world. The hospital let that happen because she was next of kin. The rule has since been changed to allow the patient to nominate their own person. Richard would have wanted his lover, the person who had loved him best from the moment they met. Instead Gary's last sighting of him was of his face muzzled by the ventilator, his eyes rotating wildly, unable to see, unable to object.

Gary can't shake that image out of his head.

The two of us see a lot of each other, sit together in slumped silence. Is it worse for him? Everybody says it is and I suppose it must be but I cannot imagine how worse might feel.

I am offered a new job, as an agony aunt. A 'sexpert', as Lauren, my new editor, likes to call it. She knows just how she wants it to be: my name will be Sue D'Enim and I'll do four letters per page, one Problem of the Month and three others. The advice will be responsible but worldly, the approach caring but sexy. Lauren is evangelical about women's magazines. It incenses her that they are disparaged, not taken seriously by the world. 'It's because they're for women,' she says. 'Baseball and car-chase movies are important, you know, but fashion and relationship advice are trivia.'

She offers me a sum of money that sounds ludicrous and when, unsure whether I want the job or not, I seem hesitant she offers me half as much again. I take this offer; I can't afford not to. The aerobics boom is dying off and numbers in the Rí Rá classes are beginning to drop. Aerobics is now an activity like any other, with its own adherents, rather than a craze igniting everyone.

Deirdre turns up at my door with a bottle of champagne, professing herself delighted with the news. This will be a better job for me, she believes, more suited to my talents. My magazine features are terrific, she loves them, this is going to be a great break, a writer at last. Being an agony aunt was hardly what I had in mind when I talked about writing but I appreciate Dee's efforts. She cares and that matters to me, of course it does.

She goes to the kitchen, takes down two champagne glasses from a high cupboard. 'I know you're Miss Healthy America and never let alcohol cross your lips any more but I don't care what you say: this is a celebration.'

She places the two glasses side by side on the table, holds the bottle at arm's length, pops the cork. As the fizzy liquid flows up and out of the glasses, spilling out over the table, she laughs. I laugh too. I take the glass she hands me: it's wet on the outside from the overflow. I put damp fingers to my mouth and lick. The alcohol tastes sharp but sweet too.

Dee is lifting her glass, smiling across at me. 'Sláinte,' she says, the Irish salutation.

'Chin-chin,' I reply.

We both tilt our heads back and drink.

The column is a success. It's because it's so different, Lauren says. So *refreshing*. I don't know why it works or what happens when I 'become' Sue. That is how I think of it. I even have a ritual for the transformation: I dress in old loose trousers and smock top, no bra and bare feet; I burn joss sticks and put Mozart on the stereo. That way, it is her perspective, not mine, that pops onto the page. This sounds silly but left to me, as me, I'd never come up with any answers. Sue believes in sexual liberation, that the heart of freedom lies there, in what we are prepared to do and think and be, sexually. And in part, I agree with her. But . . .

Dear Sue,

For most of my life I've lived monogamously with one man after another. At the same time, I've always been bothered by the world's obsession with couples and longed for love of a different kind. I dreamed of a sexual energy that could flow free between me and a variety of people at once, without guilt or shame, games or betrayal, free of the insecurity that demands ownership.

I turned thirty this year and realized that it wasn't going to happen if

I didn't make it happen. So I decided to launch an experiment. I had been living with a man for almost a year as part of a two-couple household. One night after the four of us had consumed a lot of alcohol I made the suggestion that we should extend our sexual intimacy beyond our two complacent couples. Everybody was willing and excited by the prospect, so I got together with the other guy and agreed to share 'my' man with the other woman (none of us was interested in a same-sex encounter).

All seemed to go well for a while. I thought the four of us were growing, setting ourselves free of societal constraints, having the courage of our desires. But now I've found out that while the other man and I were just expanding our relationship, breaking out of nuclear bondage etc., our respective mates were falling seriously in love with each other.

He told me last week. He loves her and wants to live with her exclusively. Sue, it hurts so much. I have never in my life been so full of rage and jealousy: I fantasize about killing them both in their sleep. The other man is devastated and spends his time either crying on my shoulder or berating me for starting the whole thing. What should I do?

Chastened

Dear Sexual Adventurer,

Forget 'Chastened.' Don't let the jealousy and possessiveness quash the spirit in you that made you start this. What should you do? you ask. What can you do except carry on living through the fruits of your experiment? Freedom is not safe. But you already know that.

Emotions pass. Later, when the rage and hurt have subsided, you will recognize that your urge to push out your boundaries is something bigger than transient pain. You are a big person, truly living. Live.

My postbag swells and Lauren is delighted with me. The publishers take note and before long the column is being syndicated to magazines in South Africa and Australia as well as the States, and in Britain, which also means Ireland. I even get occasional letters from there; their problems seem no different from anybody else's. Things are beginning to change in Ireland, Maeve tells me over the phone, but when I ask how, she talks about jobs and money, bars and coffee-houses. Racing to jump aboard the globalization express doesn't sound like much of a change to me – still acquisitive, still conservative, still mindlessly apeing other, more 'advanced' places – but if life is easier for more people, I suppose that is progress.

A minister in Idaho denounces my column as filth. I wish Richard were here to help me enjoy the accolade.

Another day, another death.

Nine weeks ago it was Granny Peg. Maeve telephoned to tell me and I stood at the end of the phone, the radio from the kitchen blaring through the open door into the hall, and asked all the right questions in a voice that didn't sound like mine while my mind whirred around the question: would I go back for the funeral? Maeve wanted me to go, tried hard to persuade me and a part of me very much wanted to be there, but I couldn't deliver myself up to Mrs D. without her even asking. And Gran, I knew, would have preferred me to come back while she was still alive.

And now today my sister has called again, this time Auntie Nora. She couldn't live without Gran, Maeve says on the phone. She willed herself to die. I hate, hate, *hate* the drama in this story, the tone of Maeve's voice as she tells it. This time, I don't even think about going back.

Sue D'Enim has all the answers but she's no help to me. I don't know what my question is.

Nothing feels real. Richard would know how to make me believe in what I'm doing. I want him here. I miss the way things were, when life was exuberant, when I had flings and relationships that gave me pleasure. Pleasure. It doesn't sound like much – and I do remember sometimes feeling that I wanted more – but it seems like all you can ask for, now that it's gone.

I used to have lovers; now I have pick-ups. I used to have fun;

now I have alcohol. Everything I'm doing is bad for me, I know it. I've done it all before and I know where it leads, to where I swore I'd never go again but I can't stop myself. I'm a vessel unmoored, out of control, with somebody else at the helm. The old me, perhaps? Or maybe somebody from further back, somebody who could have taught me how to navigate life, but never did.

46

1923

Sore-Toes couldn't take his eyes off the child. Typical of him, he had given no thought to the reality of her at all, not until she was wriggling and squirming under his nose. After they had done all the paperwork and the nun brought her in and placed her in Peg's lap, he looked set to fall off the chair. Pure astounded. But then she was astounding, the dote, with her dark tight cap of hair and her straight little back and her two big eyes, like blobs of dark ink, staring them out of it. Wondering who they were, probably.

Her nose was full of snuffles and tiny flakes of dried mucus powdered her nostrils. She had a bit of a head cold, Sister Margaret said, but nothing serious. Nothing to worry about.

Peg squirmed at Sore-Toes's stare, nervous that he was about to say or do something he shouldn't. Any thought that came into his head registered across his face and as often as not came hopping out of his mouth. At home, he was easy enough to manage – the poor chap was as aware as anybody else of his shortcomings and her pity for him usually managed to overcome her irritation – but it was a mite more embarrassing being out and about with him.

Weeks into this marriage of theirs and she was no more connected to him than she had ever been: you couldn't dislike Sore-Toes, there was not one ounce of badness in him, but . . . She got through by not letting herself think about it, about how different this marriage, this *man*, was to the man and marriage she had always imagined for herself. She felt as if she were a twig caught at the water's edge, pulled and pushed and turned over by the waves. The only way for her to keep bobbing back up to the surface was not to look at any of it too close, to stay in the minute and not fret over how she got herself here or what was yet to come.

The baby smiled a gummy smile. 'Ah, look,' said Peg.

'She's very good,' Sister Margaret said, something like a smile cracking her wimpled face. She was a formidable woman, in her black wimple. 'Sleeps from seven to seven, or later sometimes. And a great little eater. You won't have a bit of bother from her.'

Peg took the baby up in her arms. The little head smelled like something between vanilla and honey, something sweet and delectable. They got up.

'Isn't it lovely that you have her for the Christmas,' Sister Margaret said, as she opened the front door. Clearly happy to see another assignment brought to its conclusion, she handed over a bag of baby paraphernalia and waved them off.

'Fierce businesslike, wasn't she?' Sore-Toes said, as they walked away.

'Only short of spitting in her hand,' Peg agreed, 'and offering it to shake.'

Christmas again, thought Peg, settling the child over her shoulder for the walk down to the omnibus that would take them back to the railway station. She was heavier to carry than you'd think to look at her. Not a peep out of her as they walked along. No sign that she was disturbed to be so carried by a stranger. When Sister Margaret had said that about Christmas, Peg had been shocked. Nearly a year already since they lost Barney: beyond belief. And if anyone had told her this time last year that by November she'd be a married woman with a child . . . well! It was true what people said, you really never do know.

How would Nora be, this evening, when they got her home? She was fierce agitated this morning when they'd been setting off. Not that anyone but Peg would have known it, she'd held herself so quiet on the front step, watching them set off. But the turmoil was written on her, if you knew how to read it. She'd have to make a special effort when she got back to make her realize that it didn't matter who got the title of mother. That they would mother the child between them and then later on, when Nora was a bit better in herself, she could take over, if that was what she wanted.

Later too – they'd know when the time was right – the little girl would be told the truth.

The bus took a half-hour to get to the station, and when they arrived the Wexford train was already in place, huffing on its tracks. Peg led Sore-Toes into one of the small compartments, where they settled themselves in, hoping nobody else would join them. The baby's cold made her sleep noisy, punctured it with snuffly snores, but otherwise didn't seem to bother her. Off she lay in Peg's arms, her little lashes closed, tiny blue veins marbling the skin of her eyelids. The train pulled away. People rocking down the corridor smiled in at them through the window, and Sore-Toes preened under their attention, delighted with himself.

'Is she all right, d'you think?' he asked. 'She's due that feed an hour past.'

Peg smiled. 'If she was hungry, she'd wake for it, wouldn't she?'

'I suppose.'

As if on cue, she began to stir.

'Now look what you've done,' Peg chided but truth to tell, she too was pleased to have her awake.

Sore-Toes reached down to the bag at their feet, took out the bottle, held it ready for when it was needed. Sister Margaret had put everything together for them nicely; they wouldn't have thought of half the things themselves. The baby gave a small cry and when Peg handed her the bottle she latched onto the teat with a strength that would frighten the life out of you. Because of her blocked nose, she had to stop every so often to take a deep breath between sucking.

'Isn't it a grand life you have at that age, all the same?' said Sore-Toes. 'Nothing to do except eat and sleep and be ferried about the place. Isn't it a pity you don't remember it?'

Peg rubbed the baby's head gently. 'She's very good, isn't she?'

After the milk disappeared from the bottle, Peg sat her up on her knee. The child looked swollen, stupidly full. Her eyes were enormous, like two planets in her head, as she looked around her, taking it all in. Sore-Toes offered her his finger and her little hand curled around it. She stared at him so hard that Peg saw a frightened look come over him. She could see why: something in the child's look made it seem like she knew everything and they knew nothing. Then she let out a big belch and they both laughed.

'She's wet,' Peg said. 'But I think I'll wait until we're home to change her. I don't fancy doing it here, with the rocking.'

'Do you want me to hold her for a while?'

She was surprised by the request but handed her across. He rested her into the crook of his arm. Already her little eyes were heavy again with sleep. She was calm, happily sated. He put his hand on top of Peg's and when she didn't move it away, he lifted it, took it in his hold. She let him. Then she was sorry because she could see him wishing that somebody else would come along the corridor and take a look in at them. She shifted away from him in the seat, stretched out her legs. 'I'll be glad when we're home,' she said, with a small yawn. 'D'you know, I never want to see the inside of another institution. Since this thing started, it's been nothing but big houses.'

'It's over now, anyway.'

'We've a bit to face yet before we can relax.'

He turned a puzzled face to her.

'The reaction of the village, I mean.'

'I'd say we're over the worst,' he said.

'Don't talk soft, it's only starting. And it will be no frolic.'

He shrugged, which was irritating. But then maybe it was different for him. He was used to people not thinking a whole lot of him. That could be a strength in this situation. For herself, she was finding it hard. Bringing Nora back was bad, marrying him was worse – what Molly Redmond put in her letter about it was unforgivable – but now, adding the child to the mix. They would be full out for her after that. In Mucknamore it didn't matter too much what you did, so long as you kept it secret. Going open meant you had to be punished.

And she would have nobody to share the trouble of that. She had to keep a good show up in front of her parents and Nora, and not let poor Sore-Toes down either. That was the one she failed on most often – here he was again, with a face on him like one of the children in school who got a scolding, and she after saying little or nothing to him. Nothing compared to what she could say if she had a mind.

She held out her arms for him to give her back the child. She held her close, looked into the little sleeping face and immediately she felt better: the purity of the baby's repose would calm a demon. 'We'd better put a name on her,' she said. 'We can't keep calling her "she".'

'The nun called her Mary, didn't she?'

Peg snorted. 'The nuns call them all Mary.'

'Not Mary, then?'

'Nora and I were thinking of Máirín: Irish for "little Máire".'

'After your mammy?'

'Nora likes the idea. She thinks the world of Mammy. What do you think?'

'Máirín?' He put his head to one side, considering it. 'I'd better prefer Josephine.'

Josephine? Did he not realize she was only doing him the courtesy of asking? 'Where did you get that?'

'It's my own mother's name.'

'Is it? I never knew that.'

'Do you like it?'

'Em . . . I think it would be hard on the child. She's already used to Mary, Josephine might be a bit different for her to get used to. Whereas Máirín is like enough.'

'Yez have it stitched up between ye, so.' He turned back to the window. Outside, it was pure black and he couldn't be looking at anything except raindrops trailing across the window. After a time, he turned back to her. 'We'll have to think how we can keep the child away from your mammy.' The words tumbled out of him in a rush, like he had them prepared.

'What do you mean?'

'She can't be brought too near.'

So it had not been her imagination, the way she thought she'd seen him avoiding Máire. How to explain to him that you couldn't let the illness rule your life? How to explain that there was no accounting for who got struck down? Look at herself, healthy as a sandboy, after living with it for years. The disease picked its own. And all the precautions were taken, the house kept ventilated and disinfected daily. 'She'll be well minded,' she said, pulling the blanket tighter round the baby. 'You needn't worry yourself about that.'

He turned away again. Was she being fair? A child was different, he was right there – a child was more open to every class of sickness. And she didn't like the sharpness she could hear in her own tone.

'Would you like to hold her again for a while?' she asked, in a different voice.

He turned, surprised at the switch, nodded with a smile. The poor chap, it was too easy to be offhand. She'd have to watch herself or she'd end up walking all over him. Considering that none of this was his idea, that just wouldn't be fair. She'd have to pray to God for help with it.

'You don't mind the name, do you?' she said.

He couldn't resist her. 'I think it's a grand name,' he smiled. 'Fine by me.'

The train trundled onwards towards Mucknamore.

Back at the house, Máire got up from her place by the fire as they came in but Nora, who had been sitting opposite, stayed put. Peg could see the questions glowing in her eyes though she could see too that another person who didn't know her so well would probably notice nothing.

'She's here, Nora,' Peg said, looking down at the bundle in her arms. 'She's here and she's lovely.'

'Come on, Nora,' said Máire. 'Come look.'

Nora stood up but made no move to come forward so Peg crossed the room to her instead. As she took the blanket from the baby's face, the little girl's eyes opened to her new surroundings.

'Ah, look at her,' said Mrs Parle, from a distance. Nora looked like someone who'd been struck. She took a step backwards and Peg followed her, holding out the child to her. When Nora made no attempt to take her, she plonked her down into her arms. 'We've fixed on Máirín,' she said, with a smile for her mother. 'Sore-Toes liked it too.'

Nora was holding the child like you'd hold a dead animal: with straight arms, out from her body. The child, feeling the strangeness of the position, or maybe of the person holding her, was beginning to wriggle . . .

'Pull her in close, Nora, and give her a little rock,' Peg sad. 'She loved the rocking of the train and of the trap on the way home.'

But Nora didn't do anything. She made no soft words or sounds, gave her no hugs or little strokes. The child started to whimper, low first, then gathering air and noise.

'Nora! Hold her closer to you.' Peg folded her arms, mimed a rocking motion to show what she meant. 'She feels like she's going to fall, I think.'

The baby started to scream, her face growing red, her forehead wrinkling up.

'Do you want me to take her from you, Nora? Just hand her over if that's what you want. No? Then pull her into you, give her a little rock. Do it now, Nora, because she's getting very upset. You want me to take her? That's all right, that's fine, just put her in my arms. Good girl. That's it. You've plenty of time to get to know each other, don't you? Of course you do. There, there little one. No need to cry. That's your Auntie Nora. Yes, it is. Let's get you out of that wet nappy and then you'll be in a better mood for your auntie, won't you? We gave you a fright, didn't we? Silly us. No need to cry, though. No need to cry.'

The child's sobbing began to subside. When the storm had eased, Peg laid her down on the small rug in front of the fire where she could watch the flickering of the flames. Her mother heated a small bowl of water with a drop from the kettle, took the new bar of soap and new cloth that was all ready and waiting for them, and laid it on the floor beside Peg. Nora watched as Peg removed the sodden nappy. A strong smell of urine wafted up. 'There we are,' she said when she was finished, 'nice and cosy again.'

The baby was bundled into a fresh night-suit. She opened her jaws into a little yawn, stuck her fists into her eyes. From the far side of the room, Peg's mother was entranced. 'Ah, would you look, she's tired out, the creature.'

Peg asked Nora if she wanted to try again. She got no answer.

'I think I'll take her on up to bed,' Peg said.

'You're right,' Máire agreed. 'A good night's sleep is what you all need.'

'Do you want to come up with me, Nora?'

Nora was at the window now, looking out at the night. Peg exchanged a look with her mother and Sore-Toes, then went and took her by the arm. 'Come on, Nora. It's time to go up.' With her hand on Nora's elbow and the baby up on her shoulder, she led the way to the stairs.

It was only later, after she had the other two in bed, that she remembered Sore-Toes and wondered whether he was all right, left downstairs with her mother.

47

1995

At four in the afternoon, I look up from my desk and find Rory's wife is standing at the door looking in at me. A thought jumps unbidden into my head: You're too late. Too late by one day.

'I'm sorry for doing this to you,' she says.

Then don't, I think. *Don't.*

Her face is impassive but I can read embarrassment, though she is not blushing. She doesn't have the complexion for blushing.

'Can I . . . er, come in?'

I want to say no but I push my chair back instead, bring her through to the back to sit on the grass where Maeve and I went before. She is better looking than I realized: hair highlighted blonde, body exercised and groomed, good clothes. Not unlike my sister, in fact. For the first time this summer, I feel scruffy.

I take Hilde's chair. 'Pregnancy privilege,' I say, waving at the rug.

'Of course,' she agrees, awkwardly folding herself down onto the rug. 'How are you feeling?' It's a polite enquiry, woman to woman.

'Fine, never better actually. Just tired of looking like a baby elephant.'

'You're very neat. What stage are you at?'

'Heading for eight months.'

'You don't look it. That's probably from the jogging, is it?'

'I've no idea.'

The conversation dries. An awkward silence stretches.

I say: 'You better tell me why you're here.'

She opens her mouth, falters, takes a deep breath, tries again.

When she still can't find the right words, she shakes her head. 'I'm beginning to think I shouldn't have come.'

'Probably not,' I say.

She says in a rush: 'I've come because I want to know the answer to two questions and it seems like you're the only one who can give them to me.'

I wait, saying nothing. I find it impossible to make this easy for her, which isn't fair. None of it is her fault. But why come here? What a thing to do.

After a time, the question comes: 'What I want to ask you is . . . Is your baby Rory's?'

'No!' I am shocked. 'How could it be?'

Her shoulders slump and I see how tension had been holding her rigid.

'It couldn't be Rory's. I'm almost eight months pregnant, as I told you. And you must know I've only been here since May.'

'He was away for a few days in February.'

'And you thought he was with me?'

'Not at the time, no. At the time I thought he was where he said he was, on a golf trip. But afterwards . . .

'No.' I shake my head. 'The day we met at the funeral was the first time I saw Rory in twenty years.'

Things must be bad between them if that's what she thought. And things must have been bad before I came along. A golf trip: I try not to shudder. She is making me part of something I hate.

'Your other question?' I say shortly.

This one takes even longer but she tows it up and out. 'Do you want him?'

'Want him?' I echo, foolishly.

'Yes. I need to know. What's going on between you?'

I look at her, aghast. Why is she doing this? She looks back at me, and whatever she sees makes her face fall into her hands. 'Oh God!' she says through splayed fingers. 'It's true. You have . . .'

'Listen, this isn't fair—'

'You *have* . . .'

I watch her staring into the palms of her hands.

'Are you serious about him?' she asks. 'Or is this just a fling for you?'

'Now see here—'

'Please, you must tell me. I need to know. Do you want him for good or is this something you intend to move on from?'

I don't like her categories. To listen to her, you wouldn't know that we existed before she ever came along. 'Rory and I have a history,' I say, in a voice that surprises me with its calm.

'I know all about that.'

'No,' I say, stung by her tone, 'what you know is Rory's version of our history. Just like I know his version of your marriage.'

She winces and the sick look on her face dissolves my scorn. 'I'm sorry, I shouldn't have said that,' I say. 'He hardly talks about you, to tell the truth.'

I am trying to make amends but that doesn't sound much better. *I love him*, is what I want to scream. *I love him. He was mine first. Go away.*

'I don't suppose he does.' She looks at me and a lighter look, not quite a smile, comes swimming into her misery. 'He talks about himself, right?'

That surprises me. I look fully at her for the first time and in our exchanged expressions, Rory shrinks a little. Suddenly, her questions seem to be for me, as well as her. We both sit quiet, thinking our thoughts, until she says: 'I *do* want him.'

'You've got to tell him that, not me. I just—'

She frowns. 'I know, I know that. But before talking to him, it would help if I knew your plans. Are you going to stay here?'

'No.'

'I don't mean here,' she says, indicating the shed. 'Obviously you can't go on living here.'

'I knew what you meant.'

'So you're leaving Ireland?'

'I think so. Probably. Yes.'

'When?'

'Soon.'

'Before the baby?'

I resent her questions, questions I wouldn't answer from anybody else. So what bond between us makes me answer her? 'No, not until afterwards. It costs a fortune to have a child in the States.'

She hangs her head. 'If you want him, he'll go with you.'

'I'm not so sure about that.'

She nods, her face miserably certain.

'Really, I wouldn't be so sure,' I say. 'It's because he can't pin me down that he thinks he wants me.'

'*I'm* too available.' Her voice is bitter.

'You and the children are his base. Having you allows him the luxury of thinking he wants more.'

'I should go off and have an affair myself, shake him up a bit.'

That is how she persists in seeing me, the affair. And I suppose that is what I am. I look away from her angry, resentful face, out to sea. The sun shines and the cloud clusters are light and fleecy but yesterday's rainstorm has changed the weather. It's a few degrees lower today and something in the light says that the best is over for this year. Tonight it will get dark earlier than last night and tomorrow earlier again. My time here is running out. I gaze, trying to imprint the sea's serenity on my brain, trying to calm the emotions this woman is stirring with her audacity so I don't do something, say something, I'll regret.

'It's nice here,' she says, following my eyes. 'Sitting here, I can see what attracted you.'

'It was what I needed.'

'Are you over the worst?'

I look at her, puzzled.

'Your mother's death,' she says.

'Yes, I'm over the worst of that,' I say.

'It's a pity you didn't get to see her, before she died.'

In other circumstances, maybe we might have been able to have a real talk – she has listener's eyes and I'm beginning to see that she is not as insipid as she looks, as she has trained herself to be – but I cannot let us connect. Already we have gone too far.

'I better go,' she says, realizing it too. She stands, pulls her jeans straight.

'Look, I'm sorry for coming here . . . for doing this,' she says, not able to look at me. 'You must think I'm like that desperate woman in that country-and-western song: "I'm beggin' of you, pleeease don't take my man."'

'I don't think that.'

'I am that pathetic, I know I am. But—' She breaks off, looks wretched. 'He won't talk to me any more. This seemed to be the only way I could find out . . . anything.' Tears rise. 'Oh, God, no, I'm sorry.' She fumbles in her bag. 'I should never have done this. I'm sorry.' By the time she's found a tissue, she has got control and no longer needs it. She holds it helplessly, reluctant to leave. 'I feel like such a fool.'

'No need.'

'You'd think he was George Clooney.'

The sea turns over, wave after wave. *Go*, I think. *Please. Just go.*

'We were happy . . . If we don't . . . It's the children, more than anything . . .'

I say: 'Talk to him.'

She nods into her tissue, blows her nose, then brings her eyes up to mine. 'How did you get to be so strong?' she asks.

'Me? Strong?'

'I thought at the beginning, when you came first, that you must be half crazy to be holing yourself up here, like this. But you're not, you . . .'

She lets the words trail off.

'Once upon a time *I* was strong,' she says. 'It was a word my sisters used to use to describe me.'

I look at her jagged face, the fingers grasping at frayed tissue.

Maybe, I think but do not say. Maybe you were but you're not now. You're fragile. As am I. And Rory too, though he doesn't admit it. We are all, all of us, so fragile.

After she leaves, I feel raw, like my whole self is a scab that's been picked too soon but I have learned that I don't have to stay within that feeling. I can write or run or walk, all will change my mood. I check my watch – five hours to sunset – and choose to walk. Wrapping up an unproductive day, I head down the beach and out the Causeway, snarled in thought but still mindful of my balance as I negotiate the sharp rise and fall of the dunes, the weight of my bump pulling against me. To an onlooker I'm generic pregnant woman but inside I'm a Fury. All the anger that eluded me while she was there, in front of me, thrashes through me now as I walk. How dare she! How *dare* she! And as for *him* . . . If I think of him, lying off in my bed after our sex, snoring, thinking no further than his own delight, I want to kill him. I stamp my way up and down the pathway through the dunes, ranting and storming, knowing all the while that really it's my own self who is making me so angry. I am in a mess of my own making.

Why didn't I hold to what I said? 'I want us to think about what we expect from each other,' I had told him, that day we came out here to Coolanagh. 'I want us to think about where it might take us . . .' That was the right tack and I should have stuck with it instead of letting myself be swept along, all the way into bed, with nothing clear between us. After all I've learned and said and written, there I was, still an absolute *fool* for him.

Ahead lies Inisheen, fern-green against the summer-blue sea. I am going to walk all the way to the far side of the island, where the waves lash against hard rocks, exploding spray and spume. Only serious walkers and the occasional boater go so far, a long hike from the mainland. It takes me thirty more minutes of brisk, stretching strides to get to the Neck, where Causeway and island meet. From there I turn right, awkwardly negotiating the shelf that

I must climb to get up onto the outer ring path. I haul myself up and find the pathway, bracken-strewn, rising steeply on its way up to top the tall cliffs that buttress the southerly side of the island. Inisheen is granite hard, a slow eroder, even to the lash of Atlantic waves and south-westerly gales. Crags and cliffs, deep caves and extravagant rock formations hold out against the onslaught. It's a completely different landscape to the flat land and sea around the village.

I walk up the steep path in my newly careful way (it is the thing I most look forward to regaining after the baby is born: my own way of walking), mindful not to stand on a nest, remembering that this westerly path passes through a herring-gull breeding ground. A steady climb brings me in time to the plateau of the southern summit, a high rocky outcrop . The last time I was here was in the dark of night twenty years ago, the night I realized it was going to be me in my life, alone.

Today, in daylight, I can go out towards the edge of the cliff. I tiptoe forward, nervous of the height. Below me, majestic gannets sweep in and out of home and below them, two hundred feet below, thundering Atlantic waves roar and break against the base of the cliff. You'd think it a different sea to the one that politely spreads itself across Mucknamore beach.

To the east, arcs of high cliffs curve away, each covered with thousands of birds: guillemots, razorbills, kittiwakes and others that I don't recognize. My attention is drawn by an unusual bird above, soaring on an updraft of air. A bird I don't recognize, black as a raven but with a longer neck and shorter beak, gliding high and elegant. It is so completely itself, so joyous in its swoops and loops through the air, that I let my vexing thoughts fall from me to wonder where it came from and what it is doing, flying here, all alone. It is the trigger I have been seeking, taking me out of my head into the moment I am in. My ears are open to the guttural groans of the gannets, the whirring of razorbill wings, the kittiwake calls that gave that bird its name. I feel the thousands of birds nesting and preening along the cliff face, each one calling its call and feeding its young is a tiny herald of peace. Deep within me, under the tumult of my thoughts, beneath the fury of my feelings, I know what they know.

How can I be thinking that? How can I be so turbulent one moment and now, somehow, able to let it all fall away. But I am. Within this moment, I realize, I am fine. If I drop all that has already happened and all that is yet to happen, there is only here and now and, yes, it *is* fine. *Fine.* All those worries about before and after, I understand, are waves that sweep me out of whatever moment I am in. And feelings are the same. *Feelings*, which I always gave such primacy to, which I thought were the key to understanding my life, are, I see now, nothing more than thoughts held in the body. These are always there, always will be there – if it wasn't Rory, it would be something else – but underneath both is a depth that is tranquil. I rest back into it.

After a time, I get up and begin to make my way back the way I came. When I come to a turnoff that cuts down the side of the cliffside, I take it, remembering that it leads to a small cove, the only safe place to swim off the island. Somebody – I wonder who, nobody has lived on this island for a century and a half – has cut back the ferns and brambles and nettles, making it passable. The evening sun feels warmer down here: the height of the cliff behind me cutting off the breeze.

About now he is due home from work and she will surely tell him that she has been to see me. What will he do? 'If you want him, he'll go with you,' she said but I am not so sure that she is right. Does he want me the way I want him? (Oh, I *do* want him, I might as well admit it, I do. I have only been holding back to protect myself . . .) But is he really prepared to leave her? And to leave his children? Is he the type who could do that (*she*, clearly, is not) and if he is, what does that say about him? So many, too many, questions . . .

I picture him arriving home. Parking the car beside hers, putting down his briefcase in the hall, loosening his tie as he walks into the kitchen to find her waiting for him, her eyes swimming with significance. I see her sitting him down, telling him they must talk. And she's right: they must. Didn't I say so myself?

It's so quiet in this cove compared to the clamour of the birds up above. Here, the noise is distant and the waves seem hushed, like they're hesitant to turn. Stop thinking, I order myself. Feel the fading sun on your eyes and the breeze on your skin. Pull yourself out of your head down into your body, the body that can't be in tomorrow or yesterday but only here, where it is. I manage to do it: in the middle of my trouble, I let it go and when I do, it happens again, that shift in perception that makes the scene before me seem to recompose itself. Everything in my sights – the black juts of rock fingering the waves, the grains of sand being flattened by my feet, the fading light glancing off the water, the gentle evening air stroking my hot cheeks, everything – seems more completely itself than usual, full of its own living presence. And somehow, simultaneously, more connected to everything else.

I think it might be born of being pregnant, this new understanding. For the first time, I see that a mother birthed every bird and animal and person on the planet. Everything, everywhere, has been mothered into being: how had I never noticed that before? I think of all the churches holding up their God the Fathers, the men who have insisted that children carry their names through the generations, and instead of my usual anger, I feel pity. Within me is my own life and another life. I am awed to know it. I kick off my shoes, slip out of my clothes, walk into the sea and submerge myself. My skin is porous, no longer a boundary: I am melting into the water and all the world. Deep joy surges in me: the same molecules dance in me and in everything.

By the time I'm back up on the path, the light is being sucked away over the horizon, taking the warmth of the day with it. The breeze sharpens with the advance of darkness, rippling the surface of the seawater and making goose bumps stand to attention all along my arms. Further in, towards the village, the tide has retreated leaving behind hundreds of tiny sand-pools reflecting the sun, like a scattering of giant, golden coins.

He is due at my shed about now. Will he come? Maybe I'm wrong about her. Maybe she won't speak tonight, maybe she will bide her time, watch him leave to go to me as he has every other night this summer. Or maybe they'll talk and he will come anyway, maybe he is sticking his head around my shed door right now, calling my name, wondering where I am. Maybe.

About halfway back, I turn off the Causeway towards Lovers' Hollow. Ignoring the warning signs, I slide down the grassy dunes to the fencing where I prise apart the two strips of wire and, with difficulty, twist myself through. Wire barbs claw at my clothes but I get to the other side. A further slide down the rest of the slope brings my feet onto flat sand. Coolanagh sand. I am not frightened: here at the edge, I am safe. The danger is further out and it stays out there, you have to walk out to meet it.

I sit, watching darkness deepen until the sky is black, then take out my pocket torch and turn it on. The night is moonless but dry, no trace of mist or fog, but still I can see almost nothing. Beyond my puny shaft of light darkness swells, immense. It would have been the same with an oil lamp, worse in the thick fog that was down that night.

I stand up, walk forward a little, stretching for answers to a different set of questions. How far out did she make him walk? What if he had overcome her, taken the gun, turned it back on her? He was so much stronger than her, it could easily have gone that way instead. What if he had decided to make a run for it? Would she really have shot him?

I picture him quick-trudging his way out the Causeway to meet her. In his pocket is the typewritten note that enticed him into the dark wet night: *I need to talk to you*, it says, or some such words. *Meet me you know where, out the Causeway. Seven o'clock* . . . He walks as smartly as the fog permits, his head down, his shoulders staunch. He can hardly see five steps ahead but he has walked this strip a thousand times. He keeps to the centre and makes steady progress, left-right, left-right, left, soldier boy to the last.

I see him approach the light down here in Lovers' Hollow. He steps down to meet it – no barbed wire then to slow his progress – skids down the side along the top of the sand, never thinking to be fearful. As he comes close to the light, she says his name, hesitantly – 'Dan?' – and when he confirms it, she tells him to stop where he is. He does what he is told, halted by surprise. Underneath the glow of the lamp is the barrel of Barney's gun.

Poor Dan. He thought he was on his way to a tryst with the woman who once loved him, who had, he reckoned, a soft spot for him still. He went to meet her, expecting . . . what? A solution to the Nora problem? A declaration of undying love? A wish to be friends, to put the past behind? Whatever he expected it was not to find a rifle, this rifle, pointing at him, intent on revenge.

Arrogant man.

She blocks his way back to the Causeway and gives him a choice: a close-range shot in the chest or a walk across Coolanagh. He picks the chance of unsafe sands over the certainty of a bullet, just as she knew he would. The gun points him in the direction she wants him to go and he goes, walking upright, disdaining to pick his steps.

He has taken only a few strides when he feels the ground shift and then collapse.

He is down.

Then he knows fear, oh yes. Freezing, wet, chest-clutching, fear. 'Help me,' he calls out, letting up his *liugh* to her, the lady of the lamp. 'Help me . . . Please.'

Oh, sunken, shrunken man: did you really think she would?

Back at my shed I find no note, no sign of whether he came or not. I think not. I shine my torch around the door, along my table-desk where I left pen and paper handy if he should want to write. I turn on the lamp to have a closer look but there is no sign of any visit. Nothing.

I am calm, I know what I must do. Taking my torch, I cross the field, picking my way through builders' mud, to the back door of the house. It's late but there's a light glowing in the kitchen window. Even if they are asleep, I intend to wake them. I need Hilde to make the arrangements for me tonight. She will think this odd but I will insist – it must be tomorrow morning, no later – and odd or not, she will comply, not only because she is so obliging but because it will suit her and Stefan to get it done. They have been holding off for me.

Next morning, I haul my heavy suitcase up to Hilde's house, the papers weighing me down, and sit on it, underneath her new kitchen window, to wait. Regiments of cloud are mustering on the horizon, the morning air has an autumnal tang and the sea dances friskily under an offshore breeze. I sit, making myself think nothing. I know what I am doing is right.

After a time, I hear the hum of a car approaching and slowing to a stop out on the road in front of the house. A car door bangs, the engine revs away and one of the workmen comes into the field through the passage at the side of the house. The guy with the mermaid tattoos. In his hand he carries foil-wrapped sandwiches and a flask; under his arm is a tabloid newspaper. He doesn't see me.

Two demolition machines sit with their huge yellow claws expectant, waiting. He climbs into the one with the steel ball attached and ignites the motor. It coughs into a roar and lumbers across the field like a tank, pulling up beside my shed. He turns off the engine then, evacuating the air of noise, so that across the dunes the sea surf sounds again. Opening his flask, he spreads a newspaper across the steering wheel and takes a sandwich from his pack. He eats and reads. In the distance a dog barks.

Soon the others are arriving, taking out their tools: sledgehammers and mallets and picks. One of them notices me and nudges another, who says something, then they all turn their heads for a look. I stare back at them, protected by distance. The man in the crane switches the ignition again, diverting their attention. With another spluttering cough, the machine roars, primed, ready for action. It is time.

He hoists the jib on high, tugging the chains and yanking the steel ball from its mooring, so that the heavy globe plunges towards the ground. It is stopped, mid-drop, by its chain and it reels and jerks like a fish at the end of a line but the chain holds strong and it settles, a solid black orb, level with my shed's windows. The other men stand back and I rise to my feet. We all watch as the steel ball swings clumsily and strikes. One whack is enough: down she goes, my little shed, gusting up puffs of dustpowder. At the centre of the collapsed brick and corrugated iron is the bed I slept in last night, still creased with the imprint of my body. The second machine closes in, bucket tilted to scoop it away with the rubble.

Two other outhouses are also to be knocked but I don't wait to watch any more. I pick up my heavy suitcase, both hands to the task, and go round the front to rouse Hilde who has made me promise that, this time, I wouldn't leave without saying goodbye.

Peg

Dear Diary

I'm so agitated I can hardly write but I have to. I'll try to tell it all, just as it happened. The afternoon started well enough with me managing to escape for a walk on the strand. The weather is so strange these past days, like a thick cloud has sunk to earth. I could hardly see two feet in front of me, the fog was that bad, but it felt good to be out of the house, to be on my own, to breathe. I felt like the fog had been created just for me, to cut me off and aid me in my longing for a bit of time alone.

To find the sea, I had to go right down to the edge of the water. It looked like a frill of lace on a roll of grey. I walked a mile or more and soon grew warm and I was struck by the impulse to paddle in the water. It was late in the year for such a thing but unseasonably warm so I decided to risk it. I loosened my laces, kicked off one boot then the other and hitched up my skirt to unfasten my stockings. The fog gave me protection, knowing nobody could see me in my pocket of mist, and the dampness felt velvet cool on my legs' bare skin.

It was lovely but I couldn't stay long. I'd left Nora in charge of Máirín with instructions to Tess and Daddy to keep an eye on both of them. I had a string of jobs waiting for me once I got back: the evening meal to prepare for them all, reading to do for Mammy and two sheets to be repaired as well as whatever else might present itself. Little Máirín is always at her crankiest in the evenings and Nora would be put out if I stayed away too long. I had my shoes back on and was beginning to walk back across the sand when I heard my father calling me.

'What's wrong?'

'Come quick.' I hurried towards his voice. When I found him, I was so close that I nearly landed on top of him. 'What is it?'

'Dan O'Donovan is here.'

'Dan?'

'Talking to his sister. I thought I better come get you. I think he's upsetting her.'

I ran as best I could through the mist. When I got to the kitchen nobody was there, except the baby all alone, sitting on the floor having pulled anything loose down onto the floor beside her. She looked up at me all guilty as I came crashing in, one of the antimacassars stuffed in her mouth. I had no time to deal with her so I just said, 'You bold girl, what are you doing?' as I bent and scooped her up into my arms and went through into the bar. Tess was behind the counter, Pat Duggan and a few others were in. I just gave them a nod and retreated; it was obvious that neither Nora nor Dan had been there, they were all too calm.

Back in the kitchen, Daddy was coming in. 'They're not here, either of them,' I said. 'What was going on between them, Daddy? How did he get in?'

'He must have come round by the back. When I came in to check on Nora and the baby, like you asked, I found him here. I asked him what he was doing and he said, "I've come to see my sister and I want to speak to her in private." That's when I thought I'd better get you. I'd have called your mother but—' He ran a crabbed hand to smooth his thin hair across his scalp.

My mind was racing, wondering where they might have got to. Could Nora have agreed to go home with him? Would she just up and off like that? I didn't think so but she was so odd these days and if Dan wasn't taking no for an answer . . . ?

Daddy said: 'The girl was trembling, whatever he was saying to her. He's a right bully boy, that fellow.'

That made up my mind. I planted Máirín into Daddy's arms and told him to mind her until I got back.

'Where are you going?' he asked me.

'I'm going to O'Donovan's to see if he's brought her up there.'

'Peg!'

'If he can come down to our place, I can go up to his.'

'But—'

'Daddy, I'm not leaving her alone with them. She's not strong enough. Look after Máirín and I'll be back as quick as I can.'

The fog that was a comfort to me a short time before now felt like something teasing, on the side of the enemy. I was breathing water instead of air as I tried to hurry through it, as if I were drowning in my own breath. As I rounded the corner by the side of the house, a shape materialized like a ghost. My hand flew up to my heart. 'You!' I said, as if I didn't know he was about.

He was startled too but he composed himself quicker than me. 'I've come to see my sister,' he said. 'That's not a crime, is it?'

'I don't know,' I replied. 'Has the Free State made it one yet?' I was pretty pleased with that reply and didn't give him a chance to frame an answer. 'Where is she?' I demanded. 'What have you done to her?'

'She's gone running off. I tried to stop her but I couldn't see a blasted thing in this fog.'

'Running off? Where?'

'Not too far, I'd say.' Then he spoke in a squeaky voice, imitating what Nora must have said to him: 'This is my home now.'

'And so it is.'

He throws up his eyes. 'You're not doing her any favours, Peg, if you think you are.'

I snorted. 'And you are, I suppose? Why don't you just go on home, Dan? Don't you know where you're not wanted?'

'Oooooh, listen to that! We weren't always so unwelcoming, were we?'

That is what he said to me, I swear it, and he meant it as bad as it sounded. I wanted to dig my nails into his face until they drew blood. I wanted to catch his hair between my fingers and tear it out off his scalp. But I turned on my heel. Nora was the important thing. There was nothing left between me and him anyway.

'Wait a minute!' he called after me. 'You might as well know, my family want my sister placed where she can be properly looked after.'

I walked back to him. 'Return her to the asylum? Is that what you mean?'

'It's the best place for her.'

'You can't do that to her.'

'We most certainly can. It's her family's decision, as you well know.'

'And what about Nora? Is she to have no say?'

'She's not fit to decide.'

'That's not true.'

'But it *is* true, isn't it, Peg? She hasn't been right since she came home, has she? And it's not any better she's getting, is it, but worse?'

'You're only thinking of yourselves, not her—'

'And what sort of concern have you shown her, bringing her into a house with consumption? I suppose you forgot that little detail when you were talking to the asylum bosses. That mother of yours should have been sent to a sanatorium long ago. It's not right that she should be kept here, in a public house. It's not safe.'

Even after all he's done to us, I couldn't believe he was being so cruel. 'Oh, yes,' I cried, 'you'd have *her* sent away too. You'd like to send all your problems off like they don't exist.'

'It's common sense, woman. It's—'

'Get out of here now, Dan. I'm not letting you stay here one moment longer. Go back to your traitor's barracks and leave us alone.'

'*I'm* not the one going anywhere, Peg.'

Something in his voice alerted me. What did he mean?

'No, it's home I'm coming. I'm getting a transfer to the Civic Guards and, as I'm also getting married, my father has kindly donated a bit of his land to put up a house. It's not *me* who'll be going anywhere.'

So he was to marry Agnes Whitty and bring her to live in Mucknamore. 'Live where you like, with whoever you like,' I said. 'It's nothing to us so long as you leave us in peace.'

'But it's hardly that simple, is it? I can tell you that it is only with the greatest effort that I have kept my father from coming down to this house. He's not happy to let this lie and neither am I. I have no intention of living up the road from it.'

I looked at him, the man who killed my brother, the man who was once our friend, and I wondered how he had managed to tuck the knowledge of what he had done away where it cost him no trouble. 'Look at you,' I said, nearly more to myself than him. 'Look at what your foul little war has done to you.'

He burst into one of his crowing, jeering laughs. 'Jesus,' he said. 'That's a good one. Have you taken a look in the mirror lately?'

We faced each other down, the fog greying the air between us, stared each other out of it for so long that, to our own surprise, our hostility waned. We couldn't hold it up: the understanding we had once shared could not be reduced to single-minded dissension. I was first to weaken, taking a chance and appealing to the better nature I felt must be there still, somewhere, within him. 'Dan, please . . . Stop this persecution of Nora. Have some feeling . . .'

'No, you stop, Peg,' he said, but more gentle. 'Stop fooling yourself that your actions are for my sister when really it's revenge you're after, revenge against me and my family. Revenge for something I never even did.'

I let the false accusation of vengeance go because I was more struck by the possibility of his innocence. Could it be true? But he had betrayed us so often . . .

'I wish I could believe that,' I whispered.

'It's the truth, Peg. We went out that morning with the intention of rounding those boys up. I knew Barney was among them. If he had come out when I called, he'd be alive today. I'd have made sure of that. That was my full intention. And whoever fired the bullet that killed him, it wasn't me.'

Oh, I longed that it might be so.

'I can't believe you'd think that of me. Or that it's only your family who feels his loss.'

'Do you mean yourself? You grieve him?'

'Jesus, girl, what do you think? He was my best friend.'

I wanted to cry then. I wanted to tell him that I had forgotten nothing, not a single blessed thing that had passed between us.

'The problem with you die-hards is you think people who aren't going round ranting and raving have no feelings at all.'

'But Nora . . .'

'Ah yes, Nora.' With that, our moment passed. His voice changed back to that of soldier-in-charge. 'I have to tell you, Peg, that Nora is not going to be a pawn in this any longer. The asylum is the proper place for her and the asylum is where she's going.'

'Dan . . .'

He held up his hand. 'No more about it. As she won't sit still and talk to her own brother, you can pass her on a message.' Here he paused for effect, like a cowboy in a thrupenny Wild Western. 'You can tell her that I'll be back to get this sorted and soon. And this time she'd better cooperate.'

And with that he took his leave.

It took me a while after he left to get moving and then I spent nearly half an hour looking for Nora before I found her in the bottling store, hiding among the stacked cases. She wouldn't come out when I called her so I had to get in beside her to coax and plead. No matter what I said, or how I tried, she was dumb. I could get no good out of her until in the end I lost my patience. 'Please, Nora,' I snapped, 'how can anyone help you if you won't let them? Don't be so selfish.'

She cried then, the first time I'd seen her cry since she came to us from the asylum, and strange to say, they were tears I was glad to see. They felt more natural than that desperate silence of hers. After a time, as if a blockage flowed away with the weeping, she spoke. 'I'll have to go away again.'

'No, you won't. Why should you?'

'He'll make me.'

'He can't make you. How can he? You have us to protect you now.'

'He'll make me, he and Daddy between them. He makes everyone do what he wants.'

'That won't happen, Nora, I promise you. Come on back now to the house and try to forget about it. Everything will be all right, you wait and see. Things are never as bad as they seem.'

'I don't want to be here if he's here, Peg.'

'I know it's hard, and to tell you the truth, I don't much fancy the thoughts of it myself, but—'

'No, you don't understand. I *can't* stay if Dan is here.' She gripped me by the wrist and turned two wet eyes on me. 'I can't.' Whatever way she said those words knocked me back. I could feel the weight of something behind them.

'What do you mean, Nora?' I asked. 'What are you saying to me?'

'It's what he does,' she said, her fingers so tight on my wrist they seemed to be denting my bones. 'He makes everyone do what he wants.'

Again I felt it, that there was more in the words than they were able to hold and something cold and dead slithered across my skin. I looked hard at her and she held me in a horrible stare that made me want to look away, but I didn't. I let what I was seeing in her pierce me. As the certainty of what she was trying to convey to me grew, I kept my eyes up and open to her. I let the truth of it come until it was crawling all over me.

When she saw for sure that the knowledge had reached me, she let go of my arm. 'So you see, Peg, I can't stay in Mucknamore if my brother is living here. I just can't.'

The *Wexford Weekly*
12 December 1923

'FREE STATE OFFICER FOUND DEAD AT MUCKNAMORE!'

On Wednesday morning last, fisherman John Colfer of Mucknamore was taking to the sea in commencement of his day's work when his attention was caught by a body trapped on Coolanagh strand. The sands at Coolanagh are deceptive, appearing firm but in fact being subject to a 'quick' condition, and this person appeared to have got into trouble there overnight.

As the deceased was dressed in a Free State Army uniform, Mr Colfer returned to land and proceeded with haste to inform the military barracks at Wexford. The military arrived and, with the aid of planks and ropes attached to the military lorry, proceeded to try to extract the body from the sand, a scene which attracted a great number of people from Mucknamore to observe proceedings. The operation took upwards of two hours and engendered great excitement among a growing crowd.

The deceased was identified as Lieutenant Dan O'Donovan of Mucknamore, a National Army officer, and the death has caused a sensation in Mucknamore and surrounds.

It is presumed that he inadvertently wandered off the Causeway out onto Coolanagh sands in the dark. On the night in question, this area was submerged in fog, and there is much speculation as to what would have taken him out on the Causeway at Mucknamore in such dangerous conditions. While not a native of these parts, Lieutenant O'Donovan had lived here for some years and it is thought unlikely that he would not have known of the dangers associated with Coolanagh strand, notorious as it is throughout south Wexford.

The remains have been transferred to the morgue, awaiting inquest. Pending investigation, further details will be provided.

V
Reflux

Nora

Lovers' Hollow. The words hurt me too. Don't try to forget, Peg says. Remember. We can't talk of it to anyone else but we can't run away from it either. Don't be afraid, is what she means, never wondering if maybe she's too brave for her own good.

. . . He did me wrong, my brother. What he did, what we did . . . But the real wrong, the most awful badness, was what he made of it after. All to fall on me. All! And then the way he would look at me, eyes twisted up whenever they had to turn my way, as if he believed his own made-up story. Oh, the wrong of that. That was the real wrong . . .

. . . Thirty-six hours she was in the coming. The pain of pushing my insides out, pain cutting me to blood for thirty-six hours. Two nights and a live-long day. And no one to relieve me or talk to me only a cross old nun saying every few hours that I'd be another while yet and getting annoyed with me because she wanted to be in her bed asleep.

Curses to the Lord. Curses on curses and pain on pain, for a night and a day and another long night. And when she finally came, she didn't come easy. Push. Push again. Push, for God's sake, push would you, push I said, push can't you. Push.

At last the very last, when I could do no more, she gave in. 'It's coming, it's coming,' said the nun and out she slithered in a rush of blood. She was given up to me and – Oh!

She was all curled over from being inside me, her back curved like a bowl and her hands and feet like little cups. The black downy head on her and the arms and the legs, purple and fleshy like four fat eels. Bits of my body and blood stuck to her. Eyes open, open wide, half the size of her face. She couldn't take them off me and her staring drew me in. 'She's looking at me,' I said and the nun said, 'Don't be talking daft, newborns see nothing for weeks.' I didn't believe her, not with the Child's big eyes staring me out of it and I staring right back in.

Then they cut the cord. All for the best, they said, all for the best as they took her away. My bosoms filled up fit to burst, longing for little lips to ease them. Leaking from every part of me, blood and milk and tears . . .

Then the feel of my belly shrinking, closing in around the space where she grew . . .

Oh!

48

1995

No silence is ever total. Here in this hotel room, the quiet is thicker and the underlying noises more muted than the swoosh of the sea and the whine and whack of building work that was my soundtrack over the summer. Here it's corridor voices, wheels whirring over carpet, tea trays tinkling and, outside the window, the rattle and drone of Dublin street-life and traffic, muffled by double glazing. Beneath it all, the subterranean creaks and gurgles of a huge central-heating system. The air here is thicker too than the open air of my shed, clogged with faint smells of lemon polish, and carpet dust, a memory of cigarette smoke and a faint trace, despite the cleaners' best efforts, of other people.

I wonder about them, all the others who have slept in here, the business travellers and holidaymakers, as I lie between my laundered linen sheets, trying to persuade myself to get up. It's four in the afternoon and I've been asleep since two, would be asleep yet, had I not been kicked into waking by you.

But it's good that you have roused me; I should already be up and about. In less than an hour, Maeve will be sitting in Bewley's Cafe, a fifteen-minute walk away, waiting for me. I need to shower and dress and turn myself out, I need to plan what I am going to say when she asks me again why I want to 'waste good money' on this hotel room. It *is* ludicrously expensive, this square beige space with its peach-and-cream curtains and cushions, its pallid furnishings, its innocuous matching paintings (riverbank with overhanging trees and flowers from four different angles) in their identical wooden frames.

So why, my sister wonders, am I staying here instead of at her house, where she has not one but two spare rooms? Neither she nor anybody else would bother me, if that's what I'm afraid of. I could come and go as I pleased. All this she has already said on the telephone, and I know she will say it again today. She will do her best to persuade me. I will not let myself be persuaded.

This afternoon, she will want to know how the writing is progressing and all about hospitals and birthing arrangements and the question of afterwards. The prospect exhausts me, has me clinging to the mattress. I would ring and cancel our meeting – as I have once already – were it not for her saying at the end of her call yesterday that she had 'something' to tell me. Though it seems unlikely, I cannot rid myself of the idea that this 'something' has to do with Rory.

I seem doomed to repeat every action of my life. Here I am again, pregnant, having made an abrupt exit, and here he is, failing to follow me. It wouldn't be difficult for him to track me down; Maeve's name is listed in the telephone book and though it might be mildly awkward for him to have to telephone her and ask if she knows my whereabouts, it's a small test. Tiny. Is he going to flunk it? After all that he said, surely he cannot leave it like this?

I'm back where I started, that is what I find so hard to credit. Feeling that concentrated connection that I never felt with anybody else. Now I wonder whether it never left me at all, my feeling for this one man, whether it was there always, following me around, while I went about all the other business of my life. Whether all that other business was only me fooling myself? Or does the folly lie in these feelings that shook me so hard before, that have me in their grip again?

What is the real thing: my feelings? Or my ability to withstand them?

I throw aside the covers but I can't propel myself out. With a groan, I pull them back round me for a final snuggle. What I'd like to do is escape into another nap. Since coming to Dublin, that's all I seem to do: drift in and out of sleep between bouts of writing. I no longer run, have to force myself even to walk. Breakfast and dinner come to me via room service because going downstairs to negotiate waiters and other diners feels like too much bother. I'm growing heavier and slower, cow-slow. My face and arms and wrists are swollen now as well as my belly and I get short of breath just taking a shower. If I bend or reach up too suddenly, blood splurges round my head.

It's all *your* fault, especially the tiredness, not helped by your inability to tell night from day. Whenever the mood takes you, off you go on the move, kicking and nudging and poking me from inside. I have surrendered to your rhythm and spend some of most nights awake (last night I worked from 2 to 5 a.m., transcribing my hand-written work onto my new laptop computer) and some of most days asleep.

So here I am. This is as far as I've got: lying in an anonymous hotel room, teetering on the edge of sleep, feeling what I think is your heel against my rib, convulsed inside my own longing. Longing, longing, longing like a lovesick teenager, pinning my hopes on this meeting with my sister, shrinking from what I suspect will be their disappointment.

I walk in sunshine through the regimented flower-beds of St Stephen's Green to meet Maeve, past ducks that look just like the ones Rory and I used to feed when we were students. (How long do ducks live?) People sit on benches and stroll or stride along the paths but the lolling-on-the-grass season is over until next year. The park is busy, though it's mid-afternoon and the after-work crowd has not yet started to pour through. Despite the crowds – and these streets are as crowded as any I've ever walked – I can never believe in Dublin as a real city. It's about the same size as San Francisco but feels much smaller and its loudly touted, new-found cosmopolitanism always seems to me unconvincing, like a child rigged out in its mother's high heels.

I negotiate my bulk through the throngs, down Grafton Street and into Bewley's, past the pile-up of pastries at the take-away counter, into the bowels of the cafe. It takes my eyes a time to adjust to the dim light. Maeve is sitting in one of the low red booths at the back, waving at me. She looks haggard, forcing her mouth into a crooked smile as I approach. I bend to kiss her cheek and up close I can almost smell it from her: pure misery. I want to turn and run out the door.

Her skin, despite its pallor, is hot under my lips. 'You OK?' I ask.

'Sure. Fine. You?'

'Fine.'

Our eyes meet and we hover inside a moment of possibility. Then, disconcerted, I point at her cup. 'Would you like another one of those?' There's a ring of cold coffee lining the inside of the half-empty cup in front of her. She must have been here a while.

She nods. 'Please.'

'Black?'

'Lovely. Thanks.'

This is ridiculous, I think as I shuffle along the line-up at the counter, waiting to order. She is not fine. I am not fine. So after I return to the table, and hand out the coffee and the spoons, and put away the tray, I sit down opposite her and ask: 'Maeve, what's wrong?'

She shakes her head, takes a slim tin of artificial sweetener from her bag, tips two small, white pills into her coffee. Shrugs. Sighs. Shakes her head again. I wait. Eventually it comes. 'Donal's gone.'

'Donal? Gone?'

'Yes, Jo.' She wipes a hand across her forehead, irritated. 'Donal, as in my husband. Gone, as in left me.'

So there is nothing of Rory here, thinks selfish, selfish me. Goodbye my hopes. But of course I don't say that. 'Maeve, that's terrible.'

Her mouth wobbles, goes misshapen. 'I know. Of all the times . . . Now . . . Mother—'

She breaks off. I know what she means, and yet I can see how this, and her way of saying it, even her way of feeling it, could be infuriating.

'But is it permanent? What's going on?'

She reaches into her bag again, this time for paper tissues, crinkly in their plastic handipack. She takes one out, snaps the pack back into the bag. 'He blames Mother,' she says. 'While she was sick I had to go down to her, to Mucknamore, a lot. Naturally. But he resented it. And I resented him not supporting me through it.' She shrugs. 'According to him, in that time we grew too far apart.'

'And is he right?'

'If we did, there was no need for it. He always griped about Mother, you've no idea. He could be *completely* ridiculous about it. It was pathetic: a grown man jealous of an old woman and her needs.'

I recall Donal at the funeral, the sarcasm he directed at Mrs D. that I now see must have also encompassed Maeve. I realize as she is talking that I don't know the guy at all, that he has never seemed quite real to me, just Maeve's husband, slotting into his allotted place in her ordered life.

'He never made it easy for me, if I wanted her to come on holiday with us or to go down to Mucknamore for Christmas.'

'You went down every year, didn't you?'

'We could hardly have left her on her own for it.'

She catches my face. 'You think he was right!' she accuses.

'I haven't a clue, Maeve. It hardly matters, does it, what I think. I'm hardly an expert on marriage.'

'You know more than you pretend to know,' she says, a comment I could take any number of ways. She blows her nose. 'You and Donal might be happy to pretend you never had a mother,' she goes on, 'but most people appreciate their parents and look after them when they get on a bit. I was happy to do it, it was the right thing to do.' Red-faced, she shrugs. 'It's not like we had her with us day and night, she would have liked a lot more attention than she got.'

'You were pulled between the two of them.'

'I could never see why he had to make such a big deal about it. We always had at least one other family holiday, without her, each year. And as for Christmas . . . well, it's what you do, isn't it, at Christmas? The family thing.'

I grimace, recognizing my small part in this. 'It all fell on you,' I say.

'Well, yes. We were the only family she had left. She used to say that, often.'

I bet she did. I take a sip of coffee to stop my retort.

'And it's not like I didn't put her off. I did, many times. For *him*. And felt awful about it. None of that ever counted for anything with him.'

'But, Maeve, I don't understand. If Mrs D. was the problem between you, then surely things should be better now that she's . . . gone?'

Her face closes itself like a fist. 'There's more.'

I nod gently, to say go on.

'This is why I went down to Mucknamore, to you, that day two months ago . . . to try to tell you . . .'

'And you went away without saying?'

'I know, I know. I felt so wretched driving away that day. But I was so overcome by your news . . . Are you *really* feeling OK, by the way? Have you seen a doctor yet?'

'Maeve, never mind all that. We can discuss that later.'

She nods. 'You're right, I should have talked that day. Having gone all the way down, to drive back up without . . . But, Jo, I'm finding it very hard to talk about it. None of my friends know, not one. I can't seem to get it out.'

I know that feeling.

'And . . . our friends . . . I don't know how I've done it but . . .

none of them . . . I don't seem to have anybody I can bear to confide in. I hate how I think they'll be.' She screws the rumpled tissue into her eye sockets. 'Also, I can't help feeling that saying it somehow makes it more real.'

'Where's he staying?' I ask.

'He's rented an apartment.'

'Oh.'

She nods, misery creasing her face again. 'And . . .' She falters. 'And . . .'

'There's somebody else.'

Two wide eyes expand wider. 'How did you know?'

Her surprise is poignant: you'd hardly need to be Sherlock Holmes. 'I just wondered,' I say gently.

'It's the full cliché. She's only twenty-five.'

Is she indeed? I didn't think Donal had it in him.

She starts to cry then, weakly, like she's cried so much that she's tired of it but it's all she knows how to do. I watch her, uncertain. She tries to stop but fails and I say, 'It's OK,' and she sinks back into it and cries on for a long time. Then, with a grimace that acknowledges her inability to stop, she says, 'Jo, I want to ask you something.'

I nod.

'I wanted to ask if you . . .'

I wait.

'If you would come . . . and stay with us for a while?'

I turn from her wet eyes, their entreating heat. The stained glass turns the light in here blue, making the close, shabby warmth of the cafe seem cooler, airier than it would otherwise be. Above us, four wooden gargoyles, magnificently ugly, jut out from the wall, and all around, at other tables, Irish and Continental and American voices talk and laugh and clink their cups.

'I wouldn't ask, only . . . Having you there would be a distraction for Ria . . . She's such a good kid and I . . . at the moment, I'm . . .

I can't seem to . . .' She takes a steadying breath, pulls back to look at me. 'Jo, it's for Ria really that I'm asking. It's so awful . . . The pair of us . . . each trying not to crack . . .'

At the word, tears break in her again. 'Ria's heartbroken, you see . . . She doesn't understand. How can she? I don't understand myself . . .'

I think lovingly of my beige hotel room, my solitude. Inside me, I am constricting, like somebody is shrink-wrapping the inside of my neck in cling film and working their way up towards my face.

'I'm sorry, Jo,' she says into her tissue. 'I don't know what your plans are. I shouldn't . . . I don't want to be a . . .' The bag clicks open again. She takes out a fresh tissue. I find I'm putting my hand on hers. She cries a little longer, sniffles to recovery.

'It's OK,' she says then. 'I can see you'd rather not.'

'No,' I say. 'It's not that. I—'

'It's OK, Jo, I understand. I know how you value your privacy.'

'Maeve, I'm—'

'You don't have to explain, honestly. Really . . . I shouldn't have asked . . .'

'Christ, Maeve! Will you *stop* for a second?'

She stops, looks at me through those wet lashes of hers, her green eyes widened to their widest point.

I squeeze the hand that is under mine and it feels as if I am squeezing my own heart. 'Of course I'll come and stay with you,' I say. 'Of course I will.'

49

1923

The two brown doors of the public house were closed, which was strange, because it was almost twelve o'clock, well beyond opening time. Brigade Police Officer Patrick-Joe Brosnan banged on the door again with his fist, one last time – *thump-thump-thump* – no longer expecting an answer. The motor engine was growling behind and Brosnan turned and shrugged his shoulders at O'Dwyer, who was sitting at the wheel enjoying a cigarette. The private made a gesture back at him through the rain but the downpour was that thick he couldn't properly see, so he went across and stuck his head in under the car canopy, a small respite. 'What are you saying to me?'

'The door of the house, down the far end,' he said, pointing. 'You might have better luck down there.'

Brosnan nodded, raindrops falling from the peak of his cap. It was what he had intended to do, the obvious thing to try once he'd got no reply in the shop, but he didn't trouble to say so. He ran through the rain, pulling up the collar of his military coat. Since the fog lifted earlier that morning, these bitter cold gusty squalls had assailed them. Filthy weather. He put out his hand to bang the brass knocker but as soon as he touched it, the door nudged ajar. From within, he could hear a strange noise, a child's voice it sounded like, and it seemed to be grunting, querulously: *eh – eh – eh*. He gave a small cough and knocked politely, at which the door swung inwards and two frightened eyes stared back at him from the end of the stairs. They belonged to a young woman, a good-looking girl in her early twenties, sitting on the bottom step. She didn't get up, or change her expression or in any other way acknowledge that he was there. Beside her was a baby sitting up in a pram and it was from this small person that the grunts were emanating. *Eh – eh – eh*: reaching towards her toy that had fallen to the floor, one of those woollen sacks that makes a noise upon shaking.

'I'm sorry to disturb you, miss.'

She didn't answer, just carried on staring at him.

'I'm making a visit to all the houses in the area on behalf of the National Army.'

Again she made no reply. Then the penny dropped with him. She must be the loony, the dead man's sister. Kavanagh had filled him in on the queer set-up in this house. What a tragedy, a looker like her, the pale skin under the red hair was a striking combination.

'May I?' When she made no indication, he stepped in. He felt his best ploy would be to play innocent. 'I'm making enquiries about one of our officers, lost to us here yesterday. A local man, Lieutenant Dan O'Donovan. Was he known to you?'

Her stare was unnerving.

'*Eh – eh – eh . . .*' continued the child. He'd have thought no woman could ignore those sounds. He felt like going over himself – him, a man, and a stranger to the child – and picking up the thing and handing it to her. He would have, only it didn't seem right. An internal door opened and another young woman came through, about the same age. Dark to the other girl's red, not as pretty in the face. Not today, anyway: her eyes were swollen and her face blotchy, either she had a bad cold or she'd been crying, and hard. She stopped dead when she saw him there in the hall and affectedly eyed his uniform, up and down, the familiar sneer of the die-hard distorting her face. 'What do you think you're doing in here?'

'Sorry to disturb you, miss,' he said. 'This lady let me in.'

'Did you, Nora?'

No answer for her either. The child raised its voice, turning its grunts to a cry. The second girl saw the problem instantly, retrieved the toy from the floor and took the wet, pink-gummed smile that rewarded her. She turned back to him. 'I didn't hear the knocker.'

'I'm here about the dead officer found in this vicinity yesterday. You'll have heard?'

'Well, you should never have been let in here so I'll thank you now to leave the way you came.'

'I'm afraid I can't do that, miss. I've questions to put to you both, and to the rest of the household too, if I may.'

'You may not.'

'Look,' he said, trying for patience, 'a man is—'

She held up her hand. 'Save your talk.'

'I have to insist—'

'No, I insist. I insist on your respect. My mother died in the room above us one hour ago.'

Jesus God, what rotten blasted timing. 'Oh!' he said. 'I'm sorry. I didn't know, I . . .'

'We haven't had time yet to put up the card on the door.'

He found his equilibrium. 'I'm sorry for your trouble,' he said. 'May she rest in peace.'

'So we won't be receiving any Stater army sergeants.' She ran that disdainful look up and down his uniform again. 'Or answering any Stater questions. Not today.'

She was enjoying this. She was upset of course – her mother was dead – but a part of her was enjoying his discomfort.

'I'm sorry for your trouble,' he said. 'Sincerely.'

'You shouldn't have let yourself in without a by-your-leave.'

'The door was open . . . I wasn't to know . . .' He found himself, somehow, walking backwards, towards the door. 'I'll have to come back soon. You do understand that?'

She looked at him like he was a person without morals.

'We have enquiries that won't wait,' he said. 'When is your funeral?'

'We've hardly had time to think of that.'

'I'll see if I can leave it until the day after tomorrow. As a favour, like.'

Instead of being grateful, she looked at him like he was pure poison to her. 'Suit yourself,' she said. 'You will anyway.'

She turned to the other girl, put out a hand. 'Come on, Nora, let's get you two inside.' Her voice for her was so different, drenched with kindness. She helped her off the stairs, tucked the blanket in around the baby's legs. 'You can close the door behind you,' she said in the tone she had for him, 'on the way out.'

With an arm around her unfortunate friend, she steered the perambulator towards the door at the end of the hall.

Outside, O'Dwyer had the engine turned off and was smoking again, warm and dry in his vehicle and unscathed by female hostility. 'How did it go?'

'Terrible,' he said, climbing in beside him. 'They've had a bereavement. The mother of the house has died.'

'Ah, Mrs Parle, has she gone? Lord have mercy on her, she's been sick this long time. And she was only a young woman, forty-five at most.'

'They were in no mood to answer questions. I said we'd come back.'

'So where to now?'

'Have you any recommendations?'

'You could try Mrs Mythen in the post office. She's usually good for what's going on.'

Brosnan nodded. 'All right.' He didn't hold out much hopes of it but he hardly cared, he was so twisted in his thoughts of how the previous interview had gone awry. He shouldn't have let himself be put on the wrong foot like that, like he had done something bad to her on purpose. If only he'd known, he'd have done them first, yesterday, instead of spending the day on the men in the barracks and that girl from the pub. Kavanagh wouldn't be too pleased: the Parles were central witnesses.

'What do you think, O'Dwyer? Do *you* believe they – ' he nodded towards the house – 'had anything to do with it?'

'Hmmm. I'd be inclined to say no but the country's gone that mad it's hard to tell anything for sure these days.'

'They had a motive.'

'They wouldn't be alone in that.'

'Really? Was the dead man not liked? Kavanagh seemed to think he was.'

'I don't mean that, though like most men he'd have had those who didn't think too highly of him. No, what I meant was the way things are in the country at the minute.'

'Do you know her, the daughter of the house?'

'Not well. She'd know my sister.'

'She's quite a fury.'

'Really? I never heard that of her, I have to say. She was the schoolteacher here for a time and well respected.'

Yes. Kavanagh had filled him in on all that, how she'd lost her job for taking in the lunatic girl and the baby. A rare sort, to do a thing like that. She was also a Cumann na mBan and the country was learning only too well what vixens they could be when roused.

Brosnan sighed again: to think that when he applied to join the Guards it was in order to get away from killing. When he was offered this job as Brigade Police Officer in Wexford, he'd jumped at it, thinking policing milder than soldiering and that the divide was likely to be less bitter here than in Kerry. After the Ballyseedy affair, he'd have jumped at *any* offer that took him away from his own county. That whole business had sickened and shamed him. Some nights when he was falling to sleep, he'd find himself trapped in a nightmare with those boys: tied together around a ticking bomb that exploded them into smithereens, the body parts of eight of them divided into nine coffins, the soldiers not knowing that one had got away to tell the tale. He didn't want to be part of an army that did such deeds and denied them.

But he needed an income. He had a wife, two children and a third on the way.

The Civic Guards had offered him a way out. Some said the

Guards were only a tame branch of the army, others that this was not the time for their introduction, but Brosnan believed in the idea of an unarmed force and thought Ireland could not have it soon enough. That was what he wanted to be part of: the rule of law, not the rule of the gun.

Yet here he was, somehow still in the middle of the worst of it. Wexford seemed every bit as embittered as Kerry and here he found himself floundering around like a blind man who'd stumbled into the wrong house. It was a strange, closed place, this village, its people full of a strange, closed pride. Most of them wouldn't talk to him at all and those who did had a drawly, dawdly way with their words so that he had to stretch his ears to make sense of what they were saying. Even his army colleagues seemed to be wary of him. A foreigner, he'd heard himself called.

'You've *some* chance of getting something out of the people of Mucknamore,' Kavanagh had said, when he was explaining why he'd been chosen for the job. 'A local man would be devoured.'

Brosnan took off his cap, smoothed back his hair, wished himself far from here, far from Kerry, far from Ireland altogether.

O'Dwyer looked askance at him. 'Are you all right, Sergeant?'

'Have you a spare fag?'

He took it and bent to the light that O'Dwyer struck for him, inhaled the smoke deep. What he needed to do was focus, think on what to do next. They'd try this post-office woman but he hadn't any great hopes of her. It was people who knew the dead man well who were his best hope.

'A good soldier,' Kavanagh had said of O'Donovan. 'Nothing showy, but brave as he was needed to be. Good leadership ability. All qualities that would have stood to him in the Guards. I'd say he'd have made inspector.'

'Could it have been an accident, sir?'

'It could, I suppose, but I don't believe so. Why would he go out that way by night unless he was forced? Especially the night that was in it. Can you think of any good reason?'

'It's hard to, all right.'

'You know the danger good men have been living with. He was shot at before, you know, and his house set fire to this autumn gone out. Mind you, this killing has a different feel to it, more underhand. The Irregulars round here are not usually shy about using their bullets and boasting about it after.'

He had handed him over the file. 'Whatever the motive and whoever the cause, we can't have the likes of this going on, Sergeant. We have to get to the bottom of it. Because if these atrocities are allowed to go on, we'll have the English looking to come back here, claiming we can't keep control. We have to show them – we have to show the world – that such things can't be got away with in Ireland any more.'

'Yes, sir.'

'So over to you, Sergeant. Don't let us down, like a good man.'

That was a day and a half ago. The only useful witness Brosnan had turned up since was the bar girl from Ryan's of Rathmeelin, who, as far as he could make out, was the last person to see O'Donovan alive. He had taken a drink there around teatime and left, telling her that he had an appointment in Mucknamore at seven o'clock. At 7.14 his watch stopped, presumably in the wet sands. Stuck in sinking sands waiting for the returning tide to take you: what a death. If he was lured, Kavanagh was right: it was one evil act.

He gave O'Dwyer the nod to start the car. It took a bit of time, with the damp of the day, but then the machine spluttered and coughed into its workaday rumble. They were pulling out onto the road when a man came lumbering up to them and started to wave them down. He was poorly dressed but respectable looking, a farm labourer or the like.

'Yes?' Brosnan snapped, irritated by the way he stood there in front of the car, looking at them, his hands folded across his coat.

'I'm hearing that yez are investigating what went on here the night before last. Would that be so?'

'If you mean the death of Lieutenant O'Donovan, then yes, that is so.'

'In that case, I've something of interest to yez.'

'Have you indeed?'

'I have.'

He stood there, like a child waiting for a pat on the head.

'Well? Go on.'

'Here?'

'Why not?'

He looked around, over each shoulder. 'I'm thinking it would be better if we went somewhere more private. I don't want to be handing it over in front of the entire village.'

'Handing *what* over?'

The fellow tapped a finger to the side of his nose, looked about him again. The street was empty, the little windows and doors overlooking the street.

'Sit into the car,' Brosnan said. 'If you must.'

'I don't know, sir. I don't think that would go down too well with some, to see me voluntarily climbing into that particular vehicle.'

Brosnan looked at O'Dwyer who slid his eyes upwards. 'Go on, so, be off with you.'

'Don't misunderstand me, sir. Myself, I'd be entirely happy to get in. But these are dangerous times we're living in.'

'For Christ's sake, man. What is it you want?'

'It's not so much what *I* want.' He gave a slow, stupid grin. 'Sir,' he added, belatedly.

'Is this a game?'

'I'm quite disposed to satisfy you. But in order to do so, I have to ask yez to make it look as if I'm being forced.'

Forced? The devil. And he probably had nothing at all. But what if he had? So far, not one single lead . . .

He nodded at O'Dwyer to do it. The blackguard made a convincing – O'Dwyer would probably no doubt say too convincing –

attempt at resistance that went on far too long, until the private's hat was knocked askew on his head and Brosnan said, 'We've had enough of your nonsense. Get in now or we're going.'

The fellow let himself be taken by the scruff of his collar and shoved into the back of the car. 'Drive down to . . . the . . . back strand,' he said, breathless.

O'Dwyer ignored that and took the Wexford road. Once outside the village, he pulled to a stop by the ditch. 'Right,' Brosnan said, turning round. 'Let's be having it, whatever it is.'

A sly look. 'I don't know how to put this, sir. Is it a sergeant you are?'

Brosnan nodded, peremptorily.

'Well, Sergeant, I'm supposing that the army would be grateful for information about why Dan O'Donovan went walking the Causeway in the dark that night?'

The fellow had all his teeth but every one of them was black-rotten in his head. The car was filling up with an unpleasant whiff. Brosnan nodded.

'How grateful?'

So that was it. He should have known from the first.

'That would depend on the quality of the information,' he said, not looking at him directly.

'But there would be a . . . token of your appreciation?'

'Bearing in mind that it is your civic duty to help in a . . . an enquiry.' He nearly said 'murder enquiry' but that wouldn't be right. Despite what was being said abroad, they had no proof of foul play. And he wasn't going to promise this repulsive creature anything. Let's see what the fellow had first.

'I'd need to be sure, Sergeant.'

His face was as closed as a fist and Brosnan could see the future of this village written in it. From here on out, it would become even more closed and insular. Fright at what they'd shown themselves capable of doing to each other had thinned their souls, souls that were already reduced from hundreds of years of British rule. None of them – maybe himself included? – was able to face the true shame of this dirty little war, the wicked whys and wherefores of it. Some would react by making too much of small differences, because otherwise they'd have to admit they'd been killing and dying for nothing. Others would try to pretend the horrors never happened at all. Least said, soonest mended; whatever you say, say nothing. Well, he might not think their cause worth killing or dying for but he wasn't afraid of the truth. He said, 'You won't be let down, man. Not if you have something worthwhile to pass on.'

Satisfied, the creature reached inside his coat and made a great commotion of taking something from his inside pocket and presenting it with hands aloft. A gun. A Webley rifle. He held the booty under Brosnan's nose. 'I found it this morning,' he said.

Brosnan nodded. 'Go on.'

'There I was, after bringing out the cows, walking back up the road towards my house . . .'

'Which is where?'

'Down by the Tench, Sergeant.'

Brosnan shook his head.

'Don't you know the Tench?' He made a show of surprise. 'On the other side of the village, down towards what we call the Hole in the Wall.' There was that knowingness again, that simple-minded delight at knowing something that Brosnan, an outsider, a stranger – a *foreigner!* – did not. 'The strand exit nearest the Causeway, Sergeant. Which is the way out to Coolanagh, if you get my drift. There I was, strolling along behind the cattle, minding my own, when next thing I spied it, out of the side of my eye. Lying there, half in and half out of the ditch.'

'And you think it significant?'

He looked at them with feigned surprise. 'You don't?'

'Would you tell us why, please?'

'Don't you know what this is? Ser-geant?' He drawled the title full of sneer and affectation, as if Brosnan was the greatest dunce that ever walked.

'Just keep to the facts, please.'

'There was only one rifle of this sort owned around here.'

'Go *on*, man.'

'It belonged to Parle.' He flashed his sly, conniving grin again. 'Yes, Sergeant. Barney Parle. I presume you've heard of *him*?'

50

1995

'Donal drove me mad the whole time,' says Maeve, referring to her visit to San Francisco. 'I spent nearly every night after we'd gone to bed calming him down.'

'I knew he was a bit fazed by the scene but I'd no idea he took it so bad.'

'Dreadful. He was even afraid to drink out of cups that Richard or Gary had used.'

I feel the skin on my face blaze up. I think: I was right to never like him.

'I know, I know,' she says. 'But you have to remember the times. Afterwards people came to understand a lot more about AIDS but then . . . Well, he was hardly the only one, was he?'

It is Richard's anniversary: six years ago today since he died. *Six* years. *Where* did they go? It's hard not to think of them as wasted. All day, as I went about my business in Dublin, I've been dispirited, struggling against the suck of misery that always pulls me down around this time of year. None of the things that make this year different – writing, pregnancy, being in Ireland – were able to keep me buoyant today. The writing I have been so wedded to seems hollow and useless, a concoction of nothings. I am getting fearful about the baby and about afterwards, of how we will be together.

Together, alone. Rory still has not come or sent any word and is hardly likely to now.

As for Ireland, it feels as petty as ever. Here in Dublin, I cannot escape the faction fighting, the antagonism that always seems more virulent here than anywhere else. Each day, the radio brings belligerent adversaries into Maeve's kitchen and, over breakfast, we listen to them slinging their tirades at each other. Two current 'debates' preoccupy almost everybody. One centres on Northern Ireland: last year, the IRA declared a ceasefire, an occasion of great rejoicing, but the gesture was insufficient for the British government and the Unionists, who are now calling for them to destroy their guns and bombs before peace talks can begin. The IRA refuses outright – Republicans have never handed over their armoury. Not in 1921, when the British called the Truce with the old IRA. Not in 1923 after the Civil War, when weapons were dumped, not surrendered. And not now.

The second argument wheels around an upcoming referendum which, if passed, will allow for the introduction of divorce. Yes, in 1995, in a Western democracy: *divorce*. The Catholic Church is calling for a 'No' vote and the result is expected to be tight: there is a distinct possibility that it could fall. Every time I hear a bishop pontificating on the radio, I am reminded of why I fled. I have to tell Maeve this repeatedly. She keeps making suggestions about how good it would be for the baby to grow up with an aunt and cousin nearby; how raising a baby all alone is hard work; how she would be able to help me out; how, in a few years, Ria will be old enough to baby-sit . . . Tonight, such is my sense of frailty, that I almost feel I could be persuaded. Almost.

It is her thoughts on Richard that have made me warm to her. I didn't realize until this evening how much she really liked him; she has so many memories of him from her visit to San Francisco, memories that we never discussed before. All through dinner we regaled Ria with some of the more repeatable stories about him and since Ria went upstairs to bed, the two of us have been sitting together in front of the sitting-room fire, turning over memories. Maeve occupies the armchair, a whiskey and water in front of her; I recline on the sofa opposite, in the only position that is comfortable for me these days: half lying on a nestle of cushions, my belly protruding upwards like a hill. Because it comforts me to talk about Richard, because I am gratified by this comfort after days of struggling within sadness, because I don't want to ruin our growing ease with each other, I let go her revelation about Donal.

In any case, my anger is not what it was: that's you again, little baby, making me sluggish.

'Can I ask you something?' she says.

'Sure.'

'You and Richard never had a thing, did you?'

'God, no. You met him, didn't you?' Five minutes with Richard should be enough to locate him at the furthest, gayest end of the sexuality spectrum.

'Mmmmm.'

'And what is that sceptical sound supposed to convey?'

'I just find it hard to understand why his death flattened you so.'

Oh, no . . . So long, soft, sisterly feelings.

'I mean, more than your own mother's! It's unusual, you have to admit.'

'He was my friend, Maeve. Simple as that.'

She shrugs, unconvinced, and the gesture makes her neck and shoulder bones protrude through her skin. She is so gaunt, her neck could be held in the grasp of one hand. I have pity for that neck, I also have the urge to choke it.

So far, we have avoided conflict. In the morning, after she and Ria leave for school, I get up and go into town to write. I go to different cafes, most often to the Winding Stair, a rickety old bookshop cafe on the north bank of the Liffey, with wide windows (each with its window box of valiant flowers), looking out at high, complicated Irish skies. You can watch the floods of shoppers rising and falling over the Liffey's Ha'penny Bridge, crossing to the north or south side of the city, and the clouds forever clustering in from the west, bearing the next bout of rain. It's a good view of Dublin – almost soothing. I work well there, which is why I take the trouble to travel in each morning, though this house of Maeve's lies empty all day. I tried writing here, just once, up in the bedroom, but it was a disaster. All Maeve's years with Donal were in the air, all those years when I was out of the country clustered in the silence, invading my nostrils, gathering in the back of my throat. No.

No. I have even kept my hotel room, and have managed to spend the occasional night there by inventing a friend, somebody I knew in college that I 'meet' every so often. When I do, I call Maeve to say that I am spending the night at her apartment. Then I go to my beige bolthole and breathe free for eight or ten or twelve hours, refreshed enough to return. Maeve suspects the truth, I think, but appreciates the lie.

'Don't take this wrong,' she says now, 'but it strikes me that being so fixated on Richard allowed you to avoid something else.'

'Something else?'

'A relationship of your own.'

'You've been seeing too much of that shrink of yours,' I say, lightly. Maeve is attending a counsellor, to try to understand where she and Donal went wrong. Can she hear the menace under my airy tone? If she's not more careful, she will break our truce. I would like to say it straight to her, tell her that Richard gave me what I should have got from her and Mrs D.: unconditional love, as her therapist would no doubt call it. Richard's simple acceptance of me won him my undying devotion. Literally undying, staying with me even though he has gone.

Maeve, who I suspect has never had a real friendship, still thinks romantic love is the best. That it has recently – and presumably for some years now – let her down in no way diminishes her belief in it. Donal is now refusing to see her at all, asking her to drop Ria outside his apartment block for her custody visits without meeting him, but she still nurtures hope that he will come back. Half of me despises this hope but because I live with my own version of the same affliction, I want to be gentle with her. I really do, but she makes it so hard with her damn superiority. If I can be careful of her, why can't she extend me the same favour? Why always this need of hers to make me face hard questions? (Like:

how small a thing is my devotion to Richard if I could not be with him at his end?)

I want to pace the room, to punch a hole in the wall – or my sister – but it would take a crane to lift me so I confine myself to stretching out my swollen legs. The ankles are so puffy, an older, fatter woman's ankles, pooled with blood. New veins, like blue in a Stilton, have surfaced all over my legs. The skin of my abdomen is stretched to transparency: I never imagined that skin could stretch so far. You are so big now that the discomfort is constant: heartburn arrives at regular intervals to sting my oesophagus. You ripple my belly with each movement you make. You too are cramped and uncomfortable, I sense. We both want out.

But I am also dreading the labour (are you?). After years of suffering no worse physical pain than a superficial cut or burn or bruise, I am fearful.

'It's time to get closure on it, I would have thought,' Maeve says, still harping on Richard.

When she starts on like this, I think that maybe I shouldn't be here, that we are not helping each other at all. We disagree on almost everything. Yesterday it was the North. The demand that the IRA give up their weapons seems like a red herring to me, given that the British government and Loyalist groups hold the largest stocks of weapons in the territory, but Maeve disagrees. The IRA are 'terrorists', she says. It astounds me how distanced she feels from 'the North', that other country, where 'they' can't be stopped from hating and killing each other. All the patriotism in her – and she has it in plenty – is affixed to the Republic only. It stops at a border created by the British and she sees no irony in that.

I take up that topic again because, though we differ on it, it will distract her from Richard. 'I've been thinking about what you said yesterday, Maeve, about the North, and I wanted to ask you: do you not see what's going on in the North today as a continuation of Granny Peg's "War of Independence"?'

'Things were different then,' she says. 'The old IRA were men of honour.'

'All of them?' Has she not been reading the manuscript pages I've given her?

'They killed and died for an ideal.'

'The ideal hasn't changed, has it? And there were opportunists and chancers then too.'

'Not drug-dealers and knee-cappers. Not bombers who deliberately plant explosives in pubs and shopping centres to kill as many civilians as they can.'

'But that's more a matter of advanced weaponry than intent. Isn't it the same struggle, the same methods? Just that a bomb kills more people than a gun?'

'But . . .'

'Don't get me wrong, it's not that I agree with that struggle. I personally think we'd have been better off growing up in an Ireland that was part of the UK.'

This statement swings things round. Maeve stops in the act of twisting her hair up into a clip, and stares at me with green eyes aghast, wearing the exact expression that Rory wore when I said the same to him. The worst thing, it seems, that you can say to an Irish person of our background. 'You can't mean that?' she gasps.

I shrug, deliberately casual. 'Why not?'

'You're being provocative. I don't believe you mean it.'

'But I do. All the damage done by English colonization was well done by the early twentieth century. What the Irish did to themselves after that in the so-called War of Independence and the Civil War and afterwards only made a bad thing worse.'

'I *completely* disagree with you. And why do you say "so-called" War of Independence? That war *did* get us our independence. Your own book makes that clear.'

'No, Maeve. I know partial independence came out of it. But really it was just one of Ireland's little civil wars.'

'I don't understand what you mean.'

'The conflict between those who considered themselves "native Irish" and those they deemed to be settlers.'

'They *were* settlers. They came and grabbed the land and dismantled our culture and our language and tried to break our religion . . .'

'Yes, Maeve, all of that happened. I'm not denying that, though I'd question your use of "our".'

'It's your tradition too, Jo, whether you want to claim it or not.'

'I'm not denying the events you're talking about or the feelings they engendered. I'm just saying they're not very logical. *Everyone* who ever lived in Ireland came here from somewhere else. Those patriotic feelings that we're all trained to feel so strongly, they have no great logic to them, do they?'

'It's about self-respect, Jo. A dominated people achieving self-determination.'

'It is if you align yourself with the "native" Irish side, but what about those who lost?'

That's all a revolution is, a new tide rising out of the old. And though nationality likes to pretend it is the only wave in the sea, power flows through sex and class, and colour, and religion, and so many other ways. But does any of it matter?

'I'm coming to believe,' I say to Maeve, 'that the best way to deal with identity is to disconnect from it.'

'What? Decide you're not Irish? Don't be ridiculous.'

'Not renounce it, not in that way. Just disconnect from it.'

'So just when we Irish are getting confident about being who we are, we're supposed to pretend it doesn't matter? Come on! I think you're being completely naive about human nature.'

'Another friend of mine used to say that.'

Susan asking how come it was only when women and blacks and gays started asserting their identity that the very concept of identity came into question. I take the point but still . . . A part of me has always resisted identity politics, which is why I could never be the kind of feminist Susan wanted me to be.

'But nationality is only a notion,' I say. 'An abstraction, an invention of our minds. And now, with immigration into this country for the first time in centuries, Ireland will have a whole new layer of difference to fight over.'

We can fight over anything, over nothing at all: if the murderous squabble called the Irish Civil War teaches us anything, it is that. War is a parasite and it lives on our conviction that the survival of one group, 'our' group, depends on the defeat of another. Our only inoculation is to recognize this as the lie it is. Identifying too much with the thoughts that are always rising and fighting within us: that is what causes all the troubles of the world. Didn't Granny Peg say as much to me herself, once?

I think about those moments that I have felt more frequently this summer, when I found within myself a tranquillity beyond thought. 'I' am deeper than my thoughts and feelings and beliefs, and so is 'He'. Yes, and 'She' too. In the depths, we are all connected, which is why hurting somebody else hurts me. In those depths, I am suddenly sure, is where true freedom resides.

I am trying to formulate this insight into words that I can pass to my sister when the doorbell interrupts: *Ding-dong, ding-dong.*

'Good God,' Maeve says. 'Who's that? At this hour of the night?'

Ten fifteen. My stomach takes a small flip. The kind of time you'd arrive if you left Wexford at around seven thirty or eight o'clock. After coming home from work at six and having a conversation and packing a hasty suitcase . . . Then I shake myself to sense. There's no reason to think it might be him.

'Maybe I won't answer it,' Maeve says. 'You can't see the lights in here from the front.'

'I think you'd better,' I say. 'You never know.'

'I suppose.' She gets slowly out of the big armchair, uncurling her legs from under her, giving a small grouchy stretch as she goes out, leaving the door ajar. I hear her open the front door and the surprise in her greeting. She says a name but I cannot catch it. I cannot hear her words but her tone makes something in my stomach start to ferment. Then the other voice speaks, muffled but definitely male.

You give a strong kick. What do you know or sense? There's the door closing. More suppressed talk. A silence. Footsteps approaching across the tiled hallway. Two sets of footsteps. The door behind me opening. I'm afraid to turn.

'Jo?' Maeve's tentative whisper.

I look round. Her head is peeping round the door, her face flushed. 'He's here, Jo.'

'He is?' I get up out of the chair. Blood swishes into my head, probably from standing up so fast. I forgive him, I realize as I wait for the black amoebas before my eyes to vanish. I forgive him all.

Why is Maeve keeping him out there? Is she afraid that I don't want to see him?

'We'll be in the kitchen,' she says.

'Kitchen?'

'Yeah. We need to talk. Obviously.'

I give my head a waggle. When I see her clear I know what I should have known from the start. That beaming face, so irritatingly familiar.

'Why don't you bring him in here?' I manage to say, in a steady voice. 'I was ready for bed anyway.'

She opens the door wider, flourishing him in. Just like Mrs D. with Daddy, the day he came back home to us. Hence, perhaps, my anger. Because it is anger I am feeling, not disappointment. Anger, white and hard as bone.

'Hi,' I say. Then, ashamed of the pettiness I hear in my tone, I add: 'Welcome home, Donal.'

Donal's return changes everything. Now I am in the way. Maeve says this is nonsense but I am. She and Donal are shaky and he doesn't want me here, knowing what I know. I don't want to be here either, witnessing their travails. I am glad for her if he is what she wants but he is not good enough for her, I think. Things she has told me about him rankle. Also, I don't want us to lose what we have gained. Living together is straining our hard-won, tenuous bond.

But when I suggest to her that I leave, the same bond insists that she won't hear of it. I was good enough to come when she needed me, now I must stay until the baby comes. It wouldn't be right for me to have to go into labour alone, in a hotel room. What about those pains I am having in the night?

It is true that you have started to bear down inside me, that I am assailed by stabbing pains in strange new places, pains that sometimes stop me in my tracks. It is true that I am afraid to face into labour alone. It is close now, very close: a week to the due day. Even if I go over my time, it can be no further away than a fortnight, surely. Can Maeve and I live in the same house for that long without a breach? Fingers crossed, I stay.

When the fight comes, it's about Mrs D. It's evening time again and we're sitting over the remains of dinner, darkness bulked against the glass walls of her dining room. Donal has gone to the gym, Ria is in bed, Maeve is finishing a bottle of wine and since the others left, we have been fixed on the topic of our mother.

'How much of her pain was in her situation,' I ask, 'and how much in her person? That's what I could never work out. If she didn't have Daddy and all-that-had-been-done-to-her to complain about, I still don't believe she'd have been happy.'

'She was happy after Daddy died. You didn't know her then.'

'I did. Daddy was dead a year, I seem to recall, when she kicked me out of the house.'

'She did *not* kick you out, you walked. And in that first year, she wasn't herself . . . Naturally. Afterwards, she was very happy. She loved her bowls and her golf and her bridge. She liked her life then.'

'The merry widow, eh?'

She shakes her head at me. 'You're so hard sometimes, Jo. You know how unhappy he made her.'

'What about *him*? What about *his* unhappiness?' I appear to be shouting, though nothing in the conversation calls for it.

'Yes, he was unhappy too. And he too behaved badly. You never blamed him, though, did you?'

I look down at the debris on the dinner table.

'She was your *mother*, Jo. Does that count for nothing with you? Now that you're about to be a mother yourself?'

'I just don't feel like she ever gave me anything.'

'She gave you life.'

'OK. Anything beyond *life*. And bed and board and financial input, before you say it. You know what I mean . . .'

Maeve sighs. 'You were too much for her, Jo, that's the truth. She wasn't able to handle you.'

She begins to clear away the plates, scrape off the food. 'I know something she gave you,' she says, in the voice of somebody trying again. 'She gave you all the family papers, the opportunity to put this book together. Anyone can see what that means to you.'

'She wanted me to do a glorious history of our glorious family. It was for her, not for me.'

'You've got so much out of this, you said so yourself the other night. You're thinking about writing a novel. If you do, she will have given you that.'

'OK. Inadvertently, she gave me that.'

'Maybe less inadvertently than you think. Maybe she left you those papers, knowing exactly what you'd do with them . . .'

'Come *on*, Maeve. Do you honestly think Mrs D. would have passed these papers on if she knew the full story?'

'I'm not sure.'

'Well, I am. She never read Nora's notebooks: she said so in her letter to me. And you have to read Nora's stuff as well as Peg's to fully understand. No, she thought the extent of the secret that she was handing on was that she was illegitimate – that Auntie Nora was her mother, not Granny Peg.'

'That in itself was a big deal, Jo. You know how hard that would have been for her to share.'

'I do. But she did it because she wanted a glorified—'

Maeve cuts me off. 'She did it because she wanted to draw you back into the fold of the family. That's what I think. And, what's more, she succeeded.'

'You know, you don't have to defend her every move, Maeve. She was shitty to you too.'

She shakes her head.

'Maeve! She *was*. Don't pretend she wasn't.' I have to stop shouting. Why am I shouting? I long to smash her calm face of denial. 'I *remember*. And I remember the way you'd always go crawling back for more.'

'She wasn't easy, Jo, I never claimed she was easy.' Her moderate tones are a deliberate contrast to mine. 'And yes, I had my difficulties with . . . Let's just say that since she died, I . . . Well, she wasn't easy. I can agree with that. But don't you see, Jo? Nothing that she did or failed to do can alter the plain fact that she was our mother. Denying that hurts you as much as it ever hurt her.'

'No, sorry. Mothering is something you *do*, not just something you are.'

Maeve does it, with Ria. She finds time outside of her job and the work of running the house for Ria: homework, lifts, activities, treats . . . Oh, they have their arguments but Maeve always has time for her, interest in her. Sometimes I feel jealous of Ria, of the way she is so careless of that.

'Mother's failures hurt her,' Maeve says. 'Just as yours hurt you, and mine hurt me.'

I want to go on arguing but I can't think of any words. She is right, that's the problem. She is right and I know it. I know the key to a good life is not to be loved, but to love.

'Sometimes now,' Maeve says. 'I wonder whether it was because you reminded her of Auntie Nora.'

'What?'

'There is a physical resemblance, you know. Your hair: she was a redhead too. And around the eyes . . .'

'Gee, thanks.'

'Come on, Jo, just in certain ways.'

Could that be right? At least it gives her a reason.

Yes, the key is to love. But what, dear sister, if nobody wants your love? Can Maeve stretch herself to imagine how that might feel? Can I dare to ask her? I find my knees are clenching each other, alarmed at what I am about to say. My voice slides down the decibels so that this time when I speak it's only a whisper. But I speak: 'She couldn't stand me, Maeve.'

There: it's out. The shameful truth. The truth I have only ever told Richard before. My own mother didn't love me. She didn't even like me.

'Oh, come on . . .'

'*Please*, Maeve. Don't pretend. I know you knew it too.'

At last I have silenced her. Will she admit it? She never has before, it makes her – the favourite – feel too guilty. For a long moment we hover, it feels to me like forever. Then she stands up with the plates, looks down at me. 'Jesus, Jo, for once, just for *once*, could we drop the self-pity?'

I am on my feet, moving too fast, storming past the corners of the table, the kitchen units, my arms around my belly for protection. Mine or the baby's? I don't know. I can't see. My head is drowning in darkness. I am screaming again, over my shoulder as I hurtle away: 'Fuck off, Maeve. Just fuck off. Just fuck off.'

I am running down the hall room, tearing up the stairs by instinct, still unable to see clearly. In my room, the spare room that has been mine, I tear clothes from their hangers, stuff anything I can see into my bag. I brush everything that's on the dressing table in with one sweep of my arm. I'll sort it all out later, in the hotel. My hands are shaking so hard I can't get my laptop plug into its bag. Never trust them, never. Never. Never. Never.

A last glance round the room to make sure that I haven't forgotten anything. I don't want to have to come back. Out in the hall, I see Ria's door ajar and I'm sure she is inside it, watching. She possibly heard me shouting. 'Goodbye, Ria,' I say but I get no reply.

Maeve is at the end of the stairs. 'Oh, what a surprise,' she says, as I come down. 'Jo's packed her bag, Jo's decided to leave. Where to this time, Jo? Aren't you running out of places to go?'

I have to take each stair carefully, my balance unsteady. One – step – at – a – time – then – the – next. There: I've reached the bottom. Maeve is standing off to my left. Ahead is the hall door, waiting for me to open it. All I have to do is cross the hallway.

Cross the hallway.

Open the door.

'Don't stop now, Jo. What are you waiting for?'

You. You are what is stopping me. As I take the final step of the stair, you go *whompf* within me and a stabbing pain shoots through my lower belly. Now I have crumpled. Now I am folded into sitting on the step and I am crying, my face in my hands. Now I am saying I am sorry, I don't know why, but that is what I am saying, over and over again: 'I'm sorry, Maeve. I'm sorry. I'm sorry. I'm sorry.'

I say it to Maeve but in my head I'm addressing all of them: Richard. Granny Peg and Auntie Nora. Maeve, yes, and Ria and Rory. Even Orla, Rory's wife. Oh God, yes, even Mrs D.

Now Maeve has her arms around me, telling me that it's all right, that she is sorry too. I burrow my face into her shoulder, trying to explain that's not what I mean, that I am drowning in a remorse so wide and deep and sore that I think it's going to kill me. 'I had to get rid of . . . It would have been . . .' I want to tell her more, tell her properly, but I can't snatch enough breath. The skull of my forehead is grinding against her shoulder bones, my tears are wetting the skin of her neck.

'I know,' she says. She begins to stroke my head, my shoulder, my back. 'I know.'

'No, you don't.'

'I do, Jo.'

I look up and through the film of my tears I see in her glistening eyes that she does. She touches my face, nodding gently.

'How do you know?'

'Because you weren't the only one.'

Does she mean . . . ? Surely, surely not. Not Maeve.

'Yes,' she nods. 'Me too. Different reasons, but yes.'

I am without words.

'Why so shocked, Jo? Ten thousand of us take that trip, every year.'

'It's just I can't . . . Did Mrs D. know?'

'Are you mad? Of course not.'

She looks so indignant that I start to laugh. Then she joins in, and then we find that we can't seem to stop. We sit there, at the end of the stairs, holding ourselves through waves of hysterical laughter. Through it I am looking at her, at her head thrown back, at her wide, open, laughing mouth and knowing that for the first time, I am seeing her properly, in the full light of all that was.

The *Wexford Weekly*
19th December 1923

'DEAD MUCKNAMORE OFFICER'S INQUEST'
'Gun Belonging to Dead Irregular Found!'
'Mother of Deceased Calls for Murder Trial!'

An inquest into the death of Lieutenant Dan O'Donovan, National Army, was arranged by the military and held in the courthouse, Wexford, on Friday evening last. Lieutenant O'Donovan was found dead at Coolanagh, Mucknamore on the morning of Monday December 10th. Brigade Police Officer Patrick Jo Brosnan conducted the enquiry.

Evidence of identification was given by Dan O'Donovan Snr, father of the deceased. It appears that Lieutenant O'Donovan was granted a few days' leave by the army and that it was on the first evening of this break that the tragedy occurred.

John Colfer, fisherman, deposed as to how he found the body and immediately notified the military authorities. Next witness, Doctor Matthew Morris, deposed to having examined the body. There were no marks of violence, the doctor said, and he was of the opinion that death was due to asphyxia. At this point, the mother of the deceased interrupted proceedings, saying her son had been murdered whichever way you looked at it.

Police Officer Brosnan responded by saying to the jury: 'I understand the deceased man's father is here. It is open to him to cross-examine the witness if he wishes but he has not done so.' Mr O'Donovan, the father, rose to his feet and heatedly replied, 'This inquest is nothing but a farce to my mind.' The

Chair informed Mr and Mrs O'Donovan that they would have to behave themselves. If they wanted to cross-examine a witness they could do so in the ordinary way.

Miss Anne Comerford, employed at Ryan's public house, Rathmeelin, three miles from Mucknamore, testified that the deceased had called in there the night he died, between the hours of half-past five and six o'clock. He was wearing a National Army uniform, a cape and a civilian cap. He only remained in the shop long enough to drink one bottle of stout, saying he had an appointment in Mucknamore at seven.

PO Brosnan: Did he describe the nature of this appointment?
Miss Comerford: What he said to me was he had to see a man about a dog.

The night was dark and very foggy, according to witness, and the road was in a bad state but he went off in good health, sober and cheerful.

Staff Captain Sean Kavanagh, National Army, stated that he was one of the party that proceeded to Mucknamore on the morning the body was discovered, on receipt of the report from Mr Colfer. With some difficulty they had extracted the body from the sand with the aid of ropes and an army truck. It was he who identified it as that of Dan O'Donovan. There was nothing to indicate foul play. The hands had not been tied.

They took the body to the morgue. On his person, they found a typewritten letter rendered unreadable by the wet sands in which he had met his end. Also a tobacco pouch with tobacco, a pipe, a book and a photograph. There was a watch also, stopped at 7.14. 'The time of the murder,' cried Mrs O'Donovan, again interrupting proceedings.

Captain Kavanagh continued, testifying that when O'Donovan left the barracks that evening, that was the last any army personnel had seen of him until they received the emergency call the next morning. The army authorities had recently agreed to transfer O'Donovan to the new police force, the Civic Guards. He was a man with further promotion before him, most reliable, and his death a loss to the army and the country.

Final witness was Miss Margaret (Peg) Parle of Mucknamore. As this witness took the stand, commotion broke out, with much talk among the audience and again, cries of protest from the family of the deceased. After order had been restored, the police officer appealed to the jury to decide if the inquest was being properly conducted. The jury pronounced themselves perfectly satisfied that the case was being conducted in a most excellent manner by Mr Brosnan.

Testimony continued. Miss Parle said she was speaking on behalf of her family, as her father was too unwell following a recent bereavement. She was then questioned about a gun that was found in a ditch between her house and the causeway the morning after the night in question. A witness had identified this gun as belonging to her brother, an Irregular killed in action some months ago. Miss Parle said she had no idea how it had turned up where it did.

PO Brosnan: When did you last see it?

Miss Parle: Before my brother was shot, I think. I can't really remember.

PO Brosnan: We've witnesses who say it was seen at your house recently.

Miss Parle: I'd say any such witnesses were only trying to bring us trouble.

PO Brosnan: We also have witnesses who say you blamed the deceased for the death of your brother.

Miss Parle: There's those who say so, I know that.

PO Brosnan: And what do you say?

Miss Parle: I say leave us alone. I say, stop trying to make something out of nothing.

PO Brosnan then asked Miss Parle about her movements and the movements of her family on the night in question and witness gave answers that showed all had alibis for the entire evening.

Therein the evidence ended. Mr O'Donovan rose to his feet again. He wanted to know why others had not been called on to testify. He became very excitable and made a number of allegations and was again ordered to be quiet or to leave the court.

Police Officer Brosnan said that he was as aware as the next man of the horrors dividing the country in two and so he had done everything to procure all the evidence possible. If anything in the nature of foul play had occurred, he had no evidence of it. All the evidence that had been unearthed he had placed before the jury to whom he now left the case.

The jury retired and returned with the verdict that the deceased had died from asphyxiation in sinking sands. There was no evidence to show how he came to be walking in such a treacherous area so late at night. Their verdict was 'Death by Misadventure'. They extended their sympathy to his relatives.

51

1995

Let go, my sister suggested, that night after we calmed back down. Let go, the sea waves had whispered throughout my summer in Mucknamore. Let go, my own mental musings on freedom had urged. Then along you come and do it for me.

Nine months you spent dissolving my self from within and then at last you are here, out in the world. At last I am holding you and knowing that your need, your ferocious, helpless human baby need, will reconstitute a whole new self around you. From now on, I'll still be me but I will also be all yours.

What an entrance you make! It began with small contractions, well spaced, and for hours I coped well but then I end up on a hospital bed the height and width of an ironing board, under orders not to move. All I want to do is get down on all fours. Maeve is there, beside my bed, her cheerleader's face making me snap, pain growling through me. It was a mistake to bring her: I'm not going to be able to do this, I am going to fail at what she did effortlessly.

They put me on an oxytocin drip to speed the labour along: it is 4 p.m. and I have been having contractions since two o'clock this morning. When I came into hospital, after holding out at home with Maeve as long as I dared, I was only two centimetres dilated. I later learn that it is normal for first labours to be lengthy but my midwife tells me it's a problem. I hold out against her first offer of the oxytocin 'to help me along' and her second. But then she tells me you may become distressed if the labour goes on 'too' long and I capitulate.

As soon as the drip goes in, the pain becomes intolerable. I feel that the God I have always doubted has my belly in His fist and is intent on proving His power. I can no longer cope. Before long I am kitted out like something in a sci-fi movie: a drip in my right arm, a blood-pressure monitor on the left, an epidural anaesthetic in my lower spine, a catheter bag to my bladder, a foetal monitor through my cervix onto the baby's head. My limbs tremble. I am passive, jittery, useless.

Every so often a falsely cheerful midwife comes in snapping on a plastic glove to do another internal examination. I hate her, I hate them all, and their steel instruments and unfeeling machines. The foetal monitor spins slow scrolls of paper etched with stalagmites and stalactites that are your heartbeat, keeps me from wanting to die.

'*Phhhhh.*'

'And again, push,' says Midwife One, looking at the monitor screen. She stands to the left of my bed with one of my legs in her arms, her colleague on my right has the other and between them is a baby who's refusing to arrive. The epidural means I can't feel my contractions and I only know to push when they check the monitor and tell me.

'Push,' says Midwife Two.

'*Ph-ph-phhhhhhhhhhh.*'

I feel no active pain, nothing except a growing nausea in my stomach and a ferocious, dead trembling in my numbed, spread-eagled legs that extends up into my trunk. But Maeve, who's down at the other end, watching, is excited. 'Oh, Jo, there's the head,' she says. 'Black hair! Black! Thick as a brush. Go again.'

'Push,' says Midwife One.

'Good girl, push,' says Midwife Two.

'Yes, push,' says the obstetrician, two of the ten words he has so far exchanged with me in the fifty minutes he's spent fiddling with, and staring into, my nether regions. The others were, 'Hello, Mum. How are we doing? Good, good.'

Phphhh. Phphhh. Phphhh. Phphhhhhhhhhhhh. Oh God, I'm going to vomit. 'I feel sick, I'm going to be—'

I gawk and Midwife One whips a silver-tin bowl from somewhere and sticks it under my chin. My insides contract, hurtling vomit out at one end and at the other squeezing you, like I'm a tube and you are a squidge of paste. You spurt out, so that the obstetrician and the two midwives all pitch forward to catch you. It is he who succeeds, grasping you with two firm hands and for the first time I feel gratitude towards him.

'Oh, Jo,' Maeve says. 'Just look! Oh, the little darling!'

At last you are here. You are pink and purple. Your eyes are open. Your forehead is furrowed under a thatch of black hair and your hands are under your chin as if you're praying. Two fists like unbloomed buds. Four limbs curving close to the trunk, fat knees and elbows bent. A blue-and-cream woven cord attached to the stomach. A pair of distended, swollen testicles. Testicles?

'You're a BOY!' I shout it out loud, so that my surprise fills the whole room and flows out into the corridor.

Maeve laughs. 'He's gorgeous, Jo! Oh, he's beautiful. A real beauty.'

I want to hold you but my stomach is taking another heave.

'She's going again,' says Midwife Two, putting the tin bowl, still full of vomit, back under my chin. I spew again, trying to keep looking at you. A second, deeper heave and I gawk – *Auggghhhh!* – and something else spurts out of me. The placenta. It too flies through the air, as you did, but this time the medics fail to catch and – splat! – it hits the obstetrician's face like a slap of liver.

'Oh dear,' I say. Blood is dripping from his jaw. 'I'm sorry.'

'It's not your fault,' says Midwife One.

I know it isn't. Really, I'm not sorry at all. Their whole way of doing this was so awful, so heedless of my needs, so careless of my hopes. It is their fault, not mine, that I am stirred and shaken to vomiting. Though later I'll resent them and their hospital procedures for failing, utterly, to give this holy moment its due, right now it doesn't seem to matter, because now they are handing you over. Down at the other end of me they are doing I don't know what but I don't care. Here you are, up here, in my arms at last. Your skin is smooth, silky new. You give your arms and legs an awkward jerk, astonished, it seems to me, to find space where the womb wall used to be. You are wrapped in an aura of serenity, still attuned to that other place, wherever it is you came from. I pull you in close. Your first holding in this new world.

Babies are our chance, I understand for the first time, our best stab at heaven. Every day life gives us the opportunity to give, to help, to serve – the path of the good, the path of the happy – but most of us manage it only for our children.

And some fail even in that.

What about me? Your new-blue eyes are looking up at me like I'm all you'll ever want and I make a vow, into them, to strive to be enough.

Outside, light has dawned, which means it's nearly eight o'clock in the morning. That's thirty hours since the labour started.

'Do you want to try to feed him?' Maeve suggests.

I look at her and see that her eyes are glittering with tears. Outside the window, it looks like any other shell-grey, Irish day.

Maeve brings me in Ria's old swimming ring: without it I could not sit. Once the epidural wears off I realize how much I'd torn during the birth. Sixteen stitches in three layers. I walk like a cowboy on hot coals. But I will mend.

You are in my arms again. My milk has come in and is drenching my clothes. I am still euphoric. You are so beautiful, so much more beautiful than any of the other babies. I keep taking you up just to look at you and hold you, sniff and lick you. In the convex at the back of your neck is where you smell most you. Maeve tells me that when researchers gave new mothers T-shirts worn by their own and other babies, all the women were able to smell out their own baby's one. I would have found that hard to believe before but not now. Now touch and smell and taste have the solidity of sight. I run my tongue along the sweetness of your skin between earlobe and chin, dry the trail I have made with a line of kisses.

The door opens. A massive bunch of flowers comes in and behind it is Rory. He looks around the bouquet, tentatively. Nervous.

As well he might be.

'Well, look who's here,' I say.

'I'm sorry, Jo.' He hesitates in the doorway. 'I know it shouldn't have taken me so long.'

'Damn right it shouldn't.'

'I'm sorry,' he says again. His hair has got longer, he has it tucked behind his ears. 'I couldn't come until I was certain.'

His eyes are close, I can see them shining. And though I'd prefer if I could be angry with him, I know that if I were to look in a mirror I would see that mine are their twin reflection.

52

He puts the flowers on the table under the window, and sits down on the bed beside me. 'Congratulations,' he says, easing back the blanket that wraps the bundle in my arms. He smiles at the sight. 'Did everything go OK?' He is nervous but I am calm, already blooded.

'Fine,' I smile, lying the mother's lie, discounting the barbarity of the process, the three layers of stitches, the nipple that's beginning to crack.

'Do you have a name?'

'Richard,' I say, smiling.

'It's not—'

'A boy? Yes.'

He laughs.

'I know,' I say. 'So sure and so wrong.'

'You don't mind, do you?'

'Mind? No, not at all. It wasn't that I particularly wanted a girl.'

He looks back in at the little sleeping face. 'Richard, eh?' He tries it out. 'Richard. Just don't let him be called Dick.'

He takes a chair and we relax a little and I tell him about the birth, the drip and the vomit and the hurtling afterbirth. I make a good story out of it and when I reach the part about the placenta going all over the obstetrician's face, he throws back his head in a laugh, the way he does.

'And then,' I continue, keeping up the entertainment, 'when it was all over, they handed him to me and I was brought face to face with these two *enormous* purple balls.'

Why didn't somebody tell me about that in advance? I thought there was something wrong with you: such an angry colour and so huge, like an accusation.

'It was the same with Dara,' he says. 'I remember saying to Orla that his scrotum was bigger than mine.'

Dara? Orla? Is this how it is to be?

'But they're shrinking now, right?' he says. He puts out a gentle hand, strokes your black hair flat across your head. Watching his palm passing over that dip in your scalp makes my insides clench. 'Get used to it, son,' he says. 'It'll be the story of your life.'

You stir at the touch, then settle back down.

'Can I ask you something?' I say to Rory.

He narrows his eyes. 'Sure.'

'Is he the best-looking baby you've ever seen?'

'Ever?'

'Ever.'

'Em . . .'

'He's not, is he?'

'Jo—'

'No, it's OK,' I laugh at his embarrassment. 'I suspected as much. It's really strange because to me, he is. I don't just mean that as a figure of speech, he genuinely looks unbelievably gorgeous to me. Much more so than any other baby in here.'

'Don't get me wrong, he's perfectly—'

'I knew it, I knew my perceptions must be skewed. That's why I had to check.' I look down at him. 'And even though I know it for sure now, he still looks that way to me. It must a trick of the hormones, another ploy to fasten us in.'

While we're both watching, you stir again and this time you're not going to quiet down. You begin your snuffle towards my breast, knowing what you want, and I open my nightdress and nursing bra. I fasten you onto my good nipple, aware of Rory's eyes on us. Your ears move as you suck.

Rory says, 'Hungry little beggar, isn't he?'

I smile, stroke the little head that he stroked a moment ago, feel the throb of the pulse beneath the membrane and the answering thud in myself. You feed and Rory watches, the three of us wrapped in suckling sounds, rapt in a curious triangle.

'Motherhood suits you,' Rory says after a while.

'Don't sound so surprised.'

'You seem different.'

'I'm loving it.' I know why he is surprised, I'm surprised myself.

'Where have you been staying?'

'Maeve's.'

'How's that been?'

'Yeah. Fine. She's been very good to me.'

'And your work? Have you finished?'

'Almost. I'm almost there.'

'You never told me the ending.'

'No, I didn't, did I?'

You have fallen asleep mid-suck, blissed out. Your lips – lined with milk – lie open round my nipple. 'Sooo,' he says. 'What are the plans now?'

I look up at him, suddenly afraid.

'Are you going back to the States?'

I begin to readjust my clothing, fix myself up, to get a moment of time. I need to be in order for this. Then I nod.

'You've booked a flight?'

'Not yet. But I expect to leave around the 28th.'

'So . . . ?'

So . . . ? What does 'So . . . ?' mean? So . . . can I come with you? So . . . don't go? So . . . I've left my wife? So . . . what, Rory? What?

He drops his eyes. 'I'm sorry about Orla coming to see you that day,' he says. 'I had no idea she would—'

'It's all right. We got on quite well, actually.'

'That's what she said.' And he frowns, as if that idea doesn't quite appeal to him.

'Are you two going to be OK?'

He snaps back from me, narrows his eyes as if refocusing. 'Is that what you want? Me and Orla to be OK?'

'What do you want, Rory?'

He moves his head in something between a nod and a shake. 'I still don't know what I should do,' he says.

And in that precise moment, I find that I do.

I sit perfectly still then, letting him bring it up, all he has to say that he doesn't yet know, that I somehow know before him.

'I still want to go away with you,' he says. 'I like myself so much more when I'm with you. I feel so young again and free, when I'm with you.'

He is putting me in charge again. He's just the same, he'll always be the same. The younger me was right. She did what she had to do. But I can't resent him. I know how he feels, like he is splitting in two . . .

'But that's not how it's going to be, is it?'

'Oh, God, Jo. I really want to be with you.'

'I know you do, Rory. I know.'

'Then let me.'

'It's not just you and me, is it?'

'You mean the baby?'

'And your own kids. And Orla.'

'But people do it, people get over all that.'

I shake my head.

'You don't want to,' he says. Part of him, the part that thought all he had to do was ask, is stunned. Neither of us has forgotten just how fiercely I once loved him.

I reach for his hand, hold it. His fingers curl up inside mine. 'Loving you ruined me for love,' I say, wanting to give him something. 'I never loved properly again . . .'

'But now you will,' he says, miserably.

'I don't think that's what I'm looking for at the moment.'

'You will.'

He sounds so glum that I laugh, and he frowns at me, offended. He wants to keep us in love-story land, but that's not how it is, not any more. I look down at your sleeping eyes. 'Loving this little fellow properly will be quite enough for me for a while,' I say.

He opens his mouth to reply, closes it again. We sit for a long time, the three of us, in the quiet of our room, hospital noises outside.

After a long time he says: 'You never told me the end of the story.'

'I'll send you a copy of the manuscript,' I say.

'Jo, you *promised* . . .'

In the middle of our loss, he is still avid for narrative resolution, his questing eyes full of its hold. What happened? Who dunnit? Was it really Peg? Tell me, tell. Of course it's not just a story to him, any more than it was to me. He wants the ending that was our beginning.

'I'm almost finished,' I say. 'And the book will tell it better than I can.'

He shakes his head at me, disappointed but resigned.

'You're in it too,' I tell him.

'I don't know whether to be flattered or alarmed.'

'You can be flattered, I think.'

I slip from the bed to lay the baby down in his cot and he comes to stand beside me, looking in as I arrange him, wrap the blanket tight around him. The little hands are curled into fists, one on either side of his closed eyes. We stand looking at him for a long time, then Rory says, 'So this is goodbye?'

I nod, afraid to look up at him, while the feelings that the Goodbye word always bring on are welling into my throat. I think of the aeroplane that I will take next week, that will wing me and my son westwards, towards yesterday. Goodbye is sad but now I am not afraid.

'You'll come back again to Mucknamore, won't you?' Rory says. 'For a visit?'

'Sure,' I say, what I said to Hilde. But then I remember it's him. 'Actually I don't think so, Rory. You come and see me instead.'

'I will. I definitely will.' He is fervent, like it's a vow.

'I'd like that,' I say.

'And you'll send me that manuscript?'

'I promise.'

He reaches for me then and we turn to hold each other. With my bump gone I feel, for the first time this summer, the full length of him, with nothing between us. We hold each other, hard. Then our lips search the other's out and we kiss. One kiss, firm and long and deep, with eyes clenched tight. One kiss with everything in it. Then we let each other go.

VI

Spume

Nora

. . . Child made her Confirmation yesterday, all glowing all in white. Like a shiny little angel but with the devil's eyes when she looks at Nora. Nora would have liked to go to the Confirmation, to see the bishop on his throne, his hat half the height of himself, and the white flowers and the prayers, but the devil eyes that didn't want me made me stay at home.

Peg thinks Child is so good and Child wants to keep it that way. 'Isn't little Máirín such a good girl?' says Peg, never knowing that it's only like that while she's around, that behind her back it's the nasty looks and faces, and the cold hard words for Nora.

Yesterday, when the two of us were on our own in the kitchen Child told me I was to stop looking at her. I have the eye of a jackdaw, she said, always following her around, gawping at her, whatever she's doing. Like the eye of a dirty old crow . . .

. . . Mrs Duggan, the praying woman, told her Willie to keep away from us.

'Is Mrs Duggan against Fianna Fáil?' Child asked Peg.

Fianna Fáil is Mr de Valera's latest big idea, the new political party that got him back the power.

'No, Mrs Duggan is not against Fianna Fáil,' said Peg. 'She's got her eye too much on the next world to care what goes on in this one. Why do you ask?'

Child told her what wee Willie said and out it all came pouring, all the people who say all the bad things. Young Cissie Pender who said she was surprised that Child was allowed to do a Confirmation at all. Surprised she was even let go to Mass. And Rita Breen, trying to be kind, saying: You shut up, Cissie Pender, hasn't she as much right as anyone else? Miss O'Neill who is always looking at her with a frown on, as if she has done something wrong, when she's doing nothing at all. And Mr White who the other day was going to pat her on the head but pulled himself back at the last minute. And most especially Father John, who's always picking her out on his visits to the school. He once said to Miss O'Neill that there was more joy in heaven over one lost lamb than all the rest, looking at her when he said it. He was talking about her but what did he mean?

Why is she a lost lamb, Child wants to know of Peg. Why is he always telling her to keep up with her prayers? Why doesn't he say that to the others? Why is it only to her?

And Cissie Pender again, when they were talking in the schoolyard about the plaque going up to her uncle Barney, said: Uncle, how are you!

What did she mean, Mammy?

Poor Peg, her face pulled tight, didn't know what to be saying. The Child was close to crying with all her questions and Peg took her and hugged her, crushed her so tight it must have hurt her back.

'You're not to mind that one, Cissie Pender,' Peg said into Child's hair, her voice all cracked. 'Do you hear me? Pay no attention whatever to the likes of her.'

'But what did she mean, Mammy?'

'Lord above knows, child. How could anyone know what's going on in a head like that? You're not to mind her, d'you hear me? You're not to mind any of them.'

Child came out of her hug and saw Peg's face and put one hand up to touch it.

'It's all right, Mammy,' she said, after a while. 'I don't mind them. Don't worry. I won't mind any more.'

. . . Now she goes sneaking round the house, her ear pressed to doors to see what she can hear. Or through the shivery darkness after everyone's in bed, to read the diaries that Peg thinks she's kept under lock and key. Oh, Child, Child, you'd want to watch out. You're going to find more than you want to find . . .

. . . We went together, so we did. Peg and I, the two of us peering into the fog. Double-blindfolded, once by dark and twice by fuddling mist. Small and careful our steps, because under our feet was a road of slush and ahead of us who knew what?

It's hopeless, Peg said. We can't see a thing.

But we couldn't go back to the house to sit by the fire, nerves scraping, so we kept on going and we were glad we did. For it wasn't hopeless. We found what we went looking for.

They all think it was Peg who did the deed and they all go shrinking silent round. As if she would, our kindly Peg. As if she could. The country might have turned itself upside down but some things are set. The sun comes up of a morning. The sea pulls in and out with the tides. Peg Parle could not kill Dan O'Donovan. What she did to unknown soldiers gave her enough remorse.

No, it wasn't Peg killed Dan, only Peg's old talk. Too much talking, she did, up there in the sickroom with the door well closed. I didn't know she was doing that: saying those things to her Mammy. Things I never said to her. Things I never thought anyone would say.

She did it for me, Peg said, but that's only Peg trying to pull something sweet-smelling out of the muck. It wasn't for me, no. If I'd been asked, I would have told her – No. But Mrs Parle wasn't a woman for asking, always so certain sure.

. . . It was I who found her, who saw her first, like a pile of rags she looked, all in a heap by the ditch. Through the fog I saw her and I nudged Peg and pulled her over. 'Mammy!' Peg cried, a muffled cry, for who knew who might be beyond the next layer of mist. 'Mammy, is it you?'

She was lying still, a lump of black in the dimness. Peg went to her, tried to lift her, and she roused. 'Peg?'

'Oh, Mammy, yes. Yes, I'm here.'

'I . . . fell . . .'

'Are you all right?'

We could see that she'd fallen. But was it on the way to do the deed, the thing she had said to Peg she would do, if she only had the strength? Like a woman possessed she had been above in her room, Peg said. Her eyes glittering and her mouth saying all sorts of unspeakables. Was she on her way there, or on the way back?

'Didn't . . .'

'It's all right, Mammy. Don't talk. We're going to get you home.'

'Didn't . . .' She was bad for breath, very bad. 'Not shot . . .'

'Oh, thank God, Mammy. Thank God.'

'Yes, God. I let . . . God . . . decide . . .' She dribbled a bit and flopped on us, seemed to go.

'Merciful Jesus,' Peg said. 'Is she . . . ?'

But she wasn't, only passed out.

We took her up between us, our shoulders under her arms. She was heavy though dwindled with her sickness and her bones felt thin to snap.

'What did she mean?' Peg asked me. 'What did she mean, "I let God decide"?'

Between us we hauled her home, careful at first but after a while too muscle-sore and frightened of being found out to be gentle. In the end, we were pulling her along between us, her boots dragging behind. In the house the light felt bright. Child was still asleep in her pram where we left her.

Now Peg could see the state of what we had brought in: her mother, a sight to make a cat cry. But we had no time for tears. 'Lie her down,' Peg said. 'We'll have to take her up the stairs on the flat. Hurry, before Daddy comes in.'

Peg took the weight of her shoulders and chest and I took the legs. It wasn't easy getting her round the twist in the stairs. In the bedroom we took off the nightdress she had on under her coat, all mudded up and sandy at the bottom, to make her clean and dry. In the middle of it, Peg's father called up the stairs and I was left alone with the mother and the two pinpoints of red on her chalky face, like a bee stung her – once, twice – on the bones of her cheeks.

She let God decide, she said. Decide what? The question was a scourge to us. We never thought of Coolanagh, not then, not until next morning when John Colfer went out in his boat.

'She could do with Dr Lavin,' Peg said, coming back into the room. 'But I'm afraid to call him. What if he notices her wet hair?' She took a towel and lifted her mother's insensible head off the pillow to slip it under and then she broke. With the worst danger past, the full knowledge of what her mother had set out to do flooded through her, and she dropped her head into her hands. I thought she was going to cry, but it was more of a wail that she let out. 'What has she done to us, Nora? Dear God, what is ahead for us now?'

. . . She did it for me, Peg said, but I never asked for that. My brother did me wrong, the way he put it all over onto me, but I never would have wanted that. For what Mrs Parle – and Dan himself – could overlook, I never could: he was my brother. He did me wrong but he was my brother.

Author's Note

The shooting of Barney Parle superficially resembles the death, on that date, of Con McCarthy and Bernie Radford at Spencerstown, Co. Wexford. The letter written by Molly Redmond from North Dublin Union draws heavily on Dorothy Macardle's reports of May 1923 to the journal *Eire*. The casebook explanation of Nora O'Donovan's committal to Enniscorthy Lunatic Asylum and her experiences there are based on the case-notes of one asylum patient (except that the real-life inmate remained incarcerated until her death in 1978). All other events in this novel, and all the characters, are fictional.

Co. Wexford is blessed with an abundance of talented and devoted local historians. I am greatly indebted to them all, most particularly those whose work acknowledges the experience and contribution of women.

Orna Ross, January 2005